When Life Was Like a Cucumber

Greg Wyss

PAGE PUBLISHING, INC.
New York, NY

First originally published by Page Publishing, Inc. 2019

When Life Was Like a Cucumber is a work of fiction. Any similarity to any person living or dead is purely coincidental. If you still imagine yourself in this lurid tale, the author suggests that you take the time to listen to Carly Simon's classic rendition of "You're So Vain," since you probably think this book is about you.

ISBN 978-1-64462-166-0 (Paperback)
ISBN 978-1-64462-167-7 (Digital)

To Barbara
for always believing in me

1

I only met God once.

It was on a Saturday morning in late February 1972. I had just turned twenty-four, and I was on acid. My only previous experience with LSD had been two years earlier in Boston with Danny Cooper. We were living in a third-floor apartment on Buswell Street, directly across from an apartment building that had been converted to a BU girl's dorm. We spent most nights sitting on our fire escape smoking hash and listening to Led Zeppelin's first album and Chicago's "25 or 6 to 4," while we watched college girls get dressed and undressed. It was the best of times.

Danny was from Brooklyn, and whenever he returned from a weekend in The City, he usually had something new for me to try. This time he brought back two small tablets called Orange Sunshine. We swallowed our pills, left the apartment, walked to Kenmore Square, and continued down to Mass Ave, where out of habit, we turned right toward Huntington Avenue and the Northeastern Quad.

Then it happened. My head exploded. There were bright colors everywhere. We were standing at the entrance to the Christian Science Church when the door suddenly swung open and Lurch from the Addams Family appeared.

"Enter," he commanded.

We did. Once inside, Lurch led us to the back of the church, where we joined six other people who were gathered around the smallest woman that I had ever seen and who had to be eighty years old. She was barely four feet tall and was talking about Mary Baker Eddy, who, we were soon to learn, was the founder of the Christian Science Church. The next thing we knew, we were being led on a tour by this tiny woman who was all hunched over and who shuffled her feet as she walked. She showed us all the places that Mary Baker Eddy had sat and all the places that Mary Baker Eddy had received a vision. She ended every sentence with a loud gasping "Uh-huh" while she clasped her hands together and bowed her head in prayer. Then suddenly it was over. Lurch opened the door and motioned for us to leave, and we were out on the street again.

Fast-forward two years and I am living in Hubcap Harvey's house at the top of Franklin Mountain outside of Oneonta, New York. This time it is Mike Stone who shows up that morning with two hits of acid and his wife, Renee. And once again, it is Orange Sunshine. The way Mike explains it is that one hit is for me, one is for Ozzie, and he is the trip leader. That leaves Renee and Jane as the observers.

Ozzie and I sit down at the kitchen table, and Mike takes a seat across from us. He sets the two tabs on the table. I swallow mine with a glass of water. Ozzie's preference is beer.

We sit at the table for some time, waiting for something to happen. Mike talks with us, trying to prepare us for liftoff. Ozzie looks at me, and I look at him. We know something is about to happen. We just don't know what or when. Mike walks to the living room, gets down on the floor, and starts going through our albums. Savoy Brown is the winner.

What happens next is open to interpretation. What I remember is running out the front door and falling into the snow. I am laughing at everything and I am inside of a kaleidoscope and the colors are changing and Ozzie is distorted. We are running across the road and then up the hill, and then Ozzie is jumping onto a snow pile, which is not really a snow pile but instead is a pile of logs and wood with protruding nails covered with fresh snow from the day before. I am laughing at Ozzie because he is in pain, and then we run up the hill together, and that's where I meet God.

This is where it gets hard to explain.

I had never really thought that much about God before or what God might look like. I probably was expecting to see an old man with a long, flowing white beard. Instead, I found myself suddenly standing on the chest of God. I felt the hill start to breathe. I struggled to keep my balance as Franklin Mountain inhaled and exhaled. God had become the earth, or the earth had become God. Whatever. I was obviously going mad, but I know what I saw. I turned around to look for Ozzie. He was several yards behind me, on his hands and knees and trying to crawl up the hill. The next thing that I remember is that Ozzie and I were standing at the top of the hill, at the edge of the clearing, staring into the forest of birch trees. Ozzie went first. He stepped between two trees, and he vanished. I stuck out my hand and placed it between the same two trees that had swallowed Ozzie, and my hand disappeared. I pulled back my arm, and my hand reappeared. Ozzie's Head materialized between the trees.

"Follow me," said Ozzie's Head.

Ozzie's Head retreated between the two trees, and I followed. The Entire Body of Ozzie was waiting for me when I arrived on the other side. It was different on this side. The sun came straight down from the cloudless sky and turned the snow into a blinding white mirror. It wasn't one color that I saw but a lot of them weaving in and out, the bluest sky, the whitest snow, the brightest sun. The Entire Body of Ozzie had become Superman without the cape. His superpowers had taken over, and he made a giant leap to the top of a huge rock formation. He looked to the heavens, extended his arms upward, and shot lightning bolts from his fingertips. The three-dimensional world was now a memory. We saw everything through a prism, mostly in four dimensions. We ran. We laughed. We rolled in the snow. But we didn't see God again.

Later that evening, we were back at the house. Ozzie's Head went up into the attic.

"Holy shit!" Ozzie's Head shouted. "A midget lives here!"

The attic was the Entire Body of Ozzie's bedroom. The Entire Body of Ozzie was six foot three and had to crawl around on his hands and knees in order to live in this tiny space. His bed was a mattress on the floor. Next to his bed, also on the floor, were a small reading lamp and an ashtray. There was no furniture. Dirty clothes, clean clothes, books, albums, two packs of Marlboros, and a bong filled with dirty water made up the Entire Body of Ozzie's world.

"I'm a midget," Ozzie's Head cried.

I was sitting in the kitchen, watching Jane, Mike, and Renee in the living room. They were ignoring me. I did not exist. This was really odd. I felt myself coming down, but I seemed to be operating in a parallel universe, where Jane, Mike, and Renee looked like Jane, Mike, and Renee, but they were not. Were they imposters? Was this Invasion of the Body Snatchers? What bothered me most is that I did not recognize Jane. It looked like her, but her voice was different, and she seemed to be someone that I had never met before. I remembered that I had married her, but I couldn't remember why.

Six weeks later, the house burned down.

2

The house smelled of burning wood, and a thin haze of smoke filled the living room. Ozzie was lying on the couch with his sketch pad. Jethro Tull was singing "Locomotive Breath" so loud that Ozzie didn't hear us come in the front door. A bag of pot was sprawled across the coffee table, and a half-smoked cigarette and a still-burning roach were smoldering in the ashtray.

"Ozzie!" I shouted. "What's burning?"

Ozzie looked up from whatever he was drawing.

"Huh?"

I dropped to the floor and turned down the volume on the stereo.

"Don't you smell the smoke?" I asked. "What the hell is going on?"

"Hey, man, I'm drawing. What's the problem?"

Jane dashed across the room to the kitchen and opened the door to the back porch.

"The porch is on fire!" she screamed.

Actually, what was burning was the cardboard box that was full of what we thought were extinguished ashes from our kitchen stove. And it was smoldering, not burning. I pulled the box away from the wall and dragged it off the back porch and into the snow. Problem solved. We left the front door open and also opened the back door to let the smoke clear out.

Later that evening, Mike and Renee showed up, and we laughed about the smoldering box of ashes that was now in the backyard. Mike, Ozzie, and I were sitting at the kitchen table, passing a joint around, and Jane and Renee were talking in the living room, when suddenly the lights went out and the wall behind the stove in the kitchen burst into flames. Thick black smoke was everywhere, and I dropped to my stomach in order to breathe and crawled across the living room on my hands and knees out the front door onto the porch and then into the snow. Once outside, I looked up to see the back porch engulfed in flames. My feet were wet and cold. I had run out without my shoes on, and my white socks were soaking wet. Jane, Ozzie, and Mike were beside me, but no Renee. In a panic, Mike ran back into the house, yelling for Renee. Jane yelled after him that Renee had run down the road to find the nearest neighbor to call for help, but Mike was already inside. My car keys, I thought. I ran back into the house. Fire raged in the kitchen. Mike was on the floor coughing.

"Get out!" I shouted. "Renee is not in the house. She's okay."

It was unbearably hot, and I couldn't breathe. The flames were moving toward the living room. Once again, I dropped to the floor in search of oxygen. I crawled into the bedroom and felt my way to the dresser, where I always kept my car keys. I stood up, grabbed the keys, and fell to the floor. The smoke had gotten thicker, and I struggled back to the living room and the front door. As I was crawling out, Ozzie was crawling in.

"What are you doing?" I screamed.

"Getting my albums," he replied.

Ozzie was on a mission. As the three of us waited for him in the snow, we could hear sirens in the distance. A minute or so later, Ozzie emerged, dragging a box of albums. He had grabbed the wrong box. They were mine, not his. Ozzie had risked his life to save my record collection.

Renee ran back up the driveway, returning from the neighbor's house that was about a half mile down the hill. The fire trucks arrived, and it took them several hours to get the fire under control. The backyard filled with spectators. It was a freak show. They stood around talking about us like we weren't there. They watched the firemen pull burning mattresses from the house. They looked at the five of us. Some of them laughed.

"Looks like the hippies burned themselves down."

"Wonder how many were living there?"

"I heard that they were having sex orgies."

It was a festive occasion for the crowd until Hubcap Harvey finally showed up. He never approached us but instead stood with the spectators and his former neighbors. He never said a word to us. He kept shaking his head and saying the same thing over and over again: "I've lost everything. First my wife, now my house."

Ozzie looked at me.

"You burned the house down," he said.

3

Harvey Parsons had built the small wood-frame house in 1925 and lived there for nearly forty-six years with his wife, Edith, until she passed away in January 1971. Harvey owned sixty-five acres of land that was divided by Route 28 at the very top of Franklin Mountain, a few miles south of Oneonta at the western edge of the Catskills. The house was set back from the road and was shielded from view by the numerous pine trees that lined the highway. Harvey Parsons became known as Hubcap Harvey because of the collection of several hundred hubcaps that he displayed at the gravel turnoff in front of his long dirt driveway.

Hubcap Harvey could not bring himself to live alone in the house without his beloved Edith, so he decided to rent it out and move into town. Jane and I had returned to Upstate New York from Boston that summer, following my graduation from college. We were staying with Jane's parents in Unadilla, trying to figure out where we were going to live and what we were going to do when Dick Dickson told us about a For Rent sign at the top of Franklin Mountain.

Since I had long hair and no job, it made sense to send Jane and her pretty face to meet the owner. The plan was a success. We moved in the first week in September, and I did not meet Hubcap Harvey until a week later when he stopped by to see how we were doing. The house was small with only one bedroom, and the only source of heat was the wood-burning stove in the kitchen. We filled the house with furniture given to us by my parents, who had recently sold their home and most of their belongings and moved to Florida. It took a while, but we both found jobs in Oneonta, Jane as a waitress at the lunch counter in Jamesway and I on the assembly line at Corning Glass. We settled into life on Franklin Mountain. We soon had two dogs, Otto and Charlie, and two cats, Arnold and Contessa. I hated my job at Corning, but it only lasted a month. I was laid off and collected unemployment for a while until a few weeks before Thanksgiving, when Mike Stone got me an interview where he was working at Bailey Ceramics. Since I was a college graduate, Mr. Bailey hired me as bookkeeper trainee for $1.85 an hour.

Mike Stone and I had known each other since we were kids. Growing up in the town of Sidney, we played sports together, had a lot of the same friends, and shared the common experiences that kids in small towns in the '50s and '60s share. Like Ozzie and my brother Bernie, Mike was a year behind me in school. A two-time New York State wrestling champion, Mike had been the epitome of cool. He had that magnetic personality that made those around him follow his lead on most everything. He was definitely the coolest kid in Sidney. Class president and straight A student, Mike had received a wrestling scholarship to Penn State when he graduated in 1967. He had early success as a Nittany Lion, finishing second at the Eastern Intercollegiate Wrestling Championships as a freshman. Midway through his sophomore year, Mike dropped out of Penn State and returned to Sidney as a hippie. Mike and Renee were living in the basement below Palombo's Liquor Store at the corner of Chestnut and Main in Oneonta, where they operated Get Stoned Leather. The entrance to the store was in the alley behind and beneath Palombo's. Mike and Renee made leather belts, leather vests, leather wallets, and no money. To survive, Mike got a job at Bailey Ceramics, where he operated the huge kiln in the back. I spent half of my time in the front office working on the books and the other half in the back working with Mike. We became friends.

Hubcap Harvey's house became a magnet. Randy Zarin drove down several times from Boston. Danny Cooper drove up from DC, where he was attending dental school at Georgetown. Jake Fisher showed up one weekend with bags of drugs. It was the first time that I tried cocaine. Gerald Lopez had moved back to Oneonta from Boston, and he and his friends would come by. My brother Bernie, who was on his way to California with Tommy Grant, showed up over Thanksgiving weekend, along with nearly two feet of snow. He also brought with him a gray, tiger-striped cat named Farley. Farley needed a home. He had been given to Bernie by the driver who picked him up hitchhiking in Kenmore Square in Boston. The story was that Farley had been given LSD as a kitten and he had shit on Bernie's coat as he was carrying him back to the apartment. Bernie figured that Farley needed out of the big city and little bit of country living. We agreed and Farley joined the family. Soon after Bernie left for California, Ozzie McBrinn showed up, asking if he could move in with us.

The McBrinn family had moved to Sidney from England when Ozzie was ten years old. Ozzie was a skinny kid who was picked on relentlessly because of the funny way he talked. Ozzie responded by lifting weights and bulking up. By the time that he reached high school, he was a lineman on the football team and a good enough wrestler to become Susquehanna League champion at 167 pounds. He was no Mike Stone, but he was good. However, Ozzie never overcame his strangeness. In high school, he wore goofy hats and pants that were always too short. He thought he was a Beatnik, but in reality, he was just a little weird. He attended Lehigh University in Bethlehem, Pennsylvania, where he wrestled and earned a degree in biology. When he graduated in June 1971, he learned that a distant aunt in England had died and left him $11,000. At the age of twenty-two, Ozzie McBrinn figured that he had enough money to retire.

We were cool with Ozzie moving in, but since it was a small house with only one bedroom and a small living room, where was he going to stay? Ozzie surveyed the house.

"No problem," he said. "I'll live in the attic."

And he did. Each day when Jane and I left for work, he would come out of the attic with his grass and his sketch pad, stretch out on the couch, and draw. He loved M. C. Escher, whom he tried desperately to imitate. Mostly he drew strange little characters from J. R. Tolkien's *Lord of the Rings*. He had decided to become an artist, so he smoked pot all day and worked feverishly on his drawings. About once a week, Hubcap Harvey would stop by, and Ozzie would step outside to talk with him. Ozzie had good bullshit. Hubcap Harvey never made it past the front door. Ozzie would engage him in all sorts of conversations, and over time, Hubcap Harvey became confused, probably convinced that Ozzie was me.

Life on Franklin Mountain soon revolved around Ozzie. With Mike and Renee showing up every weekend, Ozzie started calling the five of us the FMLF, which was short for Franklin Mountain Liberation Front. When we were not working, we were getting high. And when we were high, we explored Hubcap Harvey's sixty-five acres.

4

The fire changed everything.

Jane was pissed. Not about the fire, but at the *Oneonta Star*. There was an investigation, and the *Oneonta Star*'s front page reported that it been an electrical fire and that the house had been occupied by a Jeffrey Hesse, his wife, and Oswald McBrinn. Jane wanted to know why she was just being referred to as my wife. She had a name, she insisted. It was the beginning of the end.

The FMLF disbanded. We had lost everything except our car, the clothes on our backs, and my record albums. Farley, Charlie, and Arnold died in the fire. Otto had wandered off, and we never found him. Only Contessa had survived, but she was badly burned. Ozzie moved into the closet in the back room of Get Stoned Leather. Jane, Contessa, and I went to stay with her parents in Unadilla. We both knew it was over. We looked around and realized that there was nothing to divide up. We had eight hundred dollars and a 1964 Ford Falcon. Jane quit her job and told me that she was planning to visit some friends in Amherst, Massachusetts. Despite the forty-mile roundtrip up and down Route 7, I continued to work at Bailey Ceramics. Then I got sick. When my fever broke, Jane was gone.

Now what? Jane wasn't coming back, and staying with her parents was not an option. Once again, Dick Dickson came to the rescue. He told me about Neal Bennett, an English professor at Oneonta State who had founded a Free School in Franklin. Dick said that Neal Bennett was looking for people to live at his school. I decided to check it out. It didn't seem like a school to me. Neal and his wife, Connie, had built themselves a house on a twenty-acre plot of land on a country road a few miles outside of Franklin. There were no classes, no students. Neal explained that we were all teachers and that we were all students and that I could have a room in the house in exchange for helping out with whatever needed to be done. That was okay with me. They had their Free School, and I had my Free Room. I moved in the next day.

Jane had let me keep the Ford Falcon. I made the drive that first Monday morning over Franklin Mountain to my job at Bailey Ceramics. When I came home that night, I discovered that there was another teacher/student at the Free School. She lived in the room next to me, and her name was Maggie. She was a big girl, probably around twenty years old. Maggie had long brown hair, wore flannel shirts, and at night, would sneak down the hall and into bed with Neal and Connie. The first few nights, I kept waiting for her to sneak into my room, but it never happened. Had Maggie climbed into my bed one of those first nights or had I been invited to join in with the three of them, things might have been different. As it was, I was getting really bored, really fast. This was not the place for me. I needed to be in Oneonta, not here.

5

Oneonta seemed like the right place for me to start over. Originally the home of Iroquois Indians, it had now been taken over by college students. Nearly half of its fifteen thousand residents attended Oneonta State or Hartwick College. It was home to a Minor League Baseball team, and a rowdy kid named Ronald Crosby, who had fled the town and changed his name to Jerry Jeff Walker. Youth ruled. The drinking age was eighteen, and life revolved around the two colleges and the fifty-four bars that always seemed to be open. I had been told that in the Iroquois language, the word Oneonta meant "place of the open rocks." Maybe so, but "home of malt and hops" was a more accurate description.

I continued to make the drive over Franklin Mountain that first week to and from the Free Room and Bailey Ceramics. On Friday night, I decided to stay in town. I stopped by Get Stoned Leather, where Ozzie was now living. Mike and Renee had gone to Sidney for the weekend, and they had left Ozzie to run their business. Ozzie had made himself a new home in the back room of the store. It was a dark room with a tall ceiling, no windows, and a large, long closet. Ozzie had gotten a mattress from somewhere and had placed it on the floor of the closet. This is where he now lived. Mike and Renee slept on a king-size waterbed in the middle of the room. They cooked on a hot plate and got their water from the small sink in the tiny bathroom. There was a toilet, but no bathtub or shower. The only lighting came from a bare lightbulb hanging from the ceiling, and two small reading lamps, one by the waterbed and one in Ozzie's closet. There was also a lava lamp next to the waterbed.

"Let's go to The Silver," said Ozzie.

Get Stoned Leather was now closed for the weekend.

Friday night at The Silver. This was my first time. The Silver was popular with both college students and the townies. The ten-cent drafts at happy hour brought in an early crowd, and it was soon filled to capacity. There was one pool table by the jukebox near the front door, and the quarters were lined up at least six deep to challenge each eight-ball winner. Ozzie immediately started working the room. Hippie chicks, college girls—Ozzie was in his element. At seven o'clock, the price of drafts jumped to twenty-five cents. That was fine with me. I had three dollars to spend, which meant that I could drink all night, buy a pack of Marlboros, and play some pool. Ozzie had bigger plans.

The more I drank, the louder and more pronounced everything became. The jukebox pounded. "Brown Sugar," "LA Woman," "Sympathy for the Devil," and "Every Picture Tells a Story" seemed to coexist in harmony with the drone of drunken conversations and the sound of colliding pool balls. It seemed like everyone had lit a cigarette at the same time. Up until now, I had not been much of a bar person, and I really did not know how I was supposed to act. I tried my hand at eight ball but got my ass kicked. Most of the time, I hung next to Ozzie, who had placed himself at a strategic corner of the bar where most everyone came to order drinks. Ozzie was relentless. He also did not discriminate.

Around midnight, it looked like his hard work might actually pay off. A tall and beautiful girl with long brown hair and big brown eyes walked through the front door of The Silver. As she squeezed between the jukebox and the pool table on her way to the bar, it seemed like every guy in The Silver turned his head to get a look, and she knew it. She was definitely older than a college girl and definitely not a regular. Trailing behind her was a tall, skinny dude with curly blond hair who wore John Lennon glasses. She walked up to the corner of the bar where Ozzie and I were standing and motioned to the bartender, who stopped what he was doing and rushed over to wait on her. Sure enough, Ozzie had found himself in the right place at the right time. He was ready.

"Your first time here?" he asked.

She didn't answer, but she looked at him with her big brown eyes and smiled. She turned to the bartender and ordered a drink that I had never heard of before, along with a beer for the dude with John Lennon glasses.

I admired Ozzie's fearlessness. Most guys would have backed off at this point, but not Ozzie. Sure enough, he managed to engage her in a conversation, and they were soon laughing and drinking together. Since I was standing next to them, I overhead most of what they said. She was a musician and singer and was booked at the coffee house on the Oneonta State campus for the weekend. She had finished her Friday night show and had asked someone where the best bar in town was. She was told that it was The Silver, so she and Sticks, who was her drummer and the dude with John Lennon glasses, had driven downtown to check it out.

Ozzie glowed with confidence. He looked at me and winked and then excused himself to go to the head. As he walked away, the Brown-Eyed Girl turned around and smiled at me.

"Do you have someplace that we can go?" she asked.

"What?"

"Listen," she said, "I have been checking this place out, and it looks like you are about the best that I am going to be able to do tonight. What's your name?"

"Jeff?" I said, hoping that was the right answer.

"Well?" she said.

"Be right back," I answered.

I hurried toward the men's room and caught Ozzie as he was walking out.

"I need to borrow the key to your place," I said.

I explained what had happened. Ozzie was pissed, but he handed over his key.

"You owe me," he said.

The Brown-Eyed Girl grabbed my hand and led me into the sea of drunks that stood between us and the door. As the waves parted and we vanished to the street, I sensed that we were being followed by every pair of male eyes in The Silver.

This must be how legends are made, I thought.

6

"Where are you taking me?' asked the Brown-Eyed Girl as we headed into the alley behind Main Street.

"You'll see," I said. "It's cool. My friends are gone for the weekend."

Man, was my luck about to change. In a matter of weeks, my house had burned down, my pets were gone, all my earthly possessions had been destroyed, and my wife had run off to Massachusetts. This was quite a recovery. I was about to get laid by a beautiful rock singer.

There was no light in the alley, and I fumbled with the key awhile before I was able to open the door. We stood in the dark confines of Get Stoned Leather. The Brown-Eyed Girl was skeptical.

"Where exactly are we?" she asked.

"This is my friends' leather store," I said. "They live in the back."

I opened the door to the back room and hit the light switch. The bare lightbulb barely lit the room. The Brown-Eyed Girl looked at the waterbed and then at the mattress in Ozzie's closet.

"Let's take the waterbed," she said.

I had never been with anyone like her before. It was also my first time on a waterbed. She did not waste any time. She stripped off her clothes and asked if I had any pot. Fortunately, I remembered that Ozzie always kept his grass and rolling papers under the lamp by his bed. As luck would have it, I found a nickel bag, a pack of Zig-Zags, and a cigarette lighter. I took off my clothes and rolled two joints. I fired the first one up, took a hit, and passed it to her. I was in love.

Her name was Emily Keenan. She was twenty-five, and she played college campuses with Sticks, her drummer, whenever she was not touring with the likes of David Bromberg, Maria Muldaur, or

Jerry Jeff Walker. I proudly told her that Jerry Jeff was from Oneonta, but she already knew that.

"How do you think I found this place?" she asked.

I was consumed by her beauty, but mostly, I was fascinated by the tattoo of a red apple just above her right ankle. I had never met a woman with a tattoo before, and my dick was as hard as a rock. Emily Keenan noticed. She pushed me down, grabbed it, smiled, and put it in her mouth. She was in complete control. I did whatever she wanted.

It turned out to be the best weekend that I had ever had. We were inseparable. The sex was great, but it was the way we were able to talk with each other that made it different. I was suddenly the little kid who wanted to run off with the circus. She laughed at me when I asked if I could go on the road with her. There was a certain sadness about her. I learned that she was living with some wealthy guy in Manhattan. He knew that she was unfaithful to him when she was on the road, but she claimed that he was okay with that, just as long as she always came back to him.

"Are you in love with him?" I asked.

"No," she said.

She was definitely out of my league, but she was kind enough to not make me feel that way. We talked about music. I asked her who her favorite singer was, and she told me it was Mick Jagger. I told her that I liked Rod Stewart better. I tried to impress her with my story of having gone to Woodstock. She knew that I didn't know what I was talking about, but she humored me anyway. I spilled my guts about the fire, about Jane, and about Neal Bennett's Free School. I gave her Neal Bennett's phone number, but she would not give me hers.

When we made love again on Saturday afternoon, she was tender. I thought that I saw tears in her eyes. No one had ever made love to me like that before. That evening she took me to her show and had me sit at her table by the stage. When she sang "Wild Horses" off the Stones' *Sticky Fingers*, she never took her eyes off me. After the concert, we went to the room that had been given to her in one of the Oneonta State dorms. We made love like it was the last time that we would ever see each other. The next morning, she left with Sticks in his VW bus.

I returned to the Free Room. I felt different now, but in reality, nothing had changed. I went to work on Monday. I did not want to be there anymore, but I needed the money. Back at the Free Room, I slept alone. Neal Bennett was sleeping with two women, yet I had none. It didn't seem fair. I wanted to leave, but I still needed the free place to stay. I wanted to run off with the Brown-Eyed Girl, but she was gone forever. Or at least I thought she was.

After work on Thursday, I called Neal to tell him that I would be staying in Oneonta for a few days. He said that someone named Emily Keenan had called for me and left her number. *Far out,* I thought, *she wants me to come to The City.* I borrowed some change from Ozzie and went to a pay phone on Chestnut Street. I was nervous. She picked up on the third ring.

"Emily," I said. "This is Jeff. How are you?"

"Jeff, listen," she said. "There is something that I need to tell you."

It was not what I was expecting. My imagination had seen her begging me to come to live with her in The City. I would travel the country with her as she toured, making love to her during the day and adoring her at night as she played before thousands of screaming fans and dedicated each of her songs to me. Instead, it turned out that she had some sort of vaginal infection and she was worried that I might have caught it from her.

Undeterred, I asked if I could come to New York and live with her. There was a long silence. Emily Keenan said goodbye and hung up the phone.

I decided to go to The Silver. It was happy hour.

7

I got totally drunk and ended up spending the night passed out on the floor of Get Stoned Leather. How I got there, I don't know. Mike woke me on Friday morning, and I rode to work with him. This turned out to be the day that I quit my job at Bailey Ceramics. I didn't realize it at the time, but the house fire was a life-changing event. It was as if someone had unlocked the door to my jail cell and was giving me the chance to break out of prison and make a mad dash for freedom.

My first escape attempt had been nearly two years earlier, when in June 1970, following the national student strikes after the Kent State shootings, Jake Fisher, Zero Lester, and I left Boston to make a cross-country trek that would end in San Francisco and Haight-Ashbury. It was the first time that I had ever been west of New York State. We camped near Niagara Falls, then outside of Des Moines, Iowa, and finally in the Rockies outside of Boulder, Colorado, where we met the Egg Man, whose photo had been displayed prominently in *Life* magazine's special Woodstock issue. Two days later, outside of Rock Springs, Wyoming, I had my first near-death experience. We were all in the front seat. Jake was driving, Zero was in the middle, and I was riding shotgun, when in a driving rain storm, Jake lost control of the car. We spun around several times and then flew off the highway. I remember bracing myself on the dashboard as we were airborne and saying out loud that this was it and we were all going to die. Instead, it was splat, and we landed in a sea of mud. We crawled out the windows and in knee-deep mud worked our way back to the highway where an eighteen-wheeler had just stopped to help us. We were a sorry sight, three wild-haired East Coast hippies rising like filthy ghosts from a landscape of chocolate pudding. This kind trucker saved our pathetic asses by wading into the sea of mud, hooking his chains to our car and pulling it back onto the highway. We drove nonstop to San Francisco, delivering our mud-caked but otherwise undamaged Auto Driveaway car to its preordained destination. It was on this trip that I learned about Auto Driveaway, a service for people who needed their cars driven for them to where they were moving or vacationing. Jake had found a car in Boston that needed to be in San Francisco, and we had seven days to get it there. We made it with one day to spare.

Although we had missed the Summer of Love by almost three years, we jumped headfirst into the Haight-Ashbury scene, happy to be alive and ready to experiment. We wandered the Haight by day and slept in Golden Gate Park at night. There were hundreds more like us. Zero met some Jesus Freaks who lived in a commune in an old Victorian house with more than twenty other Jesus Freaks, and we moved in. Zero, Jake, and I were fraternity brothers who had gone to Woodstock together, marched in the antiwar demonstrations in Washington together, and were now searching to experience the counterculture. Jake thought himself a revolutionary and was into drugs. Zero, who was Jake's best friend, was the opposite of Jake. He had a sense of humor about his politics and reveled in the guerilla theater approach of Jerry Rubin, Abbie Hoffman, and the Yippies. He had also begun to explore his spiritual side and was an admirer of Meher Baba, the Indian mystic who had died the year before. Meher Baba had not spoken since 1925 and had maintained his silence to the end of his life. Zero spoke very little now and shared Meher Baba's disdain for psychedelic drugs. He was contemplating taking his own vow of silence. Me, I just wanted to travel and experience new things. I had read *On the Road* and *Dharma Bums*, and I wanted to be like Jack Kerouac. Now I was in San Francisco, hoping to run into Ken Kesey and his Merry Pranksters. Unfortunately, my mad dash for freedom was short-lived. I was captured two weeks later.

My girlfriend Jane was pregnant. I found this out when I called her collect at her parents' house in Unadilla where she was spending the summer. I could feel the life being sucked out of me. Jane sounded calm, but I was in a state of shock. She said there was no reason for me to cut my trip short and told me to stay in San Francisco for the summer. How could I do that? My brief taste of freedom was history. When I told Jane I was coming home, she made a weak attempt to talk me out of it. She didn't say it, but I could feel it in her voice that she was glad that I was.

When I broke the news to Jake and Zero, they didn't say much, but I could see that they were sad for me. Their summer adventure would continue, but mine was over. I needed $184 to buy a one-way plane ticket to Boston, and I only had about sixty dollars in my pocket. Jake said that we should panhandle for the money, and he and I took to the streets. Zero set about hitting up all the Jesus Freaks for spare change. We told everyone my story, and after three days, we had collected enough bread to buy me a ticket. I flew out the next day. Landing at Logan Airport, I took the MTA to Kenmore Square and walked back to Mass Ave to the entrance ramp for the Mass Pike. I stuck out my thumb, and six hours later, I was in Unadilla, resigned to my fate.

It was a sad summer. I wanted to be in San Francisco with Jake and Zero and was scared shitless at the thought of the life I was about to enter. The last thing I wanted to do was get married. Still, I thought that was what I was supposed to do, so I asked Jane to marry me. We decided to take our vows at the end of August. We set the date and invited our family and friends. Two weeks before the wedding, Jane had a miscarriage.

We should have called it off, but we didn't. Jane was willing to let me off the hook and told me there was no reason for us to get married now. She knew me well enough to know how restless I was and that I wasn't ready for this. She also cared enough about me to offer me my freedom, but I felt too guilty for what she had just been through to accept her gift. Even though she was telling me that she wanted to cancel the wedding, I refused to believe her. Like a fool, I insisted we go through with it.

Jane and I were married in the tiny Saint Ambrose Roman Catholic Church on Main Street in Unadilla. The afternoon of the wedding, a crowd started to form on the sidewalk across the street. Rumors of a hippie wedding had taken over the tiny village, and a group of curious citizens had gathered to witness the spectacle. Jake and Zero were back from San Francisco, and they, along with Danny Cooper and Miles Jaffe, made the trip down from Boston. However, most of the onlookers were disappointed because it wasn't that much of a freak show. The highlight of the wedding was Christine, Jane's maid of honor, who showed up wearing a long white dress with a plunging neckline and no bra. Her tits seemed destined to fall out of her dress, but to everyone's disappointment, it never happened.

Jane and I should never have gotten married. I knew that it was a mistake the minute I insisted we go through with it, but I was too much of a coward to take it back. I was going into my last year at college, and I was ready to get that over with and go see the world. I had met Jane when I was fifteen, and we had lost our virginity together. Although we lived a little more than five miles from each other, we lived in different towns and went to different high schools. When I wasn't playing football, basketball, or baseball for mine and she wasn't cheerleading for hers, we would go parking and learn about sex together. It didn't matter where. Our weekend nights were spent parked at the Evergreen Hill Cemetery, at the Unadilla Drive-Inn, or on Plankenhorn Road, where our hormones raged awkwardly in the front and back seats of my dad's Plymouth Fury. Jane was a senior in high school when I left for college in Boston in September 1966. Somehow, we maintained our relationship over the next four years, even as we lived separate lives with separate friends and separate experiences. I don't know how it seemed to her, but to me, I was living a dual life. We were still a couple during those years, but with the exception of school holidays, we were together only about one weekend per month. The rest of the time, I lived the life of a single college guy, with all that Boston in the late Sixties had to offer. Getting married changed all that, and neither one of us adjusted to it very well. I wasn't much of a husband, and we were both still just kids. We were together because that was what we had always been. That is why when Hubcap Harvey's house burned down, it was so easy to walk away. It wasn't anyone's fault. The marriage was a big mistake, but we seemed incapable of ending it.

The fire did that for us.

8

After I quit my job, I drove back to Neal Bennett's Free School, gathered up all my earthly possessions from the Free Room, and told Neal that I was moving out. Armed with several hundred dollars, my Ford Falcon, and the albums that Ozzie had risked his life to save, I headed straight to town. Although I had no job and no place to live, I was beaming with confidence. The weekend with Emily Keenan had changed me. All that I could think about now was getting laid.

Up until now, my sexual experience had been quite limited. There was Jane and a handful of encounters during my college years. The only memorable one was the time during my junior year when I was leaving a party at a third-floor apartment in Cambridge. As I was stumbling down the stairs, the door to a first-floor apartment swung open and a tall girl with light-brown hair that hung to her waist emerged from the darkness. She looked me over from head to toe, flashed a smile, and asked if I would like to come in. Her one-room studio smelled of incense, and there was a big water pipe next to the bed. She told me that her boyfriend was in the Navy and she had not had sex in over six months. There was an eight-by-ten black-and-white photograph of him on the dresser next to the bed, and it felt like he was staring at us the entire time. In the morning, she asked me to leave and to forget that this had ever happened. She may have forgotten, but I haven't. She never told me her name.

It was spring in Oneonta, and it was a great time to be alive. The bars were bursting at the seams with college girls, and the sunshine and fifty-degree weather were filling Neahwa Park with Frisbee players and sunbathers. Before I could go see the world, I would have to conquer Oneonta. Not that I had a plan, but I figured that as a last resort, I could always sleep in the back of my Falcon. I knew that I could also count on Mike and Renee, as well as Gerald Lopez and some of his townie friends. Dick Dickson was now living in Cooperstown, and I could always crash on his couch if I needed to. However, it turned out to be Julie Tyler who first came to my rescue.

Julie was one of a group of Hartwick College students who, along with a handful of others from Oneonta State, wrote and published *Seeds*, Oneonta's underground newspaper. I had picked up a copy of the inaugural issue of *Seeds* in November 1971, two months after Jane and I had first moved into Hubcap Harvey's house. I decided to volunteer at the paper, so I asked around and learned that they met every Tuesday and Thursday evening in Life Gallery on the third floor above the sporting-goods store on Main Street. I walked in unannounced and introduced myself and my intentions, and I was accepted immediately. This was hardly a group of angry radicals, at least not that type that I was used to seeing in Boston, DC, or New Haven. They were a group of college students who seemed serious enough yet were rather laid-back and friendly. The unofficial editor was Peter Kroh, who taught history at Hartwick. Besides Julie Tyler, the core staff consisted of fellow Hartwick students Beth Allen, Alex and Nancy Kayne, Penelope Jessup, and Phyllis Van Dyke, as well as five Oneonta State students. The Hartwick students were a tight-knit group, and we gradually became friends. I stopped coming after the house fire when Jane and I moved down to Unadilla. Now I was back, and everyone told me how sorry they had been to hear about the fire. I told the group that I was ready to start writing articles again, and since Jane and I had split up, I would be hanging in town and be around a lot more. After the meeting, we all went to The Silver.

I was sharing a booth with Alex, Nancy, Julie, and a second pitcher of beer when Julie asked me where I was staying.

"I don't have a place to crash," I said. "I'm just sleeping in my car."

"You can crash at my place, if you want," she said.

Julie was sharing a house on Dietz Street with three roommates. It was after midnight when we got back to her place, and they were already in bed. We sat on the couch and talked for a while. She had some pot, so I rolled a joint while she went to the kitchen to grab us a couple of beers. Julie was from Newburyport, Massachusetts, so most of our conversation was about Boston. I was preparing myself to sleep on the couch when she suddenly grabbed the back of my neck and pulled my face to hers. It was a long, wet, and passionate kiss, and when we finished, she took my hand and led me down the long hallway to her room. She never said a word. She was a pretty girl, with smooth, soft skin and a terrific body. She was obviously not too interested in foreplay and wanted me inside her right away. Her vagina was tight, and I could not have pulled out of her if I had wanted to. Her lips clenched my dick like suction cups. When she came the first time, her body trembled in short spasms, and she broke into a deep sweat. The sheets were soaking wet, and I was just holding on for the ride. I don't know how I did it, but I managed not to come until her third orgasm. When I rolled off, I was still hard. Julie was not finished. As I lay on my back on the soaking sheets, she climbed on top of me, lowered herself onto my dick and shook and sweated her way through another orgasm. I didn't come again, but this was such a turn-on that I never lost my erection. I think that I was still hard when I fell asleep.

I liked her and I could tell that she liked me, but we never talked about it. I was always welcome in her bed, but there was never any pressure to be with her. Whenever we slept together, the orgasms were always the same. I got used to sleeping on wet sheets.

One night, Ozzie and I went to The Silver, and all my friends from *Seeds* were there. I introduced him to the group, and Ozzie and Phyllis Van Dyke took a liking to each other. Phyllis was a big girl, an earth-woman type. Like Ozzie, she wore thick glasses. And like Ozzie, she probably had not been laid in a while. Convinced I was doing Ozzie a favor, I left the bar early and went home with Julie that night. I stopped by Get Stoned Leather the next morning and found Ozzie sitting in a chair, rubbing his crotch.

"How was it?" I asked.

"I thought she was going to pull my prick off," he said. "I'm fucking sore."

"So we're good, right?"

I figured that introducing him to Phyllis Van Dyke had made up for Emily Keenan.

Ozzie gave me the finger.

"Asshole," he said.

9

I was good friends with the Hartwick students from *Seeds* that I hung with at The Silver, but most of the people that I knew in Oneonta I had met through Gerald and his band of townie misfits. Gerald Lopez was a close friend of Bernie and had once saved Bernie's life after Bernie had taken some bad acid and was wandering in a confused psychedelic haze along a busy New Hampshire highway. A former football player, Gerald made an open field tackle on Bernie just as he was about to step in front of an oncoming car. Gerald was a wiry and muscular ex-athlete with curly hair and a firm protruding jaw. I first met him in the fall of 1969 when he and Bernie drove up to Boston from New Britain, Connecticut, in Bernie's yellow VW bug and walked into an amyl nitrate party that Danny Cooper was hosting at our Buswell Street apartment.

Danny had nearly enough credits to graduate from Northeastern the following June and had already been accepted to Georgetown Dental School, so he had decided to take the fall quarter off and was working as an assistant in a chemical lab. He was smuggling out mason jars full of liquid amyl nitrate and was throwing parties at our apartment every Friday night. We always had a good turnout. We would sit in a circle on the floor and pass the jar to one another. The whole idea was to put your nose into the jar and inhale as deep and as fast as you could. Danny once even took a jar to a NU Husky football game, and we passed it around in the stands. As Bernie described his experience later, "I felt my head being ripped from my body. It raced out the door and into the street where it flew through Kenmore Square down Commonwealth Avenue into the Boston Commons before it turned around, ran through the Public Gardens, and was then jet-propelled up Newbury Street, finally blasting into the air and landing back on my shoulders."

"I thought I was going to die," he told me, "but I did it one more time because I didn't want anyone to think I wasn't cool."

After a weekend of pot, amyl nitrate, and some mind-blowing hash, Bernie drove back to New Britain, where he was attending Central Connecticut. Gerald stayed in Boston, moving in with two of my fraternity brothers, Miles Jaffe and Jon Holderman, who had just leased an apartment on Beacon Street and were looking for a third roommate to split the rent. We became friends that year. Gerald moved back to Oneonta in the fall of 1971 to be with his mother after his father died. When Jane and I moved into Hubcap Harvey's house, he and his friends became regular visitors and honorary members of the Franklin Mountain Liberation Front.

Now that I was hanging in Oneonta and living out of my car, I was becoming part of the local townie scene. There was Hank Marino and Delta McDaniel, who, along with Gerald, had been friends with Bernie when he was attending Cobleskill, a junior college about an hour east of Oneonta on Route 7. There was Groovy Mann and his brother Space Mann. Groovy's real name was Steve, and he worked at Bailey Ceramics with Mike Stone. Mike had given him his nickname because Steve, a former star running back at Oneonta High, was the straightest guy in town. Groovy's brother Larry was another story. High most of the time and often detached from reality, Space Mann's name needed no explanation. Another local character was a pale, skinny six-foot six-inch hippie named Louie O'Malley, who was nearly thirty years old. He hung with two other longhairs that were even taller than him, Jack Robertson and Phil Riker. Jack, at six feet nine, was my age and had been a legendary basketball star at Franklin High School. Phil was a muscular six feet eight with sandy shoulder-length hair. They were good friends to have in times of trouble. One night at The Silver, I was being harassed at the bar by a large dude who was mouthing off about my long hair and trying to start a fight with me. Louie, Jack, and Phil were sitting a few stools away, and when this asshole started getting loud, the three of them walked over and asked him if there was a problem. The asshole said no and bought all four of us a beer.

My other local connection was Dick Dickson, who seemed to know everyone and was plugged into the Oneonta counterculture. Dick and I graduated together from Sidney High in 1966, but we had never really hung out together. Like Ozzie, Dick marched to the beat of a different drum. During high school, he formed a band called the Mad Tones with his best friend Ted Morris. He played bass guitar, while Ted played drums and sang lead vocals. Like Ozzie, Dick fancied himself a beatnik. We reconnected accidently. I was working nights as a janitor at the Harvard School of Public Health on Huntington Avenue during my final year at Northeastern, when while stoned and mopping the front lobby, I saw someone who looked like Dick Dickson on the sidewalk outside, walking past the building. I ran out the door and shouted his name. It turned out that I wasn't hallucinating. It really was Dick Dickson. We became friends that winter. Dick was teaching at a predominately black school in Boston. He had just married Gloria, a mysterious woman with jet-black hair and gigantic breasts, but by the following summer, they were divorced and Dick was back in Upstate New York. By the spring of 1972, he was living and working in Cooperstown, having become certified as an inhalation therapist at Bassett Hospital. Unlike all my other friends, Dick did not smoke pot or do any other drugs. He also had short hair.

"Everyone has long hair," he once said. "I wear mine short as a protest."

Dick and I could talk for hours. Literature, politics, baseball, it didn't matter. He had a small apartment just a block off Main Street in Cooperstown, not far from the Baseball Hall of Fame. One night after all the bars had closed, we moved our conversation to the outfield grass of Doubleday Field. The last time that I had been on Doubleday Field was when I was seventeen and had pitched a combined no-hitter with my flame-throwing friend Henry Cable in an American Legion game. Now, seven years later, I had a six-pack of Genesee, and Dick was obsessing over alternate forms of shelter. He insisted that I learn about Bucky Fuller and geodesic domes. He went on and on about yurts, which he explained were used by nomads in Central Asia. We debated the articles that I had written for *Seeds*. We talked about Neal Bennett and his Free School. He urged me to read Richard Wright's *The Outsider*, which he claimed was the modern-day equal of Dostoyevsky's *Crime and Punishment*. Dick wondered what it would be like to fake his own death and become a new person with a new identity. We polished off the six-pack, and I slept on his couch that night.

Dick introduced me to Judd and Mary Foster, who were originally from Bainbridge but were now living in an old house in Mt. Vision, a few miles north of the west end of Oneonta. Judd was something of a pariah in the local scene, having set up his friend Joey Logan for a drug bust in order to save his own ass. Joey, a basketball teammate of mine in high school, was now serving two years in Ossining. I wasn't aware of this until Dick told me, having been in Boston when all this went down. Dick was one of Judd's few remaining friends, though I didn't know why. What I did know was that there was a free spirit named Sharon Wessel living with Judd and Mary, and I ended up in bed with her a few days later. Sharon was from Long Island and a recent graduate of Oneonta State. The girl was perpetually happy. For some reason, Sharon thought I was funny and seemed to laugh at everything I said.

"You're an optimistic pessimist," she said one afternoon as we were rolling around naked in her lumpy bed.

"What do you mean?" I asked.

"You know your life sucks," she said, "but you're convinced that it will get better."

I buried my face in Sharon's tits. They were enormous, bigger than any that I had ever buried my face in before. *Yeah,* I thought, *Sharon is right. My life is definitely getting better.*

Actually, my life was pretty good right now. I partied every day with Gerald and his friends. No one seemed to have a job. My nights were mostly spent in The Silver, and I was getting a lot better at eight ball. Three or four quarters lasted me all night. I was also getting laid more now than at any other time in my life. If all else failed, I was always welcome in Julie Tyler's bed, and that's where I ended up at least two or three times a week. One afternoon, I ran into Kim Darling, one of Dick's former girlfriends. Like Judd and Mary, she was from Bainbridge but was now living in a trailer in West Davenport, a few miles east of Oneonta. When I told her that Jane and I had split up, she invited me back to her trailer. I spent the night. Kim was pretty, petite, and very shy. She insisted that we keep the lights off when we made love, and in the morning, when the room filled with light, she pulled the sheets up to her chin. Sadly, I never got to see her naked body. My hands, my tongue, and my cock were happy, but my eyes felt cheated. She asked me to turn away when she got out of bed to get dressed. She made me breakfast, we kissed goodbye, and I drove back to Oneonta. I decided to go by Get Stoned Leather. As I turned the corner into the alley, I saw my brother Bernie standing at the door, telling his story to Ozzie, Mike, and Renee.

10

His story went something like this:

He and Gerald had gone west during the summer of 1971, camping, hiking, and doing acid but only making it as far as Colorado and the Rocky Mountains. Bernie had always dreamed of going to California, so when Tommy Grant told him that he was going to Southern California to check out the golfing scene, Bernie was happy to accept a ride.

California had not turned out to be so great for Bernie. He and Tommy ended up in a two-room, dirt-floor shack in Solana Beach, just north of San Diego. Tommy, who had been a collegiate golfer at Colgate University and seemed to have a plan, found a caddying job at Torrey Pines. Bernie, on the other hand, didn't have a plan and couldn't find a job. More importantly, he wasn't getting laid. He was collecting $1.76 a day on welfare, which was just enough for him to purchase one big meal a day at an all-you-can-eat restaurant. Hungry and horny, he decided it was time to leave Tommy and California and hitchhike to Florida.

He was almost killed in the desert outside of Tucson, Arizona. Bernie was trucking along the side of the road with his backpack and sleeping bag when a pickup truck with a gun rack, going in the other direction, slowed down as it approached him. As the pickup rolled by, the driver and two passengers began hurling beer bottles and obscenities.

"You fucking faggot!" they shouted. "We're going to kill your faggot ass."

They drove about a quarter mile past him and made a screeching U-turn. Bernie weighed his options. He could either wait to get the shit kicked out of him or make a run for it. He chose life over death. It was near dusk and would soon be dark. Bernie hauled ass through the sand and scrub brush, dodging each giant cactus and looking for a place to hide. He kept running until he could no longer hear their voices. As darkness set in, he laid his sleeping bag beside a seven-foot-tall cactus and crawled in for the long night, zipping the bag over his head. It got real cold, and Bernie was scared shitless. He never fell asleep. All night, he felt things crawling over and around him. Still, he figured that this had to be better than getting beaten to death.

Five nights later, he arrived in Indian Rocks Beach.

Our parents had moved to Florida in September of 1971. They bought a two-story, four-unit apartment motel on the beach along Gulf Boulevard and named it *Dreams Come True*. They moved into one of the downstairs apartments and rented out the other three, either by the week or by the month. At the age of forty-nine, Dad had quit his job of thirty-two years. They sold their house and most of their possessions, keeping only what they could stuff in their car, and headed off to pursue their Florida dream. Dad had lived in Sidney since he was three years old, leaving only for two years in the Navy during World War II. All their friends thought they were crazy.

Mom and Dad were not home when Bernie arrived on the scene, so he spread out his sleeping bag on their seawall and kicked back to enjoy the sweet and salty smell of the Gulf of Mexico. He fell asleep, only to be awakened by someone poking his arm.

"You can't sleep here, fella," the man said. "This is private property."

"Hi, Dad," said Bernie.

Bernie slept on the sofa bed in the living room that night, but Dad moved him to the vacant upstairs apartment the next morning.

"You can stay here until we get a renter," he said, handing him the key.

It was Bernie's lucky day. There were four college-age girls staying in the other upstairs unit. They were coming down the stairs in their bikinis just as he was heading up the stairs to check out his new place to crash. All four smiled at him as they passed him on the stairs, but Bernie only noticed the prettiest one. For Bernie, it was love at first sight. He didn't waste any time. He unlocked the apartment door, tossed in the backpack that contained everything he owned, took off his sneakers and socks, ripped off his tattered T-shirt, and raced out the door, wearing only his cutoff shorts. When he reached the beach, the four girls were lying on their towels. Two were faceup, and two were facedown. The prettiest one was on her stomach, and she had untied the straps of her bikini top, revealing the sides of her breasts. Bernie walked past them and took a seat in the sand about twenty feet away. He pretended not to notice them, but they soon noticed him.

"Hey, you!" one of them shouted. "Do you want to get high?"

Bernie turned around, only to see all four of them waving at him. The prettiest one had rolled over, but her bikini top had not rolled over with her. He waved back at the four of them, smiled, and nodded. He couldn't take his eyes off her breasts. As soon as he got up and started walking toward them, the prettiest one turned away and rolled back over onto her stomach. Two joints later, Bernie learned that they were from Ann Arbor, Michigan, and they were here for one week. He told them his story: that he had been living in California and had come to visit his parents who owned the motel. The rest of the week, he was either in their apartment or with them on the beach. It took him three days to get into bed with the pretty one, whose name was Darlene. The other three wanted to fuck him too. Whenever he was in their apartment, they were always smoking joints and parading around topless in front of him. Sometimes one of the three would step out of the shower and walk through the living room, giggle, and act surprised that Bernie was there. As much as he was enjoying the scenery, he was still only interested in Darlene. His patience and willpower finally paid off. Bernie was wasted and had gone back to his apartment when he heard a knock at the door.

After three days of topless, Bernie was staring at bottomless.

"Can I come in?" she asked.

Three days later, Bernie's Penis was on its way to Michigan, stuffed into the back seat of a Chevy Impala with Bernie, heading north on Interstate 75. Darlene had asked Bernie to come home with her. Bernie and Bernie's Penis had debated the pros and cons of leaving Indian Rocks Beach, but it was Bernie's Penis who made the strongest case. Together, they and the four girls drove nonstop to Ann Arbor, arriving at midnight in twenty-three-degree weather.

Exhausted and too tired for sex, Darlene and Bernie went straight to bed. When Bernie woke up, she was gone.

"Where did she go?' asked Bernie's Penis.

"I don't know," Bernie replied.

Darlene returned two days later. When she did, she told Bernie that they were going over to her friend Tom's apartment. When they got there, Tom pulled out a hash pipe, and they all got high. Darlene and Tom started making out, and then they got up and walked into the bedroom. They closed the door and were in there for about thirty minutes.

"What are we doing here?" asked Bernie's Penis.

"I don't know," Bernie replied.

When she came out of the bedroom, she tossed Bernie her car keys and told him that she would see him tomorrow.

Tomorrow was Thursday, and Thursday was another lucky day for Bernie. He and Darlene spent the entire day in bed. Bernie's Penis thought he had died and gone to heaven.

"Where have you been?" asked Bernie. "I thought that we were living together."

As it turned out, they were living together, but only on Thursdays. Darlene patiently explained to Bernie that she lived together with several guys in Ann Arbor and that she had asked Bernie to leave Florida and come live with her because she had an opening on Thursdays.

"I broke up with Jim last month," she said, "so I needed to find another Thursday guy. When I saw you on the beach, I knew you and I would be perfect together."

She left early on Friday morning, but to Bernie's surprise, she showed up unexpectedly on Sunday afternoon.

"Let's go," she said. "There is someone I want you to meet."

This time, his name was Michael. Once again, the three of them got high. Then Darlene and Michael headed off to the bedroom. This time, she was gone nearly an hour.

"That's it!" screamed Bernie's Penis. "I can't take this anymore."

"Hey," replied Bernie. "Coming to Michigan was your idea, not mine."

They argued for a while. As much as Bernie's Penis enjoyed Thursdays, the other six days were torture. Bernie, on the other hand, was captivated by her beauty. Darlene was a gorgeous creature, and he was convinced that he could pick up another day or two as time went on.

"No way," said Bernie's Penis. "What am I supposed to do the rest of the time?"

Bernie had lost every argument that he had ever had with Bernie's Penis, and this time was no different. The next morning, they decided to hitchhike back to the Sunshine State.

"This is the last time that I am going to listen to you," said Bernie.

"I doubt that," said Bernie's Penis.

Bernie's return trip to Indian Rocks Beach turned out to be a miserable three-day ordeal. When he stuck out his thumb that morning, he was met by a cold driving horizontal rain. It took him nearly four hours to get his first ride, and by nightfall, he had made it only to the outskirts of Toledo, Ohio, less than fifty miles from Ann Arbor. It wasn't until around midnight, when the rain had finally stopped, that Bernie was picked by an eighteen-wheeler headed south all the way to Knoxville, Tennessee, on I-75. When he scored his final ride in Tampa from a VW van loaded with six hippies smoking some killer weed, he figured he would be staying in Florida for a while. However, when he walked in the door of *Dreams Come True*, Mom handed him an envelope containing a letter from Ozzie. Bernie read the letter.

Bernie,

*Get your ass up here to Oneonta. I've got a place for you to stay. Meet me
at Get Stoned Leather. There are college chicks everywhere.*

Power to the people,
Ozzie

Bernie was back on the sofa bed. He crashed there for nearly fifteen hours, and when he woke up, he discovered that Mom had washed all his filthy clothes and had stacked them neatly on the floor next to his backpack. She made him a huge breakfast of scrambled eggs, bacon, pancakes, and toast, and as he finished off a large glass of Florida orange juice, he broke the news to her that he would be leaving the next day for Oneonta. Mom was upset, but Bernie assured her that he had a plan this time. He told her that Ozzie already had a place for him to stay and, knowing Ozzie, probably also had a job lined up for him. He left the next morning.

It took him three rides and the first day to make it into South Carolina. His last ride dropped him off near the town of Gaffney on I-85, not far from the North Carolina border. He stood there with his thumb out for almost two hours before a car finally stopped. A rusted-out Ford Fairlane with Georgia plates and a dented rear bumper pulled over to the shoulder. It was getting dark, and Bernie needed a ride. Without hesitating, he opened the front door on the passenger side, tossed his backpack into the back seat, and jumped into the front. Before he could pull his door shut, the Fairlane peeled out, jerking his head violently against the front seat. When Bernie turned to look at the driver, he knew he was in trouble. He was a short stocky man, probably in his late thirties, and he smelled really bad. He turned his head to Bernie and smiled. Most of his teeth were missing, and the few that were left were brown and rotting.

"I just killed three people," he said, "and I'm going to kill you too."

The car was already moving at seventy miles per hour, so jumping out was not an option. The man reached under his seat and pulled out a pistol. He waved the gun in Bernie's face.

"Don't try to get away," he said, "or I'll blow your fucking brains out."

Bernie had never smelled anything or anyone so foul. The man's breath smelled of vomit, and his body odor was overpowering. It was as if Right Guard had come up with a new formula for deodorant containing rotten eggs, urine, and diaper shit and then sprayed the entire can inside the car. Bernie reached for the door handle.

Jumping from a moving car at seventy miles per hour now seemed to be a better option than death by armpit asphyxiation or a bullet to the head. Unfortunately, the door handle was missing.

"That's right, you little fucker," he said. "You ain't goin' nowhere."

They got off the interstate at the next exit and spent the entire night driving along deserted country roads. Bernie had no idea where he was. When he told the man he had to pee, the man pulled over, stepped out of the car, and told Bernie to climb out on the driver's side. It was the first time that Bernie had ever pissed with a gun held to his head.

Somehow, Bernie managed to stay alive for the next two days and nights. Whenever they stopped for gas, the man told Bernie to stay in the car. If they had to piss, then they did it on a back road with no one around and always with a gun to Bernie's head. The man had several Cokes and a few bags of potato chips in the back seat, and he shared them with Bernie. It wasn't much, but Bernie's stomach was in knots, and he did not have much of an appetite. Bernie stayed awake, knowing that the man would eventually need to sleep and figuring that he would try to make his escape then. However, the man was wired on something and for two days did not appear to be getting tired in the least. Bernie kept the man talking, hoping that by pretending to be interested in his story, he could keep from getting killed. Finally, on the third day, as it was getting dark, the man pulled on to a dusty dirt road and turned off the car.

"Are you going to shoot me?" asked Bernie.

"Yes, but not right now," the man replied.

"Why are we stopping?" asked Bernie.

"Not that it's any of your fucking business," the man said, "but I need to get some sleep."

The man took his pistol and pointed it at Bernie's head. "If you try to escape," he said, "you're a dead man."

"I'm not going anywhere," said Bernie.

The man rested the gun on his stomach and covered it with both hands. He soon fell into a deep sleep, snoring loudly and drooling from one side of his mouth. Bernie weighed his options. There was no way for him to open the passenger door, but he was able to roll his window down about two-thirds of the way. He rolled it slowly, hoping not to wake up the man. It would be a tight fit, but Bernie felt he could squeeze his body through the partially open window and make his way to freedom. He would have to leave behind his backpack that was in the back seat, but that was a small price to pay to stay alive. He managed to squirm his way out the window without waking the man, and he hit the ground running. He ran into the surrounding woods and kept running for at least thirty minutes until he collapsed to the ground in exhaustion. He slept in the woods that night and the next morning walked about an hour until he came to a highway. It turned out he was in Virginia now, and his luck was about to change. He quickly got a ride to I-81 just outside of Roanoke and was picked up by a trucker who was going all the way to Harrisburg, Pennsylvania. He got another ride all the way to Binghamton, New York, where a college student from Oneonta State picked him up and drove all the way to the corner of Chestnut and Main.

The sun broke through the clouds just as Bernie stepped out of the car. He smiled, thanked the college dude for the ride, and walked to the alley behind Palombo's Liquor Store. It didn't matter that he was tired, dirty, and hungry. He was alive and ready to see his new home.

11

Ozzie pulled a joint from behind his ear and handed it to Bernie.

"Far out," he said. "Do you want to get wasted?"

Bernie nodded, and Ozzie handed him a book of matches. Mike and Renee went back inside the store. "Yeah, it's cool," Bernie said. "I lost all my shit, but I'm alive and ready to start my new life. Where is this place that you have for me to stay?"

"Light the joint, and I'll show you," said Ozzie.

Bernie fired it up, took a hit, and passed it to me. I took a hit and passed it to Ozzie, who took a hit and then motioned to Bernie to follow him into the store. Mike and Renee started laughing. Ozzie opened the door to the back room.

"This is where I'm crashing," Ozzie said, pointing to the mattress on the floor inside the closet. "Mike and Renee sleep here," he continued, pointing to the waterbed in the middle of the room.

"That's great" said Bernie, "but you told me that you had a place for me to stay."

"Hey, man, I do," answered Ozzie.

Ozzie took another big hit and blew the smoke in Bernie's face. Walking over to the entrance to the closet, he grabbed a small ladder that was leaning against the wall, looked up, and pointed.

"Hey, man, you got the Top Shelf," he said, handing Bernie the ladder.

Too exhausted to argue, Bernie accepted it and placed it against the Top Shelf.

"I need to crash," he said, starting up the ladder.

"You need a shower," I countered. "You smell like shit."

Bernie didn't say a word. When he reached the Top Shelf, Ozzie tossed him a sleeping bag, which he caught with one hand, unrolled, and pushed into the narrow opening. He crawled in and was asleep in a matter of minutes. Ozzie sat down on his mattress, picked up his sketch pad, and started drawing. I turned and walked back into the store where Mike and Renee were working on some leather wallets. I walked outside. It was a perfect day, sunny and in the midsixties, and I had a good buzz. I decided to walk over to Neahwa Park. When I got there, I found Gerald, Hank Marino, Space Mann, and two other longhairs I didn't know tossing around a Frisbee. I joined in and told them that Bernie was back in town.

"He's lost his backpack," I said, "and he doesn't have any of his clothes or other shit."

"Where's he crashing?" asked Gerald.

I told them that he was staying on the Top Shelf in Ozzie's closet at Get Stoned Leather. Space Mann thought that was the coolest thing he'd ever heard. Gerald said that they would go get him and bring him to the park, but I told them that Bernie was sleeping and that they should wait until later in the afternoon.

"He smells real bad," I said, "and could use a shower."

"He can come up to my mom's house and shower," said Gerald.

I tossed the Frisbee with them for a few more minutes and decided to split. The Silver opened at eleven, and I could get a beer and a sandwich there. I was almost to the door when I ran into Phyllis Van Dyke. She wanted to know where Ozzie was, and I lied to her and told her I didn't know. She asked where I was going, and I said that I was hungry and I needed a shower. Phyllis shared a house on Elm Street with Penelope Jessup and Alex and Nancy Kayne, and I had stayed on their couch a number of times. Phyllis said that I could shower at their place, and I told her that I would take her up on that later, but first I needed to grab something to eat at The Silver. When I walked in, Louie O'Malley was sitting alone at the bar, nursing a beer. I ordered a draft and a grilled cheese sandwich, and Gary, the bartender, went back into the kitchen to make my lunch. I chugged my beer, and when Gary came out with my grilled cheese, I ordered another draft. Louie asked what was happening, and I told him about Bernie, the Top Shelf, and running into Gerald, Hank, and Space Mann. I finished the sandwich and beer and told Louie that I had to split and go get a shower. When I got to the house, Phyllis was the only one there. She told me that Penelope, Alex, and Nancy were all in class. She handed me a towel, and I went into the bathroom, took off my clothes, and took a healthy shit. When I finished, I stepped into the bathtub, closed the shower curtain, got the water as hot as I could stand it, and stood under the shower for at least ten minutes before I started washing myself. When I turned off the water and pulled back the shower curtain, Phyllis, fully clothed, handed me the towel. She asked if she could suck my cock. Before I could answer, she grabbed my dick and pulled on it really hard. It hurt like hell. I now knew why Ozzie was so pissed off at me.

I was not attracted to Phyllis in the least, and besides still being a little stoned, it had only been a few hours since I had been inside Kim Darling. I wanted to tell her no, but she had a hold of my balls, and I was afraid of what she might do if I made her angry. I definitely was not getting hard. I figured that Phyllis must be left-handed, because she kept a firm grip on my balls with her right hand while she yanked on my soft and terrified dick with her left. Slowly, it began to rise. She spit on her left hand and began to stroke me, starting slowly and then increasing the pace, all the time squeezing my balls tighter and tighter. I was in pain, but it was starting to feel good. I screamed, and she put me in her mouth and sucked violently. I could feel her teeth scraping both sides of my erection. Horrified, I screamed again and then exploded. I kept coming and coming, and the room began to spin. My knees buckled, and as Phyllis let go of my balls and released me from the clutches of her teeth, I felt myself falling backward. I tried to break my fall by grabbing the shower curtain, but I landed on my ass in the bathtub with my legs straight in the air and the shower rod and curtain on top of me. Gasping for air, I looked down at my wounded and terrified penis. I saw blood.

"W-w-w-would you like me to eat your pussy?" I stuttered as I tried to untangle myself from the shower curtain.

"No," she said, removing her glasses with her right hand and wiping her chin with her left. She stood up, tossed me my towel, and walked out of the bathroom.

"Thanks," she said, closing the door behind her.

I sat in the tub and turned on the cold water. I could barely breathe. I splashed my dick and watched as the blood circled down the drain. I sat there for several minutes, hoping to get my strength back. Sore as hell, I finally stepped out of the tub, dried myself off, and got dressed. I opened the bathroom door and looked around. The coast was clear. I could hear Phyllis doing something in the kitchen, so I made a mad dash for the front door. I burst out the door, jumped off the porch, and ran as fast as I could to The Silver, where Louie was waiting for me at the bar, nursing another beer. He looked at me and my sweat-soaked T-shirt.

"I thought you were going to take a shower," he said.

"I need a beer."

By six o'clock, The Silver was packed, and I was on my seventh beer. Louie was playing pool and had won five or six games in a row. I had tried playing, but it hurt to bend over the table, and I scratched the eight ball on my second shot. The beers were starting to dull the pain in my crotch. I had to pee, so I went to the head. Standing at the urinal, I unzipped my jeans, gingerly pulled out my limp penis, held it gently in my hand, and took a look. It was red and raw, and I realized that I needed to give it the night off. As I was walking out of the men's room, I saw Bernie coming in the door, followed by Space Mann, Hank, and Gerald. Bernie looked like a new person. He had gotten several hours sleep, had showered at Gerald's house, and was wearing the clean clothes that Gerald had given him. I joined them at the bar, and we ordered a pitcher of beer. Ozzie strolled in a few minutes later. "Sunshine of Your Love" was blaring from the jukebox, and my head was starting to pound. I felt a tap on my shoulder, and when I turned around, Alex was glaring at me with Nancy, Phyllis, and Penelope standing right behind him.

"Phyllis says you are the one that fucked up our shower," was all he said before he turned and walked away. Phyllis just looked at me with a straight face and shrugged her shoulders. I could feel myself fading fast. The only thing that could make it worse would be for Julie to suddenly show up. She and Phyllis were friends. I turned around and tried to talk to Bernie, but he was zeroing in on a pretty college girl who was now standing next to him and hanging on to his

48

every word. She had long blond hair and big blue eyes, and Bernie was turning on the charm and trying to get her to go back with him to Get Stoned Leather. The music seemed to get louder and louder, and The Silver began to turn like a merry-go-round. I heard the pretty college girl ask Bernie where he lived, and Bernie reply that he lived on the Top Shelf. She laughed and asked again. Bernie gave her the same answer. She laughed again and told Bernie that she thought he was funny, but seriously she wanted to know where he lived. No matter how many times she asked, Bernie's answer was always the same: the Top Shelf. I chugged another glass of beer. The pretty college girl suddenly backed away from Bernie. Her face had the stunned look of someone who just realized that she might be talking to a member of the Manson family. As she moved away from the bar, Ozzie saw his opening and moved in for the kill.

"You and your weird friend stay away from me," she said as she pushed him away. She grabbed the arm of one of her friends who was also a pretty college girl with long blond hair and pulled her toward the door.

I needed to leave before things got worse, but where was I going to go? I was too drunk to negotiate the Falcon all the way to Cooperstown and Dick Dickson's couch. If I headed for Julie's place, she would want to have sex, and I wasn't about to show her my red and raw penis or explain how it got that way. Alex was pissed at me, and Phyllis scared the shit out of me, so asking to crash on their couch wasn't about to happen. I felt like I was going to puke, so I rushed toward the door, knocking Louie's elbow as I brushed past the pool table and causing him to miss his shot. He called me an asshole, or at least that's what it sounded like, as I staggered out the door. The Falcon was parked a few blocks away, and luckily, I remembered where. I got in, started the engine, and headed out Chestnut Street toward the West End. I woke the next morning to find myself in the back seat of the Falcon with a stiff neck and my mouth as dry as cotton. Confused, I looked around and realized I had no idea where I was. It took me a while before I finally figured out that I was parked on a side street in Otego. I didn't remember driving there, and I had no idea what time it was. I drove back into Oneonta but decided it would be a better idea to keep going to Cooperstown. I needed to lie low for a few days, and Dick Dickson would let me use his couch.

I stayed in Cooperstown for three days. I needed to rest and recuperate. There were bookshelves on every wall in Dick's apartment, and they were packed to the max with both hardcovers and paperbacks. I figured that I would spend my days reading while Dick was working at the hospital. Dick suggested that I read a book called *Deliverance* by James Dickey, an author I had never heard of. It was about four friends on a canoe trip down a river in Georgia. One of them gets raped up the ass by a hillbilly, and another gets killed. I couldn't put it down. I read it in less than two days, stopping only to sleep or go drinking with Dick. Rested and relaxed, I finally built up the courage to go back to Oneonta. When I arrived, I went straight to Get Stoned Leather, where I found Ozzie sitting on the steps, smoking a cigarette.

"Your brother is an asshole," he said.

When I asked him why, he told me that Bernie had been picking up college chicks at The Silver the past three nights and bringing them back to the closet. I told Ozzie that I didn't see what the big deal was, since that's where Bernie was staying. Ozzie was adamant.

"You don't understand," he said. "He and the chicks take my mattress and make me sleep on the Top Shelf. It's my closet, not his. He's an asshole."

Just then, Gerald and Bernie came racing around the corner into the alley.

"It's Race Track," Gerald said. "He's in trouble."

12

His real name was Mark Goodyear, and he had been a star baseball player at Oneonta High School. In his junior year, in a game against Norwich, he had come to bat in the bottom of the seventh inning with two outs, the bases empty, and the score tied 2–2. On a 3-0 pitch, he ignored the coach's sign to take the pitch and took a wild swing at what would have been ball 4. He connected with a line drive between first and second, which the right fielder picked up on two hops. Not content with first base and oblivious to the first base coach's stop sign, he never broke stride as he rounded first and headed to second base. He slid in headfirst as the errant throw skipped past the shortstop's glove and into left field. Not content with second base and unfazed by the left fielder who had backed up the throw and was holding the ball, Mark jumped to his feet and headed to third base as the third base coach frantically held up another stop sign and screamed for him to go back. The left fielder's throw arrived at third base well before Mark, who came sliding in with his cleats in the air like the ghost of Ty Cobb. The third baseman applied the tag but was unable to hold on to the ball. The umpire signaled safe as the ball dribbled through the coach's box and toward the Norwich dugout. Ignoring the third base coach's instructions to stay where he was, Mark got up and headed to home. The Norwich catcher was waiting for him, but Mark arrived at home plate at the same time as the throw, knocking the catcher on his ass and the ball from his glove as Mark's left foot touched the plate. Oneonta had won, and Mark Goodyear was the hero. However, Coach Gurley was not amused, and back in the locker room, he tore into Mark.

"Goodyear!" he shouted. "What the hell do you think you are doing? This is a baseball field, not a goddamn race track!"

Mark Goodyear was suspended for the rest of the year. The name stuck.

Bernie's first encounter with Race Track was during his last semester at Cobleskill when he and Gerald were sharing an apartment off campus. Race Track came up from Oneonta on a Wednesday night to stay with Gerald and party for a few days. The first night they drank beer and smoked pot until around three in the morning. Bernie and Gerald had several classes the next day, and somehow they managed to drag themselves out of bed in the morning and make it to school on time. While they were gone, Race Track decided to repay them for their hospitality and paint their apartment. When they returned from campus late in the afternoon, they discovered that every drab off-white wall had been painted a bright day-glow orange.

"What do you think?" asked Race Track, obviously pleased with his psychedelic masterpiece.

Bernie and Gerald didn't know what to say. Any hope of getting their security deposit back at the end of the semester had vanished. Race Track fired up a joint and turned on the stereo.

"Do you guys have any munchies food?" he asked.

I met him for the first time the following winter when Bernie brought Gerald, Hank Marino, Delta McDaniel, and the one and only Race Track to our house in Sidney over Christmas break. They had driven down from Oneonta in a snowstorm with a bag of weed and a craving for Dad's homemade dandelion wine that Bernie had been bragging to them about. As it turned out, Mom and Dad had gone out for the evening, leaving the house and Dad's bar in the basement unprotected.

We rolled the joints in the basement, but we had enough sense not to smoke in the house. Instead, we went outside and stood in a circle in a foot of snow in the backyard. By our third joint, we were cold, wet, and wasted. We decided it was time for dandelion wine. We went back inside and down to the basement, and the party began. Bernie put "Light My Fire" on the record player, and we played it over and over. The six of us were on our sixth bottle when we heard Mom and Dad come in the back door. Mom was the first one down the stairs, and we all tried to act normal. After Bernie introduced all his friends to Mom, Race Track immediately started a conversation with her and told her how much he liked our house. As she turned to go back upstairs, Dad appeared, pleased to see us drinking his wine. He looked straight at Race Track.

"How do you like my wine?" he asked.

"Oh, I don't know," replied Race Track. "She seems really nice."

Race Track had heard "wife," not "wine."

Dad looked around the room at this motley crew, with their long hair, bloodshot eyes, and five empty wine bottles. Not knowing what to say or what to do, he shook his head, smiled, and turned to walk up the stairs.

"It was nice to meet you, Mr. Hesse," said Race Track.

13

Gerald and Bernie were in a panic.

"Race Track is in the nuthouse in Binghamton!" Gerald shouted.

Race Track had been playing third base in a pickup game up at Hartwick College, when, for no apparent reason, he had decided to take all his clothes off and play the rest of the game in the nude. The game went on, and none of the other players seemed to mind, but a woman who was watching the game with her two small children was shocked at sight of the hairy naked third baseman and called the police. Race Track was arrested and taken to the jail in Cooperstown where they decided he should be sent to the state hospital in Binghamton for evaluation. While he was at the Cooperstown jail, a couple of deputies had tried to get him to sign some papers that would have given them ownership of a portion of the land that Race Track had inherited from his father. His father had died when Race Track was in ninth grade. His mother had been in a mental hospital since he was eight years old, and he had not visited her in years. Race Track had no job, no money, and was living in a tent on his fifty acres a few miles outside of West Oneonta. He rode his bicycle to town every day to hang out with his friends and get high.

Race Track's land had been in the Goodyear family for nearly two hundred years. Shortly after the American Revolution, Jeremiah Goodyear was among the first settlers of an area near Otsdawa Creek, which was now part of the town of Otego. Originally called Huntsville, the name was changed to Otego in 1830.

Gerald pleaded his case. "One of us needs to buy some land from Race Track. Otherwise, he is going to get screwed by the cops. He needs some money."

Gerald had gone to Binghamton to see him. Race Track had told him that he was going to sell six acres for a thousand dollars to the cops in Cooperstown when he got out.

"I don't have any money," said Bernie.

The three of us all looked at Ozzie.

"Ozzie," said Bernie, "you're rich. You have all that money that you inherited from your aunt in England. Why don't you buy the land from Race Track?"

Ozzie muttered something under his breath and then said that he was good for five hundred dollars if someone else could come up with the rest. After some thought, I volunteered to go in halves with him. A few weeks earlier, I had received a thousand-dollar money order from my parents. After the fire, I had tried talking them into making a claim with their insurance company for the furniture that had been lost. After all, I reasoned, it had actually been their furniture, and they could just tell their insurance agent that they had been storing it at my house. Whether or not they actually put in a claim or got any insurance money, I don't know, but when I called collect, Dad said that they were sending me a thousand dollars. I cashed the money order and then called Jane's mother to get her address. I felt bad because I think her mother thought that I wanted to get back together with Jane. I mailed Jane a money order for five hundred dollars. With the money I had left, I was now about to buy some land.

Four days later, Race Track rode his bicycle into Oneonta a free man. All charges had been dropped. He went straight to Gerald's house where Gerald informed him that Ozzie and I were ready to give him a thousand dollars in cash in exchange for six acres. The next morning, Gerald told Ozzie and me to meet Race Track at eleven o'clock at Karl Silvestri's law office on Main Street. When we walked into Karl's office, Race Track was sitting in a chair, holding what looked like a Santa Claus mask in his left hand. Ozzie and I just looked at each other and shrugged our shoulders. He was Race Track, after all. We turned our attention to Karl, who had handled Mr. Goodyear's will and the transfer of his land to Race Track. Karl Silvestri was Oneonta's hippie lawyer. He was around forty-five years old, had shoulder-length silver hair, and was whom you called if you were a college student or young townie in trouble. Neither Ozzie nor I had seen the land that we were about to buy, but Race Track assured us that we were getting some prime real estate.

"The section that I'm selling you," he said, "has a pond on it."

Race Track had one condition before he would sign the papers.

"I only need five hundred dollars today," he said. "I'll let you know when I need the rest."

"Ozzie," I said, "give him your five hundred. I'll give him mine later."

Ozzie reluctantly reached into his pocket and pulled out a roll of twenty-dollar bills. We all shook hands and signed the papers. Race Track grabbed the roll of bills and bolted for the door.

Ozzie turned to Karl.

"Can you draw us a map of how to find the land?" he asked.

Ozzie and I were excited. Map in hand, we ran back to Get Stoned Leather where we found Bernie and Gerald sitting on the steps.

"Let's go check out our land," I said.

Since I was the only one with a car, we piled into my Falcon, which was parked around the corner from the store. Ozzie wanted shotgun, but since Gerald was the only one who knew where we were going, I told Ozzie to get in the back seat and let Gerald have the front. Bernie jumped in last, and we headed out Chestnut Street. Gerald put my Paul McCartney tape into the tape player and turned up the volume. "Uncle Albert" took over the Falcon. Ozzie had brought rolling papers and a small bag of grass, and he and Bernie took turns rolling joints in the back seat. When we got to the light where Route 7 turned left toward Otego, Gerald motioned me to keep going straight. This was the way to the house in Mt. Vision where I had rolled around in bed with Sharon Wessel and her wonderful beautiful big tits, but instead of continuing straight toward Mt. Vision, we veered to the left a mile or so later, staying on Route 23, which was the way to Morris. When we drove into the tiny village of West Oneonta, Gerald told me to take a left onto a county road, which, according to Karl Silvestri's map, was County Road 8. We drove several miles past scattered homes and farmhouses, gradually gaining in elevation until we came to the intersection of a dirt road. Ozzie lit a joint.

"This is Mud Road," Gerald said. "Race Track's land is about a mile down from here."

I turned right onto Mud Road, and Ozzie passed me the joint. I took a hit and passed it over to Gerald. The road curved slightly to the left and then to the right. It was obvious how Mud Road had gotten its name. It was a sunny day and it had not rained for at least three or four days, but there were large ruts in the road where other cars had driven before us, and it was still a bit muddy. We seemed to be heading down into a valley when suddenly we drove through a dark, shaded section thick with trees. We came to a clearing.

"Stop," said Gerald. "This is it."

I slammed on the brakes. Gerald pointed to a large rock on the right side of the road.

"Pull out your map," he said. "This is where your land starts."

He passed the joint to Bernie, and the four of us jumped out of the Falcon.

"Far out," said Ozzie. "We're landowners."

Gerald took the map from me and set it on the hood of the car. We studied it for a while until Ozzie finally let out a war cry and took off running. He shouted something about this being where the Indians used to live, and we all ran after him. It was a beautiful piece of land, complete with tall grass, several open clearings, and clusters of pine trees. I imagined what it must look like here in the dead of winter after a heavy snowfall. It seemed that Ozzie and I now owned hundreds of Christmas trees. At the far end of the third clearing, we saw what we had come for. Bernie handed me the joint that he had been carrying, along with a book of matches. He took off his shirt, removed his sneakers and socks, and pulled down his jeans, revealing the only pair of underwear that he owned. They were white, too big and torn and tattered with several holes in them. Without saying a word, he took off running at full speed and dove headfirst into the pond. When his head popped out of the water, it was coated with a thick green scum. This was not what we were hoping for. The entire surface of the pond was covered with algae. Bernie pulled himself out of the water and sat on the ground along the edge of the pond. He stood, ripped off his green algae underwear, and tossed them in the water.

"Fuck!" he shouted and ran back to where he had left his clothes.

Bernie put his clothes back on, minus his underwear. The rest of us were laughing so hard that we could barely stand up. I lit the joint that Bernie had rolled and took a long hit. I coughed and handed it back to Bernie. The four of us sat on the ground and finished it off. Gerald pointed out that we could camp here whenever we wanted, and we could always get as fucked up as we wanted. We were in the middle of nowhere, he explained, and on private property, so we would pretty much be left alone. Ozzie wanted to know where Race Track lived, so Gerald agreed to take us there. We went back to Mud Road and then walked for almost a mile. Gerald led us through some thick brush until we came to a small clearing, where we spotted a small green camouflage pup tent next to the ashes of an extinguished fire. A few dirty pots and pans were on the ground next to the opening flap of the tent.

"Pretty cool," observed Ozzie.

We hung out for about thirty minutes and then decided to head back to Oneonta. We walked back to the Falcon and drove straight to Get Stoned Leather. When we walked in, Mike was working on a new belt. He looked up and smiled.

"You're not going to believe what Race Track did," he said.

Apparently, when Race Track grabbed Ozzie's roll of twenty-five twenty-dollar bills and bolted out of Karl Silvestri's law office, he had jumped on his bicycle and rode straight to the First National Bank on Main Street. He exchanged his twenties for ones, put the five-hundred one-dollar bills into a brown paper bag and sprinted out of the bank. He jumped back on his bicycle, put on his Santa Claus mask, drove across the street to Bresee's Department Store, and wheeled himself through the front door to the surprise of dozens of startled shoppers. As he cycled through the first floor, he reached into his brown paper bag and began tossing one-dollar bills into the air. After riding up and down all the first-floor aisles, he pedaled his bike onto the escalator and rode it up to the second floor, tossing one-dollar bills over the rails to the first-floor shoppers who were now applauding and cheering him on. When he reached the second floor, he was met by the shoppers who had come to the escalator to see what the commotion was all about. He handed each of them a one-dollar bill and wished them Merry Christmas. He then rode his bag of bills up and down the aisles of the second floor, handing one-dollar bills to each shopper he encountered. With only a few bills left in his bag, he jumped onto the down escalator and rode it back to the first floor. The shoppers had all gathered at the foot of the escalator and were giving Santa Claus a standing ovation. As he left the escalator, he waved to the crowd, shouted "Merry Christmas!" again and tossed the brown paper bag high into the air. As dollar bills floated above the cheering shoppers, Race Track rode his bicycle out the front door and onto the front page of the *Oneonta Star*.

MYSTERY SANTA CLAUS EXCITES BRESEE'S SHOPPERS

Ozzie was pissed, figuring that if Race Track was going to give the money away, he should just let us keep it. Race Track disappeared for the next three days. We looked everywhere in town that we could think of and made five trips to Mud Road and Race Track's campsite. The pup tent and pots and pans were just as we had left them. We hung out on Main Street, hoping to catch sight of Race Track pedaling his bike through town. We asked everyone that we saw if they had seen him, but it was as if he had been scooped up by a UFO and taken from the planet. By the third day we were convinced that we would never see him again. Ozzie and I decided to go to The Silver and shoot some pool. It was the middle of the afternoon, and no one was on the table. Ozzie put in a quarter and was racking the balls when Space Mann came rushing through the door, looking for Gerald. Hank Marino had spotted Race Track sitting on the curb in the Dunkin' Donuts parking lot. I dropped my pool cue and headed for the door.

"Hey," protested Ozzie. "What about my quarter?"

Race Track was okay when we found him, but he couldn't remember where he had been for the past three days. He claimed he was broke and needed the other five hundred dollars that we owed him. We set up another meeting with him at Get Stoned Leather. Gerald and Bernie pleaded with him not to give his money away this time. Ozzie and I suggested that he just let us keep the five hundred dollars if he was planning on giving it to strangers again. Gerald had an idea. He suggested that Race Track do something cool with it, like put it in the bank or invest it in something.

"Far out," Race Track exclaimed. "I'll be cool with my money this time."

The next morning, I met him at the store. Surrounded by witnesses Ozzie, Mike, Renee, and Bernie, I handed Race Track a roll of twenty-five twenty-dollar bills. With a huge smile on his face and determination in his bloodshot eyes, he took a bow, thanked me, and sprinted out the door. He jumped on his bike and rode straight up to Main Street where he took a sharp right and raced across the street to the office of Oneonta's local stockbroker Bill McMullen. Bill was not in his office that morning but his mother was. Bill paid her to answer his phone whenever he was out, but she probably was not being paid enough to handle the crazed investor who burst in the door riding a bicycle and waving a fistful of dollars.

"Where is Mr. McMullen?" he screamed. "I want to invest my money."

He dropped his bike to the floor and hurled himself onto the desk of a terrified Mrs. McMullen, who leaped out of her chair and rushed into her son's office. Race Track jumped up and down on her desk and kept shouting that he had money to invest. Mrs. McMullen called the police.

The Oneonta Police were at a loss of what to do with Race Track, who was becoming one of their more frequent guests. Karl Silvestri stopped by the jail and suggested that they send him back to Binghamton. Even the cops knew that Race Track wasn't a criminal. No one had a better idea, and the Oneonta Police were happy to wash their hands of him, so it was off to the state hospital again for Race Track.

Race Track was happy. He had free room and board, and he still had his five hundred dollars.

Ozzie and I were happy. We owned six acres.

14

Summer was on the horizon, and everything was about to change. I was making several trips out to Mud Road, but most of the time I went alone. I was excited about owning land, but Ozzie didn't seem that interested. He was spending less time in Oneonta and at Get Stoned Leather and more time in Sidney, where he crashed at his parents' house and was getting fed on a regular basis. Bernie was hanging with Gerald most of the time, but he was getting bored with living in the closet and sleeping on the Top Shelf whenever Ozzie was around.

I knew that I was eventually going to have to come up with a place to stay. I slept in the Falcon a few times, but most nights I was in The Silver until closing, looking for someone to take me home. That was getting old. When all else failed, I could always count on Julie Tyler. Now that I owned land, I wanted to be there. When I told Dick Dickson about the land, he insisted again that I learn about Bucky Fuller and build a geodesic dome on my property. Most days I just jumped in the Falcon with a bag of grass and a pack of Zig-Zags, put my *After the Gold Rush* tape in the tape player, rolled down my window, turned up the volume, and raced out to West Oneonta and up to my small piece of the American dream. With Neil Young bouncing around in my head, I would park the Falcon on Mud Road and venture into the tall grass and pine trees and finally into the third clearing and to the edge of the murky pond.

Somehow it felt right to get naked, so I did. I would take off all my clothes and spread my shirt on the ground by the edge of the pond. I would sit on my shirt, roll a joint, smoke it, and then roll another. One time after a couple of joints, I began to imagine what it would be like to have Julie here with me. I pictured us running around naked and making love in the tall grass. I ran into her at The Silver later that night.

I grabbed her hand and asked her if we could leave now and go back to her place. I was a man on fire that night, and the sex was without a doubt the best that we had ever had. As we lay on her soaking-wet sheets, I asked her if she would like to see the land that Ozzie and I had bought. She said yes but that it would have to be the next day in the afternoon since she had a test that morning. Julie left early, but I stayed in bed. Around 12:30, I heard some people come in the front door. When I walked out of Julie's bedroom, Beth Allen was sitting on the couch.

"Julie is in the bathroom," she said. "She told me about your land. I can't wait to see it."

Julie walked out of the bathroom.

"I asked Beth if she wanted to go with us. That's okay, isn't it?"

It wasn't exactly what I had in mind.

"Sure, why not?" I answered.

Beth was Julie's best friend. A short, plump, and heavy-set girl with bushy eyebrows and thick black hair, she was easily the most serious about her politics of all the *Seeds* crowd that I was friends with. Her cause was women's liberation. The three of us left the apartment and walked to the Falcon, which was parked around the corner. As we headed out Chestnut Street toward West Oneonta, Neil Young was going on and on about the needle and the damage done. When we turned onto Mud Road, he was singing about being twenty-four with so much more. When I came to the large rock that marked the boundary of my land, I pulled over and shut off the engine. I reached into the ashtray and grabbed a book of matches and two joints.

"Let's go," I said.

We headed into the tall grass through the bushes and past a number of pine trees. When we got to the first clearing, I stopped and lit the first joint. I handed it to Julie. She took a short hit and passed the joint to Beth, who took a long hit and passed it back to me. We passed it around until the roach was too small to hold, and I put it out on the ground. We were totally ripped, and we couldn't stop laughing. Excited to show them my land, I led them on a tour of the entire six acres, finally ending up at the third clearing and the pond.

Julie and Beth were laughing and telling me how great they thought my land was. I decided to take off all my clothes. This didn't seem to faze either one of them. We continued our three-way conversation for several minutes: a naked man and two fully clothed women. Julie asked me what my plans were for the land. I turned and pointed toward the clearing.

"I might build a geodesic dome over there," I said.

When I turned around, I saw that Beth had removed her blue denim shirt. Beth had large breasts, and she was not wearing a bra. She sat on the ground and removed her sneakers and socks before standing back up. She pulled down her pants and underpants and stepped out of them one leg at a time.

Beth was the hairiest girl that I had ever seen. She did not shave her underarms or her legs, and her wild and unruly pubic hair extended outward and upward, nearly reaching her belly button. When she turned and bent over to set her clothes on the ground, she offered up a bird's-eye view of the dark hair that was hiding between the cheeks of her ass.

I lit the second joint. We passed it back and forth as we walked around the pond and then back up to the second clearing. When we got there, Beth informed us that she had to pee, and she squatted down right in front of me. While she pissed on the ground, the three of us discussed what we thought should be in the next issue of *Seeds*, which was to be the final one published before both campuses emptied out for the summer.

We spent another hour or so walking the land before we decided to head back into Oneonta. Beth and I retrieved our clothes by the pond and carried them back to the Falcon, where we got dressed again. Neil Young serenaded the three of us as we drove back into town. By the time I dropped them off at Julie's place, all I could think about was having sex with Julie. As she was exiting the Falcon, I asked her if I could come in the house with her. She saw the bulge in my pants and smiled.

"Sorry," she said. "Beth and I need to study for our last final."

I watched them disappear into the house. The day had certainly not gone as I had planned.

15

My father told me that it was the day President Kennedy was shot that he knew that I was different than the other kids my age. While all my friends were playing basketball and horsing around, I spent that horrible weekend inside the house glued to the TV. On Sunday, I saw Lee Harvey Oswald gunned down by Jack Ruby on live television. They closed school that Monday for JFK's funeral, and I didn't miss a second of it.

My first recollection of being interested in politics was when I was eight years old. In 1956, I saw the Democratic convention on our tiny black-and-white TV. A then little-known senator, John F. Kennedy, from Massachusetts, challenged Senator Estes Kefauver from Tennessee for the vice presidential nomination to be Adlai Stevenson's running mate. Senator Kennedy lost, but that convention and the political process captured my imagination. I followed the 1960 election closely. Most of my classmates were for Nixon because that was whom their parents were voting for. I secretly wanted Kennedy to win. When he did, like most the nation, I became captivated by the young president and his beautiful young wife. However, what really drew me into the current events of the day were the horrible clashes that I saw on TV between the police and black demonstrators over civil rights. I was one of those kids who actually believed all those things that I was taught in social studies classes about all men being created equal and equal rights for all. When I watched the news on television, I didn't understand the Whites Only signs in front of restrooms and drinking fountains. Having grown up in a small town in Upstate New York, I had never seen anything like that before. While these events were happening far away from me and did not reach into the lives of people I knew, they left a lasting impression on me.

Although it may have taken on a different form, my journey through the Sixties was probably just another variation of the many traveled by a number of my generation. By the time I had graduated from Northeastern University in 1971, I had become completely disillusioned with everything. I was a married man with a college degree who did not want to be married or get a job. Politics seemed like a pointless exercise, and I had no desire to join the establishment.

Up until the spring of 1968, I had not been paying that much attention to the anti–Vietnam War fever that was sweeping the country. I had joined a fraternity, Tau Epsilon Phi, in the spring of 1967 and was a typical college kid with a student deferment that kept me out of Vietnam. I was enrolled as a math major in Northeastern University's cooperative education program and was working my second six-month stint at IBM in Endicott, New York, when Martin Luther King was assassinated on April 4 of that year. I remember listening to some of my short-sleeved white-shirted narrow-black-tied colleagues joking in their cubicles about how that troublemaking nigger had gotten what was coming to him. Two months later, when Bobby Kennedy was gunned down, I heard some of the same group of IBM's finest laughing about another Kennedy getting his due. When I returned to school a few weeks later, I was determined that I would never become one of *them*. I went straight to the dean of cooperative education's office and informed my counselor that I was done with IBM.

When I arrived at the TEP house, ready to start the summer quarter, I walked into a completely different universe than the one that I had exited six months earlier. My three best friends were my fraternity brothers Danny Cooper, Miles Jaffe, and Timmy Stiles; and they wasted no time turning me on to pot. Timmy drove a 1964 Lincoln Continental that Miles christened the Boo Canoe, and the four of us spent most of the summer navigating the streets and alleys of Back Bay Boston in Timmy's Boo Canoe, listening to the radio and passing around the joints that we never stopped rolling. I smoked grass every day, let my hair grow, and started skipping a lot of my classes. While I was getting high and being introduced to the counterculture that was beginning to take over Boston and Cambridge in 1968, the country was being treated to a series of rapid-fire events. Someone seemed to be firing a Gatling gun across the American landscape, and the nation appeared to be ripping at the seams. What pulled me in were the televised riots in the streets of Chicago during the Democratic convention that August. After that, I became engrossed in the presidential election. While Danny, Miles, and Timmy were only mildly interested in the politics of the time, two of my other TEP brothers, Jake Fisher and Zero Lester, were all in when it came to political activism. Zero was fascinated with Abbie Hoffman, Jerry Rubin, and the Yippies. Zero, Jake, and I went to a George Wallace rally on the Boston Commons in mid-October where several hundred Yippies carrying WALLACE FOR PRESIDENT and HIPPIES FOR GEORGE signs packed the front of the crowd. Stepping onto the stage and waving to the crowd, George at first appeared confused by his unlikely group of supporters but then suddenly realized that the joke was on him. He grabbed the microphone and shouted something about running over the next dirty hippie that stepped in front of his car. The Yippies began to chant in unison.

"WE LOVE GEORGE. WE LOVE GEORGE. WE LOVE GEORGE…"

The rest of 1968 and all of 1969, I felt like a passenger on a runaway train. The New Nixon was now the One. Judge Julius Hoffman had turned the Chicago 8 into the Chicago 7. There was the moon landing, Chappaquiddick, Woodstock, the 1969 October and November antiwar marches on Washington. As I was living in the bubble of Boston and Cambridge, it seemed like I was at the epicenter of the cultural and political revolution sweeping like a tidal wave across America. One early September afternoon, at yet another antiwar rally on the Commons, Abbie Hoffman stood on the stage and thrust his finger into the air and in the direction of the John Hancock building.

"SEE THAT GIANT HYPODERMIC NEEDLE IN THE SKY?" he screamed. "WELL, DON'T BELIEVE WHAT THEY TELL YOU. JOHN HANCOCK WAS A REVOLUTIONARY, NOT A FUCKING INSURANCE SALESMAN."

By the time the Sixties ended, I had become your typical anti-war college student. However, the antiwar movement and the counterculture were beginning to take an ugly turn. The peace and love of Woodstock was quickly being displaced by Altamont, the December 1969 free concert in Northern California, where Mick Jagger and the Stones watched helplessly as an eighteen-year-old black kid was stabbed to death by a group of Hells Angels. The peaceful antiwar marches and demonstrations were being overshadowed by newly formed groups like the Weathermen, a small but militant faction of Students for a Democratic Society (SDS), who took to the streets of Chicago in October 1969 with their three-day "Days of Rage." It was as if 1970 arrived with a scowl on its face, ready to throw a wet blanket over the previous decade.

At the end of January 1970, I was arrested and spent a terrifying night in a Boston city jail. Along with Miles, Zero, and Jake, I had attended a speech at the NU student center by Dr. S. I. Hayakawa, president of San Francisco State University. While we were inside, a large group of protesters gathered outside to protest Hayakawa's Boston appearance. Dr. Hayakawa had become a villain to groups like SDS and the Black Panthers because of his confrontational stance during the student strike at San Francisco State in 1968 and 1969. At one point, he had pulled the wires out of the speakers on top of a van at a student rally. Hundreds were arrested during the five-month strike, and Hayakawa became a hero to the establishment and a sworn enemy of the Left. We were in the auditorium when the riot started. Except for a lot of booing and one aggressive question by an SDS plant, Hayakawa's speech went off without incident. When we exited the student center into the Quad, we were met by an eerie silence and an empty campus. As we exited the Quad and crossed Huntington Avenue, we noticed a lot of debris in the street. Our plan was to go back to Miles's apartment on Hemenway Street and get high, but when we reached the corner of St. Stephens Street across from Speare Hall, we were met by a half dozen of Boston's finest in riot gear. We were on the sidewalk as they swept past us down the middle of the street. One of the cops broke ranks and moved quickly toward us.

"GET YOUR FUCKING ASSES OFF THE STREET!" he yelled and took a swing at Miles with his billy club. Miles grabbed his shoulder in pain.

This is where I fucked up.

"HEY!" I shouted. "WHY DID YOU HIT HIM? HE DIDN'T DO ANYTHING!"

The next thing I knew, I was on the ground. I was being kicked and punched. One cop had my legs. Another had my arms. The third one took a swing at me. I squirmed and twisted to cover my face.

"HERE'S ONE FOR YOUR HO CHI MINH. HOW DO YOU LIKE THAT YOU FUCKER?"

The cop who had hit Miles with his billy club was now pounding me with his fists. I couldn't free myself, but I managed to keep turning and twisting so as to avoid a direct hit to my face. As they dragged me to the paddy wagon, I caught a glimpse of his face. All I saw was pure hate. He threw another punch.

"HERE'S ANOTHER ONE FOR YOUR HO CHI MINH."

Up until now, being a pot-smoking hippie college student against the war had been all fun. I hadn't given it much thought, but I was being sheltered by the protective bubble that life on a university campus provided. Sure, I felt strongly about my views on the Vietnam War, civil rights, and the cultural changes sweeping the country, but it all was taking place in the context of the safe, intellectual confines of campus life. It was just a great time to be in college and to be part of the excitement that was Boston and Cambridge in the late Sixties. Attending a rally or demonstration was like going to a festival. It was just the cool place to be. Whether it was being among the five hundred thousand at Woodstock or the five hundred thousand at the Moratorium March on Washington, I was there. Whether it was sleeping in the mud in Bethel, New York, or crashing on the hallowed grounds of the Washington Monument, it was always a party. However, this Hayakawa thing that I was being caught up in was turning out to be some serious shit. For the simple crime of attending a speech on campus by a controversial speaker, I was being apprehended as a rioter and suspected of being a close personal friend of Ho Chi Minh. At least I wasn't alone. Altogether, there were thirty-one of us arrested.

I have to admit that I was scared shitless that night. I was thrown into a small cell that was packed with between fifteen and twenty of my co-conspirators. One dude in our cell with long blond hair wouldn't keep quiet. He seemed to want all of us to start some trouble, and he started a chant of "FUCK THE PIGS. FUCK THE PIGS." None of us joined in, and after about ten minutes of his chanting, two cops came in and pulled him out of the cell kicking and screaming. They dragged him around the corner to another cell, and the rest of us quickly got the message. We could hear them kicking the shit out of him, and his bloodcurdling screams echoed up and down the halls for what had to be more than an hour. We all kept our mouths shut for the remainder of the night, and when I was released from jail the next morning, I knew that this was one place that I never wanted to see again.

As it turned out, I was one of the lucky ones.

16

It was official. My name was in all the papers, and I was now identified to the authorities as a radical and a rioter. My poor parents were mortified. The *Boston Globe* referred to us as the Northeastern 31, but we called ourselves the NU 31. It had a better ring to it. The NU student body was outraged, and for several days, classes were canceled and rallies were held on the steps of the Ell Center. The Northeastern president told the media that the riot was the result of outside agitators and that most of those arrested were not Northeastern students. He then had the university provide free legal representation to those arrested and charged. Along with eighteen others, I was charged with disorderly conduct. Covering my face to avoid a direct hit had been a good strategic move on my part. Several of those arrested had been beaten pretty badly, and it appeared that the ones with the worst injuries received the more serious charge of assault and battery with a dangerous weapon against a police officer. On February 26, the nineteen of us charged with disorderly conduct pleaded not guilty. The case was continued to August 26. The judge told each of us that the charges would be dropped if we stayed out of trouble over the next six months.

About a week before the court appearance, two FBI agents came to my apartment and requested that I accompany them downtown to answer a few questions. They took me to an office in Government Center, where I was subjected to one of those good-cop/bad-cop scenes that I had seen on TV. The whole point of the visit was that they wanted me to become an informant for the FBI. The bad-cop dude emphasized how much trouble I was in and suggested that I could be going to jail if I didn't do the right thing. The good-cop dude explained that guys who looked like him couldn't possibly infiltrate an antiwar group but that a fine young man who looked like me could easily fit in. I was tempted to give them both the finger and tell them to go fuck themselves, but I wasn't sure what they would do to me if I did. Instead, I politely told them I couldn't do something like that and asked if I could leave. The bad-cop dude pounded his fist on the table and told me that I would be sorry if I didn't cooperate. The good-cop dude just shook his head sadly and expressed how disappointed he was in me. Since I wasn't being charged with anything, they said that I could leave. When I left the building, I was greeted by snow flurries and the strong wind whipping off Boston Harbor that made it feel a lot colder than it actually was. When I arrived at the apartment, Danny was waiting for me with his hash pipe and the Beatles' *The White Album* cranked up to full volume. We were totally wasted and listening to Jim Morrison singing "Love Me Two Times" when about two hours later, Karen and Joyce knocked on our door. It was the perfect end to an otherwise fucked-up day.

Danny and I had met them a few months earlier while walking through the Public Gardens near the Commons. They came back to our apartment with us to get high and have sex. The girls claimed to be students at Emerson College, but we had no idea if they were telling us the truth. We didn't know where they lived or when they were coming by, but we didn't care. They would just show up at our door to get high with us and fuck. Joyce was the pretty one, and she chose Danny. That was okay with me because Karen was a great lay. Danny agreed. When Karen stopped by one afternoon when I was in class, Danny did what any good friend would do and made sure that she had not made a wasted trip.

Karen was a nice distraction, but her surprise visits couldn't stop what was happening to me. My arrest, the night in jail, and my meeting with FBI agents had made me bitter and angry. I felt alienated and was becoming radicalized. The odds of me staying out of trouble until August 26 did not look very good. Sandwiched between President Nixon's announcement on April 30 that he had invaded Cambodia and the killings at Kent State on May 4, there was New Haven. On the morning of May 1, Jake, Zero, and I had hopped aboard a chartered bus in front of Speare Hall on the Northeastern campus. This was no longer fun and games. We considered ourselves members of the new revolution, a movement that would change America forever. The bus would take us to New Haven, Connecticut, where the who's who of the American Left was gathering for a May Day rally in support of Bobby Seale, who, along with eight other Black Panthers, was on trial for the murder of a government informant. The two-hour ride was filled with antiwar chants, raised fists, and shouts of "FREE BOBBY, FREE BOBBY." The electric and boisterous energy quickly dissipated as the bus approached the outskirts of New Haven. Attorney General John Mitchell had put the Marines on standby. As we rode into the city, army tanks pointed at us from both sides of the road. The chanting stopped, and the fists were lowered as an eerie calm took over the bus. The US government was expecting us. National Guard helicopters had been flown into New Haven harbor. National Guard troops were stationed throughout the city, and the streets were filled with military jeeps and troop carriers. As we passed the shops in the downtown area, we saw that most of them were closed and many had boarded up their windows. The scene was freaking me out, but when I looked over at Zero and Jake, they appeared calm. Zero looked like he was meditating.

The big rally started at five o'clock, and it was held across the street from the courthouse on the New Haven Green, a stone's throw from the Yale campus. The speakers included Jerry Rubin, Abbie Hoffman, John Froines, and Tom Hayden, four members of the Chicago 7. Yale chaplain William Sloane Coffin also spoke, along with French writer Jean Genet and baby doctor Benjamin Spock. According to news reports the next day, there were fifteen thousand of us. The rally was peaceful. Afterward, there were teach-ins scattered throughout the Yale campus. Zero, Jake, and I attended the one led by Tom Hayden. Later, about a dozen of us were sitting on the ground, smoking joints with Abbie Hoffman, when we were discovered by a CBS News camera crew. We were getting a good buzz, and it was cool to be getting high with Abbie, but I remember hoping that Mom and Dad were not tuning in to Walter Cronkite that night. Later we would find a place to crash on the Yale campus, thanks to the Yale students sympathetic to our protests who had offered to house hundreds of us in their dorm rooms. The Yale administration even opened up their dining halls for the weekend to provide us free meals. However, none of this compares to my lasting memory of New Haven.

Unknown to me on that Friday night, the New York Knicks and the LA Lakers were locked in an epic game 4 NBA Finals battle in Los Angeles. While the fifteen thousand of us were showing our support for Bobby Seale and his fellow Black Panthers, Jerry West and his Laker teammates were desperate for a win, down two games to one after losing game 3 to the Knicks in an overtime thriller. Jake, Zero, and I were in a small group listening to Jerry Rubin impart his wisdom about civil disobedience, when a skinny dude wearing a red headband raced up to our half-circle and announced that something was happening down at the Green.

"Let's go," Jerry shouted.

As we approached the Green, we were met by the smell of tear gas and a sea of protesters swarming past us in all directions. My eyes started to burn, but I could see through the incoming haze of gas that a solid wall of helmets, shields, and billy clubs was advancing toward us. We turned and started running the other way. It was chaos. No one seemed to know which way to go. The police strategy was to drive all the protesters back onto the Yale campus. In an effort to escape the expanding clouds of tear gas, Jake, Zero, and I ran into the closest building. As we burst through a side door, we heard a bunch of yelling and screaming. We were in a dormitory, and the disturbance seemed to be coming from down the hall in the main lobby area. We were not sure whether to run toward the trouble or away from it. Our instincts told us to check it out. As we got closer, we could hear what sounded like fists being pounded on a table. When we opened the door to the lobby, a huge cheer broke out. Walt Frazier had sunk a jump shot.

A large group of guys were gathered in front of a small black-and-white television. There were probably twenty of them, and they were all black. Nearly half of them wore black berets and black leather jackets. The game was in overtime, and all of them were going nuts. The half who looked like students were solid in their support of the Knicks, but it looked like four of the dudes in the black berets and black leather jackets were pulling for the Lakers. We stayed and watched. It was a wild overtime, and the Lakers ended up pulling it out 121–115. The room let out a collective groan. Jerry West had led the way with 37 points. Elgin Baylor had scored 30. The four LA fans tossed their black berets into the air and started hugging each other. Disappointed that the Knicks had lost, Jake, Zero, and I headed back outside into the tear gas.

A group of ten long-haired white guys rushed past us. They were wearing hardhats.

"Run!" one of them shouted. "The *pigs* are right behind us."

17

McGovern turns right

The headline was Peter Kroh's idea, not mine. In what turned out to be the last thing I would ever write for *Seeds*, my piece about George McGovern attempting to moderate his positions for the November 1972 presidential election was the lead article on page 1. Apparently, it pissed off the liberal professors at Hartwick College and Oneonta State, most of whom were the paper's most ardent supporters. On June 6, George had edged out Hubert Humphrey in the California Democratic primary and appeared headed to the nomination. The Vietnam antiwar movement was in full stride, and I guess that any criticism of the McGovern campaign was considered an act of treason. It wasn't as if *Seeds* was a far-out radical newspaper or that we were a bunch of crazed revolutionaries. Published roughly every two weeks, *Seeds* was a viable alternative to the existing news media in Oneonta and the surrounding area. Measuring 11½ inches by 17½ inches and selling for ten cents a copy, the ten-page paper was creating quite a stir in the Oneonta community. While it addressed national topics like Vietnam, *Seeds* was really a publication that took on local and statewide issues. It had become a thorn in the side of local officials and educators, many of whom felt it necessary to respond in writing to the accusations and unflattering stories written about them. *Seeds* represented a cultural change, not a revolution, and it was easy to understand why. After all, this was Oneonta, New York, not Berkeley or Cambridge. The paper was run by college students with few ties to the local community, and most of them would eventually leave town after graduation. The Hartwick group that I hung with practically lived at The Silver and was more interested in getting high and getting laid than in starting a revolution.

When I had volunteered to work at *Seeds* the previous November, I wasn't looking to join any political cause. I was just hoping to find some like-minded individuals in Oneonta that I could relate to. I liked the fact that this group did not take themselves too seriously. I offered to write some pieces for the paper, and Peter Kroh promised they would consider publishing anything that I submitted. I knew virtually nothing about local issues, local officials, or what was happening on either campus, so I figured that my best contribution would be to focus on national issues. The first piece that I wrote was about the current debate going on in the country about whether amnesty should be offered to the tens of thousands who had gone to Canada, Sweden, or jail to avoid the draft. The group liked it and elected to put it on the front page with the title "AMNESTY FOR WHAT?" It was a big hit with the professor crowd. Prominent politicians like McGovern, Robert Taft, and John Lindsay were offering up various proposals to forgive these guys for their so-called mistake. The premise of my article was that the Nixons and the LBJs of the world, along with the architects of the Vietnam War and their supporters, should be the ones asking for amnesty.

I counted myself as one of the fortunate ones in my generation. The first draft lottery took place on December 1, 1969, and I had lucked out. Every male in America between the ages of eighteen and twenty-six had been glued to the nearest TV to learn their fate on that historic day. It was eerie where I was. A couple dozen of us gathered around a black-and-white television in the lobby of a Northeastern dorm and watched as some congressman played God and drew 366 plastic capsules from a large plastic container. September 14 was the first date selected. No one in the room had been born that day. April 24 was next. As the drawing continued, there was a stunned silence whenever someone's birth date was announced. The first guy in the room to hear his number called was a kid from Vermont who had the misfortune of being born on Valentine's Day. February 14 was the fourth date drawn. After a while, we started to divide into two groups: those who were being selected to live and those who could soon be destined to die in the jungles of Southeast Asia. Being born in September in the years 1944 through 1950 turned out to be a bad move. September 6 was number 6. September 8 was number 7. September 26 was number 18. My birthday was announced at number 280, so I was in the happy group. Those with numbers higher than 200 jumped up and down and celebrated. Those under 150 sat alone in shock. Some said nothing. Some walked out of the room. A few guys cried. One guy vowed to go to Canada. Those who had been selected between 150 and 200 were confused, not sure which group they belonged to. My brother Bernie called me in a panic that night. His birthday had been selected number 157. Three months later, he showed up at the door of my Buswell Street apartment all freaked out.

"I just got my draft notice," he said.

We soon came up with a plan. We figured that he had a sure ticket to Vietnam if he showed up for his draft physical before the Delaware County Selective Service Board in Delhi. Since he was going to school in Connecticut, he had requested his physical be moved to Hartford. I told him that I thought this was a bad idea and that he should consider changing it to Boston. He did, and he was granted the change of venue. The hard part would be getting declared 4-F. Since Bernie did not appear to have any disqualifying characteristics like flat feet, I suggested that he talk to my fraternity brother Jake Fisher, who had just beat the draft himself.

"Just tell them that you're a homosexual," Jake said. "That's what I did."

Boston was at the center of the antiwar movement, and it was easy to find a doctor or a shrink willing to declare anyone unfit for military service for practically any reason. The most popular strategy at the time was to simply declare oneself a homosexual. A strapping and masculine six feet two, Jake had done so and was classified 4-F, no questions asked.

"It's easy," he said. "There is a gay organization here that will give you a letter that says you're gay, and all you have to do is take it with you to your physical and they give you a deferment."

That sounded simple enough. However, when Bernie went to the gay group to ask for his letter, he was told that he would have to schedule a meeting with the group's psychiatrist who himself was gay. Apparently, they were being inundated with straights claiming to be gay, and they were no longer just routinely handing out the letters. Bernie set his appointment and had ten days to come up with his plan.

Bernie was worried. "I don't know how to act like a homosexual," he said.

"We'll figure it out," I said. "Let's go get stoned with Miles, Jon, and Gerald. They've just scored some really good shit."

It was a sunny day, and we decided to walk to their apartment on Beacon Street near the corner of Gloucester. When we got there, Gerald opened the door, and we saw two chicks sitting on the floor, passing around a water pipe. Their names were Jean and Paula, and they lived in the apartment upstairs. We spent the afternoon getting wasted. When Bernie shared his story about his upcoming meeting with the shrink, we were so stoned that we couldn't stop laughing.

Bernie was planning on crashing for a few days on Gerald's couch. He learned that Jean and Paula had been getting high and getting laid with Gerald and Jon for the past month or so. Jean was the pretty one, a blonde who had taken a liking to Jon, who was also good-looking and blond. For her, it was just fun and convenient sex. Paula, however, was a plain-looking hippie chick with shoulder-length black hair who was crazy about Gerald. Jean decided that she liked Bernie more than she did Jon, and Bernie ended up spending the next two days upstairs in her bed. He never got dressed or left the apartment.

Bernie went back to Connecticut and returned to Boston and Gerald's apartment five days later. He had three days left to prepare, so he and Gerald went upstairs to get high with Jean and Paula. After her third hit, Jean had an idea.

"Let's dress you up as a girl," she said.

Bernie's problem was that he knew nothing about homosexuals and even less about the gay lifestyle that was flourishing in Boston in 1970. As far as he knew, being gay meant you were effeminate, so

Jean's plan that he dressed like a girl made perfect sense to him. He already had long hair, so he figured that it shouldn't be that hard to look like a gay guy. The four of them went into action. They went shopping at the Salvation Army, and they found Bernie a cheap yellow dress and a pair of high heels. Gerald and Bernie spent the next two days upstairs with Paula and Jean getting stoned and getting laid. Bernie practiced walking in high heels but wasn't very good at it. When he and Jean were alone, she had him put on the dress. Bernie was getting cold feet and told her that he didn't think he could wear the dress to the shrink's office. However, Jean convinced him that it turned her on whenever he wore the dress. To prove it, whenever he wore it, she would get on her knees, lift up his skirt and pull down the blue panties that she had given him to wear. She would slowly lick his balls until he was erect and then give him a blowjob. That was all it took for Bernie to change his mind and admit that he liked wearing the yellow dress and blue panties.

Bernie's appointment with the shrink was scheduled for ten thirty on Monday morning. He and Jean had stayed up all night smoking pot and engaging in oral sex. Bernie was exhausted. Jean helped him put on the dress and slip into the panties. As a finishing touch, she put some bright red lipstick on both of their lips, gave him a long, wet kiss, stroked his cock a couple of times, and sent him out the door. Bernie waited until his hard-on was gone before he went downstairs to get Gerald. He had not built up the courage to take public transportation in drag. Assuming it would prove impossible for him to drive his VW while wearing high heels, he tossed his keys to Gerald and asked if he would drive him to the appointment.

"You look great," said Gerald, trying not to laugh.

"I'm really nervous," Bernie replied. "I sure hope this doesn't take too long."

How wrong he was. First, the shrink was running late, and Bernie had to sit in the waiting room for nearly thirty minutes. It seemed a lot longer than that. Bernie tried to sit like a girl with his legs crossed so tightly that one of them went to sleep on him. When he finally stood up to greet Dr. Breaux, his right leg was so numb that he stumbled in his heels and fell to the floor. The doctor helped him to his feet. Their meeting lasted two hours, and they were the longest two hours of Bernie's life. Dr. Breaux wasn't buying Bernie's story. Bernie had practiced walking in high heels and wearing a dress, but he had forgotten to come up with a story.

Dr. Breaux wanted to know when Bernie first realized that he was attracted to men. He wondered why Bernie liked to dress like a woman. He asked why Bernie liked to wear lipstick. He asked what clubs Bernie liked to hang out in. He wanted to know what sex acts Bernie and Gerald liked to do and who did what to whom. Bernie was stumped. It had never occurred to him that he would be asked these kinds of questions.

The best that he could come up with was that he had realized he was attracted to his friend Gerald and that they had become lovers. Why was he dressed like a woman and why did he wear lipstick? Because Gerald liked him like that. What clubs did he like to hang out in? Bernie explained that he wasn't like that and that he was a one-person guy and only had sex with Gerald. The questioning went on for what seemed like forever. Bernie kept his legs tightly crossed, and they both went numb on him again. Dr. Breaux tested Bernie's reaction by placing his hand on Bernie's thigh as they talked. Bernie was sweating like a pig, and he had to piss so badly that he thought he was going to pee in his blue panties.

Finally, Dr. Breaux stood up. Bernie had worn him out.

"I've come to a decision," he said. "Yours is the strangest story that I have ever heard, but I believe you. Come back next week at the same time and pick up your letter."

Bernie was excited. He had what he wanted. He should have gone back to New Britain and back to classes, but he decided to stay in Boston for the week to celebrate with Gerald, get stoned every day, and spend as much time as possible in bed with Jean. It was a good week. On the morning that he was to pick up his letter, he and Gerald smoked two joints and drove straight to the gay group's office. The plan was to drop in, pick up the letter, and be on his way. He told Gerald to wait in the car.

Bernie identified himself to the receptionist and said that he was there to pick up his letter from Dr. Breaux. The receptionist looked through a stack of letters on his desk, but none of them had Bernie's name on them.

"Let me get Dr. Breaux," he said.

He stood up and disappeared down the hall. A few minutes later, he returned to the waiting room, followed closely by Dr. Breaux. When he caught sight of Bernie, he did a double-take. When Bernie had left Dr. Breaux's office a week earlier, he was wearing lipstick, a cheap yellow dress, and high heels. Today he was dressed in blue jeans, a green-and-blue-checked flannel shirt, and a dirty pair of sneakers.

"Sorry, Mr. Hesse," he said, "but I left your letter at my office on Beacon Hill. I'll need to go there to get it for you. Do you have a car?'

Bernie knew that his cover was about to be blown. He told Dr. Breaux that his car was parked outside and that he would be happy to drive him to his office to pick up the letter. When they got to the car, Bernie introduced Dr. Breaux to Gerald. Dr. Breaux squeezed into the back seat of the VW, and the three of them drove to Beacon Hill without saying a word. When they pulled up in front of his office, Dr. Breaux got out of the car and winked at Bernie.

"I'll be right back," he said.

He returned a few minutes later and handed the letter to Bernie.

"Look," he said, "it's obvious that you put one over on me. You really had me fooled. I probably shouldn't give you this letter, but you did such a great job and put so much effort into this that I can't bring myself to deny you your victory. Good luck, Bernie."

Bernie's draft physical was two weeks later. He went back to Connecticut and attended a few classes but decided to return to Boston three days before his physical. He had his letter, but he decided not to take any chances, just in case the letter from the shrink wasn't enough to keep him from being sent to Vietnam. Everyone he knew was giving him advice. Someone told him that he should take some speed and not sleep for several days before his physical. He asked me for help. I told him that the only person that I knew who might be able to help him score was Jake. I called Jake, and he was able to hook Bernie up with some crystal meth. Bernie showed up at Jean's apartment with the meth, and the two of them snorted speed for the next three days. By the time Bernie headed out the door for his physical, his penis was red, raw, and sore. Jean's vagina was in even worse shape.

Bernie had a few more tricks up his sleeve. He had inserted a small needle into the waistband of his underwear. He had put both his hands into a bag of sugar in order to go to the physical with sugar under his fingernails. He had not bathed in three days. With bloodshot eyes and dirty underwear, Bernie arrived at the draft board all fucked up and ready to meet his fate. At least he wasn't alone. There were twenty-five other dudes there, all as scared shitless as he was. They all were told to strip down to their underwear. A military guy was barking orders at them and lined them up in single file. Bernie was somewhere in the middle of the line and followed the short chubby kid in front of him as they were led from station to station. When he was told to pee in a cup, Bernie made sure that no one was looking and took the needle from his underwear and pricked his middle finger. Drawing blood, he dipped his hand into his urine, depositing the blood and some sugar into the paper cup. When it came time for his hearing test, Bernie did his best to convince the doctor that he had a hearing problem. He pretended not to hear about half of the sounds. There were thirteen stations in all, and no matter what Bernie did to fuck up at each station, they kept moving him along as if everything was fine. When he and the twenty-five other dudes had completed the tests, the military guy ordered them to line up, turn around, and pull their underwear down to their ankles.

"All right, you scumbags," he barked, "we're going to have each of you bend over one at a time, and we're gonna have a look at you."

Bernie wondered what they were looking for.

"Before we start," the military guy continued, "do any of you assholes have one of those fucking letters that says there's something wrong with you?"

Bernie was the only one to raise his hand. He had been clutching the letter in his left hand through the entire thirteen station gauntlet. This was his chance.

"Let me see that," the military guy shouted.

With his underwear at his ankles and his bare ass facing the military guy, Bernie held the letter over his head, which the military guy promptly ripped from his hand. There was silence as he opened the letter and read its contents. There was a loud gasp.

"Holy motherfucker!" the military guy shouted. "We have a faggot in here! Pull up your goddamn pants, Susie, and get your sissy ass the hell out of my sight."

The first stop that Bernie made after leaving the draft board was Jean's apartment. He wanted her to be the first to hear the good news. He knocked on the door.

"Who is it?" he heard Jean shout from behind the door.

Jean was sitting on a towel on her couch wearing a bright-blue blouse and nothing else. She was rubbing ointment on the lips of her vagina. It hurt to touch herself.

"It's me, Bernie. I have some great news to tell you."

"Go away," she cried.

Bernie went downstairs and gave Gerald the good news. Later, he stopped by my apartment and told me that he had beaten the draft. The next morning he drove back to Connecticut. As luck would have it, Bernie's letter from Dr. Breaux wasn't even necessary. His birthday had been selected 157, but the Selective Service only made it as high as 150 that year. However, as far as the US government was concerned, Bernie was officially registered as a homosexual.

18

Race Track only spent about two weeks in the state hospital. The shrinks claimed that they could find nothing wrong with him, and they told Race Track that they were sending him home. He begged them to let him stay. He had a comfortable bed, and he was eating better than he had in a long time, but what freaked him out the most was that there was going to be a free concert at the hospital the next weekend and he was going to miss it. Electric Mudslide, a popular bar band out of Albany, would be performing, and Race Track was hell-bent on being at the concert. When Race Track was released from the hospital, he hitchhiked from Binghamton back to Oneonta. He went straight to Get Stoned Leather, where he found Ozzie sitting on the steps drinking a Utica Club and enjoying the last two puffs of a Marlboro.

"Do you have any weed?" he asked.

"Sure," Ozzie said, pulling a joint from behind his ear. "When did you get out of the nuthouse?"

"This morning," Race Track replied.

Race Track took the joint from Ozzie, thanked him, and scurried back up to Main Street. Determined to find a way back to the state hospital, he took a right turn and made a beeline for the Oneonta cop who was standing at the corner of Dietz Street. With the joint dangling from his lips, Race Track tapped the cop on the shoulder.

"Excuse me, officer," he said. "Do you have a light?"

Race Track made it back in time to see Electric Mudslide. It was a great concert. After a long discussion, the shrinks and Race Track concluded that he should definitely stick around a little longer this time. There would be more concerts, and they agreed that the nuthouse would probably be the best place for Race Track to crash for a few months.

Race Track would spend his summer in Binghamton, but Bernie and Ozzie would spend theirs in pursuit of the West Coast. Bernie had planned on going alone, but Ozzie had pleaded his case to tag along. They stopped by Get Stoned Leather and packed up their belongings from Ozzie's closet and Bernie's Top Shelf. Ozzie moved his possessions down to his parents' house in Sidney. He stuffed a backpack full of his clothes but was convinced by Bernie to remove half of them. Bernie had lost his backpack, so Ozzie was stuck carrying Bernie's shit. It was early on a Tuesday morning when they stuck out their thumbs and headed west with the pack strapped to Ozzie's back. Mike and Renee were glad to see them go.

As for me, the summer of 1972 had arrived, and I didn't have any idea what I was going to do. However, I did luck into a place to live. Alex Kayne and his best friend Kevin Henderson had found a vacant house out on the East End. Actually, it was more like a shack than a house. It was located across the highway from the Jamesway Shopping Center, near the top of a hill at the end of a long dirt road that extended up from Route 7. The Shack had running water, electricity, a small refrigerator, a gas stove, and a toilet that flushed. Most of the floor was missing, and in order to move around The Shack, someone had put down a number of two-by-four walking planks. One narrow plank led to a small bathroom with no door, containing a toilet without a seat, a small sink, and a filthy bathtub. There were two small side rooms that served as bedrooms, and Alex and Kevin put two mattresses in each room that they supported with some extra two-by-fours. The only flooring in The Shack was in the living room, and what was left of that covered barely half the room. Alex told me that the mattress in the living room was for him and Nancy. The Shack rented for one hundred dollars a month, but for me it was free. Alex and Kevin split the rent and announced that The Shack was open to anyone who needed a place to crash. I staked my claim to the cleanest mattress in the side room closest to the bathroom.

I soon learned that Oneonta was a different place during the summer months. Empty campuses meant near-empty bars. Sure, the townies were still there and some of the State and Hartwick students stuck around for the summer, but that was not enough to keep the fifty-four watering holes hopping. Most nights, The Silver was a ghost town. After several boring nights shooting pool with Louie O'Malley and no prospects for getting laid, I decided that this would be a good time to get out of Oneonta and take a trip to Massachusetts. Jane was living with her friends in Amherst. Julie Tyler had graduated from Hartwick and had moved back to Newburyport. Randy Zarin had been trying to get me to visit him in Cambridge since Hubcap Harvey's house had burned down. I gathered up a handful of coins and found a pay phone.

My first call was to Jane, who said she was surprised to hear from me. I told her that I was on my way to Boston and that I would be stopping by to see her. I asked if I could crash there for one night, and she said that I could. I told her that I would be there sometime tomorrow afternoon, hung up the phone, and dialed the number that Julie had given me the last time that we slept together. A girl who I later found out was her roommate answered on the third ring. When I asked for Julie, her roommate wanted to know who was calling.

"Jeff," I replied.

I heard her put the phone down, and it sounded like she was whispering to someone.

"It's him," I thought I heard her say. "I told you that he would call."

Julie picked up the phone. She definitely sounded happy to hear from me. When I told her I was thinking about coming out to see her, she wanted to know when. I said that I would probably be there in a few days. Julie gave me her address and directions to find the house she was sharing with three other girls.

"I can't wait to see you," she said.

That's funny, I thought. She never seemed that eager to see me when she was in Oneonta. "Me too," I answered and then hung up the phone. I had some change left, so I dialed Randy Zarin's number and deposited the coins. There was no answer.

I thought about driving the Falcon but decided that was a bad idea. It had been giving me problems, and I wasn't convinced that it would make it to Boston and back without breaking down. I was able to drive the Falcon around town, but I had barely made it up the hill outside of West Oneonta the last time I had been out to Mud Road. I decided to hitchhike. My thumb had made this trip more than a dozen times when I was in college. It was sunny and in the midseventies the next morning when I stepped out on Route 7 with the backpack that I had borrowed from Gerald. I got my first ride in less than five minutes.

I was a little nervous about seeing Jane. I had no idea what to expect. The last time that I had spoken with her was two months earlier when I told her I was sending her half of my parents' insurance money. I had no idea what she had been doing, and she definitely knew nothing about my life since we split up. It turned out to be a good day for hitchhiking, and I made it to Amherst by early afternoon. However, finding the house where Jane lived took another hour. Finally, a longhair at a gas station told me that he knew the address and offered to drive me there in his rusted-out Chevy pickup truck. It turned out that I had been less than a mile from her place the entire time. The longhair dropped me at the sidewalk in front of the two-story gray-shingled house. I stood there for a minute, wondering if I was making a big mistake. Too late to worry about that now. I walked up the steps and onto the porch. Before I could knock, the front door swung open.

My wife looked great. She had a big smile on her face.

19

"I slept with a black man."

It was early the next morning, and I was getting ready to leave. Jane and I had just spent a disaster of a night in bed. Actually, it was me that was the disaster.

"Really?"

"Yes."

"Why?"

"I just wanted to see what it was like."

When I had shown up the day before, Jane made us both something to eat. After that, we went to her bedroom and never came out unless one of us had to go down the hall to pee. We talked for hours. Jane wanted to know everything that I had been doing since we split up. Mostly, she was curious if I had been sleeping with anyone. Like a fool, I told her way too much. I left out most of the one-night stands but told her about the Emily Keenan weekend and the many nights with Julie Tyler. It was weird. Jane never stopped smiling and seemed happy to learn that I had been getting laid. Suddenly, I had a hard-on. I didn't want her to see it, so I told her I had to piss and hurried out of the room. My whole body was tingling, and all I could think about was making love to her. I went into the bathroom and waited there nearly ten minutes until my erection was gone. I left the bathroom and walked back down the hall into the bedroom. I sat down on the bed and started making some incoherent small talk when suddenly Jane slipped her right hand down the front of my jeans.

Suddenly, I was in a time machine that sent me back to 1964, and Jane and I were in the front seat of the Plymouth Fury parked on the back side of the Evergreen Hill Cemetery. Jane's blouse was off, and her bra was unsnapped. Jane had just turned fifteen and her breasts were the most beautiful things that I had ever seen. They were firm but soft, and I loved putting my hands all over them. Jane unzipped my fly, unbuttoned my pants, and reached for my cock. I played with her breasts, and she stroked my cock until I came in my pants. The time machine hurled me back to the present and threw me back onto Jane's bed.

My hard-on returned in a matter of seconds. Jane let go of my cock, unbuttoned my jeans, and pulled down my zipper. I was all over her in a matter of seconds and couldn't get her clothes off fast enough. I still had my shirt on, and my jeans had made it down to my ankles when I pushed her down on the bed and attacked. I pushed her blouse up over her chest and up around her neck. She wasn't wearing a bra, and I licked and sucked on both her nipples while frantically trying to undo the button of her jeans. My cock was pointing straight into the air and ready to explode. I stood up and pulled off her jeans and then her panties. I slid my hand between her legs and climbed on top of her. I felt how wet she was and it turned me on even more, but it was over before I could slide inside her. My cock erupted, and I came all over her stomach. Sperm was everywhere, scattered across her breasts, on the bedspread, and all over her pubic hair. It was a mess, and I was embarrassed. I stood up. My jeans were still around my ankles. Jane was lying on her back with her legs spread apart and her blouse still crumpled up around her neck. I told her that I was sorry. She told me not to worry about it and asked me to get her a towel. After that, we each took a shower. Needless to say, we didn't try it again. The rest of the evening mostly alternated between awkward silence and more small talk. We slept together that night with our backs to each other.

"So, what was it like sleeping with a black man?" I asked.

Jane shrugged her shoulders.

"It was okay, I guess."

We hugged and said goodbye. I walked about a mile until I got to the highway and stuck out my thumb. Next stop was Newburyport and Julie Tyler. I caught my first ride on Interstate 91 down to the Mass Turnpike. I stood near the toll booth at Exit 4 for nearly an hour before I got a ride from a Boston College student who had some really good pot. I was totally ripped when he dropped me off at the Route 128 interchange at Exit 14. Newburyport was about thirty-five miles northeast of Boston along the coast.

I still had a buzz when I arrived around three o'clock. Julie greeted me at the door with a big wet kiss and even bigger hug. After taking me into the living room and introducing me to two of her three roommates, we went straight to her upstairs bedroom and straight to bed. This was exactly what I needed, a chance to redeem myself after the disaster in Amherst. Julie was her insatiable self, and as always, the sheets were soaking wet. I lasted through two of her orgasms before I came, and even then, I wasn't done yet. I stayed hard and stayed inside her until she came a third time. I rolled off covered in sweat and wondered why I hadn't been able to make love to Jane like this. I looked over at Julie and her soft, beautiful naked body. She was lying on her side and staring into my eyes. She reached over and ran her fingers through my hair. There was something different about the way she looked at me. She put her head on my shoulder and brushed her hand over my stomach, gently touching my balls and soft penis. She kissed me on the cheek and slipped her wet tongue into my ear.

"I love your cock," she whispered. "I'm glad that you came here to stay with me."

I started to get hard again. This didn't seem like the right moment to tell Julie that I had not come out to stay with her. My plan was to spend the night and then head down to Cambridge to visit Randy. When Julie moved down to kiss my penis and put me in her mouth, I began to reconsider my plan. If she kept this up, I might never leave.

Julie took me out of her mouth and climbed on top of me. She shook and sweated her way through one more violent orgasm. Afterward, we took a bath together, got dressed, and went out for a pizza. The next morning I broke the news to her.

Julie had gotten up first and brought me a cup of coffee. She had put on her bra and panties to go downstairs into the kitchen but had quickly gotten naked again after handing me my coffee. Damn, she looked good. She jumped back into bed and started telling me what a great town Newburyport was. She said it was a cool place to live with an active counterculture and knew that I would like it there. She had landed a job teaching sixth grade starting in September and claimed that I would have no trouble finding a job in or near Newburyport. The funny thing was that in all the time we spent together in Oneonta, I always felt like I was nothing more than her sex partner. I didn't have a problem with that. We never talked about having a relationship, and when she graduated from Hartwick and moved back to Newburyport, I assumed that it had been fun for her and that was it. She had given me her phone number when she left, but it didn't seem like she had expected me to call or it would be a big deal if I did.

"I was planning on hitching down to Boston today to see my friend Randy," I said.

Julie was sitting cross-legged on the bed. She lowered her head and didn't say a word. I could tell that I had hurt her. I felt bad now. Julie was a good person, and she had always been so good to me. I hadn't realized how much she liked me, and I now felt like a total asshole. I sat up and kissed her on the forehead.

"Come here," I said, pulling her toward me. I had an erection.

Julie rolled over onto her back and opened her legs. I tried to kiss her on her lips, but she turned her head to one side and I kissed her on the neck. Her eyes were open, but they wouldn't look into mine. I decided to go down on her. I kissed both her breasts and began to work my way south. Julie was motionless as I slipped my tongue inside. She didn't make a sound. As much as I tried, it was going nowhere. I finally gave up and climbed on top of her.

Julie wasn't sweating. We had never done it like this before. Her legs were apart, but she didn't shake and she didn't come. I kept thrusting and pumping, giving it everything I had. I didn't want to have an orgasm unless she did, but I was fighting a losing battle. Finally, I exploded and collapsed on top of her. I lay there for about a minute and then rolled off. Julie was staring at the ceiling. She didn't say a word. I told her that I needed to use the bathroom, and I slipped on my jeans and walked down the hall. When I got back to her room, she was gone. I grabbed a clean shirt and clean pair of socks from Gerald's backpack and got dressed. This was going to be an awkward goodbye. With the backpack slung over my right shoulder, I left Julie's room, hoping for an easy way out. When I reached the foot of the stairs, I saw Julie sitting on the couch between the two roommates that I had met the day before. A third girl who must have been her other roommate was sitting in a chair. Julie refused to look in my direction, but the other three were shooting daggers at me.

"You're an asshole," said the girl in the chair.

I couldn't argue with that.

"Bye, Julie," I said and headed for the door.

In less than twenty-four hours, I had worn out my welcome in Newburyport.

Next stop for this asshole: Cambridge.

20

Randy Zarin was probably the nicest person that I knew. He was a gentle soul. I met him when I landed a job as a janitor at the Harvard School of Public Health in September 1970. I had dropped out of NU's co-op program after a one-year stint at Arthur D. Little, a Cambridge-based think tank, and I needed some income. Jane and I had returned to Boston right after we got married and had leased a small one-bedroom apartment on Commonwealth Avenue in Brighton. One of my TEP brothers turned me on to Bob Ostrander, a fraternity brother who had dropped out of NU and was managing a cleaning crew. Bob, an Ichabod Crane look-alike, hired me immediately, and I spent every weekday night my senior year at Northeastern, mopping Harvard floors and cleaning Harvard toilets. Randy, a psychology major in his junior year at Boston University, was a fellow janitor and pot smoker, and we became friends right away. We were part of a twelve-person crew making the minimum wage of $1.60 per hour, and our biggest challenge was making one to two hours of work last four. Randy and I formed a quick bond with two other janitors, Roger Scanlon and Chris Griffin. Roger was also a student at BU, while Chris went to Wentworth Institute, a technical college just up the street from Northeastern on Huntington Avenue. Chris was also a folk singer who performed on weekends at coffeehouses in and around Harvard Square. He sounded like Jesse Colin Young and was especially good at covering songs by Cat Stevens and Neil Young, as well as the Youngbloods.

The four of us realized that if we busted our asses for the first two hours, we could fuck off and get high for the last two. Soon every night became a cat-and-mouse game with Bob Ostrander. Bob would wander the dozen or so floors for four hours, keeping tabs on his crew. At the end of the shift, he would gather the twelve of us in a group and then single out Randy, Chris, Roger, and me, wanting to know where we had been all night. We always had some lame explanation like he must have been looking for us on the fourth floor when we had been cleaning bathrooms on the eighth. Our toilets and floors were always spotless, and our waste baskets always empty, so Bob was at a loss for words when we asked him if there was something wrong with the way we were cleaning. He had to admit that we were doing a great job. Whenever we had a good buzz, we rapped about how far out it was to be taking out the trash for B. F. Skinner. Randy even had us searching for a Skinner box. We didn't know what that was, but Randy told us to look for a box with levers or keys. He explained that the Skinner box was a chamber used to analyze behavior. Apparently, BF would put an animal in the box and then reward it with food, water, or some other desired outcome if the animal pressed the correct lever or key. The four of us searched frantically for weeks, hoping to find the mysterious box, but it turned out to be a waste of time.

We were intent on spending at least two hours getting stoned, so we changed our work pattern every night to keep Bob from knowing exactly where we were. We had fun confusing him. Usually, we let Bob find us early in the evening so that he would let his guard down. In the process of cleaning offices, Chris had stumbled onto a large soundproof room on the fifth floor. We weren't sure what Harvard was using it for, but we knew that it was the perfect place to hide and get high. Each of us took turns bringing grass, and some nights Chris even snuck his guitar into the building. The soundproof room locked from the inside, so that once we were there and pressed the correct lever or key, we were safe from Bob Ostrander. We secured the deadbolt lock, rolled our joints, fired them up, and tripped out to a Chris Griffin concert. Unable to find one of BF's mysterious boxes, we instead managed to create our very own.

It took me more than two hours to hitch from Newburyport to Cambridge. Randy was home when I got there, and he was surprised to see me. Randy had just graduated from BU, and he was sharing a two-bedroom apartment with his friend Alan and Alan's girlfriend,

Shelley. This was the first time that I had seen Randy since the house fire, and we had a lot of catching up to do. Randy had become my best friend during my senior year at Northeastern, and he had only known Jane and me as a couple. He had driven down from Boston three or four times to stay with us on Franklin Mountain over the past year, and he had also become good friends with Jane. His last visit had been just two weeks before the house burned down. He and Ozzie had done acid that weekend, but I had decided to pass. I was still a little freaked out over having met God, and I wasn't sure if I was ready to meet Him again. Right in the middle of their trip, Ozzie and Randy decided that they wanted to see Frank Zappa's *200 Motels*, which was playing at the Oneonta movie theater. It had just turned dark, and since I was the only one capable of driving any kind of motorized vehicle, I loaded them into the Falcon and we headed down the winding two miles of Route 28 that descended into the big city. The night lights of Oneonta became visible as I navigated the second turn in the road, and Ozzie began jumping around in the back seat. He started screaming something about Oneonta being on fire and that the fire was dancing across the sky. Then he and Randy started giggling. They didn't stop until we hit Main Street. Both of their noses were pressed against their windows, and they stared at the quiet street in silence. We turned left onto Chestnut Street.

Finally, Ozzie opened his mouth.

"It's cool now," he said. "They put the fire out."

Ozzie didn't know it at the time, but in just two weeks, he would lose his entire collection of Frank Zappa albums in the fire. He didn't have Frank's latest album *200 Motels*, but he did have six others: *Freak Out, Hot Rats, Absolutely Free, We're Only in It for the Money, Ruben & the Jets*, and *Weasels Ripped My Flesh*. He was constantly singing or quoting Frank, blurting out the words to "Call Any Vegetable" or "Cruising for Burgers." He spoke incessantly of Suzy Creamcheese and about how brown shoes don't make it and we should all quit school and not fake it. Ozzie knew his Frank Zappa.

Since they were tripping, Randy and Ozzie probably saw a different movie than I did. Whatever it was they witnessed together, it bonded them, and they became friends that night. That's the thing about doing an acid trip with someone. You share an experience that no one else will ever understand, and that experience etches a permanent memory into each of your souls. Danny and I had the Christian Science Church. Ozzie and I had God. Now Ozzie and Randy had *200 Motels*.

I spent three great days with Randy in Cambridge and Boston. Besides being the nicest person that I knew, he was also the most laid-back. Hanging with Randy was like having my own personal shrink. He was a great listener, and nothing seemed to faze him. Randy had a lot of friends, and it seemed like there was someone either dropping in or leaving at all times either day or night. I knew his roommate Alan from the time that Randy had brought him for a weekend on Franklin Mountain, but this was the first time that I had met Shelley. I asked if we could get together with Chris Griffin, but Randy told me that he had dropped out of Wentworth and moved back to Vermont to live with his girlfriend.

I liked all of Randy's friends that I met. We stayed high the entire three days. Randy wasn't into eating meat, so we grazed on bread, cheese, rice, and spaghetti. When we got the munchies, we ate chocolate chip cookies. When we left the apartment, we hung out in Harvard Square or drove into Boston. Randy had the coolest car of any of my friends, and we rode all over the Back Bay, blowing marijuana smoke out of the open windows of his dark-blue Firebird. On the third day, we found a place to park on Newbury Street, not too far from Arlington Street and the Public Gardens. It was a warm summer day, and we enjoyed our buzz as we wandered through the Boston Commons. We ended up sitting on a bench in the Public Gardens near the statue of George Washington sitting on his horse. We fired up another joint. It was time for me to talk to my shrink.

I told Randy all about the fire and how Jane and I had split up after that. I told him about everything: Neal Bennett's Free School, Emily Keenan, the sex and one-night stands, The Silver, the Top Shelf, The Shack, Race Track, and the land that Ozzie and I now owned. I couldn't help thinking that this must be how Catholics feel when they go to confession. Being the good listener and psych major that he was, Randy let me go on and on until I was finished. He pulled a roach clip from the right pocket of his jeans. What was left of the joint had burned out during the middle of my confessional. Randy clasped the roach with the clip, took out a book of matches, and fired it up again. He took a hit and passed it to me. He exhaled, sat there for a minute, and then asked if I thought Jane and I would get back together again. I told him that I didn't think so. He wondered what I was going to do now. Was I going to stay in Oneonta? If not there, then where? What about a job? This was a conversation I definitely needed to have, but I didn't have any answers for Randy or myself. It wasn't like I was going to replace Mick Jagger as the new lead singer of the Stones. Nor was I about to move back to Boston and become the new center fielder for the Red Sox. Sure, I had a free place to stay at The Shack and enough bread to survive the summer in Oneonta. But then what? Randy saw that I was starting to freak out. He laughed and told me not to worry. He assured me that everything would work out.

I looked up at George Washington, who was still sitting on his horse. George shook his head and frowned. I lit another match and took one more hit of the roach. The match was too close to my face, and I burned my upper lip. I started coughing.

"You are pathetic," said George. "You and your hippie buddies would never have made it during *our* revolution. We survived Valley Forge and created the US of A. You idiots can't even figure out what you want to do with your lives. What the hell is the matter with you?"

I handed the roach clip back to Randy.

"Did you hear that?" I asked.

"Hear what?"

"Never mind," I said. "Let's get the fuck out of here."

21

It took me four rides and seven hours the next day to make it back to Oneonta. My last ride was with a middle-aged man on his way to see his daughter in Elmira. He picked me up just outside of Central Bridge and dropped me off at the foot of the hill leading up to The Shack. I made the long trek up the dirt road, and as I got closer to The Shack, the sound of Jethro Tull's "Aqualung" became louder and louder. As I approached The Shack, I saw Alex's green-and-white VW bus, my red Falcon, and a light-brown Mercury Comet that I didn't recognize. The Shack seemed to be shaking as Ian Anderson belted out something about sitting on a park bench and eyeing little girls with bad intent. When I opened the front door, I was greeted by a thick wall of marijuana smoke. Through the haze I could see the outline of three ghosts levitating above the living room floor. Remembering that the floor only covered about half the room, I had enough sense to search for a two-by-four with my foot before attempting to enter the room. Struggling to keep my balance, I put one foot in front of the other and maneuvered my way across the two-by-four to where the three ghosts were hovering. The music was so loud that not one of the ghosts had heard me come in. The first ghost, a startled Alex, jumped to his feet. I think he shouted something about me scaring the shit out of them, but I couldn't hear him through the music. I reached over to the stereo and lowered the volume. The second ghost came into focus, and it was Mick Jagger handing me a roach clip. I rubbed my eyes and saw that it was actually Kevin Henderson who handed it to me. Kevin looked a lot like Mick, although he wasn't as thin. He had Mick's eyes and Mick's lips, and that was enough to make me think that I was about to get high with a Rolling Stone. I took the clip from him, but the joint had burned out and what was left of the roach wasn't worth lighting. I handed it back to Kevin.

"Maybe later," I said.

The body of the third ghost belonged to a very strange and very skinny guy with stringy blond hair named Jelle Mertens. He was a Dutch dude who had grown up in Massachusetts and just graduated from Hartwick. The correct pronunciation of his name was Yell-ah, but everyone called him Jelly. He was Kevin's friend and a former boyfriend of Penelope Jessup. I assumed that the Mercury Comet parked outside belonged to Jelle but later learned that it was actually Kevin's car. Kevin told me that Jelle needed a place to crash and would be taking the other mattress in the bedroom closest to the bathroom. Kevin claimed one in the other bedroom. That left just one open mattress for me. Although Alex and Kevin had opened up The Shack to anyone who wanted or needed a place to stay, the four of us would be the only ones who slept there on a regular basis. I wondered where Nancy was, but that was none of my business.

I didn't spend much time at The Shack during the day but instead drove into town to hang with some of my townie friends. However, I wasn't seeing much of Gerald anymore. Paula, the hippie chick from Boston, had come down to see Gerald for a weekend and was now living with him at his mother's house. Louie O'Malley and Hank Marino stopped by The Shack a few times, and one time the three of us, along with Alex and Kevin, decided to go grocery shopping at the Grand Union. We piled into Alex's VW bus and rode down to the Jamesway Shopping Center. Alex, Kevin, and I had pooled our money, and we each had an assignment. Mine was to buy some beer. I bought two six-packs of Utica Club. We assumed that Louie and Hank were also buying groceries, but when they left the store, neither one of them was carrying a grocery bag. As we were piling into Alex's van, Louie yanked up the T-shirt under his blue denim shirt and pulled out a huge steak. He reached behind his back and pulled out two more.

"Let's go cook some steaks," he said.

"We need more beer," I said.

I bought two more six-packs. Kevin went back and picked up five baking potatoes, a pound of butter, and a half-gallon of Sealtest Vanilla Ice Cream. I couldn't wait to get back to The Shack. This was going to be my best meal since high school. As we headed up the hill, Alex turned on the radio. Santana was singing "Black Magic Woman." We all knew the words, and we all sang along. When we reached The Shack, Kevin jumped out, ran inside, found his dime bag, and started rolling joints. We smoked our weed, cooked our steaks, ate our potatoes, chugged our beers, and finished up with huge bowls of vanilla ice cream.

It rained steady for the next two days, and we had to move the mattresses around to avoid the roof leaks. Alex, Kevin, and I spent most of our time at The Silver, shooting pool and drinking beer until they closed down at two in the morning. The bar was a ghost town, and we usually had the pool table to ourselves. Louie was always there. On the second rainy night, Nancy and Penelope showed up with a third girl that I didn't know. Penelope liked to shoot pool, and she challenged me to a game of eight ball. She broke and sank the orange five ball. I noticed that Alex and Nancy were sitting across from each other in a booth and seemed to be having a serious conversation. I asked Penelope what was going on with them, and she told me that Nancy had split up with Alex and was staying with her for the time being. I asked Penelope about her other friend. She said her name was Colleen, and she was taking some classes at Oneonta State. We played three games, and Penelope beat me all three times. The girls left around midnight, but Alex, Kevin, and I stayed until around one thirty. On the ride home, Alex told us that he and Nancy had decided that everyone should go out to Pine Lake tomorrow.

Pine Lake was about six or seven miles outside of Oneonta on a country road near Davenport Center. It was a beautiful deep blue body of water surrounded by a lush green forest. Hartwick College had recently purchased the lake and surrounding land, but very few people knew about it yet. The school had acquired Pine Lake for some new research program to study the environment in a natural setting. All that was there now was a sauna.

I had never seen or been in a sauna before. This one was a small wooden structure located just a few feet from the lake. Someone had chopped firewood and stacked it neatly next to the entrance. Alex and Nancy and several of their Hartwick friends had been making regular trips out to Pine Lake to use the sauna and go skinny-dipping. On this day, Kevin drove Jelle and me out in his Comet, while Alex drove into town to pick up Nancy and whoever else was joining us.

This was going to be a new experience for me. Besides being in a sauna, this was going to be the first time that I had participated in group nudity. I was eager to do it, but I was nervous and I wasn't sure what to expect. I didn't even know who was going to be there.

Kevin was in charge. He said we needed to grab some firewood and get the fire started before the rest showed up because it would take about thirty minutes to get the sauna to the right temperature. We each picked up a few logs and entered the sauna. It was a small room, with two levels of wooden benches along each wall. Each bench looked like it could seat a maximum of four people. A wood-burning stove with stones on top stood on the floor near the far wall. What looked like a metal soup ladle was resting in a metal bucket on the floor. The stove felt a little warm. When Kevin opened the tiny door at the front, we could tell that someone had been here recently. The live ashes of a smoldering log were still burning at the bottom of the stove. Each of us put our logs in, and Kevin bent over and kept blowing on the red embers until the logs caught fire.

It was an unusually warm day with the temperature in the high eighties. We stepped outside and sat on the ground. Kevin said that the temperature inside would be perfect by the time Alex and his gang arrived. I took off my T-shirt and sneakers and removed my socks. The sun was bright, and it was a great day to work on my tan. Kevin and Jelle said they were going to take a walk. I decided to stay behind and put my feet into the lake. The water was cold, but it felt good. I lay back with my feet dangling in the frigid water, shut my eyes, and began soaking up the sun. I must have fallen asleep, because the next thing I knew, Alex was poking me in the shoulder.

"Hey, man, wake up. We're all getting in the sauna."

I opened my eyes. Alex was naked. He was standing between Nancy, Penelope, Colleen, and another girl that I had never seen before. The four girls were also naked. I asked where Kevin and Jelle were, and Alex said they were already inside the sauna. Alex and the girls had set their clothes down on the grass near the entrance. Alex opened the door, and he and Nancy stepped in together. Penelope, Colleen, and the other girl stood there waiting for me to get undressed. Penelope's hands were on her hips.

"What are you waiting for?" she asked.

Now I was worried. All I had on were my jeans, and I wasn't wearing any underwear. I had never undressed in front of three naked girls before. What would happen if I became aroused? *What the hell?* I thought. I slipped out of my jeans and tossed them on the ground next to my T-shirt, sneakers, and socks. I stood up in all my glory. Penelope introduced me to Amy, and I followed the three of them into the sauna. Colleen was last in line, and she turned around and held the door for me.

"Hurry," she said, "we're letting the heat out."

The sauna was dimly lit, but once my eyes adjusted, I could see everyone clearly. I was the last one in, and the only place left for me to sit was between Colleen and Amy on the bottom bench along the right wall. Alex was sitting at the end of the same bench and was closest to the stove. Kevin and Jelle were sitting on the top bench across from us, separated by Nancy and Penelope on the bottom between them. Alex stood up and grabbed the ladle. Lowering it into the bucket, he scooped up some water and threw it over the hot stones. A huge cloud of steam rose from the rocks. It had to be at least one hundred degrees in there, and I could feel the sweat coming out of all my pores. Alex threw more water on the rocks, and more steam filled the sauna. I took a deep breath and exhaled.

This was really cool. At first, I was a little self-conscious about being naked in front of this many of my friends, both male and female, as well as two girls that I didn't know. However, I was amazed at how comfortable it was. They had obviously done this many times before. We could just as well have been sitting in The Silver, drinking beer together. The eight of us sat and sweated our way through fifteen minutes of conversation and laughter until Alex stood up and declared it was time to go for a swim. One by one, we charged out of the sauna, and each of us dove headfirst into the lake. Kevin was the first one in, and he let out a war cry. I was the last one to hit the water, and after the initial shock, it felt refreshing. We treaded water for about ten minutes before getting out and spreading our bodies out on the grass. I kept thinking how natural it felt to be naked. There were no sexual vibes in the air, and everyone was perfectly at ease. Kevin had rolled a number, and we sat cross-legged in a circle and passed it around. Once the joint was finished, we filed back into the sauna and repeated our routine. After drying off on the grass a second time, we put our clothes on and headed back into town.

Pine Lake became a regular event. It was never the same people every time. Alex had started to build the frame of a geodesic dome next to The Shack, so he wasn't going as often as before. Usually, it was Penelope, Nancy, Kevin, and me. Jelle wasn't around much, which was okay because he was a little too weird for me. I never saw Amy again, but a few other friends of Penelope, Susan and Alicia, did come with us a few times. Since Kevin always had weed, we usually had a good buzz whenever we spent the afternoon at the lake.

I liked it best whenever Colleen showed up. She was a pretty girl. Tall and thin, she had fair skin and curly reddish-brown hair that touched her shoulders. I was attracted to her, but I knew it wasn't cool to come on to her or anyone else while we were at the lake. We spent a lot of time talking both in and out of the sauna, but it wasn't until one night of heavy drinking at The Silver that I made a move. Colleen told me that she had a daughter who was nearly three and that they lived with a girlfriend of hers in an upstairs apartment on Grand Street. I offered to walk her home. We started making out in the living room as soon as we got there. However, when I tried to coax her into her bedroom, she told me that she didn't sleep with guys when her daughter was there. She said she liked me, but she wasn't going to have sex with me. I slept on the couch, and when I woke up sober the next morning, I was glad that nothing had happened. Colleen was not one-night stand material, and the last thing that I wanted was to get involved with someone with a kid. Colleen was a smart girl. She had done both of us a favor.

One afternoon Kevin and I went out to Pine Lake and dropped some mescaline. I had never done mescaline before. I hadn't tripped since the time I met God on Franklin Mountain, and Orange Sunshine was the only hallucinogen that I had ever done. It was another one of those rainy Oneonta days, and there was nothing else to do, so I was game. I don't really remember much of the trip except for the part when we were coming back from the lake. Kevin's Comet was driving itself, floating several feet above the road and seeming to move at the speed of light. Kevin had let go of the steering wheel and was rolling a joint with his right hand. The windshield wipers were losing the battle as the driving multicolored rain assaulted the flying Comet. Kevin lit the joint, closed his eyes, and pushed the accelerator to the floor. The Comet shot straight up and kissed the sky, and the purple ghost of Jimi Hendrix appeared. Jimi excused himself, and few seconds later, the Comet landed at the front door of The Shack. Kevin turned off the engine, and we sat in the Comet, staring out the windows until the mescaline wore off.

I had pretty much settled in for the summer in Oneonta. Or so I thought. The days and nights revolved around Pine Lake, The Silver, and an occasional journey out to Mud Road. Whenever I needed a change of pace, I drove up to Cooperstown to see Dick Dickson. Dick drank beer, but he didn't smoke pot or do any other drugs, so it gave me a chance to clear my head and shake loose my perpetual buzz. When I mentioned to Dick that Alex was building a geodesic dome, he became very animated and insisted that I build a dome on my land. He even gave me a copy of Bucky Fuller's *Operating Manual for Spaceship Earth* and was adamant that I read it. He told me that he was considering buying some land out in Cherry Valley and building one himself.

Cherry Valley was a scenic village thirteen miles outside Cooperstown and home to less than a thousand people. Founded in 1740, it had an interesting history. During the American Revolution, it had been the scene of a huge massacre. Now, because of the poet Allen Ginsberg, it was a retreat for the likes of Gregory Corso, Herbert

Huncke, and other members of the Beat Generation. Four years earlier, Allen had bought a farmhouse and eighty acres just outside of Cherry Valley on East Hill near Sharon Springs. His vision had been to create a place where his friends and fellow poets could escape to work on their art and get off hard drugs. Dick had never met Allen, but he hung out with Stuart Blake, a guy we knew from high school who lived in Cherry Valley. Stu introduced Dick to Ray Bremser, a Beat poet who lived full-time at Allen's run-down four-bedroom house. Ray was trying to convince Dick that it was time to move out into the country and become totally self-contained and self-sufficient. Dick in turn was trying to convince me.

Since I didn't have anything better to do, I thought that it wouldn't hurt to at least look into building a dome. When I returned to The Shack, I asked Alex if he needed any help with his. He was more than happy to accept my offer, and he pointed to a pile of aluminum conduit pipes that he had cut into four-foot sections. He needed me to flatten out both ends of each section of pipe so that he could drill a small screw hole at each end. When I told him that I could do that, Alex handed me a hammer. Unfortunately, I didn't see a place where I could do the hammering. I needed a hard, stable surface where I could rest the pipe while I pounded away. I had an idea. I loaded my Falcon with as much conduit pipe that it would hold and drove into town to Get Stoned Leather. I told Mike and Renee about my plan and asked them if I could use the concrete platform and steps in front of their store to do my work. I could tell they thought I was crazy but said yes. Excited, I ran back to the Falcon and backed it into the alley. I parked it next to the steps and unloaded the sections of pipe. When I finished, I moved the Falcon back out to Chestnut Street and found a place to park. I wasn't ready to go to work yet. I figured that a cold beer would taste good right about now, so I walked down the alley and straight into The Silver. I ordered a draft from Gary and chugged it. Still thirsty, I ordered a second beer. I took my time with this one, and when I finished, my thirst was satisfied. I walked back to Get Stoned Leather to begin the task. I had no idea what I was doing or why I was doing it, but what remained of my summer in Oneonta was about to change forever. I had just flattened both ends of my first piece of conduit pipe when, suddenly, I heard the voice of an angel.

"What are you doing?" the angel asked.

Standing above me in the doorway of Get Stoned Leather was the prettiest girl I had ever seen. She looked like one of those beautiful rosy-cheek Scandinavian models with fair skin that I had only seen in magazines. She had long blond hair and blue eyes that sparkled in the late afternoon sun. The tight-fitting baby-blue T-shirt she was wearing made it obvious that she wasn't wearing a bra. Her faded blue jeans were slightly torn at both knees.

"What are you doing?" the angel repeated.

Unable to speak, I just looked up at her and smiled. The angel laughed and tried again.

"It's not that tough of a question," the angel said, returning my smile.

I finally regained my ability to speak. "I'm building a geodesic dome," I said.

Just as soon as the words left my mouth, I started laughing. It suddenly occurred to me just how ridiculous this must look to her or anyone else who happened to be passing by. Here I was, a fool standing in a back alley leaning against the steps of Get Stoned Leather, holding a four-foot section of conduit pipe in one hand and a hammer in the other. The angel started laughing with me. I made a feeble attempt to explain why I was flattening the ends of the pipe, but the more I kept talking, the more ridiculous it sounded. Finally, I dropped the hammer and pipe.

"What is your name?" I asked.

"Isadora Duncan," the angel replied.

"Do you want to go to The Silver?" I asked.

The angel had cast a spell on me. I was in love. Again.

22

It was almost five o'clock when we first walked into The Silver, and we were the only customers. I ordered two ten-cent drafts from Gary, and we grabbed the booth closest to the door. It didn't take long for The Silver to fill to happy-hour capacity, and we were soon being serenaded by colliding pool balls, a blaring jukebox, and an orchestra of loud voices. It didn't matter because it felt like we were the only ones there. I told her that I wanted to know everything about her.

"You first." She laughed.

We traded stories for the next five hours. Hers were a lot more interesting than mine. She had recently changed her name to Isadora Duncan. Dance was her passion. The original Isadora Duncan had died forty-five years earlier in Nice, France. Considered to be the mother of modern dance, Isadora was killed instantly when the silk scarf she was wearing blew into the wheel well of the convertible she was riding in, wrapped itself around the wheel axle, and broke her neck. An advocate of free love and women's rights, the original Isadora was a free spirit and artistic genius who was years ahead of her time.

My Isadora was nineteen years old. She had graduated from Oneonta High School the year before and had spent that summer traveling throughout northern Europe before returning to complete her freshman year at Bennington College in Vermont. She had come back to Oneonta for the summer and was considering taking a year off from college to clear her head and decide what she wanted to do, as well as spend some time with her father, who was in poor health. Her face lit up whenever she talked about modern dance and the original Isadora Duncan. She said that her plan was to become a professional dancer. I had never met anyone like her. She was so beautiful, intelligent, and full of life. She told me how she loved to read books and write poetry. Most of all, she was bursting with dreams: dreams of who she wanted to be, dreams of all the places she wanted to go, and dreams of the life that she wanted to live. She told me about backpacking through Europe, the lovers she had taken that summer, and how much she loved Denmark and the city of Copenhagen. She said she planned on going back.

Isadora was also a good listener. She seemed genuinely interested in me and encouraged me to tell her everything about myself. Although my life seemed boring compared to hers, I felt compelled to spill my guts. I told her that I was from Sidney, that I had lived in Boston, and that I had graduated from Northeastern. I told her about Jane and Hubcap Harvey's house and the fire on Franklin Mountain. I told her about writing for *Seeds* and the friends that I had made there, as well as the days we all spent out at Pine Lake. I told her about Ozzie and my brother Bernie and the Top Shelf and promised to show her the land on Mud Road that Ozzie and I had bought from Race Track. She asked where I lived, and I told her that I was staying at The Shack.

Finally, she stood up to leave.

"I'm really glad that I met you," she said.

I didn't want this to end. I stood up and asked if I could walk her home. Isadora smiled.

"Not tonight," she said.

She reached over, kissed me softly on the cheek, and turned to leave.

"Maybe tomorrow," she said.

I watched as Isadora Duncan and her tight blue jeans stepped out of The Silver and vanished into the night. Still under her spell, I sat back down and finished what was left of my beer. I left The Silver in a daze and wandered aimlessly until I stumbled upon the Falcon that I had parked on Chestnut Street. I thought about loading up the conduit pipe and taking it back to The Shack, but I figured that could wait until tomorrow. Besides, I wasn't convinced that the Falcon would make up the hill with all of that weight.

23

I didn't get any sleep that night. All I could think of was Isadora Duncan. When I got back to The Shack, I put Neil Young on Alex's turntable and rolled a joint. I didn't know why, but no one else was there yet. I negotiated my way along two two-by-four walking planks and into the room closest to the bathroom where I collapsed on the lumpy mattress. I took off all my clothes and fired up the joint. I had an erection. I took another hit and set the burning joint in the ashtray next to the mattress. I lay back, closed my eyes, and masturbated. I used my T-shirt to wipe myself clean and then polished off the joint. When Neil Young finished singing to me, I got up, turned off the stereo, and went back to bed. No one else came back to The Shack that night. I tossed and turned until the sun came up. I could not get Isadora Duncan out of my mind. I never lost my erection. I was still under her spell.

Around midmorning, I jerked off again to finally get rid of my hard-on. Relieved, I decided to take a bath in the filthy bathtub. Afterward, I shampooed my hair in the small bathroom sink and put on a clean yellow T-shirt, a clean underwear, and a clean pair of cutoff shorts. I raced out the door, jumped into the Falcon, and began my desperate search for Isadora Duncan. I had no idea where she lived or even if I would ever see her again. I drove up and down Main Street at least a dozen times, hoping to spot her on the sidewalk. No such luck. Finally, depressed and discouraged, I parked the Falcon at my usual spot on Chestnut Street near the alley that led to Get Stoned Leather. It was a sunny day, so I figured that I might as well get back to work on Alex's geodesic dome. As I approached the entrance to the store, I noticed a light-blue girl's bicycle leaning against my pile of conduit pipe. I walked up the steps and opened the door.

"I thought I would find you here." She laughed.

I couldn't believe my eyes. Isadora was even prettier than she was the day before. Her smile was radiant, and today she was wearing a pink blouse with buttons down the front and a pair of cutoff shorts. She was standing next to Renee and holding a leather belt in her right hand.

"I'll take it," she said, turning to Renee.

I watched as she paid for the belt. Then she turned to me.

"Are you going to show me The Shack today?" she asked.

"Sure," I said. "Let's go."

Mike was sitting at his work bench in the far corner of the store. I told him that I would come back later and pick up the conduit pipe. That was okay with him, so Isadora and I said goodbye and left the store. Isadora picked up her bicycle and wanted to know how we were going to get to The Shack. I told her that I had a car.

"Can I leave my bike here?" she asked.

I carried her bicycle back into the store and asked Mike and Renee if I could leave it there for a while. Mike laughed and suggested I store it in the back room in the closet formerly known as Ozzie's room. I thanked them, rolled the bike into the closet underneath the Top Shelf, and walked back outside where Isadora was waiting for me with her perpetual smile. She grabbed my hand, and we ran down the alley to the Falcon.

The Falcon huffed and puffed its way out to the East End. When I made the turn to go up the hill to The Shack, the Falcon stalled out. I started it again, but when I tried to accelerate up the dirt road, it stalled out a second time.

"I guess we'll have to walk the rest of the way," I said.

It took us about five minutes to walk up the hill to The Shack, and when we arrived, I was happy to find that no one was around. I didn't realize it at the time, but I was about to have the best afternoon of my brief twenty-four years on planet Earth. Before we entered The Shack, Isadora stopped to survey the property and the view down into the valley below. When we went inside, I warned her about the lack of a floor and told her to watch where she was stepping. Isadora stopped in the middle of the living room next to Alex's mattress and turned to face me. She threw her arms around my neck, and we started making out. After a long and passionate kiss, she reached down and pulled my yellow T-shirt up over my head and tossed it on the floor. She then unbuttoned my shorts, unzipped my fly, and dropping to her knees, pulled my shorts and underwear to the floor. My erect penis was staring her straight in the face. She gave it a quick kiss and, laughing, stood up and fell back into the cushioned chair that was next to the mattress. She kicked off her sandals and thrust her legs into the air.

"Take off my shorts," she said.

I stepped out my underwear and shorts. Wearing only my socks and sneakers, I bent down and unzipped the front of her cutoffs. Isadora lifted her hips off the chair, and I pulled her shorts up over her knees and off her legs. She wasn't wearing panties, and when I dropped to my knees, I saw that she wasn't wearing a bra either. Isadora's erect nipples were visible through the thin fabric of her pink blouse. I unbuttoned the blouse and removed it as quickly as I could. I then stood up and grabbed her hands to pull her to her feet and take her to the mattress in my room.

"No," she said, "let's do it here."

I let go of her hands and bent down to take off my sneakers and socks, but before I could do it, Isadora grabbed my arm and pulled me down on top of her. I could feel her soft pubic hairs rubbing against my erection as she gave me a long, wet kiss. She then put her hand on my head and gently pushed my face down between her legs. She was already wet.

When I was five years old, I spent several summer nights staying at my grandparents' house on Riverside Drive in Sidney, which was located on Route 7 on the north side of the Susquehanna River. My favorite memory is when my grandmother would walk me across the road to the Tastee-Freez and buy me an ice cream cone. Up until now, it had been the best thing that I had ever tasted.

Isadora had opened her legs and lifted each leg over a cushioned arm of the chair. My cock was as hard as a rock and I wanted to be inside her, but I couldn't bring myself to stop licking her. Isadora trembled and thrust her hips into the air. She let out a loud scream and fell back into the chair. My face was smothered with her juices. I lifted my head and stared at what had to be the most beautiful place in the world. I had never seen pubic hair as blond as hers. Isadora saw me staring and laughed. This time she used both hands to lower my head.

"You're not done yet," she whispered.

If I had died right then, my life would have been complete.

24

The funny thing about doing something right for the first time is the sudden realization that you've been doing it all wrong.

Before that glorious afternoon with Isadora Duncan, I was under the impression that I actually knew how to make love. After all, I had been having sex since I was sixteen, and I thought I knew everything there was to know. Now it was suddenly clear to me that for the past eight years, my dick had been nothing more than a misguided missile in perpetual search of a target. Getting laid was always the goal, and I was clueless when it came to knowing what the girl was feeling, thinking, or wanting. It was always about me, and as long as I got my rocks off, I assumed that the sex must be good for her too. My education began that afternoon.

I know it sounds crazy, but I am convinced that Isadora Duncan was somehow able to reach inside my brain and gain control of my cerebellum. I remember learning about the cerebellum in tenth-grade biology class. It is the part of the brain that controls fine muscle movement. Located near the base of the skull, it contains millions of neurons that relay information between body muscles and the areas of the brain that are involved in motor control. The cerebellum is critical for motor learning, fine-tuning the body's muscle groups to make fluid limb and body movements. It is how we learn to ride a bicycle, shoot a basketball, or use a knife and fork to eat our food.

Or as I was about to learn, how to actually satisfy a woman.

My face was still buried between her legs when I felt Isadora take over. I was a relative novice when it came to oral sex. It was rarely on the menu for Jane and me and not something I had done very often with the handful of others I had been with. For me, it had always been just a means to an end. It was merely foreplay, a way to get a girl ready for the main event. I was always in a hurry. This time it was different. Isadora slowed me down. I was gentle. I teased her. Isadora was turning me into Rembrandt, and I was painting a masterpiece with my tongue. Isadora climaxed a second time. I was the hardest that I had ever been in my life. Instinctively, I lifted my head from between her thighs and got up off my knees. Isadora's legs were still open, and each leg was still resting over an arm of the chair. I placed my hands just below each of her bent knees to hold her legs in place. As I lowered myself to kiss her, Isadora reached down with both hands and guided me into paradise. As I began to slide inside, I was suddenly struck by lightning. It was as if I had just inserted my dick into a light socket. Ten thousand volts of electricity rushed through my cock and sent electric currents into every inch of my body. Light flashed everywhere. I was on fire.

With my arms extended and my hands pressed against each arm of the chair, I arched my back and held myself still. The room began to spin. Isadora looked into my eyes and began to slowly rotate her hips. As I continued to hold myself still, I could feel my butt cheeks tighten. Isadora continued to rotate her hips, first slowly then faster and then slowly again. By now, my cock had turned to stone, and she was pouring delicious hot butter all over it as she tightened her grip and slid up down and around until I thought I would pass out.

I lost track of time that afternoon. I have no idea how long we made love, but I know that I had never lasted that long before. Isadora had hypnotized my cock, and no matter how swollen and excited it became, she wasn't about to let it explode until she wanted it to. Isadora moved us from the chair to Alex's mattress and back to the chair again. Completely under her spell and control, I moved in ways that I had never moved before. She had us in all sorts of positions. She took me in her mouth. I went down on her again and again. We even stopped to put on some music. Finally, like a hypnotist snapping her fingers, Isadora released my cock from her spell, and I could feel a huge tidal wave sweeping over me. We climaxed together. It was the biggest and longest orgasm of my life. I was Edmund Hillary, and I had just been led to the summit of Mount Everest by a nineteen-year old angel.

Exhausted and out of breath, I exited paradise and fell to the floor.

25

Isadora was staying in an upstairs room in a house on Cherry Street that had been converted to a small apartment with a private entrance and private bath. The first night that she took me there, we stayed in bed until the next afternoon. I couldn't get enough of her, but I knew I had to pretend that being with her was just fun and no big deal. She had taken me as her lover, and as long as I didn't let on how crazy I was about her, there was a good chance that she might keep me around for a while.

I introduced her to my *Seeds* friends, and she instantly became part of the group. She was soon close friends with Penelope and Nancy. They suggested that she join us for our trips out to Pine Lake and the sauna, and the next afternoon, Alex, Kevin, Jelle, me, and the three girls headed out to the lake crammed into Alex's VW bus. As always, Kevin brought the pot. Alex had the radio blasting at full volume, and by the time we pulled up to the lake, we were stoned, laughing and singing along to "Marrakesh Express" by Crosby Stills and Nash. We didn't waste any time. Just as soon as Alex parked the VW, the seven of us took off our clothes, tossed them in the back of the van, and ran straight for the sauna.

We stayed at Pine Lake for more than three hours, going into the sauna three times and into the lake twice. The rest of our time was spent getting wasted and walking naked around the lake. Kevin's weed was the best that I had smoked all summer, and the more we smoked, the more we couldn't stop laughing. It was one of those great afternoons. I remember stretching out on the grass next to the lake and staring up at the blue sky before turning my head to see the three girls standing together next to the sauna. I couldn't hear what they were saying, but they were giggling about something. I took a deep breath and savored the moment. I marveled at how pretty they were. Each of them could not have been more different. Penelope was a thin redhead, almost flat-chested with fair freckled skin. She was the shortest of the three with a great smile and a hairstyle like little orphan Annie's. Nancy was the tallest, around five feet ten inches with long straight silky blond hair that reached halfway down her back. Her breasts were proportionate to her height but were almost banana-shaped with nipples that pointed slightly upward. While Penelope's red pubic hair was a perfect match to the color and curl on her head, Nancy's was different. Though also straight and silky-smooth, hers was a darker, almost light-brown color. And then there was my beautiful blond angel. I was mesmerized by every inch of her body, and for the first time, I was seeing her naked from a distance. In that frozen moment, I noticed that her left breast was slightly smaller than her right. I turned my head back to the blue sky and exhaled. I was high. The three of them were beautiful. Isadora was perfect. All three of them were perfect. It was the perfect day.

Isadora was a joy to be around, and everyone seemed to like her. It didn't matter where we were. Being with Isadora was like carrying around a bottle of sunshine. She was so full of energy and joy. I spent only as much time with her as she wanted me around. I never pressed for more. We rode bikes together. We soaked up the sun on a blanket together in Neahwa Park. She read me poetry. We listened to Joni Mitchell in her upstairs room. We shot pool together in The Silver. Although it was no secret to anyone in Oneonta that we were lovers, we never acted as a couple when we were in a group. If we ran into each other at The Silver or anywhere else and she asked me back to her upstairs room, my heart would start to race and I would say yes and go. I remained under her spell, and each night and afternoon in bed with her was another magical moment in paradise.

Isadora was insatiable. My favorite moments were the times she would wake me slowly from a deep sleep by fondling and gently stroking me until I became hard enough for her to mount me. I was always on my side, and I could feel her breasts and erect nipples pressed against my back as she played with me. I would moan as she slipped her tongue in my ear and rolled me over on my back.

Maybe it was all a dream, but it was pure ecstasy that I felt, and I always seemed to wake up later to find myself sleeping on a wet spot. Sometimes when Isadora was asleep, I would try to return the favor. I was addicted to the scent of her body. Curled up behind her with my left hand cupping her smaller left breast and my continuous hard-on pressed against her lower back, I loved breathing in the soft, sweet fragrance beneath her hair at the back of her neck. Removing my left hand from her breast, I would slide it slowly down her back and along the crack of her ass, gently opening her legs. Even when she was asleep, Isadora was always ready. Inserting two fingers, I would slowly massage her until she woke up and whispered that she wanted me inside. I had no idea how long Isadora was planning to keep me under her spell, but I was hoping it would never end.

If it had not been for Danny Cooper, I might never have come up for air.

26

Danny was getting married.

Danny Cooper and I met on our first day at Northeastern in September 1966 when we were randomly paired as roommates in the freshman dorms on St. Stephens Street that were located a block from Huntington Avenue opposite the Northeastern Quad. I was the first to arrive. It was an old building with no elevator, and my room was on the top floor. My father helped me carry my two suitcases up the four flights of stairs, and when we reached the room, I noticed tears in Dad's eyes. My mother gave me a hug. I was their oldest child and the first one in my family to go to college. I was alone and on my own for the first time in my life. My first act of free will was to open the smaller suitcase and take out the eight-by-ten framed color photograph of my girlfriend Jane. I set it on top of the light-brown four-drawer dresser that was next to the bunk bed by the window. I then left to get something to eat. When I returned an hour later, I walked in to find a short kid with wavy black hair lying on the bottom bunk with his legs crossed and both hands behind his head. He looked like the actor Sal Mineo, and he was staring at Jane's picture.

"Hi," I said, "I'm Jeff."

"I'm Dan," he replied. "Who's that, your fucking mother?"

We had been best friends ever since.

I had been in touch with Danny a few times since the house fire, and I had given him Mike's and Renee's address at Get Stoned Leather as the best way to contact me. When I stopped by one afternoon to score some weed from Mike, Renee handed me a letter that she said had arrived for me two days earlier. The envelope had a return address of Alexandria, Virginia, that I didn't recognize. I ripped it open and saw that it was a note from Danny. It read in part:

118

I've met a nice Jewish girl, and I am going to get married. Any chance you might want to take a trip with me somewhere to commemorate my final summer of freedom?

He finished with a phone number and asked me to call him collect. When I did, he said that he wanted to take a trip to Canada. Danny had two things that I didn't: a reliable car and money. He was about to enter his final year at Georgetown Dental School and was driving the baby-blue Mustang that his parents had given him when he graduated from Northeastern two years earlier. We agreed to meet in Boston at the Northeastern Quad in three days. I told him that I didn't trust my car to make it there, so I would hitchhike from Oneonta and probably be there no later than three in the afternoon. After I hung up the phone, I went back to Get Stoned Leather and bought an ounce from Mike. Since I had told Isadora that I would find us some grass, I left the store and headed straight up to Cherry Street with my weed and the news. I walked in to find her sitting naked on the bed, listening to Kenny Loggins. I rolled a joint without ever taking my eyes off her, ripped off my clothes, and jumped into bed. An hour later, I was satisfied, sweaty, and stoned. When Isadora strolled out of the bathroom, I announced that my best friend Danny was getting married and that he wanted me to take a road trip with him to Canada. Isadora just laughed and leaped back into bed with me.

"Sounds like fun," she said. "Just leave me some of your pot."

Three mornings later, armed with just four prerolled joints, the backpack that I borrowed from Gerald, and a sore dick, I exited paradise and stuck out my thumb. It was one of my luckier days hitchhiking. The first ride only took me as far as Cobleskill, but I only had to wait ten minutes before I was picked up by a skinny white kid with a huge Afro driving a 1965 silver Plymouth Barracuda. His name was Andy, and he was on his way to Boston to move into his apartment before starting his sophomore year at Boston College. I pulled one of the prerolled numbers out of my front pocket and offered to light it up. Andy told me to save my weed for later because he had some great shit he wanted me to try. He reached into the ashtray and picked up a half-smoked joint.

"Try this," he said. "I grew it myself."

He was right about it being good shit. Andy was from Afton, just west of Bainbridge, and he grew his weed along the banks of the Susquehanna River. He called it Susquehanna Red and claimed that dealing pot was his summer job.

When we polished off the joint, Andy asked me to open the glove compartment.

"Hand me the eye patch," he said.

Sure enough, there was a black eye patch resting on top of the owner's manual. I handed it to him and closed the glove compartment. Andy let go of the steering wheel and placed it on his face, covering his left eye.

"Whenever I get a really good buzz," he explained, "I start to see double."

Apparently, the patch took care of the problem, because One-Eye Andy drove flawlessly the rest of way to Boston. The only thing that worried me was that he began to pick up speed once we hit the Mass Pike, and I was afraid that we might get pulled over. However, One-Eye Andy got us to Boston safe and sound and went out of his way to drop me at the Northeastern Quad.

"Thanks for the Susquehanna Red," I said as I jumped out the Barracuda.

"Be cool," One-Eye Andy replied. "If you're ever in Afton, look me up and I'll fix you up with more of this shit."

One-Eye Andy flashed me the peace sign, stepped on the gas, and vanished.

The sun was out in full force when I arrived, so I decided to take off my T-shirt and catch some rays while I waited for Danny to show up. I had gotten there with plenty of time to spare. The campus was actually quite busy for an August afternoon. It was a Thursday, and the Quad quickly filled up between classes. Unlike most universities, which divided the academic year into two semesters, Northeastern operated on the four-quarter system. As the nation's leading cooperative education university, most of NU's students were enrolled like I had been in the five-year bachelor's degree program. Most alternated quarters between classes and their paid co-op job. I reached for my T-shirt and pulled one of the joints and a book of matches out of the front pocket. I was already ripped, but I didn't care. I fired up. It was great to be back at college.

I was sprawled out on the grass with my eyes closed and had just taken my fourth toke when I heard a familiar voice.

"Hey, asshole, plan on sharing that with me?"

I sat up and handed the joint to Danny.

"Here," I said. "You finish it. I'm totally wasted."

Danny took a hit and exhaled.

"I see you had a good trip out here," he said.

"Yeah," I replied. "Some dude with something called Susquehanna Red gave me a ride."

"Is that what I'm smoking now?"

"Nope, it's some weed that I just scored in Oneonta. I've got three more joints with me. Did you bring any?"

Danny took another hit and handed me the roach. He reached into the left pocket of his jeans, pulled out a small piece of aluminum foil, and unfolded it.

"Check this out," he said. "I've got some great hash." He reached in his other pocket and pulled out a hash pipe. He looked around to see if anyone was watching us and then stuffed the pipe and hashish back into his pockets.

"And," he continued, "I have a couple hits of acid in the car."

I took another toke and passed it back.

"So," I said, "you're getting married. Who is she?"

"Her name is Judith. She is a senior at the University of Maryland, and she is great in bed."

"How did you know that she was the one?" I asked.

Danny took one last hit of what was left of the roach and tossed it to the ground.

"She showed up for our blind date with her suitcase."

"Far out," I said. "When are you getting married?"

"Next year on April Fool's Day," he replied. "I want you to be my best man."

"I'll be there."

Danny and I spent about another hour hanging out in the Quad and reminiscing about our time at Northeastern. The one thing that struck me was how calm and laid-back the campus seemed compared to how it was just a few years earlier. The NU campus that Danny and I remembered had been filled with raised fists and angry students during the national student strike that had followed the Kent State shootings in May 1970. Today, the long hair was still there, but the electricity and frenetic energy were nowhere to be seen. Just two years earlier, there would have been several groups of students sitting in small circles passing around joints. Today, Danny and I were the only ones getting high, and the handful of students sitting on the grass and around the Quad appeared to be studying for their next class. We decided to burn another joint. When we finished, we were totally ripped and in no condition to go anywhere.

"We probably ought to stay in Boston tonight," I suggested.

Danny agreed. "I'm not driving anywhere right now," he said.

"Okay, but where are we going to stay?"

"I'll bet we could crash at Club 247," replied Danny. "Let's go see if Vince is home."

27

Danny's Mustang was parked in front of 77 Gainsborough Street where the Boston Strangler had committed his first murder in 1962. We decided to leave it there for the night and walk to Vince's apartment. Danny grabbed his duffel bag from the trunk, and we walked up to Mass Ave. When we reached Newbury Street, we turned right and walked three long blocks in the direction of the Public Gardens until we were almost to the corner of Fairfield Street.

Vince Donatelli's apartment was on the first floor of the four-story Victorian brownstone that was 247 Newbury Street. Six concrete steps led up to the entrance to the building, a solid-wood black door beneath a fan-shaped arched window with twenty-two window-panes. I knew this because I had once counted them after exiting one of Vince's infamous parties in a hashish-induced stupor.

We walked into the foyer, and Danny knocked on the door of apartment number 2.

A few seconds later, we heard a high-pitch voice singing from the other side of the door.

"COMING...COMING...COMING..."

The door flew open, and there, wearing tight white underwear and nothing else, stood a six-foot-tall, athletic-looking man in his late twenties. He was holding a light-green kitchen apron in his right hand. He dropped the apron and grabbed his face with both hands.

"Oh my god," he screamed. "It's Candy and Hilda!"

"Hi, Stella," Danny said. "Do you mind if we come in?"

Donald Stanford was Vince's roommate, and everyone knew him as Stella. As Vince once pointed out, Donald had the body of a football player but the mind of a cheerleader.

Stella gave us both a hug and threw his hands into the air.

"Of course you can come in," he said. "What brings you girls here?"

"We are on our way to Canada and need a place to crash tonight," I replied. "Can we stay here?"

"Of course you can stay here," Stella said. "Vince has gone to P-Town for the weekend. You two girls can have his bed."

Danny laughed. "I think we'll probably flip a coin to see who gets the bed," he said.

Vince Donatelli was the definition of gay liberation long before anyone had even heard the term. He had lived in his Newbury Street apartment since 1965, and as Boston's counterculture began to emerge, it became known as Club 247. It was notorious throughout the Boston underground scene as a place where both straights and gays went to party. Danny and I first met Vince in the October 1966. Actually, it was Danny who met him first. Vince had enrolled at NU four years earlier but had dropped out of school after his sophomore year. Still an active member of his fraternity, he remained a fixture around campus and the freshman dorms, recruiting pledges for Tau Epsilon Phi and converts to his cause. I am not sure how they met, but Vince invited Danny to a party at the TEP house on Marlborough Street, and Danny asked me to go with him.

Although it wasn't until I returned to Boston from my IBM co-op job in the summer of 1968 that I began to experience the emerging counterculture, Vince Donatelli was my first glimpse into a world completely unknown to me. Short and stocky with a perpetual five o'clock shadow, Vince was a charismatic young man on a crusade. He was proud to be gay, and he encouraged others to rid themselves of their secrecy and shame and come out of the closet. His other mission was to change the way that straight society viewed homosexuality and the hostile and violent way homosexuals were treated. Before Vince, I thought that being gay meant being happy, and I had no idea what it meant to come out of the closet.

Vince was Boston's pied piper, drawing in straights and gays in equal numbers. His goal was to open the mind of every person he met. If someone called him a fag, he wasn't afraid to confront the tormentor head-on and defend his lifestyle. His fraternity brothers at Tau Epsilon Phi accepted Vince for who he was, and he was quite popular with most, if not all of them. Vince seemed to have special affection for Danny, and because Danny and I were best friends and nearly inseparable, I was eventually pulled into Vince's orbit during my Boo Canoe summer days of 1968. After Danny and I pledged TEP with two other friends, Timmy Stiles and Miles Jaffe, in the winter of our freshman year, Club 247 became a regular stop along our Boo Canoe route. We later become good friends with Jake Fisher and Zero Lester, two members of our pledge class who also became regulars at Vince's nonstop party scene.

Vince was certainly no saint, and he was often the beneficiary of his crusade to draw young gay men out of their closets. However, he and his gay friends were not ones to push themselves on the unwilling. His parties were open to all and included a number of NU college girls. Any sexual activity at Club 247 always took place behind closed doors, and the straight crowd was never made to feel uncomfortable. It was live and let live.

When my brother Bernie came up from Cobleskill to visit me, I took him to Club 247. When he came back with Peter Layne, his best friend from high school who was attending Holy Cross, we went to Vince's apartment. When Bernie and Ozzie lived in Boston over the summer of 1969, they were Club 247 regulars. Gerald Lopez also became a part of the scene.

Vince and his friends handed out nicknames to their straight friends. Danny became Candy Cooper. I was anointed Hilda Hesse. Since we always showed up together, Stella had started referring to us as a couple. Everyone at Club 247 knew us as simply Candy and Hilda.

The Club 247 years were an exciting and eye-opening time for me. I was exposed to so many different types of people and situations. It blew my mind the people who would gather there. We met a gay member of the Boston Bruins hockey team who, for obvious reasons, could not come out of the closet. During this period, Vince was working part-time as a maître d' at Ken's, a popular late-night restaurant on Boylston Street near Copley Square. Ken's had to be the best people-watching spot in Boston. Politicians, athletes, celebrities, and Boston's gay community packed the place to capacity after the bars closed nearly every night of the week. One night a group of us were sitting at a downstairs table when Judy Garland stopped and spoke with us. She seemed drunk to me or at least under the influence of something. She was the first famous person that I had ever met. Vince would sometimes need extra help on weekends seating customers, and he would recruit a fraternity brother to work for a few hours. The only catch was that we were required to wear a sport coat. That wasn't a problem since we all had a fraternity blazer. One Saturday night, it was my turn, and I was totally overwhelmed trying to keep up with all the people waiting for a table. I had just seated a party of four and was turning to return to the front station when I smashed heads with someone. It hurt like hell, and I saw stars. When I took a step back and opened my eyes, I was face-to-face with Senator Edward Kennedy. I was surprised to see that I was slightly taller than him. Rubbing my forehead, I quickly apologized for the collision. Ted just laughed and told me not to worry about it.

I missed the Club 247 years. Now, nearly four years later, Danny and I had popped in to see Vince again, and he was in P-Town. We could get high with Stella, but without Vince, it just wasn't the same.

Danny pulled a quarter out of his pocket and flipped it into the air. I called heads. It was tails.

Hilda Hesse slept on the floor that night.

28

Being back in Boston with Danny Cooper got me to thinking about the best summer of my life. Three years earlier, Danny, Miles, and I moved out of the TEP house on Marlborough Street and rented an apartment just around the corner on Mass Ave. By renting so close to the house, we had the best of both worlds. We could remain active as brothers and participate in all house activities, but at the same time, we were free of the restrictions of actually living there. The TEP house was experiencing the same social and political divisions as the rest of America in the summer of 1969. The differences between the older old-school brothers and the pot-smoking, antiwar younger brothers were tearing at the fabric of the fraternity. The use of marijuana was strictly prohibited in the TEP house. Tired of hiding our weed and having to leave and find a place to smoke every time we wanted to get high, we decided it was time to get our own apartment.

Danny and Miles were taking classes in the summer quarter, but I was working. I had started a new co-op job at Arthur D. Little, a consulting firm and think tank based in West Cambridge near Arlington. Meanwhile, Bernie and Ozzie had come to Boston for the summer and were renting a tiny one-room basement apartment on Beacon Street. They had found shitty jobs at a toy warehouse making the minimum wage of $1.60 per hour. By the time they paid their rent and bought their pot, they were broke. They started showing up at our apartment every night around dinnertime. Danny and Miles had money from home, and I had money from my job, so we bought plenty of groceries and made ourselves a good meal every night. We didn't suspect a thing the first time that Bernie and Ozzie knocked on the door while we were eating. Miles had made a big bowl of spaghetti and meatballs, and there was enough to go around.

By the third night, we were wise to their strategy. Danny, Miles, and I feasted on our delicious chicken breasts, baked potatoes with butter, and fresh green beans while Bernie and Ozzie sat on the couch, glaring at us and pretending not to be hungry. It took a few more nights, but they finally got the message.

I loved my co-op job at Arthur D. Little. I was assigned to a brilliant physicist from MIT. Shirley Townsend was one of the few women working there who wasn't a clerk or a secretary. I was hired as her assistant for the summer months. She didn't have very much for me to do, and I was given a lot of freedom to freelance around the facility and work on whatever came my way. An NU engineering student named David Cohen was also working a co-op job at Arthur D. Little, and he offered to drive me to work in his white 1965 Corvair if I would split the gas with him. Every day on the way home, we would share a joint. One afternoon, we wiped out the driver's side of the Corvair. David had pulled into a shopping center parking lot and was slowly driving in circles while we passed the joint back and forth with the radio going full blast. He was laughing and not watching where he was going when suddenly we were side-swiped by the only light pole in the parking lot. Poor David. The Corvair was his pride and joy, and it was a total disaster on the driver's side. He couldn't open his door, and I couldn't stop laughing. For the rest of the summer, David had to crawl in through the passenger door in order to get to his seat. David and I became friends that summer, and we both had the hots for Dorothy, a hippie chick who worked there and was five years older than us. She had an apartment in Cambridge not far from Harvard Square, and she asked David and me over a couple of times to get high. I didn't know what to expect. It was a studio apartment with a bed in the middle of the room and two chairs off to the side. Her window to the outside world was covered with dark burgundy drapes, and the only light came from a lava lamp on the nightstand by her bed and the numerous candles scattered around the hardwood floor. The smell of incense and the music of Ravi Shankar filled the room as the three of us sat cross-legged on the floor and passed around the best weed that I had smoked during my first year of getting high. Dorothy was the coolest chick I had ever met. I had been exposed to a lot over the past year, but I had never known a hippie chick. Or at least that's what I thought she was. I began to fantasize. Was she into free love? Was she going to get naked and make love to the both of us? I was a delusional fool. We were just a couple of naive college boys that she liked getting wasted with. Nothing ever happened.

The Fourth of July was a big deal in Boston. Every year, tens of thousands filled the banks of the Charles River to hear Arthur Fiedler and the Boston Pops perform a free concert on the esplanade. The sweet smell of marijuana was everywhere. Thick clouds of smoke floated like ghosts above the crowd and along the Charles. As we were picking up our blanket and taking the last toke of our last joint, two girls with English accents approached us and asked if we had any more weed. Danny was quick to respond.

"Not with us," he said, "but we have a shitload of grass back at our apartment."

The two girls turned to each other, nodded, and smiled. The skinny one with long black hair turned her head back to Danny, while the heavier one with short blond hair and large breasts feasted her eyes on me.

"Okay," the skinny one said, "let's go."

They stayed with us for seven days. We didn't know where they went during the day, but they always came back at night. Sometimes they were there for dinner, and other times they walked in much later. They liked to get high as much as we did, so every night turned out to be a pot party. The skinny one slept alone on our couch. The blond slept with me all but one of the nights, but she wouldn't let me go all the way with her. She kept her white panties on the entire night and was quite content to let me play with her tits as much as I wanted. She also let me rub her panties between her legs, but that was as far as it went. My swollen cock throbbed in pain all week long. I pleaded with her to let me fuck her, but the answer was always the same.

"Let me have your willy," she said. "I'll give it a tug."

And she did. Sometimes two or three times a night. We eventually developed a routine. I tried pulling off her panties whenever I sensed her guard might be down, only to be foiled each time I made it as far as her blond pubic hairs.

I was desperate. "I want to eat you," I begged.

"No," was all she would say as she grabbed a hold of her waistband. She would then pull her panties down a little further and tease me with a quick peek before yanking them back up. That's all it took for me to be ready. When she was through with my willy, she used the hand towel that she kept by the bed to wipe the mess off my stomach. When the English girls left the next Saturday, I was sad to see them go. I had grown used to getting two or three tugs a day.

On the third weekend in July, Jon Holderman asked me to go to the Cape with him. We ended up sharing a cheap motel room in Falmouth, and we were lucky enough to pick up a couple of girls in a bar on Saturday night and bring them back to our room and our two beds. We didn't ask their names, and they didn't ask for ours. It wasn't until two months later at our first TEP party of the fall quarter that I would learn the name of the girl that I slept with that night. My fraternity brother Dennis Staples walked into the party with his girlfriend from U Conn on his arm. Patty blushed, and I pretended that we were meeting for the first time.

When Jon and I returned from the Cape on Sunday afternoon, we were eager to tell Danny and Miles about the girls we had picked up in Falmouth. We walked in to find them glued to the small black-and-white TV.

Miles motioned for us to be quiet.

"Sssshhh," he said, "they are landing on the moon."

That was how I witnessed that moment in world history. When Neil Armstrong stepped foot on the moon a few hours later and declared that it was one small step for a man and one giant leap for mankind, the four of us were on our fifth joint.

Two days earlier, while Jon and I were cruising around Falmouth, the same senator I had once bumped heads with drove his car off a bridge on Martha's Vineyard and a twenty-eight-year old woman drowned in the accident. It was quite a weekend, but the highlight of my summer would come one month later.

On Friday, August 15, Danny Cooper, Zero Lester, Jake Fisher, Tom Fitch, and I were on our way to a music festival in Upstate New York. We had paid eighteen dollars each for our tickets. Even though I was earning a paycheck at Arthur D. Little, eighteen dollars was still a lot of money to me. When I told Shirley Townsend that I was taking Friday and Monday off to go to this music festival, she was excited that I was going and said she wanted to hear all about it when I got back. The Harvard and MIT academics, engineers, and scientists who populated Arthur D. Little seemed to be living vicariously through me. They were always asking me questions about the drugs, the antiwar movement, and occasionally the sexual mores of my generation. This blew my mind, but I played along and milked it for all I could. I was hardly an authority on anything, and I was especially not much of a spokesman for my generation. For these creatures who were much smarter than me, my unspoken role at Arthur D. Little was that of a lab rat being observed in a clandestine social experiment. A generation removed from my contemporaries, these highly intelligent creatures were being inundated daily with the sounds, images, and voices of this new counterculture. They wanted to know who these young aliens were that didn't trust anyone over thirty. I was their conduit to this mysterious world, and they were going to pay me for the two days I wasn't showing up to work. My job was to report back with all the details.

Cramming our five bodies, our drugs, and our sleeping bags into Tom's 1964 light-green Chevy Impala, we pooled our money together for gas and headed for New York State, unaware that we were about to have a rendezvous with rock 'n' roll history. Three hours later, we were stuck in a massive traffic jam. There were hundreds of cars abandoned all along the side of the road. When the traffic came to a complete halt and we could go no farther, we said goodbye to Tom's Impala and started walking. We followed the wave of humanity down the two-lane highway, not sure where we were going or what we would find when we got there. There were thousands in front of us, and when we looked back, we saw thousands following us. Sometimes a couple of lost souls would materialize in front of us, swimming upstream against the tide. "Turn around," they would say. "It's not worth it. It's too far away. It's too far to walk." We ignored their dire warnings, determined to ride this giant wave through the sea of abandoned vehicles. It was a party without a beginning or an end. Freaks were sitting on the roofs of cars, playing guitars and flutes, while scores of hippie chicks danced in the road. The side doors of VW buses were open, revealing clusters of longhairs playing harmonicas and sharing joints. We were miles from the festival, yet music was everywhere. One dude stuck out a hash pipe and asked if we wanted a hit. We did. Stoned and overwhelmed by the entire scene, we continued walking. It took us several hours to finally reach the tiny town of Bethel, later to learn that we had parked Tom's Impala nearly twelve miles away.

It was late in the afternoon when we reached the top of the hill and what had once been the entrance to the Woodstock Music Festival. Slats of red snow fence were strewn across the ground, having either been taken down by the festival's promoters or trampled into submission by the endless flow of concert goers. Either way, the entrance was gone. Below us was an open field leading to a large stage at the bottom of the hill and surrounded by tall towers that housed a multitude of lights and speakers. Our eyes scanned the area, looking for someone to show our eighteen-dollar tickets to. Finally, Zero asked a shirtless dude sitting on the ground a few feet away what we were supposed to do with our tickets.

"Hey, man." He grinned. "It's a free concert. You can throw 'em away."

Fuck, I thought, *I just wasted eighteen dollars.*

That weekend, Max Yasgur's dairy farm became the home to an estimated five hundred thousand individual experiences.

I could barely remember mine.

29

We really didn't have a plan as to where we were going, but Danny wanted to leave Club 247 early the next morning. I was exhausted, still reeling from the night before. Three of Stella's friends had stopped by, and we stayed up until almost two in the morning, smoking some of Danny's hash and drinking all of Stella's beer. Stella had been cooking a huge pot roast when we arrived, and the six of us polished it off that night while getting high and playing album after album on Stella's new stereo. Unlike Danny, who passed out the second he hit the bed, I tossed and turned for most of the night. Having lost the coin flip and won the floor, I hadn't slept a wink. When Danny hopped out of bed, he was ready to go. I had a headache and felt like shit.

We tried to leave as soon as we got up, but Stella insisted on making us breakfast. Vince called Stella the biggest drama queen he knew, and that morning Stella was in full character as he danced around the kitchen, spatula in hand, singing "The Impossible Dream" from *Man of La Mancha*.

"You need to eat," he said as he set the table. "You girls have a big day ahead of you."

We feasted on fresh strawberries, French toast with maple syrup, crisp bacon, and freshly squeezed orange juice. It was my best breakfast in years.

By the time we finished breakfast, said our goodbyes to Stella, and walked back to Danny's Mustang on Gainsborough Street, it was nearly ten o'clock, and it had started to sprinkle. As it began to rain harder, we sat in the car and discussed where we might go first. This was Danny's trip, not mine, and I was cool with whatever he wanted to do. He suggested that we start by heading up into Maine and then taking it from there. Ogunquit was less than two hours from Boston, so we made that our first destination.

We hopped onto Storrow Drive, and the skies emptied. It was pouring so hard that the Mustang's windshield wipers were barely fighting off the driving rain. It was treacherous driving, but I wasn't worried. Danny was the best driver I knew. As we headed north out of the city, Danny flipped on the radio and turned the dial until he found a station that he liked. "Soul Sacrifice" by Santana was playing. I leaned my head against the passenger window and slowly drifted into a semiconscious state. I could feel myself falling asleep, but I could still hear the music emanating from the dash. The last thing I remember was Jimi Hendrix doing his version of Dylan's "All Along the Watchtower." I slept all the way to Ogunquit. It was still raining. We had wanted to check out the beach, but we had picked the wrong day.

"This sucks," said Danny. "Let's drive up to Bar Harbor. It's only another four hours."

I went back to sleep. The next thing I remember is Danny slamming on the brakes and pulling over to pick up a hitchhiker. His name was Christopher, and he said he was from Waterbury, Connecticut. When he climbed into the back seat, I saw that he was carrying a silver flute. As soon as we pulled back onto the highway, he began to play a song by Jethro Tull. I knew the song, but I couldn't remember the name of it. When he finished, I asked him and he told me that it was called "Bouree." He said it was from Jethro Tull's *Stand Up* album, and he didn't stop there. We soon learned that Christopher had bought the flute last winter because Ian Anderson was his hero and he wanted to learn to play the flute just like Ian. He said he practiced the song every day because it was his favorite. He knew all about it. He said that the song was based on a Johann Sebastian Bach composition called Suite in E Minor for Lute and that he hoped to meet Ian one day and play "Bouree" with him. Danny asked him where he was heading, and Christopher said that he was going wherever we were going. He offered to help pay for gas.

We decided to take him up on his offer. It seemed like a good idea at the time. When Danny and I had spoken on the phone four days earlier, I told him that I was almost out of money and would have to look for a job by the end of the summer. Danny told me not to worry about money for the trip. He said he had us covered. I had a little money with me but not enough to split the gas, food, and the cost of wherever we were staying at night. Our plan was to find a free place to crash or to stay at hostels whenever we could. When all else failed, we would find a cheap motel room. Christopher's cash would definitely help our cause, and there was the added bonus of his free flute entertainment.

It started raining again, and at one point it was so bad that we had to pull over to the side of the road and let the storm pass. While we waited for the rain to let up, we fired up one of my two remaining joints. When we finished it, Christopher reached into his jacket and pulled out some rolling papers and what looked like about a half ounce of pot. Three joints and several flute serenades later, we noticed it had stopped raining. Laughing, Danny started the Mustang and peeled out. By the time we made it to Mount Desert Island and the outskirts of Bar Harbor, it was too late to do anything, but we had the munchies. We found a cheap motel, tossed our shit in the room, and went out looking for pizza. Afterward, we came back to the room and smoked more of Christopher's weed.

The next morning, we got an early start and decided to check out Acadia National Park and Cadillac Mountain, the highest point on Mount Desert Island. We drove the winding three and one-half miles up Park Loop Road to the summit and parked. There was a hiking trail that looped around the summit that was not more than a half mile long. Christopher rolled and lit our first joint of the day, and we hit the trail. We were rewarded with great panoramic views that included the town of Bar Harbor, Frenchman Bay, and some of the outer islands. The terrain and vegetation were a little different than anything I had seen before. On our way to the summit, we drove past boulders of all sizes, gnarled trees, and pines trees that were unlike pine trees I was used to seeing in Upstate New York. Just as he had known the origins of "Bouree," Christopher claimed to know all about pine trees. As we were passing the joint and walking the trail, he explained that they were called pitch pines and they usually only grew to about thirty feet in height. The branches were horizontal and contorted, and there were needles growing out of some of the trunks. It took us two quick loops around the trail to finish the roach, and when we did, we jumped into the Mustang and headed back down Park Loop Road. We had a good buzz, and we followed the road along the eastern shore until we came to Sand Beach, a gorgeous stretch of sand probably the length of three football fields. Although it was August and the sun was out in full force, it was still a bit chilly. We smoked another joint and decided we were done with Mount Desert Island and should head for Canada. As soon as Danny started the engine, he reached into the glove compartment and pulled out a map. He studied it for a minute and set it down.

"It looks like we can get to Eastport in maybe three hours and catch a ferry to New Brunswick from there," he said.

I had never heard of New Brunswick. Must be close to Nova Scotia, I thought.

"Far out," I said. "Let's do it."

Christopher picked up the flute and began to play the only song he knew.

30

We were halfway to Eastport on a lonely stretch of Highway 1 when it happened.

We probably would have heard it first if not for the fact that our windows were rolled up and Christopher was well into the second hour of what was becoming a torturous flute solo. We had just rounded a small curve when we spotted a huge cloud of smoke rising up from the middle of the road just a few hundred yards in front of us. As we got closer, we could see that there had just been a head-on collision. Danny stopped the Mustang about fifty feet from the mangled mess, and the three of us jumped out of the car and raced toward the two smashed vehicles. The driver of the larger car, which appeared to be a late-model Buick Skylark, had been thrown from the vehicle and was lying just a few feet away. His eyes were open and he was mumbling, something but his body wasn't moving. I dropped to my knees to hear what he was trying to tell us, but I couldn't make out the words. I lowered my ear closer to his lips, and I heard him mumble something about his brother. It sounded like he wanted to know if his brother was okay.

I stood up to look for his brother. What I saw next was seared into my brain forever.

The driver's window was rolled down, and I had a clear view inside the Buick. At first I thought there were two people in the car, one in the front and another in the back. However, I quickly saw that there was only one. He appeared to be a kid in his early twenties with short brown hair, wearing blue jeans and a long-sleeve blue denim shirt. His lower torso remained in a sitting position in the front, although his body was raised at least a foot above the seat. His upper body was bent down the backside of the front seat. His eyes were wide-open. It may have been an optical illusion, but it was as if his back had been broken, and half of him was sitting in the front seat with the other half was bent over staring at the floor of the back seat.

I turned away immediately and went back to his brother, who was still mumbling and still motionless. I didn't want to upset him, so I lied.

"He's okay," I said. "Help is on the way. Don't move. You'll be okay."

I heard Danny shouting.

I turned and saw that the engine of the other car, a green VW Beetle, was on fire.

"Hurry!" he yelled. "We need to put out the fire. There's a lady trapped in the car."

The front end of the VW was totally crushed, as if it had been turned into an accordion with its folds pressed tightly together. Danny and Christopher were scooping up handfuls of dirt and gravel from the side of the road and frantically trying to smother the flames beginning to grow out of the engine. I looked into the VW, and all I could see were two legs bent at the knees. They were the legs of a woman in stockings. The rest of her was tangled beneath her seat. I could hear her crying.

"Help me, help me," she whimpered.

There was no way to get her out of the car. Everything was crushed around her, and she was completely pinned in. I couldn't even see her face. The only thing to do was to put out the fire before her car exploded into flames.

Suddenly, other cars appeared. We heard sirens in the distance. We continued to toss dirt and gravel on the engine of the VW until a fire truck showed up, and they told us to get out of the way. The Maine State Troopers were next. The fire was put out. Ambulances appeared. We were in a daze. The troopers asked us questions, wanting to know if we had witnessed the accident. We had not, and we told them so. Suddenly, it dawned on us that we were carrying grass, hashish, and LSD and that the unmistakable aroma of marijuana had taken up residence in Danny's Mustang. Paranoia set in. The stars were aligned for us to get busted. Danny leaned over and whispered in my ear.

"I think we ought to split," he said. "No one is paying any attention to us right now."

We ran back to the Mustang and jumped in. Danny started the engine. A state trooper motioned to us to move over to the shoulder and then directed us around the cluster of cop cars and emergency vehicles.

Danny floored it.

"Let's get the fuck out of here," he said.

None of us said a word the rest of the way to Eastport.

Christopher didn't even pick up his flute.

31

A sign told us that we were in Eastport, Maine, the easternmost city in the United States. We were headed to Deer Island, New Brunswick. I had never been to Canada. In fact, this was the first time that I was venturing outside the US. I was a little nervous, not knowing what to expect at the border. A uniformed US customs dude asked to see our driver's licenses as we were about to enter the loading ramp to the car ferry. He barely glanced at our IDs as he waved us past the checkpoint, no questions asked. It was the same when we landed on Deer Island and were exiting the ferry. The Canadian dude just waved us through. So this is how easy it was to get into Canada? I thought. No wonder so many draft dodgers had been pouring over the border. Who knows? A lower lottery number and I might have been making this trip a year or two earlier.

Now what? After we caught another ferry to the New Brunswick mainland, we made it as far as the city of Saint John, where we found a youth hostel. We were only going to stay that one night, but our first experience with magic mushrooms extended our time in Saint John by an extra day. We were scarfing down our bowls of granola in the communal kitchen the next morning when we met Terry, a short, skinny dude from Montreal who offered us some of the mushroom soup he was preparing. Not one to turn down free food, I accepted the small coffee mug of soup and took a sip. It was the nastiest thing that I had ever tasted. I spit it out.

Terry laughed. "Haven't you ever had shrooms before?" he asked.

"No," I said. "This shit tastes awful. What is it?"

"Psilocybin mushrooms," he said. "You'll get used to the taste. Putting them in a soup makes them a lot easier to eat."

I had heard of magic mushrooms before, but this was my first chance to try them. Christopher, Danny, and I told Terry that we were all in. We each drank the vilest cup of soup that any of us had ever tasted and waited for the trip to begin.

As we soon learned, psilocybin is a great hallucinogen, but it only lasts a few hours. Terry took the lead, and he made sure that we didn't stray too far from the hostel. I am sure that the Saint John that I saw bore little resemblance to the actual Saint John. I remember running through a park and the trees turning into different colors and their almost human-like branches suddenly reaching down to tickle me as I passed by. When the trip was over, my stomach was sore from having spent nearly two hours on the ground laughing. Unfortunately, I still had that disgusting taste in my mouth.

Danny and I thought we wanted to go to Nova Scotia, but Terry was trying to get to Prince Edward Island and convinced us to go there instead. The next day the four of us drove up to Cape Tormentine and caught the ferry across the Northumberland Straight to Cape Borden on the south shore of Prince Edward Island. We learned that Terry was going to PEI to look up a girlfriend who was working for the summer at a riding stable near Charlottetown. He promised that his girlfriend Margaret would find us a place to crash. She was sharing a two-bedroom guest house on the horse farm with a coworker named Katie. The two girls seemed hesitant at first, but Terry convinced them to let the three of us sleep in their tiny living room for a few nights. We flipped for the couch, and this time I won. Danny and Christopher slept on the floor. Danny still had a little hash left, and it came in handy our first night there. The girls were into Gordon Lightfoot, and we got ripped while he serenaded us. When Christopher picked up his flute to play along, Danny finally lost it.

"Will you stop playing that fucking thing," he said. "You're driving me crazy."

I couldn't have agreed more. I was getting to the point where I never wanted to see or hear a flute again. I looked at Christopher. I could see that Danny had hurt his feelings.

Danny wasn't through. "If you play that fucking thing one more time, I'm throwing you out of my car.' He handed the hash pipe to Christopher.

The girls laughed. They were stoned and must have thought that Danny was kidding around. To me, Katie was the prettier of the two, and I was trying to come up with plan to weasel my way into her bedroom. I got the vibe that she liked me a little, but when it was time to go to bed, she went into her room without saying goodnight to any of us, and I heard the door lock behind her. All was not lost. I may have overestimated my charm, but at least I had the couch.

We found out the next morning that the girls had the day off from work. Margaret informed us that she and Terry were going to spend their day in her bed. She grabbed Katie's hand and pulled her into the kitchen. After a brief conference, the two girls came back into the living room. Katie didn't look all that happy, but Margaret announced that Katie would be taking the three of us guys to Cavendish Beach.

Katie forced a smile. "Bring some grass with you," she said.

Danny's hash was gone, and I only had one joint left, so it was a good thing that Danny had not gotten rid of Christopher yet. On the way to the beach, Katie sat in the front, while Christopher and I sat in the back, rolling until we finally ran out of papers. I counted eight joints and hoped that would be enough to get us through the day. If not, I took a wild-ass guess that Zig-Zag papers could also be purchased in Canada. I fired up the first number, took a long, drawn-out hit, exhaled, and passed it up front to Katie, who was busy giving Danny directions. Cavendish Beach was forty-five minutes and two joints from Charlottetown, and when we got there, we were not disappointed. We parked the Mustang and trucked over several big sand dunes on our way to the beach, which was bordered by red sandstone cliffs. The beach was empty. Katie insisted that we go for a swim. I thought she was crazy. I still remembered how frigid the waters of Cranes Beach in Massachusetts were from years earlier and knew it had to be even colder here. No, she explained, the water was actually warm along the north shore of PEI because of the Gulf Stream that flowed up from the Gulf of Mexico through the Atlantic and into the Gulf of St. Lawrence. We were stoned enough to believe her and give it a try. Katie slipped out of her jeans and white T-shirt. She had planned ahead and was wearing a blue-and-red striped one-piece bathing suit. The three of us stripped down to our underwear and followed her into the water. I was expecting to freeze my balls off, but Katie was right. It was actually warm enough to swim.

We spent a couple of hours at the beach, mostly sitting in the wet sand and getting high. Katie finally seemed comfortable around us. She liked smoking pot as much as we did, and she was fun to hang with once she loosened up. We burned three more roaches and then told her that we wanted to head back to Charlottetown. The wind was picking up, and the temperature was dropping. We were freezing sitting there in just our underwear. Katie asked us to look the other way while she changed out of her bathing suit and into her clothes.

"I won't watch you if you don't watch me," she said.

The three of us turned around and slipped out of our underwear. When we were done dressing, we turned around to see Katie standing a few feet from us in her jeans and T-shirt, holding her wet bathing suit. She was smiling.

"I lied," she said. "You guys have cute asses."

Danny suggested we smoke one more before we left. Holding our dirty, wet underwear in one hand, the three of us used our free hand to pass the joint. I was totally fucked up by now. Katie didn't join in this time. When we got back to the car, I dove headfirst into the back seat. She dove in right after me and started laughing.

"Want to make out?" she whispered.

Before I could answer, Katie's tongue was in my mouth. She may have caught me off guard, but my natural instincts kicked in. I reached down with my left hand and slid it under her T-shirt. She wasn't wearing a bra. Danny started the engine and turned around to look at us.

"I'll be sure to drive real slow on the way back," he said.

32

We left Charlottetown and Prince Edward Island the next day, returning on the car ferry across the Northumberland Strait to Cape Tormentine. Terry didn't come with us, choosing instead to spend another day in bed with Margaret. We made it as far as Fredericton where we found shelter in another youth hostel. Christopher had played his flute nonstop the entire day, and Danny told me the next morning that he couldn't take it anymore.

"Fuck his pot and gas money," he said. "We need to dump his ass."

Christopher was munching on a bowl of granola in the communal kitchen when Danny broke the news to him. He told him that we were going to drive to Quebec City and we were going alone. Christopher shrugged his shoulders.

"Cool," he said. "I like it here. Thanks for the ride."

It took us about seven hours to make it to Quebec City. The final leg of the trip was along a scenic stretch of the St. Lawrence River. We found a campground on the outskirts and slept in the Mustang that night. I had the back seat and didn't get much sleep. The next morning we decided to check out Quebec City. We grabbed a map of the city from the campground office. As we were about to leave, Danny reminded me that he was still holding his two hits of acid.

"It's a sunny day," he said, "a perfect day for a trip."

He pulled two small square pieces of paper from his shirt pocket.

"What are those?" I asked.

"Blotter acid," he said. "One hit for each of us. Just put it in your mouth, chew it, and swallow."

"Far out," I said, "but don't you think we should wait until we get into the city and park the car before we drop acid?"

Danny peeled out of the campground. "Okay," he said, "let's go."

I checked out the map. It looked like the coolest place to go was what the map showed as Old Quebec City. It was near the river, and there was a huge park where I was sure we could find a spot to leave the Mustang. Danny agreed, but we were starving and decided to get some breakfast first. Feasting on Canadian bacon, eggs over easy, and toast was a great way to start the day and prepare for an acid trip.

We were surprised that there weren't more cars parked along the road in the park, but then we realized it was still early in the morning. Danny turned off the engine, pulled the two hits of blotter acid from his pocket, and put one on the tip of his tongue. He handed the other one to me. I tossed it in my mouth, chewed it a couple of times, and swallowed. Danny did the same. We got out of the car and started walking.

This is what I think happened:

We were halfway across a huge open area of the park when the trip began. We were heading in the general direction of a large castle-like structure that stood alone in the distant skyline above the trees. The sun was bright, and there wasn't a single cloud in the sky. Suddenly the park came alive. People were everywhere, and we could hear them all talking at once. We couldn't understand what they were trying to tell us. I had taken French in high school, and it sounded to me like they were speaking French. The wind began to blow, and it felt like a thousand kisses on my face. That's when Joan of Arc appeared. She was on a horse, and she was thrusting a silver sword into the air. Oak trees and bright flowers surrounded us. We passed an elderly woman who was walking a dog. Danny commented how the woman and the dog looked like each other. The old woman became frightened and scurried away. We turned and saw Joan of Arc riding toward us, so we started to run in the direction of the castle. Horse-drawn carriages carrying French-speaking creatures came at us from every direction. Like magic, we landed on a long wooden board-walk. We found an empty bench and sat down. It was very warm. I told Danny that we should have worn shorts instead of jeans. The gentle breeze continued to kiss our faces while we watched at least a million creatures walk past us. The creatures continued to speak in French. We were invisible. Below us ferry boats were crossing the St. Lawrence River. I told Danny that I thought the blotter acid had taken us on a trip to Europe. Danny had an idea. He had brought his camera with him but hadn't used it yet. He said that since this was his first time in Europe, he wanted to take some pictures. The problem was that he had left the camera in his car. We had no idea where we left the Mustang. I looked down at my hands and counted: eight fingers and two thumbs. We huddled together on the bench and tried to come up with a strategy. Where was the Mustang? Was Joan of Arc still after us? Did any of these creatures speak English? The wooden boardwalk began to sway back and forth, and we both fell off the bench. We stood up and ran for our lives. We ran in circles on the winding cobblestone streets until somehow we ended up back in the park. Thankfully, Joan of Arc was nowhere in sight. We had lost her. But where was the Mustang? We ran to the open area of the park where the trip had begun. Everything looked different. The grass had turned Day-Glo green, and hundreds of cars had taken their place along the road while we had been gone. Suddenly, we heard a car honking its horn. We turned around and saw the Mustang waving at us. We couldn't get there fast enough. Danny unlocked the passenger door and opened the glove compartment. He reached in, grabbed his camera, and became more animated than I had ever seen him before.

"Did you see what I saw?" he asked.

"Yes," I answered.

"We need to let the world know," he continued.

"They won't believe us," I said.

"We have a camera," he said. "I'll take pictures."

"It won't matter," I said. "They still won't believe us."

Undeterred, Danny fell to his stomach and began pulling himself on his forearms and elbows through the Day-Glo grass. I dropped to my hands and knees and tried to keep up. One by one, he crawled up behind each parked car and took a photo of its license plate. Fortunately, we were still invisible. Danny kept snapping pictures until he ran out of film. He stood up.

"We have enough proof," he said. "Let's get out of here before we get busted."

We had ventured a long way from the Mustang. As we began to sprint to safety, the voice of Dinah Shore echoed throughout the park.

"SEE THE CHEVROLET IN YOUR USA," she sang.

We had uncovered the truth, and we had proof. Every license plate was from the United States. As soon as we returned to America, we would develop the pictures and send them to the *New York Times*.

"The US has invaded Canada," cried Danny. "We can't let Nixon get away with this."

The voice of Dinah Shore was getting louder and louder.

"Right on," I said. "Let's go to Montreal."

33

After Quebec City, Montreal was a bummer. Coming down from our trip and then sleeping another night in the car left both of us totally wiped out. It was about a three-hour drive to Montreal, and there wasn't much to look forward to. We had smoked all our pot and hash, and there was no more acid. Danny had started missing Judith, and I couldn't wait to get back into bed with Isadora. Whenever I closed my eyes, I could taste her.

We spent a few hours driving aimlessly around the city. Danny remembered that there was a TEP chapter at McGill University, and we somehow found the frat house near the campus. Since it was still summer, there were only a few brothers at the house when we got there. They gave us a room to crash in for the night, and the next morning we headed south for New York State. Since we had consumed all our drugs, we weren't paranoid about crossing the border. We pulled over a few miles outside of Montreal to check our pockets and search the Mustang in case we had overlooked something. We were clean. Not a seed or roach in sight, but then Danny remembered the hash pipe. We debated whether or not we should get rid of it but decided to take our chances. No sense throwing out a perfectly good hash pipe. Entering the States turned out to be just as easy as leaving. Danny rolled down his window and handed the agent our New York State driver's licenses. He took a quick look at the both of us, handed the licenses back to Danny, and waved us through. It seemed like a pointless exercise to me. Since our licenses did not have our photos on them, how did he know that we were who we claimed to be?

Danny offered to drive me back to Oneonta. Since he was first going to Brooklyn before heading to Judith at her mom's house in Maryland, I told him it would be easier for him to drop me off in

Albany and I would hitch the rest of the way. The Northway ended at Western Avenue in Albany, and I had made that trip out Route 20 to Duanesburg by thumb many times. Danny was cool with that. He wanted me to meet Judith, and he made me promise to visit him later in Alexandria where they had just moved into an apartment together. As an enticement, he told me that he could do all my dental work if I came to DC and it would only cost me the eleven dollars that Georgetown charged for a dental student to get some practice.

I laughed.

"That's okay," I said, "but I think I'll pass. I'm not letting *you* fuck with my teeth."

It was late afternoon when I arrived in downtown Oneonta, and I made a beeline to Isadora's apartment on Cherry Street. I knocked and knocked, but there was no answer. My reentry into paradise would have to wait. I wasn't sure what time it was, but I knew it must be happy hour at The Silver. When I walked in, I was surprised to find only five people there, and Isadora was not one of them. Louie was sitting at his usual spot at the bar, nursing a beer.

"Hey, man," he said. "Where have you been?"

"Canada," I replied.

Louie lifted his glass and took a gulp. "That's far out," he said.

I ordered a ten-cent draft from Gary, the bartender, and plopped down on the empty stool next to Louie. I asked him where everyone was. He told me that Oneonta was still dead and would be until the college kids started pouring back into town in a few weeks.

"It will be a few weeks before we can start getting laid again." He laughed.

I finished my beer and told him that I needed to split and go to The Shack. I trucked up to Main Street and started walking in the direction of the East End. I was pissed off at myself for not leaving the Falcon in town before I hitched to Boston. I continued walking with my thumb out, and just as I was passing Friendly's, I landed a ride. A few minutes later, I began the five-minute trek up the dirt road that led to The Shack. As I turned the first corner, I spotted the abandoned Falcon. It was right where I had left it, and it was covered in dust and dirt. The front tire on the driver's side was almost flat. I continued walking. As I approached The Shack, I could hear music getting louder and louder. I didn't recognize the song. Alex's green-and-white VW bus was the only vehicle there. When I walked in, I found Alex sitting cross-legged on the floor in front of his stereo. He was smoking a joint with one hand and holding B. B. King's *Indianola Mississippi Seeds* album cover with the other. Alex gave me a blank stare and passed the joint. He looked like he had been crying.

"Nancy is leaving," he said. "She's moving to San Francisco."

B. B. King was singing the blues, and Alex was singing along. Nobody loved B. B. but his mother, and he was worried that she might be jiving him too. Alex obviously felt the same. I didn't know what to say to Alex, so I just sat with him as we passed the joint back and forth. When the joint was finished, Alex rolled another. When the song was finished, Alex played it again. This went on for at least an hour. Stoned and depressed, I finally passed out. When I woke up the next morning on the floor next to Alex's mattress, I was alone. Alex and his VW bus were gone.

I checked the refrigerator for food, but it was empty. I was starving. All my clothes were dirty, and I needed a shower. Besides the Falcon and the albums that Ozzie had saved from the fire, everything I owned was stuffed into the backpack that I had borrowed from Gerald. I emptied my pockets, separated the wadded-up bills and loose change, and counted. I had thirty-seven dollars and thirty-seven cents to my name. Remembering that I kept a jar of quarters in the glove compartment of the Falcon, I tried to remember where I left my car keys. I found them on the floor next to the mattress in my room. I went back into the living room and emptied the contents of the backpack onto Alex's mattress. I counted three T-shirts, one flannel shirt, four pairs of white socks, two pairs of white underwear, my jacket, and my cutoff shorts. All this plus the clothes I was wearing had been donated to me after the fire by Gerald and his friends, and these were the only clothes that I owned. I smelled each piece one by one, trying to find something to wear that didn't smell too bad. I settled on the cutoff shorts, a yellow T-shirt, and one pair of underwear that was passable. I stuffed the rest of the clothes into the backpack and took off everything I was wearing except for my socks and sneakers. The four pairs of socks smelled so bad that I decided it would be smart to stick with the pair I had on. Next, I took a whiff of my armpits. I had gotten used to smelling myself, but even I could tell that I was in serious need of a bath or shower. Along with my belt, I crammed my dirty jeans, dirty T-shirt, and dirty underwear into the backpack and slipped into my passable underwear, T-shirt, and shorts. Then I picked up the backpack, grabbed the car keys, and headed out the door and down the hill to get the Falcon.

As I sprinted down the dirt road, I prayed that the Falcon would start. I didn't feel like making the long walk into town, and I was tired of my thumb being my only means of transportation. As luck would have it, the Falcon turned over on the first try, but the engine spit and stuttered for a few seconds and stalled out. At the least, the battery wasn't dead. I started it again, this time holding the gas pedal to the floor. Dark-blue smoke rushed out the exhaust pipe, but the engine kept running. I took my foot off the pedal and let it idle. I opened the glove compartment and pulled out the jar of quarters. I counted twenty-six. There was a Laundromat near Isadora's apartment on Cherry Street. Normally, this family of quarters would be destined for the pool table at The Silver, but today some of them would be asked to sacrifice themselves for the greater good of an Oneonta washing machine and dryer.

The first thing I needed to deal with was my nearly flat tire. The gas gauge showed that I still had a quarter-tank left, so I figured gas could wait. There was a gas station just a few hundred yards down the road, and I pulled in and put some air in my tire. Next, I stopped at Dunkin' Donuts and bought two jelly doughnuts and a small coffee. I wolfed down the doughnuts, chugged the coffee, and headed straight for Cherry Street. The Falcon was huffing puffing and coughing, struggling not to quit, and somehow willing its way to the doorstep of paradise. As the heroic Falcon rolled up to the curb in front of Isadora's apartment, it coughed one more time and then passed out. I gave the Falcon a kiss, grabbed the backpack and jar of quarters, and rushed up the side stairs that led to her room. She must have heard me coming. Before I could even knock, the door swung open. The angel was naked. Once again, I was under her spell.

34

The great New York Yankees catcher Yogi Berra once said that when you come to the fork in the road, you should take it. Well, my life was at that fork, and I didn't know where it was about to take me. The summer of Isadora Duncan and Pine Lake had now surpassed that glorious summer of 1969 as the greatest summer of my life, but it was about to come to a screeching halt. The euphoria I felt whenever I was with Isadora was now being followed by bouts of depression when I was away from her. Reality was beginning to set in. Although we never spoke of it, my instincts told me that Isadora had taken me as her summer lover, and she would soon be ready to move on to someone else. She was nineteen, and it was obvious that she had an exciting and adventurous life in front of her. Whenever we made love, it was like entering an insatiable world of mystery and magic, but it was only a fraction of the spell that she had cast over me. We talked for hours. She read me her poetry and shared her dreams. I had no doubt that she would one day become the dancer that she dreamed of being and travel the world. I knew that she would leave Oneonta and probably never return. I also knew that she was way out of my league.

I had backed myself into a corner. Isadora's dreams were becoming my dreams. I had begun to write poems and read them to her. Her stories of Copenhagen and backpacking through Europe had stirred my imagination, and I was now talking of leaving Oneonta and traveling the world. Of course, this was the same dream I had after the house burned down and Jane and I split up, but this time it was different. The problem was that I didn't have a plan or know what the hell I was talking about. To make matters worse, Isadora was taking seriously all my bravado about leaving Oneonta and traveling the world. At this point, I had no choice but to leave.

But go where?

I took stock of my situation, and it definitely looked bleak. I had a little over forty dollars to my name, no place to live, a car that didn't run, and no job. Not that I wanted a job, but I obviously needed the money. It was hopeless in Oneonta. The number of townies, longhairs, and college kids looking for work far outnumbered the low-paying jobs available. I was a twenty-four-year-old college graduate who had decided not to join the system, and I now had the job history to prove it. If I stayed in Oneonta, I was destined for nowhere, and my time with Isadora would definitely be over. I had to do something.

The first day back with Isadora was great. She took one whiff of me and made the astute observation that I could use a shower. She suggested that we take it together. I knew when it was happening that this was a shower that I would remember for the rest of my life. After an erotic thirty minutes taking turns touching, lathering up, and washing the other's most sensitive parts, we moved our wet bodies onto her small bed and spent the rest of the afternoon tenderly licking everything we had just cleansed. I was definitely going to miss this.

I fell asleep with Isadora's head on my stomach. When I woke up, she was gone. There was a note on her nightstand. She had gone to visit her father and would meet me later at The Silver. Since I had not made it to the Laundromat, I had no choice but to wiggle back into my passable underwear, yellow T-shirt, and cutoff shorts. I put on my dirty socks, slipped into my sneakers, and left the apartment. I decided to stop off to Get Stoned Leather. When I walked in the door, Mike and Renee were talking to Ozzie.

Ozzie extended his arm and gave me the power handshake.

"Hey, man, what's happening?" he asked.

"Nothing much," I said.

"Far out," he said. "You need to come to Florida with me. Your asshole brother is there right now."

35

Florida?

Until Ozzie showed up, I hadn't thought of it. Isadora had me dreaming of Europe. I saw myself in Paris hanging out on the Left Bank or living somewhere in the Greek islands. If I moved anywhere in the States, I imagined it would be some cool place like California or Colorado.

Ozzie put the hard sell on me. He stressed how great the Florida weather was and how cheap it would be to live there. He said there was a shitload of construction going on, and it would be easy to find a job and make money. He claimed there were hotels and condominiums being built everywhere up and down the beaches. Supposedly, Bernie was already looking for a place for us to live. I asked him when we were going to leave. He told me a friend of his from Lehigh University who was now living outside Pittsburgh was driving to Florida in about a week and would give us a ride. All we had to do was figure out where to meet up with him. When I told Ozzie about my trip to Maine and Canada with Danny, I happened to mention Danny's offer of eleven-dollar dental work. Ozzie was all over it.

"Let's go to Georgetown first," he said. "I'll get my wisdom teeth pulled out."

"Are you having problems with your wisdom teeth?" I asked.

"No," he said, "but eleven dollars is a great deal. How can I pass it up?"

He asked for Danny's address in Alexandria and said he would call his friend Chuck and have him pick us up at Danny's in seven days.

"Call Danny and tell him I'm coming there to get my wisdom teeth pulled," he said. "Let's leave for DC in five days."

I gathered up some coins and went up to the phone booth on Chestnut Street. Judith answered the phone. I told her that I would be visiting next week and said that I couldn't wait to meet her. When I told her that I didn't have much change to pay for this call, she handed the phone to Danny. I asked him if we could crash at his apartment on our way to Florida. I told him about Ozzie's wisdom teeth.

"Sure." He laughed. "I'll pull out his fucking teeth myself."

The thought of leaving Isadora was killing me. However, my gut told me that if I stayed in Oneonta, I would lose her anyway. It was time to take Yogi's fork in the road. When I strolled into The Silver later that night, Isadora was sitting in a booth talking with Penelope and a guy that I had never seen before. Rod Stewart was singing "Maggie May" to the near-empty bar. No one was on the pool table. I ordered a draft from Gary and slid in next to Isadora. The guy sitting next to Penelope introduced himself as Pete and reached across the booth to give me the power handshake. He asked if I wanted to shoot a game of pool. Pete was a tall, muscular dude. He was at least six-five with a long, angular nose and shoulder-length stringy brown hair. We split two games of eight ball before rejoining Isadora and Penelope in the booth.

Penelope remarked that she had not seen me in a while and asked where I had been.

"We've missed you out at Pine Lake," she said.

I told her about my trip to Boston, Maine, and Canada and said that I was getting ready to leave for Florida in a few days. I was going there to make some money so I could start my travels around the world.

Isadora smiled and gave me a kiss on the cheek.

"Let's all go out to Pine Lake tomorrow," she said.

Pete went home with Penelope that night, and I went home with Isadora. Once again, she took complete control of my cerebellum. When she was done with me, I collapsed across her bed, covered in sweat. She had etched the essence of her smell into my permanent memory, and the taste of her would linger for days on my lips and the tip my tongue. We fell asleep in each other's arms. The next thing

I knew, it was morning, and we were being serenaded by the loud honking emanating from Alex's bus. I went to the open window and looked out. Nancy, Kevin, Jelle, Penelope, and Pete were standing on the sidewalk, waving at me, while Alex sat in the front seat of the VW, honking the horn.

"Hurry up, you guys!" shouted Penelope. "We're going to the lake."

Isadora and I threw on our clothes and rushed out the door. When we jumped into the back of the van, Kevin handed me a lit joint. The seven of us passed it around while Alex navigated his way out to Pine Lake and the sauna. When we got there, we stripped off our clothes and dove into the water. Alex went into the sauna and started the fire. We alternated between the sauna and the lake all afternoon. Nancy, Penelope, and Isadora spent a lot of time together laughing and sunning themselves on the grass. With what was going on with her and Alex, I was a little surprised that Nancy was with us today. I stared at the three girls as they sprawled out on the grass and knew that I should once again savor the moment. This was probably the last time that my eyes would experience the joy of seeing all three of these lovely naked bodies together. Sadly, all good things come to an end.

The next day, it was time to deal with the Falcon. I managed to get it started and move it from Isadora's down to my usual spot on Chestnut Street. I needed money, but the Falcon barely ran, and I knew that it wouldn't make it up a hill. In an act of good conscience, I left it parked on the street with the doors unlocked and the keys in the ignition. I was giving a free car to the people. Good karma was all I wanted in return.

The day before I left Oneonta, I went to see Gerald to return his backpack. Paula was still staying with him at his mom's house. It was another lucky day for me. Gerald said he had another backpack and told me to keep the one I had. It was a good thing he did, or I wouldn't have been able to take any of my shit to Florida. Later, I went down to Get Stoned Leather to say goodbye to Mike and Renee. After that, I walked up to Isadora's for our last night together.

I was touched by how gentle and how affectionate she was when we made love. It brought back memories of my last night with Emily Keenan. We stayed up most of the night sharing our dreams together. I was hoping that she would release me from her spell, but instead I could feel the spell getting stronger. The morning light was beginning to creep though her window when I finally fell asleep. When I woke, I was lying on my back, and the angel was staring into my eyes, gently stroking my erection with what felt like wet fingers.

"Don't move," she whispered. "You don't have to do anything."

I closed my eyes and let my head sink into the pillow. I felt her climb on top of me, her soft skin covering me like a blanket. I didn't move a muscle. As much as I wanted to reach out and touch her, I honored her wishes and left both of my arms extended outward on the bed and glued to her sheets. The angel gently squeezed my erection and lowered herself slowly until she was barely touching it.

"Don't move," she whispered again.

She continued to hold on to my erection. With gentle precision, she lowered her hips slightly and began to guide me inside her. Then, just as slowly and precise, she raised her hips and reversed course, guiding me out.

"Don't move," she whispered again.

The angel continued to tease me for what felt like an eternity. Each time I entered, she let me venture a little farther in before she escorted me out. I thought I was going to pass out.

Finally, just as I thought she was about to guide me all the way into paradise, she removed my erection and redirected its voyage slightly upward. Arching her back and tossing her head from side to side, the angel turned my erection into a magic wand. I was helpless as she waved it in all directions, applying just the right amount of pressure to the source of her pleasure. I was delirious. As I was about to lose consciousness, the angel let out a scream and guided the magic wand back to its original destination. This time it traveled all the way to paradise. The earth began to shake, and the magic wand exploded in a thousand different directions beneath an endless deluge of her warm juices.

When I woke, it was the middle of the afternoon. A cool breeze was blowing through the window, and the angel was on the bed with me. She lay propped on her elbows, her chin on her hands. She was staring at me.

"I've got to go," I said.

"I know."

I looked around for my clothes. They were scattered around the room. I got dressed without saying a word. I picked up the backpack and sat down on the bed next to her. The angel reached over and kissed me.

"Write me when you get there," she said. "I promise I'll write back."

I stood up and walked to the door. I turned around and looked at the angel one more time. She looked particularly beautiful at that moment. I wanted to tell her that I was in love with her, but I kept my mouth shut.

No sense in ruining a good thing.

36

Four days later, I was in the Sunshine State. It was exhilarating. As Chuck's 1968 Ford Fairlane was launching itself onto the Howard Frankland Bridge for the twelve-mile journey across the water, I stuck my head out the window and inhaled the crisp, salty air of Old Tampa Bay. The wind ran its fingers through my hair and caressed my face as we whizzed past the pelicans and ospreys that were perched on each lamppost. The two narrow lanes that hurled us toward Saint Petersburg and the Pinellas County mainland were like a race track with no exit. There were no shoulders on either side and no place to pull over if we were to have a flat tire or car trouble. We were separated from the onslaught of vehicles coming at us from the other direction by a raised concrete barrier that seemed to be our only defense against an otherwise inevitable head-on collision. Chuck was driving sixty miles per hour, but cars sped past us like we were standing still.

Suddenly, from the back seat, I heard the voice of Elmer Fudd. "Aaaahh…rrrrr…we wear wet?" it slurred.

The pills that Danny had given Ozzie were starting to wear off. He had a mouthful of gauze and was obviously in pain. His four wisdom teeth were gone, and Georgetown Dental School was eleven dollars richer. Ozzie looked disoriented, so I asked him if he wanted a beer. He appeared to nod yes, so I reached into Chuck's cooler and grabbed two cold cans of Budweiser. I popped the tops and handed one to Ozzie.

Chuck had picked us up the day before at Danny's apartment in Alexandria, and we drove straight through the night, stopping only to piss or get gas. He was on his way to Orlando for a job interview at the new Disneyworld that had opened last year and was only planning on taking us as far as Tampa. However, before passing out, Ozzie had talked him into driving us all the way to Indian Rocks Beach and *Dreams Come True*, where we hoped to find Bernie.

I didn't know what to expect, but I couldn't wait to get there. When we barreled off the bridge onto the mainland, I realized for the first time how warm it was. It was the middle of the day, and the sun was high in the sky. I took off my T-shirt and stuck my arm out the window. It was the first week of September, and the temperature had to be at least ninety degrees.

The beer seemed to have lifted Ozzie out of his stupor. I still couldn't understand what he was mumbling about, but he reached over my shoulder and handed me a slip of paper with some directions written down. We turned onto SR 688 and made our way through Largo toward Indian Rocks Beach. Thirteen miles later, we crossed over the Intracoastal Waterway on an open grate bridge where the highway ended abruptly at the traffic light on Gulf Boulevard.

The light turned green, and we turned left. My parents' motel was located about a quarter mile south of the intersection. The light-gray two-story building was set back a few hundred feet from the road behind a cluster of shrubs and two fan-shaped palm trees. As we turned into the hard-packed shell, sand, and dirt driveway, we spotted a beat-up Rambler with Colorado plates parked next to a shiny new Ford LTD Country Squire station wagon with Georgia plates. Bernie was sitting on the seawall, staring out at the Gulf of Mexico, and he quickly turned around when he heard us pull in. Chuck turned off the engine, and Ozzie and I stepped out of the car. Bernie jumped to his feet and ran toward us. He was totally freaked out. He insisted we grab all our shit and throw it in his car. He said we had to get out of here. I asked him why, and he said that he would tell us later.

Ozzie and I grabbed our backpacks, said goodbye to Chuck, and jumped into the Rambler. Bernie ran to the door marked Manager's Office and raced inside. Thirty seconds later, he rushed out carrying a backpack, a rolled-up sleeping bag, and a No Vacancy sign. He shut the door, hung the No Vacancy sign, and ran back to the Rambler. He jumped into the driver's seat and started the engine on his second try. We peeled out of the parking lot in a cloud of dust and headed south on Gulf Boulevard. Ozzie was in the back seat, mumbling something unintelligible again. Bernie wanted to know what was wrong with him. I explained that Danny Cooper had just pulled out Ozzie's four wisdom teeth at Georgetown Dental School and that Ozzie had done it because it only cost eleven dollars.

Now it was my turn to ask questions. Where were Mom and Dad? Why did we have to split so fast from the motel? I stressed that we had driven straight through from DC, and we were tired. I wanted to see Mom and Dad and check out their place. Shit, I wanted to check out the beach and go for a swim in the Gulf. What the fuck were we running from?

Apparently, we were running for good reason. Mom and Dad had gone to the East Coast for a few days to visit friends and had made the rather dubious decision to leave Bernie in charge of the motel. They should have known better, but to them it seemed like a safe bet. Labor Day weekend was over, and only one of the apartments was rented. A young couple from Georgia with two small children was renting the downstairs unit next to theirs, and the odds were slim that anyone else would show up looking for a room. All Bernie had to do was answer the phone if it rang and hand out fresh towels to this nice family for two days. How hard could that be? How were they to know that this straight, clean-cut husband and father in his late twenties would hit up Bernie for some dope?

Bernie had landed a construction job a week earlier on Madeira Beach, and with his first paycheck, he had scored an ounce of pot. Selling a nickel bag to the Georgia dude seemed harmless enough, and he could use the five dollars, so Bernie took him up on his offer. What a mistake! This guy had never smoked marijuana before, and he wanted Bernie to show him how to roll a joint and how to smoke it. Around eleven o'clock at night, they met down to the beach to get high. Everything was going fine until the Georgia dude's fourth or fifth toke. Suddenly, he started acting all crazy, claiming to see weird colors and insects crawling all over his body. It was as if he was doing acid or peyote or some other strange shit. The next thing Bernie knew, the dude ran off the beach and disappeared into the night.

Bernie laughed and sat down in the sand, finishing what was left of the joint. That was weird, he thought. He left the beach and walked back up to the motel. The Georgia dude's wife was waiting for him at the door. Bernie's first thought was that she looked pretty hot, but then he noticed that she had been crying. She suddenly started screaming at Bernie and beating him on the chest. She demanded to know what he had given her husband. Bernie thought she was kidding and started laughing. She wasn't. She called Bernie a dope fiend and threatened to call the cops. Bernie took off running for the beach again and ended up sitting next to the water the rest of the night. He definitely didn't want to be at the motel if the cops showed up.

Bernie waited until sunrise before venturing back to Mom and Dad's apartment. There was no sign of law enforcement. He went inside and wolfed down a banana and a bowl of Cheerios. It looked like he was in the clear. He went back outside, took off his shirt, and stretched out on the seawall. Exhausted, he fell asleep.

Bernie wasn't sure how long he had been asleep, but the next thing he remembered, someone was shaking him violently by the shoulders. Convinced that this was part of the X-rated dream he was having about the Georgia dude's hot-looking wife, he kept his eyes closed and stretched out to enjoy it. The shaking became more violent until finally Bernie had to open his eyes. It was the Georgia dude, not his wife. The dude was in a panic. He told Bernie that he had kept his wife from calling the police by telling her that if the cops came out, they would probably arrest him along with Bernie. However, he wasn't sure how much longer he could keep her from making the phone call. He explained that his wife was worried that Bernie might give drugs to their two little daughters who were seven and five years old. He begged Bernie to leave before it was too late.

Bernie rubbed the sleep out of his eyes. About a hundred feet away on the beach, the dude's wife and two daughters were sitting together on a blanket. One of the little girls was holding a sand bucket, while the other played with a small beach ball. The dude's wife was glaring across the sand at Bernie. She didn't look anything like the woman in his X-rated dream.

Bernie was torn over what to do. He was expecting Ozzie and me sometime that day and wanted to be there when we arrived. However, getting busted for selling a nickel bag would be a lot worse than not being there when we showed up. He decided to go back inside and pack up his shit in case he had to leave in a hurry. There wasn't much to do. He had a sleeping bag that was already rolled up, and the rest of his possessions filled his backpack with room to spare. He left his belongings in the apartment by the front door and went outside to await his fate. When he heard Chuck's car pull in the parking lot, he assumed it was the Indian Rocks Beach Police. When he saw Ozzie and me jump out of the Ford Fairlane, he breathed a sigh of relief. At least for today he was destined to stay one step ahead of the law.

"So where are we going?" I asked.

"Madeira Beach," he answered. "I rented an apartment there a few days ago."

Ozzie reached into his mouth and pulled out the gauze.

"Is it bigger than the Top Shelf?" he asked.

37

My life of leisure was over. With no money for food, rent, or weed, I had no choice but to look for a job. Bernie claimed that in Florida, all you had to do was show up at a construction site wearing a hardhat and a pair of steel-toe shoes, and you would be hired on the spot.

The construction boom that was beginning to swallow up the nearly thirty miles of pristine white sand between Clearwater Beach and St. Pete Beach was slowly making its way toward the sleepy beach town of Madeira. Located just seven miles south of Indian Rocks Beach and bordered to the east by Boca Ciega Bay, Madeira Beach was one of Pinellas County's eleven barrier islands. There were two major construction projects underway at the time. One was a new Holiday Inn that was being erected on the Gulf near 150th Street. That's where Bernie had found his job. On the opposite side of Gulf Boulevard along the inlet of the Intracoastal Waterway, a large condominium community was beginning to take shape. Both projects were within walking distance of Bernie's apartment. Ozzie elected to help Bernie build the Holiday Inn. I decided it would be more fun to build condos.

Much to my surprise, Bernie had actually found us a decent place to live just one block from the Gulf of Mexico. The furnished one-bedroom apartment was on the second floor of a brown two-story box-shaped building at the corner of Palm Street and 141st Street. It might have been a little small for the three of us, but considering all the other places we had crashed at over the summer, it felt like we were taking up residence at the Taj Mahal. There were two single beds in the tiny bedroom and a couch in the living room. Ozzie, who had grown accustomed to sleeping in the attic on Franklin Mountain and the closet at Get Stoned Leather, volunteered to move one of the beds into the large closet behind the kitchen. Bernie and I decided to take turns sleeping on the other bed. Since Bernie had been the one to find the apartment, I figured it was only right for me to take the couch for the first week. We agreed to split the $275-a-month rent three ways. Since I was down to my last ten dollars, Ozzie dug deep into his inheritance and agreed to cover my portion until I could pay him back. With a little more prodding, I convinced him to also lend me money for a hardhat and steel-toe shoes.

Bernie was right about getting hired on the spot. It was Friday afternoon when I walked into the scratched-up white trailer near the front of the job site. As I opened the door, I was ambushed by a thick cloud of cigarette smoke and the unmistakable smell of whiskey. A rough-looking character was leaning back in his chair with his hands behind his head and both feet resting on top of a metal desk. A white hardhat with SUPERINTENDENT imprinted on the front was relaxing next to his right foot, along with an opened bottle of Jack Daniel's. A half-smoked, unfiltered Camel was dangling from his lips. He looked to be about fifty years old but was probably a lot younger. He took the Camel out of his mouth, flipped the ashes on the floor, and asked me if I had any construction experience. I told him no, and he offered me a job as a laborer. It paid $2.50 an hour. He said to come back on Monday morning.

"Don't be late," he growled. "We start at seven."

I learned later that I should have lied. Over at the Holiday Inn, Bernie and Ozzie had claimed to be experienced carpenter helpers and had conned their way to $3.00 an hour.

I hated the job. By Thursday I was ready to quit. Unfortunately, that wasn't going to happen. My debt to Ozzie and next month's rent, food, beer, and pot, though not necessarily in that order, were pushing and shoving one another, each demanding their rightful place at the front of the line. I was going to be building condominiums for a while.

The first challenge was to make it to work every morning by 7:00 a.m., and that wasn't easy after a night of killer weed, Busch beer, and maybe four hours of sleep. Making it through the entire day at work was even harder. This may not have been the worst job in the history of the world, but it had to be right up there with the most pointless and most boring. My janitor's job at Harvard may have prepared me for working one hour and fucking off for three, but I was now faced with the monumental task of fucking off for eight hours with the only break being thirty minutes for lunch. I used my math degree from Northeastern to motivate myself. Eight hours times two dollars and fifty cents equaled twenty dollars. Five days times twenty dollars equaled one hundred a week. College hadn't been a total waste of time.

Fortunately, I was assigned to a crew that had mastered the deceptive art of doing nothing but appearing to be busy all the time. These three shirtless, pony-tailed crazies knew how to turn even the most menial tasks into fierce competitions or games of danger and hide-and-seek. An assignment to clean out the trash in the newly constructed units at the far end of the property to get them ready for the drywall guys became a game of ice hockey with our brooms and shovels. Carrying iron rods across the property was turned into a game of chicken with another crew walking the wood planks and edges of buildings two floors up. Mickey, the craziest of the three, would poke at the feet of these high-wire acrobats with an iron rod, laughing as they jumped and danced to avoid a fall. Sometimes we found empty buildings where we could smoke pot and take naps. At other times, Mickey and his buddies would get bored and make a game out of sabotaging the plumbing in one of the units, seeing how many rocks and bits of gravel they could drop down the exposed pipes. I didn't take part in this. Maybe it was my small-town Honest Abe upbringing kicking in. Fucking off on the job was one thing, but fucking up the plumbing was another. I looked the other way.

By the second week, I finally got it. Hal, the whiskey-drinking superintendent, had no idea where we were or what we were doing. He walked the job site a couple of times a day but spent most of his day in his trailer, sipping Jack Daniel's or nursing a hangover. Unless we made a point of being seen, the only times he noticed us were in the morning when we punched in, at eleven o'clock when we broke for lunch, and at the end of the day when we clocked out. I had an idea. On Tuesday morning, right after we had clocked in and were heading out for another imaginary job, I checked with Mickey and his buddies to see if they had any problem with me splitting. After all, I pointed out, since we weren't actually doing any work, the three of them wouldn't be stuck picking up the slack for me. I promised to be back by lunch. Mickey laughed and gave me the power handshake.

"You're a righteous dude," he said.

I picked up the brown paper bag containing my bologna sandwich and can of Coke and hustled to the back of the property, sneaking along the seawall until I reached Gulf Boulevard. I crossed the road, trotted past the soon-to-be Holiday Inn, and walked the nine blocks to the apartment. Bernie kept a small alarm clock next to the bed, and I set it for 10:30. I took off my clothes and jumped into bed. When the alarm went off, I leaped up and got dressed. I was cutting it close, but I hurried up Gulf Boulevard and made it back to the job just as my three partners in crime were breaking for lunch. I had forgotten to bring mine.

"Way to go, man," said Mickey. "You pulled it off."

Everyone ate lunch except me. I figured that was okay, since I could split after the break and go back to the apartment where my bologna sandwich would still be waiting for me. I went to the trailer and walked in to find Hal having his liquid lunch. I didn't really want anything. I just wanted him to see me and know I was at work that day.

"What are you doing in here?" he asked.

"I just wanted to thank you for giving me this job," I said.

Hal was speechless. Apparently, no one had ever said that to him before.

This job was going to be okay after all. I made sure not to do the same thing every day, but I made sure that Hal saw me clock in every morning at seven and clock out at the end of the day. Some mornings, I stuck around until lunchtime. Other mornings, I left right away and went back home to bed. If I stayed through lunch, I usually split in the afternoon and went to the beach. I always made it back by four to punch out. On Fridays, I would sneak off both in the morning and in the afternoon but would always make it back in time to pick up my paycheck. Bernie and Ozzie were pissed. They might have been making $3.00 an hour, but I had the last laugh. They had to work all day. Or so they claimed.

Meanwhile, I was getting a great tan. Now I had to figure out how to get laid.

38

Ozzie had a new toy.

Reaching one more time into his inheritance, he hitchhiked over to Largo and purchased a brand-new Kawasaki S1 250 motorcycle. He now had his own transportation and was convinced that he had raised his level of coolness. However, as he rumbled up and down the road on his red Rice Burner, wearing his matching red helmet, no one mistook him for a Hells Angel. Always the optimist, Ozzie believed it was increasing his chances of picking up a chick.

Living just one block from the Gulf of Mexico was amazing to me. It seemed like a prime location to meet girls. The three-mile stretch of white sand from 150th Street down to John's Pass was dotted with a few small mom-and-pop motels and one ramshackle biker bar. Our view of the water at the end of 141st Street was partially blocked by a series of small sand dunes anchored in place by sea oats. These long, thin blades of grass were three to four feet in height, each crowned with a small cluster of large golden-brown seeds. Getting to the beach was as simple as stripping down to my cutoff shorts and strolling barefoot and shirtless across Gulf Boulevard. If I navigated the narrow path between the dunes, I was sure to find a flock of Florida girls in bikinis just waiting to meet me.

I was delusional. It was September, and even though the water was still warm and the temperatures were in the eighties and nineties, the beaches were mostly empty, especially during the week. Schools were back in session, and the tourist onslaught was not expected until the winter holidays after Thanksgiving. Bernie, Ozzie, and I scoured the beach every day, looking for any sign of approachable females. Weekdays, it was a waste of time. By the time we got off work, it was a ghost town. On the afternoons that I snuck away from work, I only discovered an occasional young mother with a couple of small kids or a few heavy-set middle-aged women in one-piece bathing suits. It was depressing. The weekends were a little better as the locals came over from Tampa and the mainland to catch some rays. Still, it was mostly couples or groups of guys, interrupted occasionally by small pockets of teenage girls seemingly scattered around to improve the scenery. Even with the rare sighting of one or two good-looking girls in their early twenties sitting alone on their towels, the three of us seemed incapable of doing anything. Even Ozzie was lost. We were Northern boys. None of us knew how to make a move at the beach.

We put our heads together and decided that it was time to hit the bars. We first tried the biker bar across the road. That was a mistake. All we found were three tattooed dudes with ponytails who looked at us suspiciously when we walked in. They kept their eyes fixed on us while they nursed their beers. I couldn't tell if they were looking for trouble or looking to avoid it. It didn't matter. We had one beer each and left. We had heard that the best bar for girls was Shadrack's. Nine miles from our apartment, it was located at the far end of St. Pete Beach in the small beach community of Pass-a-Grille. We went there on a Friday night, and the place was packed. Unfortunately for us, it was packed with a shitload more guys than girls. They had their pick of longhaired dudes, and they weren't picking us. Bernie saw the handwriting on the wall and left after an hour or so in his Rambler. Ozzie and I stuck around, hoping that our luck would change. It didn't. The bar was dark, and the music was loud. Rows of quarters were lined up on the pool tables, and the raucous noise of Foosball competition could be heard above the pounding rock and roll. With the exception of an occasional Allman Brothers song, the jukebox was dominated by Derek and the Dominoes, the Doobie Brothers, and Elton John. The Doobie's "Listen to the Music" was the most popular, with Eric Clapton and "Layla" a close second. I don't remember the ride home. Ozzie claimed that I passed out on the back of his Rice Burner and that he had saved my life just like he had saved my albums. According to him, he held on to my unconscious body and kept it from falling off the bike as he negotiated the grated bridge over John's Pass. What I do remember is that neither of us got laid that night.

This was going to be harder than we thought. Over the next week, we hit a different bar every night, and every night we came up empty. Ozzie was especially frustrated and determined to score. He had noticed that some of his fellow longhair construction workers at the Holiday Inn called out to and whistled at every girl who walked by on the beach. Why not give it a try? he thought. Bernie was embarrassed by the whole thing. He didn't want any part of it and ran for cover whenever Ozzie went into action. Ozzie didn't care. Whenever he had the chance, he would sneak back to the part of the open building that faced the beach and yell out at every girl he saw. It took him three days before his efforts finally paid off.

Unfortunately, they were underage.

39

I was the first one home from work on that Friday afternoon and had just stepped out of the shower and put on my shorts when they walked in. Bernie was the first through the door and was shaking his head. I could see he wasn't happy. Behind him were two teenage girls in dirty jeans and skimpy halter tops. They didn't look to be more than fifteen. Ozzie was close behind. He had a big grin on his face.

Bernie went straight to the bedroom and slammed the door. The two girls went over to the couch and sat down. Ozzie told them he would be right back and headed to his room behind the kitchen to get his pot. I followed him into the kitchen and asked him what the hell he was doing. Ozzie explained that they were from Ohio and they needed a place to crash. I told him that he was crazy and asked him how old they were. Ozzie didn't know but insisted everything was cool because they would only be staying a few days. Bernie came out of the bedroom and joined us in the kitchen. He was pissed at Ozzie and agreed with me that they were too young and we couldn't let them stay here. Ozzie countered that they had no place to go and no money for food, and the least we could do was feed them. Bernie and I didn't like it, but we reluctantly gave in to the idea of offering them a meal. After that, they would have to go. Ozzie agreed. He offered to cook his regular concoction of spaghetti and meat sauce. It was the only thing he knew how to make, but at least he was good at it. After supper, Bernie and I rolled a joint, grabbed a six-pack of Busch from the refrigerator, and announced that we were going over to the beach to watch the sunset. We wanted out of the apartment, and we made Ozzie promise that the girls would be gone by the time we got back.

I had not missed a sunset since my arrival in Florida. No two were ever alike, but each one had been spectacular. Tonight was no exception. As the sun began its slow descent into the Gulf of Mexico, the sky grew bolder and uninhibited. Light shimmered on the water while an incredible show of color exploded across the sky, mixing vibrant oranges and reds with softer and subtle pastels. Bernie handed me what was left of the joint. I took a toke and watched as a solitary pelican floated by, silhouetted against the reflection of the sun on the water. I fell back on the sand, closed my eyes, and listened to the eternal sound of the waves rolling ashore and then retreating back into the sea. It was my favorite time of the day.

Bernie didn't want to go back. He insisted that we stay on the beach and drink all our beers. He didn't trust Ozzie and was worried the girls would still be there when we got back. I popped the top of my second Busch and came to Ozzie's defense, reminding him that Ozzie had given us his word. The trailing edge of the red sun dropped below the horizon, and I saw what looked like a flash of green light. Bernie laughed and told me I was a fool. He reminded me that I didn't know Ozzie as well as he did and pointed out that they had spent the entire summer together. As the light continued to fade, we drank our beers and stalled for time. Thirty minutes later, it was completely dark. We finished off the six-pack, scooped up the empties, and headed in the direction of the apartment. As we crossed Gulf Boulevard, the sound of Led Zeppelin's "When the Levee Breaks" filled the air. We were a block from home, but there was no doubt where the music was coming from. We feared the worst but kept walking. There was no turning back now.

Bernie had been right about Ozzie. He was sitting on the couch, smoking a cigarette, and the two teenage girls were sprawled out on the floor, giggling as they passed Ozzie's recently acquired water pipe back and forth to one another. They both had wet hair. Each was wearing one of Ozzie's long T-shirts and apparently nothing else. Their jeans, halter tops, bras, and panties and two wet towels were scattered haphazardly on the floor near the bathroom door.

Bernie went ballistic. He rushed over to the stereo and turned down the music.

"What the fuck is going on here?" he screamed.

"I told them that they could take a shower," Ozzie said. "What's the big deal?"

Bernie was incredulous.

"What's the big deal!" he exclaimed. "Are you trying to get us thrown in jail?"

One of the girls stood up to go to the bathroom. She was the cuter of the two and had curly blond hair. As she rose to her feet, her T-shirt rode up to her hips and confirmed that she was wearing nothing underneath.

"Relax," said Ozzie. "I didn't do anything. I just let them take a shower."

"So what are they doing with your bong?" I asked.

"Hey," he replied. "They asked me if they could get high. I brought out my new water pipe for them to try."

Bernie glared at Ozzie.

"You're an idiot," he said. "They can't stay here. They have to go."

The girl with curly blond hair came out of the bathroom, and the other girl started to cry. She had straight black hair and small patches of acne dotting her face. When she told the blond girl that they were being thrown out, they both stated crying.

"Please," the blond girl begged. "Where are we supposed to go? It is dark out, and we have no place to stay. Please let us sleep here tonight. We promise we will leave in the morning."

Bernie and I were pissed off, but we didn't know what to do. They were laying a huge guilt trip on us and making us feel like shit. Ozzie wasn't any help. He pleaded their case over and over until we finally gave in and said they could stay for the night. We decided to give them each a sleeping bag and let them sleep on the floor in the living room. It was Bernie's week to have the bed in the bedroom, so I was stuck next to them in the living room on the couch.

When it finally came time to go to bed, Ozzie headed off to his room behind the kitchen and Bernie went into the bedroom and closed the door. I took off my shirt, kept my shorts on, and got under the blanket on the couch. Still wearing Ozzie's T-shirts, the two girls crawled into their sleeping bags and buried their heads. Before they went to sleep, there was something that I needed to know.

"How old are you girls?" I asked.

The blond girl poked her head out. She seemed embarrassed.

"Thirteen," she said and quickly slipped her head back into the sleeping bag.

It took me a while to fall, asleep but once I did, I was out for the count. If it had not been for Bernie's loud snoring, I would have made it until morning. Coming out of a deep sleep, it took me a few minutes to clear my head and collect my thoughts. Why was I hearing Bernie snoring? I didn't remember him snoring this loud before. It made no sense. He was in the bedroom with the door closed.

Or was he?

Bernie let out a loud snort. I rolled over and rubbed the sleep out of my eyes. It was the crack of dawn, and the day's first light was beginning to creep through the small opening in the curtains near the door. As my eyes adjusted, I saw that Bernie had spread himself out diagonally across the two sleeping bags. He was on his back and naked. The two girls were nowhere in sight.

I jumped off the couch, fell to the floor, and began shaking Bernie by the shoulders.

"Wake up," I said. "Wake up."

Startled and half asleep, Bernie quickly sat up and pushed me away.

"What are you doing here on the floor?" I asked. "Where are the girls?"

Bernie opened his eyes and shrugged his shoulders.

"One of them is probably in the bedroom," he said. "She came in while I was sleeping and crawled into bed with me. She started grabbing me and woke me up. I told her to get away from me, but she wouldn't leave. I finally told her she could have the bed, and I came out here to sleep."

"Which girl was it?" I asked.

Bernie thought for a second and rubbed his head.

"I think it was one with the zits," he replied.

"What about the other one?" I asked.

"I don't know," he said. "She wasn't here when I came out."

My heart sank into my stomach. I didn't need to be Sherlock Holmes to know where to find the girl with curly blond hair.

"Put your pants on," I said to Bernie. "We need to get them out of here right now."

Bernie opened the door to the bedroom and picked his shorts off the floor. The girl with black hair was asleep on the bed, facedown on top of the sheets with the T-shirt pulled up over her hips. Bernie slipped into his cutoffs and walked over to the bed. He tapped the girl on the shoulder.

"Get dressed," he said. "It's time to leave."

I looked away as she was getting out of bed and sprinted toward the kitchen. I knew that I was too late. The door to Ozzie's room was open. I looked in, and there they were. The girl with curly blond hair was resting her head on Ozzie's bare chest. Ozzie was asleep, but the girl was awake, and she looked up and smiled when she saw me standing at the door. Her T-shirt was on the floor.

"Get up," I said. "You need to get dressed and get out of here."

"Okay," was all she said as she threw off Ozzie's sheet and jumped out of bed. I stepped back to let her walk through the door. I was surprised at how comfortable she seemed as she paraded past me and through the kitchen naked. Ozzie was still out cold.

When I walked into the living room, Bernie was standing next to the two girls. The girl with black hair was already dressed, but the blond girl had just slipped into her panties and was putting on her bra.

"Hurry up," I said. "You both need to get out of here right now."

A few minutes later, they were gone. Bernie and I went into Ozzie's room and woke him up. Ozzie rolled over and reached for his pack of Marlboros. He lit a cigarette and took a long drag.

"What's happening?" he asked.

"You asshole," Bernie said. "You better hope the cops don't show up here today."

"What's the matter with you?" I asked. "She was only thirteen years old."

Ozzie looked surprised.

"Thirteen?" he said. "How was I supposed to know that? She told me she was fifteen."

40

I didn't know much about karma, but I think it showed up three days later to slap Ozzie upside the head and bite him in the ass. The same day that Bernie and I kicked out the underage girls, we acquired new neighbors in the apartment below us. We had gone over to the beach that afternoon, and on our way back, we saw a red, white, and blue Ford Econoline van with California plates parked on the street in front of our building. The door to the downstairs apartment was open, and as we started up the stairs, a pretty blonde materialized on the sidewalk. She was holding a small child. Her name was Hannah, and her daughter's name was Lindsey. Lindsey had just turned two years old and had inherited her mother's big green eyes and golden hair. Their hairstyles were identical, almost carbon copies of the one worn by the gymnast Cathy Rigby. Hannah and her daughter had been on the road for nearly two months with her best friend Sue and their mutual friend Nick.

The party was Ozzie's idea. He thought that it would give him the best shot to make a move on Hannah. It was Tuesday night. Ozzie offered to dip into his inheritance one more time and pay for everything. He asked Bernie to drive him to the nearest 7-Eleven. An hour later, they returned with two cases of Busch beer, three bottles of Mateus wine, four bags of Wise potato chips, a jar of peanuts, two packs of Zig-Zag rolling papers, a large Coleman cooler, and a bag of ice. Ozzie filled the cooler with all the beers it would hold, dumped in the ice, and put the remaining beers in the refrigerator. He then went to his room and retrieved his water pipe and bag of pot. He placed them on the coffee table in the living room and stormed into the bathroom just as I was stepping out of the shower. He handed me the keys to his Kawasaki.

"No matter what happens," he exclaimed, "don't give me my keys. I'm planning on getting fucked up tonight."

"Okay," I said as I grabbed a towel.

"No, I'm serious," he continued. "I'll get wasted tonight, and I'll want to take off on my bike. No matter how much I beg you or get pissed off at you, *do not* give me the keys. Promise?"

"I promise," I said. "Now do you mind if I dry off and get dressed?"

It was our first party in Madeira Beach, and it was a good one. Ozzie had gone to Shadrack's the night before and spread the word. In addition to Hannah and her friends, our tiny apartment eventually filled up with at least a dozen people that I had never seen before. Ozzie was in his glory. Right after we moved into the apartment, he had gone into St. Pete with Bernie and bought a new stereo system that he was now proud to show off. He had started to replace the album collection that he had lost on Franklin Mountain, and the foundation of our building was pulsating to the relentless sounds of Deep Purple, Alice Cooper, and the Stones. Ozzie's water pipe and bottles of Mateus began to circulate in unison, taking on the identity of batons in an Olympic relay race. Ozzie had produced a masterpiece. As the speed of the hand-offs increased, the Zen-like exchanges of smoke and alcohol seemed on the verge of creating a new art form.

Throughout the night, Ozzie stayed true to form, refusing to deviate from his usual life-of-the-party, storytelling self. He was the star of the show, and he was counting on his performance to help him snare Hannah. Maybe it was the effects of the weed and wine, but from where I was buzzing, the vision of Hannah was stunning. Her big green eyes commanded the room. She was wearing a sheer-white top with spaghetti straps, navy-blue shorts, and light-brown sandals. Whenever she stood near the opening to the kitchen, the fluorescent light passed through the thin material of her blouse, revealing the outline of her breasts and her erect nipples.

As the night wore on, Ozzie became more and more possessive of Hannah's attention. Whenever he spotted either Bernie or me talking to her, he rushed over and jumped between us. It pissed me off because I wanted to make a move, and I could tell that

Bernie also had his sights set on her. So that Hannah could attend the party, Sue and Nick had agreed to take turns with her, watching over Lindsey. Ozzie became restless whenever Hannah left the party and went downstairs for her thirty-minute shift, worried that she wouldn't return. When Hannah came back to the party for the third time around midnight, Sue told her that she was ready to crash and would be happy to stay with Lindsey for the rest of the night. With Lindsey now safe and secure until morning, Ozzie moved in for the kill. Rising from the ashes of his protracted state of intoxication, he now possessed the clarity of purpose. His fate was sealed. Hannah was his for the night, and nothing could stop him. Armed only with his dubious charm and what was left of the last bottle of Mateus, he coaxed her over to the couch and went into a full-court press. Confident of victory, he took her hand and offered to show her the large closet behind the kitchen that masqueraded as his bedroom. He might have made it if karma had not chosen that exact moment to make its introduction.

"Is Ozzie here?" it asked.

I didn't recognize her at first. She was wearing clean clothes, and her curly blond hair smelled like strawberry shampoo. She was prettier than I remembered, and she looked older than her thirteen years. It was probably the bright-red lipstick.

"What are you doing here?" I asked. "I thought you were going back to Ohio."

She smiled and dropped her eyes to the floor.

"I'm not from Ohio," she said. "I'm from Tampa. I just come over to the beach to party."

Ozzie and Hannah had made it as far as the kitchen.

"Ozzie!" I shouted with joy. "There's someone here to see you."

Ozzie's evening of glory was about to come to an end. Scrambling to recover, he mumbled some bullshit to Hannah and then stepped outside with the little blond girl. It took him nearly ten minutes, but he finally managed to break her heart and persuade her to leave. By the time he walked back in, I had made my move on Hannah. I reached in my pocket and grabbed the keys to the Rice Burner.

"Here," I said, flipping him the keys. "Why don't you go for a ride?"

Ozzie saw the writing on the wall. He made a great catch with his left hand, told me to go fuck myself, and stumbled out the door. A minute later, I heard the roar of the Kawasaki as it peeled out into the night. I turned my attention back to Hannah.

She didn't seem that interested in me, but I was banking on the slim chance she might be willing to take advantage of her night off from Lindsey. I noticed her exchanging glances with Bernie, who by this time looked resigned to the fact that this was not going to be his night. The apartment had nearly cleared out when I went over to him and asked if I could have the bedroom for the night. It wasn't my week, but we had an unwritten agreement to trade our sleeping arrangements whenever the opportunity presented itself.

Hannah agreed to sleep with me, but no matter how much I begged, she wouldn't let me go all the way. She stripped down to her panties and let me suck on and play with her tits as much as I wanted, but that was as far as it went. I pleaded with her to touch my cock but got nowhere. Desperate and aching to ejaculate, I mounted and dry-humped her until I squirted all over her stomach. She was sound asleep as the first morning light infiltrated the room. As messed up as I was, it was only Wednesday morning, and I needed to make an appearance at my dreaded construction job. Dragging my ass out of bed was not easy. I managed to get dressed without waking her, and after drinking three glasses of water and forcing down a bowl of Shredded Wheat, I took a disgusting runny shit, washed my face, and brushed my teeth. Bernie was passed out on the couch, and the living room floor was littered with empty beer cans and a few unwanted potato chips. Ozzie's water pipe stood majestically in the middle of the coffee table, surrounded by ashtrays overflowing with cigarette butts. Stale smoke monopolized the entire apartment, and it wasn't until I opened the door and stepped out into the world that I got my first real hit of oxygen.

When I reached the bottom of the stairs, I noticed Ozzie's Kawasaki had been dumped on the sidewalk. Beside the fact that it wasn't standing upright on its kickstand, something didn't look right. The paint on the front fender was riddled with scratches, and the rear subframe looked a little bent. Ozzie was nowhere in sight, so I assumed that he was upstairs in bed. I walked the nine blocks to work, and it felt like the longest morning of my life. After three pointless hours and my third bout with diarrhea, I abandoned the port-a-potty and decided it was time to go home and go back to bed.

When I walked in, Ozzie was sitting on the couch, smoking a cigarette and rubbing his right leg. His shin was all scraped up, and I could see that his knee had been bleeding. The door to the bedroom was closed.

"Where's Bernie?" I asked.

Ozzie flipped me the bird and pointed toward the bedroom. I walked over and opened the door. Bernie was flat on his back. Hannah looked up at me with her big green eyes and slowly released Bernie's penis from her mouth.

"Sorry," she said. "I like your brother better than you."

41

It had been six weeks.

Six weeks since I left New York. Six weeks since I left Isadora. Six weeks since I last got laid. It was now the middle of October, and I was suffering through the longest dry spell since my freshman year in college. The reality of my decision to come to Florida had finally sunk in. I was starting to doubt myself. Bernie and Ozzie seemed cool with the lifestyle here, but I felt like a fish out of water. This place wasn't me.

It didn't help that I wasn't getting laid, but it was much more than that. Sure, I loved living on the beach. I could go swimming and body surf whenever I wanted. I wore nothing but cutoff shorts and T-shirts. I went to the beach every day at sunset and smoked a joint. Except for the one week in September that something called the red tide invaded the Gulf and hundreds of dead fish washed up on Madeira Beach, it had been perfect. That wasn't it. The newness of beach life had worn off. I would be twenty-five in a few months, and here I was working as a construction laborer for $2.50 an hour with less than two hundred dollars to my name. I was in the real world now. I was still okay with the fact that I had chosen not to join the system or make use of my college degree. I hadn't wavered because I didn't want to be one of those robots. Instead, I was determined to travel the world, meet cool and interesting people, and nourish my soul with wild and exotic experiences. Now just six weeks into this journey, I was depressed. Living on the Florida Gulf Coast with Bernie and Ozzie and working this shitty job had turned out to be a far cry from any of that.

More than anything, I missed Isadora Duncan. Her letters and poems had caught me completely off-guard. She seemed to miss me as much as I missed her. Had I misjudged her feelings for me that much? Although she had asked me to write and had promised to write back, her letters to me began within hours of my departure. I ached for her. I could taste her on the tip of my tongue. Even after six weeks, I could still smell her. Whenever I closed my eyes, I could feel the warm sensation of being inside her.

It was Sunday afternoon and I was alone. Ozzie, Bernie, and Hannah had gone over to the beach. The dozen or so letters that I had received from Isadora were spread across the kitchen table in chronological order. I hadn't opened the latest letter in yesterday's mail. Before I did, I wanted to reread the first one.

> *september 5*
> *~ jeff ~*
> *I drove slowly home, looking*
> *through misted eyes into the*
> *shadows of the nighted forest, alone.*
> *fortunately the household was*
> *sleeping. i went into my old*
> *childhood room, a place of comfort*
> *to me. slowly i undressed. changing*
> *from my red bandana into my*
> *old worn print nightgown. it is*
> *so faded and torn that my breast*
> *is uncovered. it is so soft,*
> *why is it not your skin though?*
> *i remember long ago my*
> *mother bought me this nightgown,*
> *for no reason, save the only true reason*
> *for giving because she thought of me.*
> *i am empty-full and full-empty ~ ~ ~*
> *i am saturated ~ hollow ~ ~ ~*
> *if i begin this, i will not stop, for we are endless*
> *but as you said, and i know,*
> *words are only futile attempts to describe life*

I set it back on the table and fumbled through the others. I picked up the two-page letter in which she had written down the entire lyrics to "Looks Like Rain," the Bob Weir song that had been the background music to so many of our afternoons in bed. The first two stanzas grabbed me by the throat.

> *I woke today*
> *And felt your side of the bed*
> *The covers were still warm where you'd been layin'*
> *You were gone...*
> *My heart was filled with dread*
> *You might not be sleepin' here again*
> *It's alright 'cause I love you*
> *And that's not gonna change*
> *Run me round, make me hurt again and again*
> *But I'll still sing you love songs*
> *Written in the letters of your name*
> *And brave the storm to come*
> *For it surely looks like rain*

I didn't bother to read the rest of the lyrics because I had memorized them by now. I skipped to where she ended her correspondence by joking about how long the song was and adding,

> *we fuck even longer than i thought*
> *here's to our balling!*
> *love, isadora*

What the fuck had I done? Should I have stayed in Oneonta? Was she as crazy about me as I was about her? I picked up the latest envelope and tore it open. Inside was a single piece of light-brown stationery containing just a few simple words:

> *i would like to lie beside*
> *you in bed tonight, not*
> *saying a word, just touching*
> *your outlines*

It was time to make a phone call.

42

Isadora had moved out of her room on Cherry Street and was sharing a house on Thorn Street in the West End with Penelope and Pete, Alex and Nancy, and two guys I didn't know named Larry and Darrell. Apparently, Nancy had returned from San Francisco, and she and Alex were back together again. When I called, Penelope answered. She wanted to know how I was doing, and we talked for a few minutes before she handed the phone to Isadora.

I was standing at the pay phone in front of the Candy Kitchen on Gulf Boulevard, armed with as much change as I could carry. I was determined to keep talking until I ran out of coins. Isadora seemed surprised that I had called but sounded happy to hear from me. The sound of her voice was music to my ears. I told her that I would quit my job the next day and hitchhike up to see her. She laughed and told me that was crazy.

"There's nothing for you to do up here," she insisted.

I knew she was right. There were no jobs in Oneonta. I needed to stay in Florida and keep working until I saved enough money to hit the road. Still, I didn't think I could stand another day without her, and I told her so. That's when she gave me something to look forward to. She said that she was thinking about coming to see me in Florida right after Christmas and wanted to know if that was okay.

Just thinking about it gave me an erection. I was down to my last few coins. I glanced up to see if anyone was walking toward me on the sidewalk. The last thing I wanted was for someone to see the bulge in my shorts and report me as a pervert making an obscene phone call.

We talked for a few more minutes until the operator came on and asked me to deposit another thirty-five cents. Unfortunately, all I had left was one dime and one nickel. Just like that, the call was over. It was back to letter writing. Christmas couldn't get here fast enough.

I may not have gone to Oneonta, but it wasn't very long before Oneonta came to me. Two days after I spoke with Isadora, Louie O'Malley showed up at the door. A week later, it was Kevin Henderson and his light-brown Mercury Comet, accompanied by Jelle Mertens and a yellow dog named Puke. My move to Florida had sparked some interest, and a few of my friends had hit up Isadora for my address. The problem was that Hannah was now staying with Bernie most nights, and the four of us were crammed into a one-bed-room apartment. There wasn't enough room for three more guys and a dog.

That's when Ozzie jumped into action and saved our asses.

Our landlady was a thirty-nine-year-old woman named Kitty. She lived in the other downstairs apartment next to Hannah, Lindsey, Sue, and Nick. Originally from Toronto, she had been living in Madeira Beach for the past ten years, managing the apartments for her parents, who owned the building and still lived in Canada. They also owned the four-bedroom, two-story house next door. We had no idea what it rented for, but no one was living there at the moment, and Ozzie was confident we could afford it if we all pooled our money. He went downstairs to see Kitty.

He came back about thirty minutes later. He was stoned.

"Power to the people," he said. "The house is ours!"

Bernie asked him how much the rent was.

"She normally rents it for six hundred," he answered, "but she said we can have it for three hundred. That's just twenty-five dollars more than we are paying now."

"How did you get her to let us have it so cheap?" I asked.

Ozzie cleared his throat and smiled.

"Well," he said. "There is one condition."

"What's that?" I asked.

"She said that you have to come to her apartment at least once a week and have sex with her."

"Me?"

"Yes, you," he answered. "I offered to do the job, but she insisted that it had to be you."

"Are you fucking with me?" I asked.

"Nope," he said. "In fact, she wants you to start right now. She's downstairs waiting for you."

I was sure that he was messing with me, but Ozzie was adamant. He said if I didn't do it, we would not get the house. Finally, Bernie spoke up.

"You gotta do it, man," he said. "We're counting on you."

Kevin and Jelle were sitting on floor, passing a joint. Kevin handed it to me.

"Here," he said. "Take a hit and get your ass down there."

I hadn't really had much interaction with Kitty since we moved into the apartment. Ozzie liked to flirt with her whenever he saw her sitting outside on the small brown brick wall in front of the building. She had a deep dark tan and dark auburn hair and was always in a pair of tight shorts so short that they showed off the cheeks of her ass. She seemed to have an endless supply of multicolor bandannas, which she wrapped around her chest to cover her breasts. Ozzie might have felt different, but to me she wasn't very pretty. I took a toke and passed the joint back to Kevin. Resigned to doing my part, I floated out the door and down the stairs. What the hell, I thought. At least I was finally going to get laid.

I knocked three times before she opened the door. A purple-and-red bandanna was tied around her neck, hanging loose over her bare chest like an oversize napkin. Kitty was barefoot and had already unbuttoned and unzipped the front of her navy-blue shorts. The apartment was dark, illuminated only by a half dozen candles scattered strategically around the living room. She had placed a dark multicolored blanket on the floor and had lit two sticks of incense. The Moody Blues' *Days of Future Passed* album cover stood next to the stereo. "Nights in White Satin" had just started to play. Kitty untied the bandanna and let it fall to the floor. She stepped out of her shorts and motioned for me to join her on the blanket. I noticed that she did not have any tan lines. I wondered where she went to sunbathe in the nude.

"Would you like to smoke some hash?" she said.

"Sure."

I sat down on the blanket. Kitty turned and walked toward the bedroom. Her skin was very dark and had the look of leather. As she strolled out of the room, I caught a glimpse of her natural skin color beneath the fold of each of her butt cheeks where the sun hadn't managed to shine. This woman had obviously spent a lot of time in the sun. She returned a minute later, holding a hash pipe, a cigarette lighter, and a small chuck of hashish. She sat down across from me on the blanket and offered me the pipe.

"You first," she said.

I took a big hit and started coughing. I hadn't smoked hash in a while. I was still in my shorts and T-shirt. Kitty reached over and unzipped my fly.

"Don't you want to take off your clothes?" she asked.

Kitty pushed me down on the floor and unbuttoned my shorts. I lifted my hips as she pulled them off and tossed them across the room. I looked down at my penis. It had retreated for safety and taken on the appearance of a frightened turtle. *Oh great,* I thought. *Don't let me down now.* I sat up, pulled my T-shirt over my head, and heaved it next to my cutoffs. Kitty looked down at my shrinking dick and shook her head. She seemed ready for the challenge.

"Looks like I have some work to do," was all she said as she went down on me.

Try as she might, she couldn't get me hard. After five minutes of heroic effort, she sat up and massaged her chin.

"I think I'm getting lockjaw," she said. "Why don't you go down on me?"

We switched places, but even that didn't help me get an erection. Eating the pussy of an unattractive thirty-nine-year-old woman was not doing it for me. I had never been with a woman this old before, and I wasn't getting turned on. Hashish. Incense. The Moody Blues. Nothing was going to bring my penis to the party. For a brief moment, I thought I would make it and I slid on top of her. However, just as the race was about to start, my engine died.

It was hopeless. I rolled off and reached for my clothes. I apologized for my nonperformance, got dressed, and got out of there as fast as I could.

When I walked in the apartment, Ozzie, Bernie, Kevin, and Jelle were drinking beer and listening to music. Puke ran over to greet me.

"Sorry, guys," I said. "I couldn't do it."

Ozzie jumped to his feet.

"I'll do it!" he shouted and flew out the door.

An hour later, he walked back in.

"Start packing your shit," he said. "We're moving into the house."

43

"Kitty says you were terrible. She said you couldn't even get it up."

Ozzie was being an asshole. He made it a point to search me out and rub it in whenever he was about to make a service call on Kitty. It didn't bother me. As far as I was concerned, there was no shame in not being turned on by a thirty-nine-year-old woman with dark leathery skin. Ozzie, on the other hand, was ecstatic over his latest liaison and had acquired a bounce in his step. It was nearly impossible not to observe his cock frequently hoisted to full staff in his shorts as he meandered around the house. Ozzie seemed happier than I had ever seen him before, and he constantly reminded us that he was the one who had found the house and that he and his magnificent balling skills were saving us three hundred dollars a month. Although he was only required to service the landlady once every seven days, we noticed that he was adding daily surprise visits to his weekly schedule.

As much as we hated to admit it, Ozzie was the hero of our new movie. The house was huge, and it quickly became party central in Madeira Beach. Ozzie had first choice, and he picked the largest bedroom with the largest bed, which was downstairs, just off the living room. Bernie and I took the two bedrooms upstairs that had narrow beds and were separated by the shared bathroom between them. Since Kevin and Jelle were the newest arrivals, they were stuck with the fourth and smallest bedroom, which was downstairs next to the kitchen. Their room had no beds, so they spread out their sleeping bags and slept on the floor with Puke. The house had two living rooms, and the largest was upstairs with three chairs, three end tables, and two lamps. There was no furniture in the one downstairs. Louie claimed he didn't have any money for rent and asked if he could crash upstairs for a few weeks. He offered to steal food from the Winn Dixie as his contribution to our cause. The house was big enough, and there was no reason to throw him out, so we agreed. He was particularly adept at shoplifting steaks.

Kevin and Jelle found construction jobs right away, so with the exception of Louie, everyone had jobs, and every Friday everyone but Louie had money to burn. We had all the food, beer, grass, and Winn Dixie steaks that we could ever wish for. The stereo played nonstop. Marijuana smoke took up permanent residence throughout the house. Kevin had brought his chess set with him from Oneonta, and soon the six of us were engaged in fierce chess matches with the results often determined by the amount of weed and beer consumed. It didn't take long before the word got out and all the freaks and longhairs we were meeting at our jobs and in the bars starting showing up to party. However, the chicks were far and few between.

Bernie's Penis was happy. Hannah and her friends had rented their apartment until the end of November, and she was sleeping over with Bernie almost every night. Hannah was a screamer, and it was annoying as hell to have to listen to them all the time. Even Ozzie was getting laid practically every day. While I had no desire to trade places with him, I was beginning to kick myself for not at least giving Kitty a chance. Maybe I should have closed my eyes and pretended she was fifteen years younger. Hell, wouldn't I be thirty-nine one day? How was I going to feel if some twenty-four-year-old was grossed out by me? Every night I told myself that I needed to be patient. Finally, on the Friday before Election Day, my prayers were answered.

Kevin worked with Brian, a carpenter from the Chicago area who lived with his girlfriend Carol in a small cottage on a side street at John's Pass. Brian was our weed connection, and the shit that Kevin bought from him was top of the line. It was now my turn to buy pot. After smoking my last joint on the beach while taking in the sunset, I hitched a quick ride down Gulf Boulevard to score our entertainment for the weekend.

There are a few times in life when all the forces of the universe line up in just the right order and free us from our bad fortune. At first, I thought it was just dumb luck and that I had gone to the wrong cottage. Expecting either Brian or Carol to open the door, I was stunned to find myself staring at the prettiest girl I had seen in the past two months. Dressed in red shorts and a white bikini top, she had to be nearly six feet tall. Her long silky brown hair was wet and covered her shoulders. She looked and smelled like she had just gotten out of the shower, and when her big brown eyes locked onto mine, they told me that she was as horny as I was.

I was at the right cottage after all. Brian was expecting me. Before I could free myself from her eyes, Brian appeared from behind the mystery girl and invited me in. The mystery girl smiled and took a few steps back to let me pass. Two German shepherds rushed up to my crotch and took turns sniffing. Brian excused himself to go to the bedroom and retrieve the reason for my visit. Carol, who was sitting on the couch, introduced me to the mystery girl. Her name was Jennifer, and she was from Highland Park, a suburb of Chicago. She had been staying with them all week and was catching a plane back to Chicago tomorrow afternoon.

Brian walked out of the bedroom and handed me the lid. Shielding my crotch from the German shepherds with one hand, I handed him a twenty-dollar bill with the other. Now what? Everyone was waiting for me back at 141st Street. It was the start of the weekend, and the party house had run out of grass. They were counting on me. Tough shit, I thought. Right now I had something more important to do, and her name was Jennifer.

Brian knew right away what I was up to. So did the German shepherds, who were becoming more aggressive as they jockeyed for position between my legs. Brian was glaring at me as he coaxed me toward the door. I stuffed the lid in the back pocket of my cutoffs. That's when Jennifer jumped in and grabbed my hand.

"Do you want to take a walk on the beach?" she said.

Brian didn't say anything but continued to glare at me as we backed out the door. The German shepherds barked and lunged at me, just missing my crotch. The door slammed behind us.

"What's he so pissed about?" I asked.

"Don't worry about it," she said. "He'll get over it. He's my boyfriend's best friend."

I knew right then that the gang back at the house was not going to be too thrilled about me pissing off our dealer. What did they know? They weren't looking at Jennifer. If they were, they would understand. Every one of them would do the same thing.

Jennifer pointed to the small dock directly across the street from the cottage.

"Let's sit over there," she said. "Roll us a joint."

I thought we were going to the beach, but since I would have followed her anywhere on the planet, the dock was fine with me. We sat down facing each other. Jennifer pulled a pack of rolling papers from her red shorts and handed it to me. I removed the lid from my back pocket, pulled my knees to my chest, and started rolling.

"I like your balls," she said. "Can I play with them?"

I had stopped wearing underwear since coming to Florida, and I had forgotten that whenever I was wearing these cutoffs and sat with my knees up in the air, my nuts hung out for all the world to see. Tonight, that was apparently a good thing.

Before I could say yes, she reached down and very delicately cupped my balls in her left hand. Moving her fingers ever so slightly, she juggled them gently and slid her right hand down the front of my shorts. I dropped the unrolled joint. There was a slight breeze. The grass and rolling paper parted ways and blew across the dock. I didn't care. My long wait was over. After two months of suffering, this was going to be my night. As awkward as it was, I managed to reach around her back with my left hand and unclasp her bikini top. As it fell to the dock, I heard someone cough. I looked up and saw a man and woman standing just a few feet away. Next to them were two small kids, a boy and a girl.

Jennifer let go of my balls, slipped her hand out of my shorts, and laughed. She reached down, picked up her white top, and put it back on.

"Let's go to the beach," she said.

John's Pass was situated along the narrow waterway between Madeira Beach and Treasure Island that connected the Gulf of Mexico with the Intracoastal Waterway and Boca Ciega Bay. We walked up to Gulf Boulevard and over the twin-span drawbridge to the Treasure Island side, where we crossed the road and hurried to the beach. Jennifer said this was where she had been sunbathing all week. It was dark with the only light coming from the reflection of the half-moon on the water. She told me that she had loved going to the beach all week but that Brian and Carol never went anywhere at night, and she was bored out of her mind. Jennifer complained that it had been more than a week since she had sex with her boyfriend back in Chicago and she was about to explode.

"Lucky you," I said. "It's been two months for me."

We found a spot near a sand dune and took off our clothes.

44

It definitely was a night to remember. It was hard to tell who was ravishing who. I felt like a man walking into a smorgasbord who hadn't eaten in a week. I wasn't alone. She was as hungry as I was. It wasn't until I climaxed the first time that I realized how much we had been rolling around in the sand. We had started out on top of our clothes, but within minutes, all bets were off. Our raging hormones had taken control and hurled us into an erotic wrestling match. We heard people walk by us, but we didn't care. Some stopped to watch. We weren't looking for an audience, but we were so locked in to finishing what we had started that we couldn't stop. Mick Jagger and his wild horses couldn't have pulled us apart.

I was covered with sand. It was in my hair and all over my back. It had sought out every opening in my body, including my butthole and the narrow avenue than ran between the cheeks of my ass. The sand even found a home on my penis as it was sliding out, joining the team of juices and semen already there.

Jennifer had taken on as much sand as I had and in all the same places. It was getting late and we were naked, but the air was still warm. It was around nine o'clock, and the temperature must have been at least seventy-five degrees. We needed to wash away the sand before our next round, so we decided to take a break and go for a swim. The Gulf was glowing with phosphorus. It was as if sparkling diamonds were dancing across the surface of the water. I rushed after her and her long legs as she sprinted into the surf and dove in head-first. Only tourists and a couple of Northerners like us would think to enter the Gulf at this time of year. To us it was perfect. The lakes of Illinois and New York never got this warm even in the middle of summer.

The water was nearly up to her shoulders when Jennifer turned around and kissed me. She reached down between my legs and felt that I was erect again. She bounced up and wrapped her legs around my hips.

"Let's do it in the water," she said.

It was another first for me. Underwater penetration wasn't easy because the saltwater had a way of canceling out most of the lubrication she was providing. I couldn't tell if I was hurting her or not. We both struggled as she worked to guide me in, but once I was there, it was the most erotic sensation that I had ever experienced. Locked in her embrace and safely inside her, I let out a yell.

"We're like love bugs!" I shouted.

"What are love bugs?" she moaned.

I felt dizzy. I was way ahead of her this time. Before I could answer, I climaxed.

"My turn," she said. "Let's get out of the water. What are love bugs?"

First things first. When we stepped out of the water, I pushed her down on the beach and buried my face between her legs. I wasn't sure if I was tasting semen or saltwater, but I knew without a doubt that it was Treasure Island sand that was scraping against my tongue. The air was cold now that we were wet and out of the water. However, I wasn't about to quit. Jennifer was right. It was her turn, and I had a job to do.

When we were finished, we hurried across the sand to find our clothes and get dressed. Jennifer was shaking. I gave her my T-shirt to wear over her bikini top.

"So, what are love bugs?" she asked again as we were returning over the drawbridge. Her teeth were chattering. So were mine.

"They're flying insects that mate by attaching themselves to one another," I said. "They were everywhere when I moved here two months ago. They're my heroes. They fly together and fuck for three or four days until they die."

Jennifer laughed. "You're right," she said. "That sounds like us. Do you want to spend the night with me?"

"Are you sure it's okay? Brian seems pretty pissed off at me."

"It's after ten o'clock," she said. "They're probably in bed by now."

When we walked in the cottage, all the lights were off. I covered my crotch with both hands.

"Where are the dogs?" I asked.

"You don't have to worry about them," she said. "They sleep in the bedroom with Brian and Carol."

I saw that the bedroom door was closed.

"Where do you sleep?" I asked.

"On the couch," she said, "but it isn't big enough for the both of us. We can sleep together on the floor."

I didn't get any sleep that night. It was a hardwood floor, and the thin blanket underneath us was useless as a cushion. It was impossible to get comfortable. Jennifer dozed off for a while but woke up in the middle of the night, suddenly frisky and ready to go again. I was afraid to move, worried that I might roll over and hit one of the half-dozen land mines that the German shepherds had left us on the floor. Apparently, Brian had given them the green light to shit wherever they wanted. By now, we must have smelled pretty bad. The evening's marinade of sweat, sand, saltwater, and bodily fluids had formed a protective coat on us from head to toe. In a perfect world, a shower would have come first. However, there was no time to waste. We both smelled the same. Morning would be here before we knew it. Jennifer mounted me, and like two mating love bugs, we attached and never let go. And like those heroic love bugs, we were determined to fuck until we died. Or at least until Brian opened the bedroom door.

I made it back to the house around eight thirty that morning. Ozzie was sitting alone at the kitchen table, smoking a cigarette and nursing a beer.

"Where the fuck have you been?" he asked. "You missed all the excitement."

"Why?" I said. "What happened?"

Ozzie leaned back and put both feet on the table.

"Hey," he said. "We waited a couple of hours for you to come back with the weed. When you didn't show, we figured something had happened to you."

"Did you go out and look for me?" I asked.

"Fuck no," he said. "We decided to go get some booze and get drunk instead."

He stood up and walked over to the refrigerator to grab another beer.

"Want one?" he asked.

"No, thanks," I said. "So what excitement did I miss?"

I had to admit that it was a good story. At first they had gone through the house with a fine-toothed comb looking for any remnants of pot they could find. Seeds, a roach, it didn't matter. Finally, when they came up empty, they hopped in Bernie's Rambler and found the nearest liquor store. They loaded the Rambler with a case of beer, two bottles of tequila, a fifth of Southern Comfort, and two bottles of Mateus, Ozzie's favorite wine. For all they knew, I could have been busted and in jail or dead in a ditch along the side of the road. The search for me would have to wait. It was Friday night, and the party had to go on. Who needed me when Bernie was here to provide the excitement? The way Ozzie told it, Hannah had stopped by around ten o'clock to see Bernie. What she encountered was an all-dude drunk fest, which she wanted no part of. She told Bernie that she had been spending too many nights away from Lindsey and would come back another time. That freed Bernie to get as wasted as he wanted.

"It wasn't until after one in the morning that everyone realized he was gone," said Ozzie.

"So where was he?" I asked.

"That's where it really gets far out," he said. "It was probably three or four in the morning when he showed up at the door surrounded by three Madeira Beach cops."

"Holy shit," I said. "What happened then?"

"What happened next," he said, "was that Bernie proved once and for all what a big asshole he really is. He had gone across the street and passed out on the beach. Then the tide came in. He was so fucked up that he didn't even wake up when the waves started washing over him. Some tourist must have spotted him and called the cops to report a dead body. Next thing you know, the cops are poking him with their night sticks to see if he is alive. Idiot Bernie wakes up and tells the cops he lives *here*. They ask if they can walk him home, and he tells them sure, even invites them in. How fucked up is that?"

"That sucks," I said. "What did they do when they got here?"

"That's just the thing," he said. "Nothing. All they found were empty liquor bottles and empty cans of beer. We could tell they were looking for pot. That's why you're the hero, man. If you had come home last night with the weed, we'd all probably be in jail right now."

I reached into my pocket and pulled out the lid. I set it down on the table.

"Here, man, have a blast," I said. "I need some sleep. I'm going to bed."

Ozzie opened the baggie and put it up to his nose.

"Smells like some good shit," he said.

45

Instead of reporting Bernie, someone should have called the Madeira Beach cops to report George McGovern as the dead body. On Tuesday, November 7, the American people finally hammered the nails into George's coffin. His 117-day death march had begun in the wee hours of the morning back in July in Miami Beach. It had been a slow and painful demise. Even the Bataan Death March thirty years earlier was said to have lasted only five days.

My days of giving a damn about American politics were finished, but I was still going through withdrawals. Throughout the summer and fall, I was like an addict looking for another fix of depressing news from the presidential campaign. The hits kept on coming. Back in June, it was reported that five men had been apprehended inside an office building in DC. They were arrested at gunpoint at two thirty in the morning by three plainclothes cops in what was described at the time as an apparent plot to bug the headquarters of the Democratic National Committee. It was a strange story and pretty much non-news at the time. None of my friends at *Seeds* in Oneonta even brought it up. In fact, I don't remember hearing about it until more than a week after it happened. The next big event was George sacking his running mate Thomas Eagleton when it was revealed that he had been receiving electric shock treatments. George replaced Tommy on the ticket with a Kennedy brother-in-law. In August, the confident Republicans rolled into Miami for their coronation of Dick and Spiro. Meanwhile, stories began to circulate about the June break-in. For those paying attention, the story was becoming obvious. At the end of September, it was reported that Attorney General John Mitchell was running a secret fund to pay for spying on Democrats. The most recent story had the FBI saying that the break-in at the Watergate office complex was part of a campaign of political spying and sabotage on behalf of the Nixon reelection team.

This was the first time I had ever voted. I had wanted to back in 1968, but I was only twenty and the voting age was still twenty-one. It wasn't until North Carolina became the thirty-eighth state to ratify the Twenty-Sixth Amendment on July 1, 1971, that the right to vote at eighteen became law. It was possible that I might be the only person in the state of Florida casting a vote for George, but I knew I had to do it. As pointless as it seemed, this was my one and only chance to officially register my opposition to Nixon.

I wasn't wrong by that much. George got less than 28 percent of the votes in Florida. Across the country, it was a complete wipeout. Tricky Dick whipped McGovern by a score of 61–38 and carried everything but Massachusetts and the District of Columbia. It's not that I couldn't see it coming. I had not spotted a LICK DICK 72 bumper sticker in the past three or four months, and that one had been in Boston. The Revolution was over, and we had lost. Things were getting ugly. How fucked up was it that six out of ten Americans thought it was perfectly fine to have someone like Richard Milhous Nixon sitting in the White House? Was it fair that George had been forced to dump poor Tommy from the ticket just because of a few electric shock treatments? Wouldn't the six out of ten morons who voted for Tricky Dick be the ones who would most likely benefit from being strapped to a table and having a few electric currents shot through their brains? Had any of these fools been paying attention over the past four years? Who knew what Nixon and his goons would do now that they no longer had to concern themselves with another annoying election?

It was definitely time for me to apply for a passport. I felt like an alien in my own country. What began in Isadora Duncan's bed as a romantic notion of traveling the world was now starting to look like my only option. Where was my future here? Why wasn't I born fifty years earlier? Why couldn't I be living in the 1920s? Then I could just move to Paris and meet up with Ernest Hemingway and his Lost Generation. How cool would that be? I could hang out with

Gertrude Stein, John Dos Passos, T. S. Eliot, and F. Scott Fitzgerald. Even better, I could locate the original Isadora Duncan and ask her to take me as her lover.

Unfortunately for me, it was 1972. Ernest Hemingway would not be coming to my rescue. He had blown his brains out eleven years earlier.

I was on my own.

46

Isadora's letter arrived the day after the election. It contained a poem about carrying me in her heart by e. e. cummings, a few clippings of her blond pubic hair, and her plans to visit me right after Christmas. She wasn't coming alone. Her best friend Cindy was going to drive, and they would be staying with us for a week. I found a calendar and counted the days. December 27 seemed like forever. Could I make it another seven weeks?

The first thing I did was apply for my passport. I tied my hair in a ponytail for my photo, but there was no hiding my long hair. I hadn't cut it in three years. Next, I quit my job as a construction laborer. While I might have perfected the art of doing nothing and getting paid for it, the whole hide-and-seek routine was beginning to bore me. Besides, if I was ever going to save enough money to leave the kingdom of Richard Nixon, I needed to start making more than $2.50 an hour. I hitchhiked up to a condominium jobsite in Redington Beach and asked if they needed a carpenter's helper. The superintendent asked me if I had any experience. When I told him yes, he hired me at $3.25. As luck would have it, he assigned me to Bob, a thirty-year-old jack-of-all-trades handyman. Bob was an easy-going dude whose primary job was to fix any problem that popped up at any one of the six properties owned by the company that was building the new condos. My official job was to ride around all day in Bob's pickup truck and be Bob's personal assistant. All I had to do was carry things for Bob and hold things for Bob. The unofficial job was to keep him company. Bob and I got along great. He had grown up in St. Pete and was married with two kids. He had short hair and was about as straight as they come. That's why I was so blown away at the end of our third day together. Bob whipped a perfectly rolled joint out of his front pocket and asked if I wanted to get high. I knew right then that this was a job that I could handle until Christmas.

Life at the house remained its usual chaotic self. There was a party practically every night. The chess matches continued, and the music never stopped. Ozzie's obsession with Frank Zappa had followed him to Florida. He had replaced several of the albums that he had lost in the fire and the instrumental genius of Frank's *Hot Rats* echoed through the house all hours of the night. Ozzie continued to service Kitty, though he seemed to be losing interest. He was constantly lobbying us for a reduction in his portion of the rent. He claimed that he deserved a discount for his altruistic effort to keep our rent down. He threatened to stop balling her if we didn't give in to his demands. We just laughed at him. None of us wanted to change places with Ozzie, but we didn't feel sorry for him. He had the biggest bedroom, and as much as he liked to complain, we knew he wasn't about to give up getting laid on a regular basis. Meanwhile, Bernie and Bernie's Penis remained in good spirits. Hannah and her gang were staying until the end of the month. As for me, the gift of Jennifer had arrived just in the nick of time. Hopefully, it would hold me over until Isadora showed up. If not, I would have to get lucky again.

Jelle was as weird as ever and kept to himself most of the time. We made the mistake of inviting him to go to breakfast with all of us one Saturday morning. There was a café on the Treasure Island side of John's Pass that served a breakfast special on the weekends. For only seventy-five cents, we got two eggs any style, home fries or grits, toast, and as much coffee as we wanted. When the check arrived, Jelle stood up and excused himself. We thought he was going to the head, but after ten minutes, we realized he wasn't coming back. The five of us each tossed in an extra twenty cents to cover his portion. We walked out to find Jelle standing in the parking lot, smoking a cigarette. Ozzie was pissed and spoke on behalf of all us.

"Hey, man," he said. "Why the fuck did you stick us with paying for your breakfast? You owe us a dollar."

"It's not my problem," Jelle said. "You could have gotten up and walked out without paying just like I did. I never told you that I was going to pay for breakfast."

Jelle was an asshole, plain and simple. However, Bernie and Ozzie were more pissed off at me than they were at him. They couldn't understand how I knew a jerk like him in the first place and blamed me for inviting him to Florida. I tried to defend myself, explaining that I had never invited him. Besides, why weren't they pissed at Kevin? He was the one who had brought Jelle with him from Oneonta, not me. They weren't buying it. They liked Kevin and gave him a pass. He had a car and could always be counted on for killer weed. To top that off, our dealer Brian was pissed at me now and had threatened to cut us off. Kevin had talked him out of it, so as far as Bernie and Ozzie were concerned, Kevin was the hero and I was the goat.

They weren't that happy either that Louie continued to crash rent-free in the upstairs living room, but at least he was keeping us supplied with stolen steaks. I started to hang out at the beach a lot with Kevin and Puke. The two of them were inseparable. According to Kevin, Puke had named himself. Kevin had rescued him from the dog pound in Oneonta just before leaving for Florida. As they left the pound to drive back to The Shack, the dog was so grateful that he decided to leave his signature in the front seat of the Comet. Kevin wasn't sure if the dog was asking to be named Puke or wanted to be called Vomit, so he tried out both names and let the dog decide. The dog chose Puke. He seemed to know he was a lucky dog. No longer confined to a cage in Upstate New York, Puke had embraced his new life as a Florida beach dog. He loved rushing into the surf and barking at the breaking waves, and he had a special talent for leaping in the air and catching a Frisbee. The thing that was the most fun for me was getting stoned at the beach and watching the reaction of anyone within earshot whenever Kevin yelled out Puke's name. Puke seemed to get a chuckle out of it too.

Bob the Handyman and I gradually became friends. His conversation and his weed helped me make it through the long days at work. I wasn't used to working eight hours a day, but Bob kept it interesting. We drove all over Pinellas County, and I was learning my way around. Bob was a good dude. He loved his wife and his two boys but confessed to me during one of our marijuana breaks that he felt trapped in his life. Bob was six years older than me. His girlfriend had gotten pregnant, and he had married her when he was only nineteen. Before he knew it, they had two kids. I asked him how he had avoided the draft and Vietnam. He told me that because he had a family to support, the draft board classified him 3-A, which meant he didn't have to go. He confessed that he was envious of me because I was free and had no responsibilities. He said that I was lucky that I could do whatever I wanted. In Bob's eyes, I was a hippie, and he assumed that I knew all about free love. He told me that his wife was the only woman that he had ever had sex with, and he wanted to know what it was like to be in an orgy.

"I wish I knew," I said. "I'll let you know if it ever happens."

I was surprised at how fast the seven-week journey to Christmas turned out to be. Bob the Handyman was the bridge that got me there. I never missed a day of work, and I was finally saving money. I felt like a complete shithead when I announced I was quitting. I broke the news to him on Friday afternoon, just three days before Christmas. Bob didn't say much, but I could tell that I had hurt his feelings. When he dropped me off at the house after work, he shook my hand and wished me luck.

I never saw him again.

47

It was like entering into a dream for eight days. I wanted to slow it down, but it was out of my control and moving at the speed of light. Like any dream, it would soon be over.

I was alive again. Only now it was different. We had been separated by nearly four months and a thousand miles. Last summer was in my rearview mirror. I could sense that something had changed. However, the one thing that hadn't was our lovemaking. When we finally broke away from the group the first night, it was if our bodies had never separated. The marathon lasted until morning, and it ranked right up there with every one of our greatest hits. At first, I thought she had seized control of my cerebellum again, but I soon realized that I was now moving on my own. Muscle memory kicked in. Class was over, and I had earned my diploma. The angel had taught me well.

I had forgotten how beautiful she was. I was mesmerized as she removed her clothes, and I saw her naked for the first time in what felt like eternity. Her fair skin had not yet been exposed to the Florida sun, and it had the look and feel of polished ivory. She was the embodiment of beauty, a modern-day Venus De Milo with arms. If it had been up to me, we would have spent the entire eight days in bed. Unfortunately, that wasn't in the cards.

The angel continued to cast her spell over me, but I could feel her intentionally loosening her grip. She had come to Florida to have fun, and she didn't seem that eager to talk about us. I should not have been surprised, but I was. When I walked out the door of her Cherry Street apartment at the end of the summer, I thought I would never see her again. However, the letters and poems that followed me to Florida had given me hope. I began to fantasize that she might be as in love with me as I was with her. Maybe she was, but she was still the same nineteen-year-old free spirit that I had left in Oneonta. She was still out of my league, and she still had her whole life ahead of her. My gut told me that I could never have her, but that wasn't going keep me from trying. I wasn't ready to let go. After all, I was still the same lovesick fool who had been delusional enough to ask the Brown-Eyed Girl if I could come to New York and live with her when she called to tell me about her vaginal infection.

It was a wild week, and the house was rocking. I had quit my job, and Bernie, Ozzie, Kevin, and Jelle all took a few days off from theirs. Louie remained a fixture in the upstairs living room, and to celebrate the approach of New Year's Eve, he upped his steak-stealing prowess another notch. It took him three trips to Winn Dixie, but in the end, we had eight steaks to help us usher in the New Year. The only one who wasn't around was our landlady, Kitty. She had flown up to Toronto to spend Christmas with her parents. Ozzie saw this as an opportunity to make a move on Cindy, who was an attractive brunette and nearly as pretty as Isadora. She saw right through him and brushed him off immediately. Not to be outmaneuvered, Bernie's Penis urged Bernie to also give it a shot. Hannah had gone back to California at the end of November, and Bernie's Penis was getting restless. Bernie stood his ground and refused to take the bait. It was clear to everyone in the house that Cindy had standards. She had come to Florida with Isadora to get a tan, not to jump into bed with any member of this sorry band of refugees from Upstate New York. It wasn't even clear if she approved of her best friend jumping into bed with me.

Isadora and Cindy wanted to spend as much time at the beach as they could. The weather was great all week, sunny and in the low eighties every day. Between the eight of us, we had three cars, one motorcycle, and enough pot to last a month. We spent a few days across the road on Madeira Beach, but we used the rest of the week to explore the magnificent thirty miles of beaches that surrounded us. We went as far north as Clearwater Beach, spending one day there and a second day just south of there on a beautiful uninhabited stretch of white sand known as Sand Key. Our best day was spent at Fort De Soto, a county park located on five small islands to the southwest of St. Pete and across the water from the tip of St. Pete Beach and Pass-a-Grille. We found a lonely stretch of sand with no one else around. We were able to smoke our weed in the open without fear of getting busted, and the girls were able to go topless. Puke was as happy as I had ever seen him, eager to play Frisbee with whoever was willing. It was a great place to look for shells, and Isadora and Cindy both came away with an impressive collection of unbroken and colorful souvenirs to take home with them.

On New Year's Eve, we were ready for our feast. Kevin bought a large round charcoal grill and a bag of charcoal briquettes so we could grill our steaks. The girls drove up to Winn Dixie and came home with two boxes of rice, a bag of green beans, and everything needed to make a kick-ass salad. Ozzie, Bernie, and I chipped in for two cases of Budweiser and three bottles of Mateus. As always, Jelle pleaded poverty and bought nothing.

The party went on until nearly four in the morning. A thick cloud of marijuana smoke and the resounding genius of Led Zeppelin's fourth album guided us into 1973. "Stairway to Heaven" was our mantra, and "Going to California" was our escort. Isadora and I slipped away around one and locked ourselves in my bedroom. We made love until the music stopped and we were completely exhausted. It was the best New Year's Eve ever.

The night before she and Cindy left for New York, Isadora was finally ready to talk about us. She asked me to sit down on the edge of the bed and leave my clothes on. It was the moment I had been dreading.

"Jeff," she started, "you know I love you, don't you?"

I nodded, afraid of what was coming next.

"It's time for both of us to move on," she said. "I love what we have together, but we are two different people with two different lives. We come from different backgrounds, and we are going different places. This will never work. You understand, don't you?"

I did, but I didn't want to admit it. I kept my mouth shut. There was no point in arguing with her. She was right. Hell, I didn't know why she had taken me as her lover in the first place. I realized that I should just count my blessings and concede that I had been one of luckiest human beings on the planet over the past six months. Still, losing her was going to hurt.

She went on to tell me that she had taken a new lover. His name was Michael, and he was a musician. I didn't know him, but I knew who he was. I remembered seeing him in The Silver a number of times. After I had absorbed this new information, she informed me that she was moving to The City right after she got back to Oneonta. She wanted to pursue her dancing, and New York was the best place to do that.

There was nothing more to talk about. She seemed relieved that I didn't put up a fight. It was tearing me up on the inside, but I knew that I had to appear to take it all in stride. She pushed me down on the bed and devoured me. We made love one last time. Geoffrey Chaucer had predicted this moment nearly six hundred years before I was born. The English dude nailed it when he wrote that all good things must come to an end.

I was sure going to miss this.

48

It was time to get serious about leaving the country.

It was the third week in January. Dick and Spiro had been sworn in for a second term, Isadora was now living in Manhattan, and I was on my third job in three weeks. The first one was the worst and only lasted a grueling two and a half hours. Hardhat in hand, I had strolled onto a construction site on Indian Rocks Beach and was put to work immediately. My new boss handed me a shovel and walked me over to a huge hole in the ground. I stared into the abyss and observed two wretched souls who had been abducted from a Charles Dickens novel and were standing in ankle-deep water. They were covered in mud. Who were they, POWs? Indentured servants? My boss told me to jump in and start digging. I did as I was told. Once in the hole, I followed the lead of my hapless comrades, scooping up shovelfuls of mud and hurling them up to the ground above. I tried talking to them, but they wouldn't respond. Were they creatures from *The Night of the Living Dead*? Had I unknowingly volunteered to work on a chain gang? Two and a half hours into the ordeal, the ghastly head of our boss materialized in the opening above us and told us to take a ten-minute break. I was the last one out of the hole. The two zombies were slumped down on the ground next to the hole, smoking their cigarettes. Tiptoeing past them, I kept walking until I got to Gulf Boulevard. These were two and a half hours of my life that I would never get back. Technically, I was owed six dollars and twenty-five cents, but escaping this freak show was more important than the slim prospect of receiving any compensation for my time in the hole. I walked about a quarter mile down the road to the next construction site. The crew was just finishing its morning break. I found the foreman standing next to the office trailer and asked him if they were hiring. He told me they were and asked if I could start now. I would have preferred to take the rest of the day off to recover from my two and a half hours of torture, but I accepted his offer. Six hours' pay beat nothing at all. I lasted there about a week and then moved on to another construction job that was starting up closer to the house in Madeira Beach. Finally, after three weeks and three jobs, I couldn't take it anymore. I quit. My timing couldn't have been better. My US passport arrived in the mail the very next day. I told Bernie and Ozzie that I was leaving. I was done with Florida. I was going to Europe.

"Sorry to rain on your parade, asshole," Ozzie offered, "but it's fucking January. You're going to Europe in January? Are you out of your mind?"

"He's right," Bernie chimed in. "Nobody backpacks through Europe in the middle of winter."

They had a point. Now was not the time to fly to Europe. My new life as an expatriate would have to wait until late spring or summer. Besides, I had promised Danny that I would be his best man on April Fool's Day. I had received a surprise letter from Isadora telling me that she had found an apartment on the Lower East Side, but it was insane to think that just because she had written me, she would be happy if I suddenly showed up at her door. Oneonta was out of the question. It was clear that Boston was my best option. I had been exchanging letters with Randy Zarin since I got to Florida, and he was sharing a house in Cambridge with some friends. He let me know that I could crash there whenever I wanted. I bought a cool postcard of a Gulf of Mexico sunset and sent it to Randy with a heads-up that I was coming to Boston to take him up on his offer. Then I stuffed all my belongings and my passport into my backpack and converted all the money I had saved into American Express traveler's checks.

When Bernie and Ozzie heard where I was going, they thought I was crazy. They didn't understand why I didn't like living in the Sunshine State, and they couldn't comprehend why anyone would trade Florida for New England in the middle of winter.

"You'll be back," were the last words out of Ozzie's mouth.

49

The blue-and-white van picked me up on I-75 just north of Gainesville. The side door slid open, and an army of marijuana smoke rushed out and made its escape across the highway. The VW appeared to be dancing in perfect rhythm to the unmistakable sound of "One Way Out" by the Allman Brothers. As I approached the open door, a long-haired freak wearing a red bandanna stepped out and offered me a burning joint.

"Hop in, dude," he said. "We're going to North Carolina."

The journey had started slow. It had taken me almost five hours to make it this far. The first ride only took me a little north of Tampa, near Zephyrhills. Next it was another short ride up I-75 to just outside Ocala. By the time the third car dropped me off, I was beginning to worry that my once-dependable right thumb had lost its charm. It had never let me down before, and I was banking on it to come through for me one more time. I wasn't prepared for winter weather, and I was hoping that I wouldn't freeze to death trying to get to Boston. All my winter clothes had been lost in the fire. The few that I now owned had been donated to me by Gerald Lopez and his friends. I started out in the morning in my jeans and yellow T-shirt. My thin jacket and one flannel shirt were hiding in my backpack, ready to come to my rescue at a moment's notice.

My thumb had landed me a ride with a Fort Lauderdale rock band. I was the fourth hitchhiker they had picked up that day, and they stopped for two more right after we crossed into Georgia. Counting the four troubadours, there were now ten of us crammed into the van, and these freaks knew how to party. I was in the belly of the beast. The radio and the tape player joined hands in a continuous loop of Southern rock, including not only the Allman Brothers but also Leon Russell and Lynyrd Skynyrd. There was no way for any of us to consume all the Acapulco Gold that was being passed around. In spite of being swallowed up and digested by this insane orgy for nearly eight hours, I still had the good sense to turn down a hit of mescaline, two Quaaludes, and an offer to snort some cocaine through a one-hundred-dollar bill. Because I had a long way to go, the weed was all I could handle. Three of my fellow travelers were released back into the straight world on the outskirts of Atlanta, and the other two who had taken the mescaline asked to be liberated near Spartanburg, South Carolina. I was the only one going all the way to Charlotte, and I was completely ripped when they let me out of the van on I-85.

It was dark, and the temperature had dropped into the forties. I retrieved my flannel shirt and jacket and put them on as quickly as I could. The wind was blowing, and I was still cold. At least it wasn't raining or snowing. I still had another eight or nine hundred miles to go, and I was worried that no one would stop for me at night. By the time the rusted pickup truck pulled over to rescue me an hour later, I had lost most of my high, and I was freezing my ass off.

I was grateful for the ride and thankful that the heater was working. It took me a few minutes to realize the trouble I was in. The driver was in his early thirties, with short hair and a receding hairline. His head rested squarely on his shoulders like a bowling ball on a flat table. As far as I could tell, he had no neck. At first, he wasn't much of a talker, but something about him told me that I was in for a long night. When I asked him how far he was going, he evaded my question and began to ramble on about his ex-wife. I nodded in agreement as he recited his angry diatribe. He went on and on about how terrible all women were and then switched gears to deliver a sermon on how we men had to stick together and that we didn't need women anymore. Flashbacks of Bernie's hitchhiking adventure in South Carolina last year popped into my head, along with the once unthinkable image of Bobby and the hillbilly in James Dickey's novel. What little was left of my buzz quickly evaporated. I tried not to think about what might be coming next.

We drove about an hour before No Neck got off the interstate. I had no idea where we were. The more he ranted and raved about his ex-wife, the angrier he got. We drove a few miles on a two-lane highway before turning left onto a narrow dirt road. My heart was racing. Making it alive to Boston was beginning to look more and more like a long shot. The pickup continued its slow crawl along the dirt road, swerving and sometimes stopping to avoid the potholes and the occasional tree branch in its path. No Neck wanted to know if I liked women. I told him I did. Maybe it was my long hair, but he acted surprised and wanted to know why. I fumbled around with my answer, not sure of what to say and afraid to say anything that might set him off. No Neck stopped the car and turned off the engine. He reached over with his right hand and put it on my thigh.

"Are you sure?" he asked.

I didn't fumble around with my answer this time.

"No way," I said.

I wasn't going down without a fight. I grabbed his hand and pushed it away. To my surprise, he wasn't upset. He seemed to take it in stride.

"Okay," he said, "we'll talk about it later. Right now I need your help with something."

I had no idea what he was talking about. He started the car, and we resumed our slow crawl down the dirt road. No Neck had stopped talking, and I wasn't sure if that was good or bad. As we rounded a slight curve in the road, he slammed on his brakes and made a sharp right turn through a small opening between two trees. The high beam of his headlights revealed what appeared to be a small structure in front of us. As we inched closer, I could see that it was a house. No Neck put the pickup in park and turned off the engine. The headlights continued to illuminate the house.

"C'mon," he said. "We've got some work to do."

No Neck was carrying a flashlight. I followed him through the tall grass and up the front steps onto the porch.

"Careful," he said, "some of the steps are missing."

"Who lives here?" I asked.

"Nobody," he answered. "The old lady who lived here died last month."

No Neck opened the front door and hit the light switch. Nothing happened. Obviously, the power had been turned off. No Neck turned on his flashlight and pointed it to the living room.

"Over here," he said. "Help me with the couch."

So that was it. In exchange for not being murdered or on the receiving end of anal sex, I was now No Neck's accomplice as he ripped off furniture from a dead woman's house. Still, given the options, this was probably the best deal I was going to get. I walked over to the couch and picked up the other end.

The sooner we finished, the sooner I could get out of here.

50

By the time my last ride dropped me off near Boston Common, I had gone two days without sleep and food. I staggered into a tiny grocery store on Charles Street and bought a small package of cheese, a long thin loaf of French bread, one apple, and a can of Coke. It was too cold to sit in the Commons, so I went over to the Park Street Station and descended into the raucous underground for warmth and a place to enjoy my meal. I sat down with my back against the wall near the turnstiles and opened the brown paper bag. Dozens of Boston creatures scurried past me in multiple directions, but I was clearly invisible to all of them. I might have been starving, but I took the time to savor each bite of food. When I finished, the only thing left was half a loaf of bread. I stuffed it in my backpack, bought a token, and inserted it in the turnstile. Randy lived somewhere between Central Square and Harvard Square, so I skipped down the stairs and hopped on the first train to Cambridge. I was pumped. I got off at the Central Square Station and found a pay phone. Randy answered on the third ring and sounded happy to hear from me. I told him where I was, and he told me to wait there and he would pick me up in fifteen minutes.

The dark-blue Firebird was a sight for sore eyes. A lot of good times had taken place in that car. When I opened the passenger door, Randy handed me a nickel bag, a corn cob pipe, and a book of matches.

"Here," he said. "You look like you could use this."

Randy could always read me like a book. I opened the baggie, pulled out a pinch of cannabis, and packed it into the pipe. The first hit walloped me upside the head like a robust two by four. I must have coughed for at least a minute. When I stopped, my eyes were burning, and I had tears rolling down my cheeks. I could barely speak. Randy laughed.

"It's great to have you back in Boston," he said. "I knew you'd like it. It's really good shit."

I had to agree. It was a little harsh, but just one hit had gotten me stoned.

"Listen," he continued. "There's something I need to tell you. I got your postcard and wanted to write back but you had already left Florida."

"What is it?" I asked.

I handed him the pipe. The grass was still burning. Randy took a toke and handed it back to me.

"You're welcome to crash at my place as long as you want, but I need to warn you that Jane is staying there. She moved in a week ago with her boyfriend."

"Boyfriend?" I said. "I didn't know she had one. Besides, I thought she was living in Amherst."

"Well," he answered, "his name is Rick, and he's actually a pretty cool dude. He was in Nam, and I think he flew planes."

"So what's the deal?" I asked. "What are they doing at your house?"

Randy shrugged his shoulders. "I don't know," he said. "She just showed up last week and said they were looking for a place to live. We had an empty room, so I told her they could move in. That was before I got your postcard."

Staying in the same house with my wife and her boyfriend? I now knew how Bernie must have felt when he hitchhiked a thousand miles only to end up on Ozzie's Top Shelf. This was going to be awkward. However, I needed a place to stay until I could get my shit together. This definitely was not how I had planned it when I abandoned my life in Florida.

"It's okay," I assured him. "I'll figure it out."

It took us just a couple of minutes to get to Randy's place on Rollins Court. It was so close that I could have walked from Central Square if I had known where it was. It was in a rather run-down neighborhood, surrounded by a chain link fence and other homes that were probably built a hundred years ago. Randy wheeled the Firebird into a muddy courtyard and parked it between a white VW Beetle and a rusted green Chevy Impala. His house was actually one of two homes in a two-story, multifamily building with brown shingles and black window frames in need of fresh paint. Four concrete steps led to an open but covered porch that was missing its window screens and offered little protection from the elements. Randy opened the door and let me in first. I set my backpack down on the floor and looked into the living room. Jane was sitting on the couch, reading a magazine and drinking a cup of coffee. She was wearing jeans and a bright-green sweater, and she looked great. She smiled when she saw me. I walked over to her and gave her a hug. A tall, good-looking dude with short dark hair appeared from the kitchen and held out his hand.

"Hi," he said. "I'm Rick."

51

It was the strangest dream. I was standing in a Laundromat, folding my clothes, when suddenly out of nowhere Charles Darwin burst through the door. I knew immediately it was him when I saw the flowing white beard. He looked terrified.

"Quick, old chap!" he shouted. "I need to hide. They are right behind me."

No one had ever shouted at me before with an English accent. I didn't know what he was talking about, and as far as I could tell, he was alone.

"Who is right behind you?" I asked.

"I do not have time to explain," he bristled. "I need a place to hide."

If Charles Darwin needed a place to hide in order to survive, who was I to question him? After all, who knew more about survival than Charles Darwin? I had an idea. The dryer that I had just pulled my clothes out of was empty. I opened the glass door.

"Here," I said. "You can hide in the dryer."

Charles Darwin didn't hesitate. He took one giant step and leaped into the machine. He had been born way back in 1809, yet it was amazing how agile he was for his age. I closed the door. The dryer began to spin, and it suddenly occurred to me that I had pulled my clothes out before I used up all the minutes that I had paid for. I was about to open the door and rescue him when an angry mob of monkeys rushed into the Laundromat. There must have been nearly two dozen of them, each representing a different species. The largest one appeared to be the leader. Except for his hairy white belly, his fur was dark gray and was accented by two bands of color, one yellow and one black. His face was straight out of an Orange Sunshine acid trip.

It had a red stripe down the middle and blue ridges on the sides. His lips and nostrils were red, and he was sporting a short yellow beard. I glanced down and saw that he had a humongous erection. The area around his genitals had taken the same LSD as his face, offering up a psychedelic display of reds, pinks, purples, and blues. This was one pissed-off monkey. He stared directly into my eyes, bobbed his head a few times, and then slapped the ground. He pressed his face against mine and introduced himself. His name was Mandrill, and his breath was horrible.

"Where is Charles Darwin?" Mandrill screamed.

"I don't know," I said. "I haven't seen him. What do you want with him?"

"When we find the bastard," he answered, "we are going to kill him. We are going to stomp on his head and tear him apart, limb by limb."

"Why do you want to kill him?" I asked.

Mandrill raised his voice and slapped the ground again. I could tell that he was getting angrier.

"Are you kidding me?" he screeched. "The son of a bitch has given us a bad name. Have you ever read *On the Origin of Species*? He claims that humans are descended from us. For that insult, he deserves to die."

Mandrill turned to his fellow primates.

"Let's go," he said. "The asshole is not here."

The gang of monkeys quickly mobilized around Mandrill and then rushed out the door. I turned around and looked at the dryer. Charles Darwin was tumbling around in circles with his anxious face rubbing desperately against the glass. Poor Charlie looked more terrified than ever.

The loud music woke me up. I was in a deep sweat, and for a moment, I had no idea where I was. The room was dark. I looked over at the alarm clock on the nightstand. The hands seemed to indicate that it was a few minutes after nine. Now I remembered. I had shown up in the middle of the afternoon, and with no sleep for two days, I was ready to pass out. Randy told me to go up to his room and crash out on his bed. I would be sleeping on the couch at night, but I needed to get some sleep before that. I was so wiped out that I didn't remember walking up the stairs.

I was still out of it as I tried to negotiate my way down the dark stairway. As I got closer to the living room, I could hear that they were listening to Stevie Wonder. It sounded like he was singing "Superstition." I rubbed my eyes to adjust to the light. The room was packed. Seven pairs of eyes locked onto me as I attempted to reenter the world of *Homo sapiens*. I was a ghost coming back from the dead. Unfortunately, I missed the last step on the stairs. I stumbled and landed flat on my face. Everyone was laughing.

Randy came over and helped me to my feet. He handed me a cold bottle of Budweiser.

"We were wondering when you would come back to life," he said. "Are you okay?"

I was almost awake and almost ready to communicate with the human race. I took a big gulp of beer and surveyed the crowded living room. I was relieved to see that there were no monkeys and that Charles Darwin was nowhere in sight. Rick was sitting in a chair with Jane on his lap. Shelley was sitting on Alan's lap in the other chair, and two girls I didn't recognize were sitting together on the couch, holding hands. There was an unopened bottle of Southern Comfort on the coffee table and a hash pipe in Shelley's hand. I rubbed my eyes again and made another attempt to come out of my stupor. Shelley stood up and handed me the pipe. She turned to the two girls on the couch.

"Carrie and Rebecca, this is Jeff," she said. "Jeff, say hi to Carrie and Rebecca. They live in the room next to us upstairs."

"Nice to meet you," I said. They smiled back.

I took a hit and passed the pipe to Rebecca. Randy reclaimed his place on the couch, and I found a spot on the floor. I took another swig of Budweiser. I had a lot of catching up to do. As the night wore on, the room started to thin out. Alan and Shelley were the first to head up the stairs. Next, it was the two girls who said good night and made their exit. Rebecca pinched Carrie's ass, and they left the room laughing. That left me, Randy, Rick, and Jane and a lot of small talk. Finally, Randy said that he had a class in the morning and he needed to get some rest. He had started graduate school at BU back in September and couldn't miss classes like he used to. As he got up to leave, I noticed the bottle of Southern Comfort resting on the table. It was half empty. As far as I could tell, the only one who had been drinking it was Jane.

When Randy left the room, so did any pretense that the entire night had not been awkward. As long as I had known her, Jane could never hold her liquor. She was obviously drunk and had started to openly flirt with me right in front of Rick. I wanted to be anywhere but here, but this was where I was sleeping and I was stuck in this bad dream until the bitter end. To his credit, Rick was being cool and didn't get upset with her or me. He suggested they go to bed, but Jane would have none of it. I liked him. He seemed to genuinely care about her, and he was clearly the only level head in the room. Finally, resigned to how this was playing out, Rick stood up and said he was packing it in for the night. He gave Jane a kiss and withdrew from the scene. There was nowhere for me to hide.

"Do you think I'm pretty?" she asked.

That was a stupid question. She still had the same big green eyes that had captured me in the first place, and she was as pretty as she had ever been.

"You know I do," I answered.

"Then why don't you want me?"

Before I could remind her that she was the one who left me at her parents' house and ran off to Massachusetts, she came over and put her arms around my neck.

"Kiss me," she said.

As tempting as this was, my hashish-infused brain was still functioning enough to overrule my undisciplined dick. Why she still wanted to give it another go after the disaster in Amherst was beyond me. I kissed her on the forehead and gently removed her arms.

"I've got to pee," I said.

Jane stumbled backward and fell on the couch. I turned and rushed up the stairs to the head. When I finished pissing, I went looking for Rick. The door next to the bathroom was cracked open. I peeked in, expecting to find Rick, but instead caught a glimpse of the two girls. There was a candle burning next to the bed, and its glow exposed the distinct outline of Carrie under her blanket with a nude Rebecca sprawled out facedown on top of her. Both were snoring. I shut the door. Remembering Shelley saying she and Alan were in the next room, I skipped the next door and tiptoed down the hall. I knew where Randy's room was, so that left the one next to his. I knocked and heard Rick's voice tell me to come in. I stayed in the hall.

"Hey, man," I said. "I need your help."

Rick opened the door. He was naked.

"I need your help," I said. "You need to help me get her up the stairs."

Rick didn't bother to put any clothes on. He followed me down to the living room where we found Jane passed out on the couch.

"I've got this," he said.

He walked over to the couch and picked her up in his arms.

Charles Darwin had to be proud. Rick was one strong son of a bitch. There was no way I could have carried her up the stairs.

52

When I woke the next morning, Meatball was sitting on my chest and licking his ass. I liked Meatball. He was the fattest cat I had ever seen. I reached over and scratched him on the chin. He stopped what he was doing for a few seconds and looked at me with amusement before losing interest and turning his attention back to his asshole. I heard someone coming down the stairs. It was Jane. She glared at me for a moment and then stormed into the kitchen without saying a word. She was as pissed off at me as the two dozen monkeys were at Charles Darwin.

I hadn't gotten much sleep. The couch wasn't very comfortable, and trying to sleep in the living room was like trying to sleep in the middle of Grand Central Station. Crashing at Randy's was not going to work. I was already depressed, and I had been here less than twenty-four hours. It didn't take long for me to realize what the cure was, but it was a safe bet that the cure probably didn't want to see me. This time my dick overruled my brain. I decided it was worth the risk.

I went upstairs to the bathroom and took a healthy shit before brushing my teeth and jumping in the shower. As I was getting dressed, I knew I had a problem. The temperature had dropped into the twenties, and I was going to need another layer of clothing to survive the trip. I went into Randy's room and rummaged through his dresser until I found a sweater that felt thick enough to keep me warm. It fit perfectly over my flannel shirt and T-shirt. I put on my jacket and went down to the living room to retrieve my backpack. Jane was sitting on the couch, drinking a cup of coffee.

"I'm going to New York," I said. "Tell Randy I borrowed his sweater."

Jane didn't respond. She just glared at me. You would have thought that I had just drowned a litter of newborn kittens.

Determined to find my cure, I said goodbye to Jane and lugged my backpack over to the closest entrance ramp to the Mass Pike. I was smart enough to not reach out to Isadora and let her know I was on my way. I knew what she would say. I couldn't help myself. I needed to touch her. I needed to smell her. I needed to taste her. I was pathetic. I wouldn't know until I got there if she would even let me in the door.

I made it to The City just as the sun was going down. The last ride took me over the George Washington Bridge, and from there I had to solve the mysteries of the train and subway system to get my horny ass down to the Lower East Side. It was too late to turn back now. All I had with me was a slip of paper with a return address that I had torn from the last letter she sent.

It took me a few hours and a lot of help from strangers to make my way to her street and to her building. I scrolled the list of names and apartment numbers on the wall in the lobby and pushed the button with the name Duncan next to it. I was expecting to hear a voice on the intercom, but I was buzzed in without anyone asking me to identify myself. It was an old building with no elevator, and her apartment was on the fifth floor. I huffed and puffed my way up the winding stairs, set down my backpack, and knocked on her door. There was no answer, so I knocked again. A few seconds later, the door swung open, and there stood the prettiest girl on the planet. Standing right behind her was Michael, the musician from Oneonta.

My first instinct was to turn around and run. The angel saw the look on my face and spoke.

"Jeff," she said. "What are you doing here?"

Her voice was kind, and it stopped me in my tracks. I was under her spell again. I wasn't the only one. I looked over at Michael. He was as hopeless as I was.

"Sorry," I said. "I know I should have called, but I had to see you."

The angel smiled at me and then looked at Michael. With just the slight motion of her head, she directed him to move toward the door.

"Come on in," she said. "Michael was just leaving."

I could tell that this was breaking news to Michael, but he did as he was told. He shuffled past me with a sheepish look on his face and didn't say a thing. Like I had always done up until now, he was being careful not to screw things up.

Like me, he was an optimist. He was hoping for another chance.

53

And so began the Magical Mystery Tour.

It began at the only place it could. No words were necessary as the angel guided me into her bed and replenished me with the same raw passion and joy that she had blessed me with last summer. The evening turned into night and nourished me with all the mystery and excitement that blossoms whenever two bodies join together and are granted the freedom to explore each other for the first time. It took her nearly twenty-four hours to administer the cure. When she finished, I was once again ready to conquer the world. The celestial voices of John, Paul, George, and Ringo had created the soundtrack, but the angel was providing the transportation. It emerged in the form of a horse-drawn chariot encased inside an invisible bubble. Two white horses with bright-blue eyes stood side by side at the front of the gold carriage, ready to take us away. As the haunting sound of "All You Need Is Love" filled the room, the angel took my hand and whispered in my ear.

"I need to show you my new life," she said.

The white horses hustled the gold chariot out of the studio apartment and hauled us down five flights of stairs. We exited the building and came to an abrupt halt on the uneven sidewalk at the bottom of the steps. We were on East 7th Street, and it was a circus. Federico Fellini was in the middle of the road, directing traffic. Disheveled poets, struggling actors, aspiring filmmakers, and undiscovered musicians whirled past us in all directions. Lou Reed and Velvet Underground were standing on the corner, entertaining the mass of humanity with their favorite song "Rock & Roll." All five of the young dudes in Mott the Hoople were milling around on the opposite corner, smoking their cigarettes and waiting to go on next.

The chariot maneuvered its way through the poor and gritty neighborhoods, knocking over every metal garbage can that got in its way. It ventured north as far as Houston Street before turning right and making its way down to the East River. It raced along the shoreline until it reached the Manhattan Bridge and then made another sharp turn and galloped toward the Bowery. My head was spinning violently on my shoulders, trying to take it all in. I felt the angel squeeze my hand. Her warmth breath was in my ear.

"I want to take you to see the dancers," she said. "Then you will understand."

The white horses overheard her and changed directions. In a matter of seconds, the gold chariot found the nearest subway station. The earth opened its mouth and swallowed us up with one bite. As we raced through the dark bowels of Manhattan, I tried to read the seditious graffiti that ruled the subway walls and passing trains. The harrowing journey ended suddenly when, without warning, we were banished back to the earth's surface. We stepped out of the chariot and entered a small theater.

"Where are we?" I asked.

"We are going to an off-Broadway show," the angel replied.

She pulled two tickets out of her back pocket. It was a tiny venue, and the theater was packed. There were two empty seats in the front row, just a few feet from the small stage. She had found us the two best seats in the house. We were barely seated when the lights went dim, the curtains went up, and the music started.

I didn't know anything about dance and I didn't recognize the music, but I was soon mesmerized by the grace and movements of the dancers. There were just two of them: one man and one woman. It was like watching poetry come to life. Barefoot and dressed in white almost see-through Greek tunics, they moved with a free-flowing spontaneity that revealed why she had brought me here.

The angel leaned over and asked me to watch how the two young artists personified a spiritual expression of the music that combined the purist elements of classical with the raw energy of rock 'n' roll. I liked the music, but I didn't understand what she was talking about. I nodded my head and pretended I did. She obviously knew more about modern dance than I did. As they glided across the stage, their arms were extended and fluid. They turned their knees out, thrust their hips forward, and stopped at the edge of the stage right in front of us. With one effortless motion, they opened and removed their tunics and tossed them to the floor. Celebrating their nudity, their firm and flawless bodies floated around the stage for several minutes as if they were being lifted into the air by both the wind and a surging sea. When the music reached its crescendo, the gifted dancers returned to the foot of the stage, faced the audience, and took a bow. I stood up and cheered. I was excited. The theater erupted into thunderous applause. I turned to the angel who was still in her seat.

"I understand," I shouted. "I understand."

Suddenly, I felt a hand on my shoulder…

54

The Magical Mystery Tour was over. When I awoke from the dream, it was time to go. I would be saying goodbye to Isadora Duncan for the third and final time. I knew that I would never be with her again. Even though I had shown up unannounced, Isadora was kind to me and screwed my brains out for two days until my cock finally cried uncle and waved a white flag to surrender. I was so overwhelmed and delusional during the first journey into paradise that I told her I was going to stay in New York and move in with her. She just laughed and assured me that was not going to happen. I got it. This time, it really was coming to an end.

A day later, I was back in Boston and back to reality. My days as a pathetic lovesick puppy were over. All I needed now was a job and a place to live. I stopped by Randy's house first to return his sweater. To my relief, Randy was home, and Jane and Rick were not. Randy said they had gone out to Amherst for a few days to see some friends. This gave me a little breathing room. Randy told me to keep the sweater. I asked him if he knew of a cheap place that might rent to me for a couple of months. He said there was a building just a few blocks away that he drove by every day that had a Rooms for Rent sign in the window. He offered to drive me over there in the morning. Waiting until the next day was okay with me. With Jane out of town, I was cool with crashing there for the night. Besides, I needed time to recover from the agonizing farewell with Isadora and the long depressing day hitchhiking back from The City.

I didn't get that much sleep. Once again, the party went on until the early hours of the morning. Carrie and Rebecca came home late and wanted to hear Stealers Wheel, a group I had not heard of. They had a cool song called "Stuck in the Middle with You," and the girls got up and danced to it over and over again. Randy remembered that there was a little hash left over from the other night, so we fulfilled our civic duty and finished it off. By the time we went to bed, we were all pretty shitfaced.

The only person who wanted me to find a place to live more than I did wasn't actually a person. As I was regaining consciousness, I could sense that I was being watched. That's when I felt the weight shift on my chest. It was Meatball. This time he was ignoring his ass and giving me his undivided attention. When I reached up to pet him, he recoiled and leaped over to the coffee table. He sat back on his haunches and threw me a combative stare. There was no mistaking his message. I had monopolized his sleeping quarters for the second time this week, and he was losing patience with me. I tried to apologize, but Meatball just turned his head away and flipped his tail a couple of times. I was about to ask him if Jane had put him up to this, but before I had a chance, he jumped off the coffee table and waddled his fat ass and piss-poor attitude into the kitchen. I followed the feline trail and found Meatball with his face buried in his food bowl. Randy was making a pot of coffee. A bowl of granola and a banana were waiting for me on the small kitchen table. Randy handed me a spoon and a carton of milk.

"Here," he said. "Eat up. I've already had breakfast."

And so it was. Meatball and I shared breakfast together that morning, and I found a place to live. The white two-story building was a short walk from the Central Square station, and it was on a main thoroughfare, teeming with traffic all day and all night. My furnished miniscule room was in the basement and faced the alley, so the noise didn't bother me. My only window was barely a foot above street level and offered a scenic view of the legs and feet of the *Homo sapiens*, cats, and dogs who chose the back alley to come and go. I had a narrow bed with sheets and blankets, a nightstand, a three-drawer dresser, a gas stove with two burners, and a vintage refrigerator so tiny it barely stored enough food to save a starving man. The subterranean shelter was one of four on the basement floor and rented for twenty dollars a week. I shared a bathroom with the other three basement dwellers. The elderly woman who rented me the room stressed that the lobby door was locked every night at ten o'clock and that loud music and overnight guests were not allowed. That wasn't going to be a problem for me. I didn't have a stereo, and I didn't know anyone who wanted to spend the night with me.

Next, it was time to find a job. Randy was still mopping floors and cleaning toilets three days a week at Harvard and said that Bob Ostrander would probably hire me back if I wanted the job. Working twenty hours a week for the minimum wage of $1.60 was not going to get me to Europe. I had an idea. I took the train into Boston and got off at Arlington Street. If anyone could point me in the right direction, it was Vince Donatelli. I made way up Newbury Street to Club 247. It was the middle of the afternoon, and the music was already playing. This time Vince answered the door. He looked happy to see me.

"Jeff!" he exclaimed. "It's good to see you. Donald told me that you and Danny stopped by last summer when I was in P-town. What are you doing in Boston?"

Before I could answer, Stella ran up to me and gave me a big hug.

"Oh my god!" he shouted. "It's Hilda!"

I spent the rest of the afternoon there. Vince and Stella wanted to hear all about what I had been up to over the past year and coaxed the details of my escapades out of me with several glasses of wine and some ass-kicking pot. I told them I was on my way to Europe but needed to spend a few months in Boston and save some money. I asked Vince if he had any suggestions.

"Why don't you check with Jay?" he offered. "He manages a bookstore in Kenmore Square."

Jay Bouvier and I had been friends for years. He was an interesting character. Short in stature with long flowing reddish-brown hair, he possessed large seductive green eyes that were larger than life and could pierce even the thickest coat of armor. Armed with a mischievous demeanor and quick wit, Jay was everyone's favorite gay leprechaun. He was also the most promiscuous person that I knew. He once hit on me at Club 247 while I was in a drug-induced stupor. When I turned down his advances, Jay couldn't have cared less.

Hitting on every guy he crossed paths with was just part of his modus operandi. He quickly turned his attention to a more willing dude on the other side of the room.

I went by Publishers Book Market at 638 Beacon Street the next day. The bookstore, like my room in Cambridge, was located partially below street level. I left the sidewalk and descended the three steps to the entrance. I opened the door and looked around. Jay was sitting behind the raised counter next to the cash register, reading a book. I didn't see any customers. Jay did a double-take when he saw me. When I told him that I was looking for a job, he hired me right on the spot. He had some errands to run and wanted to know if I could start right then. He offered to pay me $2.50 an hour and said that since the store was open seven days a week, I could work as many hours as I wanted. I accepted the position. Jay showed me how to use the cash register and left the store, saying he would be back in a few hours. I was now the one in charge.

Things were certainly looking up. I had a job and a place to live. Only one thing was missing.

Althea Kefalas took care of that.

55

I had begun to write poetry. None of it was any good, but it was the perfect outlet for me to express my deepest thoughts and the loneliness that I had been grappling with over the loss of Isadora. I was working six nights a week at the bookstore. There were few paying customers. Most were BU students or street people who came in to either get out of the cold or lean against the bookshelves for hours and read a book for free. There wasn't a day that went by that someone didn't try to steal one. Most of the time, I looked the other way. It wasn't worth the hassle. The best thing about the job was that I got to do a lot of reading myself. I had my choice of any book in the store, and it helped me escape and pass the time.

Thea, as she preferred to be called, was a godsend. She was a good friend of Randy, and I met her when they both stopped by my humble abode to give me a ride. The weather had warmed up the day before, and Randy had asked me if I wanted to go out to Jamaica Pond the next day and play. I would have invited them to stay for a while, but besides the narrow bed, there was no place for them to sit. Randy introduced me to Thea, and I noticed that she was staring at my lonesome window and the dazzling view it offered.

"Does your window open?" she asked.

"I don't know," I said. "I haven't tried. It's been too cold outside."

Her question made me curious. I turned the latch and gave it a tug. Sure enough, it opened. The cold air from the alley rushed into the room. Satisfied, I pushed it closed and secured the latch.

I had not been out to Jamaica Pond since my days at Northeastern. Located in Jamaica Plain, it was the perfect place to get high and take a hike. Randy parked the Firebird on Perkins Street, lit one of the four joints he had brought, and led us to the one-and-a-half-mile

235

path that circled the pond. It wasn't warm enough to enjoy the walk wearing the pitiful lightweight jacket that I owned, but getting a good buzz did help a little. Randy and Thea were better prepared than I was. Randy wore a blue denim jacket over his black sweater with a dark navy-blue wool cap securely on his head. Thea, sporting baggy blue jeans and an ill-fitting blue sweatshirt, had thought ahead and covered her shoulders and back with a navy-blue cape. I hadn't even remembered to bring Randy's old sweater. By the time we killed the second joint, I was so high that the cold didn't matter anymore. I lost track of the number of times we circled the pond, but it was dark when we left and all the joints were gone.

Thea had picked my brain for most of the afternoon, and she seemed genuinely interested in what I was doing and where I was going. I liked her. She wore a perpetual smile, and her eyes gave off a warm and unique sparkle whenever she spoke. Her dark-brown hair was straight and halfway down her back and the perfect complement to her intriguing brown eyes. The day had offered a glimpse of who she was. I wanted to know more.

I didn't have to wait long. Later that night, I had fallen into a deep sleep when I was suddenly startled to hear a loud rapping at my window. At first I thought it was a dream, but the knocking continued until I felt compelled to open my eyes. The window had fogged over, so I couldn't quite tell who or what was making all the noise. I rolled out of bed and stepped over to the window. My eyes slowly began to focus. To my surprise, they revealed what was none other than the playful and determined face of Althea Kefalas.

"Open the window," she sang.

I undid the latch and pulled open the window. The arctic blast of cold air slapped me across my bare chest, rushed over my stomach, and reached down to grab me by the balls. It was at that moment that I remembered I was naked. Thea was so busy trying to crawl through the window that she didn't seem to notice. She tumbled down on the floor. I turned on the light.

"What are you doing here?" I asked.

"I want to sleep with you," she said. "Do you mind?"

"What time is it?" I asked.

She looked down at her watch. "Three thirty," she said. "Does it matter?"

I was speechless. I watched as she removed her cape and tossed it on the floor. Next, it was her sweatshirt. When she pulled it over her head, I saw that she wasn't wearing a bra and that she didn't shave under her arms. She sat on the edge of the bed and pulled off her dirty white sneakers and wool socks. Last but not least, she stood up and pulled her baggy blue jeans down to her ankles. She wasn't wearing underwear. She fell back on the bed and told me to pull off her jeans. I noticed that she didn't shave her legs either. I yanked off her jeans and threw them across the room. They landed on top of the vintage refrigerator. Thea laughed and got under the covers.

"Well," she asked. "What are you waiting for?

I was awake now. I jumped in next to her and started to kiss her.

"No," she said, "I want you to eat me."

She threw off the covers, sat up, and pulled her hips up even with my shoulders. Facing my feet, she swung one leg over my head and lowered herself on top of my face. I felt her nipples brush ever so gently across my balls before they retreated and she put me in her mouth. I had no choice but to get to work. My face was smothered in hair and I was having trouble breathing, but I wasn't about to complain. When she started to roll over on her side, I thought she was ready to move on to something new. However, it soon became clear that sixty-nine was her favorite number. It didn't matter whether we were on our sides facing each other or taking turns on top or bottom, she maintained an invincible grip on me at both ends. This was the way it started, and this was how it was going to end. It wasn't until we arrived at a simultaneous climax that her thin but powerful legs released me and let me come up for air. It was perfect timing. A couple of pubic hairs had lodged in the back of my throat, and it felt like I was about to choke to death.

Because I wasn't allowed overnight guests, I suggested she exit the same way she had entered. She was fine with that. Before she crawled out the window, she found a piece of paper and wrote down her address. She said that she didn't have any classes on Wednesday and asked me if I would come by and see her in the afternoon. I didn't answer right away because I couldn't remember if I was scheduled for the bookstore on Wednesday. She must have thought I was trying to decide whether or not to show up.

"Don't worry," she assured me. "It's only sex."

I closed the window behind her and went back to bed. It was only Monday, and I didn't have to be to work until two. I was sure that Jay would give me the day off on Wednesday if I asked.

56

Richard Nixon's problems were only getting worse. He may have been reelected in a landslide, but the rats were coming out of the woodwork and starting to jump ship. Five of the burglars had pleaded guilty, and a couple of shady characters named McCord and Liddy were convicted on charges of conspiracy, burglary, and wiretapping. The rats were beginning to squeal, and the country was starting to notice the stench. Meanwhile, the wise citizens of the Commonwealth were beginning to feel vindicated. It seemed like every other car on the streets of Beantown was proudly displaying a DON'T BLAME ME, I'M FROM MASSACHUSETTS bumper sticker.

It was a joy to be back in what had been the epicenter of sanity on Election Day 1972. I was returning home. The best five years of my life had left an indelible image on my brain. When I moved about the city, I felt like singing FDR's "Happy Days Are Here Again" at the top of my lungs. Whether it was the Common, Harvard Square, or the vibrant streets of Back Bay, I was alive again. Only now, I was free to come and go as I pleased. There were no classes to attend, no tests to study for, and unlike my final year at Northeastern, no Jane to come home to. Working at the bookstore was a breeze. When I wasn't there polishing off another book, I was venturing out to look up old friends and basically doing whatever I wanted. Althea Kefalas was the icing on the cake.

I didn't know what to expect when I made my first trek over to see her. All I knew was that she shared an apartment with two guys near the BU campus. One of them opened the door and let me into the foyer. He told me that Thea was in the living room. I stepped around the corner and found her sitting cross-legged on the large bed that stood in the middle of the room. The living room was her bedroom. Thea looked up when I walked in and closed the book she was reading. She was naked, and I wasn't sure what she was expecting me to do next. I sat down on the edge of the bed and tried to act like this was perfectly normal. Apparently, it was. A few minutes after I sat down, the dude who answered the door came into the room and passed by us on his way to the kitchen. Thea didn't appear to notice. Our conversation picked up where it had left off three days earlier in Jamaica Plain. She was asking me more about my trip to Europe when her roommate reappeared from the kitchen. He was carrying a sandwich and a glass of water. He walked past without looking at us or saying anything. It was like we weren't even there. When he was gone, my curiosity got the best of me.

"Why is your bed in the living room?" I asked.

"Because there is only one bedroom, and Steven and Malcolm are sharing it."

I guess that made sense. We went on to talk about Europe for a while. She had studied abroad in Italy for a year, so I was interested in her perspective. Finally, when it seemed like we had exhausted the subject, Thea bent over and reached under the bed. Her search produced a small bag of marijuana and some rolling papers, and she tossed them on the bed.

"Do you want to get high?" she asked.

"Sure," I answered.

"Why don't you take off your clothes first?" she asked.

We had been sitting there and talking for so long that I had almost forgotten she was naked and I was fully clothed. My eyes took a quick survey of the room.

"What about your roommates?" I asked.

"Oh, they won't come out if they hear us fucking," she said. "We just need to be loud."

I stripped off my clothes, and we smoked a joint. When we were done, I assumed the position. This time I started out on top. I straddled her face and dropped mine between her legs. To my relief, we eventually got around to normal intercourse. She was right. She made a lot of noise, and no one came into the living room. At least they didn't until we were finished. Thea asked me to spend the night.

She didn't bother to get dressed, so I didn't either. Her roommates appeared after a while, and the four of us sat around and listened to music and smoked a few more joints. They kept their clothes on. Evidently, the three of them had done this before. Right after the dudes said good night and went to their room, our bodies reverted back to Thea's favorite number. I woke the next morning to find myself lying on my side with one of her inner thighs staring me in the face. Her head was resting on one of mine. She was still asleep. I gave her vagina one last kiss, got dressed, and tiptoed out of the apartment without waking her.

I was hungry, and my tongue was numb. However, Jay wasn't expecting me at the store until one o'clock. That gave me plenty of time to grab a bite to eat and rest before going to work.

57

It was the first week in March, and I was sitting by the cash register, perusing the *Boston Globe*, when Jay walked in and told me I could go home. It was one of those rare days that he had asked me to open the store for him. It was early afternoon, and the only other person there was a scruffy-looking lost soul who was lurking behind the shelves near the back and attempting to rip off a paperback. He kept looking over his shoulder to see if I was watching him. I was more interested in the story I was reading about the acting FBI director who had testified to Congress that he had been feeding information about his investigation to the White House attorney.

As I was leaving, I asked Jay if he knew what had happened to Miles Jaffe. I had lost contact with him after graduation. I had also lost track of Jake Fisher and Zero Lester, but Miles was really the one I wanted to find. Next to Danny Cooper, he was my best friend in college. To my surprise, Jay told me Miles was living down the road on Beacon Street just below Mass Ave and sharing an apartment with a friend. He had Miles's phone number and suggested I call him. Rather than piss away a dime later at a phone booth, I picked up the phone on the counter and dialed. Today must have been my lucky day. Miles was home and answered on the second ring. He sounded happy to hear from me, and when I told him where I was, he insisted I come over to his apartment as soon as I left the bookstore. I hung up and told Jay where I was going. Jay had a question.

"Did you know he came out of the closet?" he asked.

"No, I didn't," I said.

I wasn't surprised, but it all made sense now. It explained why he had lost touch with some of old his friends. Still, I didn't know why I would be included in that group. He shouldn't have had any reason to think it would affect our friendship. I was eager to see how he was doing.

It was a fifteen-minute walk. His apartment was on the top floor of a four-story building on the Charles River side of Beacon Street. Miles looked great. He still could have passed for Elliott Gould's twin brother, but his Afro was a lot bigger than I remembered it being when I last saw him two years earlier. We had a lot of catching up to do. Miles brought out a water pipe to help us along with our recollections. I learned that he had dropped out of Northeastern and was working full-time as a maître d' at Ken's, the after-hours haunt where I bumped heads with Teddy Kennedy. His roommate, Drew, wasn't home. I asked Miles if Drew was his boyfriend. He laughed and told me no. He said Drew was just a friend and that he was playing the field for now.

That was the only time that his being gay came up in the conversation. He was surprised to hear that Jane and I had split up. I told him about Franklin Mountain and the fire, Oneonta, Florida, and my latest plan to go to Europe. We reminisced about our TEP days and the summer of '69 at our Mass Ave apartment. He asked about Danny, and I told him he was getting married to Judith on April 1. Miles asked about Judith. He had lost touch with Danny and didn't know her.

We passed the bong and talked for hours. When I was finally getting up to leave, Miles told me that he and Drew were throwing a party on Saturday night. He said it was going to be a good one and that I needed to make an appearance. I promised I would be there.

Unfortunately, I had to work on Saturday and didn't get off until ten. I locked up the store and hustled down to the party. It was going full blast by the time I got there. The music could be heard from the street. It only got louder as I made my way up the four flights of stairs. Lou Reed was imploring me "to take a walk on the wild side" as I approached the open door. Replicas of Holly, Candy, Little Joe, Sweet Plum Fairy, and Jackie were standing in the hall and beckoning me to enter. A small white pill drifted in my direction and hopped into my mouth. David Bowie's doppelganger emerged from inside to introduce me to suffragette city. I looked around for Miles. I found Elliott Gould's twin brother in the hallway between the two bedrooms, sharing a joint with a good-looking dude whom he introduced as James Dean for just tonight. The white pill seemed to be taking over. The lights were low, but I could see clearly. The David Bowie doppelganger reappeared and offered to show me where to leave my jacket. He walked me into one of the bedrooms and pointed to a mountain of coats and jackets that had planted its flag on the queen-size bed. When I added mine to the pile, the mountain moved. First, it was an arm. Then a bare leg emerged. One side of the mountain erupted, and the heads of two guys popped out. The coats and jackets continued to protect their privacy, but as far as I could tell, neither one had kept his clothes on. I wandered back out to the party where I heard Ziggy Stardust broadcast that "there was a star man waiting in the sky." I needed a drink. The white pill suggested that I try the kitchen if I was looking for alcohol. However, the path to the kitchen was daunting. It meant running a gauntlet of intertwined bodies that were so obsessed with groping one another that they remained oblivious to my attempts to get by. Rather than fight it, I decided the best approach was to join in. On one side of the hall, three pairs of dudes were furiously making out. On the other side, two chicks were wrapped in each other's arms and playfully taking turns putting their tongues into the other's mouth. Standing alone next to them was a gorgeous girl with long blond hair. Her back was against the wall. The pill told me that it was time to make a move. Love was in the air, and this orgy of decadence was turning me on. I squeezed past the cluster of kissing dudes, brushed the front of my jeans against the firm butt of one of the caressing chicks, and approached the blond beauty. I was about to introduce myself when I felt a tap on my shoulder. I turned around and came face-to-face with a dark-haired girl who was as tall as me. She was even prettier than the blonde.

"Excuse me," she said. "I need to get by."

Her voice was deep and raspy. As she squeezed around me, her breasts rubbed against my back. She had a drink in each hand and offered one to the blonde. The blonde, who was a foot shorter, got on her toes and gave her a kiss. Deflated, I turned away and resumed my quest for the kitchen. As I moved through the sea of bodies, several hands either brushed up against or grabbed my cock through my jeans. One hand made a brief attempt to make it inside. It was impossible to know which hand was male and which hand was female, but my best guess was that most of them were male. Either way, I arrived at the refrigerator with an erection.

I opened the fridge. It was packed with at least six or seven types of beer, most of which I wasn't familiar with. I picked up a green bottle. It had the words *Rolling Rock* on the label. Why not? I thought. I might as well try something new tonight.

When I closed the refrigerator door, an alluring figure with jet-black hair was standing behind it. She was wearing a black jacket over a black sweater, accompanied by black pants and a black pair of boots.

"Are you straight or gay?" she asked.

"Straight," I answered.

"Good," she said. "Let's get out of here."

58

We were halfway down Beacon Street on the way to her apartment on Beacon Hill when she popped the question.

"Do you like cemeteries?" she asked.

It was a strange question, but this was already proving to be a strange night. I played along.

"Yeah, I guess," I said. "Why?"

"I want to take you to my favorite place," she answered.

All I knew so far was that her name was Cheryl and she was from Rapid City, South Dakota. She wanted to know how I knew Miles and Drew and what I was doing at the party. I explained that I didn't know Drew but that Miles was a friend of mine and fraternity brother from college and that he had invited me. That seemed to satisfy her curiosity. When we got to the intersection at Charles Street, we continued up the incline of Beacon Street to the edge of the Common until we got to Park Street. After that we walked over to Tremont, turned left at the old Park Street Church, and arrived at Cheryl's favorite place. It was dark, and it was difficult to see where I was. The whites of my eyes were barely able to discern what I imagined to be the old and eerie outlines of hundreds of headstones.

"This is where Paul Revere is buried," she said. "Do you want to see his grave?"

By now I was 100 percent committed to getting laid, so I continued to play along.

"Far out," I said. "Where is it?"

She took my hand and led me to a large marker near the back of the cemetery. At that precise moment, the dense patch of cumulus clouds that had been stalking us like a gigantic head of cauliflower decided to break apart and shine the light of the full moon on the weathered stone.

PAUL REVERE
BORN
IN BOSTON
JANUARY 1734
DIED
MAY 1818

Five years in Boston and I had never been here. I had to admit that this was cool. She grabbed my hand again and pulled me to the left. Along the wall of the cemetery, a tall obelisk marked the site of John Hancock's final resting place. Abbie Hoffman was right. John Hancock was no fucking insurance salesman. We stood there for a moment before Cheryl became animated and pulled me back toward the front of the cemetery along the street.

"Over here," she said. "This is the place that I come to every night."

We sat down on the ground in front of an ill-shaped headstone that was covered with a grave marker that was nearly impossible to read. It looked to be made of brass that must have been exposed to the harsh elements of Boston for the better part of two centuries. Alternate streaks of green and black were smeared across its face like the maniacal vision of a mad artist.

"Lie down with me," she said.

By now, I was getting used to doing what I was told. Was I about to get laid in a cemetery? She fell back with her face to the sky and directed me to do the same.

"Can you feel him?" she asked.

"Feel who?"

"Sam Adams," she said. "He is right under us."

I looked over at the grave marker and tried to make out the writing. The moon did its thing again and illuminated the sacred words.

HERE LIES BURIED
SAMUEL ADAMS
Signer of the Declaration of Independence
Governor of the Commonwealth
A Leader of Men and an ardent Patriot
Born 1722, Died 1803

The pill that Lou Reed's androgynous amigos had slipped me back at the party was good, but it wasn't that good. Still, I was hoping to get laid, so I lied.

"Yes," I said. "I can feel him."

We only stayed there for less than ten minutes, staring up at the sky in silence while being felt up by Sam Adams, but it seemed like an eternity. Finally, she sat up. Apparently, I had passed the test.

"Let's go to my apartment," she said.

We walked back down to Charles Street. She lived at 5 Myrtle Street, which was north of Charles and just off Mount Vernon. This neighborhood was definitely out of my price range. I didn't have a single friend who could afford to live here. Her apartment was on the first floor, had a fireplace, and was nicely furnished. She said that she didn't have any marijuana but could offer me a beer or a glass of wine. I asked her what she was having, and when she said wine, I told her I would have the same. She was on her second glass when she opened up to me, and I finally learned her story.

Her name was Cheryl Prior, and she had moved to Boston the previous summer to live with her boyfriend Robert, who had just graduated from Boston College. She had applied for a job at a Boston law firm before she made the trip and assumed that she and Robert would move in together and eventually get married. Unfortunately for her, when she arrived, Robert broke the news to her that he was gay. Coming out of the closet was becoming a common occurrence in Boston in those days. Determined not to return to South Dakota with her tail between her legs, Cheryl decided to stay and make the best of it. She and Robert remained friends, and he had put her in touch with two gay friends of his with whom she was now sharing the two-bedroom apartment. She said that living with two guys made her feel safe. I asked her if she had been dating anyone, and she said no. She quickly changed the topic and began to quiz me. I told her that I had been married and about my plans to go to Europe soon, but I left out everything in between, including the fact that I was still married. She said that she really liked Miles and his friends, and if I was his friend, then that was good enough for her. When we finished our third glass of wine, she glanced up at the clock that was on the mantel of the fireplace. It was past two in the morning. That was okay. Jay had given me Sunday off. I couldn't wait any longer.

"Can I stay here tonight?" I asked.

Cheryl shrugged her shoulders.

"Sure," she said. "If you want to."

I was hoping for a little more enthusiasm, but it was late and I was all in. Cheryl stood up and walked out of the living room, motioning for me to follow. Her bedroom was at the end of the hall next to the bathroom. She said she had to pee and told me to go into her room and wait for her. I did and sat down on the edge the bed. There were stuffed animals everywhere. When she walked back in, I told her that it was now my turn to take a piss. When I returned a few minutes later, the stuffed animals had left the bed and scattered around the room. Cheryl was standing next to the bed. She still had all her clothes on, and her eyes were shut. I walked over and kissed her. She didn't move. Instead, her body stiffened. Her lips moved slightly to meet mine, but they remained sealed. She opened her eyes.

"Let's get undressed and go to bed," she said.

There was no emotion in her voice. She sat down on the bed and asked me to pull off her black boots. I did, and she stood back up and pulled the black sweater over her head. I sat down and watched her disrobe. She looked sad. There was no joy in the way she removed her black pants, took off her black bra, or pulled down her black panties. I started to undress, but I couldn't take my eyes off her body as she fell on the bed and lay flat on her back. Her arms were at her sides, and her eyes were closed again. Her skin was as white as snow, which only served to accent the well-manicured landscape between her legs. It was as straight and jet black as the hair on her head and stood in sharp contrast to the wild explosion of hair that I had become accus-

tomed to with Thea. I took off my clothes and climbed in bed next
to her. She remained motionless and kept her eyes closed. I bent over
and kissed her. Again, she moved her lips slightly to meet mine but
kept them sealed. She opened her eyes and asked me to turn off the
light. I did and rolled back over and kissed her on the neck before
moving down to her breasts. They were small but firm, and her nipples were hard. She wasn't moving at all, but the erect nipples were a
good sign. I continued my downward journey until I arrived at the
prize. She still wasn't moving, but she was wet and tasted terrific.
Another good sign but nothing I was doing was getting a reaction
from her. I dug deep into my bag of tricks, using every one that I
had learned from Isadora and a few new ones that I had picked up
from Thea. What was I doing wrong? I finally gave up and slowly
worked my way back to her face. Her hands remained at her side.
She wouldn't touch me or kiss me or grab my cock or do anything.
I was going crazy and couldn't take it anymore. Cheryl remained
motionless. I felt between her legs and she was still wet. Before it was
too late, I climbed on top of her. As if she was suddenly responding
to an erogenous cue, she opened her legs and let me slide inside. I was
balling an inanimate object, and I hated to admit that it was turning
me on. I trembled and shook until every last drop I could muster was
gone. I rolled off and fell on my back. A few minutes later, she got
out of bed and walked out to the bathroom. I heard her lock the door
and turn on the shower. She was in there for quite a while before she
returned to the room wrapped in a towel.

"I'd like you to come back tomorrow night," she said.

I'm not sure, but I think she almost smiled.

59

April Fool's Day was on the horizon. I called Danny a few weeks before the wedding, and he asked me to come down to DC at least two or three days before his big day. He said I could stay at his apartment in Alexandria.

Life was good. I wasn't sure why I was still renting a room in Cambridge since I was hardly ever there. The race track that I continually circled had only four pit stops. The first was Randy's house. Jane and Rick had moved out and were back in Amherst, so hanging out with Randy and his friends was now a lot easier. Second was Publishers Book Market. It had become my home away from home. Jay let me work as many hours as I wanted. Not only was I saving money for Europe, but I was also consuming literature at an alarming rate. Pit stops 3 and 4 were Thea and Cheryl, and the two destinations could not have been more different.

Thea was spontaneity and joy. She loved the outdoors, was a voracious reader, and possessed a sharp intellect. She never talked about it, but I sensed that she came from money. She was from Southern California and her year in Italy had given her a perspective on the world that intrigued me. She laughed when I told her that I was the grandson of Swiss immigrants. That explained everything, she said. When I asked her what she meant, she laughed again.

"The one thing about the Swiss," she said, "they think they are always right."

Sex was not a priority with Thea, but she approached each of our encounters with exhilaration and unbridled enthusiasm. It was always about the moment and always fun. She knew I was leaving Boston soon and placed no expectations on me. It was free love in its purest form.

Going from Thea to Cheryl was similar to a summer afternoon at Pine Lake. I was walking out of a hot steamy sauna and diving headfirst into freezing water. Nevertheless, I was drawn to her like a moth is to a flame. Thea was the soaring eagle, while Cheryl was the bird with the broken wing. It was always the same. We would sit and talk for an hour or two before retiring to her soft sheets to begin our ritual. The anticipation alone was enough to arouse me. She seemed to like me and always wanted me to fuck her and then spend the night, but getting her to show any emotion or feelings was like trying to find a drop of water in the desert. Each time her legs opened and she let me enter, I wondered what she was feeling. She never moved and her arms never left her sides. She never touched my cock or reciprocated in any way. I hungered for any sign of affection from her. Was my erect penis the magic wand she was using to administer her therapy, or was it the weapon to exact punishment for something she had done? Whatever the purpose, this strangely erotic coupling compelled me to keep me coming back for more.

In the days and weeks leading up to the events of April Fool's Day, the chronological order of the pit stops was dependent on my work schedule. I tried to spend as much time with Randy as I could, but my addiction to both Thea and Cheryl implored me to race back and forth between the two of them. I couldn't help myself. I was out of control. Some mornings, if I didn't have to be at the store until late afternoon, I would leave Cheryl's bed, catch the train up to BU, and go straight to Thea's apartment. On one of my days off, I spent the day with Thea, later partied at Randy's for a few hours, and then finished my personal Boston Marathon by spending the night with Cheryl. The next morning, Cheryl left for work, and I hurried back up to Thea's bed to start over again. Danny's and Judith's wedding couldn't get here fast enough. I was in desperate need of an intervention.

It was Thursday morning when I stuck out my thumb. The wedding was on Sunday instead of Saturday, which surprised me. I didn't know much about Jewish weddings. Maybe they didn't take place on the Jewish Sabbath, which I knew began just before sunset on Friday and ended sometime on Saturday night. I expected hitchhiking to DC from Boston would be a whole-day affair. I was keeping my fingers crossed that it would be uneventful. No such luck.

It was clear sailing until the New Jersey Turnpike. I was on the New Jersey side of the George Washington Bridge when I was picked up by a white Cadillac Eldorado convertible. When I got in, I was struck by the new car smell. It was not a smell that I was very accustomed to. The man who was driving looked to be in his midforties and was wearing a light-gray tweed jacket. He asked me where I was going, and I told him DC. We were engaged in some small talk, when all of a sudden, he made a quick right turn and swerved his brand-new Caddy onto an exit ramp.

"Where are you going?" I asked.

"I just need to make a stop," he said. "It won't take long."

A few minutes later, we were driving along a narrow country road when he suddenly pulled over and parked under a large oak tree. I had a knot in my stomach. Was this a "Yogi Berra déjà vu all over again" moment? I flashed back to North Carolina and No Neck and hoped that I was wrong. The dude in the tweed jacket turned off the engine and put his hand on my leg.

"Can I give you a blow job?" he asked.

I had no idea where I was. I could jump out of the car and run. But run where? I decided to try talking my way out of this before making a run for it. He wasn't a very big dude, and unless he had a weapon, I was confident I could defend myself if I had to.

"No way," I said in the strongest voice I could muster. "I'm not gay."

He took his hand off my leg and started to cry.

"I'm sorry," he sobbed. "I'm just so lonely. I don't know what to do."

I told him that it was okay and not to worry about it. He proceeded to ramble on about how he was married and that his wife didn't know about his secret life. He conceded that he was so depressed that he often thought about killing himself. I told him that he didn't want to do that. I asked him what he did for a living, and he said that he sold insurance. None of his coworkers or customers knew that he preferred men. When I suggested he talk with his wife, he broke into uncontrollable sobs.

"It would kill her if she knew," he cried. "We have two teenage boys."

We must have talked for thirty minutes before he pulled himself together and told me he would take me back to the Turnpike. He said that he lived nearby but that he would drive me as far as the Delaware Turnpike and drop me at the first rest stop. He said it would be easier for me to get a ride from there. He shook my hand and thanked me for listening.

When he let me off, I took a deep breath and took stock of my situation. I had dodged another bullet. Maybe now my fortune would change. I was having hunger pains and was about to walk over to the rest stop restaurant to get some fuel for my stomach when the hitchhiking gods came to my rescue. At first I thought I was dreaming. A bright-red Porsche 911 two-door coupe appeared out of nowhere and pulled up to the curb. A stunning redhead in a black miniskirt and long-sleeve white blouse leaned across the front seat and held the passenger door open for me. Her soft, seductive voice told me to jump in. If this was a dream, I had no plans to wake up. Her right hand was on the stick shift, and her eyes were on me.

"Get in and close the door," she said.

I obeyed. The redhead stepped on the gas, burning rubber as she peeled out of the rest stop.

"Where are you going?" she asked.

"Alexandria," I said, "just outside of DC."

"I'm going to Arlington," she offered. "That's not too far from Alexandria."

Her name was Fiona Kelly, and she drove like a bat out of hell. Each car we whizzed past seemed to be standing still. My adrenaline had kicked into high gear. I couldn't bear to watch the road or prepare myself for the inevitable crash. Instead, I concentrated on the black miniskirt that was providing me with the distraction I so desperately needed. Each time she shifted gears, it rode up ever so slightly, until finally it left nothing to the imagination. We roared through the twenty miles of Delaware into Maryland like a flash of lightning, and we were in Arlington, Virginia, in what had to be record time. Mario Andretti couldn't have gotten there any faster.

Fiona was originally from Baltimore but was now living on a yacht in St. Thomas in the US Virgin Islands. She told me that there was a pen and some paper in her glove compartment, and she suggested I write down her address so I could visit her the next time I was there. She said that her yacht was called *Yellow Submarine*, just like the Beatles song, and was docked in the Yacht Haven Marina. Not one to argue, I wrote it on a piece of paper and slipped it into my pocket. I promised that I would stop in to see her the next time I was there. I didn't dare tell her that I had no idea where St. Thomas was.

When we got to Arlington, she drove us to her friend's condominium. Her friend was not home, but Fiona had a key to her place. I asked if I could use the phone to call Danny. I wasn't in any hurry to leave, but hopefully he was home and could drive over and pick me up. We went upstairs to the second-floor condo. Her friend's phone was in the bedroom, and when I called, Danny answered. I gave him the directions that Fiona had scribbled down and asked if he would mind giving me a ride. He replied that his friend Marshall had just arrived and that it would probably be two hours before he could be here. When I hung up, Fiona walked in carrying a joint and a fancy cigarette lighter. She had disposed of the pointless miniskirt and was down to her bra and panties. She lit the joint and handed it to me.

"When is your friend picking you up?" she asked.

"Two hours," I said and took a hit.

As I exhaled, Fiona dropped to one knee and unzipped my fly.

"Hmmm," she said, "I wonder what we can do to pass the time."

60

Danny was incredulous.

"Where are your fucking clothes?" he wanted to know.

"I don't have any," I confessed.

I had never been a best man before and I had never been to a Jewish wedding, but it wasn't until Danny brought it up that the thought even occurred to me. It was probably a safe bet that my jeans, flannel shirt, and sneakers were probably not the best attire for April Fool's Day.

Danny passed me the bong. He had an idea.

"My cousin's husband is about your size," he said. "I'll call Ellen and see if Jerry has a suit you can borrow."

Jerry and Ellen lived in Arlington. Jerry was in the Navy, and I had no idea how he felt about lending his clothes to a scruffy derelict like me. On the way over, I was tempted to ask Danny to drop me off at the condo he had retrieved me from the day before. I didn't know if Fiona was still there, but it might be worth a shot. However, this was one of those rare moments where common sense kicked in and I kept my mouth shut. It was important to stay focused on the goal of tracking down some proper wedding attire.

It was probably a good thing Jerry wasn't home when we got there. Ellen was only too happy to help. I tried on a navy-blue suit, and I thought it was a perfect fit. Next, she offered up a gray-blue-and-white striped tie. Since I never wore ties, I had no idea if this was a good one or a bad one. What difference did it make? No one I knew would recognize me in the navy-blue monkey suit anyway. Ellen had me try on a pressed white shirt to complete the costume. The arms were a little short, but who was I to complain? Now that I thought about it, the arms on the suit could have been a bit longer.

Oh well, beggars couldn't be choosers. Danny advised me to pick out a second shirt and second tie, explaining that there was also a party on Saturday night where I would need to make myself presentable. I found another white shirt with well-spaced vertical gray stripes and a dark-blue tie that I wouldn't look too foolish wearing. Since I at least had the foresight to bring clean underwear, all I needed now were dress shoes and matching socks. The shoes were going to be a problem. Unlike Cinderella, when I tried on these magic slippers, they didn't fit. Cousin Jerry wore 9½, and I wore 11s. As hard as they tried, my poor feet could not squeeze into his shiny black shoes.

Even I knew that the best man could not show up barefoot, but we had plenty of time to deal with that problem. It was only Friday, and someone in the Washington, DC, area had to own a pair of size 11 shoes that would love to spend Saturday and Sunday with me. I could tell that Danny was getting tired of our treasure hunt. I suggested we go back to his place and strategize over another bowl of ganja. He thought that was a great idea.

Besides the extra time to party with Danny, the best part about coming down a few days early was the chance to get to know Judith. I liked her. Danny, with his sarcasm and dry wit, could be an acquired taste for some people. Judith got him. She was petite, cute, and intelligent, and I found her to be quite interesting. Her father had died when she was five. She and her younger brother Bruce had been raised by their mother, who was a dance instructor. Her mother ran with a creative crowd, and their home was a regular meeting place for artists, writers, and dancers when Judith was growing up. Judith had been a dancer as a child and teenager, and she seemed pleasantly surprised when I shared my knowledge of Isadora Duncan with her. I felt like that was the moment that I won her over.

I spent Friday night getting high with the two of them, listening to music, and eating pizza. Around midnight, Judith said she was tired and going to bed. She said good night to me and gave Danny a big wet kiss. Danny, who seemed pleased that his best friend and his wife-to-be were hitting it off, couldn't resist coming up with one of his smartass remarks. As Judith turned to leave, he tossed one of his trademark hand grenades into the room.

"Judith," he said, "I want you to know that you are the second-best fuck I've ever had."

Judith stopped and turned around.

"Who was the best?" She laughed, playing along.

"Jeff."

Judith forced a smile.

"Very funny," she said.

She knew he was probably kidding, but she hadn't known him that long.

The look on her face told me that she wasn't 100 percent sure.

61

On Saturday, we hit pay dirt. Danny had placed calls on Friday afternoon to at least a dozen guys he knew from dental school before he found a friend with feet that matched mine. David Rothman, who would be at the wedding, wore size 11 and offered up a black pair that he didn't need. The final piece of the puzzle was solved when Danny agreed to lend me two pairs of his blue socks.

I had scored my wardrobe just before the clock ran out. Saturday night was the prewedding party. The festivities were taking place at the Holiday Inn in Bethesda, Maryland, the same place that the wedding would be the next day. Danny and I were to head over there together, while Judith, who had left in the afternoon, would catch up with us at the party. Since they had been living together for seven months, it seemed a little silly to me that she had to go stay at her mother's the night before the wedding. Tradition, I guess. At least there wouldn't be any degenerate premarital sex happening that night. Danny's smartass comment was that Judith had left for the night so she wouldn't lose her virginity before the wedding. I countered that she was granting him one last opportunity to get fucked up with me before she turned into his ball and chain.

"Good point," he said. "I'll get the bong."

Danny's parents had booked a suite at the Holiday Inn for what they assumed would be a normal get-to-know-one-another gathering of relatives, family friends, and a few out-of-town guests. Danny, being his usual mischievous self, had other ideas. It started with his outfit, which looked to me like it had been lifted from the album cover of *Sgt. Pepper's Lonely Hearts Club Band*. I thought I looked ridiculous in my borrowed clothes, but to Danny's and Judith's relatives, I probably looked like a normal person. At least I did from the neck down. Danny, on the other hand, looked like he had just returned from an LSD trip with Peter Fonda and Dennis Hopper. His dark-blue shirt was painted with shapes and colors that could have been created by Peter Max or at least Peter Max's imagination. Gold castles, blue and white fish, red cats, a quilt of many colors, and a solitary yellow hammer were spread across the fabric like loose change accidently dropped on a sidewalk. The psychedelic shirt was tucked neatly into his mustard-colored bell bottoms and was capped off at his neck by a gigantic white bow tie. The velvet skin of his black sport coat rounded out this bizarre fashion statement. We must have looked like Woodstock Nation's version of *The Odd Couple* when we strolled into the party. Danny could have passed for a close personal friend of Andy Warhol, while I looked like an unemployed car salesman with a ponytail showing up for a job interview. Anxious to celebrate this historic occasion, we were both stoned out of our minds.

We weren't the only ones. The circus was in town, and Boston was well represented. Vince and Jay and their bloodshot eyes had made the trip down with Marcie Sher. Danny had told them to be their flamboyant selves, and they didn't disappoint him. Jay must have consulted the same fashion guru as Danny. His green corduroy sport coat was accented by a pink shirt and a blue-and-white polka dot bow tie that challenged Danny's in both size and impact. Vince was a bit more low-key, making his grand entrance in blue jeans and a purple-red-white-and-blue paisley shirt. The real party began the moment they appeared at the door. Vince and Jay were even more fucked up than we were.

Marcie, Sara, and Rachel completed the Boston entourage. All three had been among Danny's circle of female friends at Northeastern. He had known Rachel the longest, having gone to high school with her in Brooklyn. I met Rachel my first week at college. She possessed the same dry wit and knack for sarcasm as Danny and could be quite opinionated and overbearing at times. She also had gigantic tits. I really never knew much about her personal life. The only guy that I knew she ever hooked up with was Timmy Stiles during the Boo Canoe period, and that had been a rather explosive on-and-off affair. Rachel loved to dance, and she was always my fallback dance partner at our frat parties. Marcie and Sara were both from Long Island, and we met them early on at the Speare Hall dorm, where Rachel was also staying. The three girls were regulars at the TEP house, our pot parties, and occasional partakers in the clandestine festivities of Club 247. We hung out together in the Quad between classes, marched in unison during antiwar demonstrations, and were basically joined at the hip for four years of our lives. It was great to see the three of them again. It was only fitting they were here to witness Judith's capture of Danny. If he tried to escape, there were now six of his Boston accomplices to apprehend him.

I looked around the room and noticed that the walls were plastered on all sides with the puzzled faces of the older guests. What they were witnessing wasn't making sense. Judith was marrying a Georgetown dental student, wasn't she? Danny didn't look like any dental student they had ever seen before. And who were these odd people? I looked at Danny, and he had a smirk on his face. This was the party he wanted. I looked over at Judith. She seemed to be enjoying the spectacle as much as he was. They were definitely the perfect couple.

That was the green light I had been waiting for.

The best man was ready to let loose.

62

No one really knows the true origin of April Fool's Day. One of the theories is that it evolved from Hilaria, an ancient Roman festival where people dressed up in costumes. It was a religious celebration to honor the great mother Cybele, who had fallen in love with Attis, the god of vegetation. In order to guarantee that no other woman would have him, she turned on the charm and convinced poor Attis to castrate himself. When Danny told me the story, the theme of last night's party and his curious decision to get hitched on April 1 now made perfect sense.

The wedding was at one o'clock. Danny showered first. He was still naked when he walked out of the bathroom with something in his hand.

"What's that?" I asked.

"Judith's birth control pills," he said.

Danny removed a pill from the small circular dispenser and popped it in his mouth.

"I don't want to get pregnant on my wedding night," he said.

My head hurt. I was still reeling from last night, but I managed to get dressed without too much trouble. It was a team effort. My clean underwear joined forces with Jerry's white shirt, striped tie and navy-blue suit, Danny's blue socks, and David's shiny black shoes to somehow transform me into a credible best man. I was admiring myself in the mirror when Danny walked in and handed me a black beanie.

"Here," he said. "You're not done yet. You have to wear a yarmulke."

I put the skullcap on top of my head. It didn't fit very well, but since I wasn't at the Yarmulke store, it would have to do. I asked Danny why I had to wear a yarmulke since I was a goy.

"Because you're the best man," he said. "Put the fucking thing on your head."

Danny was decked out in a beige tuxedo with long tails, worn over a dark-brown shirt with a brown bow tie that was a shade darker. A yellow corsage was pinned to his lapel. He handed me my corsage. It was white and the first one I had worn since my senior prom in high school.

There was no turning back now. We drove back to Bethesda and the scene of last night's crime and whipped into the hotel parking lot. Danny said we were early and that Marshall was waiting for us up in his room. We definitely needed to smoke a joint to calm our nerves. I'm glad we did. Danny and I were both flying high by the time the service started. Today was already an eye opener for me. I never realized that Jewish weddings took place in Holiday Inns.

What little I knew about Jewish customs I had learned at the TEP house, where more than half of my brothers were Jewish. No one had ever breached the subject of the mysterious rituals of Jewish matrimony in my presence, so I was completely lost. Danny told me all I had to do was stand next to him, to not do anything stupid, and to hand over the ring when asked for it. That was simple enough. I must have passed the test because the rabbi eventually pronounced them man and wife. I was enjoying my buzz and breathing a sigh of relief when Danny suddenly freaked me out. He turned around and stomped on an empty water glass. The glass shattered, and the raucous sounds of "Mazel tov!" could be heard throughout the halls and canyons of the Bethesda Holiday Inn. That was startling enough, but the real buzz kill was the moment that I remembered I was the one everyone was expecting to raise a toast at the reception to the newly anointed Mr. and Mrs. Cooper.

I was in a panic. I skipped the reception line and rushed over to the ballroom. I made a beeline straight to the nearest bar where the bartender was setting up.

"Give me two shots of your best whiskey," I pleaded.

"I'm not open yet," he said. "Are you with the wedding?"

"I'm the best man," I said. "Please, I need a drink."

He must have felt sorry for me because he stopped what he was doing, grabbed an empty glass and a bottle of Jack Daniel's, and filled the glass to the top. I chugged it. I thought my eyeballs were about to jump out of my head.

"I'll have another," I said.

I never got his name, but the bartender dude was now my new best friend. I was counting on him to keep the liquid courage flowing while the band set up and the guests filed in. I had no idea what I was going to say, but Jack Daniel's had a few suggestions. My moment in the sun arrived about thirty minutes later. The four-piece band had just finished the song "More" when the lead singer called out for the best man to come up to the stage. I staggered away from the bar and negotiated my way to the microphone. Thank God for the mike stand. If it wasn't there to hold me up, I would have fallen flat on my ass. The room got quiet. I cleared my throat.

"Before I get started," I slurred, "I'd like to thank a few people."

I paused and took a deep breath. I had the crowd in the palm of my hand.

"First," I said, "I'd like to thank Jerry for my suit, my shirt, and my tie."

"Next," I continued, "I want to thank David for the shoes."

I paused again to wait for the applause. There wasn't any. Ignoring the silence, I continued.

"Finally," I said, "a big thank you to the groom for my clean socks."

I felt the yarmulke slipping off my head. I held on to the mike stand with one hand and made a spectacular one hand catch with the other. Someone let out a cheer. That's all it took to open the floodgates. The ballroom broke out in laughter. Bursting with confidence, I waited until the crowd quieted down before launching into my toast to the bride and groom. There was just one problem. I was the holding a yarmulke, not a glass of champagne. Undeterred, I decided to improvise and, in the process, maybe create a new tradition. I lifted the yarmulke into the air and asked everyone to raise their glasses.

"To Danny and Judith," I shouted, "the greatest couple in the world!"

Another round of "Mazel tov!" filled the room. The band began to play, and the new Mr. and Mrs. Cooper took to the dance floor for their solo performance. Nobody seemed to notice when I stumbled and fell off the stage. That was okay. This was probably how all stand-up comedians got their start. I thought that I was finished, but when the song was over, Marshall walked over and told me what was next.

"It's time for the hora," he said. "It's your job to lead this."

Two chairs were brought to the middle of the dance floor. Judith sat in one and Danny in the other. All the younger men in the room gathered around the chairs and broke into two groups. The band launched into a joyous rendition of "Hava Nageela" as we lifted the bride and groom high into the air. I was in the group carrying Danny. As the chairs were circulating around the dance floor, I feared for Danny's and Judith's safety. I would have been scared shitless if it was me being carried on one of those chairs. However, they didn't seem worried at all. Maybe it was because I was drunk and they weren't. Regardless, I was having a blast.

The next time I got married, I was definitely having a Jewish wedding.

63

It was nearly ten thirty when we caught our first glimpse of the Manhattan skyline. It was a clear night, and the bright lights of the city illuminated the sky with such brilliance that they seemed to consume every star in the universe. It may have been a Sunday night, but the Big Apple was a whirlwind of human activity. As we made our way up Broadway to the corner of West Seventy-Third, all indications were that no one was sleeping in the city that never sleeps.

I didn't know that we were stopping in New York until we had been on the road for a few hours. Marcie had offered me a ride back to Boston. She, Vince, and Jay were leaving right after the reception, and I had assumed that she was driving straight through. Apparently, Vince and Jay had convinced her to make a detour. She was taking them to a place called the Continental Bathhouse and would return to pick them up in the morning. Marcie's parents lived on Long Island, and she assured me that they had a guest room where I could catch some sleep.

The weekend had been a success. I had pulled off the best man impersonation without a hitch and had become somewhat of an authority on the customs and rituals of a Jewish wedding. When I departed the Bethesda Holiday Inn, the thought of further expanding my education was the last thing on my mind. However, as I was soon to discover, the next step on my dubious path to enlightenment was to learn all about gay bathhouses.

As Vince explained it, the Continental Bathhouse had opened five years earlier and was the place to be if you were gay. He had been there a few times before and said that it was like visiting the Roman Empire in its heyday. Jay had never been and had begged Vince to take him. The Continental was in the basement of the Ansonia Hotel and was open twenty-four hours a day. It had a pool, sauna and steam rooms, a twenty-four-hour disco, a cabaret lounge, and an endless number of private and public orgy rooms with beds where men could openly engage in sex. It was no wonder Jay wanted to go. Vince, on the other hand, was eager to get there because Bathhouse Betty was performing in the cabaret at midnight.

"Who's that?" I asked.

"Her name is Bette Midler," he said. "She's fabulous. You have to see her perform sometime."

Jay suggested that I go with them. I respectively declined.

"Your loss," he said and winked.

Jay was persistent. I had to give him that. Marcie dropped them off near the front of the hotel a little after eleven. They bolted from the car like two small boys who had just been turned loose in a candy store. She told them that we would be back at ten the next morning, adding that they should be done with their orgy by then.

I slept like a baby in the guest room that night. The weekend had definitely taken its toll on me. Marcie's mother made us breakfast the next morning. I never met her father since it was Monday and he had already left for work. Marcie drove us back into Manhattan, and we picked up our promiscuous passengers at ten like we had promised. They were sitting outside the hotel on the sidewalk when we arrived. They looked like shit but were grinning from ear to ear. It was obvious that neither one of them had gotten any sleep. Jay couldn't wait to tell us all about it. He had been snorting cocaine, and they both smelled like sex.

Jay was still in his green corduroy sport coat. He had been wearing it for two days. His bow tie had mysteriously disappeared, a casualty of his weekend adventure. His pink shirt was filthy, covered with smudges and stains. I was afraid to ask what had happened to it.

"It was unbelievable," he proclaimed. "This must be what heaven is like."

He reached inside his jacket, pulled out a joint, and handed it to me.

"Here," he said, "it's the only one I have left."

By the time we made it back to Boston, I knew more than I had ever wanted to know about what homosexual men did behind closed doors. Jay left nothing to the imagination. The vivid images of naked men, clad only in small white towels, were seared into my brain. Jay told us how he and Vince had danced, sucked, and fucked their way through the New York night. Beaming with pride, he was especially graphic when he talked about one well-endowed dude.

"He was gorgeous and had the biggest cock I've ever sucked," he said. "He was hung like a horse. It was like blowing a Greek god."

It was midafternoon when Marcie dropped me off in Cambridge. I was exhausted and needed to take a nap. As I was getting out of the car, Jay switched back to being my boss.

"Take tomorrow off," he said. "I'll see you Wednesday."

All this talk about blow jobs and fucking had got me to thinking. I hadn't been laid in more than five days. I would take my nap before heading out. Cheryl and Thea were both probably home that night. I just needed to decide where to go first.

Vince rolled down the back window.

"I've got an extra ticket to the Sox home opener on Friday," he said. "Do you want to go?"

64

I was seven years old when I fell in love with baseball. That was the year that my best friend Henry Cable and I became Brooklyn Dodgers fans. The year 1955 was also the year that I went to my first Major League Baseball game. My father was a huge New York Giants fan, and his favorite player was the great Willie Mays. It was the Sunday of Memorial Day weekend, and the Giants were hosting the Dodgers at the Polo Grounds. Dad loaded Bernie and me, along with Mr. Wozniak and his two boys, John and Jimmy, into our family's 1952 Studebaker station wagon; and the six of us made the nearly two-hundred-mile pilgrimage into New York City that morning.

The Giants were the defending World Series champions, having swept the Cleveland Indians in four games the year before. To everyone's surprise, the Dodgers were in first place and nine games ahead of them in the standings. It was early in the season, and the baseball world had no idea that this was finally going to be the Dodgers' year. My favorite team won 8–5 with Jackie Robinson, Junior Gilliam, and Duke Snider all hitting home runs to lead the Dodgers to victory. However, the highlight of the game came in the seventh inning when Willie Mays came to the plate with the Giants trailing 7–3 with a runner on base. The Say Hey Kid drove a Johnny Podres fastball into the cavernous Polo Grounds outfield and electrified the crowd by flying around the bases and sliding past Roy Campanella to score on an inside-the-park home run. It was by far the coolest day of my life.

That same year, my beloved Dodgers shocked the world and won their first-ever World Series by beating the Yankees in seven games. The same Johnny Podres hurled a 2–0 shutout, and leftfielder Sandy Amorós turned a Yogi Berra fly ball into a double play that saved the day for the Bums of Flatbush. Time stood still on that

Tuesday afternoon as every set of ears at Pearl Street Elementary School was glued to the school loudspeaker. My second-grade class was equally divided in their loyalties. Half the room cheered and the other half groaned when Gil Hodges drove home catcher Roy Campanella in the top of the fourth to give the Dodgers the lead. The radio static on the loudspeaker was in fierce competition with voice of the announcer as we waited for every pitch and every swing of the bat. We hung on every word as if the play-by-play was being delivered by God himself.

Baseball in the 1950s was practically a religion in my hometown. Pee Wee and Little League games were major sporting events. The high school team won one Susquehanna League championship after another, and the players on those teams were larger-than-life heroes to every little kid in town who one day dreamed of playing in the Major Leagues. Since New York was home to three teams, our allegiances were split three ways. We argued every day over the Yankees, Giants, and Dodgers and had fierce debates about their great center fielders. Most kids liked Mickey Mantle or Willie Mays, but the Dodger's Duke Snider was my hero. He was the player that I dreamed of being when I grew up. I wanted to hit home runs and make diving catches in center field just like the Duke.

Two years after our once-in-a lifetime Polo Grounds experience, the Giants and Dodgers played their last games in New York before fleeing to the West Coast and breaking the hearts of two-thirds of the kids in town. That same summer, Bernie and I became the proud owners of our very own baseball field. We had to be the two luckiest kids on the planet. When I was four, we had moved to an old two-story brown shingled house just outside the village limits. Located on an unpaved dirt road, it came with a big red barn, a long narrow building that had once been a chicken coop, and nearly four acres of land. We weren't there to farm, and Dad's first project was to tear down the barn. Each year he dreamed up another project. By 1957, he had run out of things to tear down or rebuild. He had an idea. The back section of the property behind the chicken coop was flat, covered with tall grass, and bordered on two sides by dense, heavy woods. Since the land wasn't being used for anything, Dad decided that it was the perfect place to build his two boys their very own baseball field. He agreed to take on this endeavor on the condition that Bernie and I agreed to mow the grass and maintain the field.

Dad never did anything half-ass. The baseball field was no exception. Everything was regulation, set to Little League standards. The bases were sixty feet apart. The pitcher's mound was exactly forty-six feet from home plate and stood six inches high. Dad got the town to donate real bases and a home plate, and he marked the first and third base lines with lime just like they did in the big leagues. He also used the lime to create both batter's boxes at home plate. The thick woods that bordered the property formed natural boundaries for left and center field, with a huge oak tree sitting in straightaway center. Right field was a different story. It was a wide-open space, with the tall grass stretching well beyond our property and as far as the eye could see. Dad solved that problem by purchasing a shitload of red snow fence and installing it from the edge of the woods in right center field to just beyond the right field line. Next, he built a backstop behind home plate, using the two-by-fours he had saved when he tore down the barn and the chicken wire he had salvaged from the old chicken coop. Finally, he constructed a small three-level set of bleachers behind the home plate backstop. It was time to play ball!

By the time I was ten, I was the unofficial commissioner of my own baseball league. Throughout the summer, the only time games were not being played was when it rained or when official Little League games were taking place across town at the Moose Field. Most of us also played on Little League teams, but the number of players in my league outnumbered the ones on the organized teams. The reasons for that were simple. Instead holding a draft and picking players for each team, I challenged different sections of town to create their own teams. The rivalries were fierce. With neighborhood pride on the line, each team was pulling in kids who would not otherwise be interested in playing baseball. The other thing that I did that wasn't being done by the Little League was to keep statistics and post them for everyone to see. Every Saturday morning, players lined up behind the backstop to see who the leaders were in batting average, home runs, RBIs, stolen bases, and strikeouts. Every player's stats were listed, and the numbers only added to the competition. We lived for baseball each summer until we all finally became teen-agers and outgrew the dimensions of a Little League field. When I was fifteen, Dad sold the land behind the house that included the baseball field. A new housing project was being built on a new street that would eventually run straight through center field. A year later, Dad sold the house and we moved into town. All I had left were my memories.

As great as they were, they didn't prepare me for my first trip to Fenway Park.

65

The year 1973 was not 1955. The Pied Piper of Boston, Everyone's Favorite Gay Leprechaun, and the former ten-year-old commissioner of Kid's Baseball were going to be at Fenway Park for opening day. As Judy Garland had once pointed out, we weren't in Kansas anymore.

For all my years in Boston, I had never been to a Red Sox game. I continued to follow baseball during my college years, but for some reason, I never made it to Fenway. Looking back, it wasn't as if it was beyond my means. If I could afford to score a lid of killer weed, I could have come up with enough bread to buy a ticket to a game. I had missed the 1967 Impossible Dream season because I was serving my first six-month sentence at IBM in Endicott, New York. Still, I scanned the box scores each day, captivated by Yaz's thrilling pursuit of baseball's Triple Crown and Jim Lonborg's dominance on the mound. I was also a big fan of Tony C as well as Kenny "The Hawk" Harrelson, the guy who was acquired to replace him during the '67 pennant race after Tony was drilled in the face by a Jack Hamilton fastball.

I was psyched. It didn't get any better than this. The Red Sox were playing their hated rivals, the New York Yankees. I checked out the sports section of the *Boston Globe* and saw that Luis Tiant was set to duel Mel Stottlemyre.

It was an afternoon game, and the plan was for Jay and me to meet up with Vince at Club 247 before heading to the park. Jay was already there when I walked in. The living room was wrapped in a cloud of hashish smoke. Jay handed me the pipe and lit the bowl. Stella danced out of the kitchen, carrying a large platter of small sandwiches, cheese, and crackers.

"Here," he said, "you girls need to eat something before the big game."

We were totally wasted when we exited the apartment. It was a sunny day. The temperature was in the low fifties, but there was a strong wind that made it feel a lot colder. We could have walked to Fenway, but the cold gusts convinced us to instead hop on the MTA at Arlington and let the train transport our altered minds to Kenmore Square. Vince was a sight to behold. A diehard Red Sox fan since birth, he was dressed for the occasion and prepared for the weather. A Red Sox baseball cap rested ceremoniously atop his receding hairline, and he was waving a Red Sox pennant as we passed through the turnstile and made our way to the cheap bleacher seats in right field. What made him stand out in the crowd was the long raccoon coat that was straight out of the 1920s. It was like we were at a Northeastern University football game. All that was missing was a jar of Danny Cooper's liquid amyl nitrate. Jay, on the other hand, couldn't have cared less about baseball. He was there to cruise. He seemed to be channeling the notorious Willie Sutton, who, when asked why he robbed banks, explained that was where the money was. There would be nearly thirty-three thousand fans in attendance that day, and Jay was keenly aware that the vast majority of them would be male. I was as excited as Jay but for a different reason. I had waited eighteen years to go to my second Major League game. I was there for the spectacle, and as it turned out, I wasn't disappointed.

The Yankees jumped out to a 3–0 lead in the top of the first, capped off by a Felipe Alou bases loaded double. Carl Yastrzemski answered with a solo homer in the bottom half of the inning. The Red Sox rallied for four more runs in the second, aided by a two-run homer by Carlton Fisk and a throwing error by Yankee third baseman Graig Nettles, who then redeemed himself by leading off the next inning with a home run.

After that, things got wild both on and off the field. It was easy to see why baseball had become America's national pastime. When Boston exploded for three more runs in the bottom of the third, all hell broke loose. I didn't see how it started, but a few rows below us, a group of Red Sox fans had gotten into a shouting match with a handful of Yankee fans. When a beer got dumped on someone's head, the fists started flying. Several bystanders jumped in, and it didn't take long for it to turn into an all-out brawl. I took a sip of my beer and leaned back to watch the show. We had the best seats in the house. Before long, one of Boston's finest came rushing down the aisle to break up the melee, only to be cold-cocked by the first drunk he encountered. As the fight began to spread, an army of his brothers-in-blue materialized and descended into the chaos. I was thankful that we had smoked hash before the game. I could appreciate the pure poetry of the billy clubs as they flew in every direction. It looked like a flock of deranged birds had taken over the world.

When it was over, there were plenty of empty seats below us. We thought about moving down to get closer to the game, but the beer-and-blood-splattered seats were too gross for us to make the switch. The Yankees went down 1-2-3 in their next at-bat, and when Carlton Fisk hit a grand slam into right center off new pitcher Lindy McDaniel, the Sox were ahead 12–4 after just four innings. We noticed several small scuffles taking place throughout the park, but in the sixth inning, the fighting moved to the field. The Yankees had brought in a new pitcher, some guy named Cox. He decided that the Yankees had seen enough of Carlton Fisk and nailed him in the back with a fastball. That was enough to empty the Red Sox bench. Miraculously, no one was hurt and no one was thrown out. However, that only encouraged the fans to get rowdier. When it was all over, Boston had won 15–5, Carlton Fisk had driven in six of the runs with two homers and a double, Cox had instigated another fracas when he hit Reggie Smith in the eighth, Vince was beaming because the Sox were in first place, and I had witnessed what had to be the most entertaining game in the history of baseball.

The only one who was disappointed was Jay. He had come up empty.

66

My job at the bookstore had turned me into an avid reader. I was a sponge. I absorbed every great writer I could find: from Hemingway to Vonnegut, from John Barth to Albert Camus, from Dostoevsky to my namesake and possible distant relative, Herman Hesse. I read everything that I could get my hands on. Most of all, I got into the two Jacks: Kerouac and London. I wanted to travel, experience the world like they did. I had a crazy idea. I would get a job on a boat and work my way around the globe.

There is always a time to stay and a time to go. My gut was telling me that if I was ever going to make it to Europe, I needed to make my move now. It was on a Monday, one week after the Boston Marathon, that I told Jay I was quitting. Counting my final paycheck and what I had brought from Florida, I had now accumulated nearly six hundred dollars. My rent was paid until the end of the week. The first thing I did was to go to a bank and convert my recent savings into more American Express travelers checks. After that, I began my farewell tour.

My first stop was at Miles's apartment on Beacon Street. It was early evening, and both he and Drew were home. They broke out their bong, and the three of us toked, talked, and listened to music for several hours. I could see that Miles was happy with his new life, and I told him how glad I was that we had reconnected. When I walked out of the apartment, I had a good buzz. Beacon Hill was not that far away. I might as well drop by Cheryl's, I thought. This was as good a time as any to say goodbye.

When she opened the door, she looked me over from head to toe and then motioned for me to come in. I must have reeked of pot. She didn't say a word, but when I sat down on the couch, she sat down next to me and put her hand on my leg. I told her I was leaving Boston. I couldn't tell if she cared one way or the other. Her eyes reflected the same sadness and distant look that I had grown accustomed to. She would always be that bird with the broken wing. She stood up and walked down the hall to her bedroom. I waited a few minutes and then followed her. The door was closed. I pushed it open and saw her standing next to the bed. She was naked. I got undressed.

I wasn't sure what to do. I already had an erection. We stood facing each other for a minute or so, just staring at each other's body. Her eyes never left my penis. Finally, she spoke.

"I want to do it doggie-style," she said.

There was no emotion in her voice or on her face. She climbed onto the bed. Facing the headboard, she got down on all fours and waited. As I focused on the juicy target, I felt my blood rushing to both heads. Cheryl had never looked sexier. Before I could jump into action, the earth came to a grinding halt and stopped spinning on its axis. Apparently, Mother Earth wanted me to record this moment for posterity. She waited for my brain to snap a couple of photos before she started to spin again.

I was completely stoned, but I honored her request with all the technique, enthusiasm, and lust that I could muster. Still, she didn't move, make a sound, or show any emotion. I probably should have been used to it by now, but I wasn't. I didn't care. What was wrong with me? Why was her lack of emotion, lack of movement, and lack of touching me such a turn-on?

When we were done, her silence continued. I tried to engage her in conversation, telling her of my plans to work my way around the world on a ship. Still, there were no words, no reaction. Finally, as I was starting to fall asleep, she put her lips to my ear and whispered.

"We'll never see each other again, will we?"

I said nothing. Seconds later, Cheryl did something she had never done before. She curled up in my arms and fell asleep with her head on my chest. Maybe I was just dreaming, but I thought that I felt her hand touch my cock during the night. When I woke up the next morning, she was standing over me, fully dressed.

"I have to go to work," she said. "Make sure the door is locked when you leave."

I fell back asleep and didn't wake up until almost eleven. I picked up her princess phone and dialed Randy's number. When he answered, I told him where I was and what my plans were.

"I'll meet you in an hour," he said, "right by the George Washington statue in the Public Gardens. I'll bring a couple of joints."

That's what I loved about Randy. He always knew what I needed. If I ever needed to go to a shrink, I would make sure it was him. Knowing Randy, there was probably a good reason that our rendezvous would be taking place in the Public Gardens with George Washington again. When we were there last summer, I was confused and unsure of what I was going to do with my life. Not anymore. I was going to travel around the world on a boat. George would be impressed with the progress that I had made.

He wasn't. I got there before Randy and took a seat on the same bench as before. George was still on his horse, but he refused to acknowledge my presence. Maybe he didn't remember me. After all, with Nixon's reelection and all the shenanigans going on in DC, he probably had bigger things to worry about. Still, he hurt my feelings.

When Randy arrived, we sat on the bench next to General George and his horse and polished off both joints. It was early after-noon and the park was flowing with people, but no one seemed to notice us. After all, it was 1973. Getting high in the Public Gardens had become one of Boston's more popular leisure activities. If George Washington didn't care if we got wasted, why should anyone else?

It was a great afternoon. Randy and I wandered through the park and crossed over to the Commons where we found a group of folksingers with guitars passing joints and playing Cat Stevens songs. We sat down with them and joined in their chorus of "Peace Train." One of the joints made its way to us, and we took our tokes and passed it on. When the song was over, we stumbled away to a quieter space so we could talk. Sly and the Family Stone couldn't have taken me higher. The Boston Common was where my heart was. I had come of age here. This was the exact spot that I had stood in many times before. I thought back to Abbie Hoffman and his giant hypodermic needle in the sky. This was where George Wallace had promised to run me over with his car. I remembered that clear October day when John Kerry delivered his powerful moral message on behalf of the Vietnam Vets Against the War. Randy and I laughed about Bob Ostrander and our toilet-cleaning days at Harvard. The Cat Stevens troubadours had got us to thinking about Chris Griffin again, and we wondered what he was up to these days.

Much to Meatball's dismay, I ended up crashing on Randy's couch that night. We feasted on macaroni and cheese and washed it down with several cans of Budweiser. Randy seemed to have an endless supply of grass, and I spent a few hours on my back with a pair of headphones riveted to my ears. The Moody Blues and their "Legend of a Mind" joined with America and their "Horse with No Name" to seduce me into a trance. I passed out around midnight to the haunting sound of Emerson Lake and Palmer as they escorted me with "From the Beginning." When I woke the next morning, Meatball was glaring at me from the coffee table. Randy walked in from the kitchen. He was wearing his denim jacket and was on his way out.

"Have a safe trip and be cool," he said. "Send me a postcard when you get wherever it is that you're going."

"I will," I said. "Thanks for everything. Can I use your shower?"

"Sure, go ahead," he said. "I gotta go."

By the time I had showered, dressed, and scrounged up something to eat, it was nearly eleven o'clock. Perfect timing, I thought. I had one more stop on my farewell tour. It was Wednesday, the day that Thea did not have classes. Randy's phone was on the kitchen wall. I crossed my fingers and dialed her number. If this was indeed my lucky day, she would still be home.

Malcolm answered. When I asked if Thea was there, he handed her the phone.

"So what do I owe the honor of this call to?" she asked. "You usually just pop in whenever you want."

I had never thought about it, but she was right. Never once had I called to tell her I was coming.

"I'm leaving," I said. "I want to stop by and say goodbye."

Thea laughed.

"I'll bet you do," she said.

Forty-five minutes later, I was knocking at her door. When it opened, Thea was standing there wrapped in a towel. Her hair was still wet.

"I just got out of the shower," she said. "Come on in. Steven and Malcolm are gone. We have the place to ourselves."

As she turned, the towel dropped to the floor. Like Pavlov's dog, I followed her squeaky-clean body into the living room. She turned to face me and smiled.

"I suppose you want to fuck me one last time?"

She looked down and saw the bulge in my jeans. She started laughing.

"No need to answer," she said.

She pushed me down on the bed.

"If I was you," she continued, "I'd be here doing the same thing. Let's have some fun."

Thea was the very epitome of fun. While we never drifted too far or too long from her favorite number sixty-nine, our afternoon was filled with more adventure and flexibility than ever before. We rolled through every room in her apartment and crashed into every piece of furniture with reckless abandon. It took everything I had to keep up with her. I held on for the ride. It was wild, but it was the perfect send-off. Thea had once mentioned that her name was derived from *althos*, the Greek word for "healing." Althea meant "Healer," and that she was. For a few brief hours, I actually forgot about Isadora Duncan.

Finally, exhausted and sapped of all my energy, I waved the white flag and begged her to stop. Thea laughed and rolled off my face.

"Don't worry," she said. "You'll do fine in Europe."

67

It was Friday morning and I had been procrastinating long enough. It was time to get out of Dodge. If I had paused for a moment, gone a few days without getting high and thought it through, I would have realized how absurd my plan was. The great thing about being fucked up all the time was that I was delusional enough to believe anything was possible. Reality was just an illusion. I was convinced that nothing could stop me from doing whatever I wanted. Where exactly was I going to find a job on a ship? What city or port would it set out from? What kind of ship or ship captain hired longhaired hippies and pot-smoking jokers like me anyway? I had no experience. Besides, there was probably a union to join. Who cared? Not me. I had made up my mind to see the world. Confident I was making the right move, I rolled up the blue sleeping bag that I had bought two weeks earlier and tied it to my backpack. I stuffed all my possessions into the pack, trucked over to the nearest Mass Pike entrance ramp, and stuck out my thumb. It was Europe or bust.

I received a letter from my mother in early March letting me know that she and Dad had sold Dreams Come True and bought another place a few miles away. It was in Indian Shores, just down the road from Indian Rocks Beach. Mom said it was called Sunset View, and it had ten units and an apartment/office where they would be living. This gave me an idea. I would head south, stop in on my parents for a few days, and then hit up some major ports. Tampa? New Orleans? Miami? Surely, someone would hire me.

It wasn't until my ride was approaching Exit 9 on the turnpike that I realized that something or someone had seized control of me. I seemed to have lost all free will. My ride was going all the way to Albany. If I had been in command of myself, I would have gotten out of the car at Exit 9 and continued my journey south toward New York City and the Promised Land of Southern Sea Ports. However, when the time came to ask him to let me off at the Sturbridge exit, I froze.

As my final ride of the day was easing into the East End of Oneonta, I understood that it was the unlikely possibility that I would run into Isadora Duncan again that had sucked me into the vortex. It was an asinine moment of weakness. I might as well have jumped into a barrel that was heading over Niagara Falls. It was ludicrous to think she would even be there. She was living in The City. Worse yet, what would I do if I bumped into her? She couldn't have been any clearer the last time I saw her. There would be no more trips into paradise.

My first stop was Get Stoned Leather. I figured that Mike and Renee would let me crash in their closet. When I turned into the alley, I knew something was wrong. Get Stoned Leather was gone. It was as if it had never existed. What was once the heart of Oneonta's counterculture scene had vanished. All that remained was the boarded-up window and locked door to the back-alley entrance of a liquor store basement. I was disoriented. I stood there for a moment before making the trek down the alley to my other security blanket. It was after five on a Friday, and happy hour would be at full strength. I was relieved when I stepped out of the alley. I could hear the jukebox from across the street. The backpack felt heavy, but I had no choice but to leave it strapped to my back as I glided through the door. The Silver was packed, and it hadn't changed a bit. As I squeezed past the pool table, I searched for a familiar face. Jim Morrison's candid observation that people are strange delivered the soundtrack as I pushed and shoved my way to the bar. I didn't recognize anyone.

Suddenly, I heard a familiar voice.

"Hey, Jeff," it inquired. "Can I get you a beer?"

It was Gary, the bartender. I nodded, and he handed me a draft. I asked him if I could leave my backpack behind the bar.

"No problem," he said. Gary wasn't the least bit curious why I was carrying a backpack. It was like I had never left. He acted like he had just seen me yesterday. I handed him the pack.

My eyes drifted over to the nine occupied barstools. I flashed back to last summer and the last time that I had been in The Silver. Was it possible? Were the same nine dudes sitting in the same nine chairs? Each one was nursing a beer, and each one had a cigarette burning its way down in an ashtray. Maybe it was my imagination, but they looked like they were slumped a little further over the bar than they were eight months earlier. It was if I had returned to my favorite garden of flowers, only to find the flowers dying a slow death.

I felt a hand on my shoulder.

"Hey, motherfucker, what's happening?"

I turned around. It was Pete, Penelope's boyfriend. It was early, but he was already drunk.

"What are you doing here?" he asked. "I thought you were in Florida."

Pete ordered another beer, and we talked for quite a while. I told him that I had been in Boston the past few months and that I was on my way to Florida again to find a job on a boat and work my way around the world.

Pete was jealous. He went on and on about how he wished he could do what I did, how he hated Oneonta, and how he and Penelope weren't getting along. I listened for probably ten minutes before offering my two cents. I suggested that if it was so bad here, he should just get up and leave. Pete listened and seemed to be nodding in agreement, but he quickly followed my advice with a long litany of reasons why he couldn't leave town. None of them seemed valid to me, but I bit my tongue. I figured that Pete would probably stay here for the rest of his life. Two beers later, I decided that I needed a break. I told Gary that I was splitting for a while and that I would be back later for my backpack.

I left The Silver and made the fifteen-minute walk up to Gerald's house. He was home, and he was surprised to see me. Paula wasn't living with him anymore. They had broken up in February, and she had moved back to Boston. I lost track of time as we sat in his mother's living room and got caught up on things. He wanted to know how Bernie was doing, so I entertained him for a while with all the misadventures of Madeira Beach, including Bernie being reported as a dead body. We had a good laugh over the Ozzie and landlady story. When I asked him how things were in Oneonta, he told me that a lot of people we knew had split. He said Phil Riker was renting a house in Hollywood, Florida, and that a lot of the Oneonta crowd had made their way down there, including his older brother Joe and Louie O'Malley. I was surprised to hear that Louie was there. I assumed that he was still in Madeira Beach. Gerald gave me the address in Hollywood in case I was ever down that way. Gerald's mother joined us for a while in the living room and asked me if I wanted to stay for supper. Of course, I said yes. Mrs. Lopez was a great cook, and it had been a long time since I had feasted on a pot roast. Afterward, I stayed around to watch some TV with them. Finally, around ten o'clock, I told Gerald that I needed to go back down to The Silver and retrieve my backpack. Gerald said that I could spend the night at his house. Since I had no place to stay, it sounded great to me. I told him I would be back in less than hour.

I didn't know it at the time, but I would never make it back there that night.

68

When I cruised into The Silver, the crowd had thinned out a bit, but the music was louder than ever. Pete was lining up a shot at the eight ball and didn't see me enter. However, Penelope was sitting in a booth and saw me right away. She waved for me to come over. I couldn't tell whom Penelope was sitting with, since the girl had her back to me. All I could see was that she had blond hair. My heart stopped beating for just a second. Could it be Isadora Duncan? However, when I slid in next to Penelope, I saw that it was Mary Lou Davies. I had crashed at her place three or four times the previous summer when I was living out of the Falcon and before I took up residence at The Shack. She was sharing an apartment with two other Hartwick students, and they had let me come by and use their shower whenever I wanted. I was attracted to her, but I never got around to making a move. When Isadora Duncan happened, I lost interest in Mary Lou and everyone else.

I ordered a pitcher of beer. When that was gone, I ordered another. Pete never came over and joined us. He was on a winning streak on the pool table, and it looked like he was hitting on a miniskirted college girl with long black hair. Penelope couldn't have cared less. After I had filled her and Mary Lou in on my comings and goings over the past eight months, Penelope told me about the problems she and Pete were having. She announced that she was breaking up with him. Mary Lou didn't have much to say. She just smiled. My guess was that she had heard all this many times before. By the time we emptied the third pitcher, the three of us had a substantial buzz. Penelope's hand was on my thigh. I pretended not to notice, but it worried me. I liked Penelope. We had been naked together dozens of times out at Pine Lake, but we were just friends. If we were going to sleep together, I didn't want it to be because she was drunk and she and Pete were having a fight. I wasn't interested in losing two friendships at the same time. Suddenly without warning, Penelope's hand was on the move. Not knowing what to do next, I turned my attention to Mary Lou. She was as drunk as Penelope. From where she sat, she couldn't see Penelope fondling my balls, but it was obvious that she knew what was happening. The smile on her face told me that she was enjoying the show and was having fun watching me squirm. As luck would have it, Penelope had to pee. I stood up, let her out of the booth and watched as she vanished into the community of endless malt and hops. I felt a little dizzy when I sat back down. It was time to make a move.

"Mary Lou," I slurred, "I've always wanted to fuck you."

I don't know why I thought that was a smart thing to say, nor did I have any idea how she would react. Hopefully, she wouldn't slap me across the face.

"Me too," she said. "Why don't we get out of here before Penelope comes back?"

I couldn't believe my ears. I jumped up and raced over to the bar to retrieve my backpack from Gary. I kept hoping she wouldn't change her mind.

We left The Silver and walked back to her apartment. Whether it was for balance or a show of affection, she held my hand the entire way. Before she opened the door, she wanted to make one thing clear.

"You're leaving Oneonta tomorrow, right?"

"Yeah, that's right."

"Okay then, let's do it."

She was still living in the same place. She asked me to be quiet since she didn't want to wake her roommates. The bathroom was on the way to her bedroom. I excused myself to take a piss. As I stood at the toilet and watched the yellow rain negotiate its graceful arc into the bowl, it felt like home. Last summer's shower curtain was still hanging from the shower rod. Tomorrow morning, I would be taking my last shower in Oneonta, and it would be here. Perfect.

Mary Lou was not into wasting time. When I walked in the bedroom, she had already gotten undressed and was waiting for me under the covers.

"Hurry up," she said.

I stripped off my clothes as fast as I could. I pulled back the covers to have a look at her. She looked gorgeous. She was fair-skinned, and she had a small mole on her chest, just above her left breast. I jumped into bed, and we embraced in a long, wet kiss. My hands were all over her as I slowly began to work my way down. I kissed her neck and then moved on to both of her nipples. I fondled one breast while I sucked on the other. My tongue's journey continued southward, stopping briefly at her bellybutton before moving ever so slowly across her stomach. As it was approaching its destination, I felt her grab my head with both hands.

"Not there," she said. "I'm having my period."

I had come too far to turn back now.

I lifted my head and our eyes met.

"I don't care," was all I said.

69

While I was on my way to Florida, Bernie and Ozzie were on their way out. Bernie's beat-up Rambler was on its last leg. It was coughing and wheezing up and down Gulf Boulevard like a terminally ill patient on life support. It was time to pull the plug. They were about to go to Winn Dixie when Ozzie noticed the For Sale taped to the back window.

"Nobody is going to buy this piece of shit," he sneered.

Bernie had to feed the Rambler a quart of oil every time they left the house even if it was only traveling a few miles to the grocery store. This time was no exception. He placed the key in the ignition and hoped for the best. The Rambler had swallowed its medicine. It coughed a couple of times and farted blue smoke out its exhaust pipe before settling into a bumpy idle. They were off and running. As they approached the corner of 148th Street, a shirtless hitchhiker in cutoff shorts caught Bernie's attention. He swerved over to pick him up. Ozzie was furious.

"What the fuck are you doing? We're only going a few more blocks to the store."

"Hey, the dude needs a ride," countered Bernie. "Let's find out where he's going. We can come back to the store later."

Fortunately, the Rambler didn't stall out while they waited for the shirtless dude to jump into the back seat. His dark-brown hair was tied in a ponytail, and his shoulders were seriously sunburned. Both Bernie and Ozzie could smell the alcohol on his breath.

"Cool car," were the first words out of his mouth. "How much do you want for it?"

Bernie turned around. "How much have you got?" he asked.

The dude looked dejected.

"Sorry, but all I have on me right now is seventy-five dollars and an ounce of weed."

"That's cool," Bernie answered. "I'll take it."

The dude reached into one front pocket and pulled out a baggie. He handed it to Bernie. Then he reached into the other pocket and pulled out a roll of bills. Bernie handed the baggie to Ozzie, who opened it and took a whiff.

"Smells like good shit to me," he said.

The dude counted the bills. He was two dollars short of seventy-five. He handed the wad to Bernie.

"That's okay," said Bernie. "We've still got a deal."

Bernie stuffed the bills into his shorts. The Rambler was still running when he and Ozzie got out. The dude stepped out of the back seat and stumbled around to the driver's side. He gave Bernie the power handshake.

"Thanks, man," he said as he jumped in the front seat, revved the poor engine a few times, and peeled out.

Bernie took the baggie back from Ozzie and put it in his back pocket.

"Let's go back to the house and check this shit out," he said.

It was only six blocks. The groceries could wait. Bernie had pulled off the deal of the century. He had driven the Rambler for over nine months, sold it for twenty-three dollars more than he had paid for it, and somehow managed to score a free ounce of pot.

Ozzie was impressed.

"Too bad you can't do this every day," he said. "You'd never get a job again."

70

My last ride dropped me off in front of Sunset View just as Bernie and Ozzie were getting ready to pull out. It was Monday, April 30, the same day that Nixon's chief lackeys Haldeman and Ehrlichman were cleaning out their desks at 1600 Pennsylvania Avenue. Tricky Dick was trying desperately to contain the impending scandal that was brewing up around him, so he fired his White House attorney and asked for H. R. Bobby's and Johnny's resignations along with that of his attorney general. Not that I gave a shit anymore, but it was fun to see how the country was receiving a strong dose of well-deserved karma. It had voted for Richard Milhous Nixon, and now it was stuck with him. He wouldn't be my problem much longer. I was about to leave.

Bernie and Ozzie had secured a brand-new dark-blue 1973 Buick Electra hardtop coupe as their Auto Driveaway car. They had four days to get it to Marblehead, a coastal town just north of Boston. Ozzie needed to get his Rice Burner, new stereo, and the rest of his possessions up to his parents' house in New York, so he rented a small U-Haul cargo trailer and hitched it to the back of the Electra. When I stepped out of the car, they were saying goodbye to Mom and Dad. When they saw me, they decided to stick around for a few hours and spend some time getting caught up. Like me, Bernie was also making plans to go to Europe. Ozzie, on the other hand, wasn't sure what he was doing next, so he talked Bernie into helping him haul his shit back to New York. Bernie would dump him off in Sidney and then continue on to Marblehead alone. After he dropped off the car, Bernie's plan was to check out flying from Boston to somewhere in Europe. He looked tired. Ozzie pulled me aside and snitched that

Bernie and Bernie's Penis had spent last night with Bernie's new girlfriend and that neither had gotten much rest.

It was midafternoon when they finally left. I spent the rest of that day and most of the next hanging out with my parents. Their new motel was far out. The property bordered a wide stretch of sand with the ten guest rooms running perpendicular from the beach up to the apartment/office next to the road. I went for several long walks on the beach and took in two spectacular sunsets. The best part was the time with Mom and Dad. I had to give it to them. They seemed happy in their new life, but what amazed me the most was how well they were handling the disappointment they had to be feeling over how my brother and I had turned out. It certainly wasn't what they were expecting when they had scrimped, saved, and gone without to put us through college. Having outwitted the draft board, Bernie saw no reason to stay in school. He had never wanted to go to college in the first place. He just wandered off one day during his final semester at Central Connecticut and never came back to obtain the credits he needed to graduate. To make matters worse for them, I received my degree but refused to attend my own graduation. At the time, I was bitter over the NU 31 and my Hayakawa arrest, the Kent State shootings, and the Vietnam War. Only later did I realize just how selfish I had been and how much I must have hurt my parents. I was the first one in our family to earn a college degree, and I had deprived them of that proud moment they had sacrificed so much for. They never got to watch their oldest son walk across the stage and receive his diploma.

Dad and I had come a long way since my days as an antiwar protestor. Our relationship had hit its low point the day I accused him of being a war criminal. His factory had received Vietnam War–related contracts from Nixon's Defense Department, so with my twisted logic, he had to be guilty by association. That seemed like a long time ago. Due to my newfound political apathy and my resignation over the road that the country seemed to be heading down, I had managed to lighten up a bit and rule him not guilty of all charges. As for Dad, moving to the Gulf Coast of Florida had definitely mellowed him and added a bounce to his step. He had shaken off the shackles of his thirty-two-year job and seemed to be having the time of his life. He obviously didn't approve of or even understand the lives Bernie and I were living, but he almost seemed ready to give us a pass. Like the rest of the country, he had begun to sour on the debacle in Vietnam. Our hometown and its surrounding communities, like thousands of other small towns across America, had been mourning the senseless deaths of their sons at an alarming rate.

"That damn war," he said over and over, "it screwed up your whole generation."

Baseball remained our Rock of Gibraltar. It was where our differences vanished into thin air. Dad was excited about the fast 18–6 start that his beloved San Francisco Giants had gotten off to this season. They were already 3½ games ahead of the Cincinnati Reds, last year's National League champs who had lost to Oakland's A's in the World Series. He was convinced that 1973 was going to be their year. Father Time had caught up with his hero Willie Mays, who had been sent packing to the New York Mets, but Dad was optimistic. He was counting on Willie "Stretch" McCovey returning to his dominant form after suffering a season-ending broken arm the year before. Stretch and the versatile Bobby Bonds would have to lead the way. I didn't share Dad's optimism. I argued that the Giants were getting old, that Juan Marichal was way past his prime, and that the Reds were the far better team. That was the great thing about baseball. You could argue all you want, but you had to let the season play out.

By the second night, I was getting restless. It was around nine thirty when I asked Dad if I could borrow his car. Before they left, Ozzie had told me about a great watering hole that he and Bernie had discovered. It was called Outlaws, and it was a St. Pete biker bar over on Forty-Ninth Street, not far from where Jack Kerouac was living when he died four years earlier. Ozzie claimed that it was the place to go if you wanted to get laid.

What did I have to lose? I figured if Ozzie could get laid there, it had to be easy.

71

It may have been Tuesday night, but the place was packed. The first thing I noticed as I was pulling in was how much of the parking lot was flooded with Harley-Davidsons. I found an open spot near the road and turned off the engine. As I made my way through the sea of motorcycles and got closer to the entrance, I encountered small clusters of shirtless dudes in leather vests who didn't seem to take notice of me. Some were passing joints around, while others were snorting what had to be cocaine off the seats of their bikes through rolled-up one-dollar bills. Blocking my path to the door was the hairy bare ass of a biker. The dude's jeans were pulled down to his knees. I tried to slip past him nonchalantly so as not draw attention to myself, but that plan went out the window when I spotted the curly headed blonde on her knees in front of him with the biker's cock in her mouth. I didn't stop for long. He was a scary-looking dude with a huge scar on his forehead, so when he glanced over at me and stared, I figured it was a good idea to keep walking. When I pushed open the door, I was greeted by the Spencer Davis Group who were offering to "gimme some loving." A giant badass with huge arms covered in tattoos asked to see my ID.

It didn't take long for my wish to come true. I had ordered a beer and had been standing around in the crowd for about ten minutes when I first noticed her staring at me from across the room. When I returned the stare, she looked away. She was sitting on a stool at the end of the bar where everyone had to pass her to go to the head. A lot of the shady characters who squeezed by her appeared to be friends of hers. The bartender had lined up four shot glasses in front of her and was filling them with tequila. I decided that this might be a good time to make my way to the men's room.

By the time I got to where she was sitting, she was polishing off her second shot. She had licked the salt off the side of her left hand, poured down the tequila with her right, slammed the shot glass on the bar, and was sucking on her second slice of lemon. As I slipped past, I felt her pinch my ass. *This is going to be fun,* I thought. I decided to play hard-to-get and kept on walking.

The men's head was a pigsty. The three urinals looked like they hadn't been cleaned since the days Eisenhower was in the White House. Two of them were stuffed to the brim with paper towels and were starting to overflow. My only good option was to point my dick into the third. As I was making my donation to the Pinellas County sewage system, I heard a loud banging coming from inside one of the stalls. Still peeing and afraid to turn around, I read the graffiti in front of my nose:

DON'T PUT CIGARETTE BUTTS IN THE URINAL—IT
MAKES THEM SOGGY AND HARD TO SMOKE

I finished my whiz, determined to get out of there as fast as I could. As I pulled the loose handle on the decaying wood door to leave, I couldn't help noticing that the door to the stall where all the noise was coming from was off its latch and cracked half open. A ponytailed dude in a leather jacket with his pants around his ankles was violently thrusting his hips back and forth while a naked pair of legs were pressed against his shoulders, pointing to the ceiling. I opened the door and split. In my rush to flee, I forgot to zip up my fly.

I was greeted with another blast of loud music. This time it was Grand Funk Railroad telling me that they were "my captain." Somehow, I doubted that. What I didn't doubt was that she was staring at me again. This time, when I returned the stare, her eyes stayed locked on mine.

Her name was Mia, and she was drunk. She had downed the two remaining shots of tequila, and the bartender was pouring her four refills as I was nestling up to her. She asked if I liked tequila. I said yes. Actually, I had only had it once before one late night in

Boston with Jake and Zero, and it had really messed me up. Mia handed me the salt shaker.

"You first," she said.

I shook the salt onto my hand, licked it off, and downed the shot. It was nasty.

"Suck on this," she said, handing me the slice of lemon. "By the way," she continued, "your fly is down."

I lost track of how many shots we did, but it got easier as the night went on. I don't remember much after that. I have a vague recollection of Foghat on the jukebox and their song about "just wanting to make love to you" taking over the bar as every biker, biker chick, and biker wannabe sang along. The next thing I recall is standing in the parking lot with Mia next to her car, holding her ass and exchanging tongues with her. Somehow she was going to drive, and somehow I was going to follow her home. Both of us could barely stand, let alone drive. She only lived a few blocks away and insisted we could make it. By now my penis had assumed command, ordering me into Dad's car and instructing me to do whatever she said.

I wish I could remember what happened in her bed that night. It was the drunkest I had been in a long time. At least I didn't puke or get sick. I must have done something right. When I woke up the next morning, I was lying on a huge wet spot, and Mia was smiling at me.

"That was great," she said. "I really needed that. Thanks."

The morning sun had lit up the room and was shining a brilliant spotlight on her. I rolled off the wet spot and gave her a kiss. I was seeing her for the first time. The smoke and haze of Outlaws was gone, as was the ill-advised bias of countless tequila shots. Seeing her naked in the light of day was a dazzling revelation. I hadn't realized how pretty she was. Her dark-olive skin was smooth and glowed like a natural tan. She looked to be of either Spanish or Italian descent. Why this lovely creature had selected me over countless others last night was a mystery. To make sure I wasn't dreaming, I reached over and touched one of her nipples. She was real.

Mia removed my hand from her nipple and placed it between her legs. I thought it was strange the way she was looking at me.

"What is it?" I asked as I began to slowly rub.

"You remind me of someone," she said.

"Who's that?" I asked as my hand began to speed up.

"My ex-boyfriend," she said. "We just broke up."

She was wet now. I slipped my fore and middle fingers inside.

"How long ago did you break up?" I asked.

"Two days ago," she answered. She opened her legs wider.

"Do you think you'll get back together?" I asked.

"I don't think so," she said, pulling me on top of her.

My dick had turned to stone. Mia reached down and guided me inside.

"Why not?" I gasped.

Mia grabbed my ass with both hands and drew me as deep into her as she could. I could feel her fingernails digging into my butt cheeks as she let out a scream.

"I don't think he'll be back," she moaned. "Bernie said he was going to Europe."

72

We had been following the Mysterious Chameleon since the trip began. She had been leading us around for hours. It felt like we had entered a perpetual carnival and there was no exit. Louie insisted that she was Julie Andrews from *The Sound of Music*. Phil Riker's three roommates disagreed. Wayne thought she was his mother. I couldn't remember the other two roommates' names, but it didn't matter anymore. They had merged into one person and were convinced that she was either Janis Joplin or Ethel Merman. As for me, I pleaded no contest. Her voice was familiar, but her metaphysical form had yet to take shape. Louie had advertised his anonymous LSD as Owsley acid, but that was doubtful. Owsley was the famous acid manufacturer that Tom Wolfe had written about in *The Electric Kool-Aid Acid Test*. As far as I knew, Owsley was in jail and his mind-blowing acid hadn't been around for years. In the end, it really didn't matter. The LSD was free, so we placed the tabs on our tongues and swallowed.

It was for the lack of a better idea that I had landed in Hollywood two days earlier. I made a feeble attempt to rationalize it by pretending that I could use Phil's place as my home base while I was getting work on ship at the Port of Miami. The truth was that I had my head up my ass and was using this as an excuse for my impotence. It was one thing to read about London and Kerouac and their exotic travels, but it was another thing to actually do it myself. I had no clue how to find a job on a boat or even where to start. I had passed on New Orleans or Tampa. Unless I was planning to swim across the Atlantic, Miami would be the end of the line for me. Last summer, George Washington had called me pathetic. He was right. I was turning out to be one sorry excuse for a world traveler.

I didn't know Phil all that well, but the word on the street was that he welcomed anyone from Oneonta that showed up. Phil was a skilled carpenter, and he had a good-paying construction job. He was sharing the rent with three other dudes who also had jobs. The only one at home when I showed up on Friday afternoon was Louie O'Malley, who didn't have a job. His by now well-established routine of freeloading off his friends had relocated to Hollywood. Louie had mastered the art of shoplifting just enough steaks to keep his rent-paying roommates from kicking him out. No one quite understood how, but for some reason, he always had enough cash on hand to score some weed. Free marijuana and free steaks were his ticket to free rent. By offering everyone free acid on that Sunday night, Louie had doubled down on his reputation as the perfect house guest. Phil opted not to trip with the rest of us because he had to work the next morning. Apparently, his roommates weren't as dedicated to their jobs as he was to his. The only thing on my schedule for Monday was to look for my imaginary job on a ship. I opted for LSD.

Louie was adamant that we wait until the wee hours of the morning before making our move. He argued that we needed to avoid the Hollywood cops at all costs. He told me about the run-in Joe Lopez had with them a month earlier. Gerald's older brother had gotten picked up on some bogus loitering charge and had spent two unpleasant nights in the Hollywood jail. When he returned to the house a few days later, he had a black eye and bruises all over his body. Joe had been swept up with three other guys, but he was the only one taken to jail.

"They thought he was Cuban because his last name was Lopez," Louie explained. "The cops around here don't like Cubans. This city was too fucked up for Joe. He split for Colorado."

We heeded Louie's warning and waited until around four in the morning to take our medicine. We paused on our launch pads for probably thirty minutes before our booster rockets thrust us headfirst into the charcoal isolation of predawn Hollywood Florida. The Mysterious Chameleon introduced herself, explaining that she had been assigned our trip leader. She suggested that we venture out on our own for a while. Without her leadership, we wandered aimlessly down the dark streets and sailed indiscriminately into a series of dormant neighborhoods, desperate for any sign of life. I was keenly aware of how each acid trip took on a life of its own. There would be no sightings of Ozzie's Head, no invitations from Lurch to follow in the footsteps of Mary Baker Eddy. As we waited for the sun to circle back around to the East Coast of Florida, we prayed together that we would find proof that there was indeed life on earth.

As dawn was deciding whether or not to break, I found myself standing precariously atop a tightrope. I was having trouble keeping my balance. One side was clearly Reality. The other side didn't have a name but seemed far more compelling. As I swayed back and forth, I felt myself bouncing out of control between the two universes. It was disorienting. It made me dizzy and confused. After a while, I couldn't tell one from the other.

That's when the Mysterious Chameleon ordered the five of us to form a circle. Standing in the center, she raised her clenched fist and yelled into her microphone. The words were sent around the world.

"GOOD MORNING, PEOPLE."

I had heard this before. The voice was familiar. A huge clock stood directly in front of me. The hands on the clock were running backward. The lysergic acid diethylamide had reached into the deepest recess of my porous mind and was sending me back to the exact moment I first saw the Mysterious Chameleon. I knew who she was. I had witnessed her arrival on an August Saturday morning as a new sunrise was reaching out to greet the newly formed Nation of Woodstock. When I opened my hashish-laden eyes, her spectral image emerged from the shadows. One hundred thousand human souls on the hill below me soared to their feet like a phoenix rising from the ashes of the night before. The human wave continued past me and lifted the several hundred thousand spirits on the hill above me to their feet. Jefferson Airplane broke into song. The queen of rock 'n' roll appeared on stage as a beautiful dream holding the Nation of Woodstock in the palm of her hand. Now nearly four years later, the sultry Grace Slick had returned to rescue me from myself.

"Go ask Alice," she sang.

I asked Louie and the roommates to stay where they were. I walked onto a chess board where a group of men were sitting. The men stood up and pointed in unison toward the main street where Hollywood shopkeepers were turning on their lights and unlocking their doors. The men chimed in with their background vocals. In perfect harmony, they repeated her words. Grace Slick followed with a new set of instructions.

"Go ask Alice," she sang, "when she's ten feet tall."

I was standing in front of a giant plate glass window. It was covered with bright-colored posters: Egyptian pyramids, Roman Coliseum, Big Ben. A sign was flashing in the window nearest the door. It read Travel Agency. The men from the chess board ran up behind me and pointed to another poster. A TWA plane was soaring into the blue sky with the caption Fly to Europe spread across its fuselage. The door was open. I looked inside and saw a woman sitting behind a desk. The name plate in front of her read *Alice*. She stood up to greet me. She was ten feet tall.

"Can I help you?" she asked.

Grace Slick was right behind me when I walked in the door. She winked and nudged me with her elbow. She told me to ask if there were any flights to Europe today. The ten-foot-tall Alice wanted to know where I wanted to go in Europe. I told her it didn't matter. Grace Slick nodded her approval. The ten-foot-tall Alice sat down at her desk and motioned for me to have a seat. She picked up a handful of brochures and leafed through them until she found the one she was looking for. She asked me how soon I wanted to leave. I told her as soon as possible.

"Well," she said, opening the brochure, "there is a TWA flight to Nassau in the Bahamas this afternoon. From there you can catch a connecting flight to Luxembourg on Air Bahamas. When do you want to return?"

By now, the *Electric Kool-Aid* had taken over my thought processes the same way that Isadora Duncan had gained control of my cerebellum. It injected my brain with a huge dose of courage and suggested that I split the country and never come back.

"I don't," was my defiant answer.

The ten-foot-tall Alice looked at me and smiled. Grace Slick nodded her approval. It was clear that the two of them were in this thing together. The ten-foot-tall Alice said that a one-way ticket was going to cost me three hundred dollars. My heart sank. I only had the five hundred dollars in traveler's checks, plus a pocketful of loose change and maybe twenty-five dollars in my wallet. If I bought the ticket, I would be running out of money before I ever got started. Grace Slick read my mind. She squeezed my hand.

"Use your secret weapon," was all she said.

I didn't have a secret weapon. Grace Slick begged to differ. She told me to reach into my back pocket and pull it out. All I kept in my back pocket was my wallet, and that certainly wasn't anyone's secret weapon. Reading my mind again, Grace Slick told me to try the other pocket. How it got there, I don't know, but when I reached into my left back pocket, I pulled out a two-by-three-and-a-half-inch white plastic card. A pair of bold interlocking circles was stamped on the front. The red circle encompassed the word *master*, while the brown one surrounded the word *charge*. My name was imprinted in the lower left-hand corner. Grace Slick took the card out of my hand and gave it to the ten-foot-tall Alice.

"He'll take the one-way ticket," she said.

Suddenly, I was having a flashback. About a month after Northeastern mailed my bachelor's degree to my parents' house, the Shawmut Bank of Boston followed suit with a plastic card. A letter was inside congratulating me on my accomplishment and stating that they were issuing me a charge card with a three-hundred-dollar line of credit. Not knowing why I would want such a thing, I handed it over to my mother and told her to get rid of it. Apparently, my mother had held on to this Master Charge the Interbank Card. It had made the trip to Florida when they moved there, and she had kept it in safekeeping for me. When I was hugging her and saying goodbye at Sunset View, she must have slipped it into my back pocket. The only thing I didn't understand was how Grace Slick knew about it. I wasn't about to look a gift horse in the mouth. I accepted the plane ticket and danced toward the door. I noticed a waste basket next to the window. I had used up the entire three hundred dollars in credit, had no way of paying it back, and definitely didn't need the card anymore. I tossed the plastic in the trash. Grace Slick tapped me on the shoulder.

"Don't forget," she sang. "Feed your head."

73

When I came down, I was seated next to Jesus.

Owsley acid or not, I had to admit this was definitely one of the best hallucinogenic journeys that I had ever taken. I couldn't prove it, but it may have been the only time in human history that an LSD trip had turned into an actual real-life trip. I was staring out the window into the darkness of the Atlantic Ocean thirty thousand feet below me. The moon had formed a perfect circle, a lightbulb frozen in suspended animation. A baby was crying. I was trapped inside the stomach of a gigantic bird, surrounded by comatose bodies lined up six abreast as it hurled its passengers through an endless black tunnel. I was confident that I could handle anything now, considering where I had been over the past twelve hours. Still, I couldn't believe my eyes when I saw who was sitting next to me.

"Are you all right?" he asked.

I had to think about it before I responded. I was having trouble remembering how I got here. Before I could answer, Jesus reached out to shake my hand.

"Hi," he said, "my name is Tony."

His disguise was a good one. Wearing faded blue jeans and a brown and rust-colored parka over a dark-blue T-shirt, he easily passed for just another hippie. His accent only added to his ruse. It sounded English, but it was slightly different. The accent and calling himself Tony made for a good cover, but he wasn't fooling me. I recognized him immediately. I had seen him in countless pictures since I was a child: in church, in books and magazines, and in black frames on the kitchen walls in the homes of my Catholic friends. His long brown hair was unmistakable. Shoulder-length and wavy, it gave off a glow that served to accentuate his closely trimmed mustache and

303

beard. His baby-blue eyes were kind, and he possessed a gentle smile. If Jesus wished to remain incognito to the other passengers, I wasn't going to be the one to blow his cover. I played along.

"Hi, I'm Jeff," I said, exchanging the pleasantry and shaking his hand.

"Seriously," he insisted, "are you all right?"

I must have looked pretty bad for Jesus to be so concerned. Should I tell him my story? I was on my second day without sleep, had just come down from an acid trip, and was on an Air Bahamas flight to Luxembourg. I didn't even know where Luxembourg was. If I couldn't tell my tale to Jesus, whom could I tell it to?

Jesus was easy to talk to. He listened patiently while I spilled my guts. He chuckled when I told him about purchasing my ticket while on LSD and complimented me on the skill I had displayed by actually making it to the airport and solving the riddle of checking in and boarding an airplane. He looked a little worried when I confessed that I had never heard of Luxembourg, admitted that I wasn't sure where it was, and revealed that I had no idea what I was going to do when I got there. He pondered my dilemma for a moment and then calmly reached out for my hand. His voice was sincere.

"You need to go to Amsterdam first," he said.

When I explained that I didn't know where that was or how to get there, he told me not to worry. He promised to help me when we landed in Luxembourg. My curiosity was getting the best of me. What was Jesus doing on an airplane? Why was he flying to Europe and going to Luxembourg of all places? Why was he pretending his name was Tony? Finally, summoning up the courage to question him, I asked Jesus what he was doing here.

I had to concede it was a convincing story. He continued to pretend his name was Tony, and he claimed to be from Australia. He said that he had been in South America for the last two years, living mostly in Peru. When I asked him if people recognized him there, he smiled.

"Only the children," he said softly.

He told me how they would often rush up to him on the streets whenever he walked alone. They were usually in small groups, and they always shouted the same words at him as they tugged at his arms and pulled on his shirt.

He laughed. "It was always Hay-zeus Kris-toes, Hay-zeus Kris-toes," he said.

"What did you do?" I asked.

"Oh, nothing much," he said. "They always asked for money, so I would give each of them a small coin. That seemed to satisfy them. They would take my coins, giggle, and run away."

"Wasn't that a hassle?"

"Not really," he said with a wink. "It was my cross to bear, if you know what I mean."

I could relax now. He knew that I knew. No more subterfuge. Now that I shared the secret of his real identity, I could sit back and enjoy the flight. I don't know why, but Jesus was easing me into my new life. I wasn't worried anymore. A thousand pounds had been lifted off my shoulders. Everything would be cool. I had left the US, and I would soon be in Europe.

I must have fallen asleep because the next thing I remember, Jesus was tapping me gently on my shoulder.

"We've landed," he said. "It's time to get off the plane."

We were seated near the back of the plane, so we were among the last ones off. I followed Jesus into the terminal and through the narrow hallways to the baggage claim area. I was relieved to find that my backpack had also made it across the Atlantic. Jesus remained true to his word. After we both retrieved our backpacks, he stayed by my side and guided me through the passport control process. I was completely disoriented. The brief one or two hours of sleep that I managed to catch before we landed had left me in worse shape than if I had not slept at all. Jesus went first and sailed right through. He had his passport stamped and then waited for me on the other side. He had probably done this several thousand times before. I wondered how many passports he had amassed over the years and how he had managed to score one from Australia of all places. I was a little nervous when it was my turn, but I was worrying over nothing. The passport dude asked me a couple of questions in English, stamped my passport, and welcomed me to Luxembourg. I was officially in Europe.

The airport was only about five miles from the center of Luxembourg City where Jesus said that I could purchase a ticket to Amsterdam. I was already freaking out about the money exchange thing. Jesus laughed. He told me that I didn't need to be converting my traveler's checks into anything right now. He explained that Luxembourg and Belgium francs were interchangeable but said that I didn't need to purchase either of them. He said that I should wait until I got to Amsterdam and then get some Dutch guilders. He reached into his front pocket and pulled out some funny-looking money.

"Let me buy your ticket for you," he offered. "I'll show you how to do it."

Jesus handed me a train schedule and showed me how to read it. First, we would take the short train ride together into the city to the central train station. There we would purchase my ticket to Amsterdam. As we rode into the city, Jesus went over the schedule with me several times. He wanted to make sure that I understood that I would be changing trains a couple of times while traveling through Belgium to get to the Dutch city of Maastricht. Once there, I would change trains one last time to complete the final leg of my journey.

I stood next to Jesus at the ticket counter and watched him procure my ticket. He then walked me over to the platform where my train was scheduled to depart.

"You are on your own now," he said. "Good luck to you."

"Thank you, Jesus," I said. "I'll never forget what you did for me."

Jesus smiled and placed a hand on each of my shoulders.

"It's Tony," he said. "Remember that my name is Tony when you tell this story."

"I will," I said. "Your secret is safe with me."

74

The Doobie Brothers were inside my head singing "Jesus Is Just Alright" as the surreal images of medieval castles, rolling mountains, and lush green farm country rushed past me. I kept pinching myself to make sure I wasn't dreaming.

I had never been very religious, and truth be told, I wasn't even sure if I believed in God. Still, the circumstantial evidence from my acid trips was piling up and beginning to tip the scales. Hadn't my very first experience led me to Mary Baker Eddy and the Christian Science Church? Didn't my second encounter land me on the breathing chest of God? And now, as I cruised through the vibrant countryside on a speeding train, how could I explain meeting Jesus on an airplane and his advice and free ticket to Amsterdam?

I was exhausted but too excited to fall asleep. The ride through Luxembourg and Belgium was exhilarating and like something I had only seen in the movies, especially when we passed through the tiny villages and mountain tunnels. My head was spinning. I didn't remember changing trains several times, but somehow my bumbling instincts had landed me on the right set of tracks. As we drifted through the Netherlands, I was struck by the dramatic change in scenery. The towns were closer together and appeared to be more densely populated the closer we got to Amsterdam. The rich green farmland was the flattest I had ever seen, with its individual farms divided by a series of canals. Windmills dominated the landscape.

I had lost complete track of time. As near as I could tell, it had taken me almost eight hours to complete my latest odyssey. It was near dusk when I arrived. I exchanged a twenty-dollar American Express traveler's check for Dutch money at a small booth inside the Central Station. As I quickly learned, the Dutch unit of currency was the guilder, and it was worth thirty-one American cents. The plural of the guilder was *florin*, and each guilder was divided into one hundred cents. I now had sixty-four florins and eighty Dutch cents to spend. My immediate goal was to score some food. I had not eaten since Jesus bought me breakfast at the station in Luxembourg City. I found a small food stand just outside the exit that was selling something called *broodjes*, which I discovered was the Dutch word for "sandwich." A *broodjes* cost one guilder, and it was basically a ham and gouda cheese sandwich on a soft bun. As darkness settled on the city, I sat down in a small grassy area across the street and gobbled down my sandwich like a man who hadn't eaten in days. When I finished, I spotted a water fountain outside the station. With my hunger satisfied and my thirst quenched, I felt invigorated and prepared for my conquest of Europe. All I needed now was a place to sleep. I remembered the last piece of advice from Jesus as he was saying goodbye.

"When you get to Amsterdam," he said, "go to the Red-Light District. It's a short walk from the train station, and you'll find a cheap place to stay."

The large plaza at the front of the Central Station was packed with people, some just hanging out and some hurrying to go somewhere. The massive building looked more like a cathedral than a train station. Emboldened by what looked like a coat of arms, its palace-like facade was flanked on each side by a tower with pointed spires. There was a large clock below the spire of the right tower, but I couldn't make out what was below the left one. I decided to ask the two longhairs in front of me for directions.

"Do you speak English?" I asked.

"Ja," answered the taller one.

"I'm looking for the Red-Light District," I said. "How do I get there?"

"De Rossebuurt?" he answered and then pointed across the street.

"It is just a few blocks that way," he said.

I thanked them, picked up my backpack, and crossed the street. I found myself sucked into a whirlpool of human bodies rushing down a river like whitewater rafts battling for the same prize. They were in large groups and in small groups, and they were mostly dudes. I had joined an unlikely coalition of drunken sailors and stoned-out hippies.

Obviously, I was heading in the right direction.

75

Jesus knew what he was talking about. If he ever wanted out of the Son of God business, he certainly had a promising future as a travel agent. I was able to find a cheap place to crash in the Red-Light District for only eight florins, which I quickly calculated to be around two dollars and fifty cents. It was a small room in a sleazy hotel. The bed was narrow and uncomfortable, and the sheets looked a little suspect, but I was wiped out and I needed some rest.

My first night in Europe had been a bit overwhelming. I may have only crossed the Atlantic Ocean, but I might as well have traveled across the galaxy. Amsterdam's Red-Light District was unlike anything I had ever seen before. I was running on fumes. It was like being on an acid trip without actually doing any LSD. I found myself sleepwalking through an endless network of narrow streets and medieval alleys that snaked up and around a series of parallel canals. The girls in the windows and behind the glass doors were the attraction. I quickly became part of the crowd, strolling with the rest of the voyeurs beneath the glow of red lights. Most of the girls in the windows were standing, but a few of them sat in chairs. While the majority appeared to be in their twenties, a few looked like teenagers and many more looked to be a lot older. What they had in common was the scarce amount of clothing they wore. Apparently, the rules did not allow them to be topless or offer a peek at the prize between their legs. Still, most of them pushed the boundaries as far as they could. I wasn't counting, but I must have walked down more than a dozen alleyways and past more than a hundred red-fringed windows before I gave in and called it a night. Exhausted to the point of collapse, I was standing under a yellow streetlamp when I saw the sign in a window. Luckily for me, it was written in both Dutch and English:

KAMER TE HUUR
ROOM FOR RENT

Despite the street noise, the narrow and uncomfortable bed, and the scratchy sheets, I passed out immediately and slept until late morning. I later learned that the price of the room came with breakfast, but I had missed out on that. There was a shared bathroom down the hall, where I took my first shit in three days. It had a bathtub but no shower. Not knowing if I was preventing someone else from using the bathroom, I took a quick bath and brushed my teeth before checking out. I was unsure of my options, but I knew that this was not where I wanted to be staying in Amsterdam. I needed to get out of the Red-Light District scene. Sleazy hotel rooms and prostitutes in windows were not why I had come to Europe.

It's impossible to describe the sense of liberation that I felt when I took my first step out to the street. I now saw my future with absolute clarity. It was a secret, a mystery yet to be written. For the first time ever, I was breathing in the heady smell of freedom. I was on my way to the life I was destined for, the life that would let me be me. The sun was bright and high in the sky, and the street along the canal was a flurry of activity. It took me a minute or two to get my bearings. I was rested, and for the first time in days, maybe in weeks, I was straight. Considering where I was, I knew that wouldn't last long. Regardless, I was enjoying the natural high and marveling at the larger-than-life scene that I had wandered into. Amsterdam was a beautiful city, clean and bursting at the seams with youth and energy. It seemed to be a cool place to live: friendly, open-minded, and extremely well-organized and efficient.

I covered a lot of ground the first day. Getting around was easy. Amsterdam was a compact and very walkable city. It didn't take me long to discover the Dam, which was a just a few blocks from where I had spent the night. I had not seen this many longhairs and hippies gathered in one place since Woodstock. Dam Square was clearly the focal point of the city where everyone hung out. Sitting in groups, both large and small, appeared to be the main activity. Hundreds of others were milling around. A variety of street musicians were scattered across the cobblestone square, creating a spontaneous and unorganized street festival. Some played their guitars, while others pounded away on their bongo drums. Longhairs waving Bibles, apparently Holland's answer to Jesus Freaks, roamed through the crowds, offering free prayers and an easy path to salvation. I watched as dozens of hash pipes circulated like free candy through the spontaneous network of street people. Within minutes, one arrived at my lips and offered to trade places with my natural high. The dude holding the matches was speaking in a language that I couldn't understand, but it was clear what he was saying. I nodded yes, and he lit the match. Firing up a hash pipe didn't require a translator. I took a deep hit and immediately started coughing. It was definitely good shit, and it kicked my ass. I hung around the Dam for more than an hour. The continuous flow of free hash made it really easy to meet people. I was getting hungry, so I asked two German dudes who spoke English where I could get something to eat that was cheap. They told me to check out a place over by the train station called Dolstra. It was only a few minutes away, and they said that I could get a great lunch for less than three florins. Man, were they ever right! I feasted on roast beef, cheese, and an assortment of breads, and it only cost me about eighty American cents. With the munchies put to bed, I decided to explore more of the city. As my backpack and I followed the afternoon sun over the canals and along the spacious avenues, I noticed that bicycles seemed to be the primary mode of transportation. There was no subway system, probably because the city was at sea level and built around water. However, tram and bus stops were everywhere. I was in awe of the old buildings, many of which I later learned were built during the seventeenth century. Canals dominated the center of the city, and small houseboats were commonplace. My westward journey took me over several canals until I reached the entrance to a park. I followed the paved footpath into a widening expanse of sprawling lawns and colorful flower gardens. The park was full of people, but it didn't feel crowded. Abandoned bicycles dotted the lush green grass, while small groups of hippies lounged nearby on their sleeping bags. I didn't see anyone waving Bibles or offering me salvation, but similar to what was happening at the Dam, there were freaks playing guitars and pipes being passed in circles. The park was gorgeous, and my hash buzz was still operating at full strength. I stared at the large oak, poplar, and cypress trees lining the winding trail and the playful reflection of pink, white, and red flowers splashing across the surface of a nearby pond. I spotted an oval-shaped chestnut tree that was wrapped in soothing clusters of white blossoms. I was so stoned that I didn't notice the three guys and two chicks sitting under it who were motioning to me to join them. I couldn't tear my eyes away from the tree. When one of them finally came over and spoke to me, I thought the voice was coming from inside my head.

"We've got some hash," he said. "Do you want to get high with us, eh?"

His name was Donnie, and he was about to become my first new friend in Europe.

76

The carpenter dude from Nazareth, in his infinite wisdom, had selected Amsterdam as my portal into the unknown. It was easy to see why. The city was the youth capital of the world. The Dutch appeared to be a kind and tolerant people who believed in freedom and made everyone feel welcome. If I couldn't make friends and enjoy life there, I probably couldn't do it anywhere.

I made my first five friends that day in the park. Donnie Lowry was a Canadian who ended every sentence or statement with "Eh." A wiry five feet, five inches tall, he claimed to be from the Yukon, or as he called it, the Bush. His face was pale and dotted with freckles, and he sported an unruly shock of curly red hair that was partially concealed by a wide-brimmed leather hat. He led me over to the chestnut tree and introduced me to the other four. The leader of the group appeared to be a guy they called Dutchy. His real name was Lucas Van den Berg, and he was also a Canadian. His father migrated to British Columbia from the Netherlands after World War II, where he met his mother. Having spent several summers staying with relatives in Holland, Lucas was nearly as fluent in Dutch as he was in English. With wavy brown hair that brushed down and over his shoulders, he had movie-star good looks and looked to be in his early twenties. The other dude had long hair that stretched halfway down his back. He was from France, and his name was Jean-Claude. He didn't speak much English and therefore didn't say much. The two chicks, Loes and Marion, were Dutch, and they couldn't have been more than nineteen or twenty. Without a doubt, they were the prettiest girls that I had seen so far in Europe. Marion, the prettier of the two, wore knee-high leather boots over her tight jeans. She was a gorgeous brunette with sparkling green eyes and a smile that never left her face. To me, Loes was sexier. She was also a brunette, and I thought her wild and frizzy shoulder-length hair added to her mystery and made her much more appealing.

Despite the sense of liberation and careless bravado I had begun to embrace, I was still quite nervous and unsure of myself. As much as I wanted to believe that I was an independent and self-sufficient traveler, I knew in my heart that I was naive and a novice at this. If I was ever going to become the person I wanted to be, I would have to engage with others who were already doing this and learn what I could from them.

Donnie Lowry became my first instructor. He, Lucas, and Jean-Claude had rooms at Hotel Ostade, which was a short walk from the park. When Donnie learned that I was wandering the city without a home, he suggested I check out where they were staying. Hotel Ostade was located on a long one-way street and one of a series of connected brick brownstone buildings. Four stories tall and reddish brown in color, it was just around the corner from a park much smaller than the one I had met them in. The modest lobby and front desk area shared the first floor with an open breakfast space. I was able to rent a room for twelve florins a night and lugged my backpack up the steep and narrow staircase to the top floor. The room was small and narrow and had two windows with no curtains, but it was clean, and the bed was comfortable. There was a small sink near the door with a mirror over it. The shared shower and toilet was a short walk down the hall. Jean-Claude's room was on the same floor as mine, while Donnie and Lucas were one story down. My education began the next morning.

My room at Hotel Ostade included a free breakfast. What I didn't know was that it also included the challenge of eating an egg. I was alone the first morning when I took a seat at the two-chair table. Along with a mixed bowl of fruit, a tiny egg-shaped cup holding an intact half-exposed egg was waiting for me next to a small plate with two slices of toast. I assumed that the egg was hard-boiled, so I took it out of the cup and banged it hard on the table. To my surprise, the egg burst in half, and a glob of runny yellow egg yolk oozed onto the table. I quickly covered the mess with my napkin and looked around to see if there were any witnesses. Apparently, no one had observed the infraction, so I sopped up as much of the ooze as I could and compressed the grimy napkin into a ball. A young girl came by and offered me coffee, which I gladly accepted. Resigned to my meal of fruit and toast, I took my time and waited for an opportunity to observe someone else eating an egg. After about ten minutes, a dude with long blond hair sat down at the table next to me. The young girl brought him his egg in a cup, his two slices of toast, and a bowl of fruit. I watched him take the egg out of the cup and place it back in with the pointy end facing up. He then picked up his spoon and used it to give the top of the egg several taps to crack the shell. Using the tip of his spoon, he wiggled his way through the cracked shell, sliced through the egg, and lifted off the top. He then dug in with his spoon and scooped up the runny inside of the soft-boiled egg.

I was confident that I could replicate what I had just witnessed, but that would have to wait until the next morning. Happy with my latest discovery, I jumped up from the table and sprinted up the stairs to Donnie's room. I was eager to continue my education.

77

The first time I smoked hash with Donnie and Lucas at the hotel, I couldn't believe how large each chunk was and how much of it they let fall to floor each time they broke off a piece. What amazed me was that they rarely picked up any of the fallen pieces. What would have been a big score for me in Boston was just unclaimed residue on an Amsterdam rug. I asked why no one was smoking pot. Donnie laughed and told me that marijuana was way too expensive in Europe because the good weed had to be imported from across the ocean. He claimed that anything grown in Europe was shitty, and although there was plenty available, not many freaks smoked it here. Hash, on the other hand, was easy to get, inexpensive, and most of the time, top-notch.

There was no way to avoid it. Hashish was the nourishment that sustained life in Amsterdam. Just as the human heart pushed blood throughout the human body, the thick dark-colored sticky substance was pumping itself through every artery and vein of the city. The elixir was everywhere, and it was cheap. A gram cost eighty American cents. The Dutch government had decided that it was easier to live with the use of soft drugs than to fight it. Donnie and Lucas warned me that selling any kind of drug or using hard drugs could get you arrested or deported, but otherwise, the police looked the other way. That was especially true in my two favorite places: Vondelpark and the government-subsidized hash clubs.

Vondelpark, where I had met my five new friends, was the largest park in Amsterdam. Hippies and locals crossed paths and interacted throughout the day in a free live-and-let-live setting. Camping and sleeping out were allowed, setting the stage for a festive twenty-four-hour-a-day celebration. The Amsterdam cops I saw in the park fascinated me. They were mostly young, and they didn't appear to be carrying guns. As we sat in small groups passing around our hash pipes, the uniformed pairs simply strolled past us, smiling and tipping their hats. Unlike their American counterparts, the Dutch *politie* were not there to bust the army of freaks for getting high or the occasional naked dude or topless chick for openly sunning themselves on the grass.

The hash clubs were even more liberating. My favorite one was Kosmos. It was like walking into a bar in America, the only difference being that it was hashish and marijuana, not beer and whiskey on the menu. Once I made my purchase at the bar, there were several small rooms with tables and comfortable chairs where I would settle in for hours and enjoy my medication and the continuous music with all the other lost souls. However, the highlight of Kosmos was on the second floor, where the sauna was located. For just five florins, I was granted access to the soothing and uninhibited world of a hot sauna, a steam bath, a group shower, and an open sitting area with a warm glowing fireplace, stuffed lounge chairs, and a cushy sofa. This was foreign territory for me, a universe far removed from my trips out to Pine Lake the previous summer. It was one thing to get naked with a few close friends, quite another to do it with complete strangers from different parts of the world. Whatever apprehension I might have been feeling was dispelled by the hashish I had consumed and was replaced with nervous anticipation. I was now in Europe where social nudity was the norm and no big deal to anyone. I was alone the first time I ascended the staircase to the sauna. I was carrying the only towel that I owned. Lucas had explained the sauna process and sauna etiquette to me the night before, so I knew what to expect. Still, I felt like an awkward sixth grader walking into his first dance. I handed over my five florins to the pretty blond girl at the front desk, and she handed me a key with a number on it and pointed me in the direction of the changing room. The room was empty when I walked in. I found the locker corresponding to the number on the key and undressed. Naked and eager to continue my education, I wrapped the towel around my waist, took a deep breath, and launched into my three-hour experience.

My first stop was the shower room, where once again, I was alone. Was it possible that I was the only one at the sauna today? The open area reminded me of my communal shower days in high school. There were three shower heads on each side of the tiled floor and two along the back of the shower. The other wall was lined with three open toilet stalls with no doors, which I didn't give much thought to at the time. Lucas had told me that it was considered proper etiquette to shower before entering a sauna or steam room. I had banked on taking a hot shower, but instead I was forced to settle for a lukewarm drizzle. I didn't have a bar of soap with me, and I didn't see any lying around, so I just stood under the slow stream for a few minutes and let the tepid water rinse away two days of dirt and sweat.

I turned off the shower and dried myself off. Just past the shower room, I saw two wooden doors. One was marked STOOMBAD and the other ZWEETKAMER. This was once again a Yogi Berra fork-in-the-road moment. I was pretty confident that *stoombad* was Dutch for "steam bath." I remembered Lucas telling me that I was supposed to sit on a towel in the sauna and leave the towel outside when going into the steam room. The five towels hanging on hooks next to the Stoombad door seemed to confirm my suspicion that my translation was correct. Placing my towel on an empty hook and opening the door, I was greeted abruptly by a huge blast of hot steam and the seductive smell of what I later learned was called eucalyptus. The steam fog was so thick that I couldn't see my hand in front of my face. I closed the door behind me and waited for my eyes to adjust. I heard someone laugh.

A male voice rang out.

"Bitte nehmen sie platz," was what it sounded like. It had been a few years since my last German class at Northeastern, but it sounded German to me. I think he was asking me to sit down. His hand was tapping on the bench.

"Here," he said, switching to English, "there's room over here."

The steam was so thick that it was impossible to see anyone clearly. It felt like a thousand eyes were on me. Slowly, the spectral forms began to come into focus, and there appeared to be seven of them, three on one side and four on the other. I couldn't make out their exact features, but I could tell by the ghostly outlines of their chests that three, possibly four of them, were female. The open space on the bottom bench was next to one of them.

"Wilkommen," the voice continued. "Are you American?"

"Yes," I said as I squeezed between him and the female apparition.

That was the extent of the conversation. Obviously, silence was proper steam bath etiquette. A few minutes later, the three figures on my side stood up to leave. When they opened the door, it created a cooling gap in the mist, offering me a clear view of the four bodies on the other side. Two were male, and two were female. I closed my eyes and tried to take a deep breath, but the air felt so wet and so thick that it was almost impossible to breathe. Drenched in sweat and moisture, I felt a little dizzy. I also felt dehydrated. I probably shouldn't have smoked so much hash downstairs. One by one, the other four got up to leave, and I quickly followed them out the door. Towel in hand, my naked body rushed around theirs and staggered past the shower room and back to the locker room in desperate search of a water fountain. Luckily, I found one.

I drank water until I couldn't hold another drop. Suddenly, I had to pee. I turned and rushed over to the row of toilet stalls, only to find two of the three occupied by females. I was stunned at first, but neither one of them looked up from what they were doing and neither one seemed to care I was there. I raced into the middle stall and began to empty my bladder. It was a piss for the ages. I was still going strong when I heard one toilet flush and then the other. By the time I was finished, they were gone. I strolled across the room and took another quick shower.

The next stop on my Kosmos journey was through the door marked *Zweetkamer*. This was more of what I was used to. The dry heat was more to my liking and so invigorating that I used the sauna three times before finally calling it quits. As I sat on my towel with the sweat rolling off my body, I was overwhelmed by what I was seeing and experiencing. It was like being in the Garden of Eden. This new path in life that I had chosen was introducing me to a collection of people from all over the world, and like them, I was high and wasn't wearing any clothes. I lost count of all the languages being spoken. I marveled at the treasure chest of beautiful bodies of all sizes and shapes that passed before my eyes. Later, when I was in the communal shower for the final time and letting the water gently massage my face, I heard the soft celestial voice of yet another angel.

"Would you like to use my shampoo?" she said.

I turned around and took it all in. She couldn't have been more beautiful. Her dark-brown hair was straight and wet and pressed firmly over her shoulders and down her back. A few errant strands reached down across her chest and caressed each of her nipples. She handed me the shampoo.

"Hi," she said, "my name is Peggy."

Lost for words, I just smiled and accepted her gift. The angel went back to what she was doing, lathering the soap under each arm and between her legs. I squeezed a huge gob of the angel's shampoo into the palm of my hand. I was washing my hair for the first time in Europe. I decided to swing for the fences.

"Can I borrow your soap?" I asked.

I loved my new life in Hash City. I knew I couldn't stay here forever, but that didn't stop me from wishing I could. For more than seven days, I had smoked hash in every corner of Amsterdam, floating from room to room at Hotel Ostade, and circulating in a surreal dance through Dam Square, Vondelpark, the hash clubs, and the saunas. I even spent a night on a houseboat.

It was time to move on.

78

It was also time to make a decision.

Even before I had stepped off the train in Amsterdam, I was dreaming of going to Scandinavia. Spurred on by Isadora's idyllic portrait of Copenhagen and Denmark, I had a burning desire to write my own story by hitchhiking through Norway and Sweden.

Donnie Lowry changed my mind.

Born and raised in the Yukon, Donnie was an outdoorsman at heart. This was his first trip to Europe, and he had been staying in Amsterdam for nearly a month. This was also the only time he had ever been in a large city. He was more accustomed to salmon fishing and dog sledding than he was to being around people. Having gone from a sparsely populated territory bordering Alaska to an urban environment with nearly a million people, I was amazed at how well he had adapted. Still, he was itching to get away.

"I'm going into the Bush," he said. "Want to come with me, eh?"

His plan was to head south and hike into the Alps. He had brought a small tent and sleeping bag with him, along with a kit that contained essential cooking gear and utensils. He was also the proud owner of a hash pipe and an ample supply of hash. I only had a sleeping bag.

"Sure," I said. "I'll go with you."

We celebrated our last night in Amsterdam into the early hours of the morning. Lucas threw a spirited party for us in his room, with Jean-Claude, Loes, Marion, and two other dudes I didn't know in attendance. It was around noon the next day when we emerged from our hashish stupor and kicked off our journey. We took a tram to the edge of the city to a spot where we could hitchhike. It must have been our lucky day. Our thumbs weren't out more than fifteen minutes before we landed a ride with a Swiss guy named Thomas, who said he could take us all the way to Lucerne, where he lived.

Thomas was an interesting dude. He worked for a rental car company that had sent him by train to Amsterdam to pick up a car and drive it back to Lucerne. He and his brother Karl had spent the previous summer hitchhiking across the United States. His English was perfect but sprinkled with counterculture and hippie slang. Instead of money, he said bread. He used the words *groovy* and *far out* in practically every conversation. He and Karl had traveled the backroads and highways of America in VW buses, hanging out with longhairs as they roamed from town to town and concert to concert, smoking pot and trying not to get busted. He said that everyone they had met in the States had been cool and good to them, offering up free food, free pot, and free places to stay. Now back in Switzerland and living their regular lives, Thomas and Karl were trying to return the generosity whenever they had a chance. He said we could crash at their pad in Lucerne whenever or for however long we wanted.

It was early evening when we drove into Heidelberg in West Germany. Thomas announced that Lucerne was another five hours away and that Heidelberg would be a far-out place to spend the night. When Donnie and I revealed that we really didn't have the bread to pay for a room, Thomas offered to pay. Donnie said no and insisted that we wanted to sleep in the Bush. Personally, I would have taken Thomas up on his offer, but I kept my mouth shut.

Heidelberg was stunning. It was a university town, and its streets were filled with young people and students. Thomas asked if we were hungry. We were, and he offered to buy us dinner. He agreed to find the three of us a place to camp outside the city, but first he wanted to eat and then show us a little of Heidelberg. We were cool with that.

We were in the heart of the city in an area called Old Town. Nestled inside a narrow one-mile stretch along the south bank of a beautiful river, Old Town was a maze of small and narrow cobblestone streets with an interesting mix of new and old buildings. It almost didn't feel real, like we had been dropped into the middle of a Renaissance painting. Looming high above us, a majestic red sandstone castle dominated the skyline. An old stone bridge spanned the rather tranquil river, whose deep-blue waters reflected the image of the green hills on the other side.

Thomas found a beer hall close to the bridge, which was packed with students drinking beer from huge mugs and singing songs, none of which I understood. We feasted on German bratwurst and sauerkraut and joined in the drunken revelry. These people loved their beer. For all the drugs that I had been doing, this was my first time getting drunk in Europe. German beer was a lot richer and more potent than American beer. By the time we got up to leave, I was totally plastered and needed help getting to the car. I crawled into the back seat on all fours and passed out. I have no recollection of our drive out of Heidelberg into the Black Forest.

It was a chilly night, but Donnie and I were too fucked up to put up the tent. We slept under the stars, and Thomas slept in the car. When my bladder woke me at sunrise, my nose was cold, and my exposed face and sleeping bag were covered with the morning dew. I took a deep breath of fresh air and saw that we were under a dark canopy of evergreens, so dense that the morning light could barely penetrate the thick pine trees. I thought back to all the black-and-white World War II movies I had seen, and I imagined Hitler's troops camping in this very spot. It was eerie.

I couldn't believe where I was. In my wildest dreams, I never thought I would one day be in the back seat of a car, being transported through the breathtaking green landscape of the Black Forest down to the magical land of Switzerland, the home of my ancestors. I was speechless for the nearly three hours it took us to get to Swiss border town of Basel. When we crossed over the Rhine, Thomas said that we were only an hour from Lucerne.

As the small villages, farmhouses, and rolling hills dotted with farmland zipped past my window, I wondered if I would ever be here again. I was mesmerized as I watched the snowcapped peaks of the majestic Alps materialize in the distance. While I was daydreaming, Donnie was grilling Thomas with questions about the mountains and the best places for us to hike and explore. He had also discovered the cure for a Heidelberg hangover. Donnie fired up a bowl and took a long, deep hit. Turning to face me, he exhaled and handed me the pipe.

"Pretty far out, eh?" he said. "That's where we'll be tomorrow."

I tried taking a toke but came up empty. Donnie noticed my predicament and took back the pipe. He emptied the ashes in the ashtray and stuffed a fresh chunk into the bowl. He passed it back to me along with his lighter. This time I hit pay dirt.

I don't know why I chose that exact moment, but I leaned back in my seat and decided to take stock of where I was and what I was doing. Life was a series of choices, wasn't it? It had been less than fourteen months since the fire at Hubcap Harvey's house, and here I was, getting wasted again and about to take a magic carpet ride into the Swiss Alps. Did I believe it was fate that had brought me here? Was it fate that explained my twenty-five years on this planet? Did fate start the fire on Franklin Mountain? Did fate bring me the gift of Isadora Duncan? What about finding myself next to Jesus on a flight to Luxembourg? Was that fate? The truth was that attributing everything to fate was a cop-out. I had chosen the path I was on. I was the one who quit my co-op job at IBM after King and Bobby Kennedy were shot. I was the one who had left Jake and Zero in San Francisco and returned to ask Jane to marry me. I chose to work shitty jobs instead of using my degree and joining the establishment. I chose to blow off my marriage after the fire. Hell, I was the one who had put smoldering ashes in the cardboard box against the wall on the back porch in the first place. It was all on me. Fate had nothing to do with any of this. No one had put a gun to my head and made me take acid and buy a one-way ticket to Europe.

I took another toke, rolled down the window, and stuck out my head. I was a dog on a joy ride. The cold, crisp air slapped me across the face. That's when Donnie tapped me on the shoulder and pulled me out of my trance.

"How about sharing some of that with us, eh?"

I exhaled and passed him the pipe.

79

Thomas was sharing a third-floor flat at Baselstrasse 7 with his brother Karl and their friend Rudi. I knew the second we walked in the door that our trek into the Bush was destined to be pushed back a day or two. A small Formica table with chrome legs inhabited the center of the room. It was surrounded by a hodgepodge of mismatched chairs and a worn-out sofa and was covered with what looked to be the remnants of last night's party. A bong filled with dirty water stood in the center, reigning supreme over the dozen or so vanquished bottles of beer and two empty books of matches. An open baggie, containing mostly seeds and stems, was resting on the floor next to a roach clip. Album covers were scattered around the room.

Donnie and I slept there for two nights, both of which involved the heavy consumption of beer, pot, and hash, along with a nonstop symphony of loud music. Thomas and Karl had been turned on to Frank Zappa and the Mothers of Invention the previous summer in the States, and they knew the lyrics to practically every song on *Absolutely Free*. Whether it was "The Duke of Prunes" or "Brown Shoes Don't Make It," they turned up the volume and were more obsessed with Frank than even Ozzie had been. A huge poster of Jimi Hendrix was taped to the wall above the black-and-white TV, and several of Jimi's albums were strewn across the floor. They turned me on to an album called *Argus* by a British band I had never heard of named Wishbone Ash. Everything was groovy or far out. It was like hanging out with American hippies.

However, there was one thing that made it clear that I wasn't in America. Hanging on the wall just inside the door in Thomas's room was a rifle. Karl explained that all Swiss males between the ages of twenty and thirty were in the Swiss army and were allowed to keep their personal weapons at home, as well as fifty rounds of ammunition. When the government drafted them into the militia, they were given both military and weapons training. I tried to imagine what it would be like if every dude in his twenties in 1973 America was given an automatic rifle and fifty rounds of ammo. It would make the 1881 shootout at the O. K. Corral look like a pillow fight. I asked Karl if I could hold the rifle.

Karl took it off the wall and handed it to me. He saw the look on my face.

"Don't worry." He laughed. "It's not loaded."

I had never held a rifle before. It was heavier than I expected.

"It's called a Sturmgewehr 57," Karl said. "It shoots over five hundred rounds per minute."

I handed the rifle back to Karl. It was obvious to me why no one had fucked with Switzerland during the last two world wars. The next day, led by our able guide Thomas, Donnie and I got to spend one full day roaming through the storybook environs of Lucerne before venturing out into the alpine wilderness.

I was in the land of William Tell. The city sat at the north end of Lake Lucerne. Like a Maxfield Parrish painting, the water was a vibrant explosion of cobalt blue beneath a ring of snowcapped mountains. We crossed over the Reuss River on the Chapel Bridge, the oldest covered bridge in Europe. Thomas pointed out that it was built in the fourteenth century and was one of two covered wooden bridges in Lucerne. Hanging from the rafters inside were more than one hundred paintings that dated back centuries and depicted scenes from the town's history.

North of the river, we wandered through Old Town, a maze of stone streets, narrow passages, and little squares with fountains. A medley of lively murals graced the walls of the medieval buildings, while some of the smaller timber-framed structures were teeming with bright-red, yellow, and pastel colors. It was like walking through the pages of a child's fairy tale.

Thomas taught me more about Swiss history in one day than I had learned during my entire life. My education continued as he took us to the Lion of Lucerne, a huge figure of a dying lion carved on the face of a cliff. He explained that it honored the Swiss Guards who were killed protecting King Louis XVI during the French Revolution. It was news to me.

It was a sunny day and one that I hoped to repeat.

We stopped for a while at the bridge where the lake, the river, and the edge of Old Town met to join hands. The spot was called Schwanenplatz, which meant "swan's square" in English. We watched a group of well-dressed schoolchildren feeding dozens of graceful white swans. When the bread was gone, the little cherubs evolved into a screaming mob of anarchists and chased the regal creatures into the water.

I could see myself living here.

80

It took us a good six hours to hitchhike about fifteen miles through little Swiss villages until finally there were no villages or roads at all. Each charming hamlet was a tidy collection of picture-book cottages, accentuated by bright, colorful flowers under each set of windows.

Before leaving Lucerne, Donnie and I had walked to the train station to get some Swiss money. A Swiss franc was worth about twenty-six American cents. I could already tell that Switzerland was going to be expensive, but I didn't think that I would need very much money to camp in the Alps. I exchanged one twenty-dollar traveler's check and received seventy-six Swiss francs in return. On our way out of town, we spotted a small market where we could pick up some supplies. We stocked up on cans of soup and vegetables, loaves of bread, and a variety of cheeses, along with bars of Swiss chocolate.

As we began our trek up Napf Mountain, my backpack felt like it weighed a ton. Besides bearing the burden of all my worldly possessions, I was also carrying most of our provisions for a week in the Bush. The tight switchbacks along the trail made me wish that I had packed lighter and had more mobility. However, I was in no position to complain. Donnie was the one with the heavy load. In addition to his tent, cooking gear, and utensils, he was carrying an ax that he borrowed from Rudi and a rolled-up clear plastic tarp. How, despite his small frame, Donnie was able to move up the trail with such ease was a mystery to me.

Even as I struggled to keep up with him, I was overwhelmed by the excitement I felt from finally escaping into the wilderness. As we hiked uphill through the patchwork of evergreen forests, it was like entering a bird sanctuary. We passed small mountain farms and were serenaded with cowbells. Everything was so green, and the trees were exceptionally tall. The giant firs appeared to reach heights of one hundred fifty feet. The beech trees, with their branches high up on their trunks, rose at least one hundred feet above the forest floor. Huge conical spruces dotted the landscape like oversize Christmas trees. A few were taller than their neighbors, extending nearly fifty feet higher than the tallest fir.

Donnie was the outdoorsman, not me, so I deferred to him when it came time to choose where to set up camp. He found us a small clearing not far from a small rapidly moving stream. We put up our tent, built a fire, and feasted on bread, cheese, and a can of beans. We washed it down with our first taste of glacial water from the Alps. As darkness settled in, so did the cold. We huddled around the fire and shared a couple bowls of hashish.

It had been a long day, and we were both tired. We decided to hit the sack early, and we fell asleep within minutes of crawling into our sleeping bags. Unfortunately, our shut-eye was cut short by the abrupt sound of rain pounding our tent like bullets from a machine gun. The storm bludgeoned our shelter for several hours in the darkness, continuing well past the first glimpse of daylight and for most of the morning. It was a bummer. We hadn't gotten much sleep, and it was raining too hard to leave the tent.

By midday, I was starting to feel claustrophobic. Thankfully, the rain let up briefly, allowing us to step out of our cramped quarters and giving us enough time to collect firewood. However, the respite from the storm didn't last very long, and we once again returned to prison inside the canvas tent.

I wasn't having much fun, but Donnie seemed to be enjoying himself. Proud of his ability to adapt to whatever Mother Nature threw his way, he was amused by my discomfort with the elements. He had spent weeks at a time camping along the sweeping tundra and wild rivers of the Yukon, and by comparison, a little rain in the Swiss Alps was a walk in the park.

Our first full day was one of basics: keeping warm, keeping dry, and eating. It was bone-chilling cold, and most of our gear was wet from the night before. The rain continued throughout the afternoon and into the night. It wasn't a downpour but rather a steady, damp drizzle. The Napf was right in front of us, but it was too wet and rainy to make the climb. Donnie decided to make an attempt, but that turned out to be a mistake. Forced to turn around, he came back soaking wet and with a bad case of the chills. Stripping off his wet clothes, he ended up in the tent for the rest of the afternoon, shaking like a leaf inside his sleeping bag.

Meanwhile, I continued to chop wood and work to keep the fire going. I thought back to that day in Mt. Vision with Sharon Wessel and her beautiful tits. She was right about me being an optimistic pessimist. It may have sucked at this moment in time, but I knew it would get better.

The fog had rolled in. I dropped the ax to the ground and shouted at the top of my lungs.

"We're in the fucking clouds!" I screamed.

I closed my eyes. Sharon Wessel was naked, and she was laughing at me. I reached out to touch her, but she turned and ran away. I opened my eyes.

Crossing my fingers, I prayed that the sun would return tomorrow.

81

"Whattaya say we go back to our camp and grab all our shit, eh?" Donnie suggested.

We had found our new home. Set back from the muddy footpath and backing up to the dense pine forest, the wood-framed cabin wasn't much bigger than the tiniest bedroom in a big city apartment. The steep A-framed roof extended well past the two outer side walls and a few feet beyond the entrance. A large peephole, in the precise shape of the equilateral cross on a Swiss flag, had been carved out near the top of the door. There was one window to the left of the door, a rectangular open-air cavity with no glass or covering. Donnie poked his head in and saw that the cabin wasn't occupied.

It was our third morning in the Bush, and the rain had finally stopped. Donnie and I had just crawled out of the tent when we were greeted by a dozen or so Swiss schoolchildren out hiking the mountain who looked to be around seven or eight years old. We were quite the attraction, especially since we couldn't speak German. They giggled and pointed and tried to talk with us, but I had forgotten so much of my college German that I was unable to understand anything they said. After a few minutes, the novelty of two grungy English-speaking hippies wore off, and the youth caravan continued on its way. When they were gone, Donnie and I took our morning pisses, shared some bread and cheese, and decided it was time for us to take a hike. The ground was still wet and slippery, so instead of attempting the Napf, we headed for a smaller mountain that was directly west of us.

We hadn't gone far before we stumbled upon the cabin. It was crazy. Had we made that turn two days earlier and walked another five minutes, we would have had a roof over our heads, a dry floor to sleep on, and a place to protect our shit from the continuous rain. Apparently, the Swiss built these primitive huts for hikers to use free of charge on a first-come, first-served basis. There was nothing in the cabin, just an empty room with four walls. I felt like we were pioneers in the Old West. This humble abode became our base camp for the next four days, four days that turned out to be my best so far in Europe.

After staking our claim to the cabin, we resumed our hike up the smaller mountain to the west. Along the way, we passed a small farm that looked to have been lifted from a postcard. I saw the biggest cows I had ever seen in my life. Unlike the normal-size black-and-white dairy cows that I had grown up with in Upstate New York, these gigantic suckers were brown in color with long fuzzy ears and huge muscular frames. The constant chaotic sound of cow-bells escorted us up the trail and echoed throughout the valley below. When we reached the top, we were greeted by our first real sunshine in days and treated to an incredibly beautiful view of the lush green valley. From where we stood, the side of the larger Napf took on the persona of a green layer cake. Starting with baby poplars, it grew to a mixture of tall palm-tree-like pine trees and full-grown poplars with tall pines on top. The pine trees looked like Christmas trees sitting on top of telephone poles.

It's hard to find the words to describe the euphoria and sense of accomplishment I experienced over those four days. After our first night in the cabin, we climbed to the top of Napf Mountain. The pan-oramic view of the surrounding snow-covered Alps was incredible. The highest peaks were to the south of us. Range after range receded into the mist, while fields and meadows alternated with swathes of forests. We had smoked the last of Donnie's hash the night before, but that didn't matter anymore. I was getting high on fresh air. It didn't get any better than this. The trail had been steep but wide and easy to negotiate. However, my cheap sneakers had not served me well. I promised myself that one day, with the right equipment and a good pair of shoes, I would tackle a much bigger mountain.

The Swiss were a healthy lot. Young and old alike were there when we arrived. At least one hundred of them were sprawled across the broad hump-shaped summit. What blew my mind was the three-story hotel right in front of us with its rows of long picnic tables. What was a hotel doing at the top of a mountain? It was like we had stumbled onto an outdoor beer fest. Children of all ages were racing around the hotel grounds, playing tag while their adult counterparts were hoisting mugs into the air and singing at the top of their lungs. Some were even dancing. Two older dudes had parachuted in from a tourist brochure. They were dressed in knee-length brown leather shorts held up by suspenders. Sporting green felt hats with white fluffy feathers, they were entertaining the revelers with their compressing and expanding accordions. Scattered across the grass were small groups of young backpackers lying down to sun themselves. A pretty blond girl in a light-brown sweater approached us and asked if we spoke English. Her name was Martina, and she looked to be about eighteen years old. She said that she wanted to practice her English with someone. Donnie and I were more than happy to oblige her.

If we hadn't run out of food, we probably could have stayed there all summer. Everyone we met on the mountain was friendly, and only a few spoke English. One was an older woman, at least seventy years old, who passed Donnie and me on the trail like we were standing still. The woman who said her name was Hilda stopped and waited for us to catch up. She was curious as to where we were from. Hikers and mountain climbers were a special breed. They seemed to dig the fact that we were out in the country just like they were and not a couple of dirty hippies sleeping in one of their parks. I loved the fact that I was forced to speak German. It was a real mental exercise to communicate in German all the time, but what I had learned in college was starting to come back to me.

We made friends with a Swiss mountain-climbing instructor named Werner, whom we talked with at length, and we invited him to have dinner with us down at our cabin. Although he was fluent in English, most of my conversation with him was in German. Before he left, he gave us his address in Willisau, a small village forty kilometers northwest of Lucerne, and asked that we send him a postcard from wherever we ended up.

On our last day on the trail, we met two ten-year-old girls with walking poles who thought we were the funniest things they had ever seen. They found my bad attempts at German to be hilarious. Outfitted with hiking boots and hiking pants, Nicola in her bright-green T-shirt and Sandra in a bright-red one seemed to think my heavy blue jeans and crappy sneakers were strange clothes to be wearing in the mountains. They were probably right.

It was time to return to civilization. We were out of food, and Rudi needed his ax back.

82

Seven days and I already had a routine. The Reuss was where I went to escape the flat and be alone. A one-minute walk down Baselstrasse brought me to Lucerne's other covered wooden bridge. Sometimes I would continue along the south bank up Bahnhofstrasse, past the Chapel Bridge to the main bridge that carried the cars and buses and where the waters of Lake Lucerne emptied into the river. However, the Spreuer Bridge was my favorite way to cross over into Old Town. I marveled at the triangular panels inside the bridge beneath the rafters, each containing a painting framed in black and representing a dance of death. Each panel portrayed death as one or more dancing skeletons urging everybody to dance with him. Each depicted a different set of people. Facing death, all were equal. Rich or poor, young or old, when death asked them to dance, there was no escaping their fate. I studied a different one every day.

The promenade along the north bank was the ideal place to spend an afternoon. I had a perfect view of the creaky Chapel Bridge and its octagonal Water Tower. Baskets of purple, yellow, and red flowers hung off both sides of the bridge. On sunny days, I claimed a small table at one of the outdoor cafés and nursed a coffee or mug of beer while I read a book or wrote some of my bad poetry. There were dozens of bars, restaurants, and cafés tucked under the arcades along the banks of the Reuss, and they were full of both tourists and locals enjoying the view across the river and Lake Lucerne. It was early June, Lucerne's rainiest month, but the showers never lasted long.

The week had been a period of intense inner thought and contemplation for me. My mind was in another world. I was talking with people but not really listening to what they were saying. Where was I going next? What was I doing with my life? Thomas, Karl, and

Rudi were great guys, but their flat on Baselstrasse was a zoo. Donnie and I had returned from Napf Mountain to find two dudes from Texas and an Australian couple crashing there. The party was never over. The music and drugs lasted into the morning hours with the six of us sleeping in the living room and not getting much sleep. I was getting burned out. Donnie was talking about returning to the Bush, but that's not where I wanted to go, at least not now. I thought of my main man Charles Darwin again. I was evolving, but what was I evolving into? The one thing I was sure of was that there was a whole world waiting for me, and I wanted to see it.

Switzerland intrigued me. It was where my grandparents were from. Grandpa Hesse had left his native country in 1920 and never returned. Apparently, he was from a wealthy family and had fallen in love with the family's maid. Determined to have her, he sent my grandmother enough money to sail to America, and she landed at Ellis Island a year after he did. They got married in Springfield, Massachusetts, and my father was born one year later. Grandma Hesse died in 1965, but my grandfather was still alive. He never spoke of Switzerland or the family he left behind. How ironic was it that I was in Switzerland and considering living there?

I was lost and I was confused, not sure of what was to become of me. I was also hung over. Thomas and Karl had taken Donnie and me out to their family's home in the suburbs the day before to attend a garden party. We had stayed late into the night, drinking beer and vodka and smoking cigars. There was a young couple from California there, LA hipsters dressed in expensive clothes. The dude with the white silk shirt and gaudy watch didn't say much, but his emaciated companion, a blond chick with cropped hair, had plenty to say. Dressed in tight jeans and an unbuttoned blouse tied at the waist that revealed the bones in her rib cage and the sunken center of her flat braless chest, she lamented what could have been.

"My gawd," she moaned, "we *tried* to change the world, but we couldn't."

I didn't have much to say to them, and they were at a loss of words for me. To them I was one of those dirty hippies they avoided back home. To me they were the very Americans I was running away from. It was probably three in the morning when we got back to Lucerne. The two Texans had left town that afternoon, but the couple from Australia was still there, crashed out naked on top of their sleeping bags.

I didn't sleep much, and I got up early to cook my now familiar breakfast. Thomas had taught me how to prepare an egg in a way that I hadn't seen before. I cut off a thick piece of French bread, carved out a doughnut hole in the middle, and dropped the bread into the sizzling butter in the frying pan. Then I cracked an egg and dropped it into the hole. As the egg was cooking sunny-side up, I took the doughnut-hole circle and placed it back into the hole, covering the fried egg. I then scooped it up with the iron spatula and dropped it on a plate. I finished it off with a glass of chocolate milk. After that, I brushed my teeth, took a runny hangover shit, and got dressed. Relieved that the sun was out, I left Baselstrasse 7 and headed for the Reuss.

I had no trouble finding a table. The going-to-work crowd had moved on, and the late-sleeping tourists had yet to invade the promenade. I settled into my favorite seat by the water in front of Mr. Pickwick's Pub and ordered a coffee. Someone had left a newspaper on the table.

It was the *International Herald Tribune*, and it was in English. Since landing in Luxembourg and making my way to Amsterdam, I had purposely avoided newspapers and any news from across the Atlantic. I considered myself an expatriate now and had no intentions of returning to the States. However, my curiosity got the best of me. The front page told me all I needed to know. Tricky Dick's ship was continuing to take on water. The *Washington Post* was reporting that his fired White House attorney was ratting him out, claiming that Tricky Dick was deeply involved in a criminal cover-up. Dick, H. R. Bobby, and Johnny were trying to pin the entire mess on the attorney, but he was having none of it. He was telling investigators that he had discussed the cover-up with the prez at least thirty-five times between January and April and that Dick had approved a payment of $1 million to buy the silence of the conspirators. Whoever had left me the newspaper had done me a favor. The news from America made my day and only strengthened my resolve to remain abroad.

Still, I had no idea where I was going. I took a sip of my coffee and waited for a sign. I watched as dozens of creatures walked past me. I couldn't relate to any of them. I identified more with the fidgety pigeons, placid ducks, and graceful swans that surrounded me. Hoping that I had a poem in me, I picked up my pen and opened my notebook. I scribbled a few lines, but none of it made any sense. I was deep in thought when I heard her voice.

"What are you doing?" she asked.

I had been down this road before. Only this time, there were two of them.

83

They were the sign I was waiting for.

Besides not knowing the next stop on my journey, I was beginning to wonder if I would ever have sex again. I hadn't been laid since arriving in Europe. I might as well have been invisible to the women of Holland, West Germany, and Switzerland. Who could have predicted that two college girls from the University of Connecticut would be the ones riding to my rescue?

They were in blue jeans and carrying backpacks. Both displayed thick crowns of dark-brown frizzy hair. The girl in the navy-blue cotton blouse appeared to be the one in charge. She was the shorter of the two. She removed her pack and leaned it against a chair.

"Well," she demanded, "are you going to tell us what you're doing?"

"I'm trying to write a poem," I confessed.

"Are you a writer?"

I paused a second to think it over. I wasn't a writer, but claiming to be one would probably help my cause. I decided to lie and say I was.

It worked. I had their attention. The American girls each pulled up a chair.

There was no changing my story now. I told them that I had come to Europe to write a novel. They asked where I was living, and I told them that I was staying with my friends in Lucerne. That much was the truth. When I asked where they were staying, they said they didn't know. They had just arrived that morning and hadn't started looking. The shorter girl, who had been doing all the talking, must have read my mind.

"Any suggestions?" she asked.

They were both cute, but she was the one I was attracted to. Her name was Silvia, and she was emphatic that it was spelled with an *I* and not a *Y*. Silvia with an *I* introduced her friend in the mustard-yellow T-shirt as Robin. They were college roommates who were backpacking through Europe for the summer. After spending their first week in West Germany, they hopped a train for Switzerland and Lucerne. This was my opportunity. In a matter of seconds, I had reinvented myself, and the girls from UConn were impressed. I had no idea how this was going to play out, but I was invigorated. No longer just a bum wandering the streets of Europe, I had recast myself as an expatriate American writer. It didn't matter that it wasn't true. Hemingway and the Lost Generation had nothing on me.

"If you want," I offered, "you can stay where I'm staying. My friends have plenty of room, and I'm sure they won't mind."

I knew I was right about Thomas, Karl, and Rudi not minding. The two dudes from Texas were gone, so there was enough room. Besides, I doubted they would be upset if I showed up at the door with two cute college girls looking for a place to crash.

Silvia and Robin were all for it. We hung out together for a few hours before making our way back to Baselstrasse 7. I took them for a walk through Old Town and along both sides of the river. We bought a loaf of bread and stopped to feed the swans. When we entered the Spreuer Bridge, I showed off my knowledge of the triangular Dance of Death paintings. I acted like I was giving them a tour of my hometown.

As we trucked up the three flights of stairs, I was hoping to be rewarded for all my hard work.

84

I was nearly asleep when I felt the skilled hand slip inside my sleeping bag.

It brushed across my arm before gently touching my chest and making its slow descent. By the time it arrived at its destination, I was already hard.

There were six bodies on the living room floor. The Australian couple was in their usual spot, passed out naked and on top of their bags. Donnie and I had stripped down to our underwear before crawling into ours. I remember the girls climbing into theirs in their panties and T-shirts.

I kept my eyes closed. If this was a dream, I wanted it to last as long as possible.

The hand was tender but methodical. It moved seamlessly between my cock and my balls.

I unzipped my sleeping bag, lifted my hips and pulled down my underwear. The delicate hand withdrew from my crotch, moved over to my far hip, and gave it a subtle tug. As the hand pulled me over onto my side, a forearm brushed against my hard-on.

It wasn't until her tongue touched the tip of my penis that I opened my eyes.

My lips were just inches away from a generous offering of dark pubic hair. I didn't hesitate when she opened her legs. My tongue was ready. I went in for the kill.

I assumed I was eating Silvia.

85

I really didn't have anything to complain about. After all, she was a great lay. I would have preferred Silvia, but Robin was the one who made the move. I was surprised when I realized it was her, not Silvia, that I was performing sixty-nine with. I knew something wasn't quite right when I reached down and felt the large breasts. Although I hadn't seen either pair yet, I had been observant enough to know that Robin was the one with the bigger chest.

Robin was committed to making it last as long as she could, and I was so horny that I didn't care whom I was fucking. However, I wasn't an exhibitionist. I felt a little awkward when I realized we were being watched by the other four in the living room. The Australians were pretending to be asleep, but I could see that their eyes were open. Donnie was staring over at Silvia, probably hoping he was next. Silvia, in turn, was watching Robin and me go at it. She was smiling and seemed to be enjoying the show. All that was missing was the popcorn.

The next three nights were more of the same. The nine of us smoked hash, drank beer, and listened to Frank Zappa and Jimi Hendrix before packing it in for the night. When the lights went out, Robin and I resumed our sex show for Donnie, Silvia, and the Australians. Donnie made a move on Silvia, but she wasn't interested. On the second night, she slipped out of the audience and went to Rudi's room. It made me wish I was Rudi.

The next day, I had a chance to be alone with Silvia. Robin was still asleep, so we took a walk down to the river. I confessed that I was attracted to her, not Robin, and asked her why she wasn't interested in me. She laughed and told me she was.

"You don't understand," she said. "Robin and I made an agreement when we decided to come to Europe together. We agreed to take turns when it came to guys. When we were in West Germany, I got it on with a guy from Turkey. So when we met you, it was her turn."

"Why can't I be with both of you?"

Silvia laughed again. "Nice try. That's what Ahmet wanted to know."

"Who's Ahmet?" I asked.

"He's the Turkish guy I was balling," she said.

"Did you like him?"

"Yeah," she answered. "I just wished that he washed his hands once in a while. It made me a little nervous whenever he stuck his filthy fingers in me."

I had nothing to add to that. We crossed over the Chapel Bridge. Silvia was holding my hand.

"Look," she finally said. "I like you. Robin got the better deal. I'd love to get it on with you, but she is my best friend and I won't do anything to hurt her."

"Would she really care?" I asked.

"Are you kidding?" she said. "She told me she was in love with you."

I was shocked.

"What are you talking about?" I protested. "We've only been having sex for a couple days."

"I know." She laughed. "It doesn't make any sense, does it?"

Things were getting weird at Baselstrasse 7. Donnie and I had drifted apart. He wanted to go back into the Bush, but I wasn't interested. Rudi was happy that he had gotten laid one night but was pissed when Silvia told him she wasn't going to do a repeat performance. The couple from Australia told Thomas and Karl that they were uncomfortable having to watch Robin and me have sex every night.

The girls wanted to go to Italy. They asked me if I wanted to go with them.

It sounded like a good idea.

86

I had never been on a road like this before. The Gotthard Pass was a treacherous and dizzying array of stunning alpine views, sheer drops, and hairpin turns. Climbing several thousand feet, it resembled a sixteen-mile tapeworm as it snaked its way up and around smooth granite rocks, blue glacial lakes, and lush green scenery. I was on the passenger side in the front seat and was scared shitless whenever I looked out the window. I closed my eyes and tried not to imagine the plunge we were about to take. The driver, a well-dressed Swiss dude in his early thirties, wasn't fazed at all. He was driving a little too fast for my tastes, but he appeared to be relaxed and taking it all in stride. The girls were in the back seat, oohing and aahing at the spectacular scenery around every turn. They didn't seem concerned or aware that we were literally inches away from death.

Robin and Silvia wanted to take a train to Italy, but I had talked them into hitchhiking. I needed to conserve what little money I had. It worked out well for all of us. They felt safer hitchhiking with a guy, and it was easier for me to cop a ride traveling with two cute chicks. We slept in that morning at Baselstrasse 7 and got a late start. Johann had pulled over for us that afternoon just outside Lucerne and said that he could take us as far as Lugano, the Italian-speaking Swiss city near the Italian border.

Even though I was paired up with Robin, I couldn't stop wishing it was Silvia. Traveling together with the two of them was going to be tricky. I knew I had to keep my thoughts to myself. Robin was sitting directly behind me and kept reaching over to the front seat to touch my arm or rub my shoulder. Whenever I thought I could get away with it, I turned my head to make subtle eye contact with

Silvia, who knew what I was thinking. Whenever she was sure that Robin wasn't looking, she glared back at me and shook her head no.

We arrived in Lugano in the early evening. Situated along the north shore of Lake Lugano, it was a striking bouquet of palm trees and picturesque boulevards with riveting views of the lake and the Alps. Johann offered to buy us dinner, and we took him up on it. Afterward, he drove us out of the town and dropped us off. We found a secluded spot on one of the steep hills above the lakefront to spread out our sleeping bags and spend the night.

Robin and I shamelessly had sex as Silvia lay just a few inches away. Being watched by her was both exciting and uncomfortable. I wanted it to be Silvia, not Robin, that I was doing it with. Still, it felt great to be getting laid again on a regular basis. Even better, I loved the enthusiasm and passion with which Robin made love to me. It was exhilarating to be so desired. I wondered what Silvia was thinking as she watched us getting it on. Did it make her jealous? Did she like how I made love? In a weird way, I felt like I was trying to impress Silvia, not Robin, with my sexual prowess. When I went down on Robin, I closed my eyes and pretended I was eating Silvia. I wondered how Silvia tasted. I had seen her in her panties and T-shirt but never naked. She was of Italian descent and had olive skin. I tried to imagine what she looked like without clothes. I fantasized about making this a threesome. When Robin finally fell asleep with me inside my sleeping bag, I thought about making a move on Silvia. Thankfully, I came to my senses before doing something stupid.

The next morning was the warmest I had experienced so far in Europe. The sun was out, and we were surrounded by lush, almost tropical vegetation. We had a wonderful view of the bay and the surrounding mountains. We walked down into Lugano and found a tiny café along the waterfront to grab something cheap to eat. Afterward, we walked across the road and strolled along the section of the promenade shaded by orderly rows of sycamore trees until we settled on one of the empty benches. We didn't see anyone who looked like us. Lugano was definitely not an off-ramp on the hippie highway. There were no backpackers or longhaired travelers in sight. The lake was full of sailboats. No one that I knew could afford a sailboat.

Although it was less than two hours away, we only made it as far as Milan that day. It took us forever to get our first ride out of Lugano, and that ride only took us as far as the city of Como at the southern tip of Lake Como in Italy. When we stopped at the border crossing, the Italian authorities took our passports and returned them to us a few minutes later. I now had the second stamp in my passport. The first had been at the Luxembourg airport. As for the other border crossings, the trains had stopped at the Belgian and Dutch borders, and I only had to show my passport to the agent who passed through the train, looked it over, and handed it right back to me. When Thomas drove Donnie and me into West Germany and then into Switzerland, we were crossing each border in a car with Swiss license plates being driven by a Swiss citizen. A quick glance at our passports and we were on our way.

Our ride from Lugano dropped us off on the outskirts of Como. I had only caught a glimpse of Lake Como's pure turquoise waters as we whizzed by on the Autostrade. As much as I tried to enjoy the scenery and experience the elation of entering yet another new country, I couldn't get over my ridiculous obsession with Silvia. I was getting aroused just thinking about what it would be like to be inside her.

What was wrong with me? I knew it was crazy. I knew that my time with both of them, whether for another day or another week, would soon be over. Why did I want to screw up what I had with Robin? What would happen if I told her what I was thinking?

I didn't care. I had to make love to Silvia with an *I* before the three of us split up.

87

It took me a while to realize where I was when I first woke up. I had a terrible crick in my neck. Even though the narrow couch was lumpy and a foot too short for me, I was too exhausted for it to matter. It was my first good night's sleep in days. I probably slept sounder than Joe Frazier did back in January when he was cold-cocked by George Foreman in the second round.

We were in Milan, the fashion capital of Europe. I had been relegated to solitary confinement in the living room. The door to the spare bedroom was open, and I could see that Robin and Silvia were passed out together on the double bed. I slid off the couch and walked over to the sliding glass door. I opened it, stepped out onto the balcony, and stretched my arms. We were on the third floor of a rather nondescript eight-story apartment building not far from the university.

It had been my first night without sex in a week. The closest I got to keeping my streak alive was the day before when the three of us were crammed like sardines into the two-person back seat of the four-door gold Fiat. My knees were pinned against the front seat, and Robin was sitting on my lap with her legs on top of Silvia. Her ass was bearing down on my jeans and crushing my nuts. I don't know how Robin did it, but I was impressed with how she turned herself into a master contortionist. She lifted her butt and twisted her arm until I felt her mischievous hand rubbing over my crotch. With the added bonus of Silvia's warm thigh pressed firmly against mine, I maintained a hard-on all the way into Milan.

We only spent one night there. We had been picked up outside Como by a couple returning from a few days in the Alps. Giovanni was driving his girlfriend Barbara back to Milan before heading two hours east to the city of Verona where he lived and had to be at work the next morning. Barbara was a graduate student at the University of Milan, and she offered to let us spend the night at her flat. She also wanted to show off her city.

Milan was a modern metropolis that was home to more than one and a half million people. While its skyline was dominated by a series of modern skyscrapers, Barbara wanted us to see Cathedral Square, the city's cultural and physical center that dated back to the fourteenth century. Its crown jewel was the Duomo, the world's largest gothic cathedral. It was a stunning sight, with its marble facade and a roof flush with thousands of statues and more than one hundred spires. There was a cool statue of a man on a galloping horse facing the cathedral from the middle of the plaza. Barbara explained that it honored the first king of Italy who came to power in 1861, the same year as our Abraham Lincoln.

Before we left in the morning, Barbara treated us to what she said was what most Italians ate for breakfast. Along with strong coffee with milk, we had a few cookies and a bunch of sweet cookie-like hard, dry biscuits. After breakfast, we thanked Barbara for the food and the place to crash and headed for the highway. Our next destination was Florence, almost two hundred miles away. On our way out of Milan, we were followed by a small group of Italian men in their twenties who had their eyes on Robin and Silvia. It probably didn't help that neither girl was wearing a bra. The Casanovas started whistling, and two of them came up behind the girls, pinched their asses, and asked them if they would like to have sex. It was like I wasn't even there. I was outnumbered, but I had to do something. I grabbed one of them by the arm and asked him if he spoke English. When he said yes, I asked him what the fuck he thought he was doing.

"Do you really think girls will have sex with you if you just walk up to them on the street and ask them for it?"

"Yes," he replied. "We know if we ask one hundred American girls to have sex with us, at least one will say yes."

Unfazed, he and his friends just laughed at me and crossed the street. They were sure of the odds and were already searching for their next targets. I was pissed. Silvia grabbed my arm and told me to calm down.

"Don't worry," she said, "we can handle ourselves. We were expecting this in Italy."

I was glad to get out of Milan. Besides the plaza and the cathedral, there wasn't really anything else about it that I found interesting. I was restless. I was getting more comfortable with being in foreign countries and starting to dig the cool places and people I was stumbling into. I wasn't afraid anymore. I was ready to expand, ready for new experiences. Jesus had been right about Amsterdam. Hash City had eased me into the traveling scene and built up my confidence. Switzerland and Lucerne had also been great, and I was sure that I would go back there one day. However, the time had come for me to embrace the road and become the person that I wanted to be.

As much as I liked Robin and Silvia, I was eager to finally be on my own.

After three days and three nights in Florence, my wishes were granted. Both of them.

88

Florence captured my imagination.

All I basically knew about the Renaissance was that it came right after the Middle Ages. Of course, I was familiar with the likes of Leonardo da Vinci and Michelangelo. Who wasn't? However, reading about it in school was one thing. Actually standing in the place where it all started was an out-of-body experience. I had to pinch myself to prove it was real. I wanted to soak it all in. If only I had come here 470 years earlier. How cool would it have been to navigate the narrow streets of what was then the most important city on the planet? Would I have become friends with Michelangelo during the time the twenty-eight-year-old genius was creating his jaw-dropping masterpiece? I learned that he spent more than two years working nonstop on his statue of *David* in total secrecy. Couldn't he have used a friend like me back then, someone to bounce his ideas off and share an occasional jug of wine with?

I could tell the minute we set foot in the cradle of the Renaissance that I had entered a new phase of my life on the road. I was venturing into new territory. Not that I had suddenly turned into a seasoned world traveler, but I could feel myself growing. I was no longer looking for someone to show me the way. I might have been a man without a plan, but I no longer needed a Donnie to guide me around Amsterdam or a Thomas to introduce me to Heidelberg or Lucerne. I had now been on the continent for a little more than a month, and I was starting to believe that I could go anywhere and handle anything. Traveling with Robin and Silvia only served to boost my confidence. While I had been hitchhiking for years, this was the first time for them. They viewed me as a street-smart negotiator of the open road and were still buying the story of me being a writer working on a novel. Even if I had wanted to, it was too late to come clean.

The first thing we did when we got to Florence was to find the American Express office and exchange some dollars for the Italian unit of currency called the lira. Cash in hand, we went looking for a cheap place to stay near the center of the city. We found a pension that rented rooms for 1,300 lire a person. Robin and Silvia shared a room, while I had one to myself. It didn't feel like I was spending real money. It was mind-boggling. I cashed one twenty-dollar traveler's check and received nearly twelve thousand lire in return. Handling Italian money was like playing a real-life game of Monopoly. It took 585 of their lire to equal just one of our dollars. I did the math and figured my bed was costing me all of two dollars and twenty-two cents a night.

I could tell that the girls had already grown tired of hitchhiking. It took us three rides and all day to make the two-hundred-mile trip from Milan, and we had to endure a steady cacophony of whistles and catcalls along the way. Thankfully, Florence was worth the hassle. I remembered that this was where Thea had studied aboard, and it didn't take me long to understand why she loved living here. When we first arrived, I assumed that we would only be staying here for one night, but the historical aura of the city swept me off my feet. If I was ever going to act like a typical tourist, I decided this was the place to do it.

Our pension was a short walk from Signoria Square. The large L-shaped piazza in front of the Old Palace was crowded all the time. It was a great place to just hang out and do some people watching. During the day, Piazza della Signoria was packed with tourists from all over the world. Surrounded on all sides by museums, it was home to a steady yet chaotic stream of the same creatures I normally tried to avoid, all loaded down with cameras, brochures, and a rabid desire to take in as many museums and sights as possible. At night, it transformed into a destination for every wandering soul, spaced-out hippie, and political exile on their way to somewhere else. It was like Amsterdam without the drugs.

I had not done any dope since Lucerne. That turned out to be a good move. The word on the street was that the Italian police were quite strict when it came to drugs. Penalties were stiff and always ended up with a stint in jail, anywhere from three to eight years. I was cool with not getting high. It actually felt refreshing to be straight for once and not laboring to function in a hash-induced haze.

Florence had me operating on all cylinders, kissing all my erogenous zones. First and foremost, it nourished my appetite for new and exotic places and quenched my thirst for knowledge. Although I had promised myself to live on less than five dollars a day while in Italy, that goal was blown out of the water the first day. A museum ticket cost about the same as one night in a pensione. That meant if I wanted to join the creatures, I would either have to go without food or eat and blow my budget. I decided to splurge. How could I come all the way to the mystical stomping grounds of immortal dudes like Leonardo and Michel-A and not check out some of their shit? My first stop had to be the statue of *David*. A smaller replica of the iconic sculpture was on display in the piazza for everyone to admire, but I decided to fork over the lire to see the real thing.

To see the actual *David*, I had to visit the Accademia Gallery. I knew that this was going to be one of the coolest things I had ever done, but I was caught off-guard as to how overwhelming my visual encounter with him would be. Blending in and shadowing the international sea of creatures, I found myself a few feet away from the most famous statue in the world. As I stood in the rotunda at the end of the long hallway, I was overcome with emotion. Naked as a Greek god, the biblical hero was standing beneath a circular skylight, protected only by the slingshot resting on his left shoulder. It gave me goose bumps. I was eye level with *David's* feet. The giant slayer looked to be more than fifteen feet tall. From the pulsing veins on the back of his hands to the flexing thigh muscles in his leg to his curly pubes and uncircumcised penis, *David* was a dazzling depiction of the male anatomy. I froze. At first overwhelmed with joy, I was soon overcome with sadness. I was only twenty-five, and I would never again in my life see anything so majestic and stimulating. I felt like a teenager losing his virginity to Raquel Welch, keenly aware that every lay for the next fifty years would never be as good. Nevertheless, I soldiered on. After all, Florence's claim to fame was that it had the best Renaissance art in all of Europe. The city itself was an open-air museum. Churches, palaces, and statues were down every street and around every corner. I stood on the Old Bridge spanning the river that cut through the old part of the city, and took in the terra-cotta-tiled dome and bell tower that dominated the skyline. I spent more lire on museum passes. Everyone I met told me to check out Uffizi Gallery, and that turned out to rank a close second to my encounter with *David*. I was particularly enamored with an artist named Sandro Botticelli and his fascinating depictions of women. Uffizi's works of art were arranged in chronological order through a series of halls that began in the thirteenth century and concluded with the eighteenth. The collection of Botticelli paintings was in the largest hall of the museum. I must have stared at his *Birth of Venus* for at least ten minutes. I couldn't take my eyes off the sensual goddess of love, who had emerged naked from the sea on a seashell with one hand covering her breast.

Basking in the glory of Florence's history, art, and sights would have been enough, but the cradle of the Renaissance wasn't through with me yet. While it was a bit of a stretch to call my interest in politics another erogenous zone, it didn't take much to get a rise out of me. Piazza della Signoria was a hotbed of heated political discourse and fervor. Students, professors, and an international assortment of zealous debaters gathered in the square each evening to argue over and defend their positions on the most pressing issues of the day.

At first I found the scene exhilarating, but it wasn't long before I was the one on the defensive. James, a University of Wisconsin graduate student who was staying at the same pensione as us, gave me a hard time when I told him that I no longer gave a shit about Richard Nixon, Vietnam, and whatever else was happening back in the States. He accused me of being a traitor to the movement. I asked him why, if he was such a dedicated revolutionary, he wasn't back in the US fighting for the cause instead of hanging out in Italy with the rest of us. That pissed him off and ended our conversation.

James was nothing compared to George, a Greek political exile who seemed to think that I was personally responsible for US foreign policy. He castigated me for America's support of his country's military dictatorship and berated me for the war in Vietnam and US imperialism in general. The more I argued with him, the more he wore me down. I'm not sure if he actually believed it, but he finally acknowledged that not all Americans were the imperialist pigs that he thought they were and that I might be one of the good ones. It was a small victory but a victory nonetheless.

Of course, my most important erogenous zone was an actual erogenous zone. Robin made sure it was attended to each night at the pensione. She wasn't about to let separate rooms keep us apart. During the day, the girls went their own way and I went mine. At night we walked over to the square together but split up once we got there. Robin and Silvia were more interested in the circles of freaks playing guitars and banging on bongos than they were in the loud and spirited debates that I was drawn to. However, once back at our shelter and under the cover of darkness, Robin made her clandestine move and slipped quietly into my room. When she left an hour later, I was spent.

As good as it felt, I couldn't stop thinking about Silvia. It was time to tell Robin the truth.

We checked out of the pensione around noon on our third day. We spent the afternoon wandering the streets with our backpacks and absorbing the sights, sounds, and smells of the city one last time. We agreed that Rome should be next. Once again, the girls wanted to take the train but reluctantly agreed to give our thumbs one more chance. The problem was that while hitchhiking was legal in Italy, it was illegal on the Autostrade. Our only option was to try the backroads. It was a great way to see the real Italian countryside but a piss-poor way to get anywhere. We landed one ride, but it only took us a few miles outside Florence.

As dusk settled in, we found a secluded spot on a hill under some olive trees to bed down for the night. We had a beautiful view of the valley. It reminded me of pictures that I had seen of California, with its rolling hills and golden fields. We were at least a hundred yards from the road and concealed from view by the tall grass. Thankfully, we had thought to buy some bread, cheese, and bottles of Coca-Cola before leaving the city. Otherwise, we would have gone hungry that night. Silvia had walked away and squatted behind a tree to pee when I broke the news to Robin.

Even before I finished my sentence, I knew I had fucked up. I watched as the color left her face, and I could tell immediately that I had hurt her. I felt like a total asshole. She had been nothing but good to me, and here I was, asking her if she minded me having sex with her best friend. When Silvia rejoined us, she knew that something was wrong. She glared at me.

"What did you do?" she asked.

"I told her that I wanted to sleep with you instead of her," I admitted.

Silvia shook her head. I could tell she was disgusted with me.

"I can't believe you told her that," was all she said before turning away.

The rest of the night was awkward. As the darkness rolled in, Robin and Silvia gave me the silent treatment. They also moved their sleeping bags to another olive tree that was about twenty feet away from the one I was under. It was a full moon, so I could see them clearly as they talked things over. I wanted to crawl under a rock. Finally, as I was slipping into my bag, they walked over and stood over me. Silvia did the talking.

"It's probably best that we split up tomorrow morning," she said.

What could I say? I knew she was right.

"Sure," I said. "That's probably a good idea."

It took me a while to fall asleep. It was a warm night, too warm to stay inside my bag. I kept wishing that I had kept my mouth shut. I tossed and turned, thinking about what I had done. When I woke up the next morning, I didn't feel any better. It was early, but the sun was already making its presence felt. I looked over at the girls, who were sitting up and finishing the last of the bread and cheese. I had to pee, so I walked behind the nearest tree and took a long piss. When I finished, I reemerged to find them standing there. Silvia was right in front of me, while Robin was a few feet behind her, refusing to look at me.

Silvia with an *I* reached down and unbuckled my belt.

"Have a seat," she said. "We've decided to give you a going-away present."

89

I was on top of my sleeping bag, flat on my back and naked. My cock was pointed straight into the air, like a radio antenna searching for a signal. I opened my eyes and saw that they had removed their clothes. Not that I deserved it, but I seemed to be living a charmed life.

Silvia was the first to jump in. She dropped to her knees and bent over to kiss me. I felt her moist hand touch my penis as she began to gently stroke it between her thumb and forefinger. Then, like she was passing a baton in the four-hundred-meter relay, she handed it off to Robin.

I didn't know what to do. I was outnumbered. I only had two hands, one mouth, one tongue, and one cock. I decided to concentrate on Silvia. As she was slipping her tongue into my mouth, I slid my hand down between her legs and slipped in my fore and middle fingers. I was finally in the place I wanted to be. I felt every ounce of energy I possessed rushing through my hand and surging to the tips of my enraptured fingers. Silvia returned the energy, pressing down so hard against my hand that it seemed like she was trying to swallow them. Our wet tongues were locked in such a fiery wrestling match that I couldn't tell who wanted who more.

Meanwhile, a second battle was underway.

Robin was pulling out all the stops. She had reached into her bag of tricks, clearly intent on making sure that she didn't become an afterthought. At first, I was hoping that she would back off and let me play with Silvia. However, it didn't take me long to realize that Robin had no intention of surrendering my cock under any circumstances. While it desperately ached to penetrate Silvia, my highly aroused weapon was powerless to escape the determined and skilled embrace of Robin's lips.

If her goal was to guarantee that I would never forget her or this moment, Robin accomplished that. She began by gently holding the base of it in her hand. At that point, her tongue took over, moving from side to side as she slowly licked her way to the tip of my spear. Having reached the summit, she celebrated her triumph by leaving her tongue there and giving it her undivided attention. Then, aided by the light touch of her hand, she guided it through her open lips with the same painless effort it took to inhale a breath of fresh air. It was like being swallowed by quicksand.

I kept my eyes closed and let my imagination run wild. In this new reality, Robin's mouth was Silvia's vagina. Instead of moving my penis in and out, Robin kept me in her mouth and used her tongue to drive me mad by swirling and twirling it up, down, and around. Each time her tongue wandered up and focused solely on the head, my body went into wild convulsions. I fantasized that I was going deeper and deeper into Silvia.

I don't remember how long this once-in-a-lifetime performance lasted. While I was pretending that my cock was in her vagina, my fortunate fingers actually were. Thankfully, my cerebellum was functioning properly and retrieving every technique it had learned from Isadora Duncan. Unfortunately, most of what was committed to muscle memory was centered on my tongue, not my hand or fingers. While Robin and her mouth were more than holding up their end of the bargain and launching me toward a physical nirvana, I wanted to make sure Silvia was on the same journey. When this was over, I would never see her again. This was my one chance, and I had to get it right.

I didn't have much time. My soldiers were preparing to run for the exit. Robin sensed what was about to happen and bought me a few more minutes. She released me from her quicksand and used her fingers to slow the stampede by applying a firm squeeze in just the right place. Silvia and I were locked in a passionate kiss. She seemed to be enjoying the mischief my fingers were up to, but I was worried she wouldn't be able to keep pace with my fleeing army. With Robin in sole possession of my weapon and Silvia in control of my mouth, my options were limited. With precious seconds left on the clock, I pleaded with my cerebellum to take the muscle memory that it was storing in my tongue and transfer it to my hand and fingers.

My request was granted. My fore and middle fingers slipped out, with my forefinger joining forces with my thumb to squeeze and move the wet folds of skin that guarded and created a sandwich around Silvia's sweet spot. My thumb then stepped away to allow my fore and middle fingers to reunite and begin the search for the pot of gold at the end of the rainbow. As my fingers continued to squeeze and probe, my suddenly skilled hand offered to assist. Determined to uncover Silvia's treasure, it experimented with different movements. It moved from side to side, up and down, fast and slow. Then, like magic, it struck gold.

Robin, who had been watching this saga, sprung back into action. She briefly massaged my balls before taking them in her mouth. Silvia had begun to move her hips, and I could feel her spasm. Her tongue dove deeper down my throat. My fingers pulled away and then returned to her sweet spot, touching it lightly and brushing over it like a feather. My hand barely moved at all. Robin put me back in her mouth and massaged my cock as she moved up and down on it with her hypnotic twirl and swirl. My soldiers were back in business. They let out a war cry and rushed for the door. Robin reduced the speed of her hand, mouth, and tongue to soften her touch. Silvia let out a scream.

That's when lightning struck.

The flow of electric current was sent in both directions. I was the object that had been struck and the one with the ability to conduct an electric current. Like any other conductive material, my current was due to the flow of both positively and negatively charged particles at the same time. My guess is that Silvia possessed the positive ones, while Robin carried the others. Whatever the scientific explanation, it was a close second to the time I had been struck by lightning with Isadora. This one may have even been a bit longer and more voluminous.

When it was over, I was speechless. Apparently, so were the girls. They lay next to me on the grass for a few minutes before picking up their clothes and walking back over to the backpacks. I watched them get dressed. Neither one said a word. Robin refused to even look at me. Silvia was a bit more gracious. As they started down the hill toward the road, she stopped and turned around. Robin and her negative particles kept walking.

"Good luck," was all Silvia said.

Then she smiled and spun around like a top.

My eyes left her for just a second, but that's all it took. I heard two loud poofs and looked up to see what had happened. All that remained were two clouds of smoke.

The girls were gone.

It was like they were never there.

90

My metamorphosis was complete. I had come a long way from my hitchhiking sagas on Route 7 and the Mass Pike. My afternoon arrival in one of the greatest cities of the world was the icing on the cake for the long day that began with my first threesome. By the time the second ride dropped me near the insane merry-go-round of traffic that was Piazza Venezia, I was nursing a natural high and convinced I was king shit. I was finally alone, a self-proclaimed world traveler no longer dependent on anyone else. Or at least I was crazy enough to think so.

When in Rome…

Rome was a trip. Not a Timothy Leary / Ken Kesey type of trip, but more like hopping aboard a time machine and returning to tenth grade in high school. Meandering through the magical city for three days made me appreciate all that I had learned in Mr. Malone's world history class. Whether it was the Colosseum, St. Peter's Square, the Forum, or the Pantheon, the twentieth-century metropolis was a mind-blowing mix of present-day Italy and the hallowed remains of the Roman Empire.

My most surreal experience was the trip I took down the legendary Appian Way and into the depths of the awe-inspiring Catacombs. It was Sunday, and the well-preserved road was closed to vehicular traffic. I took a bus to the southern edge of the city where I planted my virgin feet on the large flat paving stones that had been expecting me since 300 BC.

The ancient thoroughfare was a marvel of Roman engineering. It offered a soothing escape into the Italian countryside and a close-up view of the aqueducts, the Roman Empire's brilliant feat of engineering that delivered water to the citizens of Rome. The mystical Via Appia was flanked on both sides by green and golden fields punctuated with the ruins and other traces of Roman history. However, it was the Catacombs that really blew me away.

I turned over a few of my precious lire to join a guided tour that was in English. We were led by an attractive dark-haired girl in her late twenties who warned us not to slip away from the group and try to explore the maze of tunnels on our own. The twisting and turning system of underground passages stretched for miles and was many levels deep. One wrong turn meant vanishing into the abyss and becoming hopelessly lost, never to be seen again. As we began our descent, I could feel my claustrophobia and paranoia kicking in. If there was one thing that caused me to panic more than anything else, it was the thought of being buried alive. As we went deeper and deeper down the series of caves and passageways through the soft volcanic rock, it was like following Jules Verne on his journey to the center of the earth. I thought about those early Christians and what it must have been like to be hunted down by a sick degenerate emperor like Nero. How desperate would you have to be to seek refuge in these subterranean burial chambers? I doubt I would have had the balls to hide my happy ass down here. I probably would have just surrendered and been feed to the lions.

It was downright spooky. The bodies of the apostles Peter and Paul had supposedly been buried here. Christian images adorned the stone walls of the narrow passages. I knew it was absurd, but I could feel the eyes of a thousand consecrated souls following me through the dark and musty mausoleum. There was a macabre beauty to the ancient crypts. Lined with sculptures made from both whole and parts of the skeletons of long-dead holy men, they were disturbing and breathtaking at the same time. I hadn't been to church in probably ten years, but ingrained in my memory was the part in the Bible about walking through the valley of the shadow of death and fearing no evil. That sounded good, but the dude who wrote that probably wasn't standing where I was, staring at rib cage chandeliers, pelvis candle holders, and walls of human skulls. By the time we returned to the earth's surface, I was out of breath and eager to rejoin the living.

As fascinating as it was checking out all the historical shit, I wanted out of Rome. The city was overrun by tourists, too dirty, too expensive, and too New York-ish. Only a fool dared to step foot inside a car. When they said all roads lead to Rome, they weren't kidding. Piazza Venezia, where I was first dropped off, was the epicenter of crazy where four major roads came together to celebrate what could only be described as anarchy. Motivated by naked aggression, a blaring horn, and unyielding resolve, Italian drivers were a profile in courage as their wheels touched the slick uneven cobblestones and entered the endless loop that had no lanes or any rules. During the day, the hangouts for international travelers like me were the Spanish Steps and Piazza Navona. In the evening, the scene moved to Trastevere, a medieval neighborhood near St. Peter's Square on the other side of the Tiber River. It was a great place to meet people and get a good but cheap meal at a trattoria. I was able to get a plate of spaghetti at one of them for 120 lire, which was about twenty-one American cents. I lived off bread and cheese during the day, which cost me less than fifty cents in a small market. I also hung out at night at some of the outdoor cafés in Piazza Navona. All I had to do to claim a small table was to buy a beer or glass of wine. Nursing three of four beers cost me less than a dollar, and the table was mine for hours.

Self-confidence is a funny thing. While it's not a physical mark like a scar or a mole, the human eye has no problem recognizing it. I was wearing mine like a blanket. Whether I was sitting on the Spanish Steps, wandering through St. Peter's Square, or hanging out at Trevi Fountain, I was struck by the ease with which I was now meeting my fellow international travelers. Best of all, I was apparently no longer invisible to the women in Europe. On my last night in Rome, I was sitting alone at Bar Navona and had just ordered my third fifteen-cent glass of red wine when Isabelle sat down at my table. She said something in broken English that I interpreted to mean that she wanted to join me. She seemed to be speaking French, but I couldn't understand a word she was saying. The only things I could remember from my high school French class were "Bonjour" and "Oui" and "Ou est la bibliotheque?" and I sure as hell wasn't looking for the library.

The one language we seemed to share could only be spoken with our eyes. Hers were a bright emerald green and quickly seduced mine with a passion that was both sublime and subtle. Why someone so beautiful had chosen me was a mystery. We held hands while we took turns telling our stories, laughing continuously because neither of us understood what the other was saying. We exchanged names and addresses on small slips of paper. Isabelle Brejoux was from a suburb of Paris called Saint-Cloud, and she wore a smile that grew brighter and brighter as the night wore on. Her dark-brown hair was parted in the middle and spread out like magic tentacles to frame the outline of her face and embrace her shoulders. Her soft olive skin was remarkable, and she reminded me of the flawless Botticelli women I had fawned over at Uffizi in Florence.

We spent the night together at her room. Her pension was not far from the Spanish Steps and was a lot nicer than mine. My room was about a block from Piazza Navona and was only costing me 1,500 lire a night. It included a free shower. However, Isabelle never let me offer that as an option. When it was time for one of us to make a move, she took me by the arm and led me on a cheerful dance through the crowded streets to her fifth-floor room at a much cooler place called Pensione Erdarelli.

It was a glorious night. I was in Rome, and I was making love to a girl so stunning she could have been sculpted by the great Michelangelo. Isabelle and I were unable to exchange words with one another, but we had no trouble communicating. It couldn't have been more erotic. With no words to get in the way, our bodies performed with reckless abandon. We didn't sleep much that night, and if it had been up to me, I would have stayed there for days. However, Isabelle ushered me out the door early the next morning. I was okay with it being just a one-night stand. I had her address. I would go to France one day and look her up.

As I hit the crooked sidewalk and headed toward Piazza Navona, everything looked different. There wasn't a tourist or hippie in sight. Instead, the citizens of Rome who actually had jobs had reclaimed the streets and were scampering like colonies of ants to reach their destinations. Since this was my first introduction to early morning Rome, I found a place to sit where I could study the scene. The coughing cars, loud voices, and brisk footsteps were creating the perfect soundtrack for a new movie. The only things missing were Federico Fellini and his camera.

I had seen enough. I was an observer from another planet, and my research was done. It was time to put Rome in the rearview mirror and head for Greece.

91

I spent the entire day trying to get out of Rome. My plan had been to ride my thumb all the way to Brindisi, the port city on the Adriatic coast that had once marked the end of the Appian Way. It was more than two hundred miles southeast of the Eternal City, and everyone said this was where I needed to go to catch a boat to Greece and the Greek islands. It would have been about a six-hour drive had someone felt sorry for me and picked me up. Unfortunately, all the bad shit that I had heard about hitchhiking in Italy was true. Six hours went by and there I was, still standing in the same spot. I might as well have been stranded on a desert island. Depressed and hungry, I conceded defeat and returned to the belly of the beast like a dog with my tail between my legs.

I had two choices: I could spend another night in Rome and try again tomorrow, or I could find the central train station and see about catching an overnight train. Since my money supply was dwindling, I knew I needed to keep moving. There was no point in wasting my lire on another night in a pensione. It made sense to kill two birds with one stone. I could sleep on a train.

It turned out to be a nightmare. The main train station was both impressive and intimidating. Jesus brilliantly disguised as Tony from Australia might have taught me how to purchase a ticket in Luxembourg City, but that wasn't much help to me now. Luxembourg's station was like a pimple on the ass of God compared to the size and grandeur of this amazing display of modern Roman architecture. As I approached Roma Termini, I was struck by the gravity-defying canopy that extended well over the entrance. Once inside, I encountered a long straightaway lobby fronted by full-length glass walls and secured by a concrete ceiling that had to be more than thirty feet high. The opening at the far end of the hall led to the confusing and harried rows of ticket counters. I was no longer in the friendly confines of courteous and helpful Northern Europe. The grumpy bald dude who sold me the ticket spoke English but seemed annoyed by my very existence. I told him I wanted to go to Brindisi and tried to ask him a few questions, but all I got out of him was a grunt, a ticket, and a few lire back from the three thousand I forked over. Unsure of what to do next, I wandered aimlessly around the lobby until two Spanish dudes with duffel bags saw how helpless I looked and tossed me a life preserver. I showed them my ticket, and they told me I had better hurry because I was scheduled to leave in five minutes from platform 12. My saviors explained that my ticket was first taking me to Naples where I would then have to switch trains. That sounded simple enough. I thanked them for their help and took off running to the platforms until I reached what I hoped was number 12. I hopped aboard the first car and found a seat just as the train started to move.

I was surprised that there weren't more people sitting in the car since I assumed that Rome to Naples had to be a popular route. There wasn't anyone who looked like me. The car was half empty, and the unaccompanied women and couples I was traveling with were much older and much better dressed. I settled in a compartment occupied by a middle-aged couple who were obviously American and looked a little apprehensive when I claimed the seat across from them. I said hello, and they simply nodded and looked away. The train had been moving for about ten minutes when a surly conductor stepped in and tapped me on the shoulder. He asked to see my ticket. When I handed it over, he shook his head, raised his rather bushy eyebrows, and scowled. Launching into a volley of words in rapid-fire Italian, he motioned for me to get up and pointed to the door at the back of the car. The middle-aged couple seemed relieved and a little amused by what was happening. The husband, who was wearing a burgundy-and-white checkered sport coat, lowered his glasses to the tip of his nose and shot me a disapproving look. He seemed eager to set me straight.

"Son," he said, "this is the first-class car. The gentleman is asking you to move. You obviously have a second-class ticket."

Obviously, I did. I shrugged my shoulders, gave the conductor a sheepish grin, and picked up my backpack. When I opened the door to the second-class car, I knew I was in the right place. The car was packed to the gills with second-class riffraff like me. Each compartment contained eight seats. It took me a while, but I finally found one with only seven bodies and wiggled into the opening between two fellow undesirables with long hair.

The trip took less than an hour and half. The dude on my right was from West Germany, and the one on my left was from England. They weren't traveling together, but they were both heading down to check out Pompeii. I was tempted to follow their lead but decided against it. I already had a ticket to Brindisi. It would be far out to see the ancient ruins of the city destroyed by Mt. Vesuvius, but I couldn't afford to piss away any more money on a side trip. Besides, I wanted to get to the Greek islands as soon as possible.

It was nightfall when we reached the Naples train station. It was smaller and grungier than the one in Rome. I found an information booth and asked what train I was supposed to catch next. The woman told me that the train that went to Brindisi left in one hour from the last platform on the left. That gave me enough time to get something to eat. I found a food stall that was selling salami and cheese sandwiches for 250 lire. That and a Coke and I was good to go. I walked around the station for a while before boarding the train. The whole scene was a lot seedier than anything I had seen so far in Italy. Not that I had anything against seedy, but there was something about the vibe of the Naples train station that made me a little uneasy.

This time I found the second-class car. I was surprised that the train was so empty. It seemed a little strange. It was safe to assume that I wasn't the only person trying to catch a boat to the Greek islands. I had no reason to complain. I had an eight-seat compartment to myself. It would be easy to get some sleep. I nodded off quickly, only to be woken by a wiry conductor with a pencil-thin moustache. I showed him my ticket, but he looked puzzled. When he began speaking in his native Italian, I interrupted him and asked if he spoke English. He nodded yes, but he was difficult to understand. We struggled to communicate. Finally, in frustration, he pulled a map from inside his jacket and spread it out on the seat next to me. He pointed to a city in the middle of the country called Potenza. I realized that he was telling me that this was where this train was headed. That explained the deserted car. I had gotten on the wrong fucking train. The conductor then ran his finger along another route on the map that was farther north. I followed the finger as it journeyed across the country, going through towns called Foggia and Bari before finally ending up on the coast in Brindisi. When I pointed to Potenza and ran my finger over to Brindisi, he shook his head. He was trying to tell me that no train went from Potenza to Brindisi. He kept repeating the word autobus until it finally sunk in. Once again, it was time to make a decision. I could buy a ticket back to Naples the next day and then buy another to start over or go with the flow and catch the next bus leaving Potenza for Brindisi.

This was my first major fuck-up, and it was a doozy.

92

A day like this was bound to happen. By the time we pulled into Potenza, it was nearly midnight and I was the only passenger left on the train. When I stepped onto the platform, it was clear that I was in the middle of nowhere. The station was deserted, and everything was closed. There was no point in getting freaked out. In the grand scheme of things, this was a minor hiccup. It wasn't like I had a schedule. Life on the road was supposed to be an adventure, wasn't it? How could I be in a hurry to get somewhere when I didn't know where I was going?

I have no idea who planted the seed, but the urge to hit the road had been growing inside me since childhood. I was only six years old when I summoned the courage to launch my first trial run. My mother was in the kitchen, washing dishes. It seemed like as good a time as any to break the news to her. Determined not to chicken out, I sprinted in and boldly announced I was running away from home. Mom didn't seem all that surprised. She just had one question.

"Would you like me to make you a sandwich to take with you?"

"Uh-huh," was all that came out of my six-year-old mouth. I hadn't given much thought to what I was going to eat after I left home. Leave it to my mother to think of everything. I stood there in suspended animation as she spread generous gobs of peanut butter and grape jelly between two slices of white bread. She knew that was my favorite. She wrapped the sandwich in Saran Wrap and placed it in my Howdy Doody lunch box, along with a red apple and the handful of potato chips that she had pulled from the big round mustard-yellow Charles Chips container. Mom handed me the lunch box and kissed me on the forehead.

"Have a safe trip," she said and went back to washing her dishes.

Lunch box in hand, I scooted out the back door. I was excited. I raced down the driveway and made a mad dash for freedom. I had only gone a few hundred feet up Camp Street, when the hunger pains seized control. I stopped walking and took a seat on the hill that was on the open lot between two of our neighbors' houses. I took one last look at my house and wondered if anyone would miss me. I was sure that my little brother Bernie would. So would my best friend Henry Cable. That was okay. I could come back and visit them one day. My stomach started to growl. My sandwich and Charlie chips didn't stand a chance. I couldn't eat them fast enough. As I went to work on my apple, I began to feel sad. What was I doing? I was only six, and my lunch box was empty. Maybe running away from home wasn't such a good idea after all. Life on the road was a lot harder than I thought it would be. I finished the apple and headed home.

Who knew that nineteen years later, I would be sleeping on a wooden bench inside a deserted train station in the middle of Italy? This time, no one had packed me a lunch. Before calling it a night, I walked around the station and over to the adjacent bus terminal. Nothing opened up until six in the morning. Hungry and tired, I would have given anything for one of Mom's peanut butter and jelly sandwiches. Since that wasn't going to happen, I returned to the waiting room at the train station and tried to get some sleep.

The long bus ride over to Brindisi surely tested my cheery outlook, but it also confirmed that Sharon Wessel had been right when she called me an optimistic pessimist. Instead of treating the tedious journey as a twisted form of Chinese water torture, I saw it as an opportunity to see and feel the real Italy. The bus station opened at six, but the bus didn't leave until a little after one in the afternoon. Nine grueling hours later, me and my sore bus-ridden ass were standing at the ticket counter in the Port of Brindisi. The summer sun had just retreated behind the mountains to the west of the city, and the uniformed dude selling tickets was calling it quits. Lady Luck was still messing with my head. I couldn't catch a break. The overnight ferry to Corfu had pulled out less than ten minutes earlier. The next one would leave in twenty-four hours.

It wasn't easy being an optimistic pessimist.

93

Under normal circumstances, allowing myself get picked up by a gay Air Force captain would seem like a dumb thing to do. However, it was late at night and I was alone in a strange city in a foreign country. Sometimes you gotta do what you gotta do. I had twenty-four hours to kill and nowhere to crash. If I was going to trust someone, he might as well be an American.

I was surprised to learn that I was so close to a US military installation. Walter was stationed at San Vito Air Base, just a few miles northwest of the port. A balding dude in his early thirties, he was dressed in full uniform when he approached me outside the ticket terminal and wanted to know if I needed a place to stay. I knew right away that he was gay and where this was going. Still, my gut told me to take a chance. He seemed rather harmless, and I trusted myself to be nimble enough to ward off any of his advances.

Walter turned out to be a stand-up dude. He couldn't have been nicer. He lived alone, and his flat was only a few minutes away. He fed me and let me take a shower. When it came time to crash, I made it clear that I wasn't gay and I wouldn't have sex with him. Surprisingly, he didn't put up a fight. He only had one request. He wanted me to sleep with him, but he promised not to touch me. I decided to roll the dice. Walter had a king-size bed that was big enough for the both of us and looked a helluva lot more comfortable than anything I had slept on since arriving in Europe. I was exhausted and still suffering from the stiff neck and sore back obtained the night before at the Potenza train station. When I woke up the next morning, Captain Walter was already dressed and about to leave. I still had my underwear on, and when my hand reached in and did a quick inspection, nothing appeared to have been touched or penetrated. As far as I could tell, Walter had kept his word. Of course, I had been so tired and so out of it that Attila and his Huns could have pillaged and plundered me all night long, and I probably wouldn't have felt a thing. Walter said he had to be at his base by o-nine hundred. He thanked me for spending the night and wished me luck. He said I could help myself to anything in the refrigerator. After he left, I made myself a couple of sandwiches and watched some Italian TV. As Willie Shakespeare once said, all's well that ends well. I had been picked up by a gay Air Force officer and had managed to walk away unscathed. Instead, I had gotten a good night's sleep, taken a hot shower, and stuffed my stomach full of food.

The road was getting kinder.

Hopefully, it was a sign of things to come.

94

Sunrise over the coast of Albania and it couldn't have been any more surreal. I was on the top deck of the *Marianna*, leaning against the rail as the twisting ribbon of golden sunlight dribbled over the calm waters of the Adriatic Sea. The orange sun and its glistening reflection reminded me of a French impressionist painting as it peeked out from behind the distant mountain range and merged into the peach and pink neon sea. I pinched myself. We were cruising just beyond the territorial waters of what was probably the most brutal and isolated regime in communist Eastern Europe.

I had been awake all night. Deck passage to Corfu cost the equivalent of three US dollars, so naturally, the upper deck was jam-packed with a ragtag assortment of international characters like me. The nine-hour voyage to the popular Greek island in the Ionian Sea was a nonstop party. There were no drugs to be found, just jugs of cheap Italian wine. No one was stupid enough to be carrying hashish or pot. It wasn't worth the risk.

The entire scene was a rush. While there might have been other Americans riding the upper deck of this floating festival, I didn't notice any. Participating in the ebb and flow of bodies on the upper deck was akin to joining a perpetual game of musical chairs. Small groups formed and then disbanded in flashes of spontaneous combustion. Back in the States, I had imagined a moment like this. The sweet, salt air was intoxicating. It felt like I was finally a citizen of the world, a free spirit no longer defined by the country I was from or the person I was supposed to be. It was a clear night, and the sky was pregnant with a million tiny flashlights. It reminded me of being in Boston years ago when Danny, Miles, and I got fucked up and decided to enjoy our buzz inside the Charles Hayden Planetarium.

Only this time, I was outside and the stars were real. Every constellation known to man was flexing its muscles.

I made a lot of friends that night and soaked up a shitload of information. My fellow nomads included adventurers from France, Switzerland, West Germany, and Holland, but I gravitated to Gudrun, a gorgeous girl in her midtwenties from Sweden. She reminded me of Isadora. Blond with soft blue eyes, Gudrun was a seasoned traveler on her way to Athens and beyond. She had been to Greece several times, and she advised me to go to the island of Crete. My three-dollar ticket only took me as far as Corfu. She was traveling alone, and I thought about forking over the additional fare to stay on the Marianna and following her all the way to Athens and wherever else she was going. The problem was, she never asked. We talked under the stars for over an hour before she finally tired of me and moved on to a French dude with long dark hair, whom she obviously found more to her liking.

I wasn't surprised. As much as I had grown, a chick like Gudrun was still out of my league.

95

I knew the moment I set foot on Greek soil that this was where I was meant to be. It was more than just the rugged beauty. It was the indescribable sensation of stepping back in time. The lure of ancient Greece and the epic stories of Greek mythology were overpowering. Before she said goodbye, Gudrun had told me that Corfu was the island in Homer's *Odyssey*, where Odysseus was shipwrecked after the Trojan War. She claimed there was a beach on the west coast of the island called Myrtiotissa, where, according to legend, the hero Odysseus had washed ashore. Not being well-versed in the *Iliad* or the *Odyssey*, I had no choice but to take her word for it. Hell, I was so ignorant that I thought his name was Ulysses, not Odysseus.

I met my four British friends as we were waiting to disembark. I had planned on exploring the island on my own, but somehow these guys latched on to me and wouldn't let go. They said they were planning to camp on the beach and asked if I wanted to join them. They seemed cool enough, so I agreed to give it a shot. If it didn't work out, I could always split and go back to my original plan.

The ship docked at Corfu Town on the eastern side of the island. After clearing customs, we walked about two miles to a huge square in the center of the small city. It was halfway between an old stone fortress that loomed large on a rocky peninsula and the historic section known as Old Town. The modest skyline was dominated by a red-domed bell tower that looked more like a rocket on its launching pad than the top hat for the church that it called home. We wandered into Old Town along a narrow labyrinth of cobbled streets and vaulted passages. Tiny alleyways and small secluded squares exposed the lives of real people. Lines of drying clothes stretched from window to wrought iron balcony, while we meandered through the winding lanes. If it weren't for the nonstop hordes of tourists and their locked-and-loaded cameras, I wouldn't have been in such a hurry to blow the scene. The Americans who bundled together on their package tours were the worst, dishing out cold stares as they stepped aside and did everything in their power to avoid any contact with us dirty longhairs.

Before we left Corfu Town, we walked back to the port to do our money exchange. The Greek currency was the drachma, and it took thirty of them to equal a US dollar. My first bus ticket confirmed my initial impression of this being the right place to be. Corfu was a small island, a little less than twenty miles from east to west and maybe forty miles in length. A typical bus ride anywhere on the island cost three drachmas. Even I could afford ten cents. We found a small food market and stocked up on bread, cheese, cheap white wine, and an assortment of local fruits, including tangerines and some strange oval-shaped oranges the size of olives called kumquats. We divided the cost of our provisions five ways, and I was only out another fifteen drachmas. Greece was my kind of place.

We meant to hop a bus that would take us over to the west side of the island where we would find the mystical beach called Myrtiotissa. Somehow we jumped on the wrong bus and ended up traveling north along the eastern seashore. The scenery was stunning, but I couldn't get over how much construction was underway. Didn't these people realize the damage they were doing to their little paradise? The bus was full of tourists, and a couple of elderly women with British accents were complaining about the waiters in the restaurants not being properly trained. I couldn't believe my ears. I looked at my four British friends and saw that we agreed. We didn't want to go anywhere these people were going. We bolted at the next stop and caught another bus back to town.

This time we made sure we were on the right one. My window seat on the bus to Glyfada granted me a birds-eye view of the stunning natural landscape as we traversed the island's fertile green interior. The land was more rugged than I had imagined it would be. Spear-like cypress trees reigned supreme over the rolling mountain range and served as a backdrop for the endless groves of olive trees. The driver came to a screeching stop at a fork in the road and motioned for us to get off. He pointed to a narrow road leading to the right. Apparently, that was where we needed to go. As we watched the bus disappear down the wider road to the left, it felt like we were in the middle of nowhere. We made the right turn and had continued down the roadway for less than a kilometer when we saw a sign in Greek that none of us could read. It pointed us to the left. Moments later, we found ourselves tramping down a beaten dirt path through fiery yellow bushes and thorny shrubs. The trail became steeper and steeper the closer we got to our destination. When the pristine beach revealed itself in all its spectacular beauty, we realized we were in a special place. An unattended rowboat covered by a white cloth canopy and tied to a small makeshift wooden dock was the only sign of human life. We were amazed to find ourselves the only ones there. I couldn't help thinking that it didn't get any better than this.

Legend had it that this was the exact spot where the naked Odysseus had encountered the beautiful Princess Nausicaa and her nubile handmaidens. As we stepped out onto the golden sand, surrounded on three sides by the imposing rock-hewn cliffs, I was half expecting to see Odysseus attempting to cover his dick and balls with a handful of leaves. Behind him, I imagined a blind and furious Cyclops reaching for his wounded eye while at the same time flailing his hairy arms in a desperate attempt to exact revenge on Homer's hero. I envisioned Nausicaa's handmaidens panicking at the sight of a nude man with a blind one-eyed giant in hot pursuit. Screaming, they scattered in all directions. However, the young princess was unafraid. Smitten, she took the naked warrior's hand and calmly led him to safety.

I opened my eyes. My four British friends had ditched their backpacks and ripped off their clothes. Like wild men, they let out war whoops and dove headfirst into the cobalt-blue water.

I was right behind them.

The cold water was the perfect remedy for my lack of sleep. It was invigorating to swim in the sea again and soak up the sun. I had not done this since Florida and never in a setting so natural and unspoiled. The breathtaking cliffs and wild vegetation seemed to mystically merge together and wrap their arms around our little slice of paradise. Rocks of every size were planted in the water and resting along each end of the small cove like gigantic beach balls. It looked more like ancient Greece than 1973.

I slept on the beach for two nights. It was the most I had relaxed since landing in Europe. My new friends were good people and great storytellers, but they couldn't have been any more different from one another. Ken, the dominant personality, was extremely likeable and fit the image of the English street kid, tough and on top of it. Simon was the quiet one, a happy-go-lucky type willing to go along with whatever the group wanted to do. Jerry was outspoken and quite belligerent. He was a nice enough dude but seemed to be carrying a chip on his shoulder. Nigel was the most serious of the four. Inquisitive and sensitive, he involved himself in every conversation. Along with Jerry, he was always ready to offer his opinion. We built a bonfire each night after sundown and shared our stories. My favorite was the one Ken began about the four of them getting arrested as spies with an American a few weeks earlier in Yugoslavia.

According to Ken, they had boarded a ferry at the coastal town of Split for Hvar, an island in the Adriatic Sea that some bloke had told them to check out. With the exception of one American hippie, they were the only foreigners on board. After all, they were in Yugoslavia, well off the tourist path on one of those boats used by the local population to shuttle back and forth from the mainland to a series of small islands. Women with small children shared the deck with goats on ropes and chickens in wire cages. The American hippie was going to a smaller island just beyond Hvar called Vis. He said it was more deserted than Hvar and talked them into changing their plans.

"We never should have listened to that fucking American," offered an angry Jerry.

Nigel picked up the story there. He said that the five of them were the only ones to get off the ferry at Vis, which should have been the first sign of trouble. The American took the lead, taking them on a long scenic hike up a steep hill. When they reached the highest point on the island, they set up camp. It was near dusk as they were sitting around the campfire when the shit hit the fan. Without warning, they were surrounded by a dozen nervous soldiers and staring down the barrels of a dozen Soviet-made rifles.

Once again, Jerry inserted himself into the story. This time he was even more agitated.

"We spent two fucking nights in an army prison because of that fucking American," he said.

Unknown to the four Brits and one fucking American, Vis was the home to a secret Yugoslavian military base. The very fact that they were even allowed to get off the boat at Vis was clearly a lapse in security that the ferry boat captain would likely pay dearly for. The island was the communist government's largest base for land-to-sea missiles, complete with an underground hospital, tunnels, a command center, and army barracks. As far as the army was concerned, they had scored a Cold War victory, capturing five imperialist spies. It took them two days of relentless interrogations before they realized they had picked up five degenerate hippies from the West who were so clueless that they had camped on a hill overlooking the entrance to the secret command center. Concluding that neither the British nor US governments would trade anyone or anything for these five losers, they decided to let them go. The next morning the five useless idiots were placed in five separate jeeps, driven down to the pier and escorted onto the first ferry back to Split.

"We vowed to never go near another American bloke again," Jerry declared.

"Then why did you ask me to hang out with you?" I asked.

Simon spoke up for the first time.

"Because," he said, "we convinced Jerry that you looked a bit brighter than that other bloke."

Ken passed me the bottle of wine. Apparently, I had passed the test.

96

I couldn't believe my eyes. They were the last two people I ever expected to see again. As I was waiting to board the Marianna for Patras, the spectral images of Robin and Silvia were getting off. They both looked tired and a little sad. Robin spotted me first and quickly looked away. As they glided past me down the ramp, Silvia with an *I* tossed out a weak smile and quick hello. And then, just like Florence, a big poof and they were gone. Did I dream this? Were they just a mirage dispatched to Corfu Town to remind me of what an asshole I was? If so, it worked.

I was on my way to Athens, keenly aware that the birthplace of democracy was now being ruled with an iron fist by the military junta that had seized power six years earlier. Back in my college days, I had been moved by the movie *Z*, a political thriller that portrayed the 1963 assassination of the leader of the Greek opposition party by right-wing members of the military. It told the story of the subsequent cover-up and the events leading up to the 1967 coup. I probably should have been a little nervous, but everyone I had met while traveling told me that I had nothing to worry about. Word had it that the Greek authorities were cool with us longhairs just as long as we had enough money to spend, didn't talk politics, and didn't do or deal drugs.

The ferry ride through the Ionian Sea to Patras took nearly nine hours and included a stop at the coastal city of Igoumenitsa. I returned to the same upper deck that I had abandoned two days earlier and rejoined the party. It was early in the morning and a completely different scene than the overnight journey from Brindisi. The ebb and flow of bodies was slowly grinding to a halt, and the game of musical chairs had lost its appeal. Like water seeking its own level, each wasted reveler was gravitating back to his or her original piece of real estate. One by one, they crawled into their sleeping bags as if they were infants returning to the womb. I was in for a long voyage, and I was wide awake. I scanned the deck, hoping I wasn't the only one.

At first glance, there wasn't a soul to meet or to talk to. I leaned against the rail and watched as the Marianna pushed out to sea and Corfu faded into the background. The rising sun cast an iridescent shimmer over the open water. I wanted to remember this. I took a deep breath of salt air and stored a mental photograph of the sapphire-blue Mediterranean that I was seeing for the first time.

It wasn't long before the communal hibernation was over and the deck came to life again. Gradually, the party picked up where it had left off the night before. By the time we docked in Patras, I had acquired a new set of friends and received a crash course on the Greek islands. Besides Corfu, the islands of Rhodes, Hydra, and Mykonos were where everyone said it was happening. A few suggested Ios. I didn't know where any of these islands were, nor did I have any idea how to get there. Compared to most of the freaks I was meeting, I was clearly a virgin when it came to world travel. I tried to soak up as much information as I could. I learned that three drachmas, the equivalent of ten cents, would get me from downtown Athens to the harbor of Piraeus where I could catch a boat to most islands for no more than sixty to one hundred drachmas. I was also told that sleeping on beaches was allowed on all the islands. As for eating, food was supposedly cheap everywhere in Greece. This was good news. My money supply was dwindling, but I figured this was a country where I could make it last a while.

The group I finally settled in with included a girl from Seattle named Lisa and four dudes: a Greek, a Canadian, an Australian, and a South African. Stelios, the Greek longhair, offered us a ride to Athens once we docked in Patras. His friend was picking him up in his VW bus, and he said there was room for all of us. We were glad to take him up on it since Athens was more than one hundred kilometers away and hitchhiking there was nearly impossible because there were so few cars. I really dug Lisa, a tall girl with long brown hair who said this was her third time in Greece. Despite all the talk of Rhodes, Mykonos, and the other islands, she insisted that Crete was where it was at. This was the same advice I had gotten from Gudrun. Two beautiful girls were telling me the same thing. It had to be a sign. Hoping this was my lucky day, I asked Lisa if that was where she was heading. She burst my bubble when she said no. She was going to Athens to hook up with her Greek boyfriend whom she had met the previous summer on Crete. It was late afternoon when Stelios and his friend dropped the five of us off in the middle of Athens. We were in Syntagma Square, clearly the place where everyone hung out. Before she left us, Lisa pointed to the American Express office on the corner and said that this was where everyone cashed their traveler's checks and picked up their mail. I hadn't realized until now that I could get letters mailed to me while traveling through Europe. It was good to know. When Lisa disappeared into the crowded square, it reminded me that I had not been laid since Rome. I was getting horny again, and I wanted to believe that the birthplace of democracy would step up to the plate and hit a home run for me. The Canadian, Australian, South African, and I found a cheap pension on a street called Agiou Constantinou, less than a ten-minute walk from Syntagma Square. Each of us scored a single room for only eighty drachmas, which was less than three dollars by my calculation.

I parted ways with the Canadian, Australian, and South African the next morning and explored the city on my own for two days. It was far out meeting hip people from all over the world, but it was clear that all this marching around in groups was cramping my style. I was noticing that the most interesting people I met were traveling alone. It was time for me to break from the pack and become one of them.

The weird thing about Athens was that it could be so fucking cool and a bummer at the same time. Walking through the very heart of what was once ancient Greece had a sensuous, almost spiritual vibe to it. A person didn't have to be a history buff to feel the past reaching out to soothe the soul. Despite the crowds, the regal Acropolis with its ruins and ancient buildings was more a religious experience than a tourist ritual. When I closed my eyes and blocked out the sounds and smells of 1973, I could imagine myself somewhere between 300 and 400 BC, digging every word from the likes of Plato and Aristotle. Perched majestically on a dramatic rock formation high above the city, the ancient citadel was hallowed ground. Built at its foothill and clutching its slopes, Athens's oldest neighborhood was a labyrinth of winding lanes and narrow alleys. Lined with sidewalk cafés and small unpretentious restaurants called tavernas, the Plaka was the in-place to hang out. The sidewalk cafés in Syntagma Square were also popular. The best one there was Papaspyrou's, where ten drachmas was enough to score a Coke or a coffee and a seat on the street. It was people-watching nirvana.

The bummer side of Athens was just as dramatic. There was definitely a military dictatorship vibe to the city. Maybe I had fantasized a bit about what to expect, but Athens was different than I thought it would be. Beyond the tourist sites, it was modern with all the trappings of a big city. It was depressing to see and smell the pollution and survey a landscape dominated by Esso, Texaco, Mobil, and BP gas stations. Wasn't that what I was trying to run away from? Now more than ever, I couldn't wait to get my ass to a fucking island.

On the getting-laid front, my second and last night in Athens looked promising. I met Grace Thorn while I was climbing the steps in the Plaka on my way up for a last look at the Acropolis. She was from London, traveling alone, and asked me if I would walk with her. I have no idea why she picked me. It was all very prim and proper. Clutching a handful of tourist literature, she was hell-bent on seeing everything there was to see and knowing everything about every one of her targets.

I actually enjoyed it. I learned a lot more than I had the day before when I wandered around for hours with my head up my ass. Besides, she was pretty and a possible cure for what was ailing me. Grace Thorn was barely five feet tall with short jet-black hair and fair, almost porcelain skin. I loved her British accent, but I sometimes had trouble understanding what she was saying. When our exploration of every nook and cranny of the Acropolis finally reached its grand finale, she asked me if I would like to have dinner with her that night. There was an out-of-the way taverna in the Plaka that she wanted to try, and she said that she didn't want to eat alone. Grace gave me the name of the hotel she was staying at near Syntagma and asked me to meet her in the lobby at seven thirty. Once again, Lady Luck was on my side. Or so I thought.

I went back to my room at the pension and cleaned up the best I could. The only pants I owned were the cutoff shorts in my backpack and the jeans I was wearing, and the jeans hadn't been washed since Lucerne. Fortunately, I had a clean T-shirt. There was a small shower stall in the shared bathroom, but the shower head could barely muster a slow drizzle. The temperature of the water taunted me, jumping back and forth between icy cold and lukewarm. Showering was a slow process. I washed my hair with soap since I didn't have any shampoo. I spent extra time washing my cock and balls. I was determined to be squeaky clean for the night that I assumed was ahead of me.

She was sitting in a chair in the lobby when I walked in. The hotel was nicer than any I had ever walked into before, let alone stayed in. She looked great, decked out in a crisp white blouse, a pair of sandals, and unlike me, a clean pair of jeans. I noticed she was wearing lipstick. The lobby was full of creatures, none of whom looked like me. I was the only one wearing a T-shirt, but I didn't give a shit. At least it was clean. Grace placed her arm in my mine, and we strolled out the door like we had done this a thousand times before.

I loved the Plaka, especially at night. It was the best scene in Athens. The streets were narrow, picturesque, and jumping with spontaneous energy. Bouzouki players were everywhere, appearing to fill every corner and taverna with music that was uniquely Greek. The bouzouki was a four-string, guitar-like instrument with a pear-shaped body and long neck. The street maestros fondled their strings with tiny guitar picks, producing a sharp metallic sound similar to that of a mandolin. Most of the outdoor shops in the Monastiraiki market were still open and full of tourists searching for jewelry, inexpensive woodcrafts, and various leather goods like sandals, wallets, and belts. I had been subsisting in Athens on the grilled chunks of lamb on skewers that I was copping from street vendors. The Greek equivalent of a hot dog, a souvlaki, typically cost five or six drachmas, or about twenty American cents. At Xeno's Restaurant, Grace

Thorn introduced me to a delicious dish called moussaka, which to me seemed like a Greek version of lasagna. Served as a casserole, it contained layers of sliced eggplant in a ground beef sauce smothered on top with a thin white sauce of spices I had never tasted before. At thirty drachmas, it was a splurge for me, but one dollar felt like a good investment for a great meal and a chance to get laid. Unfortunately, all I ended up with was the great meal. We sat at an outdoor table for a couple of hours, enjoying our meals and some cheap wine. Conversing with her was easy, and I was certain she was enjoying my company. After we left the restaurant, we wandered the side streets of the Plaka before returning to her hotel. As we were walking arm in arm into the lobby, I was beaming with confidence. I might have been the only one wearing a T-shirt, but these tourist creatures didn't have a leg up on me. I couldn't wait to see what a room in this far-out hotel looked like. I was sure the beds were more comfortable than any I had been sleeping on lately. I was about to ask her what floor she was staying on when she suddenly stopped and turned to shake my hand.

"I've had a lovely time tonight," she said. With that, Grace Thorn dismissed me and headed toward the elevator alone. I was stunned. Confused and hoping that no one had witnessed my sudden demise, I spun myself around and raced out of the hotel like my hair was on fire.

When I got back to my pension, I scratched England from the list of places I wanted to go.

97

Crete was the largest and southernmost of the Greek islands. Located in the southern part of the Aegean Sea, it was all that stood between the Aegean and the Sea of Libya. As I was boarding the overnight ferry at the harbor in Piraeus, I could sense that my life was about to take an epic turn. I was ripe with anticipation, embraced by the same feeling that aroused me on Christmas morning when I was five years old and jumping out of bed to make a mad dash for my presents under the tree. I couldn't wait to rip them open and see what Santa had brought me.

I was on my third ferry ride in the Mediterranean, and I was starting to get the gist of it. It was like riding a bicycle. Once you learned how, it became second nature. By now, I realized it was impossible to get any sleep. I was beginning to view the act of sailing to a Greek island as more of an art form than a mode of transportation. The conversations, the free flow of information, and the perpetual game of musical chairs were the materials that one applied to the canvas. In the end, it was up to each of us to create our own work of art. Although I couldn't put my finger on it, my intuition told me that when I arrived on Crete, I would be crossing paths with a different breed of globetrotters. It wasn't like everyone I met on the deck that night fit the bill, but there were enough unique and solitary characters to pique my interest.

It was shortly after sunrise when the ferry pulled into the Port of Souda. While I had met some engaging pilgrims during the night, I was determined to venture out on my own. Besides, the interesting ones that I was drawn to were fiercely independent and traveling alone themselves. I watched how they steered clear of groups and avoided the slew of summer backpackers who were searching for stories to tell their friends once their summer trip was over and they were secure in the comforts of home. I'm sure the solitary souls that I wanted to be like perceived me as just another one of the summer itinerants they wanted no part of. I could relate to that because I was hoping to become as hip and independent as they were.

A three-drachma ten-minute bus ride deposited me in the old town that was the heart of Hania. The double harbor and the waterfront were a vision of unmatched beauty. The morning sky with its playful pink and soft-blue brushstrokes invoked the brilliance of a Monet painting. The broad walkways along the shore were accented by colorful old buildings whose soft reflections shimmered across the calm water like nervous schools of fish. The setting seemed more Middle Eastern than European to me. I could picture Ali Baba outwitting his forty thieves here. A stone lighthouse, located at the far edge of the breakwater and supported by a massive pile of rocks, was the signature shrine of Hania. I was intrigued by the cubic-shaped structure at the opposite end of the waterfront. Although it was no longer an active place of worship, it was the first mosque that I had ever seen. Its crown jewel was a large hemispherical dome supported by four stone arches and accompanied on two sides of its roof by seven smaller domes.

It was when I found myself squatting over a hole in a concrete floor that I realized I was in a more primitive place than I had ever been before. The public restroom was a dark open room inside a centuries-old stone building. Mine was just one in a series of holes, and I was just one of three dudes currently trying to take a shit in this dank dungeon. The stench was overpowering, and I couldn't get out of there fast enough. The half roll of toilet paper in my backpack was my lifesaver. I hate to think what I would have done without it.

My bowels emptied, it was time to take in the sights. While I knew I wouldn't be staying here, Hania was definitely worth a few hours of my time. There was a unique splendor to the old part of the city with its fascinating mix of European and Middle Eastern architecture. On the surface, Hania appeared to have preserved its charm and historical character. Wandering the back alleys and streets of the old city was like going back centuries in time. I would have spent more time in these older neighborhoods, but I hadn't slept on the ferry and I was running on fumes. What I needed was to get off my feet and get some rest. I stumbled upon a public garden in the center of town and found an inconspicuous place in the shade. I must have passed out for a few hours. The next thing I knew, the pesky sun was high in the sky, searing my eyeballs and circumventing whatever shade was left. I picked up my backpack and lumbered down to the harbor. With a little shut-eye under my belt, all I needed was fuel for my stomach. In my absence, the once-quiet waterfront had been taken over by legions of camera-toting tourists. I found a souvlaki stand where I was able to score a Coke and two of these delicious morsels for fifteen drachmas.

I had seen enough of Hania. A rolling stone gathers no moss. If the ancient proverb could inspire the likes of Mick Jagger and Keith Richards, then it was good enough for me.

It was a time to go.

98

The first two kilometers were the most difficult. The initial stair path was a series of precipitous downhill switchbacks, some bordered by wooden handrails and some not. It was slippery and steep. I had not realized until now what piss-poor condition my sneakers were in. With their treads nearly gone, it was all I could do to keep from falling on my ass and sliding over the edge.

Within the first hour, I had descended nearly two thousand feet. Up until three days ago, I had never heard of the Samaria Gorge. Now I was learning that it was a rite of passage for anyone on a journey through the Greek islands. It was said to be the longest canyon in all of Europe, and everyone I met described it in reverent, almost mythical terms.

The bus into the northern hills of the White Mountains had dodged fallen rocks and obstinate mountain goats while climbing from sea level to an elevation of nearly four thousand feet. The road was a ribbon of twists and turns as it crawled onward and upward, eventually leaving the fertile valley of orange and olive groves to blossom into a subalpine mix of oak and cypress trees. It was a clear day, and my window seat handed me amazing views of Crete's north coast. Unfortunately, it also did a punishing number on my butt cheeks. The rickety old bus and its hard seats were the remnants of a bygone era.

It was a two-kilometer walk from the bus stop to the top of the gorge. I arrived in the early evening, too late in the day to begin my eighteen-kilometer pilgrimage. I set up camp on the flat ground by the entrance, not far from the cliff and wooden handrails. It was a cold night and the first time I had needed my flannel shirt and jacket since camping in the Swiss Alps with Donnie. When I woke at sunrise, my sleeping bag was covered with frost. My exposed nose felt like a piece of ice.

I was enjoying my breakfast of bread and cheese when I suddenly heard a loud clamor of voices advancing in my direction. Like a swarm of backpack-lugging locusts, the hurried band of hikers appeared out of nowhere, their brigades swelling in numbers and surging past me in cliques of three or four. The sneak attack was over in a matter of minutes, and I was alone again. Then I remembered. Yesterday at the bus station, I caught the last ride to Omalos, the designated gateway to the gorge. When I checked the schedule, I learned that two other buses had left earlier in the day. If my memory served me, I had about three hours before the next invasion. To guarantee I was alone, I waited in suspended animation for another thirty minutes. I needed to be sure there were no stragglers. I wanted to do this alone.

It wasn't long before the morning chill was history. Even in the shade, it felt like summer again. I came to a small spring with cold, clear water. It was time to ditch my flannel shirt, jeans, and sweat-soaked T-shirt, reunite with my trusted cutoffs, and slip into a dry T-shirt. I chugged down some much-needed H_2O and refilled my canteen. The forest path had opened up, leveling off and slicing through loose patches of pine trees. The stone and dirt trail was garnished with a random mix of soft yellows and subtle whites, punctuated by occasional splashes of sun-bright orange and deep reddish purple.

The rugged natural beauty was enough to take my breath away, but it was the peaceful solitude that was so invigorating. I could sense that this was becoming much more than a simple hike through a canyon. The day was starting to feel less like a physical endeavor and more like an existential journey. Wild goats were perched high above me on the jagged cliffs. Their presence was both stoic and noble, like that of a king watching over his subjects. They moved effortlessly with an agile, almost mystical grace. Their light-brown coats were like camouflage against the walls of the gorge. What made their distant movements visible to my naked eye was the way the sunlight reflected off the horns that swept back from the heads of the holy beasts as they skirted over the uneven rocks.

I crossed over a dry riverbed three times before reaching a tributary flush with rushing water. My feet were killing me. I found a spot under a tall cypress tree and took off my sneakers. The soles had worn so thin that I might as well have been walking barefoot. It was a problem with no solution. It wasn't like I was anywhere near a shoe store. Even if I was, I barely had enough money for food, let alone a new pair of sneakers. The only thing left to do was to put the poor bastards back on my feet and keep walking.

I was at the easiest point in the hike. The path was smooth, and there was plenty of shade. The trail took a slight incline, and I was soon walking above the river. Minutes later, I was back at the riverbed, trying not to slip and fall as I tiptoed gingerly over the smooth pebbles. I came upon the ruins of an abandoned village. After wandering through the remains of the walled gardens and gutted stone buildings, I returned to the trail. I was on the riverbed again. I crisscrossed the river more than a dozen times as it made its way to the sea. While there were a few makeshift bridges along the way, my waterlogged sneakers spent most of the afternoon hopping from stone to stone or stepping directly into the water.

I was doing everything I could to avoid human contact. There were others like me, in no hurry and searching for the same solitude that I was after. They were the easy ones. Whenever they passed me or I passed them, we exchanged a few pleasantries and kept moving. The ones in groups were different. As the day wore on, I could feel them hot on my trail. In a mystifying rush to conquer the canyon, their voices always caught up to me well before they did. I was thankful that most of the encounters were brief. A quick hello in a host of different languages and they were gone. A few actually stopped and asked me to tag along, but I told them I was hiking solo and to go ahead without me.

As I descended the final two thousand feet, my journey turned inward. A striped falcon with a giant wingspan glided down to check me out. A pair of dark-brown eagles with golden washes across their crowns soared overhead. Visions of my deceased namesake Herman

Hesse flashed before my eyes. Although I didn't know shit about transcendentalism, I had read *Siddhartha*. Like Sid, I was crossing a river. Hadn't Sid chosen homelessness and fasting and renounced all his personal possessions in his search for the meaning of life? Technically, I wasn't homeless and still had some food and a few possessions to my name, but I could dig what Herman was trying to tell me. Assuming I was on the right track, was I predestined to meet the Enlightened One? Would I be as lucky as Sid and happen upon the most beautiful girl that I would ever see? Discovering the meaning of life might come in handy one day, but right now that wasn't at the top of my list. The streets of Rome and my night with Isabelle Brejoux felt like a lifetime ago. Getting laid again was the more pressing concern. Enlightenment could wait.

Here I was having all these mental convulsions, and I was doing it without drugs. The Samaria Gorge had blessed me with a natural high. As it progressively narrowed, its sheer walls reached straight upward several thousand feet into the azure-blue sky. I thought of my literary hero Jack Kerouac, dead at forty-seven, who confessed in *Desolation Angels* that he had been asking the Lord why every night and had never received an answer. If Jack didn't deserve answers, what made me think I did? I sure as hell wasn't going to find them in some book.

I passed by a small crudely built stone chapel hiding in the shadow of pine and cypress trees. There were no answers there, so I kept walking. A few moments later, I arrived at a tight passage cut between the walls. The opening through the gorge was not more than ten or twelve feet wide. It was so narrow that it blocked out the afternoon sun. There were two hikers in front of me. I watched them as they passed through this portal into the unknown.

Was the Enlightened One waiting for me on the other side? Would a beautiful girl be greeting me with open legs? I paused to reflect on this sacred day. The Samaria Gorge had swallowed me up for nearly eight hours, and it was spitting me out as I approached its grand finale.

The suspense was killing me, but I was filled with hope. Once through the narrow passage, the gorge widened and I found myself in yet another village of ruins. There was no beautiful girl to invite me in, no Enlightened One to show me the way. I pressed on. The final two kilometers were flat and should have been easy, but the sun was a scorcher. There was no shade, and my canteen was empty. I needed water.

My eyes were glued to the prize in front of me.

It was the deepest blue I had ever seen.

99

I was alone, but I wasn't lonely. I slept on the beach that night and witnessed firsthand the magic of the night sky on the south coast of Crete. I was treated to a glittering light show. One by one, the stars joined hands to form a bright cloud, creating a fiery highway that flowed like lava across the black void. The waves of the Libyan Sea added the soundtrack. I had no trouble falling asleep. The day's hike had worn me out.

I woke just as the morning sun was coming over the mountain, warming the sand and revealing the magnificent orange and rust color of the striated rock formations that surrounded the tiny cove. Small white rocks were scattered across the beach, serving to accent the gray color of the coarse sand. The hillside leading to the top of the sandstone cliffs was sparsely populated with pine trees. A series of small caves unfolded along the beach. It was easy to imagine how they once could have been perfect hiding places for the pirates of ancient Greece. I stripped down to my cutoffs and went for a swim.

I welcomed the isolation. It wasn't so much that I had become antisocial. It was just that I was evolving as a traveler. Yesterday in the gorge had been mind-blowing. Hiking it alone is what made it special. I was no longer nervous or unsure of myself like I had been in Amsterdam. I had no intention of returning to Richard Nixon's America. I had commandeered for good the same self-confidence that I had worn like a blanket in Rome. There weren't any answers yet, but there was plenty of wisdom floating around. The trick was to separate the real searchers from the summer sightseers and only make contact with those who were the true adventurers. I was faced with a baffling paradox. I only wanted to be around those who wanted to be alone. All the others annoyed the shit out of me. It was hard to be alone in a world that refused to leave me alone. I was determined to do Greece on my own terms.

I was in Agia Roumeli, an unassuming village resting comfortably between the dramatic backdrop of the White Mountains and the crystal-clear Libyan Sea. When I arrived the day before, it was late afternoon and I was just in time to watch the last boat to Hora Sfakion pull away from the jetty. The small vessel was packed full with what looked to be at least twenty bodies. I couldn't have written a better ending to such a spectacular day. I was thankful I had missed the cattle call. I was assured of the peace and solitude that I so coveted.

It was a quiet community, with only a dozen or so small stone houses, a tiny church, and one taverna to serve the daily throngs of backpackers who marched through on their way to their next hip destination. With the masses safely offshore, I headed straight for the taverna. The long hike had left me starving. I was the only one there, so I had my choice of any of the four outdoor tables. The proprietor was an old man dressed all in black with a wavy shock of white hair. He didn't speak any English, and I couldn't read the piece of paper he handed me that I assumed was a menu. Souvlaki was the only word I knew, so I blurted it out. The old man laughed and shook his head. He disappeared into the kitchen before reappearing ten minutes later holding a plate full of French fries and a large piece of grilled fish.

"Coca-Cola?" he asked.

I nodded yes. He went back inside and returned seconds later with a bottle of Coke. It was a meal fit for a king. When I had finished eating, I tried every conceivable way I could think of to ask my new friend how much I owed him. He finally understood what I was trying to say and held up five fingers on both hands. Only ten drachmas? Could that be possible? Apparently, it was. For around thirty-three cents, I had satisfied my hunger and quenched my thirst. I gladly surrendered the coins. The old man went back inside and returned minutes later with a small shot glass filled with a clear transparent liquid.

"Raki," he said, motioning for me to pick up the glass.

I obeyed his instructions and chugged it down. It had a kick to it and tasted a little like licorice. When I reached in my pocket to grab more coins, the old man shook his head and waved me off. It was on the house.

This was my kind of place. By the next morning, I was sitting on the beach, basking in the sun and serenity of my little slice of paradise. I was contemplating making Agia Roumeli my home for the summer. It didn't take long for me to come to my senses. Around midday, my illusion was shattered when the first wave of hikers emerged from the gorge. They kept coming in droves, overrunning the beach and village with their sweat-soaked T-shirts and sunburned bodies.

There were two boats leaving in the afternoon. I decided to take the first one.

100

It was a moment I'll never forget. I was on the boat to Hora Sfakion and maybe a mile offshore when I heard the Song of the Sirens. It was as if one of Homer's sea nymphs had latched on to me with a tractor beam and was luring me in. My fate was sealed. I pointed to the shore and asked the captain to drop me off.

The sea was calm as we glided into the natural harbor that was created by the small island of uneven rock standing guard at its entrance. The crescent of white-washed buildings embedded in the rocky slopes bellied up to a small pebble beach that formed a thin inverted horseshoe along the perimeter. The captain stopped his boat a few hundred yards from the shore and rang what sounded like a cowbell. The water was too shallow to go any further. A few minutes later, an old man in a small rowboat pulled up next to us and motioned to me to jump aboard. There were ten others on the boat, but I was the only one getting off.

I was in the sleepy coastal village of Loutro. Jumping off the boat was like stepping back in time. The narrow landing dock was less than twenty feet long and situated a few steps below the seawall in front of what looked to be the local gathering spot. It was midafternoon, and only one of the four thick-legged wood tables on the concrete platform was occupied. Two shirtless dudes with long hair were locked in a serious game of chess. An elderly woman in a shapeless long black dress stood in the open doorway. Her head was covered by a black kerchief tied under her chin. Seated a few feet away was a man with a gray handlebar moustache. The sleeves of his collarless black shirt were rolled up to his elbows. A black lacy kerchief with densely-sewn fringes was wrapped tightly around his head. His face was expressionless.

When I realized that no one seemed to notice me or even acknowledge my existence, I knew that I was going to love it here. The village was built into the side of the mountain, and there were no roads leading in or out. It definitely didn't look like a typical tourist destination. As far as I could tell, there were no pensions or rooms to rent. The narrow beachfront wasn't more than a few hundred yards long. I set down my backpack and took a seat at an open table. This appeared to be the only place where I might find something to eat. The straight-back chair that I chose was wobbly. There were more than a dozen others to choose from, so I tested a few until I found one to keep me on solid ground. I sat down at the table again. My stomach was growling. I glanced over to the open doorway. The man with the handlebar moustache was sitting with his legs crossed. He gave me a blank stare. The elderly woman in black had disappeared.

Apparently, the chess dudes had seen this movie before. They decided to take a break from their battle of wits and clue me in. The one who addressed me spoke English but with a heavy accent. He sounded French to me. He explained that elderly woman was Marika, and she had gone inside to wash her dishes. When I asked him when she would be back, he laughed and said that she would probably start preparing her food again in one or two hours.

The dude turned away from me and moved one of his pawns. I was starving and didn't want to wait one or two hours. As much as I hated to do it, I interrupted their game and asked if there was somewhere else to eat.

The dude with the French accent laughed again, but I could tell that I was starting to annoy him. He pointed down the beach in the direction of the rock island in the harbor. I couldn't make out what he was pointing to.

"Sometimes," he said, "Pavlos will cook for us if he is in the mood. I do not think he is at home today. We all have to wait for Marika."

I introduced myself. They both nodded, but neither one offered up their name. I thought it was a little strange, but it didn't bother me. Maybe they weren't interested in making a new friend. Maybe they assumed that I was just another hippie on my way to somewhere else. Maybe they were too into their game of chess. Maybe it was because I was an American. It didn't matter because I liked this place already.

I had some time to kill before I could score a meal. I decided to check things out.

101

I only spotted two, but there were probably more.

Barely three inches long and sandy brown in color, they blended in so well with the soil that they were able to scamper around without being noticed. I had never seen one before, let alone slept with any. I twisted and turned all through the night. It was impossible to fall asleep. I was alone on the hilltop above the village, scared to death that one of these eight-legged arachnids would crawl inside my sleeping bag and violate me with its stinger.

As I was walking away from Marika's, the chess dudes had warned me that sleeping on the beach was not allowed. That seemed like as good a time as any to search for a place to crash. After some trial and error, I was able to locate the beginning of the steep trail that led up the hill from behind the stone house that stood farthest from the shore. It was a hot, dusty climb, but the reward was spectacular: a bird's-eye view of a pint-size village clinging to a rocky coast as it was being caressed by a turquoise green and blue bay. Ahead of me were the ruins of an ancient castle. A circular tower loomed large in the distance. Narrow vertical slits were cut into the structure along the top. There were four openings in the round walls of the tower, the two smallest being side by side. The largest hole was to their left and twice their size. Crowned with a rounded arch, it was like a picture window compared to its neighbors.

I worked my way through the maze of huge boulders and scattered piles of rocks strewn between the castle and tower. My resting place would be on the hard-packed earth near an ancient circle of large stones jutting out of the soil. If I had arrived here thousands of years earlier, I might have stumbled upon a pagan ritual or some other religious ceremony. Inside the large circle were six smaller circles with smaller stones that swirled together like the coiled shell of a snail. This was where I would spend the night. I was prepared to sleep on the hard ground. What I hadn't counted on were the scorpions.

Three days would pass before I was finally accepted, but I was on day 1. In addition to the local population of twenty-five men, women, and children, Loutro was also home to a small colony of international freaks. They were rarely seen during the day when the boats dropped off the backpackers who were on their way to Hora Sfakion and points beyond. A loose-knit collection of artists, writers, musicians, and seasoned wanderers, they had settled in this sensuous paradise for any number of reasons. They were social animals but mostly among themselves. Loutro was quiet and mellow, and they wanted it to stay that way. Avoiding day trippers and summer tourists like the plague, they were in no hurry to invite just anyone into their inner circle. For this global community, life revolved around Marika's four wood tables and hodgepodge of wobbly chairs the same way the earth revolved the sun. Sunrise was Marika's breakfast, and sunset was her evening meal. The warm nights were filled with spirited debate, games of backgammon and chess, and an endless consumption of alcohol.

It was late June, and the days were long. After securing my place to sleep among the ruins that first afternoon, I left my pack and sleeping bag next to the tower and made my way back down the switchback trail to the village. By now I was so hungry that I was on the verge of collapse. Marika was back in business, and all the tables were occupied. The two dudes who had been playing chess were now sitting on the seawall next to one of the tables. Sitting between them was a middle-aged man wearing glasses and sporting a gray moustache and gray hair. The three of them raised their glasses into the air, shouted something I couldn't understand, and tossed down their shots, slamming the glasses on the table when they finished. There were ten others seated around the tables engaged in a number of conversations. One dude was strumming on a guitar. I heard mostly English and French, but one dude was speaking German. Once again, no one acknowledged my presence. Undeterred, I seized an empty chair at one of the tables.

When I sat down, the dude who was speaking English with a British accent extended his hand and introduced himself. His name was Andrew. The two girls were Americans, and they were both named Laura. Andrew, who was from London, had been in Loutro for nearly a month. Laura and Laura were students from Berkeley and had been studying together abroad in Spain for the past year. They had been island hopping through Greece since finishing classes in Barcelona and were living in the village for a few more days. Where the three of them were staying was a mystery. When I pressed them for details, all they would give me was some vague answer about sharing a house with someone. I told them I was sleeping in the ruins at the top of the hill, hoping that might inspire them to offer me a place to stay or at least a clue to where I could find one. No such luck. I didn't take it personally. Apparently, no one got an invitation to stay in Loutro on day 1.

Regardless of where I was sleeping, I needed food. Marika was standing in the doorway. Clearly, she was the sole provider of sustenance for all who made the pilgrimage to this remote village. She was our shepherd, and we were her flock. There were no menus. When I asked Andrew what there was to eat, he just laughed and explained that we could order anything we wanted but that Marika would serve us whatever she felt like preparing that day. He offered that she always had potatoes and always served pommes frites. I didn't know what pommes frites were, but at this point, I would have eaten an old shoe if that was all there was. Laura and Laura saw the puzzled look on my face. Laura, the strawberry blonde, thought it was funny. She rocked back in her chair and poked Andrew on his arm. Laura with the brown hair informed me that pommes frites was the French name for French fries. That was good enough for me.

"I'm starving," I said. "Can I order now?"

It was a simple question. I was expecting a simple answer, but Andrew and the two Lauras were silent. Finally, they decided to enlighten me. It would be the first of many lessons about life in Loutro. I learned that time stood still here. There were no clocks, no schedules. As Laura with the brown hair explained it, we were Marika's extended family. She fed us the same as she fed her own.

We ate breakfast when she made it. We ate dinner when it was ready. We ate whatever she was cooking. Each meal was five drachmas, the equivalent of sixteen cents. Sometimes she charged less. We never knew until the meal was over.

I passed the time that first evening like everyone else who was waiting for their food. It was a traditional Greek white wine called Retsina, and swallowing it was like licking the resin off a pine tree. Even worse, it smelled like the floor cleaner that I used as a janitor at Harvard. It was two drachmas a glass, and by the third one, it started to taste pretty damn good. That's when Laura with the brown hair suggested I try something called Ouzo. She seemed to like me, so I decided to follow her lead. At four drachmas a shot, it was twice as expensive, but I was into Laura with the brown hair and didn't give a shit anymore. Served in a small shot glass, Ouzo was a clear liquid with the same licorice taste as the Raki the day before in Agia Roumeli. The best thing about Ouzo was that it had the numbing effects of Novocain. My omelet and pommes frites arrived just as I was slamming the second one down.

I had a great time. The omelet and pommes frites were far out. I got shitfaced on Retsina and Ouzo, made some new friends, and spent a grand total of twenty-one drachmas. Putting my math degree to good use one more time, I calculated that it cost me all of seventy cents. As dusk began to settle in, I knew that I needed to head back up the hill before it was totally dark. Andrew and the two Lauras wished me luck. My stomach was full, my head was throbbing, and my sleeping bag was waiting for me.

So were the scorpions.

102

I never dreamed I would find a place like this. My gut told me that I had discovered Shangri-La. Of course, it was only day 2 in Loutro, and I was off to a rough start. Retsina and Ouzo had gotten me through the night. The good news was that I had slept with the scorpions and survived. The bad news was that I had a serious case of diarrhea.

As I squatted next to a large boulder, I gave thanks to the Chinese who, according to legend, had invented toilet paper nearly fourteen hundred years earlier. Besides food and water, it was the one provision I couldn't live without.

It was early in the day, but the sun was bright. With the exception of the one scorpion that was scurrying around in search of shade, I seemed to be alone. I was at the highest point on the hilltop. I left the small fortress and walked a few hundred feet to the west where I spotted what looked to be a small cove with a sandy beach off in the distance. I thought about heading down to check it out, but my thirst and hunger got the best of me.

I had a horrible hangover. My mouth was dry and tasted of cotton balls. With no food or water, I had no choice but to make the trek back down the hill to Marika's. I didn't know when she was serving breakfast, but I was prepared to wait her out. My timing was perfect. The two Lauras and Andrew were starting on their omelets. Marika was placing two more omelets on the table next to them. The couple sitting there said hello to me. He was a tall, lanky German dude with balding blond hair and cool sunglasses who looked to be in his thirties. His companion was a willowy and seductive French girl in jeans and a bright-purple top. She had short reddish-brown hair and was much younger than him. I had met them the night before but couldn't remember their names.

"You are just in time," said Brown Hair Laura. "Tell Marika you want to eat."

Marika was standing next to me with her hands on her hips. I pointed to one of the plates and nodded. Marika nodded back and went into the kitchen. A few minutes later, she handed me my omelet and a glass of water. My stomach was rumbling. I prayed that my diarrhea had run its course.

"We are going over to Livaniana Beach today," offered Brown Hair Laura. "Would you like to come with us?"

She was even prettier than I remembered her being the night before. The morning sun was poking its way through a few openings in the canopy of cypress trees and shining a spotlight on Laura's shoulder-length brown hair, turning it incandescent. Clearly, I had made a good impression on the two Lauras and Andrew. I accepted the offer without hesitation.

As it turned out, Livaniana Beach was in the same small cove I had spotted earlier that morning. It was about a thirty-minute walk from Loutro. After a leisurely breakfast, the four of us forked over five drachmas each to Marika and hustled up the switchback trail. We passed my home in the ruins and followed the winding trail down to the beach. We encountered a number of stray goats along the way. The uneven dirt path was sprinkled with stones and rocks of all sizes. The land was barren and dry, its rocky surface interrupted occasionally by an isolated contingent of scrub brush or a lonely olive tree. It was the Greece of Greek mythology. There was no sign of human life or human activity.

The sandy beach on the Libyan Sea could have been lifted from a storybook. The whole scene was otherworldly. Cast against the backdrop of a rocky ravine and a rugged mountain range, the small semicircular cove was unlike anywhere I had ever visited. I had a feeling that this was going to be one of the best days of my life.

The first thing we did was take off our clothes and race into the sea. I had never seen water this clear. The drop-off was swift. The crystal clear water was well over our heads just a few feet from shore.

There was a gigantic boulder erected in the water at the edge of the sand. It rose nearly twenty feet into the air. I felt like a primitive prehistoric man as we climbed to the top of the rock one at a time. Andrew went first, followed by Strawberry Blond Laura and then Brown Hair Laura. Pulling up the rear, I was enjoying the view.

There were no tan lines on the girls from Berkeley. Strawberry Blond Laura was fair skinned and reddish pink all over. Brown Hair Laura was golden brown, a bronze statue standing next to Andrew and the other Laura at the top of the rock. I couldn't take my eyes off her.

One by one, we dove into the sea. I was a little nervous about diving off a rock so high up, but since Andrew and the two Lauras made the plunge without hesitation, I was not going to be the one who chickened out. My headfirst descent was a success. While it may not have posed a threat to anyone's Olympic medal, it got the job done. I opened my eyes as I was entering the water. The visibility was incredible. The sheer momentum of my twenty-foot dive carried me deeper below the surface than I had ever gone before. I held my breath and went as far as Newton's second law of motion would take me.

When I returned to the surface, Andrew and Strawberry Blond Laura were already on the beach. Brown Hair Laura was floating on her back a few feet away from me. Her perfectly symmetrical breasts hovered above the water like golden scoops of ice cream each with a dark-brown cherry on top. As she wiggled her hands and hips to stay afloat, the gentle fingers of the Libyan Sea brushed over her stomach and glistened as they felt between her legs.

"Do you want to see the caves?" she asked.

We swam to shore, and Brown Hair Laura picked up her towel. Andrew and Strawberry Blond Laura were on their towels, sunning themselves. I didn't have a towel. Brown Hair Laura told them that she was going to explore the caves with me and we would be back later. They didn't seem surprised. I wasn't sure where she was taking me, but I didn't care. We were as naked as Adam and Eve, and Eve was bringing a towel.

We were barefoot. As we moved westward along the coast, the coarse sand retreated, and we were soon stepping on pebbles and sharp rocks. It didn't seem to bother Laura, but my feet were taking a beating. The first set of caves came right up to the water, and we were forced to swim around the corner to get back on land again. Laura held the towel over her head as she swam. She seemed to know where she was going. We made two more entries into the sea before arriving at a tiny cove with two cave openings. She tossed the dry towel on the ground next to the first entrance and dove underwater. I dove in right behind her, following the promise of her bronze legs as they opened and closed to lure me in.

We had entered another world. The refracted light coming through the opening was pure and magical, a kaleidoscope of blues, greens, and dazzling whites. Several irregular rock formations formed alliances along the concave edges, adorning the cave with giant replicas of rubber traffic cones. There was a long flat ledge along the back wall, large enough for two people. Brown Hair Laura burst through the liquid prism of light like a mermaid coming up for air. She landed on the ledge and held out her hand. I was Adam in the garden of Eden, and Eve was offering me her apple.

I was already hard when she pulled me on top of her. She wasn't interested in foreplay. I had a job to do, and she expected me to do it. I hadn't been laid since Rome, so I would have preferred a few preliminaries, a slower encounter with all the tasty appetizers and condiments. I wanted to go down on her, but she didn't have time for that. Still, there was no reason to complain. Whatever Brown Hair Laura lacked in variety, she more than made up for with unabashed enthusiasm. I was inside her in a flash. The ledge was slippery, and that only added to the thrill. Anyone watching might have assumed we were a pair of greased pigs acting out some supernatural mating ritual.

When we finished, my bronze seductress soared off the ledge and vanished beneath the reflecting stratums of color. Unlike her, I needed a few minutes to reflect and recover. Day 2 and I had just been given another lesson about life in Loutro. This was obviously not the first time that Brown Hair Laura had been in this cave. It was a gift she had received from someone else. That lucky dude must have been blessed with the same gift by another celestial chick. It was like a chain letter. By coming here with Brown Hair Laura, I had put my John Hancock on a sacred covenant to ensure that the chain remained unbroken.

I dove into the water and swam out of the cave. When I popped to the surface, Brown Hair Laura was on her towel, lying on her back and baking in the sun. I came ashore and sat down next to her. We stayed in the afternoon sun for a couple of hours, engaging in small talk about where we had been and where we were going. We swam a few times to cool off and explored a few more caves. I was eager to go at it again. Unfortunately, Laura seemed to have lost interest. We were getting along okay, but she acted like it had never happened. She told me that she and the other Laura were leaving Loutro the next day.

When we returned to Livaniana Beach, Andrew and the other Laura were taking turns diving off the twenty-foot rock. I couldn't tell if they had been getting it on or were just hanging out together. For all I knew, Andrew was balling both of the Lauras from Berkeley. Maybe he was not with either one. Maybe Strawberry Blond Laura would have me next. I could only dream. After all, this was Loutro, wasn't it? I had arrived in Shangri-La, and anything was possible.

Brown Hair Laura and I decided to join them on the rock, launching ourselves through the air into the blue paradise three more times. After that, the four of us sprawled naked on the sand, continuing to catch rays for another hour before calling it a day. It was depressing to put our clothes back on, but we finally acquiesced and started up the trail. When we reached the summit, I showed them where I was sleeping and promised that I would join them later down at Marika's. Andrew asked if I had seen the scorpions.

"We all slept up here our first few nights," he said.

"Bring your things with you when you come down tonight," said Brown Hair Laura. "We'll find you a place."

103

The stone building provided shelter from the elements, but with no electricity, running water, or toilet facilities, it was a bit of a stretch to call it a house. Located near the trail leading up to the ruins, the two-story structure with its fading whitewash was at the highest point in the village and somewhat isolated from the local population. The second floor was one spacious room with three large open-air windows facing the harbor. This was where everyone slept and stored their belongings. It was hard to tell how many people were living there. Laura and Laura were splitting the next morning, and Andrew said he was leaving in a few days. Sleeping bags were scattered around the room. I counted nine including mine.

I made more friends that night at Marika's. Andrew, Laura, and Laura introduced me to a slew of characters, not the least of whom was the middle-aged man with gray hair and glasses from the night before. His name was Andreas, and he was a goatherd from the nearby mountain village of Livaniana. Andreas polished off Retsina like it was water. The chess dudes were nowhere to be seen, but Andreas had found three more drinking companions. Two were Canadians. Dalton was from Ontario, and Ryan was from British Columbia. The third was an American from Westport, Connecticut, named Steve. I was happy to join their team.

It was a raucous night. Andreas only spoke Greek, and I could not understand a thing he was saying. However, drinking was still the universal language. Somewhere in all the revelry, it was revealed that Andreas had invited the four us to some sort of barn-raising in his village the following Sunday in exchange for food and drink. I was pretty fucked up and not exactly sure what I was signing up for, but I told them to count me in. It sounded like a cool thing to do.

I struck up a conversation with the couple from that morning and the previous night. Their names were Wilhelm and Juliette, and they were staying in the same house I was. So were Dalton, Ryan, and Steve. I did the math, and all the sleeping bags seemed to be accounted for. That didn't explain where the missing chess dudes and the other freaks at Marika's were crashing. I was especially curious about the dude at the other table with a chick on each arm. He looked a little like Jerry Garcia. The chicks were gorgeous and hanging on his every word. They each had long jet-black hair and, like Juliette, were slim and seductive. They were clearly out of my league.

Brown Hair Laura caught me staring at them and whispered in my ear.

"That's the American poet Dewey and his two French girls," she said. "They're staying in the house just below us with two other French guys."

"Are the French girls with the French guys?" I asked.

"No," replied Brown Hair Laura. "They're both with Dewey."

That settled it. I was on to something. I needed to become a poet. If pretending to be a writer had netted me both Robin and Silvia with an *I*, I could only imagine how fucking great my life would be if I was a real poet like Dewey.

I lost track of how many glasses of Retsina I consumed that night, but I discovered the next morning that I was twenty-four drachmas poorer. I had counted on sharing my sleeping bag with Brown Hair Laura, but I don't think that happened. I vaguely remember staggering back to the house as part of a large group. The next thing I knew, it was morning and the unforgiving sun was shining its cruel spotlight on me through one of the window openings in the wall. I was on top of my sleeping bag, naked, and the only one in the room. My testicles were on fire.

Last night's alcohol and camaraderie might have dulled the pain, but it was morning and I was awake, alone and sober. There was no escaping the fact that my balls had a nasty sunburn. So did the cheeks of my ass. Making matters worse, I sensed another bout of diarrhea about to begin. I jumped into my cutoffs, pulled a roll of toilet paper from my pack, and ran barefoot down the concrete steps.

I was in a panic. Steve the American was sitting on a wood chair on the concrete patio, sipping coffee from a tin cup. When he saw me rush out of the building, he immediately recognized my predicament. Before I could say a word, he pointed toward the trail and imparted another pearl of wisdom about life in Loutro.

"There are some ruins behind the house where everyone takes a shit," he said. "Follow your nose. It's just to the left of the trail."

It was a disgusting place but one that I would visit every morning while I was in Loutro. Calling it ruins was a generous description. All that remained was the stone foundation of a house that encircled loose patches of scrub brush and scattered tufts of dry grass. A well-worn path led to an opening in the wall where a door once stood. The smell was overpowering. The trick was to find a virgin space on the ground and hold your breath long enough to do your business. Piles of shit were everywhere. Some were fresh, while others had been there for ages. What they all had in common was the desperate look of diarrhea.

When I returned to the house, Steve was still there sipping his coffee.

"That's where we all go every morning," he said. "Dewey calls it the Proverbial Squat."

"I'm thirsty," I said. "Where can I get some water?"

"I'll show you where the well is," Steve said. "I'll get the bucket."

Steve was the teacher, and I was his student. I paid close attention as he taught another class about life in Loutro. I followed him down the path. We turned to the right and proceeded past a leafy pomegranate tree with red fruit that loomed large between two modest one-story homes. According to my teacher, the spring-fed well was thirty-five deep and was the sole source of water for the inhabitants of Loutro. Round and approximately four feet in diameter, this hole in the earth was encased by an uneven wall of laid stone that extended a foot and a half above ground. A round wood beam with a bent steel handle on one end straddled the center of the hole. It rested in the cradle of two Y-shaped posts. A crumpled body of thick rope slept in a pile on the ground next to the well. One end of it was fastened to the beam. The other was tied to the handle of a large wood bucket sitting on the wall that looked to hold up to three gallons of water. Steve picked up the bucket and tossed it down into the dark chasm. The pile of long rope leaped to its feet and began to unravel as it took off in hot pursuit of the fleeing bucket. A few seconds later, we heard the soft echo of a distant splash. After pausing to let the bucket fill with water, Steve grabbed the handle with both hands and began cranking. As the heavy bucket made its slow but steady climb to the surface, the rope wrapped itself around the wood beam like it was trying to choke it. When it arrived, Steve poured the fresh water into the tin bucket he had brought with him. As we turned to leave, he offered me the honor of carrying it back up to the house. I accepted. When we got there, he told me to set it in the shade just inside the door. He emptied his tin cup, dipped it in the bucket and offered me a cup of water.

It was a good start to another good day. It was morning, I was barely awake, and I had already received two more lessons about life in Loutro. Knowing where to take a shit and where to find water, it didn't get any more basic than that. Ready for whatever was next, I decided to venture down to Marika's for yet another omelet.

When I got there, Andrew and the two Lauras were just finishing theirs. The girls' backpacks were resting against the seawall. Brown Hair Laura had saved me the seat next to her. She handed me a slip of paper with her full name and an address in Pacific Palisades, California, scribbled on it.

"If you are ever in California," she said, "look me up.

104

Loutro was as much a state of mind as it was a place. I was like a watch that someone forgot to rewind. I seemed to be floating along in slow motion, prepared to stay there as long as I could. There was no reason to go anywhere else. The USA and the life I left behind were performing a vanishing act in my rearview mirror. I didn't have anything or anyone to go back for. Still, I had a lot of shit to sort out. I was running out of money. How was I going to solve that problem?

My needs in life had become primordial, and my senses were on high alert. As I was about to discover, life in Loutro would pass each test with flying colors. Here I was, living on a Greek island in a remote village reached only by foot or boat. I would find food, water, and a place to sleep. I would be interacting with flawed saints and enterprising sinners from a multitude of countries, as well as immersing my heart and soul in the local culture. The solitude I was so desperately searching for would rest at my fingertips. I would swim with the fish in the pristine waters of the Libyan Sea and run naked like a child with the ghosts of ancient civilizations on deserted beaches. I would explore supernatural caves and visit tiny hamlets that had been forgotten by time. I would read books, write poetry, and even get laid once in a while.

All this and I would be living on less than a dollar a day.

Of course, there was no way for me to know that morning what the future had in store for me as I watched the small passenger boat push off from the dock and whisk the two Lauras away to Hora Sfakion and out of my life. I planted my flag at Marika's until midday, absorbing as much as I could about the village, its people, and how to survive and thrive there. I started out sitting alone with Andrew, but we were soon joined by the Canadians, Dalton, and

Ryan. Andrew and Dalton would be leaving in a few days, but Ryan said he was thinking of staying most of the summer. When I revealed my plan to make Loutro my home for the next month or two, it was clear that I had been accepted. The three of them were a wealth of knowledge, opening up and sharing all that they had learned while staying there. They also reminded me that we had volunteered to work in Andreas's village on Sunday in exchange for food and drink.

I learned that the people of Crete and the citizens of Loutro were proud and independent. The island had been home to the Minoans, the earliest advanced European civilization that peaked nearly two thousand years before the birth of Christ and centuries before the birth of modern Athens. We were sitting in a region known as Sfakia, which had been a hotbed of resistance for the past two centuries. Two hundred years ago, the brave citizens of the nearby mountain village of Anopolis had risen up against the Ottoman Empire and managed to function as an independent nation for more than a year before their revolt was finally crushed. Ruled over by both the Turks and Greeks, the people of Crete had fought viciously for their independence every step of the way. In addition to their involvement in the Greek War of Independence that began in 1821, they had staged five uprisings between 1841 and 1898, at which time they finally achieved complete independence from Turkey.

According to Andrew, emotions were still raw when it came to World War II. Hitler's Third Reich had launched a major assault on the island in the spring of 1941. Crete became the home to a major resistance movement throughout the entire war. The land was rugged and dominated by a massive mountainous backbone with peaks stretching into the sky nearly eight thousand feet. The Germans never really gained a firm foothold on the island. The guerilla fighting was fierce, and the brutality of the Nazis was unspeakable. Hundreds of men, women, and children were lined up in front of firing squads, and the homes of entire villages were razed to the ground.

Ryan shared a mind-blowing story about an incident involving a German tourist that occurred just a month earlier. It seems that the middle-aged dude was on holiday with his family and was showing them around the island. They were in a nearby mountain village when the dude was said to have remarked to one of the locals that he had been there during the war and had always wanted to return because the place was so beautiful. An elderly man who heard what was being said went into his house to get his rifle. When he returned, he proceeded to gun down the moron in front of the moron's wife and two daughters and several other witnesses. By the time the police arrived, the old man had gone into hiding, and none of the locals would admit to witnessing the shooting or identify the shooter. The story was that the Nazis had slaughtered dozens of families in that village during the war, and the old man had lost both parents and his younger sister.

Steve the American pulled up a chair just as Ryan was finishing the story.

"Hey, man," he said. "These people have a strong sense of right and wrong, and they have their own code of justice."

"Are they cool with us being here?" I asked.

"Sure," he said, "just as long you respect their village, their families, and their culture."

Ryan had another story.

"A few days before you got here," he said, "some American asshole was skinny-dipping at the end of the beach in full view of everyone in the village. Giorgos walked down, pulled him out of the water, and beat the shit out of him. Giorgos was pissed that this dude was swimming naked where everyone could see him, including Giorgos's wife and two young daughters."

"Is it okay to swim naked over at the beach on the other side of the ruins?" I asked.

"It's cool," offered Steve. "The people here have a live-and-let-live attitude. They are okay with whatever you want to do on your own or behind closed doors. Just don't fuck with them or their families."

Ryan chimed in. "It's why we don't do drugs here," he said.

"Yeah," Steve laughed, "but you can drink all the rotgut Retsina you want."

Andrew turned serious again.

"There is still plenty of political unrest in Greece today," he said, "especially here on Crete."

He went on to tell me about all the shit that had been happening in the country over the past few months. Back in May, a Greek commander had docked his naval destroyer in Italy and refused to return to Greece after learning that several of his fellow officers had been arrested and tortured while he was participating in a NATO exercise.

"Papadopoulos has just declared himself president," he said. "He is holding a referendum at the end of July to legitimize his new authority. The people here are not happy about it. This is Crete. They do not like to be ruled by anyone. There may be some unrest."

Like it or not, I could see there was no escaping the real world. I had not been paying attention to American politics or world events since dropping acid in Florida and hopping on a plane to Europe. Was I delusional enough to think that just because I was so fixated on this personal journey of self-discovery that I would find a place untouched by all the bullshit? I was living in a country ruled by a military dictatorship. The depressing part was that it had the full support of Tricky Dick and the US government. That asshole seemed to be following me everywhere.

It was enough education for one day. I wanted to go for a swim and clear my head.

I thought of Brown Hair Laura. I couldn't get the vision of her luscious golden-brown body out of my mind. I owed her big time. I had gotten laid again, and for that I was eternally grateful. Livaniana Beach and the caves were just the icing on the cake.

"I'm going over to the beach this afternoon," I said. "Anyone want to go with me?"

Steve was game. So was Andrew.

"I'll see if Wilhelm and Juliette want to come with us," he volunteered.

That sounded cool to me. Even better, I was hoping that someone would pry the other two French girls loose from Dewey the American Poet and bring them along. It would make for another perfect day in paradise.

105

Andreas handed me the leather flask and gestured for me to take a swig.

"Poly krasi, kala ypnos," he said.

It was a phrase that he had repeated many times down at Marika's. It meant if you drank a lot of wine, you would sleep well at night. We were sitting under the solitary olive tree that provided the only shade between the beach and the ruins. I had spent the entire afternoon diving off the mighty rock, swimming in and out of caves and sunbathing on the coarse sand. Livaniana Beach was where I would go every day to read, write, and search for inner peace. Some days I was joined by four or five other naked souls, and I felt a spiritual connection with each of them. Like me, they were celebrating the noble pursuit of pleasure.

On this particular day, I had gone to the beach alone. As I was taking it all in, it felt as if I was the only human within a million miles. There was nothing to indicate what century I was in. It wasn't until I slipped into my shorts and started up the trail that I realized I was being watched. I wasn't sure how long he had been watching me, but he was sitting in the shade and smiling as I approached the tree. A few dozen goats were grazing nearby. I offered my greetings.

"Yassou," I said.

"Yassou," he replied, handing me the goatskin leather bag. I took a hit. The wine was warm and tasted bitter.

"Efharisto," I said and passed it back to him.

Knowing how to say "Hello" and "Thank you" in Greek wasn't much, but it was a start. If I was going to live here for a while, it was important that I learn a little of the language. The locals seemed pleased whenever I tried to speak to them in their native tongue. I knew the word *parakalo* which meant "please." I could say "Kalimera" and "Kalinikta," which was how the Greeks wished one another "Good morning" and "Good night."

Andrew, Dalton, and a few other regulars were gone. The village had suddenly become a flurry of activity as backpackers from the gorge descended on Loutro each afternoon. Most moved on to Hora Sfakion, but the steady flow added an occasional adventurer to the mix to replace one who had departed. Lucky for me, one of them was Mel.

Her full name was Melanie, but she went by Mel. She was Canadian, and she had arrived in Loutro with her Greek friend Nea, whose full name was Cornelia, and two dudes, Robert from Scotland and Joe, an Italian from Rome. It was early evening when I ventured down to Marika's. I had spent most of the day alone on the beach, rereading *Desolation Angels* and feeling a special kinship with Kerouac's alter ego Jack Duluoz. I found comfort in Jack's solitary life as a fire lookout on Desolation Peak and how the months of isolation and meditation prepared him to rejoin the world of human contact. I could relate. I had an all-over tan, a clear head, and a strong desire for a glass of Ouzo. I was also in the mood to make some new friends. I could tell that the four of them had been drinking for a while. They looked like an interesting group, so I pulled up a chair and joined the party.

They had already found a place to stay. Dewey the American Poet had offered my new friends the questionable comfort of his stone patio. Nea, Mel, and Joe would only be staying a few days. I gathered that Robert was planning on staying longer. He was hard to understand. Being from Scotland, he was supposedly speaking English, but his heavy accent made his words nearly incomprehensible. Mel was from Alberta but was living in Athens where she had met Nea. The hirsute character named Joe wore a curly black Afro and didn't speak any English. It was like going to a United Nations cocktail party without a translator.

It was definitely a *poly krasi, kala ypnos* kind of night. I woke up early the next morning with a craving for pommes frites. When I got to Marika's, Nea and Mel were the only ones there. They were drinking coffee and breaking bread. Marika walked out, and I asked her for pommes frites. She shook her head no and walked back inside. Ten minutes later, she returned with an omelet. While I was wolfing it down, I noticed Mel writing in a small notebook. When I finished eating, she tore out a page and handed to me. It was a poem.

Blue eyes
What ja thinkin'
Blue eyes
Where ja going
Hey—
Blue eyes
What's your name?
Blue eyes.
Alberta?
Brecky's on the table.
Blue eyes
Omelet again.
Alberta
What ja thinking?
Blue eyes
What's your name?

It wasn't a very good poem, but I got the message.

"Would you girls like me to show you the beach that I go to every day?" I asked.

Mel turned to Nea, and they both nodded.

"Can we go now?" Mel asked.

Brown Hair Laura had taught me well. I knew she would be proud. I led the girls up the hill, past the ruins, and down the path. Andreas was sitting beneath his olive tree, sipping on his flask.

"Yassou," I said.

"Kalimera," Andreas replied. He had a big smile on his face. He knew what he would be watching today.

When we reached the beach, we took off our clothes and ran into the water. I was amazed how my life kept getting better and better. What had I ever done to deserve this day? I still wasn't convinced there was actually a God, but just as I had observed on the train from Luxembourg to Amsterdam, the circumstantial evidence was tough to ignore. Standing on what appeared to be the chest of God on Franklin Mountain? Mary Baker Eddy and Lurch? Jesus disguised as Tony from Australia? Emily Keenan? Isadora Duncan? Robin and Silvia with an *I*? And now this, a deserted beach on a Greek island with two beautiful naked women? Granted, it may not have been God doing His thing, but someone was sure as hell looking out for me.

They were both in their early twenties. To me, Nea was mesmerizing. Blessed with the curves of a voluptuous Greek statue, she had thin shoulders with wide breasts and wide hips and was slightly overweight in her lower body. The clear and precise shape of her face was the work of a master sculptor. She owned a brilliant pair of turquoise eyes. With her dark hair, high forehead, straight nose, and olive skin, she was the Mediterranean ideal of classical beauty. Mel, on the other hand, was several inches taller with fair skin and blond hair. She looked Scandinavian and reminded me a little of Isadora. I would have been happy making love to either one or both of them, but only Mel seemed that interested in me. Still, it was worth a shot, so I asked them both if they would like to explore the caves with me.

Nea looked over at Mel and smiled. They had already discussed it.

"You and Mel go without me," she said. "I think I will stay here on the beach."

106

Dewey was throwing a party. He and the two French girls were leaving the next day. There seemed to be a changing of the guard. More and more transients from the gorge were coming ashore, and this was turning off many in the international community of freaks who had been staying there a while. Some of them concluded it might be a good time to split. The house had taken on at least five or six new residents I didn't know. Mel was gone. She and Nea had left two days earlier.

Dewey was going out in style. He had gone to Hora Sfakion that morning and returned with a boatload of food and alcohol. In addition to all the bottles of Retsina and Ouzo, he brought back a case of FIX, a popular Greek beer. Everyone including the locals was invited. Loaves of French bread were there to absorb the alcohol, along with six large watermelons and several blocks of cheese to feed our faces.

Since I loved Ouzo, had acquired a taste for Retsina, and hadn't had a beer since Switzerland, logic dictated that I should drink all three. I took turns, taking great care not to play favorites. My memory of that night is a bit spotty. I had my fortune told by a gypsy fortune-teller who predicted I would be leaving in eight days. It might have been the best party I had been to since Miles Jaffe's mad orgy on Beacon Street back in March. I remember grooving to a couple of dudes playing guitars. I have a vague memory of rapping with a few fresh arrivals, but I have no recollection of their names, faces, or even what we talked about. What I was doing when I hit the pavement is a total mystery.

When I regained consciousness, I had no clue where I was or how I ended up there. I was facedown on a slab of concrete and drooling from one side of my mouth. I struggled to get on my feet. It took me a second or two to focus, but when I did, I saw that I was on Dewey's patio. The party was over, and I was the only one still there. I stuck my head in the door and saw what I assumed to be the outline of a naked Dewey sleeping on a mattress between the two French girls, who were also naked. Apparently, no one had tried to revive me or help me home. I had been left to fend for myself. I didn't know what time it was. The village was sound asleep, dark and void of human sound. The silence was broken only by the mating calls of male cicadas. The electric buzz of the high-pitch serenade was roaring through the village like a passing train. I felt like shit. It was as if someone was driving a railroad spike into my head. I stumbled off the patio onto the dirt path that I hoped led to my sleeping bag. My memory pointed me in the right direction, but it didn't have the decency to point out all the damn rocks. After stubbing my toe a few times, I decided I had to piss. I unbuttoned my cutoffs and let them fall to the ground. Holding my cock with both hands, I pointed it over the one-foot wall that marked the path up to the house. That's when I heard her voice.

"HEY, YOU DUMB BASTARD!" she yelled. "DON'T PISS ON ME."

I looked down and saw that my dick was pointed directly at the vague outline of a woman sitting on a rock.

"Sorry," I said, spinning into an abrupt one-eighty. I couldn't hold it any longer. I started peeing.

"Jesus," she said. "When did you piss last?"

I didn't have an answer. All I could do was moan. I just kept pissing and pissing. I couldn't wait to find my sleeping bag and pass out. This had to be a dream. I finished my business, pulled up my cutoffs, and put away my cock. That's when I felt a hand on my waist.

"You look like you could use some help getting home," she said. "Where are you staying?"

"Over there," I confessed, pointing to the two-story structure up the path.

"Come on," she said. "I'll help you."

Who was this mystery woman that I had almost urinated on? It was too dark to make out her face, and I didn't recognize her voice. She sounded American, but her accent was one I hadn't heard before. What did I have to lose? We staggered up the rocky trail, neither of us saying a word. We reached our destination, stumbled across the cracked patio, and entered the house. We heard snoring.

"Where are you sleeping?" the mystery woman whispered.

"Upstairs," I whispered back.

I was hoping no one had copped my sleeping bag or the beat-up mattress that I had inherited a day earlier when one of the regulars left. Seniority had its benefits. The mystery woman led me to the foot of the stairs and whispered for me to go first. She planted her hands firmly on my ass and pushed me up the steps. When we arrived on the second floor, I was relieved to find my sleeping bag and quasi-mattress unoccupied. We tried to be quiet as we stepped carefully over and around the comatose souls, some of whom were sleeping there for the first time. The trick was to get undressed and get in bed without waking anyone. She was way ahead of me. While I was fumbling around, trying to unbutton my shorts, she pulled off her blouse, slid out of her jeans, unzipped the bag, and slipped inside. It was pure poetry.

My entrance wasn't quite as graceful.

"Careful," she whispered. "You'll rip the sleeping bag."

I still had not seen her face. I didn't know her name, where she was from, or what she looked like. Her hand was on my cock, and that's all that mattered. She had her work cut out for her. The room was spinning, and I was having trouble getting it up. Attempting to fuck in my present condition bordered on the absurd, but I was just like any other dude on the planet. It was too good an opportunity to pass up. She was trying to jerk me off, so I placed my hand between her legs to return the favor. I heard a few bodies shifting and coughing on the floor in that universal way people have of letting you know they are in the room. I didn't care, and neither did she. Our hands were working in unison. The mystery woman was heaving back and forth on the mattress and causing quite a commotion, but I could tell she was getting impatient with me. She kept stroking me faster and faster, but I still wasn't up to the challenge. Frustrated that this might be going nowhere, she changed her strategy. She let go of my unresponsive manhood, yanked out my wet sloppy fingers, and sent her mouth into battle. That turned out to be the magic formula. I had an erection in a matter of seconds. When she was convinced it was real and could stand the test of time, she climbed aboard. That's when I saw her face for the first time.

The next morning, I was the first person in the room to awaken. I managed to untangle myself from the arms and legs of last night's encounter and put my shorts on without waking anyone. I felt awful. I wasn't sure if I had to vomit or take or shit. I looked down at the guardian angel. She was lying on her side at the edge of the mattress, half out of the sleeping bag. Her breasts were small, and one of them was touching the floor as she slept. She couldn't have been more than eighteen or nineteen. She had straight red hair, and her face was lac-quered with such innocence that I found it hard to believe she was the same creature I had almost pissed on the night before.

I stepped quietly over the lifeless bodies and tiptoed down the stairs. If this had been a movie, my grand entrance into the morning sun would have been accompanied by a powerful blast of music from Stanley Kubrick's *2001*. As it was, I simply hurried off the patio and raced up to the ruins behind the house to do the Proverbial Squat. I made it just in time before the diarrhea kicked in. Unfortunately, I had forgotten to grab my roll of toilet paper before I ran out. It was too late to do anything about it now. As the flies began to circle, I accepted my self-inflicted fate and pulled up my shorts. I stumbled out of the ruins and burst into a trot when I hit the path. The rocks that had given me so much trouble the night before were now a piece of cake. Dodging them like I was O. J. Simpson heading for the end zone, I darted past the white-washed houses, a barking dog, a couple of chickens, one pine, and two fig trees and dove headfirst into the cold water. This was becoming the regular routine for me after a night of drinking. The ten-minute swim each morning was the clos-est thing to a cure for my hangovers. It had a way of shocking me into a new day. Today, there was the added bonus of personal hygiene.

It was early, and I was the second one to arrive at Marika's. My Canadian friend Ryan was drinking coffee and reading his book. He was an extremely likeable dude. Twenty-three years old, he was an engineer from Vancouver who designed heating systems before quitting his job to travel the world. Ryan wasn't a lost soul. Unlike me, he was well-grounded and didn't seem to be running away from anything or searching for some unattainable meaning of life. He also liked to play chess. We had just finished our second game when she appeared at the table and pulled up a chair.

"Are you a faggot?" she asked.

It suddenly hit me whom she reminded me of. With her freckles and red hair, she was the spitting image of my mother. And just like my mother, she wasn't all that impressed with me.

"I think the word is *gay*," I said. "Why do you ask? Was I that bad last night?"

"Oh, I was just wondering," she said. "It's your mannerisms, you know, the way you walk and the way you move your hands. You seem, if you don't mind me saying so, a little effeminate."

Her name was Elena. She was Greek, but her parents had packed up the family and moved to Weston, Massachusetts, when she was thirteen. That explained the unique accent. She was spending the summer in Greece and was sharing an apartment in Athens with her older sister. It was my turn to ask questions.

"Tell me something, Elena," I said. "What were you doing sitting on that rock last night?"

"Waiting for you," she answered. "I knew you had to wake up sooner or later and walk home."

"How did you know where I lived?"

"I've been watching you," she said. "Even though you're a little on the faggy side, you are kind of cute. I bet you get laid quite a bit around here."

I guessed that was her idea of a compliment. A repeat of the last night's performance looked promising. I asked her if she would like to go over to Livaniana Beach that afternoon and explore the caves with me.

She just laughed.

"Listen," she said. "You need to try that line on someone else. Last night was a lot of fun, but I'm leaving tomorrow and I'm not going to screw you again."

With that, she turned her attention to the one-arm fisherman who was on the dock about to get into his boat after dropping off his morning triumphs. It was amazing to me how much control this one man had over everyone's diet. He seemed to be the sole supplier of fish. Some days he showed up empty-handed. This morning his boat was full. Today would be fish day at Marika's.

"How did he lose his arm?" she asked.

"I don't know," I said. "The rumor going around is that he lost it in a fishing accident before the war."

Elena stood up. "I think I'll ask him," she said.

She ran after him and shouted out something. The old man stopped and turned around. He looked annoyed. Elena kept talking. I couldn't hear what she was saying, but she was speaking Greek, so it didn't matter. The one-arm fisherman listened to her without saying a word, but it was obvious he was getting pissed off. Even from where I sat, I could see the large vein twitching in his neck. When Elena finished talking, the old man glared at her in silence. Finally, he spoke. Waving his one hand in the air, he ranted and raved for a good minute and then stormed off to his boat. Elena walked back to the table, shrugging her shoulders.

"What did he say?" I asked.

"He said that little girls like me should mind their own business."

107

The gypsy turned out to be a shitty fortune-teller. Three weeks came and went and I was still in Loutro. Each day brought something new. This tiny village, with its primitive lifestyle and steady stream of international characters, provided the perfect setting for my pursuit of pleasure. Hedonism fit me like a glove. There was no reason to leave. I was convinced I had found the utopian balance between free will and inertia. I woke up each sun-drenched morning and did whatever the fuck I wanted unless I was acted upon by an external force. Life revolved around the basics. I knew where to relieve myself. Beyond that, it was about food and shelter.

When it came to food, it wasn't just omelets or pommes frites. Marika cooked us the fresh fish caught by the one-arm man whenever he hit the jackpot. There were also contributions from Steve. He owned a spear gun and a dive mask and was quite skilled at spear fishing. Steve liked to free-dive along the perimeter of the small rock island protecting the harbor. I dove with him a few times just to observe and learn. I didn't have a mask, so I couldn't see as well as he could. Steve let me borrow his, along with the spear gun, and gave me the chance to try my luck. With the mask on, it felt like I was swimming inside an aquarium. I aimed and shot several times but came up empty. Nailing one of these slippery bastards was definitely harder than it looked.

Spearing a fish was a simple and sanitized way to score a meal, but slaughtering an innocent lamb revealed the true nature of the Loutro food chain. I was playing chess with Steve late one afternoon when Andreas's drinking buddy Manoli strolled onto the dock in front of Marika's, pulling the condemned creature at the end of his rope. The sad look in the lamb's eyes told me that it knew what was about to happen. Lifting the lamb's head high into the air with his left hand, Manoli held a long knife in his right and, with one effortless motion, slit the poor thing's throat. That's when the work began. Manoli cut a small hole in one of the lamb's hind legs and blew into it, pushing the blood to the next leg. After that, he began the slow process of skinning the animal. After pulling the skin back over the hind legs, Manoli cut off its head. The lamb was then hung by its hind legs from the closest tree branch. What followed was a slow tugging process, aided by a smaller knife that pulled away at the skin between the wool and body. Once the skin was off, Manoli split open the chest cavity and removed the spaghetti-like intestines. He then spent a long time blowing through the condom-like intestine lining to make sure it was clean, causing it to flap violently in the air. When he finished, he pulled out the stomach, cut it open, and dumped its contents into the water. Manoli tossed the stomach lining to a skinny black dog who had been sitting patiently beside him on the dock, waiting for its treat. He then removed the heart and liver and carried them into Marika's kitchen. In less time than it took me to drink a glass of Retsina, the meek, cuddly lamb had been transformed into a large slab of meat. Manoli carried the slab inside where it would be cut into portions and become that night's meal at Marika's.

As a last resort, there was the market in Hora Sfakion. Every three or four days, a few brave freaks in the international community volunteered to leave their sanctuary and gather supplies for the others who stayed behind. Everyone's money was pooled, and the fearless souls always returned unscathed with the communal necessities in hand. Soap, toilet paper, watermelons, French baguettes, and beer were the most requested. Since no one really wanted to go there, they took turns biting the bullet. There were two ways to get to Hora Sfakion. Catching a boat ride over in the morning was the easiest, but the two-hour hike along the coast was more popular. When it was Sean's or Steve's turn to go, they chose the latter. Sean was a handsome Irishman in his midtwenties who had been staying in Loutro for over a month. An artist who had quit his job at an advertising firm in Dublin, he was now traveling the world and painting landscapes. He wore a distinguished-looking moustache and was extremely likeable. He spoke with a firm voice, yet the words were soft and melodic, akin to poetry being put to music. Like so many of us, Sean had discovered the magic of Loutro and was calling it home. Since I had not yet had the privilege of making the journey to Hora Sfakion, he and Steve suggested I tag along.

"Bring a bar of soap," Steve said.

I had not had an actual bath or washed my hair since Athens. I was relying on my dips in the Libyan Sea and an occasional bucket of water from the well dumped over my head for my personal hygiene. I hated to admit it, but I didn't own a bar of soap.

"That's okay," Steve said. "You can borrow one of mine."

The coastal trail was a treacherous goat path that hugged the side of the cliffs approximately two hundred feet above the water. I was nervous walking so close to the edge. I broke off a crooked branch from an olive tree and used it as a crutch to keep my balance. My sneakers were in the final stages of life. The shoelaces that I had borrowed from Steve and tied around my feet were all that kept them from falling apart. The scariest portions of the hike were when the path snaked around a section of the cliff that jutted out over the water. We negotiated two of these headlands in the first hour. Both times, the open breeze rushed up to greet me, and I was too afraid to look down. I was paranoid that I might get dizzy and plunge over the side. After we conquered the second one, the trail descended the full two hundred feet down to the sea and exposed the real reason everyone chose to walk to Hora Sfakion.

I had been told stories of the legendary freshwater beach, but they didn't prepare me for the beauty and absolute grandeur of this coastal oasis. Situated at the halfway point on the trail, it presented the ideal time and place to take a break. As I was soon to learn, it was more than just another deserted cove seemingly untouched by the hands of time or human activity. There were a few stretches of sand, but the beach was mostly a mixture of smooth stones and small pebbles. What was unusual was the shade provided by the rows of cypress trees growing not more than fifty feet from the water. There was very little breeze. Nestled in a semicircular cove, the beach was sheltered from the wind by the sheer cliffs of the mountain backdrop.

We didn't waste any time. We stripped off our shorts and sneakers and raced into the sparkling blue water. The sea was icy cold. It felt refreshing but was a whole lot chillier than what I had grown accustomed to on Livaniana Beach.

I had never seen water this clear. The sun danced along the surface, and the schools of fish rushed between my legs and flew around me like flashes of light. The water felt warmer the longer we swam. When we finally got back on the beach, Sean and Steve wanted to show me something. They were standing about twenty feet apart when they dropped to their knees and started digging with their hands. They scooped up and tossed aside the stones and pebbles until they reached a thin layer of coarse sand and gravel. They continued to dig. Steve was the first to hit pay dirt. As he dug deeper and wider, the hole began to fill with water. Sean followed suit, and in a matter of minutes, they each created a pool of water the size of a small bathtub. Steve walked over to his abandoned shorts and pulled two bars of soap out of a pocket. He tossed one over to me.

"Start digging," he said. "This is your one chance to get clean."

I dug my man-made bathtub midway between them. It was amazing how quickly I found water and how surreal it felt to be washing my hair and taking a bath in a hole on a deserted beach on the southern coast of Crete. The fresh water was cold at first but was soon warmed by the hot sun. I was ready to attribute the phenomena of fresh water to some supernatural force, but Steve was the one who set me straight. His explanation was logical and similar to one I might have heard on TV from Mr. Wizard when I was a kid. The fresh water was from the snowmelt of the White Mountains and was carried to the sea through a series of underground water routes with a single-minded purpose of joining forces at this one magical spot. It was why the water was so cold and why the trees were able to flourish there.

Clean, refreshed, and ready to take on the world, we got dressed and continued on our crusade. The initial slog up the footpath was a bit more precarious than earlier. We passed a few athletic mountain goats that seemed to defy gravity while they foraged for food along the side of the mountain. After a scary hairpin turn near another secluded beach, we reached a paved road that let us cruise the rest of the way into Hora Sfakion. As we approached our destination, I saw why my fellow nomads in Loutro avoided it like the plague. Hora Sfakion was a small village of not more than one or two hundred people, but compared to where we had just come from, it felt as if we were walking into Grand Central Station. This was where the deluge of hikers from the gorge were deposited before hopping aboard a bus to carry them back to the north coast and the port cities of Hania and Iraklion. I was suddenly surrounded by the very creatures I had been trying so hard to avoid. Steve saw the freaked-out look in my eyes.

"Hey, man," he said. "This place is a trip. Don't flip out. We've got three hours to kill before the boat leaves to take us back. We'll get some food in our stomachs, drink a few beers, and buy our supplies. Just be mellow and enjoy the show."

He was right, of course. Mingling with creatures for a few hours was no big deal. I had been doing it my entire life. There was no reason to have a nervous breakdown.

108

The first thing I did each morning was pinch myself. I wanted to make sure this wasn't a dream. But that's what it felt like. Was I kidding myself? Had I really fallen into the arms of Utopia? Could I live here? I tried to imagine what life would be like if the summer was over and I was the only foreigner left in the village. Would I be accepted? Would I even be happy here? Although I cherished my solitude and went out of my way to avoid the vast majority of humans who crossed my path, I wasn't so delusional to think that I could completely cut myself off from the outside world. As idyllic as life had become, I knew nothing lasted forever. I vowed to make every second of every minute count while I was in Loutro.

My favorite time of the day was just after sunrise. The early morning hours were the most beautiful. The air was cool, and the village evoked the serenity of its ancient past. I loved the precious moments before everything came to life. Ryan and I were the only foreigners who awoke this early. The Greeks had already eaten breakfast and were milling about. The women were sweeping their steps and washing their clothes. The men were preparing their boats. My morning plunge into the sea had become a ritual. It made for a quick recovery from the heavy nights of drinking. Why was I drinking so much? A good question perhaps, but what did it matter? If there had been any drugs floating around, I would have been doing them instead. After all, wasn't my life here all about the camaraderie?

I was back in the same house after a brief attempt to escape the revolving door of bodies that called it home for a night or two. I had moved out with Wilhelm and Juliette the same day that Elena left. They had discovered an abandoned building perched above the water just beyond the beach at the far end of the village. We had become friends, and they asked me if I wanted to move in with them. Like me, they had grown tired of all the commotion and noise and were searching for some semblance of privacy.

The one-story structure was dark and dusty. It was a mess, filled with broken chairs, a long table missing one of its legs, and two sets of bedsprings without mattresses. We decided to spend the night there and start the clean-up the next morning.

It probably qualified as one of the worst nights in my twenty-five years on the planet. I didn't get a wink of sleep, and neither did Wilhelm or Juliette. The bedsprings were uncomfortable, but that wasn't the problem. It was the rats. It was unnerving. I zipped my sleeping bag up over my head and prayed for hell night to be over. I had no idea how many rats there were. I could feel the brazen storm troopers racing up down and around me like it was Memorial Day and I was the track at the Indianapolis 500. They were relentless. Thankfully, I had trained for something like this when I was in grade school. My teachers had taught me how to hide under a desk and survive a nuclear attack from the likes of Nikita Khrushchev and the Russians. While they had not specifically prepared me for the invasion of rats on a Greek island, the same survival techniques applied. I kept my head down, closed my eyes, and hoped to live through it.

When morning broke, we came out with our hands up and surrendered. To the victor go the spoils of war. I was exhausted, my eyes were swollen, and my stomach was upset. The rats had won, and the broken chairs, three-legged table, and discarded bedsprings were all theirs. It was back to the old house. To our surprise, no one had even missed us. It was like we had never left.

The old house became my permanent residence. It belonged to one of the taverna owners in Hora Sfakion who didn't seem to care who or how many stayed there. All that mattered to him was that one of the transients showed up at his taverna each month with seven hundred drachmas. There were seven of us living there when the time came to pay the piper. My share worked out to be three dollars and thirty-five cents. Renting a house for less than twenty-five dollars a month seemed like a steal, but all we were really paying for was a two-story empty shell with a roof on top. There was no kitchen and no furniture. No doors. No windows. No water. No toilets. Still, no one was complaining. As far as we were concerned, we were living in a seaside castle.

The faces changed almost daily, but the core remained intact. Pierre, the French Canadian with a master's degree in linguistics, called it esprit de corps. Whatever it was called, it was real. An undeniable spirit and sense of community existed among the coterie of wanderers who were making Loutro their home. It was a unique and diverse group. Each person had a story, and each of their stories was embraced by the others, enthusiastically and free of judgment. The ones who stayed for just a day or two were afforded the same respect. Everyone had something to offer, be it wisdom, music, or sex.

There was massive turnover in the village during my first two weeks back in the old house. I was already starting to feel like an old-timer. No longer classified as one of the two-day or three-day transients, I had moved into that nebulous world between long-term foreigner and backpacker just passing through. Besides Pierre, the only ones who had been here longer were Wilhelm and Juliette, Steve the American, Ryan the Canadian, Sean the Irishman, and Robert from Scotland. Wilhelm and Juliette had taken over the house once occupied by Dewey and his two French girls and were sharing it with Pierre and Robert. That left plenty of room in the old house for Steve, Ryan, Sean, and me to welcome the next wave of new characters. A British couple were the first to move in, followed a day later by three women, one Greek and two Israelis. All five split after three days and were quickly replaced by the next ensemble. My attitude about interacting with people was coming full circle. Rather than avoid them, I was beginning to welcome all the new faces with open arms. I was more comfortable with myself and who I was. While many of those I was consorting with were more worldly and experienced than me, I no longer felt intimidated by their adventures or personas. I was continuing to evolve as a traveler. It had been a gradual assimilation of knowledge and confidence, but the osmosis was complete. I had become one of them. The number of international pilgrims who chose to stay was dwindling by the day. The village was thinning out, and the few who were trickling in were good people: mellow, creative, and intelligent. It was important to feed my mind as well as my body. I strove to create a social equilibrium, one that maintained a perfect balance between intellectual and physical stimulation. I spent most afternoons at Livaniana Beach. Nothing was more sensuous than lying naked on a smooth rock and letting the water caress my body with a thousand erotic fingertips. I felt a rush each time it washed over my thighs and ran up between my legs. Whether I was alone, with another lover, or with a few of my friends, the sensation was always the same. It was as if the Libyan Sea was making love to me. The days might have been lazy and rapturous, but the nights were uplifting, filled with guitar music, stimulating conversations, and ungodly amounts of alcohol. Politics, the upcoming plebiscite, and the state of Mother Earth dominated the spirited debates.

One night, I counted eight nationalities attempting to shape a world without borders. Each individual's life experience and country of origin fostered a unique perspective and a different opinion. We sometimes disagreed, but there was never any animosity. American, Canadian, Irish, Swiss, French, German, Belgian, and Greek: if we could all get along in this tiny village on the southern coast of Crete, then why was it so hard to do back in our real worlds? What bound us together here as one? Was it the rugged strength of the land and its people? Was it the eroticism of the sea? Was it the Retsina?

Whatever it was, I felt alive in this sensual paradise.

109

When I first met him, I thought he was American. His English was perfect, with an accent that suggested he might be from the Boston area. Only later did I learn he was Greek and that he was somewhat of a Renaissance man. The son of an Athens doctor, he was thirty years old and had been educated in Switzerland. Besides Greek and English, he was fluent in German, French, Italian, and Spanish. He was a published writer, the former lead singer of a popular Greek rock band, and a recently released political prisoner. Papadopoulos and the ruling military junta had considered him such a threat that they tossed his ass in jail for eighteen months. The time he spent behind bars had only strengthened his resolve. It was only fitting that Vassilis Dimitriou found his way to Crete, the breeding ground of Greek resistance for the last two centuries.

Vassilis would become a friend and a pivotal figure for me in the months to come. He was the very definition of charisma. A force of nature, his very presence in Loutro changed the social dynamic of our international band of seekers and the way we interacted with the locals. He was larger than life without aiming to be. That was his appeal. He wasn't trying to draw others in or lead anyone anywhere. It was an unassuming charm. Everyone loved his wry sense of humor and unique brand of cynicism. Barely five feet five inches tall, he was a little on the plump side and possessed a full scraggly beard that covered a face bursting with life and mischief.

He quickly became the intermediary between the foreigners and the villagers, explaining us to them and them to us. Expanding our conversations and interactions, we were soon able to form real relationships no longer premised on the ordering and delivery of food and alcohol. Most of the locals had never even been to the north coast of Crete, let alone left the island. While they appeared to take our being there in stride, I couldn't help thinking how we must have seemed like visitors from another planet to them. I posed the question to Vassilis.

"What do the people here think of us?" I asked.

Vassilis just chuckled. "They don't understand you," he said.

"What do you mean?" I replied.

Vassilis shook his head and laughed again.

"My friend," he said, "they don't understand why you come here. They don't understand why anyone would want to come here. You all come from other countries, from faraway places. They don't understand why you would leave your homes to come here."

"Don't they realize how beautiful it is here?" I asked.

"My friend," he said, "this is where they have lived their entire lives. It is the place where they work, where they raise their families. It is all they know."

"Do they like us?" I asked.

"They don't think like that," he said. "They just want you to respect them, their families, and their way of life. None of you will be here that long. In the winter, when the tourists are gone, many of them return to their homes in Anopolis."

Vassilis was a bona fide Zorba the Greek, a flesh-and-bone version of that larger-than-life fictional character created by Crete's native son Nikos Kazantzakis. Spending time with him made each day brighter and every night richer. His zest for life was contagious, and his energy was boundless. Whether it was music, literature, religion, or politics, he seemed wise beyond his years. I would have expected someone who had been imprisoned and tortured by his government to be angry and bitter, but he was just the opposite. He was cheerful and seemed not to have a care in the world.

Wisdom has a way of sneaking up on you when you least expect it. Late one night, as I sat alone with him just a few steps from the sea, Vassilis gave me a glimpse of what I assumed to be the guiding principle in his life. I was admiring the silhouette of a palm tree as it splashed across the full moon that was hurling its reflection over the water when he suddenly stopped strumming his guitar. He paused a moment before uttering a few words that I didn't understand. I asked him what he had just said.

He smiled at me with that now-familiar twinkle in his eye.

"I zoi einai san ena angouri," he repeated.

"What did you say?" I asked.

"My friend," he answered, "there are no English words to explain it."

I could have given up right then, but I was intrigued.

"Try me," I countered.

Vassilis used his hands whenever he spoke. They were as indispensable as his words when he was communicating a thought. This time, without them, it would have been impossible for him to explain what he was trying to tell me. He clasped them together and furrowed his brow.

"You see, my friend," he said. "In Greece, we say that life is like a cucumber."

"Life is like a cucumber?" I asked. "What does that mean?"

Vassilis hesitated. I could tell that he was struggling to find the words that someone like me would understand.

"It means, my friend," he said, "that some of us taste it and enjoy it..."

His voice tailed off, and he began wringing his hands together in a slow but forceful manner.

"While others," he continued, "others...they..."

He was lost for words. The muscles on his face mobilized in painful contortions as he gripped and squeezed what I imagined to be a very large cucumber. As he continued to twist and turn it, he emitted several grunts and groans. He looked to be in severe pain, as if someone was forcing the oversized cucumber up his ass.

He dropped his hands to his sides and let go of the cucumber.

"You see, my friend," he said. "There are no words to explain it in English."

110

Her long fingers were like golden pencils as they whispered the notes on her guitar.

Her magnificent blond hair concealed her face and fell over the strings like the low sweeping branches of a weeping willow tree. All that was visible were the gentle slopes of the narrow shoulders that guided my eyes down the skeleton arms so warmly camouflaged in golden flesh and fuzzy blond hairs. Her yoga stance implied serenity, and her soiled feet spoke of many journeys and a rich, full life. When she turned her head, a smooth freckled nose jumped out from beneath her golden locks. Her blue eyes were soft and bright, yet they seemed tired and wise beyond their years. She wore a strapless peasant dress that extended from her bosom to her knees. The dress was yellow with tree-branch patterns of lipstick red and what resembled leaves falling in faded greens. Her breasts were not large but more like ripened melons in correct proportion to her gracefully thin frame. Thick yellow hair crept from beneath her armpits with unbridled passion. Her legs were long, her calves slender, and her feet too large to belong to a woman. Her name was Jenny, and I was obsessed with her.

Jenny was from Florida and twenty-five years old. Beyond that, the details were a bit sketchy. She had done her college thing and West Coast thing and was now traveling the world alone. There was a reckless mystique to her. She had that same spaced-out distant look in her eyes that I had witnessed in Cheryl Prior. While outwardly warm and friendly, she could also be detached and cautious. At times, she seemed a little sad. As with Cheryl, someone must have really hurt her. Why did I want her so much? Was it because I couldn't have her? She was not the least bit impressed with me. We might have been the same age, but she was obviously more experienced and more mature than I was. She had crossed paths with hundreds of guys like me. The only male in Loutro who met her standards was Vassilis.

I was thrilled when she moved into the house with us. Vassilis was my best friend, and she was his lover, so we spent a lot of time together. There were the idle days when we traveled in groups over to Livaniana Beach. She was even prettier without her clothes on. I tried not to stare, but I couldn't keep my hungry eyes off her. At night, when Marika closed up shop, our international posse retreated back to the house where we listened to Jenny and Vassilis play their guitars and sing together. The painful part was sleeping a few feet away from them and having to watch and listen as they made love.

It took every ounce of willpower to keep my desire in check. It finally bubbled to the surface one night when a group of us were sitting in Marika's, solving the problems of the world with the help of Retsina and Ouzo. I had reached the point where I was slurring my words so badly that I was barely able to string them together in a coherent sentence. It was one of my asshole moments where my mouth neglected to consult with my brain. Vassilis had left the table to find Marika when, for some inexplicable reason, I thought I saw an opening. I asked Jenny if she wanted to sleep with me. That was bad enough, but I didn't stop there. I wanted to know why she was sleeping with Vassilis and not with me, what she saw in him that she didn't see in me. For Christ's sake, she was at least six inches taller than him, wasn't she? I told her I was crazy about her and was still babbling on in earshot of everyone when Vassilis returned to his chair.

It was an ugly performance. I had to hand it to both of them, the way they laughed it off and handled it in stride. To them, I must have seemed like a child. I might as well have asked Jenny why there was no tooth fairy or no Easter bunny. As for Vassilis, he was my wise friend and too cerebral to be upset with me. He understood that I would one day unravel what was presently a mystery to me, much the same way a curious child eventually learns there is no Santa Claus.

The next morning was worse than most. I woke with a demon hangover and such a splitting headache that it felt like I had stuck a fork in my eye. My diarrhea was more pronounced than usual, and I barely made it up to the ruins in time. When I took my ritual plunge into the sea, my facedown dead man's float lasted so long that it was amazing no one raced into the water to see if I had drowned. What amplified my pain was the shame and embarrassment that I felt when I recalled the previous night's fiasco. I was shocked to learn that no one cared or even remembered that I had made such an ass out of myself. We were a family, a giant amoeba capable of altering our size, shape, and makeup without sacrificing our shared affection for one another. Vassilis even gave us a name. He said that we would forever be known as the Loutro Order of the Amphibious Chicken.

Jenny stayed for ten days. After she left, Vassilis quickly filled the void on his mattress with Simone, a petite and sexy French girl with long jet-black hair. Her eyes sparkled like the stars that came out on a clear night, and she was no more than twenty years old. I was as obsessed with her as I had been with Jenny, but the outcome was the same. Simone didn't speak English, and Vassilis spoke perfect French. I didn't stand a chance. All I was left with were the naked afternoons at the beach with her and Vassilis and a ringside seat for their nocturnal lovemaking.

During those first early days in Loutro, I was bursting with confidence when it came to women. While Elena had confessed she thought I was a little on the faggy side, she also conceded that I was cute and assumed I would be getting laid a lot. I had no reason to doubt her. I was way too cocky. Before my drunken encounter with Elena, there was Mel. Before Mel, there was Brown Hair Laura. I was on a roll, ready for my next liaison. Or so I thought. Unfortunately for me and my ready-at-a-moment's-notice dick, there was a new sheriff in town. I was forced to accept the new reality that as long as Vassilis resided in Loutro, the prettiest and most intelligent would always gravitate toward him.

My winning streak might have been over, but it wasn't for lack of effort. There was Nelleke, the zany Dutch girl from Amsterdam. I spent an entire day at the beach trying to apprehend her. It was like chasing Tiny Tim through the tulips as her lithe body pranced naked along the shore, performing pirouettes to music that only she could hear. I never caught up to her, which was frustrating but probably a good thing. A few nights later at Marika's, I found myself at a table with a large group of new arrivals while being teased by a Swiss girl named Clara. She had short dark-brown hair and a colossal set of tits. I was sure that I was going to get laid. Her English was limited, but most of her phrases were gift-wrapped with sexual innuendo. I was having trouble concentrating on all the multilingual conversations because she kept playing footsie with me under the table. It began with what I first thought was an accidental touching of my foot but soon blossomed into a not-so-subtle come-on. As the night wore on and the drinks kept coming, her magic toes morphed into an advancing army, slowly crawling up my leg until they found what they were looking for. Emboldened by their success, they turned whimsical, juggling my balls in the air like a playful street performer. When she confirmed my erection, Clara giggled and let her foot drop to the floor. She had me right where she wanted me. Pushing her chair back, she rose to her feet and blew me a kiss. "Guet Nacht," was all I heard as she slipped past me and vanished into the night. I wanted to run after her, but I wasn't about to jump up in front of everyone until my cock eased back into hiding. By the time it calmed down and realized this wasn't going to be its night, the Swiss girl was long gone.

It was time for a little soul-searching, time to come to grips with my sense of isolation. As happy as I was living in Loutro, I was fighting bouts of depression. There were moments when I felt so alone, convinced that there was not one person on the planet with whom I could share my deepest thoughts. It was an awful feeling, a gut-wrenching loneliness that reached into the deepest corners of my stomach. Where did I belong? Did I belong? Was there anyone for me? Why couldn't I make it work with Jane? Why couldn't I get Isadora Duncan out of my brain? Why was I so obsessed with getting laid that I would say and do almost anything to make it happen? What the hell was wrong with me? It was more than just a physical need. It was a sickness, a disease without a cure. It was all I ever thought about. I was infatuated with women like Jenny and Simone, whom I could never have. I seemed incapable of saying no to any girl who offered herself to me. The ones like Nelleke and Clara, the temptresses who taunted and teased me, were irresistible. The more they strung me along, the more I wanted them. I knew that I had a serious problem, but it took an afternoon at Livaniana Beach and a fifteen-year-old German girl for me to realize just how fucked-up I was.

About a dozen others accompanied me over to the beach the next morning. While group nudity had become as commonplace as my morning swim or one of Marika's omelets, I continued to look forward to feasting my eyes on the latest female arrivals. I marveled at the enigma that was the human form. My days of frolic the previous summer at Pine Lake had freed me of my inhibitions. Being naked with a few friends or with a group of strangers seemed as natural as scratching an itch or taking a walk. I felt more comfortable without clothes than I did wearing them. It fascinated me how the recipe for every woman contained the same ingredients, yet each dish served up was slightly different. Each woman's mind formed a unique set of thoughts. Arms and legs, asses and breasts came in all sizes and shapes. Particularly intriguing were the vaginas. They were like snow-flakes. No two were alike. My obsession with them was getting worse by the day. I seemed incapable of resisting them. I wanted to see, touch, and taste as many as I could before I died.

The newest members of the group were my Swiss tease Clara, a teenage brother and sister from West Germany, Peter and Angelika, and the latest French couple, Guy and Danielle. Clara was the obvi-ous target. Her body was as tantalizing as Swiss chocolate. This had to be her first time swimming and sunbathing nude. She had a slight summer tan, but her large breasts and firm, perfectly shaped ass were as white as milk. Reaching into my limited bag of tricks, I pulled out the Brown Hair Laura tactic and offered to show her the caves. While Clara knew what I was up to and turned me down, the naked teenag-ers were a different story. They overheard my invitation to Clara and asked me if they could go. I was stuck. All bets were off with Clara, and I couldn't very well refuse the brother and sister team.

I had been so obsessed with Clara that I had barely noticed them. They could have been pulled off the cover of a magazine. Sixteen-year-old Peter was six feet tall, with broad shoulders and a wiry, athletic frame. His wholesome sister was fifteen and was four inches shorter but endowed with a physique as lean and muscular as his. Both were blond and blue-eyed and graced with modest patches of identical straw-colored pubic hair. Their long noses were interchangeable, with matching small bumps along the bridges. The siblings were ideal portraits of adolescent innocence and as comfortable with their nudity as Adam and Eve must have been before taking a bite of the forbidden apple and getting their asses tossed out of paradise.

The soles of my feet were as tough as nails. They had come a long way since that first afternoon with Brown Hair Laura. My sneakers were useless. Most of my time in and around Loutro was spent barefoot. The way my soles had adapted to their new environment was a perfect example of Charles Darwin's theory. By laminating themselves with a leather-like coat of armor, they were impervious to the sharp rocks and pebbles that dominated the path leading to the caves. It was a cakewalk for me but not so for the German teenagers. Their unaccustomed feet were having trouble keeping up with mine, forcing me to stop several times so they could catch up. It was early afternoon, and the bright sun was high in the sky. As they hurried to keep up with me, their young bodies glistened like classic portraits of Nordic beauty. When we reached the cove with the two cave openings, I explained where we were going. They didn't hesitate. They dove into the water, disappearing like a pair of playful dolphins into the liquid prism of color and refracted light. I stood there for a minute or two, debating whether or not to let them go alone. *What the hell?* I thought. *Why not enjoy the magical caves?* I dove in.

As soon as my head popped out of the water, I knew I was in trouble. I was staring between the open legs of Angelika, who was lying spread-eagle on the flat ledge along the back wall. Her brother was nowhere in sight. Apparently, he had moved on to the next cave. Why had he left Angelika behind to greet me like this? What was he thinking? What was she thinking? Maybe this was a trap. Maybe the Greek gods had convened a summit and were taking stock of my character. Whatever it was, my head was swirling. My perpetual pursuit of copulation was now leading me down a rabbit hole. It wasn't fair. I was a starving man staring at a mouthwatering plate of food. I was a thirsty man being offered a glass of water. What the hell was I supposed to do? I was drowning, and this teenage beauty was throwing me a lifeline. I took a deep breath and tried to gather my wits. What was wrong with me? How sick did I have to be to even consider this? The only fifteen-year-old girl that I ever had sex with was Jane, and I was sixteen at the time. I was being offered a delicious piece of cake, and I knew I had to turn down dessert. The nubile temptation lifted her head and smiled at me. She reached down with two of her fingers and gently touched herself.

My head continued to spin on its axis. It was time for me to get the fuck out of there. I allowed my eyes one last look before dropping into the liquid escape hatch. Mark Spitz couldn't have split the scene any faster. As I was swimming for redemption, I flashed back to the apartment in Madeira Beach. I thought of Ozzie McBrinn. I knew what Ozzie would have done if it had been him instead of me.

When I came up for air on the other side, Ozzie's Head was waiting for me.

"Hey, man," it said. "What's the matter? Need some help?"

Ozzie's Head was grinning. If this was God's way of testing me, then I must have passed.

"No, thanks," I said. "I'm cool.

111

When it came to religion, I wasn't sure what to believe. I counted myself among the terminally confused. I had met God on an acid trip, so how could I claim to be an atheist? Agnostic? What the hell was that? Christianity? Just because I was born to Christian parents and was fortunate enough to be assigned a seat next to Jesus on an airplane, how did that make me a Christian? All I knew was that none of the major religions made much sense to me. Thank God for the mischievous mind of Kurt Vonnegut. I owed Kurt big time for showing me the way. If push came to shove and I was forced to choose, I probably considered myself a Bokononist.

Kurt was one of three dudes that I wished I could smoke a joint with, and the other two, Ernest Hemingway and Jack Kerouac, were dead. The man was a genius. Who else could have dreamed up a religion that made so much sense and was so easy to understand? I first read *Cat's Cradle* in college, and it was the one book that I carried with me everywhere I went. When it was the only book to survive the fire on Franklin Mountain, I suspected it might be a sign from God. The front cover of the ninety-five-cent red paperback was slightly singed, and Kurt's first name was charred beyond recognition but the pages and wisdom inside remained intact.

His *Book of Bokonon* had taught me not to worry and fret over things I had no control over. Life was a series of random events, most of which I would never understand or be able to affect. Yes, I could usually choose to walk out a door whenever I pleased, but I had no way of knowing what the consequences of walking out at that particular moment in time would be. Suppose I left five seconds earlier or a minute later, would I be run over by a car or be struck by lightning? Conversely, would I be spared of some disaster because I departed at that exact moment? Each random event spawned a new series of random events, which in turn spawned yet another series of random events. The possibilities were endless. Had my father ejaculated a minute earlier or three days later, a different sperm would have latched onto a different one of my mother's eggs and another person would have entered this life instead of me. Just thinking about shit like this was enough to make my head explode.

What drew me to Kurt's imaginary religion was that unlike all the others, he freely admitted it was based on shameless lies, or as Kurt called them, harmless untruths. Assigning those people I crossed paths with into one of his two groups, a *karass* or a *granfalloon*, seemed simple enough. According to Kurt, if I found my life intersecting with someone else's for no logical reason, there was a good chance that they were a member of my karass. They were the ones who charted my path in life, the ones who stirred the pot and sent me on my way. With no Jane, no Danny Cooper, no Vince Donatelli, no Isadora Duncan, no Jesus disguised as Tony from Australia, I would not have become the person I was. I would have ended up in a different place with a different life surrounded by different people. I didn't have to be a rocket scientist to recognize these life changers as members of my karass. On the flip side, a granfalloon was a little trickier. It was easy to be fooled and believe that someone belonged in one group when they actually were part of another. According to the astute Mr. Vonnegut, a granfalloon was nothing more than a false karass. These were the irrelevant ones who might share an identity or purpose with me, but that perceived association would reveal itself to be meaningless. His example of a granfalloon was the people from Indiana who thought they were in a karass simply because they called themselves Hoosiers.

As my time in Loutro approached its inevitable conclusion, I began to think a lot about fate and destiny, my karass and granfalloons. Was it my destiny to have ended up here in this unique village with these specific people? Who among these nomads had slipped into my karass? Was this experience and the entire village of Loutro just one gigantic granfalloon? What did fate have in store for me next? Was I in control of my destiny, or was I simply being pushed through a playful series of twists and turns that were designed to entertain me before dropping me off at some preordained locale as my predetermined self?

I really didn't care one way or the other. After all, wasn't it Lao-Tzu, the Chinese philosopher and father of Taoism, who claimed that a good traveler had no fixed plans and was not intent on arriving? And then there was Lao's modern-day soulmate, New York Yankees philosopher Yogi Berra, who, when asked why he was running late for a party, acknowledged he was lost but insisted he was making good time. Lao-Tzu and Yogi Berra were wiser men than I am. By their standards, I was on the right track. As a Bokononist, I recognized the folly of pretending to understand anything. However, one thing was abundantly clear.

Vassilis Dimitriou had joined my karass.

112

The Libyan Sea was angry.

I had gone over alone that afternoon. The water at Livaniana Beach was normally quite calm. The curling fingers of the small waves usually brushed over the sand with very little force. Today was different. The water was rough. No longer willing to maintain its silence, it seemed determined to voice its displeasure over the unsettling events of the past twenty-four hours. Like a swollen train rolling into the station, the rhythmic percussion of the incoming tide was overpowering. The roaring and pounding obliterated all other sounds. I watched the waves rush violently toward the rocks and grab them with authority. The white salt spray crashed and growled before retreating to prepare for its next salvo. Just two days earlier, it had been incredibly hot here. Vassilis explained that it was because of the winds that were blowing in from the desert sands of Africa. He called them *Livas*.

Papadopoulos's referendum was less than a week away. Any illusion that Loutro might be some sort of utopian enclave immune to the forces of the outside world had been shattered the night before. It was late, and we had returned from yet another night of festive drinking at Marika's. At first, we didn't know what it was. It started slowly, like a distant drum roll. As it got closer, we realized we were hearing footsteps coming down the hill behind us.

Vassilis raised a finger to his lips and signaled for us to be silent. I glanced over at Steve and Ryan. They looked as bewildered as I was. The cadence got louder and louder. I froze when the first two soldiers rolled in marching side by side. The rifles on their backs were strapped to their right shoulders with the muzzles pointed toward the sky. Dressed in olive-green fatigues and sporting dark-green helmets, they looked to be younger than me. The parade continued as disciplined

451

pairs of emotionless young warriors stomped past us in a silent but transparent attempt to be heard. When they reached the water's edge, they took a sharp left, their soldier boots punishing the startled sand before heading up the perilous goat path that would lead them past the freshwater beach and on to the unsuspecting citizens of Hora Sfakion.

When it was over, the three of us turned to Vassilis for guidance.

Vassilis shrugged his shoulders and turned to go inside.

"Life is like a cucumber," was all he had to say before entering the house and climbing the stairs to be with Simone.

Steve and Ryan were puzzled. They had no idea what he was talking about.

It wasn't over. The action picked up the next morning right where it had left off. I had just returned from my daily Proverbial Squat and finished my morning swim. I was standing on the patio with Steve, sharing his tin cup of hot coffee, when I heard the roar. The ground shook, and the air exploded like a bomb going off in my ear. Two fighter jets dropped out of the sky and swooped down so low that it looked like we could reach up and touch them. Then, like a pair of single-minded bullets, the silver birds turned and soared upward into the heart of God's blue canvas. The hot exhaust from their engines collided with the atmosphere, leaving two long artificial clouds in their wake. I turned to Steve, who looked as shaken as me.

"What the fuck was that?" I asked.

Vassilis was standing in the doorway, rubbing the sleep from his eyes.

"My friends," he said, "that is just Papadopoulos reminding us he is everywhere."

It suddenly occurred to me that things might be getting serious. While the signs of trouble had been there all along, most of us who had found refuge in Loutro had chosen not to notice. Each of us had been swept up in our individual versions of reality, convinced that we were immune to the influences and events of the outside world. The solemn procession of soldiers in the dark of night and that morning's aerial assault were a swift kick in the balls. The peace had been broken. However, the message from Papadopoulos wasn't meant for us. It was being sent to the citizens of Loutro and the island of Crete.

Papadopoulos knew the history here: the revolts, the years of resistance, and the fierce torrent of independence that ran through each and every vein of the local populace.

Vassilis put it all in perspective that morning. A group of us gathered down at Marika's, staying long after breakfast to discuss the upcoming plebiscite and understand what Papadopoulos had up his sleeve. We had talked about it many times among ourselves but never with our Greek Renaissance man. As a recently released political prisoner, Vassilis was able to shed light on the ruthless mind-set of the ruling junta in Athens and the events about to take place. He reminded us that King Constantine had been forced to flee to Italy back in 1967 after the military coup. While on the face of it the upcoming plebiscite was to confirm the end of the monarchy and establish Greece as a republic, it had nothing to do with democracy and was nothing more than a charade to give legitimacy to Papadopoulos declaring himself president. Adding insult to injury, Vassilis stressed, was that the vote itself was meaningless.

"A yes vote," he declared, "means you support Papadopoulos and the job he is doing as president. A no vote means you think he should stay in office but needs to show some improvement. Either way, he remains the president."

Vassilis went on to warn us of the approaching storm. Everyone of voting age in Greece was required to vote. Even in tiny Loutro, there were signs of defiance. Crusty and cantankerous Pavlos had made it well-known that he had no intention of voting and would shoot any fool who showed up to force him to the ballot box or arrest him. He was the old man at the end of the village who fed us whenever Marika didn't feel like cooking. Pavlos had a gruff exterior that was impossible to penetrate. He was said to have fought the Germans during the war and had killed more than his share of Nazis. At least seventy years old, he was lean and mean. He didn't take any shit from anyone, and everyone in Loutro was content to leave him alone.

"There will be trouble," Vassilis warned, "if they come for Pavlos."

My bet was on Pavlos.

113

I was about to scarf down the last of my pommes frites when she put her hand on my shoulder.

"Ora gia sas na pate," she said. There was a hint of sadness in her voice.

I turned to Vassilis and asked him to translate.

"My friend," he replied, "Marika says it is time for you to go. She is worried about you."

I knew she was right. Everything was about to change. An invisible cloud was casting a long shadow over our up until now free and easy existence. For someone like me, this was simply a loss of innocence, just another intellectual reminder that there were no Utopias in this world. For Marika and the people of Greece, this was reality. This was their country. This was their government. This was their life.

I was going to miss her. She reminded me of my Grandma Hesse, who died of cancer when I was in high school. Marika was the matriarch of Loutro. She had been the source of sustenance for all of us who were passing through this tiny slice of heaven. While she cared for and nurtured everyone equally, I felt a special connection with her. I would miss her omelets, her pommes frites, her independent spirit, and the black kerchief that was tied under her chin and never left her head. More than anything, I would miss her kindness.

My gut told me that I would never again feel so carefree, never again be surrounded by people like this. Life here might only have been a state of mind, but it was a state of mind I desperately wanted to hold on to. I thought back to the day that had the greatest impact on me. Although we had postponed our trip for a few days, Andrew, Ryan, Dalton, and I had kept our word and hiked the steep path up to Andreas's village to help him and his neighbors put a roof on a house in exchange for food and drink.

We made the rigorous hike in the early evening and spent the night in Livaniana eating and drinking with the small number of inhabitants. Being in this tiny hamlet was like stepping back in time. Had it not been for the telephone poles stretching up the hill, we could have been standing in any century. The eight stone houses were quite basic. Andreas seemed proud to show off his village. His neighbors welcomed us with open arms. They treated us like visiting royalty, inundating us with more food than we were accustomed to consuming, and drowning us in beer and wine. Had I known we were going to work so hard the next day, I would have eased up on the alcohol. It was the most physical labor I had ever done in my life. Mostly relegated to wheelbarrow and bucket duties, we mixed the powdery cement with sand, gravel, and water and transported it to the ones who knew what they were doing. Comparing my construction jobs in Florida to this labor was like comparing a clerical job to working on a chain gang. Andreas's older brother Apostolis was the most interesting character we met. Although he looked to be no more than fifty-five or sixty years old, we learned that he was approaching his eightieth birthday. Working side by side with us, his strength, stamina, and work ethic put the rest of us to shame. The rumor was that Apostolis was on his fourth wife and was looking for a fifth, preferably a young American girl. I was learning how Crete was such a rugged land that the people had to be tough to survive and thrive. It was impossible to guess the age of a man. He could either be young and look old from the hard life he lived or be old and look young because of his healthy and rugged lifestyle. One day of hard labor and I was worn out. It was a great experience, but I was glad to get back to my life of leisure in Loutro. My entire body ached, and my muscles were sore for the next three days.

I was going to miss the *poly krasi kali ypnos* days and evenings with Andreas. I had spent many an afternoon on my way back from the beach, sharing rotgut wine and laughter with him beneath the solitary olive tree while he supposedly watched over his goats. Whether I was completely alone, traveling solo with a woman, or joining forces with a group of friends, Andreas knew better than anyone how I spent my days. His seat in the shade was the ideal spot to monitor my carnal activities.

It was easy to get depressed at the thought of leaving, but I really had no choice. Besides the political firestorm that was looming on the horizon, I was running out of money and needed to head somewhere in Northern Europe where I could find work. I figured that I could make some bread and then return for the winter. Vassilis told me that he and a Dutch dude named Jan were going to rent the house for another six months. He suggested I come back down to Loutro for Christmas. There had been long conversations over Ouzo about how to create a utopian society among ourselves. Marika had stood over us during one of our drunken gabfests, waved her hands in the air, and tossed in her two-cents.

"Chalazi Trela!" she exclaimed.

When I turned to Vassilis to ask what she had said, he was laughing harder than I had ever seen him laugh before.

"My friend," he said, "she thinks we are all crazy."

I wanted to know exactly what she had said. I pressed him for a translation.

"Hail lunacy!" was his reply.

114

I didn't realize it at the time, but a German woman named Gretchen had also joined my karass.

Gretchen and her friend Eva arrived in Loutro a few weeks before the plebiscite. They quickly became part of the inner circle and contributed to our nonsensical musings of creating a secret utopian society. Something about Gretchen intrigued me. She was tall, muscular, and big-boned, with dark-brown hair that was parted in the middle and tied off into two long pigtails. I wasn't physically attracted to her, but I was drawn to her mind. A published writer, Gretchen was the intellectual equal of Vassilis. Like Vassilis, she was endowed with a wealth of knowledge about an endless number of topics. I learned that she was currently living in a sleepy farming village twenty miles outside of Heidelberg called Oberschonbrunn. It had a population just under five hundred. Gretchen had moved there a year earlier and established a free school for the town's children. When I told her I was considering heading into Northern Europe the following month, Gretchen suggested I come to her birthday party in Wurzburg on the nineteenth of August. I had no idea where I would be in August or where Wurzburg was, but I wrote down her address and promised I would show up for the festivities if I found myself anywhere near there.

The final days before the plebiscite were depressing. A hushed acceptance settled over Loutro like a wet blanket. Papadopoulos had gotten his message across. With the exception of Pavlos, the villagers were quietly preparing for the long haul up to Anopolis where they would dutifully cast their meaningless votes. Meanwhile, what remained of the international community and the Loutro Order of the Amphibious Chicken was slowly disbanding. One by one, the people who had become such an integral part of my life were now hopping into the small rowboat and heading out into the harbor to catch the boat to Hora Sfakion. Steve, Wilhelm, and Juliette were the first to depart, followed the next day by Eva, Simone, Sean, and Pierre. They were being replaced by clueless day trippers. First, there was a boisterous boatload of camera-toting Italian tourists decked out in nice clothes and dark sunglasses who seemed puzzled over the lack of things to do here. Right behind them was a loud invasion of Greek Boy Scouts who dropped into the sea like rats deserting a sinking ship or, as Vassilis wryly observed, like grapes falling into the water.

I was packed and ready to go the morning of the vote. Ryan, Gretchen, and I would be leaving together, taking the bus from Hora Sfakion to Hania and most likely the same boat to Athens. The thought of hitting the road again was freaking me out. I promised Vassilis that I would return for Christmas, but I knew that would never happen. There would be no more pommes frites or omelets at Marika's. No more lazy afternoons under the olive tree with Andreas sipping wine from his goatskin flask. No more bounty from the sea from Kostas, the one-arm fisherman. No more gruff and intransigent Pavlos. No more Manoli and slaughtered lambs. No more icy baths at the freshwater beach. Most depressing of all, no more glorious days at Livaniana Beach. The sad truth was that I would never again have it so good.

It was late morning when Ryan, Gretchen, and I caught the boat to Hora Sfakion. Loutro was a ghost town. The entire village had cleared out earlier to go to Anopolis. As the boat moved away from the harbor and out to sea, the image of whitewashed houses and the pebble beach began to fade. I don't know how Ryan or Gretchen felt, but I had a knot in my stomach. It was as if a part of me had surgically removed itself and stayed behind to lure me back in one day.

When we pulled into Hora Sfakion, we discovered that we had missed the bus to Hania by a few minutes. The next one wasn't scheduled to show up until around six in the evening. The village was bursting at the seams, alive with a carnival atmosphere that I had not seen before. It was electric. This was where everyone had gathered together for the bus rides up to Anopolis, and every man and woman was dressed to kill. Democracy Day was serious business on Crete even if the vote was meaningless. When we spotted Andreas and Manoli sitting at a table by the dock, sharing a carafe of white wine, we rushed over to join them. I could tell that this wasn't their first carafe. Apparently, they were in no hurry to vote. They were laughing and toasting each other, and their faces were flushed with the telltale signs of too much alcohol.

When he saw us, Andreas raised his glass into the air and shouted, "POLY KRASI, KALA YPNOS!"

We all laughed. Great minds think alike. We had six hours to kill before the next bus arrived. We pulled up three chairs and sat down.

115

Three days later, I was being detained at the border in Yugoslavia.

Returning to civilization was definitely a shock to my system. It began with the harrowing bus ride over the mountains to Hania. I tried to relax, but there were no guardrails and the driver seemed oblivious to the steep drop-off that loomed but a few feet from my seat next to the window. It was a miracle we made it without taking a nosedive off a cliff.

I knew there was no going back, but the collective insanity that greeted me in Hania was enough to make me want to turn around and race back to the primitive shores of Loutro. I wondered if this was how John Glenn felt as he was re-entering the earth's atmosphere. The unholy marriage of noise, cars, tourists, and Western culture hit me like a ton of bricks. I wasn't ready for any of this. Hania had not changed, but I had. I was no longer the novice traveler, in awe of the architecture, colorful old buildings, and historical charm. I was back in the real world again, engulfed in its chaos and surrounded by strange creatures. Paul Simon claimed that the words of prophets were written on subway walls. What he neglected to mention was that they were also served up with omelets and pommes frites. Hail lunacy! The prophet Marika had hit the nail on the head. I decided to embrace the madness and drink as much Retsina as I could before boarding the passenger ship *Kydos* for the overnight voyage to Athens. It turned out to be a smart move. There was nothing I could do but kick back and roll with the punches. We were herded together like cattle in a cowboy movie and hustled up to the upper deck where lumpy sleeping bags transformed the ship's surface into massive rows of oblong pimples.

I was still traveling with Ryan and Gretchen when *Kydos* docked at the Athens harbor of Piraeus. We paid three drachmas each for the bus ride into the heart of the city where we got off near Syntagma Square. We headed straight to the American Express office. This was where every traveler passing through Athens stopped to pick up any mail from home. At least a dozen backpackers were hanging near the front of the building and milling around on the sidewalk. To our surprise, there were a number of familiar faces. I recognized the British couple Graham and Patricia, who had stayed at the house in Loutro for three days with Steve, Sean, Ryan, and me. One of Dewey's French girls was also there, but there was no sign of Dewey. She was beautiful, but I couldn't remember her name.

We were exchanging hugs and enjoying the mini-Loutro reunion when I saw the front door to American Express swing wide open. She was wearing the same yellow peasant dress that she always wore. The strapless frock with its tree-branch patterns of lipstick-red and leaves falling in faded greens had been seared into my memory. Even more vivid was my recollection of what lay beneath the thin material: the tan lithesome frame, the flawless breasts, and the triangular patch of light blond hair. As she got closer, my heart skipped a beat. I could feel the blood rushing to both of my heads. Her sudden appearance was a cruel reminder that it had been weeks since she had left Loutro and I still had not been laid.

"Hi, Jenny," I said.

"Hi, Jeff," she answered, giving me a quick hug and a smile before inching past me to join the rest of the reunion.

And that was it, the last time I would ever see or talk to her.

Hoping no one had noticed my temporary arousal, I walked over to Ryan, who was talking with a short bespectacled hippie-looking dude with curly reddish-brown hair making a feeble attempt at growing a goatee. His name was Nicholas, and he was from England. Ryan was excited.

"Nicholas has a van and, he is leaving in a few minutes for Dubrovnik," he said. "He's offered us a ride."

"Okay," I said. "Let's go."

I had heard of Dubrovnik and knew that it was in Yugoslavia. I also knew that Yugoslavia was a Communist country. What the hell? I thought. What did I have to lose? I needed to get out of Greece and back up into Europe to find a job. The thought of retracing my steps back through Corfu, Brindisi, and across Italy was depressing. This seemed like a good shortcut and a chance to experience something totally different. In what felt like a hundred years ago, my four English friends on Corfu had left me with a cautionary tale about Yugoslavia, so I knew that I needed to be careful and not place myself in any stupid situations. I was eager for new adventures with new people. I had not planned on traveling with Ryan or anyone else I already knew, but this ride out of Athens was too good to pass up.

I said goodbye to Gretchen and promised I would try to make it to her birthday party. I could tell by the way she looked at me that she didn't believe me. Ryan and I then bid farewell to the Loutro alumni, found a nearby souvlaki stand to grab a quick bite, and then piled into the escape vehicle. I noticed the steering wheel of the VW bus was on the right side, not the left. Nicholas and his VW bus had taken a ferry across the English Channel months earlier and somehow managed to drive across Europe and make it all the way to Greece while learning to drive on the right side of the road. He had met a Norwegian girl named Inger in Northern Italy, who was staying in Dubrovnik for the summer. Seeing her again had become his obsession. He claimed that she was his dream girl. When I asked if he had gotten it on with her, he admitted that he had not. However, he was convinced that since Inger had given him her address in Dubrovnik, she must have felt the same way about him. I didn't have the heart to tell him that I also had collected a shitload of addresses, but that was no guarantee I would get laid if I showed up on one of their doorsteps. Poor Nicholas couldn't get to Dubrovnik fast enough. His prospects for coitus sounded shaky, but who was I to be giving advice? I understood why he was making the pilgrimage. It certainly wasn't any dumber than some of the trips I had taken. *The penis wants what the penis wants.*

It took us most of the day to travel up through the mountainous regions of Northern Greece to the border. Along the way,

Nicholas picked up a couple of Swiss dudes who were on their way to Thessaloniki. They seemed interesting, but I was too wasted after the overnight voyage from Crete to spend much time rapping with them. I attempted to get some sleep in the back of the van, but the road was bumpy and I didn't have much luck. After dropping off the hitchhikers from Switzerland, Nicholas picked up another English dude named David, who was also on his way to Dubrovnik. What was it about the Brits and Dubrovnik? I sensed that we were passing through some incredible scenery, but it was difficult to see or enjoy it. It had been raining steady since we left Athens, sometimes so hard that the windshield wipers had trouble keeping up. It was the first rain that I had seen in almost two months.

It stopped raining, and the sun reappeared when we were just a few miles from Yugoslavia. Since we were about to cross into a Communist county, I took the break in the weather as a positive sign of what was to come. My optimism was short-lived. When Nicholas rolled up to the checkpoint, we saw several armed guards. They ordered us to pull over and made us get out of the van. They took our passports and led us inside a small concrete building. The four of us were then placed in separate rooms.

My room was empty, dimly lit and tiny, not more than ten feet by ten feet. Neither of the two guards who escorted me in spoke English. The heavy-set one brought in a small wood chair and motioned for me to take a seat. The other official was tall and thin, and he was leaning against the wall, thumbing through my passport. It's funny. I should have been nervous, but I wasn't. This was like a walk in the park compared to the wild night I spent in a Boston jail. I wasn't worried. I had not done anything wrong, and I was not carrying any drugs. Still, if I had thought to pull my head out of my ass, I would have considered the possibility that I had no rights. I was in Yugoslavia, and they could do whatever the hell they wanted with me.

I knew I was entering a different world, but everything I had heard from word of mouth told me that the country was well worth the hassle. It was said to be blessed with beautiful scenery and a gorgeous coastline. It also had a reputation for being the most open of all the Communist regimes in Eastern Europe. The government supposedly had a liberal travel policy, permitting western tourists and their money to travel freely throughout the country. Marshal Tito had been ruling it since the end of World War II and was the one Communist leader who remained independent of the Soviet Union. Rumor had it that Tito and the Yugoslavs were tolerant of hippies and longhairs.

It didn't feel that way as I was sitting in the chair. The guards took my backpack and left me alone in the room for more than an hour. I had plenty of time to think. I wondered if Nicholas, David, and Ryan were faring any better than I was. I wondered if being an American was good or bad for my situation. I wondered what I would do if they turned me away. My imagination was running wild. What would I do if they put me in prison? Would anyone know I was there?

My paranoia was laid to rest when they walked back into the room. The double spectacle of drab uniforms caught my eye for the first time. The gray-green shirts, trousers, and field caps were punctuated with black leather ankle boots. A small round silver badge was displayed prominently on each left pocket. The heavy-set sentry motioned for me to stand and handed me my backpack. The tall, thin dude who had been so interested in my passport handed it back to me. They both pointed to the open door. When I walked out, Nicholas, David, and Ryan were waiting for me on the other side.

"What happened in there?" Ryan asked.

"Nothing," I said. "They left me in there alone the entire time. What about you guys?"

"They didn't bother us," Ryan answered. "They just stamped our passports. We've been waiting out here for you the entire time."

Nicholas seemed agitated.

"We've wasted enough time here," he growled. "Let's go before the blokes change their bloody minds."

116

I wasn't sure what had just happened, but I was glad to get out of there. I was plunging headfirst into the unknown, thrilled to be entering a new phase in my search for something I couldn't explain or understand. Still, I had mixed emotions. Where was I going? Where would I end up? The newness of being on the road, being out of the US, and hitchhiking through Europe was starting to wear off. While I knew where I didn't want to be and what I didn't want to do, I was grasping at straws when it came to guessing what life had in store for me. I was nearly broke and slipping into uncharted territory. It was one thing to thumb my way through Western Europe and another to be making my way through a land ruled by the Communist Party. Greece might have been under the thumb of a military dictatorship, but it was an American ally with Western rules that I could navigate. Where I was going, I figured all bets were off.

The sun was calling it quits as Nicholas pulled us away from the checkpoint and semicircle of humorless armed guards. The narrow road was deserted and barely visible in the twilight. The VW had shitty headlights. We talked it over and decided to toss in the towel and surrender to the darkness. Nicholas found a secluded spot to pull over a few miles north of the border, and we crashed in the van for the night. When we woke at sunrise, we were surrounded on all sides by plush green mountains. It reminded me a little of Upstate New York.

It would take us the entire day to make it over to the Adriatic Coast.

Driving north, the road followed the churning chocolate Vardar River along a grassy valley that made a deep cut through the mountains until we reached a large city called Skopje. After that, the landscape evolved into sprawling farmland, rich with golden fields of hay, miles and miles of yellow-green cornfields, and acres upon acres of bright-yellow sunflowers. We encountered very few cars, and the ones we did appeared to be driven by tourists. The narrow highway belonged to the local farmers and peasants in their horse-drawn and ox-drawn wooden wagons. It was a strange mixture of old and new. The small cities were industrial and modern, while life in the rural communities seemed timeless. There were square and rectangular concrete-block houses with pointed brick-orange roofs. The peasants riding in the carts were aggressively friendly, waving at us each time Nicholas slowed down to pass. We even received a raised pair of clenched fists from two teenage boys eager to show their solidarity to a van full of Western hippies.

I was mesmerized by what I was seeing and lost track of time. Eventually, we reached the city of Mitrovica, which sat at the intersection of two rivers: the Ibar and the Sitnica. Nicholas seemed to know where he was going. He turned to the west and followed the Ibar River valley past a series of small farms into an imposing group of mountains that were an explosion of emerald green against a backdrop of red dirt. As we climbed higher and higher, I felt my ears pop. The road was an engineering tour de force, a magnificent work of art that followed the curvature of the mountains and carved out endless rows of tunnels. Each time we exited a tunnel, it was like entering a painting. The Ibar resembled a turbulent pea-green soup as it tumbled through the valley of red-brick houses and wooden chalets. Conical mounds of hay dotted the landscape like invading armies of Walt Disney characters. As we crawled up and down the winding marvel, the river was reduced to a slithering, greenish-brown garden snake working its way between breathtaking gray cliffs whose unreachable caves peered out at us like dark eye sockets. We descended into the valley near a sleepy but modern village called Rozaje. The hillside was sprinkled with tall pine trees, and the once-mighty Ibar retreated to a crawl, with the August sun creating an illusion of diamonds dancing on its surface. We continued along a winding two-lane road through farm country that easily passed for the foothills of the Catskills and climbed up gentle mountains that were a mirror image of the

Berkshires. Any illusion that I was journeying through Upstate New York or western Massachusetts was quickly shattered when Nicholas reached the finish line of the swirling maze leading down to the city of Ivangrad. We arrived in a valley ruled by grotesque factories generating thick gray clouds of sulfur-smelling smoke. We couldn't get out of there fast enough. Holding our breaths for as long as we could, we turned north and followed the sea-green waters of the Lim River.

The scenery was spectacular the rest of the way, especially the ride down the mountain from Kolasin to Titograd. It was equal to anything I had seen in the Italian or Swiss Alps. It was late afternoon when we reached the coastal town of Kotor. As eager as Nicholas was to reach the Promised Land of Inger, we were too exhausted and hungry to keep going. Dubrovnik was still a few hours up the coast. I had heard about Dubrovnik but not Kotor. It was well worth the stop. Cradled within a calm and protected bay, it was a fortified town. Nestled against the steep limestone cliffs that dropped straight down to the water's edge, Kotor was defended by a formidable stone wall that twisted and turned its way up the imposing precipice. Since we were in the land of Communism, I was surprised by the number of churches and cathedrals that seemed to dominate the medieval setting. There was even an ancient church on a small island in the middle of the bay. We wandered the narrow streets, squares, and markets for a few hours and found an outdoor café where we each ordered a bowl of porridge-style soup containing barley and mushrooms. My lack of money was becoming a problem, but I had to eat something substantial. I couldn't just live on bread and cheese. As night was rolling in, we drove outside of town and found a secluded place to park and sleep one more time in the van.

We blew into Dubrovnik around ten the next morning.

As cool as Kotor was, the city of Dubrovnik with its natural beauty was in a class all by itself. Positioned below a steep hill along a thin strip of coastline, it rose above the celestial blue waters of the Adriatic Sea, more like a jaw-dropping mirage or magic mushroom trip than an actual place. Protected by an irregular pentagon of high stone walls with angled fortifications at each corner and more than a dozen towers, Dubrovnik's historic town center was a dazzling display of Renaissance architecture. The city was small enough to get around on foot, and the walk along its stony rampart and through its labyrinth of little streets was surreal. The massive number of churches, monasteries, palaces, and fountains were a Rorschach test. The inkblots that I saw were the German tourists. As beautiful and awe-inspiring as Dubrovnik was, the city was expensive, highly commercial, and in the midst of a massive tourist infestation.

While Nicholas and David were in Dubrovnik for the long haul, Ryan and I were planning on making our way through Yugoslavia into Northern Europe. Hitchhiking up the coast would likely be a long, difficult slog. With my cash running low, it made sense to get closer to Switzerland and Germany where I might find work. The three of us parted ways with David and ventured down to the harbor where Nicholas waited while Ryan and I purchased tickets to Rijeka, a port city near the top of the country. The next boat didn't leave until ten the next morning. That meant we would need to find a place to crash for the night. It also meant that Ryan and I would have the rest of the day to explore the city. Nicholas had other ideas. He didn't give a damn about checking out Dubrovnik. He was but a stone's throw from his object of desire. He pulled the slip of paper with her address on it out of his pocket, and the three of us set out to locate the Promised Land of Inger.

Inger was staying in a tiny one-room flat that was just off the main street and not far from the harbor. Her roommate, a fellow Norwegian named Solveig, answered the door and said that Inger was out for the day and would return later that afternoon. Solveig suggested we stop back around seven. Nicholas, bursting with optimism, promised her we would. We decided to fill the time trucking around the city. We circumnavigated the stone walls, taking in views of the town, the tile roofs, and the clear turquoise sea below us. The walls stretched for what had to be more than a mile and a half and rose as high as eighty feet in some places. We explored a medieval monastery where we wandered through cloisters replete with animal and human heads adorning their dual columns. We found a small market where we bought some bread and cheese. Before heading back to the Promised Land of Inger, we ran into a couple of English hippies who directed us to a hostel where we could spend the night. Even though it was only a couple of dollars, I hated to do it.

There would be no pot of gold at the end of Nicholas's rainbow. I felt bad for the dude. It had to be a real bummer for him. His penis had sweet-talked him into making the two-day pilgrimage from Athens, only to discover that he had driven all the way to Dubrovnik for nothing. When we showed up at her flat that evening, Inger was friendly to us as a group but showed no interest in Nicholas. The Norwegian girls had plenty of Ouzo and an abundant supply of hashish, and we partied into the wee hours of the morning. It was the first hash I had smoked since Switzerland and my best buzz in months. Nicholas was as high as I was, but he was distraught. Inger ignored him completely and spent most of her time talking with me.

Maybe it was my imagination, but Inger could have passed for Isadora's twin sister. I couldn't believe my eyes. She wore her soft blond hair the same length, and her blue eyes were bright and sparkled with the same magic. Was every tall, blond, blue-eyed beauty destined to remind me of Isadora? Hadn't I also imagined her in the Swedish chick Gudrun aboard the overnight ship to Corfu? Would I ever be able to get Isadora Duncan out of my mind?

Whether or not my eyes were playing tricks on me was irrelevant. I had a decision to make. Inger was coming on to me and not Nicholas. It wasn't my fault that she was attracted to me and not to him. He should have known better than to expect that some Norwegian chick he had met along the road would be waiting for him in Yugoslavia. Still, Nicholas had become a friend over the past two days. He was being rejected, and for me to ball the girl he had come to see would be a shitty way to thank him for the ride.

As the night rolled on and I continued to smoke hashish and consume more Ouzo, I engaged in a silent debate with my cock. I understood where he was coming from. Elena, Mel, and Brown Hair Laura were a distant memory. It had been light-years since we had gotten laid. My cock was in a state of frenzy, jumping up and down, waving his arms and legs, and demanding to be heard. He insisted that he had waited long enough and made it quite clear that his sights were set on Inger. I felt the same way he did. I too was captivated by her beauty and wanted more than anything to get it on with her. When he dropped to his knees and starting begging, it took every inch of willpower I had to overcome his objections and fight him off. I stood my ground and explained that Nicholas was my friend and I couldn't do this to him. My cock became angry and countered that I should make it up to him because he had taken a pass on the fifteen-year-old girl from Germany.

"Yeah," I said, "so what? It was the right thing to do."

It wasn't until the hashish and Ouzo beat us both into semiconsciousness that the dispute ended. The Norse beauties closed up shop and sent us packing back to the hostel. The next morning, Nicholas and I parted as friends.

117

Were there any Yugoslavians in Dubrovnik? It sure didn't feel like it. Everyone was speaking in German. I was lucky to know enough of the language to understand most of what was being said to me and carry on some simple conversations. It felt good to learn that my two years of German classes in college had not been a waste of time after all.

It would take me three more days to make it out of Yugoslavia. As jaw-dropping beautiful as the country was, I couldn't escape it fast enough. The creatures were everywhere. I assumed that if I headed north, I could outrun them. Was I ever wrong! The boat to Rijeka was named *Liburnija*, and it was literally packed wall to wall with hundreds of creatures. It was nearly impossible for Ryan or me to move around. We might not have been washed or cooked or had our heads removed, but other than that, we were like oily sardines packed tightly in a can. I had never seen so many tourists in one place. As far as I could tell, I was the only American on board. The last American I had seen or spoken to was Jenny back in Athens. There were very few young backpackers on the ferry, and most of them were Hungarian dudes in their late teens or early twenties. I learned that Hungary had one of the more liberal travel policies in Eastern Europe for its citizens, and these dudes were taking advantage of it. They were excited to meet an American hippie, and all they seemed to want to talk to me about was hard-rock music. They were really into Led Zeppelin.

The *Liburnija* arrived in Rijeka early the next morning, and again I had not gotten any sleep. However, I was relieved to get off the cattle boat and hopefully leave the creatures in my rearview mirror. This is where Ryan and I parted ways. He was determined to reach the Italian border near Trieste as quickly as possible while I wanted to check out some of the beaches along the western coastline before bolting this strange Communist playground. Ryan was a good dude. I had known him longer than anyone else I had met in Europe. We wished each other luck and exchanged our addresses back home, but we both knew we would never see each other again.

Hitchhiking was impossible, so I spent a few more of my precious dwindling dollars and purchased a bus ticket to Pula, a coastal town near the southern tip of the Istria Peninsula. Once there, I bought some bread and cheese and caught another bus up to Rovinj. The ride took less than an hour. I had been told it was home to a famous art colony and an even more famous nude beach. It seemed like a cool thing to check out. The problem was that I stuck out like a sore thumb. I was in the land of wealthy vacationers and jet-setters. As I was walking through a public park and heading in what I was certain was the direction of the beach, I was stopped by two policemen who demanded to see my passport. They were my age or younger.

"Sprechen sie Deutsch?" one of them asked.

"Ich spreche nur ein bisschen Deutsch," was my reply, which meant that I could speak it a little.

What followed was a conversation that could have passed for an Abbott and Costello routine. These strict guardians of Yugoslavian law and order proceeded to explain to me over and over in slow, methodic German that I wasn't allowed to sleep in the park. I, in my broken German, tried to explain that it was the middle of the afternoon, and I wasn't looking for a place to sleep. This absurd dialogue went on for several minutes. I flashed back to my border crossing and started to worry that the very presence of someone like me in this playground for the rich might actually be a crime. Fortunately, they came to the conclusion that I was harmless and that I understood that I couldn't sleep in the park and would not return. They handed me back my passport and sent me on my way. I could feel their official eyes glued to me the entire time as I strolled out of the park with my backpack and out of their lives forever.

It only got stranger after that. It was a long walk. The beach was maybe two to three miles from the center of town. I was startled to find so many yachts and so many naked people gathered in one place. The coastline was mostly rocky but did contain a few sandy coves. Pine trees growing near the shore provided the only shade. The magnificent yachts were like competing floats in a Rose Bowl Parade. Attractive nude women with all-over tans graced each bow, while the proud captains, wearing nothing but their white captain's hats with embroidered gold emblems and shiny black brims, stood watch at the helm. The beach was swarming with people of all ages. Entire families basked in the sun together. Small children splashed in the turquoise water under the watchful eyes of svelte young mothers and plump gray-haired grandmothers. Fathers and grandfathers gathered in small circles, laughing and joking among themselves, secure in their good fortune.

It was clearly a when-in-Rome-do-what-the-Romans-do moment. I may have looked out of place when I got there, but as soon as I ripped off my clothes, I was one of them. That is the great thing about nudity. All differences are stripped away when we return to the innocence of Adam and Eve. I still had my all-over Loutro tan, and with the exception of my long hair, I could have passed for any one of these rich bastards.

I had only been there about ten minutes when I realized that I was an integral part of a popular tourist attraction. Several boats, each carrying between twenty and thirty gawking creatures, were taking turns coasting as close to the shore as they could get without running aground. Most of the creatures had cameras around their necks and seemed to be snapping photos until they ran out of film. There was even a dude in a small rowboat who paddled out to meet the creature flotilla and sell them cold soft drinks.

I spent the rest of the afternoon soaking up the sun and savoring the moment. It was bizarre. Here I was in a Communist country, yet I was surrounded by more wealth than I had ever been around in my life. My eyes feasted on the beautiful bronze women. They all seemed younger than the men they were with.

I wondered what it would be like to make love to one of them.

118

It was a miserable night, a night that ranked right up there with the harrowing one I spent in Loutro sleeping with the rats. I was in the Austrian Alps, hunkering down in a ditch just a few feet away from a deserted country road. It had taken me more than fourteen hours to travel less than one hundred kilometers, and it had been several hours since the last car passed me by. There was nowhere else to go. I was learning the hard way just how cold it could get in the mountains at night even in August. It was pitch-black, and it was raining. I was glad that I was traveling alone. I took solace in the fact that at least I didn't have to listen to someone else complain about the wretched conditions. Still, I was chilled to the bone and praying for the morning sun to ride to my rescue.

The hitchhiking had been terrible. I was in tourist country. I had not seen a backpacker, hippie, or hippie van since Rijeka. I felt like an exotic animal on display at a zoo. The creatures whizzed by in their shiny cars, slowing down just long enough to get a look at me before stepping on the gas and speeding off into the void. I could sense them passing judgment on me, trying to decide whether or not I was fit to be part of the human race. They didn't want to dirty or infect their prized vehicles with any of the filth or germs I might be carrying. I would have been stranded in Tito's Yugoslavia forever if I had not been lucky enough to catch a ride out with two German kids in a small VW who were on their way home. They crammed me and my backpack in and transported us over the border into Italy and then into southern Austria where they dropped us off near the medieval town of Lienz. I probably should have stayed the course and bonded with them all the way into West Germany, but for some stupid reason, I felt the need to dive deeper into Austria and head up to the city of Vienna. Now, a day later and huddled inside a soaking-wet sleeping bag, I was fighting the rain, the cold, and a creeping feeling of loneliness and depression.

I tried to remain positive, tried to see the cup as half full and not half empty. However, I could sense a subtle change washing over me. The pure, unbounded joy I felt when I first set foot in Europe was slipping away. This dark moment, this lying in a ditch in the pouring rain in the middle of the night was my new reality. I was down and out. My clothes were torn, and I was filthy. The only thing I had for my feet was a pair of sandals, and they kept falling apart. I was down to my last ninety dollars and had no idea how I was going to solve that riddle. No longer the wide-eyed American kid who had greeted each new experience and place with a naive sense of wonder, I was coming to grips with the person I had become. There was no getting around it. This was the life I had chosen. The sad part was that I had lost the only thing I really ever owned: my optimism.

Somehow, I made it through the night. The rain stopped around dawn. My clothes were wet, but my options were limited. The blue jeans I was wearing were the only pants I had, and it was way too fucking cold to change into my cutoff shorts. I pulled off my soggy T-shirt and traded it for the damp one in my backpack. What few clothes I had were dirty and smelled musty. My only defense against the cold was my puny jacket. My teeth were chattering, and my sandal-wrapped bare feet were turning blue. What could I do? The buck stopped with me. I was being sucked into the downward spiral that I alone had created. How was I to know that divine intervention was on its way in the form of Eddy, a member of the Austrian National Ski Team?

I heard the dark-blue sports car long before I saw it. The primal scream of its engine bounced off the mountain walls and echoed into the valley. Eddy the Skier was in a hurry. He was flying out the next morning for an international competition in Argentina, and he was hell-bent on getting laid before he left. Eddy didn't speak English, so I did my best to communicate with him in my limited German. I learned that he was racing to a girl in Vienna whom he was sure was waiting to open her legs the way a flower opens to the sun after several days of rain. He drove like a bat out of hell, and his driving scared the shit out of me. Eddy's blue phallus sped around one hairpin turn after another like it was flying into the sun. I begged him to slow down.

"Du fahrst zu schnell, du fahrst zu schnell!" I shouted.

Eddy just laughed. He explained that everything he did, he did fast. There was nothing I could do but hold on and place my fate in his hands. The G-forces pressed me back into my seat. Eddy had a full tank of gas and was racing against his own clock. He was not about to stop for food or a piss. By the time he dropped me off on the outskirts of Vienna, it was late morning, and I knew how the Apollo astronauts must have felt when they first reentered the earth's atmosphere.

My first reaction to Vienna was disappointment. It was much more expensive and modern than I expected. I literally walked into the city from the outskirts and spent several hours along the way, looking for a place to stay. I couldn't find anything I could afford. Exhausted, hungry, and thirsty, I hauled my ass into a small pub in a residential neighborhood. There were about a dozen men in their forties and fifties scattered around a few tables, nursing large mugs of beer. They stopped talking when I walked in. I was probably the first unbathed longhaired hippie shrouded in filthy clothes and carrying a backpack to have ever had the balls to stroll into their sanctuary. I was too tired to worry. I grabbed a seat at the bar and set my backpack on the floor. I was greeted by a rather stern-looking middle-aged woman standing behind the bar.

"Kann ich dir helfen?" she asked. It was going to be another chance to practice my German.

"Ein Bier bitte," I said. "Kann ich etwas essen bestellen?"

That broke the ice. The woman smiled and grabbed a large mug. She placed it at a forty-five-degree angle about one inch below one of her three taps and filled the glass. After she set the beer in front of me, she pointed to the black chalkboard on the wall next to the clock. I ordered the only thing I recognized.

"Gulasch bitte," I said.

The last time I had eaten goulash was in a school cafeteria. Although I was so hungry that it didn't matter, I was praying that the goulash in Austria was better than the goulash that was churned out by the cooks at Sidney Senior High School.

I could feel my luck changing. The reddish meat and vegetable stew was a delicious concoction, with large chunks of beef and a rich amalgam of onions, carrots, potatoes, and tomatoes with a splash of seasoning that hinted of garlic and red wine. It was the best food that I had tasted in months. Not only was it my best meal since Crete, it was also the best afternoon since I had left the magical island. Curiosity must have gotten the best of them, and several of the dudes in the pub joined me at the bar. None of them spoke English. I must have seemed strange to them, but they took turns asking me questions about who I was, where I was going, and where I had been. They were impressed by my use of German and amused by all the mistakes and bad grammar that came out of my mouth. It was a glorious afternoon, and when I staggered drunk out of the pub a few hours later, I had a full stomach, a spinning head, and the same amount of money that I had walked in with. I must have provided good entertainment. The dudes picked up the tab for my goulash and all my beers.

I wasn't planning on it, but I stayed in Vienna for three nights. I found the coolest place to crash, a tiny but private room in an underground hostel that had once been an air-raid shelter during World War II. It was in a bunker beneath a huge concrete and steel tower in Esterhazy Park that the Nazis had built to house anti-aircraft weaponry to counterattack the Allied bombing raids. The best part of my stay was that I was able to take my first real shower in two months. It felt good to clean up my act. I found a *Waschsalon*, the German word for Laundromat, to wash my tattered clothes. I did a lot of walking and finally broke down and invested six of my disappearing dollars in a pair of shoes to replace the pathetic sandals that had brought me this far. I didn't care for the hostel scene. I met a few Americans there but none that interested me. Vienna was a pleasant city, with plenty of palaces, formal gardens, gothic churches, museums, and art galleries. Mostly, I just wandered around and took in the surroundings. I couldn't afford to spend money on anything but food and shelter. There was a splendid shabbiness to the city, but it was clean and efficient. It was also very straight. Even the few young people who were traveling through Vienna and staying in the underground bunker were straight. There was no drug scene, no freak community. Vienna was much bigger and more Westernized than I had expected. However, the Austrian people were not hustling the tourists all the time, and that was a pleasant change from cities like Rome or Athens.

The time I spent in Vienna gave me time to think and catch my breath. With the little money that I had left, I was pinching pennies. Still, I was showering each day, eating some real food again, and sleeping in a comfortable bed. It was a refreshing change of pace but one I knew wouldn't last long. I thought of my brother Bernie and wondered where he was and where his head was at. Was he in Europe like I was? We were both restless animals and similar in many ways, yet we approached our lives differently. Bernie's emphasis was on nature. I could picture him living somewhere out in the woods, away from cities and people. He and my friend Donnie from the Yukon would have dug each other. While I was into nature and scenery, I still needed to interact with people. The trick was to avoid creatures and only interact with the real ones: the kindred spirits. They were out there. I had learned at least that much on my journey.

It was during my last night in Vienna that I sat on my bed and tried to unravel the mystery of my inner self. The more I reflected, the more isolated I felt. I was starting to feel my age. The hostel scene was nowhere. The cutoff age for entry was twenty-five, which made me the oldest person every time I crashed at one. I wasn't some asshole college kid making my way through Europe for the summer on a Eurail pass. I was a disillusioned American adult with a college degree and no future who had left behind my country and was grasping for some intangible truth or path of enlightenment, which I seemed incapable of identifying or explaining to anyone, including myself. The only two times where I had felt true happiness were last summer in The Shack in Oneonta and the halcyon days I had just abandoned on Crete. What they both had in common was that I had no money, no job, and I was getting laid. Maybe that was the secret formula.

The next day produced a relatively effortless day of hitchhiking. The sun was out in full glory, and it took me four rides and seven hours to reach Innsbruck. My last ride was with two Israeli dudes from Jerusalem, Giora and Yehuda, who wanted to spend the night at the youth hostel before taking me all the way to Zurich the next day. The hostel was another nowhere scene, but Innsbruck was nicer than I thought it would be. The surrounding mountains with their jagged rock spires were beautiful, and the alpine city was much smaller, much slower, and less touristy than I had been expecting. It was a cool evening, and I stayed up late to bask in the perfect weather.

We left early the next morning.

119

Reality was a bitch.

I was back in Lucerne, ascending the three flights of stairs at Baselstrasse 7. I had come full circle. I was counting on Thomas, Karl, and Rudi to once again take me in. I was down to three twenty-dollar traveler's checks and a pocketful of change. My traveling days were over. Unless I solved my money problem, I wasn't going anywhere. Even if I wanted to, I couldn't return to the States. I could barely afford to eat, let alone buy a plane ticket.

Nobody was home, but the door was unlocked. I was in familiar territory, returning to the womb. The usual suspects, the empty beer bottles and the bong filled with dirty water, greeted me from atop the Formica table in the living room. The inspired collection of Frank Zappa and Jimi Hendrix albums that had dispersed themselves across the floor remained the same, but it was a new competitor that caught my eye. A naked woman with wavy blond hair, blue nipples, long blue fingernails, and a patch of blue pubic hair was splashed across the cover, wearing a blue peacock feather headdress and standing in a circle of blue feathers. The album was called *Moontan* by a group that I had never heard of: Golden Earring. I was curious. There was a small chunk of hash waiting for me in the bong and a half-empty book of matches beckoning me from the table. I placed the mystery record on the turntable and the needle on the record. I struck a match, fired up, and took a hit. "Radar Love" filled the flat.

And so it began. If it bothered Thomas, Karl, and Rudi that I had returned to crash, it didn't show. It was just the opposite. They greeted me with open arms like I was some long-lost relative returning from a faraway land. I wasn't the only one they took in. Curtis, an eighteen-year-old from Chicago, had already been staying there for a few weeks. His plan was to live in Switzerland for one year and get into his photography. Curtis had a camera called a Canon F-1, a shitload of lenses, and a compulsion to keep a photographic record of the daily happenings at Baselstrasse 7.

I was back in the same old scene I had left months earlier. The flat was a continuous party, a nonstop carnival of music, German beer, and hashish. Thomas still had his job with the rental car company, disappearing and returning at odd times of day and night. Karl also had a job, although it wasn't clear what it was. His on and off schedule made no sense to me. Rudi, on the other hand, didn't have or need one. He sold a few grams of hash to friends that stopped by and played the drums in his bedroom whenever he was bored or high. He was the perfect party dude because he never seemed to sleep. Thomas and Karl had a younger sister, Marianne, who stopped by nearly every night to join in the festivities. She and Rudi didn't seem to be an actual couple, but they sometimes retreated to his room to have sex. Thomas and Karl kept the music loud so they didn't have to listen.

I quickly reverted back to my old routine of hanging out along the north bank of the river, claiming a small table at an outdoor café and nursing a beer. Only now it was different. Every beer brought me one step closer to destitution. Summer was on its last legs. The days were warm but getting shorter. The summer transients were gone, and there were no Robins or Silvias with an *I* to pick up. Rudi was getting laid, but I wasn't. I was becoming the "nowhere man" that John Lennon had written about.

I had been there about a week when Karl burst through the door, claiming to have found me a job. The only problem was that foreigners were not allowed to work in Switzerland without a work permit. Karl didn't seem overly concerned. His ability to bullshit his way through anything reminded me of Ozzie. He insisted that because I had a Swiss name and my grandparents were from Switzerland, he could get me hired at Keller Moving Company in Lucerne. He turned out to be right. He went with me the next morning to meet the owner. Mr. Keller, a kind man in his fifties, was skeptical, but Karl was a force of nature to be reckoned with. He convinced Mr.

Keller that I had been granted a work permit and was waiting for it to arrive in the mail. Mr. Keller gave in reluctantly and said that I could start the next day.

The job paid fifteen Swiss francs per hour. It was more than I could have hoped for in my wildest dreams. It was hard work. I was paired with two husky, muscular dudes who spoke no English and appeared to have been born without necks. Up until now, my stabs at speaking in German had been fun, a chance to practice what I had learned in college. Now it was critical to my well-being.

The German words for "up," "down," "right," and "left"—*oben, unten, rechts*, and *links*—were the most crucial commodities in my survival kit. There were no elevators in the flats we visited, and moving desks, dressers, and pianos up and down several winding flights of stairs was often a high-wire act of epic proportions. The no-neck dudes fired their instructions to me at Gatling-gun speeds, and there was no room for error. One slip, one stumble and one of us could find ourselves crushed beneath the weight of a five-hundred-pound piano. I returned each evening to the party at Baselstrasse 7 as a bruised and battered member of the Swiss working class.

I was fired after one week. Mr. Keller called me into his office and asked me to produce my work permit. When I told him that I was still waiting for it to come in the mail, he just smiled and said that he would have to let me go. He was an honest man who knew that he had been duped. He could have stiffed me but instead handed me a roll of bills that totaled more than five hundred francs. I was rolling in the dough again and had bought myself more time.

I stayed in Lucerne through the end of August into early September. Most nights, I drank and smoked myself into oblivion. My downward spiral continued, and it was only made worse by the letter I received from Jane toward the end of the month. I wrote my parents when I arrived in Switzerland and told them that I would be staying in Lucerne for a while. Apparently, Jane had been trying to track me down and had reached out to them for my address. My past was hot on my trail, and her words hit me like a ton of bricks. She was pregnant and expecting some time in November. That breaking news was heavy enough, but what followed next blew me away.

She asserted that since we were still married, I might legally be the father. I did the math and concluded that she had conceived back in February around the time I had crashed at Randy's in Cambridge. I may have been a little fucked up that night, but my memory was clear. I distinctly recalled a naked Rick swooping in as her knight in shining armor and carrying her up the stairs. This was on him, not me. Jane knew it, and I knew it. Yet here she was, sending a warning shot across my bow. She ended her uplifting letter by suggesting that she might be forced to file desertion papers against me.

When I told Thomas and Karl the news, they decided that a change of scenery was in order. Thomas somehow managed to score a French car called a Peugeot free of charge from the rental car company, and we were ready to roll. The five of us piled into the burgundy four-door sedan with our sleeping bags, Rudi's trusty ax, and enough food, alcohol, and hashish to get us through the weekend. We headed into the mountains. Rudi's uncle owned a small log cabin about an hour away near the tiny village of Emmetten, not far from the southern shores of Lake Lucerne. We chopped wood, cooked bratwurst and beans over a campfire, and hiked for miles. We encountered dozens of those gigantic Swiss cows, reveled in the gorgeous vistas, and stayed high throughout the days and nights. When we returned to Baselstrasse 7, I felt like a new man.

Still, I needed to make a move. I was once again back where I started, a nowhere man trapped in a nowhere scene. Thomas, Karl, and Rudi were good dudes, and they were generous and good to me, but just getting high and listening to music all the time was a dead-end street. I wanted to get my creative juices flowing again, experience new places and new people. If I wasn't going back to the US, I needed to make a new life for myself somewhere in Europe. Was Gretchen and West Germany the answer? I had missed her birthday party in Wurzburg, but I still had her address. I could easily hitchhike to Heidelberg in a day. It wasn't more than a three- or four-hour drive from Lucerne.

I broke the news to Thomas, Karl, and Rudi on Friday, August 31, that I was going to head up to West Germany and look for work. They were cool with that but insisted that I stick around for a few more days. They reminded me that Frank Zappa and his Mothers of Invention were playing a concert outside of Zurich on Sunday. There was no chance that they were going to miss it, and they assumed that I felt the same way. I didn't argue. What were a few days one way or another? When would I ever have a chance to see Frank Zappa again?

The concert was at night at an inside venue called Mehrzweckhalle Wetzikon. It was a raucous crowd. Frank was apparently popular in Europe. The audience responded well to the songs they were familiar with, like "The Dog Breath Variations," "Uncle Meat," and "Brown Shoes Don't Make It," but seemed perplexed by the new stuff that none of them, including me, had heard before. You could have heard a pin drop as he was introducing a new song that he said was about moving to Montana and raising up some dental floss. Regardless, it was a great concert and a great time. Rudi's hash pipe circulated in perpetual motion and was never empty.

If this was my last time in Switzerland, it was one helluva send-off.

120

Before leaving Lucerne, I picked up a copy of the *International Herald Tribune.* I had not read a newspaper in over two months, and it was time for me to catch up on what was happening in the world. There was some stuff about recent nuclear tests performed by the French and by the Soviet Union, but that wasn't the news I was looking for. I was more interested in whatever questionable behavior might be emanating from the United States of Nixon.

Plenty of shit had happened since I last checked in, but none of it surprised me. The fish was rotting. Tricky Dick and his sycophants were now under serious investigation, and they were starting to circle the wagons. Some dude named Butterfield had let the cat out of the bag and revealed that paranoid Richard Milhous had been recording all the conversations and phone calls in the Oval Office. Dick had then doubled-down and was refusing to turn over his tape recordings to the Senate committee or the special prosecutor trying to nail his ass. America was preparing for another old-fashioned gunfight at the O.K. Corral.

The news from the land of Nixon was predictable. It only served to remind me why I had left in the first place. It was time to put up or shut up, time to move beyond the romantic notion of being an expatriate and actually become one. I was determined to remain abroad. I had no idea where I would end up living, but I figured that I might as well give West Germany a try.

Would Oberschonbrunn be the place I was searching for? The tiny hamlet was far more quaint and charming than I had imagined it would be. Although only about twenty miles outside of Heidelberg, I was entering a world that had been created by the Brothers Grimm. Maybe this small village with its Hansel and Gretel gingerbread

houses was the right place to start over. The fresh air, lush green forests, small farms, and nearby Neckar River seemed the perfect anti-
dote for what ailed me. I had no trouble finding Gretchen's house at
Steinbruchstrasse 1. As I strolled into town, I was met by an elderly
woman wearing a scarf and carrying a small sack full of fresh vegetables. Before I could even say Gretchen's name, the woman knew who
I was looking for. Who else would someone who looked like me be
coming to visit in this remote community? She pointed to the fairy-
tale house on the corner. A white VW Beetle was parked along the
wall next to it.

Gretchen smiled when she saw me.

"I knew you would come," was all she said when she opened
the door.

The first few days were great. It had been a long time since I last
had my own room and my own bed. I loved Gretchen's house. It was
a timber-framed structure with a steeply-angled A-frame roofline.
From a distance, it looked like a giant game of Tic-Tac-Toe. The
diagonal bracing of the dark-brown beams formed a series of trian-
gles and Xs across the white outside walls. The section in front of the
house was a triangular patch where Gretchen had planted a vegetable
garden. It was bordered on both sides by a short brown cross-picket
fence that came together at the corner.

I was convinced that this was where I needed to be. Gretchen
had her gardening, her writing, and her free school to keep her
busy. I loved the solitude. I took long walks in the countryside and
started writing poetry again. I was feeling a spiritual connection with
Oberschonbrunn and was in no hurry to look for a job. My furni-
ture-moving venture had provided me with a little money and had
bought me more time. When Gretchen offered to let me stay rent-
free as long as I wanted, I was ready to settle in for the long haul.
However, as I soon discovered, nothing is ever really free. The rules
quickly became crystal clear.

I really liked Gretchen. I loved her mind, her intellect. I loved
the person she was and the way she lived her life. However, I wasn't
physically attracted to her. I had not come there to become her lover.
Even so, the first time was great. It happened innocently enough. I

had only been staying at her house for two days when she asked me if I would like to go into Wurzburg. She was meeting some friends at a club, and it sounded like a cool idea. I had missed her August birthday party, so this would be a chance for me to check out the city. The drive in took a little more than an hour. Wurzburg was a university town with a population of slightly over one hundred thousand. We arrived in the early evening just as it was getting dark and met four of her friends at a dimly lit jazz club in the old section of town. It was the hippest bar that I had ever been to. The jazz trio was led by a black dude playing the saxophone. An opaque cloud of cigarette smoke drifted over the small tables like a thin blue veil. It was the sort of place that Jack Kerouac would have dug if he were still alive. We drank beer. We discussed politics and literature. The lively conversations and the alcohol, combined with the low light, improvisations of the sax player, and the syncopated rhythms of the room, were intoxicating. They combined to jump-start my senses and my intellect and give me the best high I had felt in ages.

I don't remember much of the drive home that night or getting undressed or jumping into bed. I had just fallen asleep when I felt the warmth of her body pressed against mine. For all I know, she might have been there all along. The fact that it was Gretchen was irrelevant. It could have been anyone. Since abandoning Loutro, my testicles had been producing and storing several hundred thousand sperm cells a day. The boys were restless and wanted out in the worst way.

A volcanic eruption is caused by molten rock rising through the cracks or weaknesses in the earth's crust. The pressure in the earth builds until it becomes so great that the molten rock explodes to the surface, creating the flow of lava. That's about the best way to explain that night in bed with Gretchen. She instinctively knew where the cracks and weaknesses were in my crust. She knew what I needed, and she needed the same thing. She was all over me like a storm trooper, and I returned the favor. It had been a long time. The room was dark. I could feel her and I could smell her, but I couldn't see her. It was like balling an apparition. I released enough semen to fill an empty milk bottle.

I was alone when I woke up the next morning. The sheets were still wet. When I walked into the kitchen, I found Gretchen sitting at the table, drinking coffee. She offered me a cup. We didn't talk about the night before. It was as if it had never happened. It wasn't until I was heading to bed two nights later that I understood how she was expecting me to pay the rent. She called me into her room and asked me to take off my clothes and get into bed with her. Before we got started, she wanted to make sure that I understood our arrangement. The rules were simple. She wasn't looking for a lover or interested in having a serious relationship with me or anyone else. She had her needs, and as long as I was staying in her home, she expected me to satisfy her sexual appetites whenever she asked.

At first, I didn't mind. I was finally getting laid again. My attitude changed by the third night. Gretchen was a big girl with a big appetite and a big bush. She always insisted that I eat her before we did anything else. Since this was my favorite thing to do, I initially approached the task at hand with unbridled enthusiasm. I took the job seriously. Each headfirst plunge became a leap of faith, a blind foray into a dense forest. As I blazed each new trail and whacked my way through the shrubbery, I was reminded again of the Chinese philosopher Lao-Tzu, who said that a journey of a thousand miles must begin with a single step. I approached each headfirst dive as a preliminary bout, a warm-up drill before the main event. I was determined to get the job done, and each time I dove in, I maintained my focus until I reached my destination and tasted victory.

I didn't know what to do. All my plans to stay in Oberschonbrunn, find work, and start a new life were beginning to look like a pipedream. As much as I liked Gretchen and admired her intellect, I was quickly losing interest in having sex with her. Finally, on night 7, things came to a head. Hoping to avoid the inevitable, I told Gretchen that I was tired and slipped off to bed early. I had almost dozed off when I heard the door open and saw her walk into my room. Before I could tell her that I wasn't up for it, she removed her clothes, tossed them on the floor, and jumped into bed with me.

What transpired next was reminiscent of that ill-fated liaison in Florida with Kitty the landlady. Gretchen went right to work, convinced she could make me rise to the occasion. She yanked, licked, pulled, and sucked for what seemed a lifetime. Nothing she tried worked. I was as limp as a dead fish, and there wasn't anything she could do to change that. Exasperated, she sat up and pulled a couple of pubes from her mouth.

"I give up," she said. "All I'm getting is a mouthful of hair."

With that, she abruptly jumped out of bed, picked her clothes up off the floor, and stormed out of the room naked.

When I met her in the kitchen the next morning, I told her I was sorry about the night before. She didn't seem upset.

"That's okay," she said. "It happens."

Whether or not she meant it was unimportant. I needed some time off, to get away for a few days and clear my head. I decided to tell her that I was going to hitchhike down to Lucerne. The lame excuse I came up with was that I had to pick up some things that I had forgotten to bring with me and check to see if I had received any mail. The story about the mail was true. The flat at Baselstrasse 7 was the only address that anyone had for me. I promised I would be back in a few days. I didn't take all my shit with me because I did intend to return. I could decide my next move once I got back. I knew that Lucerne wasn't the answer. I just needed a break.

The break turned out to be Jill Jackson from Lafayette, Louisiana.

121

I barely gave them a second thought. They were just another hippie couple hitchhiking in the same direction as me. I had thumbed into Heidelberg that morning so I could pick up the main expressway heading south toward Basel and the Swiss border. While it was illegal to hitchhike on the Autobahn, it was perfectly legal to stand at an entrance and stick out my thumb.

Since they had gotten there first, I observed one of the cardinal rules of hitchhiking etiquette and planted myself a reasonable distance past them at the entrance. As I went by, I asked the dude how long they had been waiting for a ride. He looked to be in his early twenties, had shoulder-length black hair, movie-star good looks, and a golden tan. He said they had been standing there for more than hour. I introduced myself and asked where they were going. He glanced over at his companion before answering. The chick, who I assumed was his girlfriend, appeared to be a little older than him. Her light-brown hair was straight and nearly reached her waist. She just shrugged her shoulders as if to say she didn't know or didn't care. She had a pretty face, but I was struck by how thin and pale she was.

"Lake Geneva," said the dude, "and then maybe down to the French Riviera."

They were Americans, but I never got their names. It didn't matter because as soon as they scored a ride, I would never see them again. My day didn't look too promising. If the two of them had been waiting for more than an hour, what were my chances of making it out of Heidelberg anytime soon? Once I had reached an acceptable distance from them, I placed my backpack on the ground and took a seat. I mentally prepared myself for the long wait.

I must have been living a charmed life. I had barely sat down when a shiny silver-blue four-door Mercedes Benz pulled up and offered the hippie couple a ride. The driver, a well-dressed man in his forties, got out of the car and opened the trunk. I watched the hippie couple toss their backpacks in and then pile into the back seat together. I was happy for them and happy for me. I stood, picked up my pack, and started for the now-vacant spot at the entrance. To my surprise, the Mercedes pulled up beside me and stopped. The back window on the passenger side was rolled down.

"Get in," she said. "He said that he would give you a ride too."

It was definitely my lucky day. The man, whose name was Siegfried, was going all the way to Lucerne. My backpack got to join its siblings in the trunk of the Mercedes while I got to ride shotgun in the front next to Siegfried. I was in the lap of luxury. I had never ridden in a car this high class. There were no speed limits on the Autobahn. It was like being shot out of a cannon and soaring through the universe at the speed of light. I could hear Golden Earring screaming in my ear about radar love. It was more than just a ride. When it was over, I understood what it meant to be *hypnotized and speeding toward a new sunrise*.

Siegfried was the one who brought us together. He engaged all three of us in lively conversation as he flew by other vehicles like they were standing still. He was eager to hear our stories and learn of our adventures. Darrell was from California and Jill from Louisiana. They had met two weeks earlier in Spain and had traveled through France and West Germany together. I opened up about my exploits and talked of my summer on Crete, as well as my travels through Holland, Germany, Switzerland, Italy, Yugoslavia, and Austria. My German was gradually getting better, and I was able to carry on some conversations with Siegfried in his native tongue. When we got to Basel, he offered to buy the three of us lunch in a restaurant nicer than any I had ever been to in my life.

Siegfried seemed to relish the stares he got as he escorted three scruffy characters like us into such a fine establishment. All the stories of my time on the road had picked up my spirits. I was starting to see myself as worldly for the first time, and I was feeling cocky. When it came time to order, I spoke to the waitress in German. Siegfried was impressed. Apparently, so was Jill. When we were about fifty kilometers south of Basel, Siegfried pulled the Mercedes over and told Darrell and Jill that this was where he needed to exit for Lucerne and they needed to get out and catch another ride. Darrell opened the door and jumped out, but Jill stayed put. Darrell looked a little confused and stuck his head back in the car.

"What are you doing?" he asked. "We have to get out here."

Jill came across the seat and met him halfway. She kissed him on the cheek and then sat back down. She turned and pointed to me.

"Darrell," she said, "we had a great time, but I am going to go with him."

122

It was the seventh day. Or maybe it was the eighth, I can't remember.

We were alone in the flat. I was on bottom and had a clear view of the Jimi Hendrix poster in the living room. A tingling sensation swept over my arms and legs and briefly touched every nerve in my body. Reality was beginning to warp. I was in a twilight zone where my ability to distinguish what was actually happening was on a collision course with the physical interaction of my imagination. Untethered thoughts swirled in my head like debris inside a cyclone.

Jill was on top. She was a 78 record slowing down to 33 rpm's. Her right hand was waving in the air above her head while the fingers of her left were pressed against my stomach. It was a slow-motion rodeo, and she was the bull rider, casting a long shadow across the Sturmgewehr 57 on the wall behind her. We were melded together, and nothing could pull us apart.

Quaaludes were a wonderful thing. I was continuously aroused and able to stay erect for heroic amounts of time. Each performance was an epic event, an existential snowball. This physical union was no different. It began as a single snowflake rolling down a hill and reaching out to pick up other snowflakes along the way. As the snowball gathered steam, its sheer size and strength caused it to crescendo. I let out a scream. Jill's was even louder.

Jill was the spring thaw, and I was the bear coming out of hibernation. Her lithesome body was now my playground. An unfolding mindscape of distant sounds and tumbling thoughts had seized control of me. Kidnapped inside my own body, I was still semihard when she raised her hips, gripped my penis at its base, and cajoled it to slide out. She collapsed next to me on the mattress but refused to let it go. It had been like this for days. What had begun for me as a three- or four-day sabbatical in Lucerne had evolved into an ongoing fondle fest. I had lost track of time and the number of times we had done this. I closed my eyes for a few minutes and drifted off. When I opened them, Jill was sitting up near the foot of the mattress. Her knees were drawn to her chest, and her arms were clasped around her shins. She looked sad.

"I'm going to Turkey," she said. "I want you to come with me."

I had found another wounded bird. Or had the wounded bird found me? Maybe she saw me as a kindred spirit, another lost soul just like herself. My gut told me that we were different. Jill was clearly running away, fleeing something that had left an indelible scar on her. As close as we had grown and as much as we had shared our inner thoughts, her pain was buried so deep that it was impossible to pry loose. I wanted to believe that I wasn't like her, that I was running *toward* something, not away. Regardless, we had managed to give each other an emotional transfusion. I didn't give her an answer right away. I knew that I wasn't going to Turkey with her, but I didn't want this sensory submission to end. She had an endless supply of Quaaludes, and her desire for me was insatiable. I was in a permanent state of euphoria, tasting a hundred different pleasures that had eluded me up until now.

We had very little privacy, but we didn't care. Thomas, Karl, and Rudi had opened their home to me when I showed up again, this time with Jill. Since Curtis was sleeping on the couch in the living room, Thomas pulled a mattress into his bedroom and said it was ours as long as we wanted. We shed our clothes and spent most of our time on top of it, rolling in and out of my sleeping bag. His bedroom didn't have a door, so we were in full view most of the time. If the four of them were growing tired of watching us get it on, they never said a word. The credit for their laissez-faire attitude belonged to Jill. Besides sharing her Quaaludes with them like it was Halloween night and she was passing out candy, Jill was quite comfortable wandering nude around the flat no matter who happened to be there. We normally put our clothes on for a few hours in the evening and joined the party in the living room where the music was blaring. Rudi had bought *Over-Nite Sensation*, the new just-released

Frank Zappa album. We listened to it over and over, smoking our hash, popping our Quaaludes, and washing it all down with bottles of German beer.

My favorite moments were the quiet ones when we were alone in the claw-foot bathtub. Words were unnecessary. The Quaaludes took over. We conversed with our eyes and verbalized with our hands. Our conscious thoughts dissolved into early stages of dreaming whenever we explored each other with our gentle yet uninhibited zeal. No orifice or body part was ignored. Jill's desire for me was unrelenting. She understood my body in ways no one ever had before, and she possessed an intuitive grasp of how to guide it toward nirvana. We would sit in the tub facing each other, with our knees bent and our legs wide open. Each time was better than the last. One hand would be in the water, swim under the submerged testicles, and insert a finger. Her other hand acted as a velvet glove, massaging the mast sticking out of the water with soft strokes until her head fell forward and it was in her mouth. Each climax was a high-speed nuclear reaction, a sexual energy that transcended both space and time.

I tried to return the favors whenever I could. Jill was a pliable partner who encouraged me to go wherever my imagination took me. Exploring her was infectious, much like catching a ride on a euphoric rainbow in a Peter Max painting. Her skin was fair, almost chalky. When I first saw her in the flesh, I was surprised at how thin she actually was. Her ribs were showing, her breasts were small, and she looked a little emaciated to me. She was the happiest when we made love, but even her playful laughter contained no joy. I could feel her pain, but I was helpless to do anything about it.

Finally, after another record-setting oral encounter, I broke down and confessed that I wasn't venturing off to Turkey with her. I tried to talk her out of going, not to get her to stay with me but because I was concerned for her safety. Hitchhiking through the Middle East seemed risky enough for a longhaired dude like me. I hated to think what might happen to an American girl traveling alone. She said she didn't care. She would not come out and say it, but I sensed she had a fatalistic attitude about her future. Life had dealt her a bad hand, and she was prepared for whatever was in store for her next. She put her head on my chest and snuggled in my arms. When we woke up an hour or two later, she suggested we take another bath.

By day 12, I was completely spent. Jill had squeezed, pulled, and sucked all the toothpaste out of the tube. My balls were reduced to a pair of low-hanging balloons with all the air let out. The very essence of my being was in jeopardy. Jill had lodged herself under my skin. Her sexuality and her Quaaludes were addictive. Neil Young was in my brain, singing "I love you baby / can I have some more." If I didn't split now, I never would.

I told her that I was going back up to Heidelberg to look for work. I wasn't thinking clearly when she asked me how she could get in touch with me. The Quaaludes had softened my brain.

Like an idiot, I gave her Gretchen's address and phone number.

123

It was about time I stopped kidding myself and admit that I was a bum. As much as I wanted to believe the path I was carving out was in the tradition of London, Kerouac, and Hemingway, the sad truth was that I had become nothing more than a derelict. When I left the States, I carried with me a sense of complete freedom and optimism. Now, months later, I was drifting without direction or purpose. The idea that I was going to Heidelberg or anywhere else to look for a job was a joke. I had been using that line since Miami. If I was being honest, I would concede that my ambition in life was to work as little as possible. I drank all the time, did drugs at every turn, and was a sucker for a pretty face. It sounded romantic and adventurous now, but where would I be in ten or twenty years? Would I even be alive?

I knew I was in trouble when Gretchen opened the door. Her arms were folded tightly beneath her sizable breasts while her big green eyes were shooting daggers at me.

"Someone named Jill called for you earlier."

"What did she want?"

"She asked me to tell you that she missed you."

With that, she turned and walked away. There would be no late-night visits to my room, no more headfirst dives into the furry undergrowth. I was relieved. My head was still in the ozone, less than twenty-four hours removed from the effects of my last Quaalude. My nether regions were pleading with me for a time out. Nevertheless, I clearly had a problem. The cool reception was a sign of things to come. My days in Oberschonbrunn were numbered.

Gretchen didn't ask me to leave, but it was obvious she wanted me gone. She ignored me most of the time, and we barely spoke to each other when we occupied the same space. I tried to break the ice, but it was pointless. I was in my room counting the days and contemplating where to go next when I heard a loud knock at the front door. I wasn't sure where Gretchen was, so I decided to hop out of bed and see who was there. I was stunned when I opened the door.

"My friend," he said, "it's good to see you."

He was wearing black jeans and a black wool sweater, but there was no mistaking the scraggly beard and tan face bursting with life and mischief. I couldn't have been any happier if Mighty Mouse himself had shown up singing "Here I Come to Save the Day." The high tide of destiny had washed up in Oberschonbrunn and left him in its wake. It was Vassilis, and he had come to the rescue.

Or so I thought. Gretchen greeted him warmly at first, and for a while it seemed like the Loutro Order of the Amphibious Chicken was getting back together again. This sentimental journey lasted but a few days. This was Gretchen's home, and she had a life to live: writing, gardening, and running her free school. What she didn't have patience for were a couple of derelicts hanging around her house, getting high all the time, and neither one fucking her. My friendship with Vassilis picked up right where it had left off on Crete. We discussed music and literature and the current state of affairs in Greece. Papadopoulos and his thugs had carried the day in the plebiscite, and the monarchy had been abolished under the cynical guise of reform. Vassilis had left his country because he wanted no part of life under the brutal military regime that US vice president Spiro the Zero had declared the best thing to happen to Greece since the golden age of Pericles in ancient Athens. Vassilis predicted that the shit was about to hit the fan. He was sure that an uprising of students and workers was about to happen and that Papadopoulos would respond with brute force and bloodshed. When I brought up what was happening with Nixon and his cohorts, Vassilis just shrugged it off. He claimed it didn't matter who or what political party was running my government because every one of them supported the military takeover of his country.

There was no Ouzo or Retsina to guide us through the days and nights, but Vassilis was carrying enough hashish to make up for it. Most of our time was spent at Gretchen's kitchen table, and most of our focus was on getting wasted and writing poetry together. I had been jotting down poems, verses, and my thoughts since the day I arrived in Europe, and I was comfortable enough to share them with Vassilis. He told me he thought I was talented, and he encouraged me not to give it up. It lifted my spirits, and for a few days, I actually felt good about myself again.

By the fourth night, Gretchen had had enough and threw us out. At first, I thought she was a mirage standing beneath the languid cloud of smoke that was hovering over the kitchen. Vassilis was holding the pipe and laughing at a verse that I had written, and I was trying to fight off the incessant cough that the last protracted hit had left behind. Gretchen was pissed.

"I think it is time that the two of you left," she said.

Vassilis looked over at me and shrugged.

"Where should we go now, my friend?" he asked.

"I have some friends in Switzerland," I said.

It was all I could think of on such short notice.

124

It was the night of the Black Lung. Shakespearean comics sat at mustard-stained tables while magic chessboards wiggled through the crowds. Carnivals came to life in the form of paper mannequins, and five-dimensional spirits were afraid to go out in the world because it was raining. Double-knits pranced by with their hairspray revolution. In the solitude of madness, a virgin deer trembled while the armies of derange sneered. The candle burned while outside lunatics with pushbuttons played almighty, never consulting, only deciding. The world was a holocaust, but inside crumpled cigarettes floated methodically and outside it was still raining.
Energy raged with nowhere to go. The night of the Black Lung was upon us.

I wrote these words in the waning hours of the acid trip before I crash-landed and the events of the night evaporated into the ether to be lost forever. Memory can be a soothing companion, a gifted sculptor capable of kneading the clay of our malleable past into a comforting work of art. I didn't want to sugarcoat what had happened and the effect it was having on me. There was no meeting God, no Mysterious Chameleon or Jesus disguised as Tony from Australia showing me the way. My pilgrimage was throwing a monkey wrench into any theory of evolution. I doubted whether Charles Darwin would recognize the path I was on. The ground below me was ceasing to exist, and there was no net to catch me. Allen Ginsberg wrote that he saw the best minds of his generation destroyed by madness. My generation had been dying in the leech-infested rice paddies of Vietnam, sticking needles in their arms, and fleeing to Canada. Some were like me, racing round and round on a hamster wheel, unsure of where it was taking us but afraid to jump off. I didn't know what to do next. I was in a downward spiral, tumbling through a rabbit hole into a bottomless pit. I sensed there were darker times ahead.

The dudes of Baselstrasse 7 were surprised to see me but were nevertheless happy to welcome me back into the fold. Jill and her Quaaludes had vanished, but I had brought with me a worthy replacement, a Greek bearing the gifts of killer hash. I lost track of time. Like Yogi Berra, I was experiencing déjà vu all over again. The music and the drugs were locked in a perpetual duel. Deep Purple was singing "smoke on the water," but there was no "fire in the sky." I was back in the living room, trying to sleep in a room that never slept. September was approaching its grand finale. The days were shorter, the nights were getting colder, and the walls were closing in.

The Black Lung was an assailant lying in wait.

Purple-gray smoke had formed a permanent layer of dancing smog near the ceiling of the flat. The cloud hung in the air like fog in an alley, ready to greet anyone brave enough to open the door and enter. Once inside, there was no escaping its reach. The smell permeated every hair, invaded every pore, and clung to every fiber. We sucked the smoke particles deep into our air passages and felt the sweet burning sensation curl throughout our lungs and throat until we could no longer hold them in and were forced to let them escape. Ribbons of Death swirled upward, twisting and turning like garter snakes.

The Black Lung was now in control.

We were listening to Pink Floyd's new album *Dark Side of the Moon* and lamenting our dwindling supply of drugs when Karl barreled through the door and announced that he had received the trips in the mail he had been waiting for. We weren't sure what type of LSD Karl had scored, but we didn't care. It seemed like a good way to break the monotony of smoking the remains of Vassilis's killer hash.

And so it began.

There were five of us who dropped acid. My trip companions were Thomas, Karl, Rudi, and Vassilis. Curtis took a pass. He had met an eighteen-year-old American girl earlier that day and had invited her to stop by the flat. He didn't want to be freaking out when she showed up. Karl tried to change his mind, but Curtis had the good sense to stick to his guns.

We had just crossed over the threshold when Pink Floyd offered us a glimpse of our future.

"Us…us…us…us…us…and them…them…them…them…them."

We should have heeded the warning from Roger Waters, but we were at the point of no return. Karl suggested we leave the safe confines of the flat and venture into the crazed carnage of the outside world. The cold chill had set in, and the dark sky was pissing rain. It was the start of Oktoberfest, and we were about to be thrust into the calamity of creatures already thronging the streets. Words were useless. We descended the three flights of stairs at Baselstrasse 7 like a colony of ants marching in single file. Spellbound by a trail littered with irresistible pheromones, we crossed over the cool breeze of the Reuss River beneath the rafters of the Spreuer Bridge. Each dancing skeleton of death came to life and urged us to keep going. When we reached the promenade along the north bank, we were met by a dude who called himself Lewis Carroll. He was a short elderly man in an Abe Lincoln top hat, chatting the jabberwocky of a sidewalk saint and warning us to shun the grotesque creatures we were about to encounter. We ignored his advice and soldiered on without fear through the rain. The intoxicating trail of pheromones led us to the heart of Mr. Pickwick's Pub. We rode in on a magic carpet like wet aliens from a distant planet. We were in the land of polyester. Women wearing high-cut boots and low-cut pants were being pursued by men in two-button checked sport coats, tight white slacks, and platform shoes. All the women, in their late twenties and early thirties, wore gold-button earrings to accent their close-cropped hair and upturned bangs. Peach, tangerine, and pistachio were the polyester flavors of choice. There was a piano in the far corner but no piano player. Karl seized the opportunity, bullying his way through the crowd of creatures to bang on the keys. The polyester creatures froze. Mr. Pickwick's Pub grew silent. Karl climbed to the top of the piano and stood up. Then, in a booming voice that could be heard throughout the Swiss Alps, he began to yodel. As his voice launched into dramatic leaps of low-pitch chest sounds and high falsetto notes, Karl reached down and scooped the creatures into the palms of his hands. One by one, they joined in. Soon, every polyester creature was yodeling. Each assumed that Karl was the entertainment that Mr. Pickwick had booked for the evening. They applauded and cheered. Karl took a formal bow and performed an acrobatic leap off the piano. The sea of creatures parted as he ran for the exit. We followed him into the waterlogged night. We could hear the fading cheers and yodels trailing us as we raced in swift pursuit of Karl over the Chapel Bridge. A giant Ferris wheel and a merry-go-round of wooden horses were waiting for us on the southern banks of the Reuss. We were near the train station where dapper dudes wearing knee-length leather trousers with ornamental buckles were playing oompah music on gigantic tubas. Busty women danced over to offer us large mugs full of beer. They wore low-cut blouses with long puff sleeves, full skirts, and long colorful aprons. I accepted a frosted beer from the prettiest one and chugged it down. When I finished, I handed her the mug and freed my eyes to survey the scene. My companions were gone. Had they been swallowed up by the polyester creatures? Had they melted in the rain like the wicked witch of the West? The woman holding my empty mug motioned to an open door. Her ivory breasts had fallen out of her blouse, and she was blushing. She pointed to the sign that read Haus der spegel. Unable to resist the temptation, I stepped into the portal and emerged on the other side.

There was no turning back. I had lost all contact with reality. LSD had fried my brain, and I was in a house of mirrors, being confronted with confusing and frightening images of myself. Mirrors were obstacles that I would have to overcome in order to solve the puzzle I had stumbled upon. If I was to escape the maze and return to reality, my focus would have to be on a true path, not the glass panes put there to trick me into seeking places I could never reach. I would need to smash through them, blow them to smithereens, and assert my autonomy. I wanted to cry for help, but I knew that no one could hear me. Everything was distorted. I fought my way through the mirrored jungle. I was a schizophrenic polygon, unable to decide whether I was convex or concave. My contorted face frightened me. I touched it to see if it was real. It was, but I wasn't convinced it was mine.

Then, in one fell swoop, the Black Lung reached into my nightmare and pulled me out.

Vassilis was waiting for me. He was standing next to the woman whose breasts had fallen out of her blouse. The mug was full of beer again, and she handed it to me.

"My friend," Vassilis said, "did you enjoy your trip through the house of mirrors?"

My legs were wobbly. My head was spinning, and I was trying like hell to get my bearings. The street was full of polyester creatures. I chugged my beer and handed the empty mug back to the woman whose breasts had fallen out of her blouse.

"Where are Thomas and Karl?" I asked.

"My friend," he said, "I believe they have returned to the flat to smoke more hash. Would you like to go there now?"

I nodded yes. Vassilis had never looked so wild, so untamed. His eyes were dancing like sparks in a fading candle. He and I were the only ones on the street, speaking English. I could no longer understand German. The polyester creatures were now speaking gibberish. I covered my ears and followed the blurred outline of Vassilis down the path along the river, where I hoped to return to the comforting womb of Baselstrasse 7.

We could hear the music before we entered the building. As we climbed the stairs, Pink Floyd was singing about money and telling us to keep our hands off their stack. The door to the flat was half open, and wisps of the Black Lung danced into the hallway, greeting us with outstretched arms to invite us to the party. Tendrils of silver smoke swirled around our heads and accompanied us into the living room. We had accessed a world of four, possibly five, dimensions. Karl and Thomas were sitting on the floor sharing a bag of magic potato chips. Rudi was in front of the stereo, studying the surreal artwork of the *Over-Nite Sensation* album cover. The Formica table was littered with empty beer bottles, dirty plates, Rudi's reliable bong, and a small chunk of black hash. In the world of three dimensions, Curtis was sitting on the couch, holding court with a virgin deer. He was clutching his Canon F-1, but it was impossible to hear what he was saying because the music was so loud. She was a pretty girl, a picture of innocence in a den of iniquity, who looked younger than her eighteen years. Curtis and the fair young maiden were not prepared for the madness about to ensnare them. *Dark Side of the Moon* and *Over-Nite Sensation* traded places on the turntable. By the third song, Frank Zappa was begging for *dirty love* and Vassilis was circling the room like a predator stalking his prey. Bloodshot eyes fell from the faces of madmen and rolled across the floor. Sensing the danger, Curtis and the virgin deer scampered for the exit and disappeared into the uncertainty of darkness. It was still raining. Hints of daylight began to converge outside the room's only window. It would soon be morning. As my heart raced toward the rising sun, an avalanche of emotion washed over me. The armies of the Black Lung had completed their task and were in retreat. It was the dawn of a new day.

I knew what I had to do.

125

Vassilis had an idea.

"My friend," he said, "why don't you come to Berlin with me? I have some friends there we can stay with for a few weeks. After that, we will travel to Afghanistan."

"Maybe," I said, shrugging my shoulders. "I dunno."

The very fact that I was considering it showed what a vagabond I had become. Was I out of my fucking mind? Afghanistan? Where the hell was that? Berlin? The thought of traveling the one hundred mile stretch of barricaded highway through East Germany to reach the city divided by a wall sounded thrilling enough to me, but I was nearly out of money. This wasn't Yugoslavia. Would the commies even let me past their checkpoints?

"I don't have any money left," I said.

"Do not worry, my friend," Vassilis replied. "I have enough money for the both of us."

"Besides," he continued, "there are ways to make money along the way."

So there it was. Yogi Berra was dropping another one of his forks in the road. I was once again at a crossroads. I had changed over the past few months, and it wasn't for the better. Whenever I looked in the mirror, I saw a face that I barely recognized. The hair was longer, the eyes were colder, and the smile had lost its joy and optimism. It was strange. A few months earlier, I was admiring the solitary ones, the seasoned nomads who wandered the world without a country or a place to call home. It seemed romantic at the time, and I longed to be one of them. I had not looked into their souls and considered the dark side. In order to survive in this underground arena, I would have to become a different person. I would need to get by on my wits, live a much seedier existence, and subsist like an outlaw. Afghanistan? Was I really prepared to travel through the Middle East and deal with all the dangers that awaited a longhaired drifter like me? I had heard the horror stories. Others who chose this route had ended up broken in brutal prisons. Some simply vanished from the face of the earth. Was this the kamikaze path I wanted to go down?

Vassilis saw the indecision in my eyes and tried to assure me.

"My friend," he said. "You will love West Berlin. It is a wild, sophisticated city with students and radicals from all over the world. There is a free university, an underground press, and all the drugs you could ever want. The women are beautiful and outnumber the men. We will go to a bar called the Resi, where the women ask the men to dance and we will get laid. The next night, I will take you to the Old Eden Saloon. It is where everyone goes, and it has everything you could want: jazz, disco dancing, and light shows. You can order a drink while you sit in a school desk and watch pornography that is being projected on the ceiling."

It was tempting, but Yogi was waiting for me to pick up his fork.

I shook my head.

"Sorry, Vassilis," I said. "I want to go back to the States."

If he was disappointed, it didn't show.

"The problem is," I continued, "I don't have any money to buy a plane ticket."

Vassilis smiled. "Don't worry about that, my friend. How much do you need?"

I thought about it for a minute. A ticket back to Florida would probably cost at least two hundred dollars, maybe more. That and I needed money to survive on for a while.

"I dunno," I offered, "maybe three hundred dollars?"

"Okay, my friend," he said. "We will get you three hundred dollars."

126

His plan was simple.

The next morning we strolled along the Reuss up to the Bahnhof, where Vassilis bought a pair of round-trip tickets. Twenty minutes later, we hopped aboard the train. An hour later, we were at the main train station in Zurich. It took us another hour to find the American Express office. Vassilis handed me three hundred dollars and instructed me to go inside and purchase fifteen twenty-dollar traveler's checks. Checks in hand, I signed each one on the line in the upper left-hand corner. Mission accomplished, I walked out the door to find Vassilis leaning against a lamppost and smoking a cigarette. His face was full of mischief.

"Write down the serial numbers of your checks on the paper they gave you, and keep it separate from your checks," he said.

The plan was to return to Lucerne, cash the checks at a bank, and give Vassilis his three hundred dollars back. The following day, I would go to the American Express office in Lucerne and report the checks as stolen. American Express would then issue me fifteen new checks, and I would be on my way to the USA.

"Won't they know it was me who cashed the checks?" I asked.

"My friend," he said, "it happens all the time. They will never know it was you. Besides, look around. This is Switzerland. What does three hundred dollars matter to them?"

It made sense to me, so I did as I was told. When we exited the train in Lucerne, I went straight to the Credit Suisse Bank near the station and cashed all my checks. I had to show the teller my passport in order to make the transaction. That worried me. When I handed Vassilis his money, I asked if the fact they had written down my passport number was going to cause a problem for me. Vassilis laughed.

"My friend," he said, "you worry too much. Remember, *i zoi einai san ena angouri.*"

How could I forget? Vassilis was right. Life was indeed like a cucumber, and it was up to me to taste it and enjoy it. The bounce was back in my step. I would soon have money in my pocket. It was late afternoon when we returned to the flat. Curtis and Rudi were passing the bong. The music was loud, and Frank Zappa was claiming to be "the slime oozing out of our TV sets."

It would be my last night in Lucerne, so we partied until early morning, polishing off the last of the killer hash and all the beer in the refrigerator. When I woke around noon, I took a bath in the claw-foot tub and put on a clean shirt before heading over to the American Express office. Replacing the traveler's checks was as easy as Vassilis said it would be. I walked out a free man, with three hundred dollars and a new lease on life. It was sad leaving behind the new friends that I had made, but I knew I was making the right decision. Thomas, Karl, and Rudi had been good to me. There was no way that I could ever repay them. I tried to convince myself this was just a temporary setback. I would return to the States, find work, and save enough money to leave the country again. I would be back, stronger and wiser than ever. I was now a citizen of the world.

I traveled overnight to Luxembourg. The trip took twelve hours, and I had to change trains in Basel. From there we crossed into France and rumbled through the darkness of the countryside before crossing into the grand duchy of Luxembourg. I had a compartment to myself and tried to sleep, but it was hard. My mind was racing with the uncertainty of what was to come next. The train made a number of stops along the way, and the attendant passed through the car each time to check my ticket. At the French and Luxembourg borders, a customs official came through the car to check passports. The train arrived in Luxembourg City around nine in the morning at the same platform where I had said my goodbyes to Jesus more than five months earlier. I wondered where he was now. Was he still pretending to be Tony from Australia, or had he assumed a new identity?

I needed some Luxembourg currency. I cashed a twenty-dollar traveler's check at the central train station and received 891 francs in return. I bought a train ticket to the airport, and I was soon in the same place where it had all started. Only now it was different. The last time I was here, I was coming down from an acid trip and only had a vague idea of where I was and how I had gotten here. This time, my acid trip had ended three days earlier, and I was a seasoned traveler. I no longer needed Jesus in disguise to show me the way. I found the TWA ticket counter and learned that there was a direct flight to Miami leaving later in the afternoon. A one-way ticket cost two hundred twenty dollars. I whipped out eleven traveler's checks and scored a ride home.

Did I believe in divine intervention? Bokonon, according to my buddy Kurt Vonnegut, wrote that "anyone who thinks he sees what God is doing is a fool."

I didn't consider myself a fool.

I had no clue why I was once again being assigned the best seat on the entire plane.

127

It was an aisle seat at the back of the plane near the toilet. She had the window seat and was staring out the window. There was no one between us in the middle seat.

Her name was Elizabeth. She didn't say much at first. When I sat down, we exchanged names and pleasantries, but after that we didn't speak for at least two hours. I could see that she wanted her space, so I left her alone. She was a pretty girl with bright-green eyes and straight light-blond hair that reached the middle of her back. She looked to be about my age, maybe a year or two younger. She definitely wasn't a hippie chick. Her dark jeans appeared to be brand-new, and the white short-sleeved blouse she was wearing was crisp and shiny. She was holding a paperback book but never opened it.

I must have dozed off. The next thing I remember, the stewardess was asking me if I wanted something to drink. I rubbed the sleep out of my eyes and looked over at Elizabeth, who was staring out the window and sipping on a glass of orange juice. It looked like a good idea to me.

"I guess I'll have some orange juice too," I said. "Thank you."

That's when Elizabeth Summers broke through the ice and entered my life.

"You must miss Florida orange juice as much as I do," she said.

And that was all it took. Her voice was warm, and her smile was contagious. I was drawn to her like a moth is to a flame. The way she opened up to me suggested the attraction was mutual. We shared our stories and our innermost feelings over the next eight hours like we had known each other most of our lives. When we needed a break, we took turns napping across the middle seat with our head in the other's lap. The warmth of her thigh was as soothing as a cup of hot chocolate.

"I'm Mennonite," she said. "Do you know what that is?"

I told her I did not.

"Have you heard of the Amish?" she asked.

I had heard of them but had never met one in person. I remembered seeing pictures of men in broad-brimmed straw hats and suspenders riding in horse-drawn buggies and walking behind plows being pulled by horses. The women in the pictures were in long dresses covered with aprons and wore white bonnets on their heads to cover their hair. I knew there were a bunch of them in Pennsylvania and that they lived simple farming lives, shunning modern life and all modern technology. Elizabeth didn't look very Amish to me.

"We're like the Amish," she explained, "except that we believe in living in the modern world."

She went on to explain that while Mennonites, unlike the Amish, embraced technology, they were careful to maintain their spiritual and moral values and not fall for the temptations of modern society. If that was true, I wondered, why was she talking with me?

Her story interested me. Born and raised in the heart of Pennsylvania Dutch country, she had recently graduated from the University of Virginia and gone to Europe for the summer with her boyfriend from college. Her parents, who were practicing Mennonites, had sold their home near Lancaster and moved to the Miami area. Thanks to Elizabeth, I learned that there were quite a few Mennonite communities in the state. Most were near the Sarasota/Tampa area, but their numbers had been growing in South Florida. Her parents disapproved of her going to Europe with a boy she wasn't married to, but they didn't try to stop her. After all, it was 1973. The temptations of modern society were everywhere. There was no place to hide. They loved their daughter and had faith that the values they had instilled in her would keep her on the right moral and spiritual track.

What they hadn't counted on was Elizabeth breaking up with her boyfriend a few weeks into their summer trip and staying in Europe by herself until October. She told me that she had not broken up with him because of a fight. She just wanted to be independent and do something on her own for the first time in her life. She said they parted as friends. He reluctantly flew back home while she journeyed through most of Northern Europe for the next few months, taking trains and staying in hostels. She wrote her parents several times, letting them know that she was safe and hoping they would understand.

Elizabeth was bright, beautiful, and confident. She was also a good listener. By the time we arrived in Miami, she had absorbed most of my convoluted story. She was curious to know what I intended to do with my life now that I was back in the US. That was a tough question that I couldn't answer. She asked where I was going when we landed. When I told her I was hitchhiking over to the Tampa area and the beaches, she reminded me how late it would be when the plane got there. She suggested I spend the night at her parents' house in Miami and start hitchhiking the next morning. They were picking her up at the airport, and I could stay in the guest bedroom. I doubted that her mother and father would be thrilled with the idea, but it was clearly the best, maybe the only option I had. I accepted her offer.

Elizabeth's unsuspecting parents were waiting for her on the other side of the customs door. Whatever they were expecting to see, it definitely wasn't me. Their discomfort was obvious. They were not sure what to make of me. It was unsettling enough that their free-spirited daughter had been traveling on her own through Europe for the past few months. Now, like a little girl bringing home a stray dog she had found wandering the streets, she had landed on their doorstep with a rather dubious, scruffy-looking character needing a place to sleep. They were understandably freaked out.

Whatever their misgivings, they made me feel welcome. They fed me, made polite conversation, and provided me with a shower and a comfortable bed. I slept like a log that night. I had no idea where in Miami I was staying. The next morning, a relieved Mrs. Summers served me a hearty breakfast of piping-hot oatmeal full of blueberries and nuts, whole wheat toast with butter and blueberry jam, and two large glasses of Florida orange juice. I thanked her and Mr. Summers for their hospitality, and they wished me well. A radiant-looking Elizabeth offered to drive me to a main highway where it would be easier to hitchhike.

Although our lives had crossed paths for barely twenty-four hours, it hurt to say goodbye to her. I knew she was special, but it was time to confront the next chapter in my journey. I tossed my backpack into the trunk of her 1970 silver-blue Ford Maverick, hopped in the passenger side, and off we went.

Elizabeth dropped me off just outside of Miami on US 41. Before I got out of the car, she handed me a piece of paper and a pen.

"Is there a way to get in touch with you if I want to?" she asked.

I knew we would never see each other again, but I pretended we would and wrote down my parents' phone number in Indian Shores. Elizabeth stepped out of the car and opened the trunk so I could retrieve my backpack.

We kissed for the first time.

I missed her already.

128

I landed in America the same day that the vice president resigned from office. Dick's partner in crime had gotten his proverbial tit caught in a wringer. Agnew had been busted for accepting bribes going back to his days as governor of Maryland. He continued to take the kickbacks even after he arrived in Washington, just a crooked Nixon heartbeat away from the presidency. The Feds let Spiro plead no contest to federal income tax evasion and resign in exchange for dropping all the political corruption charges against him. The news caught me off guard but didn't surprise me. Nixon's Potemkin village was continuing to crumble.

Being back in America was disorienting, a sensory overload of familiar images and retrieved memories. Pizza Huts, McDonalds, 7-Elevens, and Burger Kings dominated the flat landscape. Each Florida town struck me as a Xerox copy of the one I had just passed through. There was nothing to distinguish one from the other. Each contained the same fast-food restaurants, the same gas stations, and same convenience stores. It was a shock to my system. Everyone was in such a hurry. I felt like a visitor from another planet. I missed the distinct personalities and slow pace of the timeless villages I had left behind. I worried that the cobblestone streets, medieval castles, and centuries-old buildings would one day be nothing more than blurred images of a dream I would struggle to remember. I caught a series of rides that skirted the northern edge of the Everglades over to Naples and then propelled me up along the Gulf Coast to Tampa. I didn't know what was in store for me, but I already regretted my decision to return to America. I was a stranger in my own country. Florida was the last place I wanted to be, but here I was.

It was midafternoon when my last ride dropped me off in front of Sunset View. Since they had not seen me in more than five months and had no idea I was returning to America, I expected my parents to be both excited and surprised to see me. If they were, they made a concerted effort not to show it. When I walked in the door, I found Mom at the kitchen counter drying dishes and Dad reading the sports section of the *St. Pete Times* in his recliner in the living room. Mom set the dish towel down and greeted me with a hug. She asked if I was hungry and offered to make me something to eat. Dad just looked up from his paper and asked me how long I had been back. They acted like I had only been gone a day or two. It was clear they were becoming impervious to the aimless wanderings of me and Bernie. Any hope they had of either one of us ever amounting to anything was quickly fading away.

The first few hours were great. Mom treated me to her world's greatest meatloaf. After supper, the three of us walked the beach together at sunset. Dad didn't have much to say, but Mom was full of questions about my trip and the places I had seen. I learned that Bernie had returned from Europe in August and was living in a small cottage over in Seminole. They weren't sure what he was doing, but they thought he was probably working a construction job. It wasn't until we were back at Sunset View and I was having a beer with Dad that the shit hit the fan.

"So who do you think is going to win the World Series?" he asked.

"I don't know," I said. "Who's playing?"

Dad was disgusted.

"You don't know who's playing?" he said. "You know what your problem is, Jeff? You need to get back into the real world."

The thought of returning to the real world was depressing, but I understood why Dad was so pissed off at me. Our shared love of baseball was hallowed ground, the sacred bond between us that was supposed to be unbreakable. Bernie and I had been raised on baseball. For Christ's sakes, hadn't Dad built us our very own baseball field when we were kids? Through all the turmoil of the Sixties, all the drugs and long hair and all the bitterness over the Vietnam War that tested our family and tore at the nation's fabric, hadn't baseball had been the one safe place we could gather in peace? The World Series was set to begin in two days with the New York Mets taking on the Oakland As. By not knowing who was playing, I had committed the ultimate sin in the eyes of my father.

As I soon learned, baseball wasn't the only thing that had sailed past my head without making contact. What I read in the *St. Pete Times* was a revelation. While I had been tripping my brains out in Switzerland and navigating the minefields of the Black Lung, war had broken out in the Middle East. Armed by the Soviet Union, Syria and Egypt had launched a surprise attack on the nation of Israel. Nixon had to be sweating bullets. His vice president was dead meat, and a determined federal prosecutor was hot on his trail. On the bright side, the World Series was about to begin.

The next day was Friday, and it was a busy one for both me and the president. Dick decided to airlift weapons and supplies into Israel and anoint Congressman Gerald Ford to be his next VP. As for me, I decided to head over to Seminole and crash at Bernie's place. I promised Dad that Bernie and I would be back the next night and we would all watch the first game of the World Series together.

Bernie's one-room cottage was a dive, but I had less than fifty dollars left over from my rip-off of American Express and nowhere else to go. His lumpy couch would have to do until I got my shit together. But could I? It was sinking in that I was right back where I had started. My future in America looked bleak. I had escaped her shores and eluded capture for more than five months. I had even been foolish enough to believe that I was destined for an exciting new life. The joke was on me. I was back in the same nowhere land, with even less to look forward to. I had become a third-rate performer in my own Theater of the Absurd. I was struggling to find a purpose in life. Mostly, I felt like jumping off a bridge. Lucky for me, my brother was there to catch me.

Bernie was working as a carpenter's helper in Largo at a condominium construction site. He said that they were hiring laborers and convinced me to go in with him on Monday morning to get a job. I hated every minute of it, but it paid $2.50 an hour, and by

Friday, my stash of cash had increased another eighty-five dollars. I was amazed at how upbeat and positive Bernie was about life. While he was as unsure about his future as I was about mine, he didn't seem to have a care in the world and wasn't overly concerned about what was to come next. Bernie was the type of person who tasted the cucumber and enjoyed it. We went to the beach during the day on Saturday and Sunday and watched the World Series both nights with Dad. Oakland won the first game 2–1, but the Mets were able to even the series by besting the As in extra innings in game 2. Dad was happy that we came by, and for a few hours each night, he was able to set aside his disappointment in us. Bernie and I spent the weeknights sharing our stories while smoking pot and drinking beer. Bernie's journey had been different than mine. He had flown from Boston to London and spent some time in England before moving on to the continent. His favorite country was Spain, where he had been invited to live with a local family outside Barcelona for a few weeks. He had even ventured down to Northern Africa, traveled into Morocco, and been deported from Tunisia. That was interesting enough, but my jaw dropped when he told me what happened to him in Yugoslavia.

"I was busted with four English dudes and spent two nights in a military prison," he said.

"You're shitting me!" was all I could say.

"No, man, I'm not," Bernie continued. "We were camping on a small island off the coast when we were arrested. We had no idea we were near a secret military base. The commie assholes interrogated us for two days before finally letting us go."

"That was you?"

"What do you mean?"

"I met those four English guys on Corfu," I said. "They told me the whole story."

We had a good laugh over it. What were the chances of us meeting up with the same four dudes on our travels overseas? We were already high, but this just added to the buzz. As long as we were talking about unlikely encounters, I figured this was as good a time as any to tell Bernie about my night with Mia from the biker bar.

"Far out," he said. "That's as unbelievable as us running into the same English guys."

My first week back in the States was an adjustment, but I had survived. I had reentered earth's atmosphere and was adapting to its gravitational pull. Meanwhile, the earth continued to spin on its axis. I read the *St. Pete Times* every day. The Arab assholes that controlled the oil in the Middle East were now pissed at Nixon and the US and decided to cut their oil production, more than double the price, and impose an oil embargo on the West. By the time the weekend hit, every Arab country had joined the embargo and the Oakland As had tied the World Series at three games apiece. On Saturday night, King Richard fired the prosecutor who was on his ass and accepted the resignations of the attorney general and deputy attorney general, who refused to do his dirty work and quit in protest. On Sunday afternoon, while war continued to rage in the Middle East, Bernie and I journeyed over to Sunset View to watch game 7 with Dad. I didn't care who won. I was consumed with depression. All I could think about was how much I hated my pathetic job and how desperate I was to get the hell out of Florida.

Had I been paying attention that day, I might have noticed that the stars were about to align again. When I walked in the door, Mom handed me a small piece of paper and rolled her eyes. The piece of paper had a phone number written on it.

"Some girl named Elizabeth called for you," she sighed. "She wants you to call her back."

129

"I'm driving up to Pennsylvania to visit some friends," she said. "Would you like to go with me?"

Once again, the winds of fate were swooping down from the heavens to save me. I had no idea where I would be a week from now or what I would be doing, but I didn't care. Like the white bird in the song by It's a Beautiful Day, I had to fly or I would die. There was no yesterday or tomorrow, only today. This is who I was. I only existed for the moment. I chased shiny objects and followed pretty faces. I hated the idea of having a job and only worked at a shitty one long enough to put a little cash in my pocket and move on. I was incapable of coexisting with all the creatures that surrounded and suffocated me. I wanted to run away, but to where? Sex was my only refuge. The need to be wanted, to be desired by a woman, had become more important to me than food or water. It was the fuel that was powering my self-worth and keeping me alive.

So off I flew into the wild blue yonder, this time a passenger on the soaring wings of an angel with bright-green eyes. I thought of Vassilis and his words of wisdom. Life was indeed like a cucumber and I was still enjoying it. Elizabeth picked me up at Bernie's cottage on Tuesday afternoon. Her silver-blue Maverick blew in like a winged stallion, a modern-day Pegasus embracing my freedom. I assumed that we would be driving straight through to the Keystone State, but Elizabeth informed me she was in no hurry. Her plan was to take up to a week to get there and dig the backroads and the scenery along the way. I told her I was cool with that and even had a few dollars to contribute for gas, but I didn't have enough money to help much with food or motel rooms. She just laughed.

"Don't worry about it," she said. "I've got enough money for the both of us."

And with that, we blasted off, climbing high into the sky.

It would begin as a week of slow-motion ecstasy. Elizabeth and I picked up right where we had left off on the flight from Luxembourg. We were barely out of Seminole when our minds locked arms again. No thought was too private. No feeling was off-limits. My body trembled with anticipation. I felt light-headed. We made it as far as Gainesville before we both confessed we couldn't wait any longer. We were a few miles from downtown when Elizabeth pulled into a Quality Inn motel and dished out nineteen dollars for a room on the second floor.

It was even better than I expected. Every encounter, from my teenage discovery of Jane to my glorious education with Isadora to my carnal self-indulgence of Jill, flashed before my eyes. Each experience had prepared me for this very moment. When I entered, my entire being melted like butter on a warm stove. It felt both supernatural and familiar, like it wasn't our first bite of the apple. The intimacy was organic, as natural as breathing or sleeping. It was as if we had tasted each other a thousand times before. No drugs or alcohol were needed to start the fire. Foreplay was effortless. There was no learning curve, no trial and error. It was the perfect union. Time stood still. Once again, I had placed my heart and every ounce of my self-worth in the hands of a beautiful girl. I knew it was insane, but I couldn't help myself. I was bound to end up like Icarus, the dude in Greek mythology who ignored warnings not to fly too close to the sun. When his wings melted, he fell into the sea and drowned.

Mine was a slow, steady burn over several days, a descent so gradual that I didn't know I was falling until I hit the water. When we floated out of the room that first morning, I was ready to follow my newest lover to the ends of the earth. I was under another spell and wasn't even sure what day it was. We grabbed some breakfast at a small diner across the road before jumping into the Maverick and hopping on Interstate 75. When we reached the outskirts of Atlanta early that afternoon, Elizabeth left the interstate and pointed us toward the mountains of North Georgia and Tennessee, a part of the country I had never seen before.

Why she was so attracted to me was a mystery. I had no job, no money, no car, and no plans for the future. Everything I owned was on my back. Elizabeth was the polar opposite. She wore nice clothes, drove a nice car, and knew where she was going. She impressed me as someone who could do whatever she wanted in life and get it right. Was there something about her I wasn't seeing? I had grown so accustomed to the wounded birds landing in my lap that I wasn't sure what to make of my good fortune. Maybe the roles were being reversed. Maybe I was her wounded bird. I had enough sense not to ask questions and to go with the flow. If my life was on the road to nowhere, this had to be the best way to get there. What began with the Brown-Eyed Girl on the waterbed in Get Stoned Leather had come full circle. Only a fool would now refuse to jump aboard and go for the ride.

Elizabeth was into nature and the great outdoors. Late October was the perfect time of the year to be making this trip through the mountains. The days were warm, the evenings cool and crisp, and the colors were eye-popping. The nights were even better. We bedded down in austere rooms in tiny motels in out-of-the-way villages. We talked, made love, talked again, and made love again until we finally passed out. During the day, while the Maverick inched its way along the meandering roads and highways, I was taken aback by the sheer beauty of all I was seeing. We stopped at nearly every scenic overlook to marvel at the warm blanket of red, yellow, and orange that covered the arresting landscape. We passed pumpkin farms and apple orchards and ventured out onto a number of the hiking trails that we stumbled upon along the way. The sweet smell of the autumn air was intoxicating. The trails were lined with red-tinted maples, glimmering yellow oaks, and dogwoods flush with reddish purple leaves and glossy red fruit. We discovered a beautiful canyon and were treated to cascading waterfalls. By the time we entered Great Smoky Mountains National Park on the third day and ventured onto a section of the Appalachian Trail, I was convinced I was dreaming. I was so enamored of Elizabeth, so swept up in the slow-motion ecstasy that I was unaware of my surroundings, unaware of the black bear standing right behind me.

The picnic was her idea. We stopped at a small store just outside the park and bought a picnic basket, a loaf of bread, one package each of cheese and sandwich meat, and small jars of mustard and mayonnaise. The park straddled the border of Tennessee and North Carolina, and the entrance to the trail was near the highest elevation point on the Tennessee side. We were probably a half mile onto the trail when we found what we thought was the perfect spot to stop and have our lunch. We had just spread our blanket out in a small clearing a few feet off the trail and set down our food, when I saw the color rush out of Elizabeth's face. Her mouth was wide-open, but no words were coming out. She slowly lifted her right hand and pointed a trembling finger over my shoulder.

I think I smelled him before I saw him. When I turned, he was standing upright just a few feet away from my face. His eyes were small, and they were staring directly into mine. He was the same height as I was. With the exception of the coarse brown hair covering his long nose, his entire body was covered with jet-black fur.

Elizabeth's voice returned but was barely audible.

"What are we going to do?" she whispered.

I assumed that our guest had stopped by because he was hungry. There was only one question. What was on the menu, us or the food on the blanket?

I turned back around to face Elizabeth and tried to act like nothing was wrong.

"H-h-he probably just wants our food," I stuttered. "Let's back away slowly and let him have it."

We backed off the blanket and shuffled backward onto the trail, never taking our eyes off the bear who, never took his eyes off us. Lady Luck was on our side. As the saying goes, even a broken clock is right twice a day. I didn't know shit about bears, but somehow I had guessed right. We were not on today's menu. We were about fifty yards down the path when our new friend took a seat on the blanket. Lunch was on us.

After treating the black bear to his feast on the Appalachian Trail, we filled the next two days roaming the blue mists of the Smoky Mountains and scoping out Elizabeth's college stomping grounds in Charlottesville, Virginia. When it dawned on me that Alexandria was a mere three hours away, I suggested we take a detour. Why not? It was a free place to stay and as good a time as any to drop in on the newlyweds I had not seen since April Fool's Day. Danny always had the best weed, and it would be great to see my best friend again. It was a great move. Danny was his usual funny self, and his weed didn't disappoint. Elizabeth fit in like a comfortable pair of shoes. I couldn't have asked for a more perfect day. It was the happiest I had been since Loutro. I was hanging with my best friend and traveling with a beautiful girl. It didn't get any better than that. Later that night, when Elizabeth and I were on the couch, the lights were out, and our clothes were on the floor, I was expecting the perfect night.

I could not have been more wrong.

After John Glenn orbited the planet three times in 1962, his capsule made a fireball reentry into the earth's atmosphere and parachuted into the Atlantic Ocean near the Bahamas. Fortunately for John, he and his charred capsule were fished out of the ocean by a naval destroyer twenty minutes later. I wasn't going to be so lucky. When my wings melted and I fell into the water, no naval destroyer would be coming to rescue me.

It had been nice while it lasted. I had no illusions that it we would orbit the planet forever. Still, I didn't expect to be as lost as I was when the curtain came down. I was in a coma. I had placed reality on a back burner for six days, and the outside world had ceased to exist. I had absorbed Elizabeth into my skin. She was the oxygen I was breathing. For six days, our union moved seamlessly between the physical and emotional. Our minds and bodies were in sync, as playful at night in bed as they were during the warm daylight hours we spent wandering the mountains and forests along the spine of the East Coast.

I was clearly vulnerable. Like Icarus, I ignored all warnings and had flown too close to the sun. Sex had become my sole purpose in life. Nothing else mattered. For six days, making love to Elizabeth had stoked the fires and lighted my passion. Until this fateful moment, our union had been my *Mona Lisa*, my Leonardo da Vinci masterpiece. I believed I had the only skill I would ever need. I was confident. I felt invincible. Expecting perfection each time had not prepared me for my failure. When reality smashed through the door, when I couldn't bring Elizabeth to orgasm on our last night together, I knew I was living in a fool's paradise. It was bad enough that I had no discernible skills to offer an employer or any useful talents to help me become a productive member of society. That wasn't a problem. I could handle the thought of having no money, no job, and no future. What was the point of living if I couldn't satisfy a woman each and every time?

It was a quiet ride the next morning. The Maverick's windshield wipers were no match for the torrential downpour as we crept along a slippery Interstate 83 up through Maryland into William Penn's Commonwealth. I was devastated. I knew once I stepped out of the car, I would never see her again. The angel with bright-green eyes tried her best to cheer me up, but I knew the only way that would happen was if she put me on her wings and took me with her. I didn't know where she was going, but I didn't care. I had nowhere else to go.

When she dropped me off outside of York, it was like being tossed under a waterfall. There was nothing to do but tread water and hope for a naval destroyer to pick me up. The icy-gray sky was relentless. Raindrops were pelting the pavement like bullets from heaven. I swam and sloshed my way north along the interstate for more than an hour before a Good Samaritan pulled off the road and threw me a lifeline.

I struggled to reach the waiting vehicle. The rain was beating me with a thousand tiny hammers, and my body was being dragged down by the weight of my soaked clothes and waterlogged backpack.

Where was I going?

What was I going to do next?

Did I even care anymore?

130

I had reached a permanent state of limbo, stuck between a past I could never return to and a future that had no use for me. I had no place to go, but I was in a hurry to get wherever it was that I was going. I was overwhelmed by a complete and utter sense of isolation, like I was floating away from my body. Was I defective? My mind was drifting far out into space, whirling around inside an invisible spaceship. It was observing the world, watching the millions and millions of robotic creatures, who, unlike me, had all been neatly assigned to their place in the universe. Back on earth, I continued to taste the cucumber and was trying desperately to still enjoy it. Doing so was becoming harder by the day. I was a man in a rowboat crossing the sea alone. Life was reduced to the basics: food, shelter, and sex.

My first stop was Oneonta and The Silver, a journey I had learned by rote. I was just in time for another happy hour. Much had changed, yet so much hadn't. God had introduced a new player or two and a new deck of playing cards, but the game remained the same. Quarters, dressed as silver soldiers preparing for battle, were lined up on the pool table, but the trusty jukebox was still the star of the show. The Allman Brothers were singing the praises of a ramblin' man, while Gary the bartender manufactured ten-cent drafts at the speed of light. I scanned the garden of dying flowers, hoping to see a familiar face. The town had planted a fresh crop of college girls, but that harvest would have to wait. This was not the right time to be on the prowl. I probably smelled as bad as the bear on the Appalachian Trail. My clothes were still wet, and I was in dire need of a shower. Just as I was about to give up hope, salvation appeared in the form of two old friends of mine making out in the Naugahyde booth nearest the door.

Mary Lou Davies might have graduated from Hartwick and moved on to greener pastures, but her roommates Joe and Holly were still an item and still living together in the same apartment in this home of malt and hops. After ribbing me about my last night in Oneonta back in April, they graciously offered me their shower and said I could crash there if I needed to. Apparently, Mary Lou had filled them in on our one-night dalliance and how I had insisted on eating her out while she was having her period. Joe thought it was gross, but Holly disagreed. She winked at me and said it was sexy. As for me, I couldn't remember. Joe informed me that a Hartwick dude I didn't know was staying in Mary Lou's old room, but he said I was more than welcome to sleep on the floor in their living room. It sucked, but it was shelter and the only offer I had.

I only stayed one night. Before I fell any farther down the gaping hole I was digging for myself, there was something I had to do. Reality was about to rear its ugly head. I had a wife living in Massachusetts who was more than eight months pregnant and carrying a child that wasn't mine. Like it or not, I had to go to Amherst. Burying my head in the sand and pretending this wasn't happening wouldn't make it go away. What I would do or say to her once I was there was the $64,000 question. What choice did I have? I found a pay phone and made the call.

My mind continued to travel inside the invisible spaceship. It existed solely as a stream of consciousness, a flowing series of images and ideas running through it like a herd of wild horses. There were no yesterdays, no tomorrows. The moment I was stuck in was all there was. When Jane opened the door, I was shocked to see how radiant she looked. Pregnancy had wrapped its loving arms around her and given her a warm, almost ethereal glow. Still, it was unsettling to see her like this. If this was the real world that my father had insisted I rejoin, it wasn't a world I wanted any part of. It was a moment of clarity for me. I saw for the first time just how much of a misfit I was and how serious my inability to be like everyone else had become. I already knew I was incapable of getting a straight job and living among the creatures. What I hadn't realized up until now was just how averse I was to bringing another person into the world.

If I couldn't take care of myself, how could I be expected to take care of another human being? I was glad that we were no longer together, glad that the baby wasn't mine. Society was a round hole, and I was the square peg that would never fit in.

Jane was remarkably nice to me. It was as if she had never written that letter threatening to file desertion papers against me. I had never seen her this happy. My uncomfortableness seemed to amuse her. I honestly didn't know how to act. I was a bumbling idiot the entire afternoon we spent together. I had never been in such close contact with a pregnant woman, let alone one who was just weeks away from delivery. When she suggested we walk down to the sandwich shop at the corner, I was terrified. What would I do if she fell? What if she went into labor? I held her arm. I helped her down the steps of her front porch. I held doors open for her. I could tell she was enjoying it. She was also prepared to let me off the hook. When I finally summoned the courage to ask her if she would agree to sign some legal papers stating I was not the father, she surprised me and said she would. I couldn't believe my ears! I was so ecstatic that I told her I would pay for the attorney. It was a bold move considering I barely had any money left to feed myself. When I got back to Oneonta, I would need to plead my case to Karl Silvestri. Hopefully, Race Track's attorney would feel sorry for me and cut me a deal.

Nothingness was washing over me like a sluggish wave. Every road I had taken had come to a dead end. This wasn't fun anymore. I could no longer pass myself off as some world traveler searching for some higher meaning or greater purpose in life. At this point, did it matter where I chose to hunker down? Why Oneonta? Why not? If it was now about survival, about food, shelter, and sex, then this was as good a place as any to throw down the gauntlet. College towns were the last refuge of hangers-on and lost souls like me. At least here I had a small network of friends, knew the bar scene, and understood the rules. A job would be hard to come by, but there would always be food and a place to crash. Most importantly, there was an endless supply of college girls.

November had always been one of my least favorite months. Having spent the previous one on Florida's Gulf Coast, I had forgotten just how depressing the weather could be. Winter was on its way, and the sun was in full retreat. Cold, wet mornings were followed by gray afternoons and dark ragged clouds. Bare trees and the absence of color dominated the landscape. Snow flurries made their first appearance. The prevailing gloom was enough to numb the soul. It was like being wrapped in gauze and unable to break free.

An oasis is a sanctuary in the middle of a desert, an island of life that makes it possible to survive long treks through wastelands devoid of sustenance. The Silver was mine. Old friends jumped up to greet me, buy me beers, and offer me places to stay. Fresh faces of college girls took notice, curious as to what the fuss was all about.

It would be a long winter, but I wasn't worried. I was back in the womb.

131

"Can I have a hit?" James asked.

Jane blushed and shook her head.

"No," she said, "I don't think so. That's not going to happen."

Baby Adam was hungry. He was resting on her left forearm with his head in the crook of her arm. Jane had just unbuttoned her blouse and exposed her left breast when James walked into the living room. True to form, she wasn't wearing a bra. She tilted the baby's head back slightly and tickled his lips with her nipple until his mouth was wide-open. Guiding his lower jaw on first, well below her nipple, she guided the mammary gland into his mouth. Then, tilting his head forward, she coaxed his upper jaw firmly onto her breast, making sure he took in her entire nipple.

James only expressed what the rest of us were thinking but were afraid to ask. Watching Jane breastfeed her six-week-old son was fascinating. It was the middle of January, and she had come down from Amherst to sign the separation agreement. The Chestnut Street apartment was rocking on all cylinders. It was the middle of the afternoon, and James and his band were rehearsing in the kitchen while Bernie, Gerald, and I were smoking a joint in the living room. The jamming had just stopped when we heard a loud knock at the door. The three of us were too wasted to move. Penelope, who had just gotten out of the shower, ran into the room, waving her towel. If she was trying to get our attention, it worked. She was dripping wet and naked.

"Hey!" she shouted. "Is anyone going to answer the door?"

Penelope and I had been friends now for more than two years going back to our days at *Seeds* and that glorious summer out at Pine Lake in the sauna with our bare-ass playmates. Thanks to Penelope, I had shelter and the means to pay for it. We had a sidesplitting laugh together over that now-infamous night in The Silver when I opted out of her friendly hand job and exchanged it for a headfirst dive into Mary Lou Davies's menstrual cycle. Hand job aside, she and I knew that we were never meant to get it on. There was no point in ruining such a good friendship. Penelope had dumped Pete over the summer and was living with James, a tall handsome dude who played lead guitar for a local bar band called the Missing Heads. Their upstairs apartment had two empty bedrooms, and they offered to rent me one. James worked as a welder at Miller Trailer, the company that had recently opened up shop out in the West End where the old Lyncoach plant had once operated. Miller manufactured bodies for Ryder trucks and was about the only place in Oneonta that was hiring. I rode in with James one morning and applied for a job. I started the next day and was assigned to the assembly line as a trained monkey to stand there all day and put decals on the side of each Ryder truck that passed in front of me. It was mind-numbing, but it paid two dollars an hour. That was all the money I needed for the basics: food, shelter, and seven nights a week at The Silver in my dogged pursuit of sex.

Karl Silvestri had come through for me. He was only charging the filing fee of seventy-five dollars, which was just a few dollars more than one week's take-home pay. It was a small price to pay to get off the hook. The two-page document spelled out that Jane and I were legally separated, that Baby Adam wasn't mine, that Jane released me forever of any responsibility or liability, and that I forever waived any claim to be the father. Technically, we were still married, but it was the get-out-of-jail free card that I needed. As an extra treat, Gerald Lopez, my brother Bernie, and James the guitar player were granted an extended period of time to admire Jane's beautiful tits as she breastfed her baby boy. No one else got to take a hit though.

I had been living there for two months, caught up in a strange dream. Each day was the same yet its own event as I continued to swirl down the rabbit hole. My mind remained a prisoner inside my invisible spaceship, detached from the physical world as my body pursued pleasures of the flesh. I existed to taste the cucumber and worked feverishly to enjoy it. My days began at night when I crossed over the threshold and entered The Silver. I was flush with cash, enough to live on the pool table and consume all the beers I wanted. There was no shortage of both townie and college girls, no shortage of willing partners. The goal was to never leave alone, and most nights I didn't. I had stopped being choosy. I no longer made love. I just fucked. When it was over, I tried to cop a few hours' sleep in their bed or mine before catching a ride in James's 1955 pea-green Ford pickup and staggering into work by seven in the morning. The long days at Miller Trailer were unbearable. Living on fumes, it took every ounce of energy I had to stay awake. Thankfully, applying decals to truck bodies required no thinking. A chimpanzee could have taken my place on the assembly line, and no one would have noticed. When the whistle blew at three thirty, I cruised home with James and collapsed. Three to four hours was all the sleep I ever needed. I showered, found a clean shirt, and ran out the door to begin the pursuit of pleasure all over again.

This was my life, a meaningless existence interrupted by brief moments of physical gratification. It was a repetitive exercise in futility, one that I tried not to dwell on. What was the alternative? A sinister chill seemed to have drifted over the nation and the entire planet and set up shop for the winter. There was no place to go, no place to hide. Whenever I attempted to pry open the door of my invisible spaceship, my mind was met by fierce headwinds. Catching a slice of news on TV or picking up a newspaper were acts of self-flagellation. The entire USA had the blues. Egypt and Israel might have signed a ceasefire, but the asshole Arabs and their oil embargo were continuing on their merry way. Gas was becoming scarce and more expensive. Long lines of distressed cars were starting to form at gas stations around the country. President Nixon was comforting a worried nation by declaring he wasn't a crook. We had a new vice president and a new Nixon stalker from Texas named Leon. No one could explain why there was an eighteen-and-a-half-minute gap in Tricky Dick's White House tape recordings. Unemployment and the cost of just about everything were on the rise. Bob Dylan had proven himself to be a prophet when he declared "we didn't need a weatherman to know which way the wind was blowing." Ominous black clouds were forming in the sky. It was clear that a storm was on its way.

It was time to batten down the hatches.

132

At least I wasn't alone in my debauchery.

It was the winter of drugs, sex, and rock 'n roll. The Chestnut Street apartment morphed into a living, breathing organism as earthlings, both known and unknown to me, entered the lair. They were escorted by marching armies of cannabis. The music was live and loud enough to be heard both day and night from the street. The Missing Heads were the most popular band in Oneonta. Their rehearsals in the kitchen served as an excuse for dozens of friends and fans to wander in from the cold, get high, and kiss the sky. Besides James and his lead guitar, the band consisted of Melissa, the lead singer and fiery redhead with the sultry voice; Richie, the spaced-out drummer; and Michael, the bass guitarist whom I had last seen the winter before shuffling out of Isadora Duncan's Lower East Side apartment with his tail between his legs. Michael and I never spoke of that awkward afternoon. It was ancient history. We were at peace with the special afterglow we shared from our separate journeys into paradise. We had never been rivals. We had been chosen. We were happy to count ourselves among the lucky ones.

Bernie showed up right after Thanksgiving and claimed the empty bedroom. I had lured him to the Oneonta winter with promises of a job and a room of his own. Bernie was hesitant at first. He wanted to make sure that he wasn't having another Ozzie trick played on him, that he wasn't being enticed into another Top Shelf moment. I assured him that the offer was on the up-and-up. Bernie's Penis weighed in and reminded Bernie of all the college girls they would have to choose from. That information was enough to tip the scales and convince Bernie to leave Florida and search for a new pot of gold in the wintry north. Bernie's arrival on Chestnut Street energized his friends in the townie community and ushered them into the growing circle of decadence. Gerald Lopez and Hank Marino were frequent guests in our den of iniquity. Even Race Track, who was now living in a small trailer out on the frozen tundra of Mud Road, had wandered in a few times to groove on the music and smoke some pot. Louie O'Malley was back from Florida and once again finding places to crash for free. He spent several weeks on the couch in the living room before striking pay dirt one night at The Silver and moving in with a tall, long-legged beauty of Russian descent named Nadia. He still stopped in most nights to get stoned. Louie wasn't about to pass up free grass.

It was a different Oneonta than the one I had left behind in 1972. The darkness that was now gripping the USA was reaching into every soul and grabbing it by the throat. No one was immune. Optimism was in short supply. I fantasized about jumping into H. G. Wells's time machine and returning to that summer that was so full of promise and freedom. I wanted to feel alive again, have a future to embrace. I missed the friends who had moved on to greener pastures. I missed Mike and Renee and Get Stoned Leather. With the exception of Penelope, all my *Seeds* friends and Pine Lake playmates were gone. I missed Alex and Nancy. I missed Julie Tyler. I missed The Shack. Most of all, I ached for Isadora Duncan.

For me, it was a brave new libertine world. The rock 'n roll apartment was never empty. There was always someone getting wasted or getting laid. I was a fool running in place, just existing to exist. Keeping my cock happy was all that mattered. I did whatever it instructed me to do and with anyone it wanted. We prowled The Silver together in search of prey. Sometimes we hit the jackpot, and we experienced ecstasy. Our grandest prize was the hometown girl I met through Gerald. Debbie was pure joy and a sexual contortionist. Nearly six feet tall with big hazel eyes and short jet-black hair, she was a recent graduate of Oneonta State who had selected me to explore a series of erotic fantasies with her before she left town and moved to Boston. Debbie's pubic hair was exquisite, a gift from the gods. Straight and soft as silk, it was as luxurious and fine as a cashmere sweater. Each time we balled, I felt like I was being turned loose inside a candy store. Debbie's playful laughter and exuberance were contagious. Her pliable frame bent and twisted in every direction, and our bodies glistened with sweat.

While marijuana and beer were the medications that dulled my senses, sex was the one drug that I was dependent upon. I did whatever it took to feed my addiction. If it meant closing down The Silver at two in the morning to find a female as desperate as me, that's what I did. Whether I reached high or I sank low, it was all the same to me. If Debbie was the yin, then Gwen had to be the yang. She was one of Penelope's friends whom I had met once in the sauna out at Pine Lake. I saw her in The Silver most nights, but she existed on the periphery of people that I hung out with, and I had never really had a conversation with her. She was living with Charlie, an auto mechanic who worked at the gas station near the movie theater. I should have known better, but I had become so depraved that I no longer cared. It was near closing time, and The Silver had cleared out. Gwen was sitting alone at the bar. She looked drunk, and Charlie was nowhere in sight. My cock was egging me on. I figured it was a long shot, but what did I have to lose? I moved in for the kill.

"Hey, Gwen," I said. "Wanna come back to my place?"

And with that, the trap door opened, and I tumbled farther down the rabbit hole. Gwen looked at me and nodded. Her pock-marked face was expressionless. When she slid off the barstool, she lost her balance, but I was able to catch her before she hit the floor. I looked around and saw that there were no witnesses. Gary the bartender had seen and heard everything, but he could be trusted not to testify. The walk along Main Street and up Chestnut was an adventure. The sidewalks were icy, and Gwen could barely stand. I was nearly as drunk as she was, and it took every ounce of strength I could muster to keep her upright and get her back to the apartment and maneuver her dead weight onto my mattress on the floor.

What was I doing? How low could I go? Was I so desperate to get laid that I would sink to this level? Obviously, I was. I stripped off all my clothes and tiptoed down the hall to take a piss. When I returned, I was stunned to find Gwen sitting on top of my sleeping bag on the mattress. She was wide awake and alert. Like me, she was naked. She looked me over from head to toe and spoke for the first time.

"What are we waiting for?" she slurred. "Let's do it."

I was starting to sober up, and my brain was urging me to come to my senses. However, my cock had already made up his mind and come too far to bail out. He had a way of functioning all on his own, without any help from me. And I was definitely no help. I was balling another dude's old lady, and I wanted no part of it. I wasn't attracted to her. Gwen was a hippie chick with a bad complexion who didn't shave her armpits or legs, but I was cool with that. What made this a challenge was the body odor. Apparently, bathing was not one of Gwen's favorite activities. My cock wasn't concerned. He was getting what he wanted. I decided not to ruin his fun. I held my breath as much as I could and did everything he asked me to do.

Penelope was not happy when she saw Gwen walk out of my room the next morning. Charlie wasn't too happy either when I ran into him at The Silver the next night. He glared at me with a red face for several hours. He looked like he wanted to kill me, and no one would have blamed him if he had. The verdict was in, and it was unanimous: I was a complete lowlife.

I could feel the cucumber sneaking up on me from behind. How would I know when I reached rock bottom? There was no way to predict what loomed ahead or to what depths I would sink. Naturally, I was worried. My head was spinning with visions of Vassilis and the muscles on his face mobilizing in painful contortions as he squeezed, twisted, and turned the imaginary vegetable in his hands. Would I continue to taste the cucumber and enjoy it, or was there a brutal penetration in my future?

I needed someone to break my fall, to catch me before I fell so far into the abyss that it would be impossible to climb out. James seemed to be the most likely candidate. I saw him as the North Star, a guiding light to follow out of the wilderness. He seemed to have his shit together. He had a steady job, owned a truck, was lead guitarist in a local band, and the dude Penelope wanted to fuck every night. His hair was short, he didn't do drugs, and I could always count on him to rustle my sorry ass out of bed in the morning and give me a ride to Miller Trailer. James was everything I was not.

That's why it was such a letdown when he revealed his dark side.

133

We were on a dirt road in a heavily wooded area at least ten miles outside of Oneonta.

"Where are we going?" Bernie asked.

"You'll see," replied James. "We're almost there."

It was a Saturday morning. James had asked us to do him a favor and help him move some shit. We weren't sure what it was we were moving, but since he was our ride every day of the week to and from Miller Trailer, we couldn't very well say no.

The run-down house was set back just a few feet from the road. James pulled his truck alongside the front porch and killed the engine. Bernie and I looked at each other. What had we gotten ourselves into? James sensed our apprehension.

"Don't worry," he assured us, "no one is here."

That much was obvious, at least from the outside. The wood-frame structure was clearly the victim of serious neglect. Paint was peeling from its weathered sides, and the roof was missing several shingles. Snow had fallen overnight, and it was a cold, windy morning. Except for the traces of powder from the last night's dusting, the trees were bare, freeing the wind to whistle through the limbs unencumbered. The branches of the oak, sugar maple, and birch trees that surrounded the humble abode resembled skeleton arms reaching out to touch it. Bernie and I had no clue why we were here and what we were doing. We asked James to explain.

"The old woman who lived here died a month ago," he said. "No one has come to claim the house or anything in it. There's a lot of cool shit in here. Stuff we can sell for a lot of money."

Bernie and I looked at each other again.

"You're shitting me," I said. "We're going steal things from this house?"

"It's not stealing," insisted James. "The woman had no family. No one is coming to claim what's inside. If we don't grab what's here, someone else will."

This definitely sucked, but Bernie and I were already committed to helping him. We were on a lonely dirt road in the middle of the nowhere, and James was our only ride out of this impending nightmare. It was what it was. At this point, the smartest thing to do was to load his truck as fast as possible and get the hell out. James opened his door and jumped to the ground.

"What are you guys waiting for?" he said. "Let's go."

Bernie and I were now accomplices. Whether we were committing grand larceny or petty larceny was irrelevant. If we were busted, either crime would land us in jail. We piled out the passenger side and followed North Star James. Dead branches snapped beneath our feet as we touched down on the soggy mass of fresh snow and dead leaves that led to the porch. One of the steps was rotting and loose, causing Bernie to stumble. I was right behind him and caught him before he fell off and landed flat on his face.

"This is what you had me leave Florida for?" he snapped.

What could I say? He had every right to bitch at me. Each time I thought I had reached the bottom floor, another trap door sprung open and I plummeted farther down the hole.

There was no reason to take Bernie with me.

134

Bernie wasn't long for Oneonta. He hated the cold, dreary days of winter and complained every chance he got about the pointless existence we all seemed to be living. He missed the Florida Gulf Coast, its sugar-sand beaches, its orange and pink sunsets, and all the tanned girls in their skimpy bikinis. He was getting laid most nights like the rest of us, but he was irritated by all the layers of winter clothes he had to fight through to reach his destination. He griped that the girls he met in The Silver were so bundled up that it was impossible to know what they would look like once they were undressed. More often than not, unwrapping the package and opening the gift was a big disappointment.

His tenure at Miller Trailer lasted two days short of two weeks before he finally had enough and walked off the job. He claimed that he had better things to do with his life. It was a few weeks before Christmas when he got together with Race Track and the two of them came up with a foolproof plan to make some quick cash. Race Track's remaining forty-four acres were home to hundreds, maybe thousands of pine trees. Most were white spruce, but there were also dozens of scotch pines, our family's Christmas tree of choice when we were kids. Bernie saw dollar signs. He convinced Race Track that he was sitting on a gold mine.

"Far out!" Race Track exclaimed. "Let's rent a Ryder truck and fill it up with trees. We can drive down to The City and make a fortune. We'll be rich!"

Race Track suddenly had a purpose in life. It was a match made in heaven. Race Track had the trees, and Bernie had the bread to rent a big truck. Race Track suggested they split the profits. As far as he was concerned, the plan was a stroke of genius. He claimed it was the greatest idea he had ever heard. Race Track owned one ax, and he borrowed a second one from Gerald. They rented the biggest Ryder truck they could find and spent the next day from dawn to dusk out on Mud Road, chopping down defenseless pines. When they were finished, they realized that they had no idea how many Christmas trees they had crammed into the bowels of the yellow truck. Race Track took a wild-ass guess and decided that there had to be more than a hundred. He was pumped. Bernie took a rare night off from The Silver. The City was a good five-hour drive from Oneonta, so they needed to get an early start. Race Track crashed on our couch, and they split the next morning before sunrise.

Life is always full of surprises, so it shouldn't have been a surprise to Bernie and Race Track that their surefire plan ended up biting the dust. Robert Burns, the eighteenth-century Scottish poet, tried to warn anyone who would listen that the best-laid plans of mice and men often turned to shit. The derelicts-turned-businessmen returned two days later poorer than when they left.

"This place sucks," Bernie said. "I'm going back to Florida."

"What happened?" I asked, passing him the joint.

It was a long story. Bernie took a couple of hits before recounting his real-life version of a *Fabulous Furry Freak Brothers* adventure. It seems that neither he nor Race Track knew their way around The City, where they were at, or where they were going. They piloted the Ryder truck like they were blindfolded and playing pin the tail on the donkey until they settled on what they thought was a perfect spot to sell their wares. It was a vacant lot on the corner of a busy street with lots of people walking by. They unloaded two dozen trees, leaned them against both sides of the truck, and waited for the money to start rolling in.

"We stood there all day until it got dark, and we didn't sell a fucking tree!" Bernie said.

The joint had burned its way down. I took what was left and clamped it to the roach clip.

"Shit," I said. "How's that possible?"

"It's possible," Bernie said, "when you try to sell Christmas trees in a Jewish neighborhood."

"What did you do?" I asked, trying hard not to laugh.

Bernie grabbed the roach clip. The roach had burned itself out, and what was left was too small to smoke. Bernie picked up the book of matches on the coffee table, struck a match, and lit the remains. He held the clip under his nose, inhaled, and handed it back to me.

"We slept in the truck that night," he said, "and headed up to Harlem the next morning."

It was Race Track's idea. He was positive that black people liked Christmas trees.

"How many did you sell?" I asked.

"Not a fucking one," said Bernie.

They might not have sold any trees on that cold day, but Bernie and Race Track nevertheless created quite a scene in Harlem. They found another vacant lot to set up shop and emptied every white spruce and scotch pine from their truck. Race Track had reached his stride. He was in his glory, as if he was again riding his bicycle through Bresee's Department Store giving away one-dollar bills or jumping up and down on a desk in a stockbroker's office shouting that he had money to invest. He climbed to the top of the truck's cab like Moses had climbed Mount Sinai to receive the Ten Commandments. Acting as both prophet and snake-oil salesman, Race Track beckoned all who would listen to come forth and purchase a Christmas tree. It wasn't long before a huge crowd gathered. Word spread that two crazy white dudes had come into the neighborhood peddling trees. The more Race Track jumped up and down on the truck's cab shouting about his Christmas trees, the larger and louder the crowd grew. They applauded and cheered. It was a historic moment, like nothing they had ever witnessed before. Unfortunately for Bernie and Race Track, no one stepped forward to buy a tree.

"What did you do?" I asked.

"What do you think we did?" he answered. "We left the trees there on the ground, got in the truck, and drove away."

What a far-out story, I thought. It called for another joint. I picked up the orange pack of Zig-Zag papers and reached for the baggie. Bernie wasn't finished.

"As we were driving off," he said, "we saw several people moving onto the lot and picking up trees. Some had already started dragging them across the street."

"That's cool," I said. "You did a good thing, giving away free Christmas trees."

"Up yours," Bernie said. "I hate it here. I'm going back to Florida."

He left the next day.

135

I wasn't the only one staring at her ass, but I was the only one playing pool with her. She was left-handed, and each time she bent over the table to take her shot, the black miniskirt rode up just far enough to expose the pink panties and grab the attention of every dude in The Silver. When it was my turn, I took my sweet time lining up the shot. Like everyone else, I was enjoying the scenery and wanted the show to last forever. Seven quarters had suddenly lined up on the table. Every guy in the bar wanted in on the action. I thought about losing to her on purpose so she would stay on the table, but that wasn't necessary. She was a better player than I was, and she kicked my ass convincingly. I accepted my defeat with grace and secured a front-row seat in the audience.

Her name was Rose, and this was her debut appearance in The Silver. Watching her bend over the pool table had brought me back to life and gotten my juices flowing again. Rose was a fresh face in a sea of familiar ones that I had already slept with, and I was determined to go home with her. I hovered close to the table and kept our conversation going while she proceeded to chew up and spit out all comers. I could tell she was into me. When she finished wiping the floor with her seventh and final victim, she asked me if I wanted to go to a party at Bobby Bong's house. I didn't know who that was or where he lived, but that wasn't important. I was prepared to go wherever this fresh face in a black miniskirt wanted to take me.

We weren't leaving alone. Rose had ridden downtown with her roommate, a tall and strikingly beautiful girl with smooth olive skin and wavy brown hair named Michelle. Her almond-shaped blue-green eyes were what struck me first. There were natural lifts at the outer corners, which made the lower lids look slightly longer than the ones on top. Michelle didn't say a word to me but instead let her piercing eyes do the talking. They let me know that she was on to me. She was driving a white 1967 Pontiac Lemans with bucket seats and a dark-blue vinyl roof. Two dudes that I didn't know were going to the party with us. One jumped in the front seat with Michelle, and the other in the back with Rose and me. The dude up front flipped on the radio. As we raced out to the West End, Dr. John was warning me about being in the right place at the wrong time and then about being in the wrong place at the right time. Which was it? I didn't care. All that mattered was that Rose was sitting on my lap and I was making out with her.

Entering Bobby Bong's house was like being admitted to a secret society. No one knew his real name, but his persona and his afterhours parties were legendary among those allowed to enter. How could I have lived in Oneonta for so long and not known of Bobby Bong and his parties? The small one-story house was packed with at least thirty revelers, all there to receive the material and spiritual nourishment of Bobby Bong's holy communion. I counted four glass water pipes, the largest of which had a drawtube at least twelve inches long. *Goats Head Soup* had commandeered the two large speakers on the floor, and the defiant Stones were belting out "Dancing with Mr. D" to the anointed congregation. I scanned the room for somebody I knew but came up empty. I bent down and whispered in Rose's ear.

"Who are these people?" I asked.

"They all go to Oneonta State," she whispered back, "just like Michelle and I do."

It was at that exact moment that Bobby Bong entered the living room. He was a large dude with a round face and short black hair. Dressed in tight black jeans and a plain white sweatshirt, he was carrying a clear plastic bag full of grass. The room let out a cheer. Bobby Bong smiled, took a bow, and moseyed over to the four bongs anticipating his arrival. He placed a large bud in each bowl and tossed a handful of matchbooks onto the coffee table. Mick Jagger continued his dark serenade, begging the Lord for mercy. Within minutes, the room was filled with smoke.

Smoking a water pipe at Bobby Bong's was an art form. Each thespian knew to wipe his or her mouth and dry their lips before placing them on the mouthpiece. They knew that proper bong etiquette called for them to purse their lips and push them inside the tube instead of around it. Each was experienced enough to take a deep breath and fill his or her body with oxygen so as to make it easier to inhale all the smoke from the bong without much coughing. Each anointed soul inhaled slowly as they lit the bowl, drawing the vapors up into the chamber and watching it get cloudy as it filled with smoke.

Billy Bong's spiritual sanctuary was still going strong when Rose whispered to me that we were going to leave. I had no idea what time it was, but I was flying high and ready for what I assumed was coming next. Dawn was beginning to break when Rose and I jumped into the back seat of the Lemans and started making out. Michelle hopped in and started the engine. Thankfully, the two dudes who had ridden to the party with us had gotten lost and were nowhere in sight. Rose and I had the back seat to ourselves and were all over each other. Michelle turned on the radio, spun the car out into the street, and peeled out. I had just unbuttoned Rose's blouse and slipped my hand into her bra when the Lemans came to a screeching halt and flung me against the bucket seat in front of me.

"This is where you live, isn't it?" she said without turning around to look at me.

She was right. The Lemans had stopped across the street in front of the house where my apartment was. Stupid me. I had pointed it out to Rose when we passed it on the way to Bobby Bong's, and Michelle had obviously overheard me. I looked at Rose, who just shrugged her shoulders and smiled. My hand was still inside her bra, and her nipple was hard. Michelle stared straight ahead and said nothing. I didn't have to be a genius to see the handwriting on the wall.

I pulled my hand out of Rose's pink bra and slipped it out of her blouse.

"I guess I'll see you around," I said as I opened the door.

I wasn't about to give up. I sat there and waited for Rose to say something and stop me from getting out. Michelle revved the engine. Her blue-green eyes were glaring at me from the rearview mirror.

"I hope so," was all Rose had to say.

Her blouse was still unbuttoned, and her black miniskirt was high on her hips. I'm sure she saw the bulge in my pants when I finally threw in the towel and climbed out of the car. The door was barely closed when Michelle stepped on the gas and almost ran over my foot. It was probably my imagination, but I thought I saw Rose wave at me from the back seat. I looked around. There wasn't another car in sight. Chestnut Street was a ghost town.

It was Friday morning, and I had to be at work in a few hours.

136

All birds of prey have remarkable vision. An eagle can see a rabbit moving from almost a mile away. A hawk can spot a mouse from a hundred feet up in the air. Ospreys feed only on fish and hunt over shallow bodies of water. They scan the water's surface for telltale ripples before diving down feetfirst to snatch the cold-blooded vertebrate from the sea.

I wanted to believe that I was the predator, but in truth, I had become the prey. It didn't take the eye of an eagle, a hawk, or an osprey to spot me. My reputation in The Silver was etched in stone. The telltale ripples were everywhere. Everyone knew why I was there. I was a sitting duck, as easy to snare as any rabbit, mouse, or fish. Trapdoor after trapdoor was opening. I was in a freefall, continuing to plummet so far down the hole that all any bird of prey had to do was ask. When she tapped me on the shoulder, I was ready to go even before I turned around and saw who it was. Another Friday night and I was there for the taking.

Bobby Bong's weed had taken its toll. It was the best I had smoked in ages, and I was still ripped when I rode into work that morning with James. Of course, not having slept didn't help. Even on a good day, applying decals at Miller Trailer was an eight-hour descent into hell. With no sleep and a monster buzz, it was like working on a chain gang. Somehow, I managed to survive the torture. When I got home, I stumbled into my room, stripped off my clothes, and collapsed on the mattress on the floor. It was ten o'clock when I regained consciousness. Naked and still in a stupor, I staggered out of my room into the hall. The apartment was dark and empty. If I had any sense, any shred left of self-control, I would have stayed home that night. But that's not who I was. I was incapable of sleeping alone. I was the heroin addict who needed his fix. Getting laid was my drug, an affirmation of what little value I was to society. The lines between the good and the bad had blurred. Whether it was a Debbie or a Gwen was irrelevant. Missing out on Rose the night before was nothing more than a temporary setback. I needed to return to the arena and feed my habit.

I shuffled bare ass down the hall to the bathroom and stepped into the standing water in the shower. The drain had been clogged since the day I moved in, and it always took at least two hours after every shower for the dirty water to make its glacial getaway. The red pubes floating on the surface indicated that Penelope was the last one here.

The Silver was packed when I made my entrance. I placed a quarter on the pool table and made my way to the bar. "The Joker," a new Steve Miller song, was on the jukebox. I ordered a draft from Gary and surveyed the landscape. The garden was teeming with the same dying flowers, the same faces from yesterday that would be here tomorrow. The tired conversations would be the same, but the carnal couplings would continue to change until every possible combination was exhausted. I had indulged most of them, and there were none here tonight that I wished to repeat. The thought of remaining forever on this island of repetition was depressing, but I was determined to make the best of it. Life was like a cucumber, wasn't it? When my quarter was up, I jumped into action. With a little luck, I might shoot well enough to stay on the table for a while and medicate the melancholy with a sufficient number of beers. As fortune would have it, this looked like my night. I was on a roll and had just sunk my fifth straight eight ball when I felt the hand.

I turned around. It was Michelle. The gods must have sent her to rescue me.

"Would you like to come back to my house?" she asked.

Before I could answer, she turned and headed for the door. I rolled my pool cue across the table and turned to the dude I had just demolished.

"You can have the table," I said. "I'm outa here.

Yogi Berra would have been proud of me. I had come to another fork in the road, and I had not hesitated to take it. The blue-green eyes were lying in wait for me when I exited the womb. They remained silent when I opened the passenger door of the white Lemans and slid into the bucket seat. The radio was on, and Led Zeppelin was declaring that "it had been a long time since they had rock and rolled." Michelle turned left on Main Street and then right on Chestnut. We zipped past Oneonta's radio station before taking another right onto West. Michelle was sharing a house up near the campus with Rose and two other girls. The two-story Victorian was on Spruce Street, and her tiny bedroom was in the converted attic above the second floor. The bed was in the middle of the room directly below the highest point in the A-shaped ceiling. The room was colder than hell. There was so little heat that we might as well have been camping at the North Pole. Fortunately, her bed was layered with several thick wool blankets and a plush dark-green comforter. We wasted little time getting out of our clothes and jumping into bed together. If I was being forced to choose a place to hibernate for the rest of winter, this was definitely my first choice.

It was a long night that turned into an even longer weekend. For some inexplicable reason, we seemed unable to pull ourselves apart. For me, making love with someone for the first time was like sampling a strange new food that I had never tasted before. Sometimes it was delicious, and it was impossible to get enough. More often than not, it was simply nourishment, and one small helping was all that I wanted. With Michelle, I sensed right away that it was more complicated. She exerted a strange gravitational pull over me that was confusing. I sensed that something special was happening, but I couldn't put my finger on it. She didn't talk much about herself, and getting her to reveal anything personal was akin to pulling out teeth with a pair of pliers. The sex was more primordial than passionate. It seemed to have a higher purpose, as if we had been sent to each other by a higher power to fill in the empty spaces in the other's life. We buried ourselves under the pile of blankets. Our bodies absorbed each other the same way plants absorb water. We left the artic chill of the attic and the refuge of her warm bed just long enough to use the bathroom or wander down to the kitchen for sustenance.

I was in familiar territory. How many times had I done this? How many times had I injected sex into my veins to make my stay in this world tolerable? How many times would I flip head over heels and rely on a pretty girl to validate my self-worth? It didn't take long for Michelle to become my latest drug. I definitely had a type, and she seemed to fit the bill.

I was clearly attracted to pretty faces, but for some unknown reason, it was ones who were the wounded birds that were drawn to me as much as I was drawn to them. The ones like Isadora Duncan who had their shit together saw me for what I was. To them, I was simply a brief stop along life's journey, and they knew not to stay for long. The free spirits like Thea Kefalas found me amusing. For them, I was just another playmate in the sandbox and there were plenty more to play with where I came from. It was the damaged ones like Cheryl Prior and Jill from Louisiana who reeled me in. They were impossible for me to resist. Michelle wasn't as obvious as the others, but all the clues were there, and I was hooked. Her sorrow was definitely under lock and key, hidden deep below the surface in a place I was reluctant to go. For all I knew, she might have thrown away the key.

I knew not to press her on it. If it was meant to be, I would learn about it in due time.

137

Although I was sleeping there less and less, the Chestnut Street apartment continued to be the center of the universe. The Missing Heads and their nightly rehearsals owned the kitchen. The playlist was inspiring, and the perpetual flow of friends and admirers made it the perfect place to get high. Melissa's seductive vocals saturated every room, and Richie's drums could be heard from the street. The guitar work of James and Michael was flawless, but the cherry on top was all the new music and artists I was being introduced to: Fleetwood Mac and *Bare Trees*, Steely Dan and "Bodhisattva," the folksy blues of Bonnie Raitt. Everyone in attendance was hypnotized by what was in the air. Louie and his voluptuous benefactor Nadia were there almost every night. Gerald and his new girlfriend Pam rarely missed a rehearsal. Michelle sometimes stopped by and spent the night, but more often than not, we withdrew to the protective cover and privacy of her Spruce Street attic.

I was so immersed in Michelle that I could not see that my time in Oneonta was nearly up. Unbeknownst to me, I would soon be following Bernie's footsteps out of town. The irony was that by sleeping with her every chance I got, I was speeding up my departure. I couldn't help myself. As much as I loved her body, her long legs, and the smooth texture of her skin, it was the mutual comfort our desires rewarded the other with that transported me. We didn't seem to have much in common and rarely engaged in intimate conversation, but I was in the grip of an obsession I was powerless to resist. Michelle was a month shy of twenty-one and on track to graduate at the end of May with her teaching degree. I, on the other hand, was a month shy of twenty-six and clueless as to what life had in store for me. My consuming passion for her might have been the reason I was tasting the cucumber and enjoying it again, but it was also what finally cost me my job.

My supervisor Paul was just doing his job when he asked me into the break room and ordered me to sign the confession. I had strolled into work nearly two hours late that morning, and it was the third time in a week I had failed to show up on time. The drugs and the alcohol were not the problem. I could handle them with ease and still get my happy ass out of bed. The real struggle was getting out of bed with Michelle still under the covers. I loved sex in the morning. While I considered this a legitimate excuse for tardiness, Miller Trailer wasn't buying it. I didn't give a shit. I wasn't a fool. Why would anyone in their right mind rather apply a decal to the side of a Ryder truck than get laid first thing in the morning?

Poor Paul was probably making seventy-five cents an hour more than I was and was clearly mystified as to why I wouldn't sign the one-page document in order to keep my precious job. From what I could tell, I was fucked either way. Threatening to fire me unless I surrendered and signed the full-blown confession was no threat at all. If I did, I was admitting to an unsatisfactory work performance and agreeing to my immediate dismissal if I ever missed work or showed up late again. The chances of me never skipping a day or lingering an extra hour or two in bed with Michelle were zero.

When I told Paul that I wouldn't sign, he said he had no other choice but to fire me. He asked me to hand over my work belt that contained my decals and the retractable box cutter knife.

"Fuck you!" I shouted. "It's all yours."

I unbuckled the leather belt and flung it across the room through the open door. Paul freaked out. He called for help, and two other supervisor dudes rushed into the room. Each enforcer grabbed an arm, and they dragged me out the door with Paul in hot pursuit. The assembly line had come to a complete halt, and you could hear a pin drop as they escorted me toward the outside world. Suddenly, there was a clap. Then another clap. Then another. As the two goons dragged me along the factory floor to the exit, the applause inched forward until it reached a thunderous crescendo. My fellow inmates were giving me a standing ovation. When I raised the clenched fist into the air, the floor erupted.

The support was uplifting, but I didn't give it much thought as I was making the long walk back along the West Side to my apartment. When I got home, I ate a bowl of cereal, smoked a joint, and went back to bed. It wasn't until I walked into The Silver around happy hour and Dickie Jensen ran up to me that I understood my place in Oneonta history. Dickie worked next to me applying decals and played drums in a bar band called Back Seat Drivers.

"Hey, man," he said. "That was far out. Everyone's talking about it."

So this is what Andy Warhol was talking about. This was my fifteen minutes of fame. I drank for free that night and was everyone's best friend. Thankfully, Michelle waltzed in around nine and dragged my ass out. If she hadn't, I might have gone home with someone else.

138

Maybe it was a dream. Maybe it wasn't. Either way, it was a test.

It was one of those rare Oneonta days in early February when the clouds vanished from the sky. It had snowed the night before, and the sun's reflection seemed determined to blind me as it danced like a giant spotlight over the sea of fresh white powder. No longer required to waste time at a ridiculous job, I was starting my drinking a lot earlier in day. It was the middle of the afternoon when I stepped through the door and heard the pool balls collide. It took a few seconds for my pupils to open wide enough to restore my vision. Once they adjusted to the subdued lighting, I thought I was hallucinating.

I flashed back to that fateful day on the steps of Get Stoned Leather. I remembered every detail: the fair Scandinavian skin, the long blond hair, the sparkling blue eyes, the nipples protruding like searchlights through the tight-fitting baby blue T-shirt. A year had passed since the Magical Mystery Tour, and I had resigned myself to the harsh reality that I would never see her again. Yet here she was, just a few feet away.

"Hi, Jeff," she said. "How have you been?"

Isadora's smile was as wide as the room. I froze, as powerless to speak as I had been the day she entered my life. The past year had been kind to her. How was it possible? She was even prettier than she was the last time I saw her. I felt the ground shift below me, but I managed to maintain my balance. This was no time to come unglued. I decided to lie.

"I'm doing great," I said. "How about you?"

Mine was a dumb question. The stars always aligned for Isadora. She just smiled again, took my hand, and led me to the empty booth that was standing guard over two full glasses of beer. She saw the puzzled look in my eyes.

"The other beer belongs to him," she said, pointing to the tall dude bending over the pool table to line up his shot.

The kid didn't look to be more than eighteen or nineteen. He sank the purple four ball with authority and turned around to smile. Isadora smiled back.

"Who's that?" I asked.

"His name is Robert," she said. "He's my new boy."

Isadora's boy reached in the breast pocket of his blue denim shirt and pulled out a smoke and a book of matches. He fired up the cigarette and bent over to take his next shot. The Marlboro dangled from his lips like he was the second coming of James Dean. His face was delicate, the fine features reminding me of the Renaissance statues in the museums of Florence. From behind, the straight blond hair extending halfway down his back made me think of Gregg Allman. I was jealous. I remembered what this felt like. Isadora's boy had no idea of what was on his horizon. This was his moment in the sun, his temporary admittance to paradise. Like me, Michael the bass player, and countless others before and after us, he would one day look back at this time in his life and realize that it would never be this good again.

"So, tell me, Jeff," she said. "Where have you been, and what have you been doing? Did you ever make it to Europe?"

I wanted to spill my guts, open the spigot, and tell her everything I had done and felt over the past year. I wanted her to believe that our time apart had expanded my horizons. I wanted her to believe that I had grown, that I was no longer the inexperienced dreamer she had known before. I wanted her to believe that I had become a citizen of the world. Was I trying to impress her? Was I hoping against hope that she would welcome me back into paradise? If this was a dream, it was one where I was falling off a cliff. What was my mind trying to alert me to? I had let go of Isadora Duncan once before. Was it the fear of letting go one last time?

Isadora's boy sunk the eight ball. His next challenger inserted his quarter and was racking the table when Robert wandered over and grabbed his glass. Isadora introduced us to each other and then asked her new boy to leave us alone. He looked a little confused, but he obeyed her command. He went back to the table and broke the rack. The balls scattered, with the red-and-white eleven ball dropping in one side pocket and the yellow-and-white nine in the other. He was off to a good start.

"You've got solids," he said to his challenger as he looked to line up a shot at the maroon-and-white fifteen ball. He glanced nervously over to the booth, unsure of what Isadora was up to.

"He's young," she said with a laugh. "He'll get used to it."

We sat there for more than an hour, and I did most of the talking. I told her about following the Mysterious Chameleon while I was on acid, about hopping on the plane to Luxembourg and meeting Jesus disguised as Tony from Australia. I talked about my early days in Amsterdam and my time in the Swiss Alps and Lucerne. I went on and on about Loutro, Vassilis, and the island of Crete and how I was hoping to return there one day. However, when she asked me to tell her about my lovers, I hesitated. What was she getting at? Why did she want to know?

Before I could answer, Isadora's boy skipped over to the booth. Isadora looked up and shooed him away with her hand. He backpedaled awkwardly toward the pool table, dragging his tail between his legs. Isadora turned her attention back to me. She was waiting for my response.

I wasn't a Catholic, but I always wondered what it would be like to go to confession. If this was what she wanted, then I felt compelled to step into the confessional booth and tell my story. Was she reconsidering me? Would she take me back? I knew I was deluding myself, but what did I have to lose? I shared as much as I could remember, right up to Michelle the night before. So much had happened in the past year. Thanks to Isadora, I was a better lover. I was hoping that my travels abroad and my sexual exploits would make me more attractive to her. Would she see it that way, or would she see me for the degenerate I had become? Could she tell how far I had fallen down the hole? Would she absolve me of my sins? Would she try to save me?

I would receive no answers that afternoon. Isadora would leave with her new boy right after happy hour, and I would stay at The Silver, getting sloppy drunk until Michelle showed up after ten and drove me back to my home away from home on Spruce Street. I fucked her with a vengeance that night, keeping my eyes shut the entire time and pretending she was Isadora.

The final test and all the answers would come two days later. I had been on a binge, starting my drinking when The Silver opened for business at eleven in the morning. I had finished off my second glass of Novocain when Louie walked in to keep me company. We pounded down a few cans of Utica Club together and commiserated our circumstances for over an hour until we grudgingly admitted we had hit the jackpot with Michelle and Nadia. What these delicious young beauties saw in a couple of derelicts like us was puzzling.

Around three, I decided I needed to grab a nap and catch a second wind in order to have any chance of lasting until the bars closed at two in the morning. I bid Louie farewell and staggered back to the Chestnut Street apartment. When I walked in, Penelope was coming out of the bathroom wearing nothing but a towel around her head. I mumbled something to her about going to bed and went into my room. I shut the door, stripped naked, and slid inside my sleeping bag on the mattress on the floor. I passed out in a matter of seconds.

I'm not sure how long I had been sleeping when I heard the door open. The room was dark, and the light coming from the hallway startled me. What startled me more was when I squinted to see who it was. Music was coming from the living room, and I could hear Jim Morrison begging someone to love him two times because he was going away. I didn't know if I was dreaming, but I decided not to take any chances. I closed my eyes quickly and pretended to be asleep.

Isadora Duncan closed the door and sat down on the floor next to me. I didn't move. Her clean, sweet smell commanded the room and began to slowly seep into my pores. I could feel her looking at me, but I was afraid to open my eyes. As tempting as it was to reach out and touch her, my gut told me it would be a mistake to make the first move. I felt paralyzed. I ached for her, but I didn't know what to do. I just wanted her to answer my prayers and whisk me off to paradise.

Isadora watched me for what felt like eternity. Her presence was overpowering. I tingled with anticipation. I was on my back, and I was becoming aroused. The down lining of the sleeping bag lifted into the air like a phoenix arising from the ashes to form a tepee over the middle of my body. What was she waiting for? What was I waiting for? My mind began to drift. As it faded and floated away, the tepee gradually collapsed until it ceased to exist.

Neither of us spoke. There was nothing left to say. If this was a dream, it was over. If it was a test, I had failed. Isadora kissed me on the forehead, stood up, and opened the door.

I never saw her again.

139

We were on a lonely stretch of I-75, just south of I-10, when the headlights caught my eye.

My mind had been traveling inside my invisible spaceship for so long that it was becoming nearly impossible to distinguish between what was real and what wasn't. I was sane enough to know that I was behind the wheel of the Lemans. I had taken over the driving outside of Atlanta, and I was dead set on making it to the Florida Gulf Coast by midnight. Michelle was out cold, her body slumped against the passenger door like a folded accordion. Louie was unconscious in the back seat surrounded by empty beer cans. I was playing with the radio dial and had finally picked up the weak signal of a station in Gainesville when I sensed that the shit was about to hit the fan. Cream was singing "Tales of Brave Ulysses."

The car left the northbound lanes of the interstate and was bouncing like a basketball on the grass after hitting the dip in the middle of the median. The approaching headlights grew in size, morphing into a pair of fireballs eager for their date with destiny.

I had arrived at another Yogi Berra fork into the road. Was the smart move to slam on the brakes and hope the car crossed in front of us, or should I step on the gas and pray that the Lemans had enough juice to propel us past the point of contact?

My baseball instincts kicked in. I'm in center field. Bottom of the ninth. Tie game. Runner on second. Two outs. Batter swings. Line drive into right center. I move at the crack of the bat. Where will the ball land? Can I get there in time to make a diving catch? Do I play it on one hop and take my chances throwing the runner out of the plate? If I dive and come up short, the ball skips past me and the game is over. If the ball drops in front of me, there is no guarantee I'll be able to nail the runner. I have a split second to decide. I put it all on the line and go for the game-winning catch.

I gunned it and held on for dear life. Time slowed to a crawl. What wasn't more than a second felt like one hour. I held the gas pedal to the floor. The Lemans was all that stood between us and the angel of death. Seizing the moment, it lunged forward like a sprinter making the extra effort to cross the finish line in first place. I braced for impact. The rogue vehicle was out of control as it shot past my side window, missing us by a couple of inches. The opposing driver was slumped over the steering wheel. A smiling skeletal figure wearing a hooded black cape was in the passenger seat. He was holding a large sickle-shaped blade in one hand and a sign in the other. It read SEE YOU NEXT TIME, ASSHOLE. My eyes darted up to the rearview mirror just in time to see the marauding vehicle careen off the pavement and disappear into darkness.

My slick A. J. Foyt Indy 500 maneuver brought my traveling companions back to life. Michelle opened her eyes and sat up. Louie rose from the ashes and yelled at me.

"What the fuck was that?" he demanded.

I didn't answer. I was in shock. It had happened so fast that I wasn't even certain that it had actually happened. What was the point of telling them that I had just saved them from the Grim Reaper? Was this brush with death a figment of my imagination? Was my invisible spaceship taking my mind farther and farther away from reality? Wasn't it better to blow them off and say nothing?

The truth was that I had been paying very little attention to the world around me. The ten-cent drafts, constant weed, and habitual sex had consumed me. I hadn't read a newspaper in months and frankly didn't care if I ever read one again. My brain and my body were coexisting inside a giant whirlpool that was sucking them down a ruthless drain. I was oblivious to current events. The long gas lines and stations that had run out of fuel were the smelling salts I needed to snap out of my coma. Clearly, the USA wasn't doing any better than the last time I checked in. Gas, when it could be found, was approaching sixty cents a gallon. It was the middle of February, and the price of everything was continuing to climb. A nineteen-year-old newspaper heiress had been kidnapped by a group calling itself the Symbionese Liberation Army. On a lighter note, the House of Representatives was on a scavenger hunt, searching for grounds to impeach the clown at 1600 Pennsylvania Avenue who was still claiming he wasn't a crook.

I was returning to Florida not because I wanted to but because it was the only move that made sense. Upstate New York was killing me. I was running out of money, and the prospects of landing a job in Oneonta were nonexistent. Boston? I loved the city, but how would that be any different? Besides, I was freezing my ass off. At least I would be warm in Florida and have a fighting chance of feeding myself. There were plenty of shitty jobs to be had for a drifter like me. Getting there was the issue. The thought of battling the freezing temperatures, wet snow, and icy roads was a bummer. I wasn't too excited about hitchhiking thirteen hundred miles, so I borrowed a page from Tom Sawyer and lobbied Michelle to drive me to the Sunshine State. If Tom could convince a bunch of kids to whitewash a fence for him, how hard could it be to talk her into going south and hanging with me for a few days on a sandy beach? Michelle agreed to do it, but only if she didn't have to make the return trip alone. Desperate to hit the road, I asked Louie to come along for the ride and then drive back to New York with her. It made sense. Like me, Louie was a bum with no place to be and nothing else to do.

It would turn out to be a colossal blunder.

140

The knock at the door surprised me. I had moved into the cottage that morning, and besides not expecting anyone, I didn't know a single soul in Madeira Beach. When I opened the door, I did a double take. If I hadn't known better, I would have thought it was Charlie Manson.

"Hey, man," he said, "I need a favor."

He raised his right hand and reached out to give me the power handshake. His left hand was holding the plug of the extension cord that was hanging off his arm and dragging behind him.

"I'm Abraham," he said. "I'm your neighbor."

We clasped hands. The Charlie Manson look-alike was probably a foot shorter than me. His hand was small, but his grip was firm. Like Charlie, he was a slender dude with an unruly shock of dark dirty hair. He didn't have Charlie's moustache or beard, but he had the same crazy eyes. What leaped out at me was the small circular scar in the middle of his forehead. It looked like an old bullet wound to me.

"Listen, man," he continued, "the Pigs have turned off my power. Do you mind if I plug this into one of your outlets?"

Abraham didn't seem like the kind of dude that you should say no to. I backed away from the door and motioned for him come in.

"Sure, man," I said. "No problem."

The one-room cottage was tiny, and there were not a lot of electrical outlets. Abraham zeroed in on the unoccupied one under the laminate dinette table that stood next to the small stove.

"Thanks, man," he said. "Anytime you want to get high, just come over to my place. Me and my old lady Janet always have some good shit to smoke."

Abraham plugged the cord into the wall and reached out to give me another power handshake. We shook again, and he turned to leave.

"Don't forget," he said before walking out the door, "you're cool to stop by anytime."

All I knew about the Hindu concept of karma was that it originated in India more than a thousand years before the birth of Christ. There was a huge difference between good karma and bad karma. Allowing Abraham to rip off my electricity definitely qualified as good karma. Since I had not found a job yet and I had no weed and no money to score any, it seemed like a fair trade. I didn't want him to think I was desperate, so I waited an hour before I wandered over to take him up on his offer. I followed the extension cord out the door and around the corner. My cottage was one of six forming a circle around the courtyard that was mostly sand haphazardly landscaped with scattered clumps of coarse bladed grass. I was in a great location, at the corner of 146th Street, just a block from Gulf Boulevard and the beach. Abraham's power line led me to the cottage diagonally opposite mine. There was a black chrome-plated Harley-Davidson parked a few feet from the wide-open door. I stuck my head in and saw him sitting at his round dinette table rolling a joint. Abraham licked the sticky strip of the Zig-Zag paper and sealed the doobie, twisting it lightly at both ends to keep any precious reefer from slipping out. When he looked up and saw me, he lit the joint with a match and motioned for me to come in.

"Hey, man," he said, handing me my reward, "I want you to meet my old lady."

Abraham's old lady Janet looked to be in her early twenties. She was sitting sideways in her chair with both legs hanging over one of the cushioned arms. Her hair was shorter than Abraham's or mine, cropped short like that of a young boy. Her face was round and feminine. An open book was resting on her stomach just above her cutoff shorts. Janet had a dark tan, and she was topless.

I took a hit and coughed. It was some strong shit.

"Hi," I said. "I'm Jeff. What are you reading?"

Janet just smiled and held up the book. The word *SERPICO* was splashed in bold letters across the top of the white cover. Below it was a black-and-white photo of a dude with long dark hair and a full beard and moustache. I offered her the joint. She shook her head no, so I handed it back to Abraham.

I tried not to stare, but I couldn't help myself. Being exposed to one more pair of tits was not that big of a deal, but Janet's were just different enough to pique my interest. It wasn't that they were big. In fact, they seemed smaller than average for a girl with her solid frame. It also wasn't because they were as tan as the rest of her. What caused me to stare were her nipples, larger than silver dollars and the darkest that I had ever seen. They seemed more an artist's rendering than real. Each areola was airbrushed the same dark-brown color as its nipple neighbor and the perfect complement for each golden-brown breast.

Janet either didn't notice that I was ogling her breasts or, if she did, seemed not to care and went back to reading her book. For his part, Abraham was proud of his old lady and appeared to get off on my fascination with her and her tits. We rapped with one another for about an hour, killing the joint in short order and polishing off a second one for good measure. Abraham was a drug dealer who mostly sold marijuana but also had access to speed. I confessed I wasn't into speed but would like to score some weed from him once I landed a job. He just laughed and assured me he would give all the weed I wanted free of charge. Janet didn't speak the entire hour I was there, but Abraham told me she worked as a waitress in a restaurant up the road in Redington Beach.

"If you need food," he said, "my old lady is far out when it comes to sneaking some out of the restaurant."

I couldn't believe my good fortune. Free food and free pot. Even when their power was turned on two days later and Abraham retrieved his extension cord, their generosity continued. The Harley parked outside told me he was home. It was all the permission I needed to make the trek over and get high or cop some food from a restaurant I could never afford to enter.

Abraham's open-door policy was far out. It had no hours or any boundaries. One afternoon in particular blew me away. The Harley had come roaring into the courtyard thirty minutes earlier when I decided I needed a buzz. I was halfway to their cottage when the sound of War drifting from the cassette player reached my ears.

The Cisco Kid was a friend of mine
The Cisco Kid was a friend of mine
He drink whiskey, Poncho drink the wine
He drink whiskey, Poncho drink the wine

The door was half open. I knocked.

"Who is it?" Abraham shouted.

"It's me," I answered. "I wanted to get a joint."

"Come on in," he said. "Help yourself."

I pushed open the door and stepped inside. Abraham's lily-white ass was the first thing I saw. It was bouncing up and down on Janet to the beat of "The Cisco Kid." Abraham lifted his left arm and pointed to the round dinette table.

"The baggie and the papers are over there," he said without missing a beat. "Roll yourself a doobie."

This was awkward.

"Sorry, guys," I said. "I didn't mean to walk in on you like this."

"Hey, man," Abraham replied, still not missing a beat. "It's cool. Have a seat and roll one for yourself. There's some lasagna in the fridge if you're hungry."

What the hell? I thought. *If they're both cool with me sitting there while they're fucking, why should I care?* Janet didn't seem concerned. She never looked over at me or acknowledged my presence. Her tanned legs were wrapped around Abraham's hips, and her undivided attention was on the open book she was holding above his head.

Abraham was still grinding away when the song ended. Janet turned the page and kept reading. I wasn't sure how long the show was going to last. What did I care? I had two new friends and all the food, drugs, and entertainment I could ever hope for.

The cool part was that there was never any cover charge.

141

Mine was a pointless existence. While the warm weather and sandy beaches made it easier for me to survive as a derelict, all the sunshine in the world couldn't wash away the melancholy and darkness I felt. As bummed out as I was in frigid Oneonta, my life in sunny Madeira Beach was more depressing. If I was hoping that Florida would be my salvation, I was sadly mistaken.

It had been nearly three months, and I was swimming in Jell-O. I was barely getting by. After giving three different construction jobs a try, I switched gears and took a shot at restaurant work. That was even worse. I washed dishes and bussed tables, but all they paid was minimum wage. It was hard work for too little money. I noticed that the waiters and waitresses seemed to be the ones living the good life, so I lied about my experience and applied for a waiter's job. It was a fancy restaurant just over the bridge from Treasure Island on Blind Pass Road. I had to buy a pair of black slacks and a white shirt, but I figured it was worth depleting my life savings in order to swim to the surface and start raking in the tip money. I was one of three underlings assigned to the team of a waiter captain named Dominic, a short dude with slick black hair and a receding hairline who wore a pleated black cummerbund around his sizable waist. Since I was lowest flunkey on the totem pole, my primary task was to transport food from the kitchen on a large tray to the stand by the table so that the higher-ranking servants who knew what they were doing could pass the expensive dishes to the well-heeled diners. The first few hours of my new career went smoothly. I figured that I was on to something. I grew excited, wondering what my share of the night's tips would be. My dreams were shattered in a matter of seconds. I was carrying a tray of dirty plates and glasses back to the kitchen when catastrophe struck. I had never carried so many plates stacked so high. I should have known better, but I didn't want to let on that I was a virgin at this. I was about to go through the swinging door when someone suddenly pushed it open from the other side. The impact drove me backward onto my ass and hurled my dirty cargo into the air. My cover was blown. It was the sound heard 'round the world. I tried to maintain my composure as I was bending down to pick up the broken mess. The dude who had burst through the door and ruined my first day on the job offered to help.

"You know," he said. "You'll have to pay for this. They take the cost of the plates out of your paycheck."

"You're shitting me, aren't you?" I said.

"No, man," he said. "That's the way it works around here."

It wasn't even a tough call. I took the easy way out and bolted for the exit. My career in the restaurant business was over before it ever started. There was no way that I was going to work for free for who knew how many days to pay for this shit. I hitchhiked back to my cottage. I saw that Abraham's Harley was home and the lights were on. I didn't even have to knock. He must have seen me coming. He opened the door and handed me the burning joint. I took a monster hit and coughed just as Janet walked out of the bathroom. She was wearing a white tank top but was naked from the waist down. Considering what I had just been through, Abraham's pot and Janet's sweet all-over tan were just what the doctor ordered.

I staggered out a little past eleven and was halfway across the courtyard when I decided that the night was still young. I was completely wasted, but the thought of returning to the solitude of my pint-size living space was depressing. The truth was that nearly everything about my life was depressing. Stuck in a hopeless rut, I was bouncing from one pointless low-paying job to another and scraping by day to day on what little money was in my pocket. I didn't own a vehicle. Abraham and Janet were my only friends. Each day was both a physical and mental struggle, an existential battle just to make it to the next. It was a battle that I was losing. I was isolated from everyone and everything around me. I was twenty-six years old and still felt like a stranger in my own country. I was surrounded by creatures. There was no place to run, no place to hide in Richard Nixon's 1974 America. However, I knew that blaming Dick for my downward spiral was an exercise in futility. I had chosen to live like this. Whatever was waiting for me down the road didn't matter. If I was going to taste the cucumber and enjoy it, I had no choice but to learn how to cope.

Sex had always been the one drug I could rely on whenever I felt this disconnected from the world around me. Yet now when I needed it most, it was nowhere to be found. I could tolerate the constant poverty and the dehumanizing jobs, but not getting laid no matter how hard I tried was crushing me. What had always been so easy in a college town like Oneonta had become an impossible mountain to climb in a Florida beach bar. I was a misfit, a square peg trying to fit into a round hole. Still, as futile as it seemed, I wasn't going to throw in the towel. I needed to get the monkey off my back, so I ditched the black slacks and white shirt for a clean T-shirt and clean shorts and stumbled the seventeen blocks down Gulf Boulevard to John's Pass and the Sand Bar. The long walk and warm breeze killed my buzz. By the time I arrived, I had regained consciousness and was ready to break the curse.

The music gods had read my mind. Foghat was pleading my case from the jukebox:

> *I don't want you, be no slave*
> *I don't want you, work all day*
> *I don't want you to be true*
> *I just want to make love to you*

I spotted Kerri. She was sitting on the same barstool that she sat on every night. Nursing a beer, she was talking to a longhaired dude who was indistinguishable from at least ten other drunk longhaired dudes who were searching for action. When she saw me walk in, she nodded and motioned to the empty stool next to hers.

Kerri always had her pick of the litter. I had been trying to get into her pants for the past two months. Was this finally going to be my night? I knew that I wasn't her type, but I was coming to the conclusion that I wasn't anyone's type in Florida. Being a derelict wasn't the problem. The bars and beaches were full of derelicts, and most of them were not having much trouble getting laid. While at first glance I might have looked like them, I might as well have been an alien from another planet. The Sixties were over, and the cruel Seventies had swept across the land like a huge tsunami, leaving only drugs and cynicism in its wake. Idealism was relegated to the ash heap of history. There would be no more Woodstocks, no more Summers of Love. I was a refugee from another era, a college kid from the East Coast who had come of age during the antiwar movement and a time of seismic cultural shifts. Hippies were a thing of the past. I was in the South now, and I was having trouble adjusting. Everyone had long hair, and the longhairs along the beach were not the ones I was used to. They were partying, hard-living bikers and construction workers whose sole purpose in life was to get as fucked up as possible every night. They did hard drugs and got into fights. This was not a scene I could relate to or a scene that related to me. These fucked-up dudes with their biker tattoos and hair-trigger fists were the ones that Kerri and all the chicks like her wanted to ball. A guy like me didn't stand a chance.

Kerri had befriended me months earlier when I first walked through the door, but I was likely the only dude in the Sand Bar she hadn't screwed. I think she found me a little odd but not odd enough to let me jump into bed with her. She wasn't beautiful, but she was pretty in a rough sort of way. I assumed that she was about my age, but it was hard to tell. She was one of those sandy-blond Florida girls with the sort of weathered dark tan that told me she had spent her entire life in the sun. She was probably younger than she looked.

Kerri lost interest in the indistinguishable longhair she was conversing with and turned her attention to me. The dude took the hint and shuffled off with his beer in hand.

"I haven't seen you in a few days," she said. "What have you been up to?"

"Not much," I said. "Just quit another job."

Any illusion that my latest hard-luck story would score me points was quickly dispelled.

"Shit," she said. "You've got a serious problem, don't you? You can't hold a job."

It was downhill after that. We talked for a few more minutes until she got bored and turned away to interview the next indistinguishable longhair who had just stepped up to the plate. When I finally accepted the fact that this was a lost cause, I settled in and focused on getting shitfaced. Unfortunately, I didn't have enough cash on me to purchase the necessary alcohol. After three beers, I decided to call it a night. I might as well have been invisible. When I got up to leave around one in the morning, not a soul in the Sand Bar seemed to notice. I wandered out to Gulf Boulevard to begin the long slog home. I had gone about four blocks when the car raced up next to me and slammed on the brakes. The back door on the passenger side swung open. All I could see was a flurry of arms and legs.

"Jump in, motherfucker!" some dude shouted.

It looked like one of those photos I had seen as a kid where a group of college students stuffed as many of themselves as humanly possible into a phone booth. There didn't appear to be any room for me.

"That's okay," I said. "I'm just going about a mile. I can walk."

Someone rolled down the passenger window in the front seat. A cloud of smoke emerged, and the skunk smell of burning marijuana drifted over to where I was standing.

"Get in, asshole. We'll take you home."

I recognized the voice. It was Kerri. She was sitting across the laps of two dudes who were crammed in next to the dude driving.

I decided not to fight it. This was a free ride home and, if I was lucky, a few hits of some wicked weed. I wormed my way through the open door and squirmed atop the massif of bodies. I was twisted like a pretzel, and I couldn't get a direct look at any of the faces. I felt a hand brush over my crotch, but I couldn't tell if it was accidental or intentional. Someone cranked up the volume of the radio. The Edgar Winter Group was singing "Free Ride." By the time I realized where we were, it was too late. The vehicle turned right and headed over the Causeway to God knows where. I tried shouting, imploring the driver to stop and let me out, but I was competing against Edgar Winter, and Edgar Winter was winning. I had entered a sensual snake pit. Hands were crawling all over me. Fingers rushed through my hair. I felt a wet tongue slip into my ear. A burning doobie touched my lips. I took a hit. I didn't know where I was going, but now I couldn't wait to get there.

The car pulled into a driveway, and the four doors flew open. Bodies tumbled out and ran for the house like salmon returning to spawn. We were in a residential neighborhood. I stood on the front lawn and watched as the sea of humanity poured into the house. The rest of the street was quiet. The houses were dark. I sensed we were about to disturb the peace.

I waited until everyone was inside before I entered. The front door was wide open, and Lynyrd Skynyrd's "Free Bird" was blasting through the air. The living room was filled wall to wall with bikers, biker chicks, and other assorted miscreants. I was halfway across the room when I was stopped by a shirtless dude with glazed eyes holding an open can of Busch. He was wearing a red bandanna and handed me a pill.

"Here, man," he said. "Take this."

I flashed back to my brother Bernie and the infamous amyl nitrate party on Buswell Street. Like Bernie, I didn't want anyone to think that I wasn't cool. I grabbed the dude's beer, popped the pill in my mouth, and took a swig.

The next thing I remember, I was on my knees in a strange bathroom hugging a dirty toilet. The room was spinning, and a crowd had gathered. I couldn't make out the faces, but I could hear the voices.

"Who is this guy?" a female asked.

"I dunno," a dude replied. "Anyone know who he is?"

I emptied my guts into the porcelain bowl. It felt like my stomach was ripping apart.

"Who brought this asshole here, anyway?" another spectator wanted to know.

That's all I remember until the sun tiptoed through the half-open curtains and forced open my eyes. I was lying faceup on the shag carpet. Dried spittle had solidified on one side of my mouth, which was now nothing more than a desert filled with cotton balls. The living room was empty except for the legion of crushed beer cans, empty liquor bottles, and overturned ashtrays that the mob had left behind. My fly was open, and I had no idea where the fuck I was.

First things first. I had to pee, so I struggled to my feet and wandered down the hallway in search of a bathroom. I passed two open doors along the way and peeked in. Naked bodies were everywhere. Shoes, shirts, dirty jeans, and torn panties were strewn across the carpet in both rooms. Each bed was a tangled mess of arms, legs, hair, and flesh. The second bedroom had a spare mattress on the floor inhabited by a hairy overweight dude branded with multiple tattoos who was reaping the spoils of war. Three nude chicks with bronze tans and lily-white asses were sprawled across various parts of his body. I kept quiet and kept moving. My head was throbbing. I found the bathroom, unbuttoned my shorts, and let them fall down to my feet. The floodgates opened. My disoriented dick had shriveled up, allowing a rogue pube to jump in front and send my urine flying in two different directions. I rotated my hips so that at least one yellow arch made it into the bowl. The other was on its own and raced to the floor.

I wasn't sure what day it was, but what did it matter? I didn't have a job, so I didn't have to be anywhere. I needed to find my way home, but where the hell was I? What had I done? What drug or drugs had I ingested? What level of lowlife had I sunk to now? These were all fair questions, but I wasn't about to wake up any of these dubious strangers and hassle them for answers. I yanked up my shorts, zipped my fly, and hurried back down the hall to make my getaway. All that stood between me and the front door were the beer cans, liquor bottles, and upside-down ashtrays. I bobbed and weaved my way through the living room like Mercury Morris dodging tacklers in the open field on his way to a game-winning touchdown.

My head was still killing me, and the morning sun was lying in wait. It emerged from its resting place and slapped me across the face the moment I stepped outside. A soft chorus of birds was there to greet me, but the street was void of human activity. I was no longer accustomed to being up this early, and I was surprised how warm it already was. The humidity was stifling. Had I fallen into enemy territory? I suddenly wished I could return to that magic time in Loutro. It had been less than a year, but that dreamlike summer felt like a million years ago. I held my head and closed my eyes. I wanted to scream. I wanted desperately to take my morning plunge into the Libyan Sea. I was nostalgic for one of those Retsina or Ouzo hangovers that always felt better than this.

I wandered up and down the streets looking for signs of where I might be. It was impossible to tell. I was in one of those generic Florida neighborhoods, strolling past modest one-story homes that had been built in the Fifties. Despite trying to differentiate themselves with their choices of white, gray-pink, and gray-green colors, the asphalt-shingled concrete houses all looked the same to me. It seemed hopeless. Stevie Winwood was inside my head, pretending to know what I was going through. He claimed, like me, he was wasted and couldn't find his way home. If life came with identifiable low points, this definitely was one of mine. How much longer could I live like this? Any pretense that my life had meaning had vanished into thin air. How could I have fallen so far in such a short period of time? A year ago, I was setting out to see the world and full of optimism. Suddenly, life was no longer an adventure. I had entered an advanced state of decay, decomposing like a dead animal along the side of the road. I was two years older than James Dean was when he crashed his Porsche and bought the farm. James had nothing to worry about. He would live in posterity. As for me, I had done nothing worth remembering. Hemingway might have shot himself, and Kerouac might have died a bitter drunk, but at least Ernie and Jack had pursued meaningful lives and left us their brilliant work. Even the original Isadora Duncan, who met a horrific ending, left a lasting impression on the generations that followed. Would anyone notice or care if I suddenly vanished from the face of the earth?

I walked in circles, listening for something or someone to show me the way. I passed homes with orange trees in the front yard, and I couldn't resist stealing an orange from one of the sleeping Floridians. I heard what sounded like flies or mosquitos buzzing around my head but could not tell where it coming from. I followed the faint whispers, hoping it was traffic that had caught my ear. Where there were cars, there had to be a road out of the wilderness. I made a series of wrong turns, but I eventually reached a highway. It was my lucky morning. I recognized where I was. I now knew the rush that Chris Columbus must have felt when he first laid eyes on the New World. I was on Seminole Boulevard in Seminole, not far from the beach. I stuck out my thumb. It took me more than thirty minutes, but I finally caught a ride.

I laid low for the next three days, keeping busy by contemplating my pathetic life. I hung at the beach during the day. At night, I wandered over to get high with Abraham and watch him ball Janet while she tried to finish *Serpico*. Finally, I gathered the courage to return to the Sand Bar. It was after ten when I walked in. Kerri was sitting on her personal stool, interviewing another indistinguishable longhair.

I turned around and left before she saw me.

142

Shakespeare called it the green-eyed monster. Why I thought I was immune to it is puzzling. All it took was Michelle's "Dear Jeff" letter to expose my capacity for self-deception and send me into a tailspin. While I may have been a late arrival to the sexual revolution, once the fire on Franklin Mountain hurled me into the age of free love, I assumed that I had evolved to a higher state of being and was incapable of a bourgeois emotion like jealousy. It was a brutal wake-up call. Michelle was sharing an apartment with Hank Marino and Louie, and she made sure to mention that she was *with Louie*. She ended by asking if I was coming back to Oneonta anytime soon.

I couldn't eat. I couldn't sleep. All that I could think of was Michelle in bed with Louie. My stomach was in knots. I was pummeled by a burning sensation, and it felt as if my entire body was crumbling around itself. I wasn't as liberated as I thought. Karma was a bitch. My cavalier attitude toward sex was rising up and biting me in the ass. For the past two years, it had all been fun and games. What began with a weekend with Emily Keenan had degenerated into a sexual safari, a perpetual pursuit of big game that was now an obsession. My rootless life was reduced to a series of conquests and encounters. But to what end?

As freaked out as I was, I only had myself to blame. It wasn't Louie's fault. He was a lowlife opportunist just like me. I would have reached for the prize too if the situation was reversed. How could I be pissed off at Michelle? Hadn't I had abandoned her, conned her into driving me to Florida, and then offered her up to Louie on a silver platter? Still, why was this consuming me? From Althea Kafalas to Brown Hair Laura to Jill from Louisiana, I didn't care who they were balling before or after me. Had I not been oblivious to whatever damage I might be doing to anyone who crossed my path of destruction? Had I cared how I treated Julie Tyler? Did I even consider how Randy would have felt if he had known about me and Thea? What about Robin? How had I hurt her, and what harm had I done to her friendship with Silvia? Could I have been any shittier to Gretchen after she had offered me shelter in Oberschonbrunn? And then there was Jane. What had I done to *her*? My philandering road was littered with asshole behavior.

Maybe I was overreacting. Was it possible that I might be in love with Michelle and not know it? I didn't think so, but how could I be sure? Would I even care if Florida was kinder to me and I was getting laid? The only one I had fallen hard for since the fire was Isadora Duncan, and even then, I had managed to handle the loss of her in stride. Whether it was desperation, anger, or jealousy that I was feeling now, the letter sealed my fate. I no longer had free will.

It was the middle of the afternoon when I stuffed all my clothes into my backpack and prepared to hit the road one more time. The refrigerator was barren except for a half-full carton of milk, a jar of mustard, and three cans of Busch beer. It was hardly a payback to Abraham and Janet for all the free pot and graphic entertainment, but I didn't want what little I owned to go to waste. I gathered up the last of my provisions, put them in a grocery bag, and carried them across the courtyard. The Harley was home and the door was open, so I walked in without knocking. Janet was leaning back in her cushioned chair, reading a new book. Apparently, she had finished *Serpico*. Abraham's face was buried between her legs. As usual, their clothes were nowhere in sight. I placed my offering next to the open bag of weed on the dinette table.

"Sorry to bother you," I said, "but I'm splitting. Thought you might like to have this."

Abraham lifted his head and gave me the peace sign.

"Far out, man," was all he said before taking a deep breath and diving back in.

Janet closed her book and glanced over in my direction. She flashed me a smile. I took one long last look at those gorgeous dark-brown larger-than-silver-dollar nipples. I wasn't going to miss Florida, but I was sure as hell going to miss them.

I remember very little of the twenty-eight hours it took me to hitchhike up the East Coast and descend one last time on the home of malt and hops. My mind was once again riding inside the invisible spaceship, fueled by adrenaline as it drifted farther and farther into space. Working its way up the spinal column of America, it offered me a bird's-eye view of all the interlocking and fused vertebrae that were trying desperately to hold the country together. The former VP was being disbarred. The former attorney general was pleading guilty to something. The House of Representatives was beginning hearings on removing Richard Milhous from 1600 Pennsylvania Avenue. The cost of everything was surging upward, and it was impossible not to notice the veil of darkness that was threatening to enshroud the entire nation. I worried that I was about to crash and burn. I thought of Doris Lessing's novel *Briefing for a Descent into Hell*. I might not have been as insane as Professor Charles Watkins, but I was heading in his direction. In poor Charlie's mind, he spun endlessly on a raft in the ocean before being carried away on the back of a white bird across the sea of the dead and then abducted by a crystal that sent him whirling into space on a cosmic journey. It sounded more like a bad acid trip to me, but I seemed to be as out of control as he was.

It was early evening when I reached Oneonta. I hadn't slept a wink. My only nourishment had been a couple of Snickers bars and a handful of potato chips. My heart was racing. Even if I had known where Michelle and Louie were living, I was in no condition to make an appearance. There was something I needed to do first. I headed straight for Nadia's apartment.

She didn't say a word when she opened the door. She knew why I was there. She fed me, let me take a shower, and was waiting in bed for me when I got out. I was a total wreck, but I was determined to make this a night that would live forever in *The Guinness Book of Records*. The fact that I was beyond exhaustion worked in my favor. My poor dick had been living in exile for the past few months and was eager to get back in the game. While I was obsessed with lasting forever, he was a volcano threatening to erupt at any moment. It created the perfect union, one that lasted for more than an hour. Nadia was spontaneous and unrestrained, as committed to our endeavor as I was. She let me explore her, allowing me to follow my desires wherever they might lead. The only time she hesitated was the first time I went down on her.

"I'm having my period," she whispered as she lifted her hips and pressed hard against my face.

It was the sweetest one I had ever tasted.

143

While revenge may not be one of the seven deadly sins, it is certainly a worthy contender for number 8. I believe it was Gandhi who once said that an eye for an eye only ends up making the whole world blind. I knew what I was doing was wrong, but I could not help myself. I tried hard to remember the person I used to be, but he was nowhere to be found as I tumbled deeper down the rabbit hole in a malicious effort to even the score.

Michelle, Louie, and Hank were living in the upstairs half of a two-story house on Walnut Street that had been converted into two apartments. A set of wooden steps at the back of the building led up to their private entrance off the kitchen. My resuscitated cock and I were now partners in crime. We had tasted the cucumber together and basked in its glory. It was late morning when we finally tore ourselves away from the rapture of Nadia and prepared for our next battle. We had the element of surprise on our side. We were rested and ready to go.

I didn't knock at first. The kitchen door with its four panes of glass gave me a chance to suss out the situation before I made my move. Louie was sitting shirtless in his underwear at the kitchen table, sifting through a small pile of weed that was mostly seeds and stems. I was about to open the door when I saw Michelle enter the room. She was wearing her baby-blue teddy, and she looked gorgeous. I felt the blood rush to my head. Was this a mistake? "Go forth, Nimrod," I said to myself. It was too late to turn back now. There was only one question. Would I be the mighty hunter from the Old Testament or the hapless Elmer Fudd that Bugs Bunny loved to mock?

Michelle spotted my face through the glass and jumped. I opened the door and set down my backpack. Louie stood up and walked over to give me a hug.

"Hey, man," he said. "What's happening?"

Michelle was frozen in place. She stared at me without saying a word.

"I missed Oneonta," I said, not taking my eyes off Michelle.

"Far out," Louie continued. "Did you just get here?"

"No," I said. "I got here yesterday. I spent the night at Nadia's."

If someone had dropped a thousand pins at that very moment, I would have heard every one of them hit the floor. Louie recovered first. He asked how long I was staying. I told him I didn't know. He walked back to the table and sat down. He picked up a pack of Zig-Zags.

"Wanna smoke a joint?" he asked.

It didn't look like there was much to smoke, but if anyone could scrape it together, it was Louie.

"Sure," I said. "I'm always up for getting high."

Michelle's eyes were locked on mine. A nervous smile inched across her face.

"Where's your room?" I asked.

"It's the last room down the hall," she said, speaking for the first time.

I picked up my backpack and carried it down the hall. I passed two bedrooms before I reached hers. They both had mattresses on the floor, but the one closest to the kitchen didn't appear to be lived in. The one in the middle must have been Hank's. Books and clothes were scattered around the room, and the mattress, with its blanket and crumbled-up sheets, looked slept in. Michelle's room was the biggest of the three.

Michelle's clothes were hanging in the small closet. There was a small two-drawer dresser against the wall near the door. What caught my eye were the messed-up sheets on the mattress on the floor and a couple of men's shirts, a pair of men's jeans, and dirty men's underwear in a pile next to the dresser.

I poked my head out into the hall.

581

"Hey, Louie!" I yelled. "You need to come get your shit outa here."

Louie knew his time was up. He came down the hall and picked up what little shit was his. He didn't seem upset either with being replaced by me or with the fact that I had fucked Nadia the night before. He had a wry smile on his face. His playtime with Michelle had been fun while it lasted. We were kindred spirits. In an alternate universe, I could have been him, and he could have been me. We were more alike than I wanted to admit.

After he left and I was alone, I unzipped my fly and stood over the mattress. I was the alpha dog, and I was here to mark my territory.

144

Obsession is a sun that never sets. It can gnaw at one's soul the way a frightened animal chews off his leg to free himself from a trap. With me, it was more like a sickness. I knew I should have stopped with Nadia but felt powerless to rein myself in. I wasn't thinking clearly. What began as an eye for an eye was now an eye, nose, arm, and leg for that one eye. Getting laid was the only way that I knew to keep score and know that I was winning.

The challenge I accepted from Hank brought it all to a head. I had been living there for almost two weeks. Michelle and I were getting it on every night and getting along great. I could tell she was still a little pissed at me, but she was doing her best to let it go. She wasn't around during the day. She was the only one of us who had something to do or anywhere to go. She had finished all her classes and was on her final student teaching assignment before she graduated at the end of the month. While her days were spent herding second graders, the three of us were getting high and listening to music. We had very little food and even less money. We were dependent on Michelle to bring us any nourishment she could steal from the school cafeteria and for whatever handouts we got from friends who stopped by to smoke our dope. Gerald and his girlfriend Pam were regular visitors. Joe Lopez, Gerald's older brother who had been roughed up the year before by the Miami cops, was in town for a few days. He came by with some potent weed he had scored in Mexico and to strum his guitar. Even Race Track, who was living in a tent out on Mud Road, made a few surprise appearances. Louie came and went, reduced to prowling The Silver each night in search of a new victim. He made a futile attempt to get back with Nadia, but she told him to fuck off.

Meanwhile, Michelle and I were growing closer by the day. No one seemed to miss us when we slipped away to the bedroom.

It was one of those rare afternoons when Hank and I were the only ones there. Michelle was corralling her ankle-biters, and Louie had made a daytime trek down to The Silver. We were listening to Alice Cooper and smoking our second joint when Hank began to whine about how he never got laid. He wanted to know why it was so easy for dudes like me and Louie. I just laughed. Hank had an exaggerated image of me. He had only seen me in action in the bars of Oneonta and really only in The Silver. He had no idea what a loser I was in Florida.

"Hey, man, can you show me how you do it?" he asked.

"Show you?" I answered. "What do you mean?"

"Let me hang out with you and watch you pick up chicks," he said.

I thought he was joking, but I played along. Hank was high, and he had a plan. Michelle and her second graders were taking a school camping trip out to Goodyear Lake in a few days, and she had been designated as one of the chaperones. She would be gone for two nights.

"She'll never know," he said. "I want to watch how you do it."

"Okay," I said without thinking. "I'll do it."

What was wrong with me? What made me accept his challenge? Michelle and I were growing closer by the day. The sex was good, and I had no reason to stray. The fact that I would risk what we had without giving it a second thought just went to prove what a sick bastard I was. Maybe I was still trying to exact revenge on her for screwing Louie, but my problem ran deeper than that. My obsession was rearing its ugly head again. I was addicted to the chase and ultimately to the conquest. I could no more resist the urge to screw a girl I had never screwed before than a heroin addict could resist another needle.

I was sitting in the kitchen on the day Michelle came home from school to pick up her things before she headed out to the lake. Driven by equal parts guilt and desire, I followed her down the hall and into her bedroom, hurrying to unbutton my pants along the way. I knew she had to get going, so I needed to make it quick and skip the foreplay. I pulled her jeans and panties down to her ankles and pushed her onto the mattress. Grabbing both knees, I opened her legs and jumped on for the ride. It was over in a matter of minutes. I have no recollection of how long Michelle waited after I rolled off her before she stood up and pulled up her panties and jeans. She seemed more surprised than upset.

"What was *that?*" she asked.

I didn't have a good answer. I wasn't sure myself. I hadn't bothered to take off my sneakers or my T-shirt, and my jeans had only made it as far as my knees.

"Just wanted to say goodbye" was all that I could come up with.

Michelle gave me a long, wet kiss. She grabbed my limp dick and gave it a quick squeeze.

"See you in a couple of days," she said and walked out of the room.

I knew I should drop out of the challenge, but I didn't. Getting laid one more time with one more woman was a drug I could never say no to. I needed the rush, that profound exhilaration that lifted my spirits and boosted my self-esteem. No matter the cost.

My first fix appeared in the form of a sophomore from Hartwick College. Hank and I left the apartment around nine thirty. If I was going to pull this off, it would have to be somewhere other than The Silver. Besides having slept with a number of the regulars, practically everyone in the bar knew me, knew my reputation, and more importantly, knew that I was living with Michelle. I needed a fresh start, a place where I was a new face and no one was wise to my act. The Brass Rail was just down the street, and it was the perfect bar to reinvent myself. It boasted a straighter crowd, with straighter college kids and less townies and lowlifes like me. It was the favorite watering hole for Hartwick jocks. I'm not sure why I felt so confident I could get laid there, but I figured it was worth a try. Hank was egging me on. He thought I was crazy to make my move there, but he couldn't wait to see me in action.

We were sitting at the bar, nursing our beers, when I first noticed her. The jukebox was trotting out the Paul McCartney single

"Band on the Run" for the third time since we had been there. She was petite, less than five feet tall, with wavy blond hair that fell to her shoulders. She was wearing tight blue jeans and a snug yellow blouse. Her smile was infectious, and she carried with her a bright pair of blue eyes that seemed to shimmer as she worked her way toward the bar. I didn't think she looked old enough to buy a drink.

Sometimes it just pays to be in the right place at the right time. The short-haired dude on the stool next to me had just gotten up to go to the head. The blonde answer to my prayers squeezed into the open space between me and the empty seat and bellied up to the bar.

"Hi," she said. "I'm Heidi. What's *your* name?"

"Jeff," I answered. "Are you sure you're old enough to be in here?"

Heidi giggled. "I'm nineteen. How old are you?"

It was a calculated risk, but I told her the truth.

"Twenty-six."

"You don't look twenty-six."

"You don't look nineteen."

Heidi giggled again. Meanwhile, Hank was taking all this in. I doubt he was gleaning any insight or sophisticated technique from what he was witnessing. I didn't care. I liked where this was going. Apparently, so did Heidi.

"I don't live too far from here," she said. "Do you want to go back to my place?"

This was why I loved Oneonta. It fed my addiction. It massaged my ego and made it easy to forget that I even had an addiction. The mystical effects on my body were akin to those I felt when I was doing Quaaludes with Jill in Lucerne. Oneonta hypnotized me and soothed me with a sense of euphoria. It made my muscles relax and induced numbness in my fingers and toes. Most importantly, it elevated my sexual prowess. There was only one problem. Like with any drug, the more I consumed, the more I needed to increase the dosage.

I was in another world that night. Time ceased to exist. I forgot about Michelle, forgot about the sorry life I was living. We played together like two kids in a sandbox. I laughed. She giggled. When morning came, I wanted more.

Heidi brought me breakfast in bed. She was lying facedown on top of the sheets as I savored the English muffin with its load of butter and let my eyes wander over her wondrous body. She had a tiny waistline, and her ass had to be the sexiest on the planet. Firm yet soft, it was in the shape of a perfectly formed, upside-down heart. Michelangelo couldn't have sculpted it any better. It was impossible to resist. I swallowed the last of my muffin and slipped a hand down between her legs. It was time for dessert.

Heidi giggled and let me entertain myself for a few minutes before abruptly pulling my fingers out and jumping out of bed. I was hard and ready. It caught me off guard.

"Rafael will be here in an hour," she said. "You need to leave."

"Who's Rafael?"

"He's my boyfriend," she said. "I need you to be gone before he gets here."

I quickly learned that Rafael was the captain of the Hartwick College soccer team and would be returning from an away match the day before.

"Can we do it one more time?" I asked.

"Sorry," she said. "It's been fun, but you don't want to be here when Rafael shows up."

I understood. I wouldn't want to be here if Michelle showed up. Still, it was worth one more try. I reached over and fondled her breasts.

"Are you sure we don't have time?" I pleaded.

She must have felt sorry for me because she let me play with them for a few seconds before pushing my hand away. She giggled one last time.

"Get dressed," she said. "You need to go."

When I returned to the apartment that morning, Hank and Louie were sitting in the living room, listening to music. It was Alice Cooper again. This time he was lamenting being eighteen and not knowing what he wanted.

"Hey, Louie," I said. "He's playing your song."

"Fuck you," said Louie as he gave me the finger.

Hank had told Louie about last night in the Brass Rail. They both wanted details. I wanted no part of it.

"It was great," was all I said.

"You're in deep shit now," Louie gloated. I sensed that he was already plotting a path back into Michelle's bed. I couldn't much say that I blamed him. I went into Michelle's room, took off my clothes, and collapsed on the mattress. I needed to get some sleep. When I finally rose up from the dead, it was five o'clock. My legs were twitching, and I was sweating and shivering. A cold chill had grabbed hold of my body, and I felt nauseous. I went down the hall to the bathroom and filled the tub with hot water. I soaked in it for more than an hour and contemplated my next move. The drug that was Heidi had worn off. I needed another fix.

Hank was waiting for me when I walked out.

"Let's go," he said. "I want to see you do it again."

I felt a bit groggy as I was getting dressed. The hot bath had helped, but I was still fighting the cold sweats. At least I was clean. Out of habit we headed for The Silver. I was a migrating salmon swimming upstream to return to where it all began. What was driving me? Did I even care who was next? I suspected that I was about to discover how low I could go.

The Silver proved to be a waste of time. Happy hour was over, and the crowd was surprisingly thin and devoid of any plausible candidates. Hank suggested we try the Copper Fox. I had never been in there, but it was a short walk from the Silver, around the corner next to the Italian restaurant owned by former Boston Red Sox third baseman Frank Malzone. Why not give it a shot? I was in the home of malt and hops. If I couldn't score at the Copper Fox, Oneonta offered me fifty-one more opportunities to satisfy my hunger.

I didn't recognize a soul. That was a good thing because it increased my chances of success and minimized the odds that Michelle would learn of my depravity. I was conflicted. I didn't want to continue the challenge, but at the same time I lacked the will-power to stop myself. As Hank and I sat at the bar drinking our beers and making small talk, my mind left my body and returned to my invisible spaceship. It drifted aimlessly until it realized it was time to focus on what was about to unfold. We were surrounded by a mixed crowd, equal part townies and college kids with a few older alcoholic dudes hanging together near the back end of the bar. The lighting was dim. My eyes had settled on a group of eight to ten girls standing and sitting at a table near the door. Mine was a blank stare, unable to focus on any one of them in particular. All I could see was an odd mix of tight blue jeans and equally tight miniskirts. That's when trouble appeared out of nowhere and tapped me on the shoulder. When I turned, the first thing I noticed was the bright-red lipstick. It wasn't something I was used to seeing in Oneonta.

"I saw you staring at me," she said. "You want to fuck me, don't you?"

Poor Hank. When he heard what she said, he lost his mouthful of beer. I was as stunned as he was, but I kept my cool. I had never seen her before, and as far as I knew, I had not been staring at her. Maybe I had. I decided to play along.

"Sure," I said. "How did you know?"

The bright-red lipstick ignored my question.

"I'll bet you want me to give you a blowjob, don't you?"

That was easy enough to answer, but before I could, the bright-red lipstick had more questions.

"Do you live around here? Do you have a place we can go?"

These were tougher questions. Taking this girl and her bright-red lipstick back to Walnut Street and Michelle's room seemed like a bad idea. I countered with a question of my own.

"Can't we go back to your place?" I suggested.

"No," replied the bright-red lipstick, "I share a bedroom with a roommate."

I didn't care if her roommate watched, but the bright-red lipstick did. I had a decision to make. I could reject the offer, or I could risk taking her back to the apartment. I looked over at Hank, hoping for some guidance. He just shrugged his shoulders. The girl with the bright-red lipstick grew impatient. She grabbed my hand, pulled me off the stool, and led me out of the Copper Fox like I was a dog on a leash on my way to the gallows.

It had all the qualities of a nightmare. Paralysis. The sensation of falling. Beads of sweat hanging on my forehead. My heart pounding in my ears. Attempting to speak but no words coming out. Part of my skull had cracked open, and the contents were cascading like a parade of miniature waterfalls in search of a final resting place. Would I die if I didn't wake up before hitting the ground? The demon was in its glory, riding me bareback and screaming for all to hear. Its hips were wide, its thighs were heavy, and its legs were as thick as tree trunks. Lurking in one corner of the room, a menacing dark shadow was pointing a Kodak Instamatic.

I wanted to believe that I was a better person than this, but I clearly wasn't. We were assaulting Michelle's mattress, soiling Michelle's sheets. We were surrounded by Michelle's books and Michelle's clothes. If the girl with the bright-red lipstick didn't care, I should have. When I woke the next morning, she was still there. Last night was a blur. The skirmish had taken place in the dark, and I was getting my first real look at her. She was bigger than I remembered. More big-boned than overweight, she had toned biceps that were more like those of a dude. That explained why she had been in complete control of me for the entire night. The bright-red lipstick had lost its luster, with smudged portions circling her mouth and brushing both of her cheeks. I looked over at Michelle's alarm clock. It was nine thirty in the morning, and Michelle would be home by ten. In a panic, I nudged the girl with the smeared red lipstick.

"Wake up," I said. "You need to get out here."

It suddenly dawned on me that I didn't even know her name. She hadn't bothered to ask for mine either. I nudged her a second time, and she opened her eyes. I could tell by the surprised look on her face that she was also getting her first look at me. I got the impression that she was regretting this as much as I was.

She rubbed her eyes and glanced around the room, seeming to take stock of all the things that belonged to Michelle.

"Whose room is this anyway?" she asked.

"My girlfriend's," I said. "You need to go. She'll be home any minute."

Neither of us spoke while we got dressed. For me, it was easy. All I had to do was slip into my jeans and put on a T-shirt. Her task was a bit more complicated. There was an awkward silence as I studied her efforts to put herself back together. It was taking way too long. I sensed that trouble was on the way. The bra, the panties, and the stockings were the easy part. Squeezing her haunches into a black miniskirt that was at least one size too small for its contents was another story. It was like watching a sausage maker struggle to stuff ground meat into the skin of intestines. Mission accomplished, I hurried her down the hall toward the kitchen where we were met by the Cheshire cat grins of Hank and Louie.

Any hope that I was out of the woods was short-lived. I was seconds away from the girl with the smeared red lipstick disappearing from my life forever when the sky opened up and the walls came tumbling down. She was halfway down the stairs and blowing me a kiss when Michelle turned the corner. The girl with the smeared red lipstick continued her descent, twisting ever so slightly to avoid a collision. Michelle turned and inspected the jam-packed miniskirt as it tiptoed past her. Satisfied she had seen enough, she began her ascent. When she reached me at the top of the stairs, she shook her head.

"Big ass," she said, stating the obvious.

Louie let out a whoop that could be heard for miles.

I had never seen him so happy.

145

According to the Bible, an angry God rained down burning sulfur from heaven to punish the cities of Sodom and Gomorrah for the depravity of their inhabitants. When Lot's wife made the mistake of turning around to feast her eyes on the destruction, the poor woman was turned into a pillar of salt. Michelle had a worse punishment in store for me.

"I'm going to sleep with Hank," she said.

It was the first time she had spoken to me in almost two days. It was a punch in the gut. Not that I didn't deserve it. I had become a one-man Sodom and Gomorrah. Turning me into a pillar of salt qualified as one form of divine retribution. Michelle sleeping with Hank was another. What better time than now to seek absolution.

It was a long shot. I had screwed things up so bad that my road to redemption was bound to be more an obstacle course than a straight-ahead interstate highway. My invisible spaceship had been traveling at warp speed, and the time had come to apply the brakes. I knew there would be twists and turns and a few detours and potholes along the way, but if I wanted to hold on to Michelle, what choice did I have?

"But...why?" I whimpered.

"Why not?" she snapped. "I feel sorry for him. He never gets laid."

I grappled for the right words. This was another one of those Yogi Berra fork-in-the-road moments. The madness had to stop, so I fell on my sword.

"Look," I pleaded, "I'm sorry. I really am. Please don't do this. I promise I'll never do it again."

I expected her to toss me out on my ass. To my surprise, she was willing to keep me around. Not only did she accept my apology, but she opened up to me for the very first time. I realized how little I knew about her. I hadn't known what made her tick or why her emotions were kept under lock and key. We didn't leave the apartment that day. We stayed in the bedroom, only venturing out when one of us had to pee or when the hunger pains forced us into the kitchen. We made love one time. Mostly, we just talked.

My mind drifted back to that first long weekend we spent together in the Spruce Street attic and the strange gravitational pull I felt her exerting over me. My gut told me at the time that she was yet another wounded bird and that we had been sent to each other to fill the void in the other's life. Was I ever right! I needed her, needed her if I was going to continue to taste the cucumber and enjoy it. Michelle's need was more serious. Unlike mine, it was a desperate cry for help. With each hour that passed, I learned how she had been damaged and why she was drawn to me. Like me, she wanted to get away. Like me, she had no idea where she wanted to go or where she wanted to end up. While I may have been searching for some illusive meaning or bullshit purpose in life, her desire to run for the hills was no intellectual exercise. What she was running from was real. The final destination was irrelevant. Escaping was all that mattered.

I hated Robert Adams before I even met him. To my ears, he sounded more like a coward than a monster. How else do you describe a man who beats his wife and daughter and uses a twisted interpretation of the Bible to justify it? A God-fearing Baptist born and raised in Missouri, her father enlisted in the Navy near the end of World War II. He met Michelle's mother, a devout Catholic, during the time he was stationed at the naval base in Bayonne, New Jersey, and their improbable marriage took place right after the war ended. Michelle had an older brother who was spared the beatings. A year older than me, he was married with two daughters and worked at an accounting firm in The City. Robert Adams was a recently retired New York City firefighter. Michelle and her brother had both been born and raised in Queens, but their father had moved the family out of the city to escape a neighborhood that he saw going to hell. He had bought a house on Long Island in New Hyde Park, and the family assumed that Michelle would move back home after graduation and get a job teaching at one of the local schools. It was the last thing in the world that she wanted to do.

The idea that someone as screwed up and as lost as me could be anyone's knight in shining armor was ludicrous. Yet here I was, being cast in that role. I think it was the Greek philosopher Plato who first observed that necessity is the mother of invention. Frank Zappa was so taken by this pearl of wisdom that he named his band after it. Frank's "mothers of invention" were now passing the torch to Michelle. Her need to make a run for it was pushing her boundaries and forcing her to invent a savior. Another Greek dude once claimed that desperate times call for desperate measures. Michelle's ill-conceived choice of me was the proof in the pudding.

I hadn't made any actual plans to leave Oneonta, but I had been grumbling off and on for weeks about hitting the road again. Michelle had been listening. She told me that it didn't matter where I was off to next; she just wanted to go there with me. She said that we could leave right after graduation, and we could take the Lemans. There was only one thing that we needed to do first. She wanted me to come home with her and meet her father.

Sure, I thought, why not? What could possibly go wrong?

146

I had to hand it to her father. He might have been a real asshole, but he knew his shit when it came to working on car engines. The Lemans was a fine-tuned machine. It shot up Franklin Mountain like a rocket with whirring wings until it encountered the charred remains of Hubcap Harvey's house. When I saw the still-standing collection of hubcaps at the gravel turnoff, I was hit by a wave of nostalgia. I thought about asking Michelle to pull over. Thomas Wolfe was on the money when he wrote *You Can't Go Home Again*, but that didn't mean I couldn't sneak a quick peek at where my journey had begun more than two years earlier. I thought better of it and kept my mouth shut. Before the Lemans conquered the summit and began its graceful glide down Route 28 toward Delhi, I glanced across the road and caught a glimpse of the sacred spot where I had once stood on the holy chest of God. The hill was smaller than I remembered.

There was no turning back. I was a moth making a kamikaze dive into an open flame. My body settled in for the ride, embraced by the bucket seat the same way a protective mother clasps an infant child to her bosom. My mind elected to return to the invisible spaceship for a bird's-eye view of the looming disaster. What was I walking into? Why was I doing this?

Did I really have a choice? I thought of Kitty Genovese, the woman in Queens who had been stabbed to death ten years earlier while the dozens of people who witnessed the murder did nothing to help her. I wanted to believe I would have done something had I been there. I had been on the run ever since the house burned down, so maybe it was time I thought about someone other than myself. I was a sorry excuse for a savior, but I was all Michelle had. As we cruised down Route 17 toward The City, I tried to prepare myself for

Robert Adams. The son of a bitch would hate me the second he laid eyes on me. Who could blame him? His only daughter was bringing home a longhaired drifter in scruffy clothes with whom she was about to run off with. Robert Adams could have been Robert Young in *Father Knows Best*, and the reaction would be the same.

The more I learned, the more I knew I was doing the right thing. It didn't matter that I was still married to Jane or that I would never escape the spell of Isadora Duncan. Michelle needed her freedom, and I needed a companion. She told how her mother would jump between her and her father and take the beating that was meant for her. She told me how shocked her mother was to learn about her sexual freedom and how the poor woman could not comprehend her daughter having sex before marriage, let alone with so many different boys. Michelle repeated the explanation that had reduced her mother to tears.

"When I'm hungry," she said, "I eat. When I'm thirsty, I drink. When I'm tired, I sleep. And when I'm horny, I have sex."

It was a five-hour drive, but I lost track of time. I remember passing by the town of Liberty on Route 17 and thinking that we were less than fifteen miles from the ghosts of Woodstock. My mind began to bounce around inside the invisible spaceship. Had it really been five years? Was Max Yasgur still a dairy farmer? Where was Grace Slick? I still had the hots for her.

It was early afternoon when we pulled in the driveway. Robert Adams was doing what he had been doing most days since he retired from the New York City Fire Department. His head was under the hood of a car. Michelle put the Lemans in Park and turned off the engine. We each looked over at the other and took a deep breath. I could tell she was nervous. So was I.

It was at moments like this that I realized how lucky I was to have an invisible spaceship. It afforded my mind a comfortable seat at a safe distance to watch the nightmare unfold. Like with any other bad dream, I can only remember bits and pieces. I remember her mother crying when she learned I was five years older than their twenty-one-year-old daughter. I remember her father asking me a lot of questions that I had no answer for. I remember being surprised at how long he managed to keep his cool. I couldn't tell him where we were planning to go because I didn't know myself. Colorado? California? I couldn't tell him what I intended to do for work, and I definitely couldn't explain why, in the three years since I had graduated from college, I had never looked for a real job.

The debacle ended the only way it could. Robert Adams eventually lost his cool, but I stood my ground. I was never worried that it would turn violent. He was a coward who only hit women and children, so I knew I was safe. The closest he got was when he grabbed my shirt and got up in my face.

"Listen, buster," he growled, "the next time you walk in this house, you had better be wearing a wedding ring."

Before I could respond, Michelle grabbed my hand and pulled me out the door.

147

George Harrison tells us that *all things must pass...*

It was the summer of 1974, but the Sixties were still hanging on by a thread. America was exhausted. The creatures were growing restless. A new word, *inflation*, had entered the nation's consciousness. The price of everything was continuing to rise, and a global recession was knocking at our door. The draft and America's involvement in the Vietnam War might have ended, but the damage had been done. The final numbers were still coming in, but close to sixty thousand American soldiers had been killed and hundreds of thousands more wounded. No one was quite sure how many of our generation had fled to Sweden or Canada or how many had just dropped off the face of the earth or lost a battle with drugs.

Probably the only ones who were tasting the cucumber that summer and enjoying it were the people of Greece. Papadopoulos's military dictatorship had collapsed under its own weight. The future didn't look quite so bright for the rest of us. Irish Republican Army bombs were going off in London at the same time the French, the Soviets, and the Americans were openly testing their nuclear arsenals in order to establish which country had the biggest dick.

Here at home, King Richard, like the Sixties, was also hanging on by a thread. Nixon's thugs were ordering John Lennon to leave the country at the same time the Supreme Court was telling Tricky Dick to turn over his tape recordings and the House of Representatives was preparing articles of impeachment to toss his happy ass of out of office. The bookies were taking bets on who would be around the longest. The smart money was on John.

There were several ways to cope with the insanity. The Franklin Mountain Liberation Front and its fellow travelers chose to scatter around the country and across the globe. Ozzie migrated to New Zealand and became a scuba diver. Mike and Renee folded their tent and vanished to parts unknown. Jane was rumored to be somewhere in western Massachusetts, preparing to raise her infant son in a world with an uncertain future. Bernie had tripped off to Oregon in search of his fortune, while Gerald and his girlfriend Pam had fled to Colorado to hide out in his brother Joe's cabin in the mountains high above Breckenridge. The only one staying put was Race Track, who was hunkered down on Mud Road and waiting for the revolution that would never come.

Michelle and I hit the road, determined to run as fast and far as the Lemans would take us. We traveled south and spent a few days in the Smokies before moving on to Florida. We needed to make some money so we could head west and start over. We settled in a cheap motel room on Treasure Island just down the road from the new Ramada Inn. Michelle picked up a waitress job at the Ramada restaurant while I found another one of my shitty construction jobs on Sunset Beach. We went up to Indian Shores a couple of times to visit my parents. I had pretty much stayed away from them since returning from Europe. It wasn't that I didn't want to see them. I wanted to spare them the embarrassment of me. It took Michelle and me until the middle of July to scrape together what we hoped was enough cash to make it across the country without running out of gas or starving to death.

But go where?

The poet Robert Penn Warren once noted that west is where we all plan to go some day. It had been four years since Jake Fisher, Zero Lester, and I left Boston and made the cross-country trek to Haight-Ashbury. Michelle was up for going anywhere just as long it wasn't back to New York. I wanted another shot at California, but I also hungered to see more of the USA. Gerald Lopez had given us directions to his brother's cabin in Colorado, so heading for the Rocky Mountains was another option. Going west was all that mattered.

The Lemans was a blessing. It hummed its way through the Florida Panhandle and the Ozarks in Arkansas. It cruised through Oklahoma on what was once Route 66 and was now Interstate 40.

We wanted our money to last, so we slept in it at rest stops. When we headed into Colorado and up into the Rockies, it soared like an eagle.

Joe's cabin was just a few miles outside of Breckenridge, but it might as well have been light-years from civilization. The Lemans negotiated a pair of tight switchbacks on the narrow dirt road like it was born to the task. As we worked our way through the patchwork of majestic pine trees and open meadows, it felt like we had entered a painting. The welcoming pines, with their eclectic mix of blue, light-green, dark-green, and yellow evergreen needles, were offering us refuge from the outside world. I was mesmerized by the wildflowers, a dizzying array of Monet-inspired rose purples, yellows, and bright pinks that must have been placed there by a higher power to soothe our souls. If we wanted to go into hiding, we could not have picked a more perfect spot.

And that it was. There were six of us sleeping in the small cabin. Michelle and I shared the downstairs floor with Gerald and Pam, while Joe and a cute blonde named Vickie slept in the tiny loft above the open room. We cooked over the wood-burning stove and relieved ourselves in the nearby outhouse built with maple two-by-fours. We took our communal baths together in the frigid waters of the fast-rushing stream that was a ten-minute walk from the cabin. Joe was an avid chess player. There were two tree stumps a few feet apart that we used for seats that were directly in front of the outhouse. Joe brought out a large wooden crate to use as a table and placed it between the stumps. We played for hours. Joe was a better player than me, but I did manage to win a few games.

Michelle and I stayed there for a week. It was an idyllic existence, but we knew we had to move on. The great boxer Joe Louis once told his opponent that he could run but he couldn't hide. There was no point in pretending that we could continue to live like this. America was a big place. There had to be somewhere we could go to make a life. We talked it over and decided to head up through Idaho and into Oregon. We would keep going until our money ran out and set up camp wherever that was.

Maybe it was my imagination, but the sun seemed brighter the morning we left. There wasn't a cloud in the sky. It was a spectacular day, the kind where anything was suddenly possible. We loaded our sleeping bags and the rest of our things into the Lemans and said our goodbyes. Gerald wished us luck. I wondered if I would ever see him again. Michelle and I didn't know where we were going, but the fresh mountain air had filled our lungs with optimism, and we were ready for whatever 1974 America had in store for us.

We decided to grab a bite to eat in Breckenridge. It was a small town with maybe six hundred residents. Main Street was lined with clapboard and log exterior buildings dating back to the mining days of the nineteenth century. We found a small diner that was serving breakfast and parked the Lemans. We passed a coin-operated newspaper vending machine on the way into the diner, but I was too hungry to notice the headline. It wasn't until we were leaving that I spotted the bold print.

The photo on the front page of the *Rocky Mountain News* showed him hugging his youngest daughter Julie.

Epilogue

Friday, August 9, 1974: The line started to form before sunrise. It began at the northwest gate of the North Lawn and spread like a wildfire down Pennsylvania Avenue. It circled the Washington Monument and snaked its way along the reflecting pool to the Lincoln Memorial. By the time the sun peeked over the horizon, the line had split in half a dozen times like a crazed amoeba on a crusade to keep reproducing itself. By midmorning, the lines had fanned out across the country and taken residence in the Lower 48. Every US citizen wanted in on the action. Alaska and Hawaii were begging not to be left out. Each had issued an urgent plea for a ship or a plane to carry one of the lines to their shore.

The president was alone in the Oval Office. He got out of his chair and walked around to the front of his desk. He unbuckled his belt, unbuttoned his navy-blue suit pants, and let them fall to the floor. He grabbed the waistband of his boxer shorts and pulled them down to his ankles. He seemed prepared for what was about to happen. Before he bent over the desk, he pulled his shirt, undershirt, and suit jacket up far enough to fully expose his hairy ass.

The crowd at the northwest gate was growing restless. The Secret Service had been tasked with procuring every cucumber in America in less than twenty-four hours. Somehow, they managed to pull it off. At exactly twelve noon, they opened the gate and handed a fresh cucumber to each citizen who entered the grounds.

It was Michelle's turn to drive. I tossed her the keys and jumped into the passenger seat.

It was a glorious moment. The Sixties were finally over. Along with two hundred million fellow Americans, I was tasting the cucumber and enjoying it. The president, on the other hand…

603

Michelle started the engine, and we pulled out of the parking lot. I was in the mood for some music, so I turned on the radio. We were in the mountains, and the reception sucked. I kept playing with the dial, hoping to find a station. Finally, through the relentless static, I heard what sounded like a Beach Boys song. I turned up the volume.

And she'll have fun fun fun
'Til her daddy takes the T-bird away

The Greeks were right.
Life was like a cucumber.

About the Author

Author, entrepreneur, and businessman, Greg Wyss was well-known on the small-press scene in the 1970s where his poems and stories appeared in dozens of literary publications. A collection of his work, *Sit Down Have a Beer*, was published in 1977 by Realities Library in San Diego, California. A graduate of Northeastern University, Greg retired in 2015 to resume his writing after the wireless communications company he cofounded was purchased by a competitor. Greg and his wife, Barbara, live in Houston, Texas. This is Greg's first novel.

CPSIA information can be obtained
at www.ICGtesting.com
Printed in the USA
FSHW020614050419
56948FS